Lessons in Love

OTHER BOOKS BY LAUREL OSTIGUY

THE ONONDAGA STATE SERIES

Last Goodbye
Longing to Be
Lying in Wait

Lessons in Love

LAUREL OSTIGUY

Visit my website at www.LaurelOstiguy.com

www.facebook.com/AuthorLaurelOstiguy

http://twitter.com/authorlaurelo

Email: authorlaurelo@gmail.com

Cover Layout by Qamber Designs

Cover Branding by RBA Designs | Romantic Book Affairs

Cover model: Travis Bendall and Brooke

Photographer: Lindee Robinson Photography

Editor and Interior Designer: Jovana Shirley, Unforeseen Editing, www.unforeseenediting.com

ISBN-13: 978-0-578-95395-3

I dedicate this book to Rachel R. *Kupillas.*
I wish you health and happiness, always.

Acknowledgments

Thank you to Sara Miller, Cielo Bellerose, Cat Skinner, Zara Dash, Jesse Savage, and Gaby Michaelis, and Jenny Patel. Your feedback was greatly appreciated.

A special thank you to Lindee Robinson and Najla Qamber for a beautiful cover and my deepest gratitude to Jovana Shirley for your patience, support, guidance, and exceptional editorial skills.

Thank you to everyone who has read my series and for your continued support!

A Note to the Reader

Lessons in Love picks up where the series left off during the students' sophomore year circa 1996. Part One begins on the evening *prior* to the ending of *Lying in Wait.* And Part Two picks up moments after the ending of *Lying in Wait* when Laura finds out the tragic news regarding her dear friend Travis Taylor.

While the two parts of the book run parallel to one another and share similar storylines, I purposely changed the details, dialogue, and some of the events in order to align more with Abigail's specific thoughts in Part One and Laura's take on some of the situations in Part Two.

Think of it this way: if you asked two of your friends to recall a situation, you'd most likely get a similar yet slightly different version of the story. The main premise would be there, but the details could be exaggerated or downplayed, depending on the person telling the story.

It's much like the saying goes: *There are two sides to every story.*

The same applies here.

I hope you enjoy following Abigail, Laura, Kelly, Nathan, Tank, and the rest of the gang at OSU as they plow ahead in the fourth installment in the Onondaga State Series!

Part One

One

Eye Candy

The honeymoon dating phase was over. But for Abigail and Nathan, that was okay because it just meant their bond was stronger than the typical college student hook-up. And besides, if history teaches us anything, it's that things change in every relationship. You settle in. You move beyond the shy, polite phase, and you get real with one another. In fact, no relationship ever remains the same.

The same would be boring, right?

At least, that's what Abigail has tried to convince herself this past month. Nathan's demands on the football team and his popularity throughout campus have pulled him away from her more times than she can count. But then again, it was only a matter of time until his status at Onondaga State University grew. Their freshman year, he was named Rookie of the Year and was recognized all over the school for his accomplishments. Now, as a sophomore, he's halfway through an even better football season. In fact, the Hawks are off to their best start in over twenty-six years. After every game, the fever seems to grow, and more fans wait for the players to congratulate them. Abigail included. She always waits for him. She wants to. She can't help herself, but sometimes, that's all she does.

Wait.

But it seems like the thing to do when you're head over heels for Nathan Ryan. They've been together for almost a year, and it's been amazing. He's kind, considerate, and loving, and he treats her as an equal.

And he tries to balance the stresses. But like most people they know in college, balance doesn't always come easy to students. It's something you must work at.

He's got a bigger list than most college students, with his academics constantly hanging over his head in order to keep his football scholarship. He has to work extra hard at keeping himself healthy, and when he's not in the gym, he's studying or doing his best to spend time with me. But I can see him struggling to maintain it all.

She often daydreams about the hours they used to spend together, curled up on her twin bed in the dorm room, eating pizza, watching a movie, or enjoying the quiet moments alone. Two lowly freshmen no one really cared that much about.

Fast-forward to a year later, and she's found herself spending more time alone. She does keep herself entertained while he's away. She's not necessarily alone; she's got the best friends a girl could ask for. Her floor mates get together for movie nights and parties, and they often meet in the common room to watch TV after a long day of school and hitting the books. These distractions seem to take her mind off missing him.

But here they are, trekking across campus to the Union, and she knows their time together will quickly be coming to an end.

She stops on the brick pathway in front of the Union and squeezes Nathan's hand. "Can't you come into the Union for a cup of coffee?"

"If I could, I would. But I need to go workout and talk to Coach about Saturday's game," he says before letting out a wide yawn.

"Nathan, you look exhausted, and it's only Tuesday. Can't you skip one workout?" she adds, her navy eyes softening.

"Don't do that, Abby," he says playfully. "You know I can't resist you when you look at me that way."

"That's the point." She stretches up onto her tippy-toes to close the distance between her and Nathan's six-three frame to brush her lips onto his.

He has strong, distinct features—a hard jawline but a perfectly proportioned nose and pouty lips. His cheeks are always flushed like he just went for a run, and his naturally wavy hair is a darker brown, which makes his steel-gray eyes stand out even more. With his glasses, he resembles a young Clark Kent. He literally makes Abigail swoon with just one look from him—he's *that* good-looking.

With a winning smile, he says, "Dinner. Later. I promise."

"I'll take what I can get," she says with a spirited laugh. "As long as you promise to take care of yourself."

He releases her hand and slowly backs away from her as he mouths the words, *I love you, Abby.*

Her feet urge her to run after him and steal one more kiss, but then she halts as she notices a beautiful blonde girl approaching Nathan at the edge of the street. He peps up, smiling ear to ear as he speaks to her. He no longer appears tired as they interact like old friends. Enough to continue to walk down the street together toward the field house. An uneasy feeling ripples in Abigail's gut as she watches them disappear out of her view. Now, her feet won't move underneath her. But then a rush of students, desperate for coffee, swarms the Union, forcing her to enter the double glass doors.

Don't freak out, Abigail. You can't possibly know every single person that he knows. He's popular. It's a fact. Go about your day and just count the minutes until you see him tonight. It's what you do because he's worth it.

She heads to the main area near the fireplace. After scanning the room, she finds an empty table. The Union is packed today.

So much for a quiet study session.

Removing her sweater and draping it over the back of the chair, she pulls out her textbook and leans back, relaxing her shoulders. Her legs stretch out on the empty chair at her table as she gets as comfortable as she can. Scanning the introduction to her *Veterinary Anatomy and Physiology* book, she twists the long tendrils of hair around her finger, memorizing the information in front of her.

After about fifteen minutes, Abigail senses someone standing over her. Glancing up, her eyes meet his. Her cheeks immediately fill with heat. She'd be hard-pressed not to recognize the handsome guy with the unforgettable piercing green eyes; strapping, tattooed build; dark hair; and slightly tanned skin, who accidentally knocked on her dormitory door a few weeks back. He was looking for their new floormate, Alex, who transferred this year to OSU. Alex resides in her dormitory at the opposite end of the hall and lives with Abigail's friend Casey.

"Hey," he says. "Thought that was you. It's a little crowded in here. Mind if I sit?" he asks.

Swiftly, she regains her composure. "Kelly, is it?"

He grants her a phenomenal smile. "Yeah, it is. Good memory."

She takes her boots off the chair and watches as he dusts it off before sitting down in his perfectly torn jeans.

He pulls off his leather jacket and tosses it on the table. Abigail watches as he takes out his book from his worn messenger bag.

She spies the cover to comprehend what he might be studying. *Criminal Law.*

"What's your degree?" she asks.

"Prelaw."

She surveys the tattoos up his well-built arms as he shows her the cover of his textbook.

"You?" he asks.

"Veterinary science."

With a devilish grin, he says, "Nothing hotter than a beautiful veterinarian."

She inhales so sharply that it causes her to choke.

His green eyes ignite, making her skin prickle, as he adds, "But you're not a veterinarian yet."

She wishes now more than ever that Nathan were here with her. *If Nathan were here, would Kelly have asked to sit with the two of us? Of course, he would have. As he said, it's crowded in here, and he simply needed a place to sit. Right?*

"It's cool. I'm an animal lover, too," he continues, pulling up the sleeve over his massive muscles. There is an outline of a black dog on his bicep. "This was Iggy. The best dog ever."

Trying to compose herself, she says, "Black Lab, I presume?"

"Yes, good guess. Maybe you're closer than I thought to becoming a vet." He laughs.

She can't help but watch his full lips part as the most incredible smile spreads across his face. *What the hell, Abigail? Get it together!* "I have a dog, Skyler," she blurts out. "But obviously, she's at home with my parents," Abigail adds, finally contributing to this seemingly one-way conversation.

"Bummer. Maybe next year, you can bring her?"

"Never thought of that. I suppose if I live off-campus, I could," she says.

"Definitely. Alex and I want to bring ours soon, too, if we can. We have a new Lab, Seltzer."

"Seltzer?"

His expression remains neutral as he repeats, "Yeah, Seltzer."

Abigail can't help but laugh. "How did you come up with *that* name?"

"Alex did. And I do what she says," he replies with a smirk.

Somewhat perplexed, Abigail asks, "But why Seltzer?"

"Alex said it's because she's got a bubbly personality," he says with a roll of his eyes.

Abigail covers her mouth, trying to hide her giggles.

He cocks his head as his expression softens. "I'm going to grab a coffee. Want one?" The edginess in his voice is sexy.

She's not used to intense strangers. Alex must be one cool girl to be able to handle this guy.

Nervous about this unplanned coffee date, she barely gets her voice past her lips. "Yes, I'd love a latte, skim. And thank you."

He doesn't say a word as he gets up and walks away. She lets out the biggest breath of relief possible and tries to play it cool by returning her eyes to her textbook. She came here to study, and that's what she needs to do. Study. Science. Not Kelly Conrad.

Five minutes fly by, and he is strutting through the crowded Union toward her. She notices the girls he passes do a double-take as they admire him. Something about being here with him makes her uneasy, as though she were doing something wrong.

Am I? Should I politely tell him I need to leave? But he bought me a coffee, so it would be rude to vacate, right? It's just a cup of coffee. Besides, he's dating my floormate. I'm sure I'll run into him again. I'm just being a friendly neighbor.

Before he can place it in front of her, she thanks him.

"You're welcome, Abigail."

Abigail. Only my girlfriends call me that. I guess that's a safe sign.

He returns to his textbook. But there is a burning question inside of her that she needs to ask. The puzzle is not quite fitting. Abigail clears her throat. "Um, how long have you known Alex?"

He smiles wide. "Forever, but now, it feels longer since she transferred here this year."

"Oh, right. Totally get it. *Can't be apart.*" She laughs awkwardly.

"To be honest, it was a little strange at first to have her transfer here. I like my freedom and all that, but we get along, so it's hard to be mad about it. In some ways, it's cool."

"Yeah."

"It's not a common occurrence. Not that I'm aware of."

Abigail tilts her head and narrows her eyes at him. "Not common?"

"Yeah, my parents are psyched."

"They are?"

"Yeah, they only have to come to one university to see their kids. Brother and sister under one roof, like old times."

Abigail tips her head back but regains her composure. *How in the hell did I not catch on they are brother and sister?* The eyes, the tattoos, the deeply involved conversations filled with details—it's because they are kin, as simple as that.

Why am I also relieved? He's incredibly hot, but so what? So is Nathan, and that's all that matters. I'm easily distracted by all the commotion happening on campus. Regarding the trial of the Campus Creeper, with Laura being involved in uncovering a poorly and almost criminally run school administration, and unfortunately, how this all ties to Bree's encounter with the Campus Creeper. It's too much. So, a little eye candy can't hurt anyone, right? Not that it's tit for tat, but the number of girls that swarm Nathan after games and at parties is, well, more than I'd prefer, but I deal with it.

"That's great. Your parents must be thrilled."

He leans back in his chair, eyes penetrating through her. "Tell me about you."

"Me?"

"Yeah, you."

"There's not much to tell."

"That's not true." He crosses his arms over his torso.

Her guard goes up, so she replies, "What are you insinuating?"

Eyes narrowing, he says, "I'm *insinuating* nothing."

She tosses her long hair to the side. His stare is more than she can take.

She glances at her watch, and before she can say a word, he interjects, "You've gotta be somewhere?"

"I—yes, I do."

"I understand. Please don't let me keep you."

She eyes him. His tone was deliberate. As is his unfamiliar style…at least within her circle, aside from Alex, but that makes sense now.

It's not Kelly's good looks, his sharp green eyes, his brawny build, or his dark hair that particularly draw Abigail in. Not at all. She is surrounded by good-looking men—hell, she has access to the entire football team. Yet something about him makes her nervous, and she's unsure if she even likes him.

He has a very confident air about him.

She slides on her sweater as he eyes her intensely. Her hands tremble as she tries to shove her textbook into her bag. "I'll answer one question about me. Fair?"

He contemplates her offer. He glances at the clock on the wall, and then with complete confidence, he replies, "Nah. I'm never good at *just one.*"

She tries hard not to react, but Abigail is not the type of girl to be able to hold her reactions in. She wishes she could but, damn, she has never been good at it.

Her skin pinks upon his stare, and with good intentions of leaving, she stops, grabs her coffee, and boldly says, "I'm not known to disappoint, but I guess you've proven me wrong."

His muscles twitch, and something about that eggs her on.

She stands and slings her bag over her shoulder as she says again, "Thanks for the latte."

He doesn't turn to acknowledge her departure. He simply picks up his textbook and continues to read. "See you later," he calls after her.

Thankfully, he can't appreciate the sheepish smile that graces her beautiful face, and that's probably a good thing for her.

The last thing Abigail needs is trouble.

Two

Wash It Away

Abigail hurried to grab her roommate, Laura, from their dorm room in Willis Hall just in time to switch on the television to catch the afternoon news and coverage of the final sentencing of Jeremy Gordon—aka the Campus Creeper. Laura takes a seat next to Abigail on the couch as they eagerly wait for the news reporter to announce that the court will be in session.

The judge has allowed cameras in the court for only the sentencing phase.

"We are going live in the courthouse," the woman from Channel 8 News announces. "The judge should be entering the courtroom momentarily."

The lounge room starts to fill up with students from her dorm as the minutes tick by.

Abigail shudders at the mere glimpse of Jeremy Gordon as he is escorted in, shackled in handcuffs and legcuffs.

Laura, ever the supportive roommate, grabs her friend's hand. "Are you okay?" she asks.

"Just seeing him makes me feel nauseous. I've never really hated anyone before. That alone bothers me, but I despise him so much," Abigail says.

"We all do. No one blames you for hating him. He did terrible things to you, Bree, and countless others. He's a monster, and I, for one, don't feel bad about saying that or feeling that way." Laura reassuringly squeezes her hand.

The bailiff stands before the packed courtroom. "Please rise. The Court of the Second Judicial Circuit, Criminal Division for Oswego County. October 22, 1996. The people of New York versus Jeremy Gordon is now in session, the Honorable Judge O'Connor presiding."

Everyone promptly stands and waits for the judge to take his seat. He carefully eyes the crowd before sitting down.

"You may be seated." He pauses. "Would the defendant like to make a statement?" he asks his attorney.

"Do you think he'll say anything, Laura?"

"I doubt it. Would you? I mean, what can he say? That he's sorry? What would that even mean at this point?"

"I guess you're right. And do I even want to hear him say he's sorry?"

"No, Your Honor," his attorney finally says.

Coward, Abigail thinks. *Although hearing anything from him other than his admittance of one hundred percent guilt would just be a waste of everyone's time. I can't believe the jerk had the gall to plead not guilty. I don't think he'll admit to any wrongdoing now.*

"Would the counselor for the state like to make a statement?"

"Yes," Claire Marion says as she rises. "Considering the number of crimes and the predatory nature of each count, we feel Mr. Gordon would continue to be a threat to society should he be eligible for parole in the future. Therefore, the state is requesting the maximum sentence for each count, Your Honor."

"Very well, then. Let's not delay this any longer. Please rise, Mr. Gordon. The state of New York has found you guilty of sixteen out of eighteen counts of battery and sexual assault. After careful consideration of your case, I've noted the Three Strikes statute, for which you have *not* been convicted of any felony or misdemeanors in your short time on this earth."

Abigail swallows hard. She can feel the beat of her heart pounding within the cavity wall of her chest.

He continues, "While I've taken the Three Strikes statute into consideration, I've also looked at the disproportionately harsh crimes you have been convicted of. This, by most standards, would be considered a crime spree. Therefore, for the sake of the safety of others and by the power bestowed upon me by the state of New York, I am sentencing you to seven years, the maximum allowed, for each count, for a total of one hundred twelve years to be served consecutively."

The roar can be heard in the courtroom, the dorm lounge area, and practically across the campus. Abigail, fixated on the back of Jeremy's head, watches his knees drop as his lawyer tries to hold him up.

The judge bangs his gavel. "Order in my court."

The courtroom hushes.

"You may be eligible for parole in ninety-eight years."

Considering he is only twenty-two years old, he'll be over a hundred, which means he won't see a parole hearing.

"Holy shit," Abigail mutters. "That's, like, forever. I can't believe it. He's actually going away for the rest of his life."

"Unbelievable. I'm speechless."

Laura and Abigail rise from the couches in the recreation room and push through the crowd of cheering students in their dormitory, unsure why they're unable to celebrate along with their peers. They somberly return to their room, not sure how to digest the good news. They sit at their desks, both searching for words to sum up the ordeal but fall silent instead. Then, the phone rings, waking them both from their thoughts.

Little does Abigail know that she is about to receive the most unimaginable phone call, direct from the courthouse, from the district attorney, Claire Marion.

"Hello?"

"May I speak to Abigail Price?"

"This is she."

"It's Claire Marion, counselor for the state."

Abigail clears her throat. "Oh, yes, of course. How are you?"

"Much better after today. More importantly, how are you?"

"You know, it's been an emotional few days."

There is a long pause, making Abigail's stomach turn with an uneasiness that is becoming all too familiar to her.

"Yes, I understand. I wanted to speak with you about a few items, if I may?"

"Of course." Her voice shakes.

She can hear the counselor ruffle some papers in front of her. "Yes, I wanted to call you personally now that the sentencing is behind us to inform you that the two counts he was found not guilty of pertained to you."

Abigail tries to breathe in, but it's like the wind has been knocked out of her. "Me?" she chokes out. "But how? It was Tank—Thomas was the one who caught him, and I was the…"

"I understand completely. It was a surprise to all of us."

"Does Thomas know?"

"No, we wanted to come to you first because if you choose to pursue a civil case and testify again, that is the only way that we will end up contacting Thomas. Without your consent, we have nothing."

"I don't understand. How could that happen? He…he attacked me." Tears well in her eyes. "I told the truth on the stand, and they didn't believe me?"

"Listen, this will be hard to comprehend now, but someday, you will. The jury did their job. There *was* reasonable doubt that it wasn't just an encounter between two college students gone wrong."

Abigail gasps. Laura grabs onto her arm, a concerned expression on her face.

"And in fairness, who's to say Jeremy Gordon never had a consensual relationship in his life? So, in my professional opinion, the jury did exactly what was asked of them."

"How can you say that?" she cries.

"The sexual assault charge was hard to prove since there were no physical markings, if you will, besides the ones from what they believe was the altercation with Thomas and you and him on the ice. Understanding that this was, of course, by accident. Plus, your medical records showed a fall, and hospital stay not long before. The second count of sexual battery was again hard to prove without reasonable doubt. The jury believed it was tough to prove with little physical evidence. They felt, despite Jeremy's history, that Thomas got jealous, and an altercation took place."

Abigail huffs in sheer disgust.

"I know. It is heartbreaking—"

"Heartbreaking? It's a lie! I never left with him. I never did anything to warrant his advances…and Tank, he's my friend—that's all."

"Miss Price, we didn't doubt your story at all. My team and I fought to have this overturned. We believe that is why the judge was harsh with his sentencing. Mr. Gordon could have gotten the minimum of forty-eight years and been out at the age of seventy. If he makes it that long. Prison is tough. Usually, inmates are tougher on those who commit sexual assault, especially on young women. It will be extremely hard for him."

Abigail hangs her head. "So, Tank will only know they didn't believe me *if* I agree to pursue this further? But if I let it go and walk away, he might never know?"

"Yes."

"So, if I don't testify, that means Tank will never know that a retrial was an option? Is that what I'm hearing? I'm just trying to understand this all." Abigail's voice shakes.

"That's correct. New York State is only interested in what you want to do. However, if you choose not to pursue a civil suit, we have an agreement that the defense will not ask for leniency, nor will they try to contest the sentence that was handed down today. They feel that at this point, justice has been served. There is enough mounting evidence against him that a new trial could cause additional years in prison for him. There's not much else that anyone could do to make this any better for him. He will be going to prison for a long time, and everyone feels that is satisfactory."

Abigail's head is spinning with so many questions and information that it is almost hard to comprehend this is happening. But if there is one thing she does know, it's that testifying—putting herself on the stand, facing that monster—was *the* hardest thing she's ever had to do. The minute she walked out of the courthouse, she knew unequivocally that she would never do it again.

As though her voice leaks out of her unknowingly, she admits, "I don't ever want to do that again."

Claire's voice softens. "I know, Miss Price. It's for the best to walk away. I would advise you if it weren't. I have a daughter around your age, and I'd tell her the same."

"You would?"

Abigail hears Claire sigh deeply. "Yes. There is nothing to gain here but more heartache. He's gone, out of society, and he won't be coming back. We all believed you. They just got it wrong. It happens all the time."

Abigail knows Tank's strong will, his temper, and his competitive nature and, drive to always be a winner won't allow him to see this clearly.

I love him too much to put him through all of this again. He's a hero. He's the reason we're all safe. I can't let him think that the night he put his career and his life on the line for me was all for naught.

That is something Abigail cannot do to him. She will gladly bear this pain if it means sparing his. "You promise Tank will never know?"

"Yes. You're an amazing young woman, Abigail."

"I don't feel amazing right now," she says, dabbing the corner of her eye with the tissue Laura handed her.

"I know. It will take time. But you are strong. You all are."

"Thank you. May I go now?"

"You have my number. If you need anything, please call me, and in the meantime, if anything changes, I'll be in touch."

"But it won't."

"Most likely not."

"Thank you for calling," Abigail whispers.

"Take care, Miss Price."

Abigail sets the receiver down.

Laura places her hand over the top of the phone and picks up her friend's hand and squeezes it. "I don't know what to say, Abigail. I can't believe they were unable to convict him on the charges *you* testified for."

"I'm so damn pissed, Laura," she says with a thump of her fist on her desk.

She abruptly stands as the comfort of her bed calls to her. Laura quickly follows her dear friend to her bedside. She crawls in next to her, cradling Abigail in her arms, and that's all it takes for Abigail to lose her anger and replace it with tears.

"Oh, Abigail, I'm so very sorry."

"I feel like such a fool." Abigail sniffles.

"I don't blame you. I can't believe it."

"It was so hard for me to stand up in court in the first place, and knowing they didn't believe me or that there was a lack of evidence or whatever, it all sucks," Abigail says.

"So ridiculous."

"Please don't say anything to the others, okay? I need to talk to my parents. Wrap my head around this. I can't have the school thinking I was caught up in some stupid jealousy triangle with Tank, Nathan, and that jerk. That would kill Nathan and Tank. The school can't know about this."

"I promise." Laura again pats her hand reassuringly.

Abigail raises her head to look at Laura. "You can *never* tell Tank. No matter what, okay?"

Laura's eyes dance over Abigail's concerned expression. It's clear this means something to her. "I-I won't," she stutters. "I promise you, Abigail. You're my chosen sister. I would never betray your trust."

"I know. It's just...you know how tough he can be, and if he finds out I made this decision without him..."

"You did it for the right reason. I would have done the same."

"Thanks. Means a lot, coming from you," Abigail says as she snuggles deep into Laura's comforting arms.

The two lie together in silence for another hour, just holding on to one of the only things in this dark world that feel like home.

Finally, Laura stretches her arms over her head and lets out a much-needed yawn. "You going to be okay if I go shower before the party at the Ridge?"

"Yeah. Don't worry about me. I think I'll go grab some of the girls and head over early. Take my mind off this."

"Okay, I'll get ready quickly, and Melissa and I will meet you guys there."

Laura climbs off her bed and exits the room while Abigail changes and tries to cover up her tears with makeup.

As the floor mates come upon the Ridge, they don't get the typical vibe that usually emanates from the football house. It's more hush-hush versus the typical loud house party. Nonetheless, Junior, the large doorman with rippling muscles, is still holding a clipboard at the front door. He nods his head in acknowledgment of Abigail and her friends. Everyone who has anything to do with the football team is aware of who Abigail is at this point. All the girlfriends of the players dress up on game days with jerseys that have their boyfriend's number on them.

"Ladies, I wish you a wonderful evening." Junior grabs Abigail by the arm. He whispers, "How are you doing?"

"Who, me? Never been better," she says flippantly.

He eyes her strangely and then says, "Okay, honey. If you need me, I'm here."

The girls enter, and for the most part, it is already packed. Abigail immediately sees a few of the players—Marcus, the team captain, and Jason, the backup quarterback—and goes over toward them.

"Hey, Abby," Marcus says.

"Hey, guys. Thanks again for having this party," she says.

"Glad we have something to celebrate," Marcus says without hesitation.

Jason pats Abigail on the arm. "We all are."

She barely acknowledges their remarks because she told herself before she left tonight that she had to put on *her* game face. She can't let on that she knows anything more than anyone else does. She simply has to swallow it down and smile.

She peers past them toward the backyard. "Thanks, guys."

"No problem. And Nathan and Tank are out back," Jason adds.

Abigail pauses and looks up at Jason as Bree enters. At some point last year, Bree and Jason might or might not have had a little connection one night. Ask Bree if it ever happened, and she brushes it off. But as Abigail watches Jason eye her up and down, there is no doubt he wishes it would happen again.

"You look gorgeous," he whispers to her, slathering it on thick.

Little does he know that she is dating her assistant professor. A scholar—a wildly handsome one—who is already on the path to big things with a private cabin in the woods. Bree and her hot professor boyfriend, Adam, might as well be glued at the hips—if only they were allowed to be seen together in public. Bree does a great job of socializing with her friends and then finding extra time to sneak away with Adam. She is completely satisfied with their arrangement. And her friends fully support her relationship, which helps Bree keep her secret safe, as it would undoubtedly be frowned upon by the university.

"Thank you," Bree says. She glances at Abigail. "Want to venture out back?"

"Let me at least get you girls a drink first," Jason says.

Bree links her arm with Jason, and he escorts her to the bar.

The girls grab drinks and then step out onto the back deck. Nathan is surrounded by not one, not two, but six girls. One Abigail immediately recognizes—the gorgeous blonde from the other afternoon. Her blood pressure rises with disappointment. She's had a terrible day, and she arrives at a party, only to find her boyfriend's time consumed by female fans.

But of all the friends Abigail could be standing with, Bree is the one who would understand this the most. She leans into Abigail's ear and says with complete conviction and bitchiness, "Smile like I'm telling you something funny."

Abigail smiles despite herself.

Bree continues, "One, get used to it. He's popular and sexy as hell, and girls want that. Two, he picked you, and if I recall, he *chased* after you. You remember that."

Abigail glances up at Bree.

A smile spreads across Bree's beautiful face. Then, she says out loud, "He picked you over me, and look at me, for Christ's sake!"

This sends a wave of laughter over Abigail. "God, I love you, Bree."

"Love you, too, sweetheart. Now, stop hunching your shoulders. They'll notice and think they have some play on you."

Abigail straightens up, and with a little sway in her step, she moves down the stairs and onto the grass.

"Don't rush over. You'll appear desperate," Bree whispers again.

"Jesus, you write the book on man-eating?"

"Nah. Didn't have to."

Abigail and Bree turn quite a few heads as they make their way through the groups of students. In the distance, she can hear Tank holding court. Abigail shudders at the sound of his voice.

Will I be able to keep my poker face on? she wonders.

Bree and Abigail stop and talk to a few friends here and there as they maneuver through the crowd toward the back of the fence.

As they arrive in the dimly lit yard, Nathan finally notices Abigail has arrived. She smiles, though inside, she wants to scream.

She waves at him as Bree whispers, "Part the sea of women. He is yours."

"Hey there!" he says with conviction.

"Hi!" she says eagerly back. She hates that it's forced on her end.

"When did you get here?"

Before she can respond, Tank comes over, grabbing her by the waist.

"Hey," he says, pecking her on the cheek.

Tank is Nathan's teammate and one of Abigail's best friends. And while some might agree about Nathan being the most eligible guy on campus, Tank's a star on the team, too, and the girls go wild for his six-foot-four-inch frame and enormous muscles. He also keeps his blond hair just above his shoulders, and his silver eyes sparkle with every smart-ass remark that flies out of his mouth. Which is often. It's part of his charm. So, depending on your type, you could easily be smitten by either one.

"You okay?" Tank asks.

"Awesome," she says, taking a big sip of her drink. She finds her spot next to Nathan.

Bree says her hellos to everyone and ends up standing next to and talking to Jessica, Tank's on-again, off-again girlfriend. This being an on-again time.

Nathan leans in. "You look beautiful."

She peers up and smiles at him. As soon as she does, a few girls immediately say they need more drinks or must go to the bathroom or whatever and leave. This is unsettling to Abigail, but the look on Bree's face says she smells a victory.

"Thank you. You look as handsome as usual."

He winks and then wraps his arm around her waist, pulling her in.

"When did you guys get here?" she asks.

"Oh, about an hour ago. We got out early, so we decided to come right here."

"You know the sentencing was today," she says.

"I'm sorry, Abby, but you know how it is. All the guys headed over, so…"

"No, I get it."

"I should have stopped by. I realize that now. I'm sorry. I wasn't thinking." He pulls her into his chest. Leaning in, he whispers into her ear, "Are you okay?"

"It's been a strange day," she admits, yet she's unwilling to tell him much more than that. She peers up at him, forcing a smile. "How was your day?"

"Practice was tough today. Coach had not been pleased with us yesterday, so he pushed us hard."

They all stand together for a little while longer until Tank and Nathan announce they need another drink.

"I'll get you one, too," he says.

"Thanks." Abigail cozies up next to Bree and Jessica. "Jess, I feel like I haven't hung out with you in forever," Abigail says.

"We can meet at the game tomorrow if you want."

"I'd like that."

While their relationship started off rocky due to Abigail's friendship with Tank, the two are now in a good spot.

Bree, always straight to the point, asks Jessica, "You know these girls who were hanging around?"

Jessica's expression darkens. She snarls as she replies, "Not really, but they sort of remind me of groupies." She rolls her brown eyes. "I hate groupies. They are desperate to attach themselves to whatever they think *this* is." She uses her hands to trace an imaginary circle around the party.

Abigail's pulse quickens.

"How'd they get invited?" Bree asks.

"The guys invited them."

"The guys?"

"Yeah. I guess they asked the girls to come tonight," Jessica says.

Jessica, while confident and unaffected by them being here, is the opposite of how Abigail feels.

Nathan never mentioned anything to me. Is he into the groupie thing? He never was before. He used to be shy and put off by the attention.

Abigail watches the back door as Tank and Nathan come out, and the girls are following them. The blonde girl is gabbing incessantly in Nathan's ear as he carries the drinks. He motions for her to follow him. And like a little pack of devotees, all the girls follow Nathan right back over to where they were before. Nathan immediately takes his spot next to Abigail.

Bree says with an edge, "You guys are so rude. Aren't you going to introduce us to your new friends?"

Nathan hesitates. "Oh, this is Poppy." He introduces the blonde girl first. "And Morgan and Shelby. This is Bree and Abigail, my girlfriend. And you guys met Jessica."

Tank takes Jessica by the shoulders. "She's my girl," he says with a friendly chuckle. "Shelby here is in my English Lit class," Tank adds.

"Nice to meet you guys," Bree says with a flick of her hair.

Abigail joins in. "Yes, nice to meet you." Inside, she is dying to ask how they all became friendly.

Poppy grants the girls a smile, although it's quite fake. "How long have you two been dating?" she asks Abigail.

Dating? "We've been together for about a year." She snuggles into Nathan's chest and is pleased when he wraps his free arm around her.

"Yep, it's gone by fast," he says.

"You?" Bree asks.

"Me what?" Poppy replies.

"Dating anyone?"

"Nope. Waiting for the right guy." Poppy peers over at Nathan and Abigail as they snuggle.

Bree hurriedly distracts her when she notices the longing look on Poppy's face. "He'll come along eventually. The *single* ones are out there!"

Poppy lends her attention back toward Bree, and with eyes narrowed, she asks, "You?"

"Me? Nah. I like to be casual. I'm not looking for anything serious," Bree says, giving Abigail a wink.

Tank interrupts the conversation by asking the group, "Game of beer pong, anyone?"

Jessica rolls her eyes. "You and your beer pong."

"What, babe? I like it, and I'm good at it."

"I'll give you that," Jessica says.

Before anyone else can chime in to play, Marcus, Jason, Troy, and lo and behold, Colin—Laura's beau—come out of the house.

"We'll play!" Marcus bellows.

"Hey, come be on our team," Nathan calls to Colin.

Colin swaggers over to Tank and Nathan as Laura, Melissa, and Alex join the girls. Colin hasn't hung out with this crowd before but, thankfully isn't too shy. He is on the radio every day, so he does not lack in personality or conversational skills.

"Hey, good to see you. Been a while. I hear I'll be running into you a lot more in Willis." Nathan winks, referring to Colin's solidified relationship with Laura.

"Ha. Yes, you will." Colin chuckles.

"This is Tank." Nathan points to him.

Tank shakes Colin's hand. "Hey, buddy. Hear you a lot on the radio. Super cool and"—he smiles wide—"Laura is an awesome chick."

"She's the best." Colin glances over at Laura and can't help but grin.

"Let's do this," Tank says with an enthusiastic clap of his hands.

Marcus, Troy, and Jason are at one end of the table while Tank, Nathan, and Colin are at the other end, filling up the Solo cups with beer.

All the girls loosely gather around the table. Light introductions are made, but Bree and her crew kind of find themselves on one side of the table while Poppy and her friends stand on the other.

After about thirty minutes of watching the boys toss balls into the cups while high-fiving and shit-talking, Abigail announces, "Hey, I'm going to the bathroom and then grabbing another drink. Need anything?"

They wave her off, so she slips away and back into the house.

She uses the bathroom and touches up her lip gloss before exiting. Then, she makes her way to the bar. She leans up, and on edge, orders a heavier drink than usual. She stands there, talking to some girl from one of her classes, and then orders another one. By the noise she hears outside, it's clear they are still playing beer pong and therefore not missing her. It's not necessarily Nathan's fault for carrying on per usual, but it would be nice to get some extra attention this evening.

Her body floods with all kinds of emotions as she replays the conversation with the lawyer. Then the boost she felt when Bree empowered her with just her words to bring her back up to a higher level. But then the scene with the girls, the uneasiness she felt standing there. And she is right back down again. She doesn't like it one bit.

She steps onto the porch after getting another drink. Poppy is standing at the other end, right near Nathan.

Ugh. What is this girl trying to do? Unfortunately, she isn't harsh on the eyes. In fact, she is the prettiest out of her friends.

Abigail spins on her heel and turns to go back inside. *I need a much stiffer drink after the day I've had.*

"I need something a little stronger," she says to the bartender.

"The lady has spoken," a voice from behind her says.

She looks to her left. "Kelly, I didn't see you. Um, what are you doing here?" Her cheeks flame up.

"Can't a guy go to a party?" His green eyes slice through her.

"I'm…sorry. That came out wrong."

He motions to the new drink that's been placed in front of her. "I'll have another beer," he says.

Kelly steps away from the bar with his drink. Maybe it's the tumultuous ride her emotions have taken today, or the unlikely acquaintance that appeared at the party, or the stronger than normal drinks she's consumed that makes her want to follow him, but her mind and body seem to be separate creatures this evening, and before she knows what's happening, she's following him toward a vacant corner of the room. The music is loud but bearable. The distinctive voice of Soundgarden's front man is wafting through the speakers, asking you to follow him into the desert, and as "Burden in My Hand" continues, the banging of the drums resonates through the crowded room of students.

Kelly leans up against a far wall. "My sister here?"

"Yes, outside. Watching beer pong."

"She must be bored to tears." He laughs.

"They get quite the crowd," she replies with a roll of her eyes.

"You mean, because of the girls surrounding them?"

Abigail peeks up under her long eyelashes. "Yeah. I suppose it comes with the popularity."

He shakes his head.

"What? You don't agree?" she asks.

"I don't know much about it. I don't typically come to these kinds of parties."

"What kind of parties do you go to?" The alcohol swirls in her brain.

"I like a good house party but with more of a mix of people, if you catch my drift."

"Yeah, when they say football party, it's a football party." She laughs as she observes all the Champion sweatshirts and Adidas running jackets.

"Yeah, wouldn't be top on my list."

"Then, why come?"

He's about to answer when Alex comes bounding into the room. "There's my brother. I was wondering if you were going to show or not!"

He smiles wide at her, and it warms Abigail's heart. Being an only child can be lonely. It's refreshing to see siblings genuinely like one another.

He winks at her. "I always have my reasons," he replies rather coyly.

"And where have you been hiding?" she asks Abigail. Before she can answer, she adds, "You shouldn't leave those boys to the wolves."

Abigail sighs. Despite her pep talk from Bree, she doesn't have the energy right now to fight for what is already hers. She's embarrassed in front of Kelly, too. Like she must defend her turf in order to keep someone satisfied. "They're just fans." She laughs.

"Let me grab us some drinks," Alex says.

"Thanks, sis."

The music changes to a much slower and softer song, and as it does, overheard in the background are two guys laughing loudly.

Then, one says with complete disregard, "Those stupid jurors couldn't find him guilty on all charges. What's the freaking difference between one charge and a hundred of them?! Isn't one crime all the same? The guy was a total stalker."

The other guy laughs and slaps him on the back. "I mean, they called him the Campus Creeper. Stupid hicks. What'd we expect in this part of the world?! How could they not just make a straight flush, go right through to the end? Guilty on all!"

The guy raises his drink to his friend and shouts, "Guilty on all counts!"

Much to Abigail's disappointment, the students in the room hear this, and everyone starts to cheer just as Alex comes back with their drinks. Abigail grabs hers and downs half of it quickly.

Alex raises her cup to the crowd. "Yeah, guilty on all counts!"

Abigail, with little warning, says, "Will you excuse me?"

She bolts toward the upstairs. Hurrying up the rickety wood planks two at a time. She rushes down the darkened hallway and out onto the balcony that barely juts out on the side of the house. A slight peek of the backyard is the only view. The harder she tries not to burst into tears, the more she feels it coming on. Tears start to rain down her cheeks. She wipes what she can away with the back of her sleeve. Her chest heaves with heartache. That horrible feeling of loneliness wraps tightly with melancholy.

She stares off to the side as she hears the roar of a good time below her. It might as well be a hundred miles away from her. She takes a gulp of her drink. Drowning out the pain.

"Abigail," a whispered voice says.

She steps close to the side of the house, shielding herself from view.

"Abigail?"

She holds her breath. She can hear the steps getting closer. Kelly comes out onto the tiny deck, and at first, he doesn't notice her hidden in the shadows. Then, he turns. He pads closer to her.

"Please don't." Her voice trembles.

"What's wrong?" Kelly asks with concern.

"I…I—" Sometimes, it's the simple gesture of someone innocently asking if you are okay that can send a person over the edge. Or, in Abigail's case, *back* over the edge.

He reaches out an arm to her. "I'm here as a friend, 'cause for some reason, it appears to me like you could use one."

She bursts into tears, and instead of standing in front of him like a fool, she buries herself into his open arm. With extreme caution, he gently holds her. And he does for more than a few minutes. She can't worry right now about the fact that a mere stranger is holding her tightly. It's the kind of embrace that friends give to one another. She can't consider the fact that Nathan is below her, having a great time, while another man consoles her. All she can muse about is the pain in her heart. The lack of validation for what she endured. The flippant words by two drunk students who basically stomped on the fact that Tank put his life on the line for her. She can only feel that hurt. That deep pain she has been harboring secretly for the past five hours.

As her breathing slows, she almost jerks back as the realization of Kelly holding her hits her. "I'm so sorry. I'm embarrassed you had to see me—"

"No need to explain."

She sniffles. "I'm not *that* girl who cries at parties, just so you know."

He takes a step back. In a slightly cautious tone, he adds, "Never said you were."

He leans over the railing and breathes in deeply. Abigail watches him, enthralled by this person she barely knows, yet they've caught one another's attention a few times.

She takes another sip of her drink.

He cocks his head to the side. "I get the sense that you're trying to wash something away." He chuckles. "It doesn't appear to be working."

His strange but accurate remark makes her smile a tad.

"You think?" She steps close to him and leans on the railing.

Another roar from the drunk students below fills their silence.

"Wish you were down there?" he asks.

"They can't see me like this," she confesses.

His eyes flicker when he gazes at her as though he wants to say something but hastily changes his mind. "The other day, you offered to answer one question about yourself. Do you remember that?"

"Yes," she says softly.

"I regretted not letting you."

"You did?" *I'm surprised he thought about it.*

"Yeah, but now, I don't."

Oh.

"Because now, I get to ask you again. Tell me something about you. Why did you get upset back there?"

She stares forward into the darkness as the urgency to release this demon inside of her gets stronger. And sometimes, a little liquid courage helps, too.

"Why do you want to know?"

"Because I do."

Her eyes well again. She lowers her head, and as she does, his hand caresses her chin, drawing it up to meet his stare.

"It might make you feel better," he says.

She glances around her, but she's certain there is not one person remotely within earshot. She watches his eyes, which look eager to take in what she is about to say. "I found out today…that…" She struggles for words. "That the guy…he was found not guilty on two counts."

"I heard that, too."

"Those…those counts," she stumbles, bracing herself on the railing.

He places his hand on top of hers.

"What?" he asks.

"Those two counts were the ones *I* had testified for."

He gasps. "*You*?"

"Me."

"I had no idea you were involved. I'm so sorry."

"Well, now, you know something about me." She pauses and then whispers, "The worst part about me."

"I feel awful. Are you okay?"

"Obviously, I'm not handling the news well." She shakes her nearly empty drink. "Tank doesn't know yet—at least, I assume by his partying tonight that he hasn't found out."

"Wait, the two counts. Tank? You were the reason the Campus Creeper was caught, and they didn't find him guilty of what exactly?"

Abigail can sense his confusion and frustration rise, much like hers did.

She wipes a tear from her eye. He carefully steps closer.

She drinks the rest of her watered-down cocktail and continues, "Before you run and rid yourself of the mess that is me…"

"I asked because I wanted to know," he says with an edge. "You see me running?"

"No…"

"Okay then."

She sighs. "See, I had met him—the jerk—earlier at the party. He told me about his girlfriend, blah, blah, blah," she says rather incoherently. "Then, I went to leave, and I did. I left alone. *Sooooo* stupid of me. I used to regret it every day until I realized," she says, pointing her finger at herself, "that I'm the reason—or I should say, Tank and I are the reason that asshole got caught. When I left the party, he called my name, and innocently, I believed it was okay to walk back to the same dorm with him, right? Nope. He lured me into a path, pinned me against a tree, and then, *BAM!* Tank hit us both, and we all went flying on the ice. How did Tank not get hurt? No idea. You've seen the size of him, but still, his football career could have ended, all because of me." She drops her head and then says quietly, "And the jury found insufficient evidence to convict on both charges. Total bullshit."

"It definitely is, and what I've learned in many of my classes is that it happens and often, unfortunately. Reasonable doubt can be so vague, depending on who is sitting in the jury."

She glances up at him. "It was so hard for me to get up there. To face him. And to think, someone didn't believe what I said."

"They believed it. I mean, in general, or he would have walked free."

"I'm devastated," she whispers.

"Jesus Christ. How are you even holding up tonight?"

She chuckles. "Let's be honest, I'm not. And obviously, when I heard those guys downstairs say such stupid things, I lost it."

"Abigail, I feel awful. Those guys are insensitive idiots. What can I do?"

"Nothing. Go have fun at the party. I'll be fine," she replies.

"I'd rather stand here with you, if that's okay?"

She doesn't respond. In fact, they don't speak for a few minutes. All they can hear is the party happening below their feet.

He breaks the silence with his curiosity. "When will Tank find out?"

"He's got a game tomorrow. I don't want any of them to know."

He sighs. "I get that. I guess it's a good thing I decided to come, huh? At least you had someone to talk to."

She turns to him. "What's your story?" There is an obvious edge to her voice.

"Excuse me?"

"You," she says with the brazenness of alcohol running through her veins. "You've got these tattoos, you're here and give off a vibe like you couldn't care less about this scene, but you're asking me questions about myself and…"

"One, no idea what my tattoos have to do with anything. You put makeup on, no?"

"Yeah, but…"

"How is that any different? Your skin, my skin." He steps a little closer to her. She can smell his cologne, an aromatic woodsy note interwoven with citrus. It's unexpected and rather nice. "What's your question exactly?"

What is my question? Why do I want to know more about him? I shouldn't want to. I should have never confided in him. But it felt good to tell someone. Someone not so close to all of this.

Although somewhat embarrassed, yet again her mouth runs away from her as she says, "I was curious—that's all."

"About me." His tone is conceited. She watches as the outline of his broad shoulders straightens back. "I'm thinking tonight isn't the night for getting to know me."

"Sorry I asked. You asked me, so…"

"Don't get offended."

"I'm not."

"It sounds like you are."

"You don't know me well enough…" She starts to brush past him toward the door when he grabs her wrist.

"Hey. All I meant was, you've got a lot to process tonight. I didn't want to make it about me."

"Ha! By the looks of you, you like it to be about you." She gently shakes her arm free.

His eyes widen. "The looks of me? How so?"

"You know."

He smirks. "No, I don't."

"You're brooding, and your piercing green eyes and muscles…"

He starts to laugh.

She crosses her arms over her chest. "What's so funny?"

"You," he says.

"Me?" Her voice screeches. She has had way too much to drink.

"My piercing green eyes and muscles."

"I meant…"

"I'm attractive." He grants her a devious grin.

"No, I didn't say that."

"Okay then, I'm not."

She is silenced. Then, frustrated beyond her limits, she barks, "Why are we discussing this?"

"No clue what the hell we are discussing anymore."

"I should have never told you…"

With slight annoyance in his voice, he says, "Now, wait a second. Please don't say that. We have gotten off on the wrong track here, and I'm sorry."

She lowers her head and then glances up. "No, I am. I'm pissy and drunk, and it's a bad combination."

He chuckles. "It must have been meant to be that I knocked on your room that day by accident."

"How so?"

The roar of the crowd below and the chatting of students, mixed with the loud and pulsing music, reminds Abigail of why she came here to begin with—to forget about her problems. But here she is, dealing with them head-on.

"So, tonight, you'd have a friend you could talk to." He pauses. "It's fate."

Fate. Here I go again.

"You are full of layers, aren't you?"

He smiles, and it strikes Abigail like lightning. "Yeah, and I've been told the layers underneath all this"—he motions to his body—"are actually attractive."

She starts to respond but decides it's best to leave that comment alone. "I'd better get back to the party. They're probably wondering…"

"You mean, Nathan," he says point-blank.

She whips her head up. "Yeah," she says quietly.

"It's not like I don't know."

But why haven't I spoken his name at all tonight? I talked about Tank but not Nathan. It's not a secret.

She hesitates before stepping through the door and into the hallway. Kelly is right behind her. They make it down the stairs in silence. As she nears the bottom, Nathan is standing there, a concerned expression on his face. She gives Kelly a sideways glance.

"Thanks," she whispers right about the time Nathan says, "There you are. We've been looking for you."

"Sorry. I was hanging around." She notices Kelly glance at her. She's lying, and it's obvious to him.

"You okay?" he asks.

She wipes her cheek, and some makeup gets on her fingertips. "Yeah. Had something in my eye and tried getting it out. I was using the bathroom upstairs."

"Oh, okay. Do you want to head out? I've got to get some sleep for the game tomorrow."

Exhausted and in desperate need of solitude and to sleep away this day, she eagerly agrees to leave with him. He grabs her hand, and out of the corner of her eye, she sees Poppy and her friends watching them as they leave.

"She's always right there," Abigail whispers.

As they exit the door, she turns as Kelly strikes up a conversation with Poppy and her associates in crime. Kelly makes a remark, and Poppy laughs, flipping her hair to the side. There's a distinct pang in her gut, but Nathan brings her back to reality.

"Who was that guy you were coming down with?"

"Oh, Casey's new roommate, Alex, it's her brother."

"Oh, cool."

"Yeah...cool."

Once at his dorm room, Nathan unlocks the door, pulling her inside by the hand. He doesn't flip on the lights. Instead, he spins her around, pinning her up against the wall. With one hand behind her head, he kisses her deeply, pressing his body tightly to hers.

Breathlessly, he whispers as their lips part, "I've been wanting to do that all night." He kisses her again, as though he is charged up on a different level than usual.

Does all that attention from the girls at the party fire him up in a way that might end up benefiting me?

She is too confused tonight to further question anything that the universe might throw at her. She needs to focus on herself. Taking his hand in hers, she squeezes it, and he can't help but pull back and regard her.

Before he can ask her what is wrong, he leans toward his desk, switches on the light, and lowers into his chair, pulling her onto his lap as he does.

She rests her head on his shoulder. "I got some bad news today," she begins.

And for the second time tonight, Abigail unburdens her soul—if only that meant it would wash her pain away. For good.

Three

It Gets Worse

The following afternoon, Bree and Abigail stand at the gate of Menton Field, waiting for Laura to arrive. When they hear the roar of the crowd, indicating the game is beginning, they decide to join the others in the stands. But within moments of joining their floor mates, Abigail spots Colin as he desperately searches the crowd.

No Laura? What's going on?

Abigail yells his name, "Colin!"

He locks eyes with her and hurriedly waves for her to join him on the sideline.

"I'm coming with you. He looks worried," Bree says as she excuses herself through the students and follows Abigail as she, too, jumps off the end of the bleachers.

Colin hurries toward them.

Before they can ask, he says, "It's Laura. She needs you. In the hospital." His voice is strained, and Abigail can see his eyes are dilated from adrenaline.

"What's wrong?" Bree asks.

"Come on. Let's get out of here, and I'll tell you on the way."

They ask zero questions as they hurry to his waiting car, which is parked, still running, in a tow-away zone in front of the stadium gates. Abigail is trailing Bree and Colin as they push their way toward the latecomers to the game. Suddenly, there's a tug on Abigail's arm. She whips around.

"Hey." Kelly smiles.

"Kelly, hi." Her cheeks turn pink.

"You're blushing," he says with a killer grin.

Snapping back to reality, she states, "I can't talk. My friend is in the hospital."

"Can I help?" He touches her arm.

It's so nice of him to offer to help, but I can't accept it.

"No, but thank you." She hurries away from him but not before glancing back in his direction.

She hops in the backseat of Colin's car. Bree is already fastened in the front. Abigail slides into the middle of the seat and leans forward.

"Is she hurt?" Abigail blurts out.

Colin does a three-point turn and then pulls out onto the main road. "She's okay. I took her to the hospital. She'd passed out."

"Jesus, what happened?" Bree asks.

Colin chokes out, "Her friend Travis…he died in a motorcycle accident last night."

Abigail gasps, clutching her hand over her heart.

Bree's chest heaves as she tries to catch her breath. "Oh my God. That is horrible," she whispers.

Abigail didn't know Travis all too well but knew he was a junior at the school and had been involved with *The Weekly Blue*, the school newspaper. But more importantly, Laura fell for him, and from what others have said, Travis returned her feelings twofold.

But during all this, Colin appeared in the picture, and ultimately, Laura chose him.

"She is not doing so hot. They'd like to keep her for observation. She's sedated because once she woke up, she had what they called a panic attack. They gave her some medication to calm her. But she keeps trying to leave the hospital. She needs you guys. I didn't know what else to do." The strain in his voice not only indicates his adoration for her but also acknowledges that he gets this is something that will take her a long time to recover from.

"I'm glad you got us," Abigail whispers. "She has been through so much…"

"With us. She's our rock." Bree's voice quivers.

Colin looks in his rearview mirror at her. "I'm sorry. To both of you. It's been a hard year for you guys."

Abigail sits back, resting her head on the seat. She ponders her issues with the trial, the not-guilty verdicts, and Laura's involvement in uncovering the conspiracy surrounding the lack of urgency by the dean around Jeremy Gordon, the Campus Creeper. Laura's friendship with Travis was crucial to her survival on the radio. And both Bree and Abigail, in their own ways, comprehended that Travis was the one to break all this wide open. He wanted to ensure everyone was held accountable. Not just Jeremy.

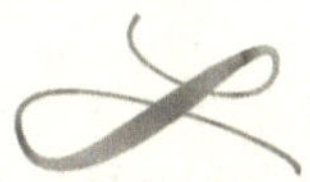

The three of them rush into the hospital, and with trepidation, they enter Laura's room. The beeps emanating from the monitors fill the otherwise silent room. A heaviness hangs in the air as the girls approach Laura's bed. Her body is still, but soon, she realizes she has company. She panics, trying yet again to leave the confines of her hospital bed by pulling on the wires connected to her. A nurse rushes in from the hallway as the monitors go berserk.

"Slow down, Laura," she warns. "Lie back."

Another nurse rushes in and inserts a syringe into her IV. Quickly, Laura begins to retreat into a catatonic state. Abigail grabs her hand and strokes her hair with her other hand as she watches Laura's eyelids lower.

"Laura, we're here," Bree whispers. "But you need your rest." Bree leans into Laura's ear and whispers, "I promise I'll find Wolfie. I'll make sure to bring him back to you." She fights back her tears as she watches her friend, obviously in pain and unable to comprehend her heartache.

Bree glances at Abigail, and with only a look, Bree knows she needs to leave and find out more about what happened from Wolfie.

"I'll be back as soon as I can," she says softly.

Abigail nods her head as she watches her leave.

Abigail, on the other hand, can't get herself to go despite Colin's encouragement to do so. She stays until it is clear from Colin that there is nothing more Abigail can do while Laura sleeps.

"It could be hours until she wakes again," he says.

"I know. But I'll be back soon."

"Thanks, Abigail."

"You'll be okay, Colin?"

"I think so." He tries to muster a smile.

She takes his hand and gives it a squeeze before exiting the hospital.

As the doors to the building slide open, she notices Kelly is leaning against his black Mustang at the end of the ramp.

She approaches him, concerned by his presence. "Everything okay?" she asks.

"You said your friend was hurt."

"Yes, but weren't you just at the game?"

"When I saw your friend's car peel out of Menton Field, I figured you might need some extra help—that's all," he says.

Oh, how nice of him to come and help.

"Gosh, I'm sorry. Yeah, my roommate's okay for now."

He looks around the lot. "You have a car?"

"No. I'm walking back to campus."

"Come on. I'll give you a ride." He shakes his head, laughing slightly.

"I don't want to impose. You should enjoy the day."

"Get in." He opens his door and unlocks the other door.

Abigail climbs into Kelly's car.

"She okay?"

"Yeah, they're releasing her tomorrow. But for now, they gave her something to sleep. Colin thought it was best we not all sit around her in silence."

"He's right. Tomorrow will be an entirely new reality."

"That's what Colin said."

He roars the engine to life. "You hungry?"

"I feel guilty," she confesses.

"For being hungry?"

"Kind of."

He puts the car in drive and pulls out of the lot. "You need to eat."

"Okay." *Interesting. Is he telling me or asking me?*

He pulls into a parking lot about fifteen minutes west of the hospital. By Abigail's calculation, they are about twenty minutes from campus. During the ride, she was stuck in her mind, thinking only of Laura and Travis. How heartbroken she must be to lose someone she cared so deeply for.

How will she possibly recover from this? How can I help her?

Kelly pulls his car into a parking lot, and as he kills the engine, Abigail snaps back to reality.

"We're here," he says.

As they get out of the car, she reads the sign on the front.

"Diesel Food?" she says.

"Yeah, get it? Like diesel fuel but food. It's a bar, but they have great eats."

And she knows exactly why it's called that as she enters. The clientele sitting at the bar and tables are mostly tattooed, wearing leather jackets, and talking about the mechanical customizations and modifications to their cars. Their prized possessions. They sit at a table, and a scantily clad waitress comes over. She gives Abigail a serious once-over. She puts the menus in front of them with little enthusiasm.

"What can I get you to drink?" the waitress asks as she flips her pad to the next page.

"Can we have two of the Carbon Calms?" Kelly says.

"Sure thing." She steps away toward the bar.

"Carbon Calms?" Abigail asks.

"It's good. Ever have a Long Island iced tea?"

"No. Not that I know of."

"You'd know if you had one. But this has this lemon balm tea in it that is calming, but it also has a little vodka, tequila…"

"Oh, a *drink*, drink."

"Thought you could use it." His smile makes her skin flush.

"Thanks," she says.

"Been a rough couple of days for you, hasn't it?"

"It's been something else." She picks up the menu. "What's good to eat?"

"I'm vegetarian. I get the pasta dish. It's amazing," he says.

She tips her head and is unable to hide the confused expression as she glances up at him.

"What?"

"I just, um…nothing."

Again, he smiles and says, "*No*, I don't eat meat."

"I didn't know that about you—that's all. I'm surprised if I'm being honest."

"There is a lot you don't know about me…yet."

She immediately returns her eyes to the menu. She can't stand the sensation in her gut right now. Guilt, deception, uneasiness, curiosity, contentment, interest, confusion. *I'm going to need that drink after all.*

The waitress brings over two drinks in very cool, tall blue glasses. "You having something to eat?" she asks.

Kelly nods toward Abigail.

"I'll have the Unleaded Salad," she says.

"You?"

"I'll have the Power Pasta." He takes Abigail's menu and hands them both to the waitress.

Abigail takes a sip of her drink. *He's right; it's delicious.* "So good."

"Right? I love it."

She takes another sip and sits back in her chair, trying to relax. She looks around the bar. The decor has a Motor City vibe to it. She glances down at her dark jeans, navy sweater, and Converse sneakers, and she feels incredibly out of place. She chuckles to herself as she remembers her first time at the No Nickname bar with Tank.

"Boy"—she laughs—"do I stick out like a sore thumb."

Without hesitation, he says with a seductive tone, "Yes, you do."

Don't blush. Don't blush.

Dying for a distraction from his piercing eyes, she blurts out, "Why are you helping me?"

"Why wouldn't I?"

"You must have other people you could be hanging out with?" she asks.

"Yes, I do," he replies, somewhat offended. "But I thought I could help you instead."

"But you hardly know me."

With a furrowed brow, he asks, "I'm confused. Isn't that what we are doing? Getting to know one another? Isn't that how these sorts of things work?" She opens her mouth to respond, but he adds, "Aren't you friends with my sister?"

"Yes, I am." She starts to fold her arms over her front in a defensive manner when he shakes his head. She unwraps her arms. "What?"

"Nothing," Kelly says.

"You can't say nothing," Abigail hastily responds.

"Look, don't take offense. You're going through a lot, so take this for what it's worth."

She takes a massive gulp of her drink, and his gorgeous eyes get wide.

Would I feel uneasy if he were, say, not as attractive and less mysterious than he appears to be? Abigail wonders. "It's just…I have a boyfriend, you know."

Now, it's his turn to cross his arms over his chest. His icy stare sends a shiver down her spine. He slowly leans forward, his chiseled face merely a few feet from hers, and whispers in a cool tone, "You honestly think I'm not aware of that?"

Okay, in the last forty-eight hours, I've felt sad, confused, maybe even a little depressed, and now, I can add completely stupid to my list of emotions. Oh, and embarrassed, too.

She swallows hard. Her brain is blank. She has no comeback.

He continues, "But I haven't seen him around the past few days, so I thought I'd step in as a friend, obviously." His demeanor is cocky, and his words are somewhat admonishing. He keeps his eyes locked on hers as he takes a sip of his drink.

Needing to say something instead of sitting there like an idiot, she replies, "He plays football. And can be very busy."

"I'm aware of that fact, too."

She glances down at her drink, picks it up, and finishes it.

"Let me get you another one." He waves to the waitress, and within minutes, another drink is in front of her.

"Trying to get me drunk?" She laughs at her poor attempt at a joke.

"Not my style," he says forcefully. "I'm trying to get you to relax."

"It's hard. It's been—"

He cuts her off, "Let's sit here like old friends having lunch and be on our way."

His coolness bothers her because deep down, she knows in some way—although she's not exactly positive how—she has offended him.

Trying not to add to the situation, she says, "Sounds good."

"Okay then." He pauses as if searching for a topic of conversation. "How do you think Alex is doing here?"

Relieved to talk about someone else, she replies, "Really well. She has a great roommate, and all the girls on my floor like her."

"Good. I was worried," he says.

"Why did she transfer?"

"She didn't love the school. The classes weren't right for her, and she knew how much I liked it here," he says.

"Hopefully, she's as happy as she appears," Abigail says.

"I get the sense she is."

The waitress brings over their lunch.

"How long have you been vegetarian?" Abigail asks.

"A few years now."

"You like it?"

"What's not to like?" He chuckles as he swirls the pasta on his fork. "I had a friend who was vegetarian. I sort of went for it and have been doing it ever since."

Famished, Abigail takes a bite of her salad. "This is good," she acknowledges.

"I like it here. Good food, good drinks. A little out of the way."

"Yeah, I always pick Cool Beans, the coffee shop that is the farthest away from campus. It's nice to get away from all of it sometimes."

"Yeah, the Union gets too crowded. Like the other day," he says.

"I was glad you asked to sit with me," she admits.

He can't mask his surprised expression. "You were?"

"Yeah, most people would have given up, walked away. I know I probably would have."

Getting a sense for what she's saying, he adds, "You're right. We don't tend to intermingle enough unless we're one hundred percent comfortable."

"Exactly what I mean."

Once they finish with lunch, Kelly insists on paying. Abigail protests about fifty times before she realizes she's simply annoying him. He leaves a tip on the table as Abigail rises and walks toward the exit. Then, without warning, the door to the kitchen flies open. Kelly reacts by pulling Abigail into his arms and out of harm's way. Frightened, she gasps as the heavy wooden door narrowly misses her. The young dishwasher boy profusely apologizes as he tries balancing the large stack of plates in his arms.

Kelly speaks for her, "It's okay, but be more careful."

Abigail, without realizing that the moment has passed, is still wrapped in his arms. She peeks up at him, her face crimson. "Thank you," she whispers.

He releases her rather abruptly. "Don't mention it," he says, pushing open the front door and holding it for her as they step out into what is left of the afternoon sun.

Her eyes adjust as she makes her way toward his car. They climb in without speaking. He fires up the engine and pulls out of the lot.

As they get closer to campus, she finally speaks, "Thank you again, Kelly." He glances at her. "I appreciate your help."

"You're welcome." His expression is sad. "I hope everything with Laura goes okay tomorrow. I'm sure my sister will be around to help you if you need her."

As they pull toward her dorm, droves of students are hiking back up from the field.

Abigail missed the whole game, and a part of her realizes how insignificant this part of her life is. Especially now that her roommate is lying in a hospital bed and the editor of the student paper has died tragically.

He pulls in front of her dorm.

She doesn't want to reach for the handle, but she must. "I, um…I don't know what to say other than thanks again."

"You guys take care."

"We'll try," she says.

"I'll see you around, okay?"

"Yeah, I'll see you around." She gets out, closes the door, and waves as he pulls away. She hates the confusing feelings that shower over her as he leaves.

See you around. But why am I wondering…when?

Four

Misled Actions or Words

The days have proven to be incredibly difficult after Laura arrived home from the hospital. She won't leave the room. She barely eats or showers. It's clear to all their friends that she's suffering from a broken heart. And no one has a clue how to help her heal. The melancholy in the room is stifling, and the darkness from the drawn shades makes what was once a happy place feel like anything but. Laura barely stirs in her bed; some of this is due to the medication they gave her, and the other is just her body's inability to admit another day has passed without her dear friend Travis.

Depression can be like an infectious disease, spreading to those around you when their life, too, is hanging somewhere in the space between happy and sad. Abigail pushes her chair back from the cafeteria table. Once again, she finds herself without Laura as she tosses her napkin on her tray. Another dinner without her friend. Another day of trying to do whatever she can to make Laura feel a little better.

Today was awful since it was Travis's funeral. Abigail had never seen Laura cry the way she did today. And she hopes she never does again.

Abigail puts her tray on the belt and grabs the sandwich she made for Laura in the hopes that some sustenance will help her not feel as lousy as she currently does. As she is departing the cafeteria, she sees some of the football players sitting at their usual table in the back room.

Tank immediately gets up and puts his tray on the belt. As Abigail is about to say hello, he places his hand on her arm. "Can I talk to you—in private?"

Slightly alarmed by his approach, she nods her head as he leads her outside.

"You don't have a coat?" he scolds.

"No, I wasn't planning on standing outside for long."

"Come on. My truck is right here."

She follows him to his dark green Ford F-150 truck. He climbs in and starts the engine. He pulls out onto the main road.

"Um, where are we going?" she asks.

"You'll see."

He pulls his truck off the road after a few miles of driving. "You remember the day I took you here to tell you about Jonathan?" he blurts out. "How I said I would always protect you?" He shifts his body toward her, so he can see her better.

She swallows hard. "Yes. Of course, I remember. How could I forget? Jonathan is the reason you and I are connected…forever," she whispers.

"I have protected you, haven't I?"

She notes the heat in his voice. She swallows hard, fearing this conversation is going in the one direction she is hoping to avoid. "Yes, Tank, you have."

"Then, why, Abby"—his voice rises—"did I have to hear secondhand about the not-guilty verdicts?"

Shit. Double shit. She catches a glimpse of the old Tank. The one who was dark and intimidating, like he used to be their freshman year. She thought they were past this in their relationship. "I'm sorry. I was going to tell you."

"Going to tell me? When?"

Never. I planned to take it to the grave. To spare you the pain that I carry with me. "When I could," she lies.

"Don't you think I should have been the first person to tell?" he barks.

"I was afraid."

"Afraid of what?"

That you'd try and force my hand. "Afraid you'd get upset and fly off the handle."

His eyes grow dark. "Well, now, I *am* upset!"

"I can see that." She tries to come up with an excuse, but she doesn't have one. At least, not the one that is the truth.

"Well, now, what are we going to do?" he asks, obviously agitated as he runs his hands through his shoulder-length blond hair.

"Nothing," she whispers.

"What?!"

"I'm not going to do anything, Tank."

"Why the hell not?!" he says, raising his voice high enough that it could be heard outside the truck.

"Tank, please stop yelling at me," she begs.

"I'm pissed off at you. Am I not allowed to be pissed off at my friend?" he asks in a slightly lowered tone.

"I want to forget all about it. Please, just let me leave this part of my life behind me," she says as her body shrinks into the corner of the truck.

"Behind you? We were the reason he was caught. This school did nothing to protect you. But I did, and you sit here and tell me you're throwing in the towel?! I want the courts to acknowledge the truth—that he attacked you. Plain and simple. It's bullshit, what they did—you know it, and I know it. How can you let them get away with being so reckless with your testimony?!"

With wide eyes, she leans back toward the door.

"Well?"

"Tank, I need to move on."

"No civil suit, no nothing. Just like that? You get to decide that what happened in the courtroom can be cast aside? I'm even angrier with you, Abigail."

"Oh, *Abigail.* So, now, you're going to call me that to stress your point? I think you've made that loud and clear." Tears sting her eyes.

"Don't start to cry," he says harshly.

She can't help it. He's just being cruel to her.

"Take me home, Tank."

"Listen—"

"Now!" she yells, crossing her arms over her chest as she turns to face the window.

I can't talk sense into him when he is like this. History has shown me that. He only wants me to do what he wants, and I won't. I'll never step foot in a courtroom again with anything pertaining to Jeremy Gordon. Never again.

A big guy like Tank doesn't flinch when a girl of Abigail's size yells. He leans into the wheel and turns the key. The engine roars to life. Abigail stares out the window the entire ride back as they wallow in their dislike for one another.

He pulls in front of her dorm. She grabs the food for Laura, and that's when it hits her. Neither Tank nor Nathan has bothered to ask about Laura, the funeral, or anything.

She throws open the car door. "If you see Nathan, tell him to call me."

"Haven't seen him since this morning," he replies through gritted teeth.

Before slamming the door shut, she barks, "Yeah, I know, and thank you to both of you for asking how Laura is. Really appreciate your concern. Today was Travis's funeral. There are more important things going on right now. And now, maybe you know why I haven't told you all of this. I've had other people to worry about. And so should you." She slams his truck door shut. She can hear him yell after her, but she spins on her heel and marches toward the front door.

The two of them are unreal these days. An absent boyfriend too caught up in his popularity to ask about how his girlfriend is doing—or more importantly, his friend Laura. Doesn't he realize how lonely I feel in all of this?

And then there is the other one. How dare Tank yell at me like that! He might have protected me, but that doesn't give him control over my decisions. And where is his trust? Doesn't he trust me enough to make the right choices? But it's clear by his reaction that he's only interested in what he wants. Not what's best for everyone. Typical.

All of the commotion from the prior day made for a terrible night's sleep, which unfortunately caused Abigail to oversleep. And today might be the worst day to miss her alarm, as she has a full day of classes. She rushes toward the Union as quickly as she can while trying to tuck her flannel shirt into her jeans.

Thankfully, the coffee shop is empty.

"Can I have a bagel with cream cheese and a latte, skim, please?" she says.

She rummages around in her bag for her wallet and pays the barista as he places her order on the counter. Putting her jacket on, she slings her bag over her shoulder and rushes to class.

Abigail hurries across campus as the sun is rising in the east. It's going to be a beautiful day but cooler. She's trying to focus on the day ahead and not the night before. Her argument with Tank kept her up most of the night, seething.

That, and the fact that Nathan and I have not been able to connect as much lately. Football practice, classes, studying, and me taking care of Laura.

Poor Laura. She doesn't want anyone around or anyone in our room, especially Colin. I'm playing the part of her boyfriend and her girlfriend. So, that leaves me little time to see Nathan. But she's my priority right now. She has to be.

She enters the science building and heads up the stairs, taking her usual seat near the aisle next to Webber. "Phew," she says, placing her hot coffee down first. "I didn't think I'd make it."

"Ready for another riveting class?" Webber asks with a devilish grin.

His sarcastic wit is refreshing when she needs it most.

"I'm starving and in desperate need of caffeine." Sporting a halfhearted smile, she opens her notebook.

"Don't worry," he says. "Relax, sip. You know I'm an excellent notetaker. Your partner has got your back."

Webber and Abigail have been lab partners for the better part of their collegiate time. They are both the same major and try and take all the core classes together. They just clicked academically from the beginning.

Professor Sparks begins the lecture with the endocrine system in canines. Unable to help herself despite Webber's offer, she jots down every word as she desperately waits for the caffeine to kick in. When she finally glances up, she notices Webber watching her.

Turning toward him, she whispers, "What?"

"You okay?" he asks, glancing at her notebook.

Her notes are scattered and illegible, which he knows is unlike her typically neat and orderly transcripts.

"I'm just tired—that's all."

Professor Sparks clears his throat, and when they both look up, he is staring at the two of them. "A question perhaps?" he says.

"No," she mumbles as her cheeks pink.

Snapping to reality, Abigail forces herself to pay attention, and thankfully, the rest of the class flies by. Before Abigail knows it, Professor Sparks is giving them a few questions to answer for homework.

"I also want to remind you all that Thursday's class will not be meeting in this classroom but rather in the lab, which is located in the basement of the building. If no one has anything else, then the class is dismissed. Have a safe and wonderful weekend."

Abigail walks out of the lecture hall with Webber hot on her heels as she makes a beeline for the little café on campus that sells coffee and quick snacks for on-the-go students in between classes.

"Want a coffee?" Abigail asks.

"No, thanks. I've gotta run to Econ. Call me later, okay?" he says with a sympathetic smile as he pushes his wire-rimmed glasses back up on his nose.

"I will. See you later."

Abigail orders another latte and then wanders over to the Draper building with about fifteen minutes to spare before her next class. She finds a quiet bench in the sun. Sitting down, she is finally able to eat her bagel and sip her second latte. She reaches into her bag and retrieves her sunglasses, placing them on her face. She watches the crowd of students shuffle in and out of the buildings as she enjoys her breakfast in silence.

Moments later, the quiet is broken as loud screeches and laughter are heard nearby. Abigail turns toward the commotion. She notices six long legs strutting down the pathway in perfect succession. There is a definitive bounce to their steps, only allowed by the high-heeled boots they all must have purchased together. Students entering the building they are exiting, men and women alike, stare at the entourage of Barbie-like figures as they continue on without an ounce of care to their surroundings. And then Abigail recognizes Poppy smack in the middle of them.

As Abigail is about to turn her stare as quickly as she can, Poppy lowers her shades, and with a trickle of her polished fingers, she waves at Abigail, all the while moving her lips to her friends, saying, "There's Nathan's girlfriend."

This prompts them to quickly spin their perfectly coiffed heads in her direction.

Abigail briefly freezes, and then with the power of dark sunglasses on her side, she pretends she sees nothing and continues sipping her latte.

When you get a sense in your gut that something isn't right, it usually means something isn't right. She felt that way last night with Tank's reaction and now with just a simple look and a few whispered words by a girl she's very uncertain of.

Poppy acts like a girl who gets exactly what she wants, and my biggest fear is what she wants right now is my boyfriend.

She watches as they gossip and giggle their way across campus like they own the land they're walking on, and Abigail can't help but wonder to herself why Nathan or Tank would hang with girls like that.

They just don't seem like their type of friends, and no sooner does Abigail think this than she sees the girls laugh as someone drops their paper on the pavement and the wind carries the piece away.

Anyone I know would stop to help, but this pack of girls keeps walking on by.

Something begins stirring in Abigail's mind. She is determined, now more than ever, to see individuals by their actions, and therefore, she will never be misled by their words.

Five

Losing More Than the Game

A week later, Abigail waits outside the metal doors of the field house for Nathan. The Hawks lost in the postseason in a dramatic fashion. Therefore, she's expecting the players coming out of the arena will not be happy. This is something she hasn't quite gotten used to as the girlfriend of QB1 because she knows how much winning means to him, and a loss in the final seconds is very tough to swallow.

She stands against the wall, nervously fiddling with her fingers. One by one, they exit the building, many meeting fans or friends, congratulating them on a successful season. Most of them mumble in acknowledgment and head toward their cars.

Abigail sees Tank and Nathan exit through the doors, side by side. Her breath catches while she watches them approach her. She has not spoken to Tank since their verbal altercation in the car after Travis's funeral.

"Hey, Abby," Tank says, barely able to make eye contact.

She can't quite place his tone. It could be displeasure from the loss or from seeing her.

"Hey. I'm really sorry about the game."

"Sucks," Tank mutters.

"You, too," she says to Nathan. "It was a tough loss."

Both downhearted, they simultaneously voice their complaints about the game.

When they have nothing left to remark about, Nathan asks her, "Ready to go?"

"Sure."

"See you later," Tank says as he walks off ahead of them toward his truck with Jessica, his fickle girlfriend, leaning on it.

They literally break up every other week and then get back together. How they've managed to make it this far is anyone's guess.

Nathan and Abigail climb in his car. He pulls out of the parking lot. "Do you want to go home?" he asks.

Unable to place his mood, she replies, "Do you want to be alone?"

"I'm not sure," he admits. "Things have been so strange lately."

"Tell me about it. If I'm being honest, you seem very distant. Is something wrong?"

"With us? God, no," he says, placing his hand on her leg. "I've just been feeling overwhelmed, I guess. It's hard to explain."

Surprised, she says, "I do see that, Nathan, and I'm here for you. But I'll leave it up to you what you feel like doing tonight." Deep down, she's hoping for some time with her boyfriend and to get a break from being in her dorm room with Laura. And in fairness to Laura, she all but begged Abigail to get out of the room, too. To go have some fun and to try and get back to her normal life prior to Travis's passing.

He drives for a minute in complete silence. "You up for going to a party?"

"Are you?"

"Yeah. I think it might be what I need."

"Okay, where to?" she asks.

"I'll park my car, and we can walk."

A little perplexed by this sudden change of plans but not wanting to push him on such a terrible day, she simply answers with a smile. "Sounds good."

He pulls into the student lot on campus, parks, and gets out of his vehicle. He hurries around the front of the car to open the door for Abigail. Once she is out, he locks his doors and then takes her hand as they stroll across campus. They approach a run-down colonial-style house and walk up the stairs. The deep beat of the bass pulsing through speakers gets louder as they enter the front door.

"Who lives here?" she asks.

"Some of my friends from the team."

"I see," she replies with skepticism, having never been to this house before.

The place is packed wall to wall. Abigail is introduced to a few people before they make their way through the crowd toward the bar.

"Are those your friends?" she yells over the music.

"Sort of. One of the guys is a student trainer for the team. He's cool. Come on. Let's get a drink." He cozies up to the bar and orders two beers.

Within moments, there is a high-pitched scream. "You made it!"

Nathan spins around, and Poppy throws her arms around his neck. Abigail watches his cheeks pink and his eyes bashfully lower. He grabs her arm, releasing them off his neck.

Quickly, he turns to Abigail. "You remember my girlfriend, Abby."

With the fakest smile, she says, "Of course, Gabby. Nice to see you."

"It's Abby," he yells over the music.

"Hello," Abigail says, trying desperately not to show how uncomfortable she is.

Poppy grabs a few beers from the bartender. "Follow me. We're over here," she says as she spins around in her skintight Guess jeans and crop top.

"We're?" Abigail whispers to herself.

Nathan, without checking with Abigail, agrees and starts to follow her toward the back corner.

Standing under the speaker near the back, wearing dark sunglasses, is Tank. This gives Abigail an unsettling feeling as neither of them mentioned this party, nor did they seem as though they were in the mood to go out. Nathan receives his usual round of high fives and hugs from everyone. It's never bothered Abigail…until recently. More and more, people are paying attention to him, and this makes Abigail want to retreat away from the limelight. They both weren't into it before, but now, it seems they can't escape it. Abigail takes a big sip of her beer as she waits out all the hellos. She is anything but antisocial, but the manly high fives and hugs belong to the athletes in the group.

Nathan, on the other hand, has no choice, according to him. He's mentioned to Abigail that he's always felt, as QB1, his teammates expect him to be a leader off the field, too. To be the virile athlete who comes into a room and takes center stage. He gets embarrassed when recognized on campus, however, and mostly by the women, but the older guys on the team have told him to just get over it and accept it. There is nothing he can do about it. Embrace it. He seems to be doing that more and more. In the same breath, being popular on campus does come with its perks—there is no debating that. Free coffee, drinks, whatever. Never waiting in line at bars, never waiting in lines, period. The list goes on and on. Tank, too. Heck, all the players. This school loves its athletes.

A few of their friends bring several more beers over and pass them out. Abigail takes another one and observes the cheerleaders and players interact, and it makes her more uncomfortable as she notices how well they all seem to know one another.

This, of course, is news to her.

She finishes her beer and then motions to Nathan that she is stepping away.

This party is way too crowded for me, and I literally know no one. Oh, wait, is that the girl from my Biology class who always asks the same question every single class? Yes, thank God. Maybe she'll recognize me. At least I can chat with her and kill some time away from Poppy and her Barbie army.

A full beer down the hatch and a relatively intelligent chat with my new Biology friend has left me in desperate need for the ladies' room. Ugh, why is the line always so long? she thinks as she ventures toward the bathroom to wait in the dreaded line.

She stands there for five minutes until she hears, "It must be so hard," directly in her ear.

She spins around. "Pardon me?" she says.

"It must be so hard, dating Nathan," Poppy says, her frosted-pink lipstick shimmering in the pale glow of the basement lights.

"Why would you think that?"

"He's so popular. It can't be easy to watch him be the center of attention." Her remarks, while odd, are said with cruelty to them that Abigail does not take kindly to.

"I'm very proud of him. So, no, Poppy, it isn't hard when you love someone like I love him."

"If you say so." She laughs with a flip of her long blonde hair. She motions for Abigail to move. "It's your turn."

Abigail turns and sees the bathroom door is open. As she walks in, she can hear Poppy yell, "Don't worry; I won't bang on the door."

With tense shoulders, Abigail hurries in the bathroom, and then as she pulls open the door, she notices Poppy is not in line.

Did she get in line simply to bug me?

As she nears the group in the corner, she catches Nathan's eye as he stands with Poppy and some of her friends. He motions for her to join him, and as she is about to approach him, there's a tug on her arm.

A deep voice says, "Can I talk to you?"

She looks up at Tank hovering over her with his sunglasses still on. "Only if you take off those glasses."

"Fine." He lifts them off his face and rests them on his head.

"What's up?" she asks, not masking her agitation.

"Did you change your mind about the lawsuit?"

"No, Tank. And I'm not going to."

"I think you should."

"I'm aware of that."

"What's with the attitude?" he barks.

Me? Are you serious?

She'd never admit it, but being around them all the time might be getting old for her. Tank seems to think he can tell her what to do, and neither one of them has asked about Laura. And the worst part of this terrible evening is being around their cheerleader friends.

They're not my friends, and I don't think I care for them. Quite honestly, Poppy's nasty to me and then as sweet as pie to Nathan. Classic.

"I'm pissed off, too, Tank. You tend to be adamant about your feelings in all of this, but you don't seem to acknowledge mine."

He laughs. "Is that so?"

She straightens up, brushing her hair back off her shoulder. "It feels that way."

His eyes soften as he asks, "You think I don't care about your feelings?"

"I didn't say that. But you don't seem to respect my opinion."

"Jesus, Abby. All I do is think about your feelings. What is right for you, and how I can help. How do you not realize that by now?"

"Tank, you've barely spoken to me. You don't say hello. You haven't called me in the last few days, nor have you asked how Laura is doing. What am I supposed to think?"

Frustrated, he asks, "Can we talk about this when we are not at a party? I think you and I should do that."

"You brought it up." She pauses and takes a sip of her beer. She can feel the wall between them going up and hates more than anything that it is happening to them. "Where's Jessica?"

"I dropped her off at the dorm."

She cocks her head. "She didn't want to come?"

"Not really."

"Huh."

"What?"

"Why didn't she want to come?"

Glancing around the crowded room, Tank says, "This scene isn't really her thing."

"And what scene is that exactly?" Abigail asks.

"This." He motions to all the girls surrounding them.

Abigail's skin crawls. "I see. So, you'd rather be here with *them*?"

"No," he huffs. "I'd rather be here in general. To get my mind off the fact that our season is over."

Abigail peeks over at Nathan, still surrounded by Poppy and her friends, and shakes her head. "I get it."

Following her gaze, Tank chimes in, "Listen, you know he's only into you, but you had to think this would happen. You can't let it bother you."

"Easier said than done. There is something about them—*her*—that I don't trust."

"It's harmless flirting," he says.

"Easy for you to say."

He places his arm around her shoulders and squeezes. "Hey, the holiday break is almost here. And before you know it, all this crap will be done for the rest of the year."

Again, easy for you to say.

Across the room, Poppy leans into Nathan's ear. "What's the deal with those two?"

"What two?" he asks.

"Abby and Tank. They always seem like they are in some deep conversation, and from where I'm standing, they look to be in the throes of a lovers' quarrel."

"What? That's ridiculous." He leans away from her, visibly agitated.

"Look at them."

Nathan peers over toward the two as they appear to be arguing. He watches with a different lens, but quickly, he shakes his mind free. "They're good friends. Nothing wrong with that."

"I suppose you're right. Having friends of the opposite sex is what college life is all about. It's good to have another perspective in your life. Wouldn't you agree?" Her smile, while beautiful, does show signs of a more sinister disposition.

But regardless of her expression, he can't argue with the importance of friends. "Unquestionably."

"Like us." She laughs as she links her arm in his.

After Abigail witnesses Poppy link arms with Nathan, she decides that she needs to step away and get some fresh air. "Hey, I'm going to the bathroom. I'll be right back," she lies to Tank.

"Sure."

Abigail spins on her heel and heads straight for the front of the house. She steps onto the porch and breathes a sigh of relief. The tension in her body is undeniable, and she contemplates continuing to walk right down the steps and back to her dorm.

"Didn't expect to run into you."

Abigail whips around as Kelly steps out of the front door and onto the porch. "Oh, hey. I didn't see you before."

I wish you didn't always see me so vulnerable. But then again, you seem to be right there when my friend card is empty.

"I know," he replies with a killer smile.

"How—I mean, who do you know here?"

"One of my old floor mates from the dorm lives here."

"I see."

"And you?"

She sighs. "No one, really. One of the student athletic trainers for the football team lives here."

"Yeah, that's Mike. Nice guy. And I heard about the big loss. Too bad."

"It was a tough one."

"Are they here, celebrating a great season or wallowing in the loss?" he asks with a chuckle.

She smiles for the first time in hours. "I'm not sure what they are doing."

He steps closer. "Why are you out here, in the cold?"

She pauses, considering how much she should say. "I needed some air."

With a sympathetic glance, he adds, "What were you arguing with the big guy about?"

"How did you know that?"

"I saw you."

She tips her head. "You were spying on me?"

"No. I was going to say hello, but I noticed you were in a rather deep conversation."

She stares down the street, her mind filled with thoughts. So many that she can't think of one word to utter.

"We don't have to talk about it," he says.

A crisp wind blows across the porch. She shudders. He takes off his flannel and wraps it around her shoulders. This startles her. He stands before her, wearing only a T-shirt. His muscles push the limits of cotton against his skin.

"Now, you'll be cold," she says. She can smell his scent on the shirt before she can feel the warmth. Subconsciously, she breathes in deeply, and the splash of aftershave mixed with soap hits her nose.

"I'm fine. But are you all right?"

She knows the decent thing to do when he is being so kind is to answer him. "Tank knows about the not-guilty verdict, but unfortunately, with everything going on with Laura, he found out before I could tell him. He was not happy about that. And we don't see eye to eye on how to handle it, moving forward."

He tips his head. "Ouch. That can't be easy."

She sips her beer. "No, it's proving to be anything but. It's driving a wedge between us."

"Go with your gut. You guys are coming at it from two different angles, and you must do what you think is right. I mean, if I had advice to give, that's what I'd do," he says with a slight laugh.

"Right, but only if you had advice to give." She smiles.

His eyes get wide as the moon overhead reflects off her face. She seems to light up in his presence.

"What?" she asks, touching her cheek.

"Oh, nothing. It's just the moon is beautiful tonight. Wouldn't you agree?"

She chuckles. "My middle name is Luna, so I tend to always think the moon is quite spectacular."

She could have sworn that she heard his breath catch when she spoke.

"Abigail Luna—how different."

"Different?"

"Yes, in a good way."

"It's a long story."

"You can tell me someday." His expression dims. "But I did want to ask you, how is Laura? Alex mentioned she's struggling, as I imagined she would."

"She's okay. Hanging in there, but it's going to take her some time to heal. I think she's finding the right people to help her, so I feel good about that. Thanks for asking." Abigail places her hand on the railing and accidentally touches his. "My God, you're cold!" she barks. She pulls the flannel off her shoulders. "While I appreciate this, it won't be at the expense of you freezing."

He laughs, and as he is about to pull his shirt on, the door opens.

"There you are," Nathan says.

They both turn and watch as he approaches.

"It's chilly out. You okay?" Nathan asks.

"Yes, I'm fine. Um, Nathan, this is Kelly, Alex's brother."

An oddness hits her as Abigail watches the two of them exchange their first words.

"Hey, man," Kelly says, extending his hand to shake Nathan's.

"Hey, Kelly. Nice to meet you. I see your sister around quite a bit."

"I would imagine so," he says, giving Abigail a sideways glance. "Anyway, I was going to head back in." He slips on his shirt as Nathan watches with a confused expression.

"You're brave to be wearing just a T-shirt." He chuckles.

"Yeah, something like that. I'll see you around. It was nice meeting you." He steps back through the doorway.

"Come on. Let's get back inside."

"Nathan, wait." She pulls on his hand to stop him.

"You okay?" he asks.

"Are you?"

"I've had better days than today, but there is nothing I can do to change it, except work harder."

It wasn't quite what she was asking, but since he answered so honestly, it does make her wonder if all her strange thoughts are merely in her head. Confused by his popularity. Insecure by her own misfortunes lately. Taken aback by her friendship with Kelly. Saddened by the heartache her roommate lives with. Many of these contributing factors could play a role in her mood swings. At least she's willing to admit that.

What she won't admit is that she can't handle the attention he gets from Poppy. She senses when someone is on a mission.

But I don't know if I have the energy for another battle in my life.

Six

Second Year, Second Semester

Winter break was agonizing for all the girls on the sixth floor of Willis Hall. With so much going on at school, it proved difficult to be away and relax when there was still so much work to be done.

Abigail went home and spent as much time as possible with her best friend, Rebecca. She was able to get in a little skiing, too, when she wasn't volunteering at the local animal shelter, like she had been doing for the past three years. It's something that has always been near and dear to her and an obvious reason why she wants to study veterinary medicine. Spending her days caring for the animals is the best medicine for not thinking about her drama at school. Caring for anything without a voice can put lots of trivial things into perspective rather quickly.

Nathan was able to visit her for New Year's Eve. Being away from school seemed to be the recipe for their happiness. This renewed sense made her eager to return to school in the hopes that the second semester would be far better than the first.

Laura asked for a leave of absence from the station for the break and opted to go home to Stockbridge instead of staying at school and working. She wanted to continue her mission with the news by working with Travis's right-hand man, Wolfie, but she needed a break first.

After that, they returned to school.

Abigail convinces Laura to leave the dormitory to help her get a few extra provisions for their room before the semester starts. The bags under Laura's eyes are a telltale sign that time is not healing her wounds despite her outward attempt at pretending to be "normal." Whether that is for Abigail's sake alone, it's hard to tell so soon upon returning to school.

Abigail and Laura rush into the Union as a whip of cold air hit them. The Union is packed with students getting ready for the spring semester. Laura pulls her baseball hat down tight, shielding her identity as they enter the student store.

Immediately, Abigail gasps.

"What?!" Laura whispers.

Hanging above the student merchandise section is a massive poster of Nathan in his football uniform.

"Oh no. Did you know about this?" she asks.

Abigail can't take her eyes off the life-sized photo above her head. The one of her boyfriend *and* Poppy in her cheerleader uniform, draping her pom-poms over his shoulder.

She chokes out, "No, he never mentioned it."

Laura places her arm around her shoulders. "Look, we can go shopping later, okay?"

"Yeah, I want to get out of here."

They exit the Union door and wander back along the brick sidewalk toward their dormitory.

"So, what's going on?" Laura asks.

"I feel like something is up with them. I can tell by the way she acts around him that she likes him."

"Duh," Laura says.

"What?"

"Abigail, he's the star quarterback and named captain for next year. He's bound to get attention."

"So, what do I do?"

"If I were you, I'd ask him why he didn't tell you about the posters with her and go from there."

"How can I ask him without coming off as insecure and jealous?"

"You might not be able to, but at least he'll know how you feel, right?"

"Maybe I'm afraid I'll get my answer, and it won't be what I want to hear," Abigail says.

"Abigail, I very much doubt that. In fact, why don't you ask him right now?" Laura peers over Abigail's shoulder, and as Abigail herself slowly turns, her heart rate increases as she watches him walk toward his dorm. "Nathan!" Laura yells.

Abigail hits her on the arm.

"It's now or never," she whispers.

Nathan stops and looks in their direction. Abigail waves as he catches her eye. She swallows hard as the image of him and Poppy rushes over her while he jogs in their direction.

"Hey!" he says with a killer grin. "Laura, how are you doing?"

Laura gives him a hug. "I'm okay. I guess. Did you have a good winter break?"

"It was okay. How was yours?" he says with an empathetic smile.

"Same, I think. It depends on the day, I guess," Laura says.

"I know. I went through lots of ups and downs the first year after my mom passed away," Nathan says. "These things take time." Nathan pats Laura on the arm and then leans in and kisses Abigail on the cheek. "How's my girl?"

At a loss for words, she just nods. This catches his attention immediately.

But before he can speak, Laura interjects, "Hey, I've got to run. I'll see you guys later." She takes off toward their dorm.

"Everything all right?" he asks.

"Yes, of course," she lies.

He takes her hand and says, "I was going back to my room. Have some time to hang?"

"I'd like that."

"Good."

They walk in silence to his dormitory. The entire time, Abigail searches for a way to start the conversation, but her foolish emotions run rampant.

I have to give him the benefit of the doubt that he just forgot to tell me, right?

They walk up to his room. She is disappointed to see that Webber, Nathan's roommate and one of her dear friends, isn't home. He would've been an easy distraction for them.

Nathan closes the door. He leans up against it as it shuts. "Want to tell me what's bothering you?"

She spins to face him. He grants her a crooked smile. When she doesn't return the gesture, he crosses toward his desk and sits in his chair.

"Sit," he says, pointing to Webber's empty desk chair.

"I'm okay." She steps away.

"Abigail, talk to me," he pleads.

She turns to face him, fighting back her emotions with all her might. "Laura and I were in the Union."

"And?"

"We walked into the bookstore…"

"Yeah…"

"I saw the posters of you…and Poppy."

"Oh." The color drains from his face.

"And I didn't like the way it made me feel."

He rubs his face and moans.

"And I think what bothered me the most is that you never told me about it."

His eyes lower toward the ground. "I screwed up," he admits.

"How?"

"Because I meant to talk about it, and it slipped my mind once the shoot was over. I've done so many of them the past year that it seemed inconsequential…until now."

"Were you afraid to tell me?"

He shakes his head. "I don't know. Maybe…subconsciously…I didn't because I wasn't looking forward to the conversation."

"But this is far worse. For me. Us. Don't you see that?"

"I do."

"To walk in with Laura and have that literally hanging over my head and know nothing about it."

"Yes, I get it. I guess they wanted her in the picture because she was named captain for next year, like me."

Abigail swallows the lump in her throat and then blurts out, "I think she likes you, Nathan."

His eyes grow wide.

"Don't you?" she asks.

"I haven't spent much time thinking about it," he says flippantly.

In a huff, Abigail crosses toward the door.

"Don't go," he begs.

She turns. "Do you like her?" Asking him hurts. And deep down, she realizes he might not admit it if he did. But she took a chance and asked regardless.

"No. We're friends—that's all."

"Friends?" she repeats.

"Yes. We're friends with a lot of the squad. It's kind of how it works."

Feeling stupid, she retorts, "Well, I wasn't clued in on that either. And they're always looking at me."

"Of course they are. Aren't girls always sizing up other girls? Are you surprised by this?"

"Well, now that you put it that way, no, I guess not. But they're just not welcoming. So, it makes me very uneasy, and I feel like I don't belong."

"I can see that, and I'm sorry. But for me, it's hard, too. It's sort of what I have to do on campus—the posters and stuff. You get that, right? It kind of comes with the territory of being on the team."

"They're always around you," she whispers. "And I don't like it, Nathan."

"Abby, are you jealous?" He can't help the smile on his face.

"You think this is funny?" She frowns.

"No." He chuckles. "But I know the feeling. You do remember our freshman year, right? Before I knew about the situation with Tank and Jonathan, I was jealous of him, and it sucked."

He's right. I know it was hard for him. It made a mess out of our relationship, and that is what I fear will happen to us. History will repeat itself. I insisted Tank and I were just friends. Because I meant it. But Nathan doubted it. And we ended up apart.

Her cheeks pink, and with marked frustration, she blurts out, "It does suck. And I feel so stupid and confused."

"Please don't."

"I can't help it. I wish I could. But I think she has a thing for you."

"Really?"

"*Nathan.*"

"What?"

"You honestly think I'm the only person at school who thinks you're hot?"

Now, his cheeks pink. He stutters, "You think I'm hot?"

"Nathan, don't joke."

"I'm not."

She fiddles with her hands, unable to meet his gaze.

"Come here."

She peeks up as he takes her hand, pulling her onto his lap.

"I should have told you about the picture. I can't imagine how that would have made me feel. I'm sorry. I'll do a better job of telling you things."

She leans her head on his shoulder. "It's like we're not as connected lately," she admits.

"I've been busy, and I need to do better and make time for you."

"But I don't want it to be hard."

"It's not. I promise."

She picks up her head. "You'll tell me if it gets to that, right?"

He touches her chin with his fingers and stares directly into her eyes. "I would. I absolutely would."

She sighs. For some reason, she doesn't feel better. But words are words. Actions speak much louder, and with that in mind, she'll have to wait and see.

He leans in and brushes his soft lips on hers, allowing her shoulders to relax as the welcome feeling overcomes her hesitations.

"How about you and I go out to dinner tonight? To our favorite Chinese place?"

She smiles. "I'd like that."

"Good. It's settled." He wraps his arms around her and pulls her toward his trunk for a deep hug. "I love you, Abby."

She breathes in his scent as she closes her eyes. He rocks her gently side to side as they sit in silence, no doubt hoping they can finish the last semester of their sophomore year a little better than it began.

Seven

Are We Friends?

Abigail returns to the dormitory with a heaviness she can't quite place. Despite spending the afternoon with Nathan, there is a continued feeling of nagging at her core.

And simply stated, Poppy is trouble. No matter what Nathan says. Abigail can't shake the feeling she will cause more problems for them.

She lets out an audible sigh, trying to release her stress.

Sensing there is something behind her roommate's demeanor and dying for a distraction from her misery, Laura asks, "Tell me what's going on. This about Nathan?"

Abigail plops into her chair. "Yeah, I talked to him about the posters, and I just feel unsure. He said he forgot to tell me and that he thinks of Poppy as his friend, but it still doesn't sit right with me."

Laura cocks her head and says, "I think you should trust your gut."

Abigail continues, "You're his friend, and Bree, Melissa, Jen, Casey…those are his friends. Not some girl who pines over him and is always touching him and looking for him at parties. I get a bad feeling."

"She ever talk to you?"

"Not really. You can tell she prefers I'm not around. Although at a party once, she made some strange comment to me about how dating someone so popular must be hard for me. It was a weird statement."

"Planting the seed of doubt—that's what she is doing."

"But I trust Nathan."

Laura, trying to remain honest, adds, "He does seem more distracted, so I don't think that's in your mind."

Abigail sighs. "Thank you because for a while there, I was thinking maybe it was."

"When we first met him, he was shy, a little reserved, and definitely not into the *big man on campus* mentality. But that was bound to change. We've all changed, right?" Laura says.

Abigail leans back in her chair and gazes out the window. "You're absolutely right. We've all changed quite a bit, I'd say. Even Tank. I thought he'd gotten past the brooding and tough-guy attitude with me but not when he doesn't get his way. It becomes a one-sided friendship, and that has been hard for me, too. He's one of my best friends. We have such a connection. Or at least, I thought we did."

"He'll come around. He always does."

"I suppose I should sit down with him, too. Talk it out."

"At least then you can say you tried," Laura says.

"True."

"Want my advice about Nathan?"

Abigail tips her head. "Of course I do."

"Don't worry about it until there is really something to worry about. It will drive you crazy, and in the end, our destiny is already determined; we just have to live to get there." And just like that, a tear falls on Laura's cheek.

Abigail leans forward and takes Laura's hand. "Sounds like good advice to me. For both of us."

Laura wipes the wet from her skin. With forced determination in her voice, she adds, "Exactly. Now, I suppose I should put some makeup on if I'm going to face the world."

Abigail and Laura enter the Union the following Tuesday. The first week of classes is always relatively painless. Abigail hasn't stepped foot in the Union since their last attempt to shop, only to be stopped by the large poster of Nathan that hung above their heads. But Laura promised Professor Tucker, the head of the radio station, that she'd meet him for coffee, and Abigail was finally able to make plans with Tank.

"I'm heading to the café to see Professor Tucker. I'll see you later, okay?"

"Sure thing. Enjoy your time with him. I know he'll be so happy to see you."

"Thanks, and good luck with Tank," Laura says.

"Appreciate it." Abigail moseys toward the tables and chairs near the fireplace. She grabs a seat toward the back wall and patiently waits for Tank to arrive. She has been dreading this conversation all day. But on the other hand, she is hoping she can get her best friend back, and they can finally put this behind her.

She pulls out her *Advanced Chemistry* textbook and starts reading the first chapter.

A few minutes pass.

"I thought that was you," a deep voice says.

Abigail looks up from her book, and immediately, her flesh heats up. "Hi, Kelly."

He pulls out the chair across from her. He places a bag on the floor next to him. He's comfortable with her, which is nice but also a tad unsettling.

"You have a nice break?"

She crinkles her face. "Sort of. You?"

"It was okay. I stayed here. It was quiet, but I put in more hours at the garage."

"Garage?"

"Yeah, I work part-time at an auto body shop on Route 20."

"Oh, that's good."

"Gives me play money," he says with a wink. "You studying?"

"Yes, reading, really. I'm waiting for Tank."

"The big guy?"

She leans forward and whispers, "Yeah, we're finally going to talk."

"About the lawsuit—or lack thereof?"

She nods her head.

"You change your mind?" His brow furrows.

She nervously twists a strand of her hair around her finger. "No. But I need to close this conversation in a civilized manner."

Kelly smiles, and Abigail notes her skin prickle as they lock eyes. She looks away.

"When is he meeting you?" he asks.

"Soon. So, what brings you here?"

"I needed to grab a few things for my Contracts Law class. Man, that is a large poster of Nathan they got hanging in there. What's that girl's name in the picture, Pippa?"

Her skin burns red at the thought of the picture. "Poppy." Her lips form in a hard line. "I'm proud of him." Her words sound forced, and she hates that.

"Well, I'm glad I ran into you," he says, easily changing the subject. "My roommate, Tom, and I are having a party this weekend, and I wanted to invite my sister's friends."

His sister's friends?

"I see, well, I'm sure they'd love to go."

He narrows his eyes. She returns an equal stare. The corners of his mouth turn upward. Abigail smiles with her eyes.

"I see what you did there."

"Did you?" She smirks.

"I'm inviting you all as my friends, too."

"Then, I'll consider it."

"I won't hold my breath. But tell the others for me in case I don't see them."

"I will."

He stands. "Maybe I'll see you around."

He turns and marches toward the back doors. Abigail stares ahead, unable to take her eyes off him until Tank steps into her view.

"Hey," he says. "Can we go for a walk?" He peers over his shoulder at the mass of students invading the Union.

"Sure." She stands and puts on her coat. She grabs her bag and follows him out the side door. "Where are we going?"

"You'll see."

She walks alongside Tank to the west end of campus in virtual silence.

Suddenly, Tank comes to a standstill, past Montgomery Hall. He faces her, placing his massive hand on her shoulder. "You remember that night, the night I scooped you up in my arms and carried you back to my dorm, to Nathan's room?"

When she realizes she is standing at the edge of the path where Jeremy Gordon attacked her, a lump forms in her throat. "Of course I remember."

"Nobody, except you and me, knows why I was there that night, watching out for you. We've kept that our secret. But you and I are the only ones to comprehend that had it not been for the bond formed between us after Jonathan's death, the situation could have been far worse."

"I never doubted that."

"Then, why are you unable to fight for what we both know to be true?"

"Tank," she sighs, "I don't have the answer you want to hear."

He takes her hand. "Tell me, please."

With the sting of tears in her eyes, she whispers, "Because I don't have it in me. It's just not me."

"But I'm asking you to try to fight." He gently squeezes her hand.

She looks up at her friend. "Can you try to understand where I'm coming from?" she asks. "It's over. We have no other options." *And therefore, I could never tell you I had a choice; you'd never have let it go. And I have to. It's for the best. For all of us.*

"I have tried, but it doesn't make sense to me."

"Isn't the fact that Jeremy Gordon was caught and found guilty on all the other charges good enough for you? Is this about Jonathan? Because no one knows but us, Tank. Isn't that enough? That *we* know?"

"No. No, it's not. It negates everything he did to bring us together. And I thought you'd feel the same."

"I'm sorry, but I don't, and I don't see it that way at all," she replies.

He drops her hand and steps back; his appearance is wretched.

"Tank, what are you doing?"

"I—I think that maybe right now, I need some space."

"Space?"

His silver eyes redden as he whisks his blond hair behind his ear. He glances toward the sky, and then with the saddest expression, he says, "From us."

Abigail gasps. She's at a loss for words. She was not expecting him to leave her in her time of need. Nathan is drifting away. Tank is, too. Laura is in agony, and Abigail suddenly feels terribly alone. Jeremy Gordon continues to cause her pain, which is exactly what she thought him going to jail would end. But his actions continue to play a role in her tortured relationships.

A tear falls on her cheek. "You'd leave me?" she chokes out.

Tank, never being the best at reining in his emotions, turns to leave. "You had your time to think about what you wanted. Now, I need my time."

Abigail tries to grab his arm, but he pulls away. She's stupid for wanting him to stay, knowing he doesn't want to be near her. This is a first for them, for her. Her guardian is stepping down, and never in her wildest dreams did she imagine that he would.

"Don't put Nathan in the middle, okay?" he says coolly.

Her eyes widen. "I wouldn't."

"Good." Visibly agitated, he storms off back toward campus, leaving Abigail heartbroken.

She stands where he left. Her legs won't allow her to move. The hard thud of her heart within her chest is all she can feel.

He left me? What does that mean for us? I have no idea what to do next.

She finally turns and rushes back to her dormitory. She knows exactly where to go to get away. She knocks on Bree's door.

"Come in!" Bree yells.

Abigail enters. "Hey, can I borrow your car?"

Bree, never flinching, says, "The keys to the Benz are on my desk."

"Thanks." Abigail goes to the other side, grabs them, and turns to head out.

"Need help?" Bree asks.

Abigail stops dead in her tracks. "No, I'll be back later."

"Take all the time you need," she replies.

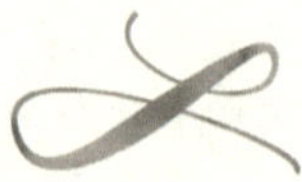

Abigail finds herself driving beyond campus, past the hospital, and for another ten minutes. She passes the sign that reads *Diesel Food*, and before she realizes it, she is doing a U-turn and entering the parking lot. She is half-expecting to see Kelly's Mustang in the parking lot and hates, particularly now, that she's disappointed it is not.

He's been a neutral party to talk to over the past few months. I sure could use that now. Tank told me not to involve Nathan, so I won't. That's the least I can do.

She climbs out of Bree's Mercedes and enters the front door of the establishment. She asks to be seated near a window. She sits and stares out across the road, watching the cars pass by. The waitress comes over.

"Can I get ya something?" It's the same waitress she had when she was here with Kelly. Feeling brazen, she replies, "Carbon Calm."

"Coming right up," she says, never asking for ID.

Moments later, Abigail sips on her drink as she continues to stare out the window. Her mind races with questions, one being why she is not more outraged at Tank. If anything, a great sadness washes over her, not anger. But why?

Is it because I never once considered how my decision would make him feel? He was watching me that night because of Jonathan. It's so much deeper than anyone realizes. I should have sat down and told him everything. I should have consulted him. But I didn't. And he's hurt. But then again, it was my decision, right? I couldn't go through it all again and risk the same outcome. I know in my heart that I did the right thing. But maybe now that I've lost him, I can see that I went about it the wrong way.

"This must be my lucky day," a deep voice says.

Abigail is yanked back to reality from her thoughts. Kelly stands before her.

"What, um…what are you doing?" she asks.

"Was going to order takeout. Then, I saw you."

"Oh."

"Mind if I sit?" he asks.

"I guess you can, sure."

He crinkles his brow as he lowers into the seat. "That was not a resounding welcome." He chuckles.

"I'm sorry. I'm not very good company right now."

"Who says you are otherwise?" He laughs as he gestures to the waitress.

Abigail smiles for the first time in hours. "Got me again."

"I'm gathering by you sitting here alone, things didn't go well with your friend."

"You could say that." She takes a big gulp of her drink. "You could also say that it went terribly, and I'm pretty sure he doesn't want to see me anymore."

"Friends, they come and go. Sometimes, they come back."

"Speaking of, it's rather uncanny that you always seem to be right around the corner in the moments when I could use one, don't you think?"

He smiles. "I guess you're just lucky—that's all."

She huffs, "Not so much today. I mean, with, Tank, that is. It's complicated."

He cocks his head. "How so?"

"Tank and I, we have history."

His eyes glimmer. "History?"

Her face flushes. "Not like that. It's complex, he and I, and—"

"I get it. Say no more."

She's relieved not to have to explain the saga that is her friendship with Tank, and her shoulders relax. She takes another sip of her drink.

"What does Nathan have to say about all of this?"

Her shoulders tense back up toward her ears. "Um, he doesn't know about it."

"Really?"

She thinks of Tank's comment about not putting Nathan in the middle. It did give her pause. The least she can do is not confuse things further by involving her boyfriend and the issues she's having with one of their best friends.

"Yeah, for now." She averts her eyes.

"Interesting."

"It's best for now. Meaning right now. He's busy with stuff, too, and—"

He cuts her off, "He seems to be busy a lot."

"He is."

He puts up both his hands. "I meant nothing by it."

She takes a big gulp of her drink. "Can we change the subject?"

"How old are you anyway?" he asks, eyeing her drink.

"I turn twenty soon."

"Soon?"

"Yes."

"Care to fill me in?"

She laughs. "Your sister could fill you in if you really want to know."

"I get it. Shy about your birthday. I won't ask again."

The waitress brings over two drinks and places one in front of Kelly and one in front of Abigail.

"Thank you," he says. When the waitress steps away, Kelly picks up his drink and says with a huge smile, "To my birthday."

"What?!" Abigail laughs.

"We're not celebrating yours." His matter-of-fact remark makes her return a smile.

"No, we're not," she notes with a clink of her glass with his.

He takes a sip. "How'd you get here?" he asks.

"I borrowed Bree's car."

"That's nice of her."

"Yeah, she's good like that."

"Let me guess…a girl like her, at this school, money…does she drive a Jaguar?"

Abigail laughs. "No, a Mercedes."

He whistles. "Nice."

"It sure is. A real beauty."

His eyes widen when she says *beauty*, and Abigail must turn her eyes down to the table. The way he looks at her makes her uneasy, to say the least.

Kelly finishes his drink and orders his takeout.

Abigail excuses herself to use the restroom, but when she comes back, he is standing near the back, holding his food.

"The check is all set. Consider it an early birthday present."

"Thanks, Kelly."

He nods his head and walks toward the door. She stands there, like an idiot, not sure whether to follow him or let him leave without saying good-bye. She finds her legs following him out the door and toward the parking lot. His car is parked next to Bree's.

"This it?" he asks. "It's nice."

"Yeah, this is it."

He opens his car door. "Well, glad I ran into you, but I have to study for my Constitutional and Business Law class. It's a big one." He starts to climb in.

"Kelly, wait." She walks around the car toward his driver's side. "I, um, just wanted to say…"

"Yeah?"

"Thanks. For the drinks and advice…I do appreciate it."

"Anytime. And like I said before, maybe I'll see you this weekend." And with those few words, he's in his car, turning the engine to life, and he pulls out but not before granting her one final glance good-bye.

She stands in the empty spot where his car once was, and wonders how this day could be any more confusing than it is right now. She senses the loss of one friend yet recognizes the addition of an unlikely friend.

Are Kelly Conrad and I truly friends? It sure seems that way these days, considering he knows more about my life than anyone else does. Including my own boyfriend.

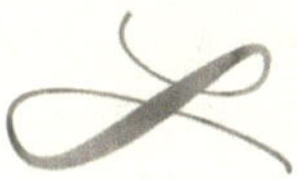

Abigail hears a knock on her door. "Come in!"

"Where've you been? I was worried." Nathan's tone is rather alarming as he steps into her room.

"I went for a ride—that's all."

"But Bree said you left hours ago."

"I needed to clear my head." She scans his face, wondering if he's privy to her conversation with Tank. *Did Tank tell me not to run to Nathan, so he could?*

"Okay, I just got concerned. I think Bree was, too."

"Well, I was driving her car. Can you blame her?" She chuckles.

He releases his breath and then looks her over. His eyes narrow. "Have you been drinking?"

"What? No?" she lies.

"Oh, thought maybe you were out with Tank."

Her skin crawls. "Nope."

"I ran into him on my way over, and he seemed a bit tipsy."

Oh, Jesus. Here we go again. Tank finding his feelings at the bottom of a glass.

"Yikes. But you know Tank."

Nathan shrugs his shoulders. "Anyway, I was thinking, for your birthday, we could go out for dinner at the Italian Farmhouse."

She smiles. "I do love that restaurant. That sounds really nice."

"Then, there's a party at the Ridge after. All the guys would love to see you. And we have that recruit, Dylan, coming in, too."

She tries not to freeze or react. A party at the football house does not sound that enticing in the moment, but instead of shaking the tree, she nods her head.

"Awesome."

He takes her hand and drags her over toward her desk. He takes a seat and pulls her onto his lap as he does. His size allows her to fit her slender frame within his. He envelops her in his long arms and pulls her into his chest. She rests her head on his shoulder.

"Listen," he begins, "I know things have been off lately."

"Uh-huh."

He tightens his embrace. "The fact that you needed to clear your head tells me there's more going on in that beautiful brain of yours than you're letting on."

She sighs. *If I told you right now that the one and only thing I ever wanted was to be happy, you'd assume that means you don't make me happy, but you do. But what is happening around us is not making me happy. We're drifting. I need more from you, and I don't know how to ask for it because it's not just more time together that we need; it's the feelings from our time together that needs to be better, different, like it used to be.*

"If I am the reason for any confusion you might be having, I want to say that I'm sorry and that I'm always here for you."

"I wish we had more time together, Nathan. Didn't things used to be less"—she searches for the right word—"complicated?"

He kisses her on top of her head. "I know what you mean. But we can get through this. I know we can." He places his fingers gently under her chin.

His eyes locking with hers, he says with a tender voice, "I love you, Abby Luna Price."

Her heart recognizes the connection to his, and without hesitation, she says, "I love you, too, Nathan."

Eight

Happy Birthday

"Happy birthday, Abigail," Laura bellows, waking her from her slumber.

Abigail turns her head and faces her roommate, who is genuinely smiling for the first time in months. "Thank you," she replies sheepishly.

"I got you a bagel and coffee to start your day off right."

Abigail swings her legs over the edge of her bed. "You shouldn't have."

"For the world's best roommate, of course I should have."

"Thank you. I love you, too. How did you sleep last night?"

"Better than I have in a few weeks. So, I'll take any small improvement." Laura turns to her mirror to finish fixing her hair. "You have dinner plans with Nathan and then the Ridge, right?" She pauses and turns to face her. "You definitely have to go?"

Abigail puts up her finger. She takes a big sip of her coffee and savors the taste as she swallows. She peers up at Laura. "I told Nathan I'd go with him. You guys are all going with Alex to Kelly's party?"

"Yeah. Kind of have to. We were all invited, and it means a lot to Alex that we go to her brother's."

"I'll see what I can do, but I'm not promising anything."

"I get it. We can always celebrate tomorrow with a nice, greasy breakfast at the diner."

"You seem chipper today," Abigail adds.

"I'm trying. Some days are better than others. And today, I have a reason to be happy. It's *your* birthday!"

Abigail smiles. "I'm glad. It's nice to see you smile."

"It feels good."

Abigail stands and wraps her arms around Laura, squeezing her tight. "See you after classes, okay?"

"Sounds good."

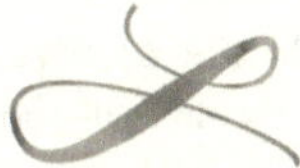

Abigail painstakingly puts on her makeup. Her hand trembles as she tries to apply eyeliner.

Why am I nervous? she thinks. *Is it because I actually get some uninterrupted time with my man? Or do I fear he might be slipping away and tonight will be a telltale sign of it all going south? So much pressure placed on one evening.*

Nathan should be arriving any minute to pick her up. The butterflies in her stomach are doing nothing to help quell her jitters. She examines her outfit again. Skintight dark jeans, a black silk blouse, and black ankle boots. She grabs Bree's red leather bomber jacket she loaned her and shoves a few more items into her purse after she applies her dark red lipstick. Too nervous to sit down, she paces her room. Catching a glimpse in the mirror again, she fiddles with her hair.

Do I look okay? More importantly, will he think so?

The girls are down in Casey and Alex's room for a little pre-party. She flips on her radio; Colin's announcing the next song. Finally, there's a soft knock on her door. She leans forward and turns the handle. When she opens the door and locks eyes with Nathan, her world comes to a standstill. His hair is slicked back from his shower, and he is wearing a fitted button-down shirt, black pants, and a long black wool coat. He's gorgeous.

The feeling is mutual because his eyes enlarge as he takes her in. "You're beautiful," he gushes.

"So are you." She can finally exhale.

He steps toward her, closing her door behind him. With conviction, he approaches and seductively wraps his arms around her waist. Pulling her toward him, he presses his full lips onto hers. Her heart rate skyrockets as he leans her back on the wall, pressing his body firmly against her frame. She braces her arms on his pecs as he kisses her again and again. Then, he stops and rests his head on her forehead.

"Too bad we have reservations," he breathes.

"It sure is." She smiles.

"Come on, before we're late." He takes her hand as they exit her room, out the side stairwell, and toward the student parking lot.

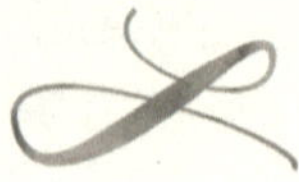

Two hours later, a sated expression adorns her face as they walk hand in hand out of the restaurant. "Dinner was wonderful. Thank you."

"You're welcome, Abby. Happy birthday." He smiles as he opens the car door for her.

She stares out the window as he drives the car back toward campus. Parking in front of the Ridge, they can hear the loud beat of the grunge music before even opening their doors.

"You're still cool with coming to this party, right?"

"Yeah, of course I am. I wish my friends could come, but I understand."

"Come on," he says with a wide grin. "We'll make the best of it."

She smiles in return as she opens her car door. He takes her hand as they enter through the front door. Many of the partygoers turn to see who is walking in.

Then, despite her gesturing *please don't*, many of them holler, "Happy birthday," to her, and her skin flames bright crimson.

"See, told you they'd want to see you," he says, placing a quick peck on her cheek. "Come on. Let's get a drink."

He pulls her through the crowd toward the kitchen. As they enter the dimly lit kitchen, Abigail is struck by the scene in front of her. The room is filled with what appears to be the entire cheerleading squad and a group of players playing some drinking game. The sexual tension in the room could be cut with a knife; it's so thick.

"I see things are getting rowdy," Nathan says in her ear.

Abigail has no retort. But what she wants to ask him is if it's always like this when she is not around.

"Let's go to the bar, and we'll get out of here."

No sooner do they move into the room do they hear a screech and then, "Nathan! You're here!"

Poppy comes running over, slightly inebriated, and whisks her arms around Nathan for a desperate hug. Nathan still has his hand locked with Abigail's. But quickly, Abigail drops her hand out of embarrassment.

Nathan steps away from Poppy and places his arm around Abigail's shoulders.

But as soon as he does, Marcus, the team captain, comes over, "There's the birthday girl!" He gives Abigail a big hug, lifting her up as he does.

"Thanks, Marcus."

Poppy interrupts, "Wait, it's your birthday? Oh my God. Girls, the birthday girl needs a shot!" She takes her hand and pulls her toward the table.

Someone is already pouring a shot as they approach. "Nathan, we need you for this!" She motions for him to come over.

Curious more than anything, he walks up behind Abigail. "What's up?"

"Here." She hands Abigail a shot of tequila. "Now," she says as the crowd gathers closer, "lick his neck."

"What?" Abigail replies, obviously uncomfortable, as all eyes are on them.

Poppy rolls her eyes. "You have to lick his neck." She moves Nathan in between them.

Nathan, not helping, looks at Abigail with a sheepish grin and then shrugs his shoulders. "So you can put salt on him."

Abigail freezes.

"Here," she barks, "I'll show you." She puts her hand on Nathan's shoulder and starts to spin him toward her.

Something in Abigail snaps, and before she knows it, she puts her hand up over Poppy's and replies, "No need to. I got it."

She reaches up on her tippy-toes, licks Nathan's neck, salts it, licks it again, and then tosses back the shot. She looks up at Nathan. Between his lips is the lime. He is grinning ear to ear. Hastily, she leans forward and tries to take the lime from his mouth, but he whisks it away and kisses her instead. The whole room erupts in applause, much to Abigail's chagrin. She tries to smile as he finally gives her the lime, but she can't help but notice Poppy storm out of the room, like a dejected teenager.

"Now, let's get that drink." He laughs as he approaches the bar, leaving Abigail standing, dumbfounded.

After he hands her a drink, she asks, "Can I talk to you?"

"Shoot."

"Someplace private."

He tips his head and then notes her stern expression. He says, "Sure. Yeah, of course. Follow me."

They walk into the living room, and then he takes her hand and escorts her down the hallway to an empty bedroom.

He closes the door behind them. "What's up?"

Abigail releases her frustrated breath. "No idea what I might have to say?"

He steps closer. "No. What's going on?"

"Nathan, the scene, just now."

He averts his eyes and takes a big sip of his drink. "Well, it's…I don't know what to say."

"She screams when you come in and practically throws herself at you. She—and I can't believe I'm going to say this—tries to lick your neck, and you didn't seem like you planned to stop her."

He immediately puts his hand up in protest. "Now, wait a second. I didn't do anything to provoke her."

"It's not the point, Nathan. Do you really not see how she acts around you?"

Shrugging his shoulders, he asks, "What am I supposed to do?"

Abigail stares at him, trying to find the words but all she feels is stupid. Stupid for making a big deal out of what happened, but it bothers her, and she wishes now more than ever that it didn't. "No clue. Maybe tell her to go away?"

He steps closer. "For the record, I felt weird about what happened. And would I have *let her* lick my neck? *No*, of course not. I would have stepped away or something. I'm glad it didn't get to that. And"—he raises his eyebrows—"I was glad you pushed her aside…"

"Well, I'm not going to let her do whatever she wants."

He smiles. "I won't either. Deal?" He takes her hand.

Feeling like this conversation could go in circles, she decides to drop it. "Okay, deal."

But mark my words, Nathan, that girl is one hundred percent into you. And she makes no bones about it. But I refuse to let her ruin my birthday. She'll not get that satisfaction from me.

He pulls her into him and hugs her tightly. "Good. Now, we are here to celebrate your birthday, right?"

"Yep," she mumbles.

"What?" When she doesn't speak, he adds, "Come on. Tell me."

"Seeing her storm away like that and with all her friends here and none of mine, I feel out of place. I want to see Marcus, Jason, and the guys, but Tank is mad at me, Poppy hates my existence, and I just…"

"Want to leave. I get it."

She steps back. "You do?"

"Yeah, of course. I knew this wasn't your top choice tonight, but being without you wouldn't have felt right," he says.

"I know."

"But we had a great dinner together, and it sounds to me like you need your girls."

Abigail smiles. "I would like to see them."

"We have that new recruit here tonight, and I'm supposed to show him a good time. I feel bad, but I should stay. It's only for an hour, maybe two? Why don't you come to my dorm later, say midnight? It'll give us some time alone together."

"I totally get it."

"You sure? I feel badly."

"Don't. I promise I'll be there at midnight."

"Good. I won't be late. It'll just be you and me."

"I'd like that."

"And I promise I won't let anyone else lick my neck…well, maybe not until later." He gives her a sexy grin.

Her heart quickens. "You'd better not, Nathan Ryan."

"Come on. It's time to see your friends."

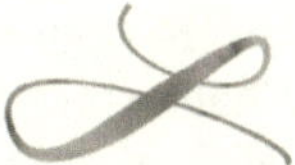

Abigail doesn't bother knocking on the door. The music is so loud that they wouldn't hear her anyway. She opens the door, nearly knocking into a few people squished behind it. The party is packed wall to wall. She maneuvers her way through the living room, desperately searching for any sign of the girls. She stops at the table off to the side and pours herself a drink. She hears a screech and immediately spins to see it's Laura.

"You're here!"

"Yes! Yes, I am!" she yells over the music.

"Damn, girl, you look hot tonight," Laura announces.

Abigail blushes. "Thanks. Bree loaned me her jacket."

"Oh, it's not the jacket!" She laughs.

"Thanks, Laura," she bashfully replies. "You look amazing, too."

"I can't tell you how good it feels to be among the living. Even if this wave is only short-lived, I'm riding high!" she hollers as she pours herself another drink.

"Where is everyone?"

"Downstairs—not as loud. Follow me!"

Abigail follows Laura through the crowd and toward the basement stairs. As they descend, the noise lessens as the music pumping down here is at a much more tolerable decibel. It's still crowded, but not nearly as much.

Standing at the bottom of the stairs, leaning up against the wall, is Kelly. There's a tall brunette pressed against him with her hand clasping the edge of his shirt. They're conversing as Abigail steps on the last step. He looks up and catches her eye. A lump forms in her throat, and uneasiness passes through her. Abigail smiles, but then he nuzzles into the girl's ear and whispers something, to which she tips her head back and giggles. Abigail looks away from them and continues to follow Laura over to their friends.

He didn't even acknowledge me, which is strange in itself, but seeing him with her, that girl, it makes me feel…I don't know…funny? As in I feel funny about it because I know I shouldn't. Ugh, why is everything so complicated? It's my birthday, and of all the days to not have any complications, it should be today. But I suppose I'm just not that lucky.

The girls are all pleasantly surprised to see her and welcome her with hugs and birthday wishes. Alex—with a bright floral tattoo peeking out of the sleeve of her Luscious Jackson T-shirt, nose piercing, and funky, newly dyed dark brown spiked hair—grabs a bottle of vodka from a back closet and offers up a birthday shot for all of them. As they clink glasses and down the shot, the girls erupt into a quick rendition of the "Happy Birthday" song.

Abigail tries not to look toward her right, where Kelly is standing. It was probably rude of her not to say hello, but something about his reaction to seeing her made her want to recoil. She can't help but wonder if he was whispering about her. Showing up on her birthday alone. Without her boyfriend.

But they don't know the story.

"Where's Nathan?" Maddie asks.

"At the Ridge. A new recruit's here to entertain, and besides, I really wanted to celebrate with you guys." She smiles. "I plan to meet up with him later."

"Cool. We're so glad you came," Bree adds. "Loving the jacket on you."

"Thanks for letting me borrow it. And, boy, this party is packed."

"My brother throws a good party, I must say," Alex replies.

The girls chat and drink for another hour until Abigail must venture to find the bathroom. She weaves in and out of the crowd and waits her turn in the line for the bathroom.

Once inside, she touches up her lipstick and takes a good look at herself. Then, she smiles. *I do look good tonight.*

She tries to find her way to the back of the room as more people fill into his house. She gets bumped around as a bunch of big guys come charging in with twelve packs of beer hoisted on their shoulders. She gets jerked again. Before she can say anything, someone takes her hand and pulls her toward the side.

She tries to free herself but hears, "Come this way."

She turns as Kelly motions for her to follow him. He's still clutching her hand as he guides her toward the side hallway.

"Where are we going?" She tries to release her hand.

"They're in here," he says.

"Kelly," she blurts out.

He stops and turns to her. She looks down at his hand, still holding hers. He drops it. "Sorry."

"No, it's just, um…where are you taking me?"

He steps closer to her. "My sister and the others are back here now."

"Oh."

"And happy birthday."

"Thanks," she says and bashfully glances toward the ground.

"I would have said it sooner, but you didn't say hello before." His tone is somewhat scolding.

"I'm sorry about that. You seemed to be…well, in a conversation."

He squares his shoulders. "And that means you can't say hello? I'm trying to understand."

Feeling foolish, she shrugs her shoulders, saying, "You could have said something."

He narrows his eyes at her, and then he gives her a full once-over and blatantly says, "You look hot tonight, by the way."

"Oh, um, thanks," she says, making her forget all about hellos and whatnot. "Bree let me borrow her jacket."

With a laugh, he says, "It's got nothing to do with the jacket, Abigail."

Someone must've turned up the heat in here because a bead of sweat forms on her forehead.

He motions for her to follow him back down the hallway. Before opening the door, he asks, "Where's that boyfriend of yours?"

Quickly, she says, "At a party. I'm meeting up with him later."

He pushes the door open as she passes into the room. "What time?"

She spins to face him. "Midnight. Why?"

"Wondering how long we have you for."

Abigail notices the tall brunette impatiently awaits Kelly on one side of the room, and on the other side of the room are all Abigail's floor mates, waving her over.

"I should go," she says. Peering past Kelly, Abigail adds, "And you'd better get going, too."

Kelly turns to glance behind him, and Abigail slips away to her friends, so they'll stop yelling, "Birthday girl," over and over, embarrassing her to no end.

Abigail doesn't need to convince Bree and Laura to walk her to Nathan's dormitory. They'd had enough of the party, and they were both eager to call it a night.

In front of Boyd Hall, they kiss each other on the cheek.

"Now, go enjoy the rest of your night," Laura says.

Bree, never shy from spitting out the truth, chimes in with, "Yeah, you have fun with that gorgeous boyfriend of yours."

Abigail laughs and then waves to them as she dials Nathan's extension on the call box outside his dorm.

"This'd better be my girlfriend," he answers.

She hits the talk button. "It is."

He buzzes her in.

She arrives on the floor. His door is cracked open a bit when she arrives.

"Nathan?" she whispers.

As she pushes open the door, the soft hum of Mazzy Star fills the room. The same song that was playing the first night they spent together. Smiling as she walks in, she removes Bree's jacket and places it on the chair. Then, she strides to the other side of the divided room. Nathan's lying on the floor on top of sleeping bags with pillows propped up behind him. It reminds her of that evening their freshman year by the cabin. They spent the entire night snuggled in sleeping bags in the back of the OSU football practice van with nothing but the moon above their heads.

"Come here." His silky voice gives her a chill.

"Nathan," she says as she takes his outstretched hand, and he gently pulls her toward him. "This is a nice surprise."

She leans on her side to face him. His eyes dance back and forth, taking in her face as though for the first time.

Brushing her hair off her shoulder, he then delicately traces her jawline. "I'm sorry about the party earlier."

She lowers her lashes. "Don't be. It's over."

"Yeah," he says.

"What is it?"

"It's nothing." He leans forward and starts kissing her neck, up to her jaw, on her cheek, and then presses his lips firmly onto hers. He pulls back. "Happy birthday, Abby."

As his eyes dance over hers, there is an uncertainty in his expression that he can't mask. Abigail wishes he could. But he's too kind to hide it, even from himself.

But Poppy has already taken up too much of her birthday to now enter her alone time with Nathan. So, instead of asking him to explain the look on his face, she chooses to appreciate the gesture to bring her back to a simpler time—back to the night in the van, two freshmen madly in love, with nothing standing in their way.

She traces the tip of her finger over his lips. A soft moan escapes his throat. He wraps his arms around her and rolls her onto her back, so he is resting on top of her.

"You're all that matters to me," he says.

Before she can respond, he hastily presses his lips onto hers. What she would've thought was merely a passionate kiss from her doting boyfriend on her birthday is coming off as a desperate attempt to remind her of his love.

As Nathan clings to her, Abigail wants to whisper in his ear that she'll always try to be an understanding girlfriend, but tonight left her with a feeling that other women won't hesitate to throw themselves at him, whether she is around or not, and she wonders if he is strong enough to handle that. The scene at the Ridge left Abigail with a true sense of the raw magnetic pull some people feel toward him.

Potentially despite his wishes.

Yet she still left. And when she did, she found herself locking eyes with another man.

Desperate to shake her thoughts loose, Abigail squeezes her eyes shut tighter, wishing for less complication and more birthday attention before the sun rises. As she runs her hands through the soft waves of his hair, she kisses him deeper and hugs him tighter, unwilling to let him go, only wanting more. Because here and now, no one else can enter their world.

It's here in his arms that Abigail won't admit to finding herself in a similar situation tonight.

That would be no way to end a birthday.

Nine

Springtime Disappointment

To say the past months have been a bit ho-hum at OSU is an understatement. Abigail and Nathan, despite numerous conversations, have been slowly spiraling into an uncomfortable place neither of them ever truly saw coming. But their love for one another is keeping them afloat. College relationships are hard—no one would dispute that. But add Laura's depression into the mix, and Abigail has found herself just as distracted as Nathan has been with his growing status on campus.

Laura was asked to give a speech at the Associated Collegiate Press College Media Liberty Award ceremony honoring Travis for his years of service at the student newspaper. She does an exceptional job, but everyone who knows her well knew it was a gut-wrenching ask but one she could not decline. Particularly since the request came from his parents.

After the conclusion of the awards ceremony, Abigail and their friends accompany Laura to the coffee shop downtown to try and reconnect after what has been a difficult day for her. Alex invited Kelly and the girl he is apparently dating to join them. The same girl from his party a few months back. So, it must be serious.

This aggravates Abigail, although she's unwilling to admit it. During the frequent times she and Kelly have spoken, he's never mentioned her, which seems odd to Abigail. If you have a girlfriend, one would think you'd talk about her. But maybe it's the fact that her boyfriend is noticeably absent on one of the most important days for Laura.

The football team had some post-season meeting they were required to attend, followed by a team workout. Abigail thought this was ill-planned by the coaches, considering what Travis did for the school. She tried to convince

Nathan to skip the meeting as a sign to the coaches that sometimes, football must come last, but they were wasted words on her part.

Abigail and her friends duck out of the rain and fill up a few tables at the coffee shop and sip on their drinks. Laura sits in silence, staring blankly at the floor.

"Your speech was wonderful," Melissa says.

"Truly," Bree adds. "What a nice tribute to him."

Laura snaps out of it. "Thanks, guys. I appreciate all of you being there."

There is a moment of silence, and then Bree pipes up, "Didn't the football team have a mandatory event or something?"

Abigail's cheeks pink at the mention of the team. "Yes, they did," she mumbles apologetically.

"Oh, because I saw them walk by," Bree says.

Without warning, Abigail sees a figure slip by the second window. She pushes back her chair and heads for the door. Like a slow-motion movie playing, she steps out into the rain and sees Nathan, Tank, and a few other players walking down the sidewalk. And they are following some of the girls, clad in their cheerleader jackets. Naturally, her blood boils.

"Nathan," she yells over the loud drops of rain on the steel roof above.

His shoulders tense as he turns toward the sound of his name. Tank turns, too, pushing his hood off his head, giving her a faint smile before walking over to Laura, who stepped outside for some fresh air. Nathan comes jogging back to her as the others duck into a bar.

"Abby. Hi!" he says. He leans in to kiss her, but she turns her cheek. "What's wrong?"

"What's *wrong*?"

"Yeah."

"What's wrong is, I'm in the coffee shop with all *our* friends, supporting Laura, and apparently, you're going to a bar with your team and the *cheerleaders*."

His cheeks burn red, and she notices him swallow hard. "I—we got out early and decided…"

"Yeah, I can see that. Why would you not try and find me first?" She looks up as the rain comes down harder.

"I figured it was all over."

"Whether it was or not, it's the effort that would have mattered."

"You're absolutely right."

"But it's too late now. They all saw you walk by, and I feel like shit because of it," she admits.

"Abby, you're misunderstanding."

She shoots icy daggers at him.

He takes a step back. "I can tell you're very upset with me. What can I do to make it up to you?"

Laura hurries back inside, and Tank heads toward the bar. As Abigail glances in that direction, Poppy peeks her head back out, smiling at Tank as he approaches.

"Don't keep them waiting. I need to get back to Laura." She whirls around, and yanks open the door to the coffee shop, leaving him in her wake.

Abigail hurries into the restroom. She doesn't want her friends to see her this angry.

Nathan pulls open the door and faintly smiles as he enters. "Hey, guys."

"Hey," they all mumble back.

He looks right at Laura when he says, "Sorry we—I was unable to make it today. We had a mandatory football thing."

"It's okay," she says.

"I really am sorry. I hope it went well?"

"It did, thank you."

"Good." He glances nervously around at all of them. He quickly adds, "The team is up the street. Tell Abby I'll call her later."

"Bye, Nathan," they reply.

Abigail hears this and then waits another minute before exiting the restroom. She tries to calm her annoyance because she doesn't want them to know what they argued about, especially in front of Kelly.

She awkwardly exits the restroom by attempting not to make eye contact with anyone specifically. She grabs her coat off the back of the chair. Clearing her throat, she blurts out, "I'm not feeling all that well, so if you don't mind, I'll see you guys later."

Melissa stands up. "I can walk back with you."

Without hesitation, Abigail says, "That's not necessary. Stay, please." She puts on her coat, pulling her hood over her head. As she passes by Laura, she whispers, "I'm sorry. I hope you understand. I'll see you after the dinner with Travis's parents." Then, she vacates the coffee shop in a hurry.

Ten

Rainy-Day Blues

As Abigail shuffles her way back through campus and the rain pours down on her, she is struck by the feeling that something is shifting within her. She has been feeling different lately. Jealousy, meaninglessness, and complacency all come to mind. But Nathan seems to have changed to her as well. The excitement around the team is infectious, but there is a part of it that can alter a person. He's the face of the team. The quarterback. The good-looking, friendly leader that everyone loves to love. He's revered on campus.

When Abigail and Nathan are alone is when she finds their relationship pleasurable. Out at parties or events, he becomes a celebrity in a small pond, and it can be overwhelming to be a shadow in his light.

Maybe it's me who's changing.

What doesn't help is her crumbled relationship with Tank. They don't talk like they used to. Ever since they fought, he has undoubtedly treated her contrarily.

Deep in thought, Abigail passes by a house party. Someone calls her name. She turns.

"Abigail, is that you?"

She pulls back her hood and sees Jessica standing on the porch with about ten other people. Music can be heard from the speakers in the slightly cracked open window.

"Hey, Jess."

"Come here. Get out of the rain!"

Reluctantly, Abigail steps up the stairs and onto the porch.

"What are you doing, wandering around in the rain?" Jess says with a laugh.

"Drowning my sorrows," she mumbles.

"Here." She hands her a beer. "This is how you drown your sorrows."

"Thanks." She shakes the rain off her shoulders. She cracks open the beer. The taste is a welcome one.

"So, what's up?" she asks.

"Not much, just having a bad day."

"Well, you're more than welcome to hang here and have a good time and forget all about your problems," she says with a drunken smile.

"Thanks," she says, taking another sip of her beer.

Under her breath, Jessica asks, "You see Tank lately?"

"No. Why? Haven't you?" Abigail gives her a concerned expression.

"No, we broke up."

"What?!" She can't believe she didn't know they had broken up. Wow, she's really on the opposite end of where she was with him months ago.

"Yep. He didn't say anything to you?"

"No. We don't talk like we used to."

"He still pulling that *he's mad at you* crap?"

"Yep. Saw him about twenty minutes ago, heading to a bar with Nathan and all the cheerleaders, and he hardly acknowledged me."

"Wait, why are you here?"

"They were happy without me. I was at the coffee shop with the girls and Kelly after Travis's award thing, and I happened to see him walk by. Felt like I caught him doing something wrong. It was really weird."

"Those guys. Man, I have to say, I don't miss the guessing. *Will I see him? Will I not?* I feel freer if that makes sense."

Abigail ponders her words for a moment. She does guess a lot and put things on hold for Nathan's schedule, but he is a hard habit to break. But maybe Nathan's feeling like he needs to be free, too. After all, he didn't stay with her in the coffee shop. He left. Even knowing she was mad at him.

"Besides," she continues, "Tank is a grump, and it's all about him. I don't miss that."

Abigail nods her head. "So, are you dating anyone?"

"Everyone." She smiles. "It's nice to be out in college and not tied down anymore. I mean, for Christ's sake, we're almost juniors."

"I can't believe it," Abigail sighs.

"And speaking of, that Kelly is one fine piece of ass!"

"He has a girlfriend," Abigail quickly replies.

"Who cares? He's sensational to look at."

He never introduced the girl to anyone, and she just sat there, like his plaything. Meanwhile, over the past few months, he has been finding Abigail all over campus. Sitting with her for coffee. Working on schoolwork together. Giving her rides when he sees her walking downtown. Hanging out more and more with his sister and the girls at parties and such. But he has been seen with that girl on more than one occasion, yet he's never introduced her.

Disgusted by this whole day, Abigail says, "Got any vodka at this party?"

Jessica's sinister smile is all Abigail needs to see as she grabs her hand and pulls her toward the front door of the house. "You've come to the right place."

It's about damn time!

Abigail stumbles down the stairs, clutching Jessica's arm. "You are a troublemaker," she slurs.

"I am," Jessica agrees with a laugh.

"I'd better get back. They're probably wondering where the hell I went."

"Tell them you were abducted by aliens," Jess jokes.

Abigail laughs. "No, I'll tell them I got asked to star in a movie, and I've been rehearsing lines."

"Ha! Tell them you joined the swim team and have been doing laps in the pool."

"Oh, good one. Would explain why my hair is wet." She touches her soaked strands, nearing stumbling on the sidewalk as she does.

"Or you joined a convent but decided it wasn't for you." Jess snorts at her own joke, making Abigail burst into a bout of uncontrollable laughter.

They bounce back and forth between these ridiculous scenarios as they walk arm in arm back toward campus. Finally, the girls come to a split in the walkway to their dorms.

Abigail turns, and with sincerity, she says, "Thanks, Jess. I needed this tonight."

"I did, too." They hug, and then like atoms, they split and go their separate ways but not before Jess yells, "Let's do it again," with a slight wave of her hand.

Abigail smiles as she approaches her dorm. She takes the elevator up to the sixth floor, and as she steps off, she almost immediately stops dead in her tracks. Sitting on the floor at the end of the hallway is a figure, leaning up against her door. She approaches and can tell by the narrowed eyes Nathan is giving her that he's not happy. He slowly stands. She fumbles to get her keys out of her pocket, and after a long time, she unlocks and pushes the door open. The room is empty. Abigail's not surprised that Laura is not home. She probably went to see Wolfie before their dinner.

He closes the door behind him as she tries, albeit poorly, to get her soaked jacket off.

"Where have you been?"

She chuckles. "Where have *I* been?"

"Yeah."

"At a party."

"Obviously."

"Where have you been?" She steadies herself on the wall.

"After the bar, I came here and was waiting for you."

"Oh, I see. *You* had to wait for *me*."

"What does that mean?" he asks.

"Nothing," she mumbles. She plops on her bed and kicks off her shoes.

He crosses his arms over his torso. She hates more than anything that he looks good right now. Despite his anger, he is damn hot.

"You've had a bad day, I get that, but this is nuts, Abby."

"Bad day? How would you know? You were at a bar."

"For an hour. Otherwise, I was sitting here, waiting."

"Why?" she barks.

"You know why."

"No, actually, I don't."

He yanks off his jacket and tosses it on the chair. "Because I knew you were pissed, and I hate that."

"You hate that I'm pissed? That's why?" she says with an icy stare.

"You know what I mean."

"So, if I weren't pissed, you'd not be here? Is that how I have to get your attention?"

"My attention? Are you serious? You have *all* my attention."

"Nathan," she slurs, "I think you believe that but…"

"But what?"

"It's not true, and deep down, you know that."

With a frustrated sigh, he says, "I'm here, aren't I?"

"Too late. Don't you get that? If I'd actually believed you'd show up, I would have been here, too. But once you're with them, like, all bets are off, right?"

"Them?"

"You know who."

"The team?"

"I don't care about the team, Nathan. You know that, so don't ask me that again. It's never about them. Never will be about them."

"I see what this is about," he says, pacing in front of her.

"Do you really? Let me hear it," she challenges.

"No matter how many times I tell you that we're just friends, you'll never be happy about it, but that is all we are. The whole team, Abby. Not just me. So, what do I do? Am I the only one who has to be separated from them?"

"So, you do get it."

"No, actually, I don't because I thought you trusted me."

"Trust you? I *needed* you today," she says as her eyes well.

"Jesus, Abby. Don't cry, please," he begs.

He steps closer to the bed and kneels in front of her. He inches in closer. Confusion washes over her. Their connection is deep, and their love is deeper, but she wants to be mad at him to make him understand.

She puts her head in her hands. "Don't. I can't do this. Not now."

"Let me see your face." He reaches for her hand, and as he does, she yanks it free.

"No," she says. She tries to stand but staggers and lands back on her bed. "Of all the days to not be around, Nathan. You could have tried." She pushes back her hair from her face. "I have been by Laura's side for months. I'm exhausted. I needed you. But you were out with them. It's so hurtful."

"I apologize I wasn't there for you. I should have been," he whispers.

"Other people can make the time. Why can't you?" *Even Kelly can.*

She lowers her eyes as a tear rolls down her cheek. He wipes it off, and as he does, she rests her tired head in his hand. He pulls her in closer. She places her head on his shoulder as he strokes her long blonde hair.

"You're soaked," he whispers.

"And drunk," she says. "And mad at you."

"I know. But can you at least let me get you some dry clothes?"

"Fine," she says as he releases her.

Nathan rises to his feet and opens her dresser drawer, pulling out a T-shirt and flannel pants.

"Did you know Tank and Jessica broke up?"

He turns toward her, and with sad eyes, he replies, "Yes, I did."

"Why won't he talk to me?"

"He's stubborn. You know that. But I've tried."

He takes her hand in his and pulls her up. Grabbing the edge of her shirt he guides it over her head. She unbuttons her pants and slides out of them. His eyes grow wide, and heat fills her cheeks. Nathan's giving her that look, and it's one she can't resist. Pushing her wet hair off her shoulders, he steps closer. She swallows hard as his large frame towers over her. She shivers, so he wraps his arms around her.

He places a warm kiss on her cheek and then whispers in her ear, "I'm sorry, Abby."

She gazes up at him. It's nearly impossible to stay mad at him. "Me, too."

He tosses her dry clothes on the bed. He pulls his shirt up over the back of his head and throws it on the floor. She watches as his muscles twitch. She runs her fingers over his skin. The soft, perfect skin that is Nathan Ryan. She is drawn to him. There is no denying it.

Oh, Nathan, I remember when loving you was so effortless. Or at least, it seemed that way. Was it just that I thought nothing of it because it was so easy? But you are like a drug. I can't imagine not wanting you.

He embraces her, and with intensity, his lips meet hers. His tongue twirls around hers, almost desperately. A moan catches in the back of his throat. Before her mind can get ahead of her, she unzips his jeans. She traces her fingers over the textbook arches of his hips, allowing his jeans to drop to the floor. He steps out of them as he presses his full lips harder onto hers. He spins her back toward the bed and cradles her as he lays her down, allowing the weight of his body onto hers. He works his kisses down her neck, moving his way to her breasts, easing the straps from her bra off her shoulders. Her skin's like velvet as his lips trace the curve of her bosom. Kissing each one with appreciation, he unhooks her bra swiftly and removes it, tossing it across the room.

"I promise to be there for you more," he whispers as he lightly traces the tips of his fingers down her flesh.

"I need more, Nathan," she admits.

"I know."

His hands find their way in between her smooth legs, and goosebumps on her skin let him know his touch excites her. She moans as his fingers reach into her panties. She gasps. He glances up at her with a devilish grin. He knows exactly how to make her feel good, and he's damn good at it. It's why he waited outside her door for hours. He needs her—sometimes more than she realizes.

But she's sensing he's being pulled in another direction. It's a feeling she can't seem to shake despite her love for him. She knows his life is moving at a rapid pace, full speed ahead, and she can only hope that she will be coming with him.

But odds are…well, just that—odds. And no one likes anything but a guarantee. But in love, there are no guarantees.

Eleven

Don't You Miss Me?

Abigail glances at her watch for the fifteenth time in the past thirty minutes. After their talk the other night, Nathan and Abigail committed to spending more time together. And he planned to meet her at the Union to study. But she's been waiting abnormally long for him.

One more minute, and I'm leaving, she repeats to herself.

Then, ten more minutes pass.

Finally frustrated to the point of tears, she starts to gather her books and shoves them into her bag.

"I take it, he's not coming?"

Startled, she jumps. "Kelly, Jesus." She places her hand over her heart. "What makes you say that?" she asks.

"You keep looking at your watch." He gives her a sympathetic look, only she takes it as he is giving her a pathetic look. As in she's pathetic for waiting around for Nathan.

"I'm not," she adds defensively.

"Don't get upset."

"I'm not upset, Kelly." She starts to walk toward the west exit.

"Hold up," he calls after her.

"What?"

"I'm not trying to piss you off. I was merely making an observation."

More embarrassed, she asks, "Are you watching me or something?"

He laughs, frustrating her more. She lets out a sigh with marked exaggeration.

He places his hand on her arm. "Abigail."

"What?"

"It's late. Let me at least walk you home."

"Who says I'm going home?"

He tilts his head, as if to say, *You don't know where Nathan is.*

This makes her want to burst into tears. But she must remain steady.

"Are you going to see your sister?"

Quickly, he reacts. "Yes, that's why I was coming through the Union."

Somewhat disappointed that he *wasn't* watching her, that it was merely a coincidence, she says, "Fine, I'll walk with you."

"Jeez, do me a favor, why don't you?"

She wants so badly to say to Kelly, *Can we not do this thing tonight—whatever this is between us? Because it's tiring.*

Instead, she walks alongside him to the doors and enters the cool spring evening.

They walk in silence until Kelly breaks the ice by asking her the one thing she wishes he hadn't, "Nathan stand you up?"

Her shoulders tense. "He…he must have gotten tied up with football stuff."

"Right," he whispers.

Desperate to change the subject, she asks, "How is your Constitutional and Business Law class going?"

"You remembered that?" He smiles.

"Well, yeah. Isn't that what you study?"

"Yes. And well, I might add."

"How do you mean?" she asks.

"Currently, I'm top of my class."

"Wow, I had no idea."

"My father is a lawyer. It's kind of in my blood. He graduated from Harvard Law. I hope to go there, too, after graduation."

"Oh, that's impressive," she says with a genuine smile. "What an accomplishment that would be."

He pulls open the side door to Willis Hall. Immediately, he yanks on Abigail's arm, pulling her into the laundry room, slamming the door shut behind them. He quickly raises his finger to his mouth and motions for her to shush. Her eyes get wide as he ducks slightly, shielding them from the window.

"What's going on?" she whispers. Abigail notices a figure pass by.

Kelly is silent until whoever it is exits the side door. "That was close," he murmurs.

"What?"

"I did *not* want to run into her."

"Who?"

"No one."

She rolls her eyes at him.

His eyes narrow despite the darkness. "I wouldn't roll your eyes," he warns.

"Seriously?" She tries not to laugh in his face.

"You don't have the backstory," he scolds.

"No, I don't, nor do I care to." She continues to fight back her grin.

"Sure you do." His tone is cocky.

He straightens back up from his crouch, puffing his chest as he does. She goes to yank open the door when he grabs on to her arm.

"Please, don't go." His tone is much softer, which piques Abigail's attention.

Glaring at him, she says, "You don't want me to blow your cover, is that it?"

In a contemplative state, he replies, "No, that's not it at all."

"So, what is it then, Kelly?"

His expression softens. "You just seem upset—that's all."

She lowers her eyes and nervously fiddles with her hands. "I'm fine. Really."

"Fine?" He steps closer toward her.

She backs up, bracing herself on the concrete wall. "Yes," she whispers.

He comes nearer. He pushes a long, thick wave of blonde hair off her shoulder.

"What," she says as he touches her hair.

"You have such beautiful hair," he says.

Her breath catches, and she swallows hard. It's difficult to meet his eyes, but when she finally does, he adds, "And your eyes are like faraway oceans. Has anyone ever told you that?"

She can smell the cologne on his skin as he traces his hand down her hair, touching her cheek as he does. Confusion and anxiety wash over her as his hand rests on her arm.

"What—" she stutters. "I mean, who were you hiding from?"

His lips part, but he doesn't speak. She finds herself staring at his mouth. She's frozen, yet her breathing is heavy.

"Is it the girl you're always with?" she presses.

"She," he barely chokes out. "I've wanted to tell you…" He's now within inches of her.

"Kelly, I, um…" *Oh my God. What is happening? Run. Move. Do something. He's so close. This is so inappropriate.*

Naturally, Nathan comes to mind, and within an instant, she is pushing off Kelly as the tears of guilt well in her eyes.

"I'm sorry," she says as she whips open the door and runs up the stairs to her room.

She hurries down the hallway and quickly unlocks her door, slamming it shut behind her. The room is dark. She tosses her bag on her desk and paces her room. The adrenaline coursing through her veins is making her feel queasy. She prays silently that he doesn't find his way up to her room. He knows where she lives. The last thing she needs is trouble.

She peers over at the machine and notices there is no red light indicating a message.

Nathan hasn't called to explain why he stood her up. Maybe something's wrong with him. She snaps back to reality. She reaches for the receiver and dials his number. She slows her breath as best she can.

Webber, his roommate, answers.

"Hey, Webber. It's Abigail."

"Hey. How are you?"

"Oh, fine. And you?" she asks, although she is in no mood for small talk.

"Not bad. What's up?"

"Is Nathan around?"

"No, he went to some party with some of the guys from the team."

"A party at the Ridge?" She would have heard about a party at the Ridge.

"No. Some of the cheerleaders were hosting an end-of-the-year gathering. Thought you were with him."

Gritting her teeth, she replies, "No, I was waiting for him at the Union."

Webber sighs, "Oh, Abigail. I'm sorry. I'll have him call you as soon as he gets home."

On the verge of tears, she says, "It's okay. I'll see him tomorrow."

If he calls me tonight, I might do something I'll regret. I definitely need to cool down first. How could he do this to me? Again! He'd better have a really good explanation.

She places down the receiver. "How could you, Nathan?" she says as an angry tear finds its way onto her cheek.

She paces her room yet again. Her irritation rises and falls and is replaced with hurt and confusion. She was just moments ago in the company of a gorgeous man, filling her with compliments. Only to rush home to find out her boyfriend is out partying with Poppy and her clones.

Am I a fool to ignore someone like Kelly when my own boyfriend doesn't seem to even care anymore? But I do owe Nathan at least an opportunity to explain himself. He told me to trust him, but that doesn't give him the freedom to just ignore me. This is becoming too hard. It used to be so easy.

Her eyes deceive her and land upon the framed picture of the two of them from the football banquet their freshman year. Two smiling faces now mock her, and she can't take it a moment longer. Hastily, she flips the frame facedown on her desk, wondering what she should do with herself and all these awful feelings she is having.

Nothing.

I'll do nothing.

She wipes a tear from her eye.

If you don't know you're missing me, then I'm in no position to try and remind you.

Twelve

The Truth Always Hurts

The next day, Abigail, Bree, Melissa, and Laura walk into the realtor's office. The woman behind the desk greets them with a smile.

"We're here to sign our lease for next year," Bree announces.

"Wonderful. This way, please." She shows the girls to a back room.

They each sit at the long table, and she hands a folder and pen to Bree.

Bree convinced the girls to look off-campus for a better apartment than the cookie-cutter ones in Parkers Village, the on-campus student apartments.

Bree lit up the moment the girls walked into the old Victorian on Charlotte Street, and before anyone could ask how much it was per month, Bree was telling the relator to draw up the papers and to take the listing down.

In typical Bree fashion, she picked the best house they saw that day and assured the girls that her father would insist the Van Tousen family pay most of the rent, considering the house was way out of their price range.

The house is central to campus but tucked back on a beautiful side road. The colonial has been upgraded and modernized with top-notch amenities, and each girl gets their own massive bedroom. A far cry from the dorm rooms they currently live in.

They sign the papers for the house on Charlotte Street, and Bree leaves a check to cover the first month's rent, last month's rent, and the security deposit.

As they leave the office, Laura asks again, "Bree, are you sure about this?"

"Of course. Are you kidding? That is the only place we can live. It's worth it."

"Well, we do appreciate it," Laura says.

"What good is money if you can't spend it?" She laughs with a flip of her hair.

"Thank you, Bree," Abigail adds.

Noting her friend's lack of enthusiasm, she asks, "You okay?"

"Yeah. Would you guys mind if I cut out? I need to do something," Abigail says.

They give her the same pained expression. It's obvious to those around her that things with Nathan are on the rocks.

"See you for dinner?" Laura asks.

"Sure, I'll be there," Abigail says.

"Okay, bye," they all reply.

Abigail parts ways and heads toward Nathan's dorm. As she approaches his dormitory, a sinking feeling rests within her stomach. She has been on edge for weeks, and last night's events of being stood up haven't helped her to feel better, only worse.

She drags her feet through the entryway of his dorm, dread looming within her. She takes the stairs to his floor, only because it takes longer, and then heads down the hallway and can see that his door is open.

She knocks. "Hello?"

She can hear movements, and then Nathan appears around the corner.

His expression is despondent. "Hi."

Abigail walks in and closes the door behind her. She doesn't remove her jacket; instead, she stands near the desks. He approaches, taking her hand in his.

"You're mad," he begins. She doesn't respond. "I'm so sorry for last night. It completely slipped my mind."

I slipped his mind? There was a time when all he thought about was me.

"I realize I screwed—"

"I slipped your mind?" she whispers, almost subconsciously.

"Abby, please," he begs.

"Please what?" she replies, yanking her hand free.

"I'm so sorry. Can you forgive me?"

Abigail exhales, "What am I to forgive?"

"That I messed up. I was supposed to meet you, and I didn't."

"But why?"

She can tell he's nervous.

He steps back as his face flushes red. He runs his hand through his hair. "I…I, um…was at a party."

"What party?" She needs to hear him admit it.

He glances up at her and then finally says, "There was an end-of-the-year party at Poppy's house."

Bam! A ton of bricks hit her. "And?"

"We went, the whole team. It was sort of the right thing to do for the team."

"Was it?" she asks. "Because it didn't feel that way to me."

"Abby, you know what I mean."

"Don't most people plan parties in advance?"

"What?"

"When did you find out about the party?"

"Right before, I swear."

"And you didn't think of me at all?"

He hangs his head as he admits, "No."

Her chest feels as though someone was sitting on it. Bouncing up and down, knocking the wind out of her repeatedly. Her eyes well with tears. "I see. Well, I'm not sure what else to say, so…" She leans over to pull the door open when he reacts quickly, shielding her from leaving.

"Please, don't go."

Another confusing man in her life is begging her not to go. But she's unsure if she's even wanted. By anyone. Is she merely a hard habit to break? Or worse, like a favorite key chain you just can't get rid of?

She wipes a tear from her cheek.

He steps closer. "I don't want you to go."

"Nathan," she pleads.

"I screwed up. I was so nervous about you coming here because I don't want to hurt you, and I know that I have."

"Are you hurting me?" she asks.

He grabs her hand, and with pleading eyes, he says, "No, I swear to you, I am not. I wouldn't do that to you."

She swallows hard. Since the first time she encountered Poppy, she has painfully imagined her and Nathan lip-locked. It kills her to think of it, but she can't help it. Desire is a hard emotion to overcome. She knows this because she, too, has fantasized about what it would be like to kiss Kelly Conrad. She almost did. Her guilt surfaces. She stares into his honest eyes, and her heart softens.

Then, he pulls her in closer, and with a deep voice, he adds, "I love you, Abby. Only you."

She must admit, she saw this talk going in a whole other direction. She can't say she wanted it to.

No, of course not. I still love him.

But she thought with certainty that this was the beginning of the end. Maybe this is the perfect time for the semester to be commencing and for summer to come upon them. The distance between her and the men in her life might be to her advantage.

He leans in. Embracing her in his long, lean arms, he squeezes her. She can feel the tension in his body. He's uneasy. She peeks up at him. His concerned expression tells her of his sorrow at his marked omission.

She needs to let him off the hook. "I love you, too. But I can't keep doing this. I'm sorry."

"What?! Oh, no, please don't do this. You can't mean what I think you do. Please, Abby. I screwed up, and I promise it will never happen again. It was a stupid party. Everyone went. Coach was there, which never happens, and it was just like we all left the field house, and it was so…"

She watches him nervously drone on and on about every detail about the entire night and how they dragged him to go and wouldn't take no for an answer. And while he wasn't thinking clearly about meeting her, the time just slipped away. He repeats a hundred times that he walked home with Tank only. And then, once in the dorm, he saw the message from Webber, and he remembered. Webber told him how upset she'd sounded and *not* to call. He's been in agony all day, waiting for her.

"Abby, I might screw up, but I would never cheat on you. Ever," he says, taking her hand. "Please, you mean everything to me, and I completely get that I have done very little to show you that, but don't throw away what we have because I'm an idiot."

Their eyes lock, and she can tell without a doubt that he is telling her the truth. She just knows this about him. "Please, Nathan, this is the last time."

Acting as though she'll change her mind, he quickly seals their love with a passionate kiss. Her knees weaken as he eagerly displays his adoration for her.

"Nathan," she mumbles.

He pays no mind to her. He kisses her again and again.

"Nathan," she says breathlessly.

He grabs her face in his hands. "Please, Abby, I need you."

"I need you, too," she whispers. "I've needed you."

"I know." He takes her hand and guides her over to his bed. "I know. And I've failed you horribly. Believe me, I get it." He embraces her tightly as he lowers them together onto his mattress. He pulls her onto his chest while he strokes her long blonde hair. "I'm so sorry," he whispers. "Just please don't give up on me, okay?" he says, peering down at her. "Okay?" he asks again.

"I won't," she says.

The rise and fall of his trunk and the soft strokes of his hand on her head relax her. She can sense her anger dissipate with each motion of his fingers, and it's replaced by sadness. But what she can't seem to shake is the notion that he didn't think of her. She wants to question him again. To hear it again.

But as she peers up at him to ask him, his eyes are closed. He looks exhausted as a tear falls down his cheek.

Truly exhausted. Like he's being pulled in a thousand directions. Am I making things worse for him? I don't want him to feel so stressed about being perfect for everyone that he has to walk on eggshells around me—or anyone for that matter. People around here ask a lot of him. Am I asking too much of him when he needs more space to be free and not less?

This unusual moment tells her that he is more saddened by all this than relieved. And while she admires him for his ability to admit the truth, doesn't he know it still hurts her?

The truth usually does.

Thirteen

Nothing Happened?

Abigail knocks quietly on the front door. She takes a step back and waits to see if anyone is home.

A guy with average height and build answers. "Can I help you?"

Her heart beats hard, and she stutters, "Um, yes, I'm here…"

"Let me guess…to see Kelly." He smirks.

Her cheeks burn with embarrassment. *Of course he has a parade of girls coming through here. I must look like some joke to this guy.*

Before Abigail can turn around and run for the hills, Kelly comes to the door.

"I thought that was you," he says as he greets her with a sly smile.

She's blushing, and she hates it.

"This is my roommate, Tom."

"Hello, Tom."

"This is Abigail. She's a friend of my sister's."

Ah, so I'm a friend of your sister's. I feel even more ridiculous for coming, unannounced.

"Come in," he says, pulling open the door. "Can I get you a drink?"

"No, can't stay," she says.

"Okay." His eyes narrow at her. "What's up?"

She glances at Tom, who has plopped down on the couch and resumed watching television.

"This way," he says.

She follows him toward the kitchen and out onto his back deck.

"What's up?" he asks casually.

"I, um, wanted to, um…" She nervously pulls on the edge of her shirt.

She can't look at him. His stare makes her unfocused. The way he appears makes her swoon, and she can't swoon over him. She simply must ignore her desire.

"Wanted to talk about the other night?" he says.

She peeks up at him. His green eyes flash mischievously.

"Yes, that's why I'm here."

"I'm glad you came," he adds.

Ugh, he makes this so hard. Focus, Abigail.

"I'm sorry about what happened, and it won't happen again," she blurts out.

He cocks his head. "Nothing happened."

Embarrassed beyond comprehension, she says, "Right, well…"

He leans up against the railing of the deck. He looks like he is about to say something, but then he doesn't.

As the moment for discussion passes, Abigail says, "I should go then." She walks down the stairs of his deck. The sadness she feels is eating away at her, and she hates that he has any effect on her at all.

All the things he said to me the other night. How they made me feel. Renewed. Like I mattered again. And in the end, to him, they were just words he threw together to try and hit on one of his sister's friends. Boy, I really am a fool.

"Have a nice summer," he calls.

She stops deep in her tracks and turns to him. "I hope you have a nice summer, too."

There are a thousand other ways she would have liked to end their conversation.

Did you mean all those nice things you said? Who am I to you? Are we friends? Or maybe, if I was really being honest with myself, I'm confused. Are you? Or is this just a fun game to you? Because if it is, find someone else since I've got a boyfriend that I'm trying to work on things with, and it's complicated enough without you in the mix.

But she is incapable of saying any of those things.

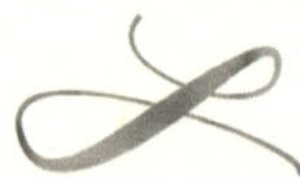

The girls enter the party at Delta Chi for the last time as sophomores. There is a sadness to ending a year none of them can quite put their finger on. Maybe because it is Maddie's last hurrah that left them all with a sinking feeling when she announced she would be transferring to a new school next year. Maddie has been their floor mate for the past two years and has always been a great friend. She'll be missed very much.

Maddie puts her arms around Laura. "I'm sad to be leaving," she announces.

"We are, too," Melissa adds.

"I hate the end of the year. I'm away from Adam, and I have to go back to the Hamptons and hang with all my bitchy friends," Bree adds.

"I get to wallow in my own misery, not working at the station. I hate the summer," Laura chimes in. "I feel like I have so much to do."

"Jesus, what is with everyone these days? You sound like my brother. Last week, he was all happy, and now, he's all freaking bummed out," Alex says as she plays with the new piercing in her eyebrow. "Moody boy."

"Where is your brother? He still coming?" Casey asks, glancing around the room.

"Changed his mind about coming. I think he's sick of hanging out with us." Alex laughs.

Only Abigail doesn't. Her conversation with him went horrible in her eyes. But the last thing she wanted was to alienate him from hanging with his sister. She can't leave it this way and wonder about it all summer. It will eat away at her if she has offended him.

"I'm going to use the bathroom. I'll be back in a bit," Abigail announces.

She steps away from the girls before anyone can join her. She heads up the stairs but passes right by the long line for the bathroom and goes straight out the front door.

She walks for a few minutes and then arrives at Kelly's house. Like a record playing over, she knocks on his door. She can hear movement inside, and nervously, she pulls at the end of her shirt. Then, the door swings open. Kelly is standing before her, wearing only a pair of athletic shorts. His chest muscles bulge as the sweat drips down his body.

Gulp.

He resembles an Adonis.

She can barely find a word to speak. "I, um, hey."

"Abigail? What's going on?" he asks, peering around her.

"I'm sorry," she says, her heart fluttering. "Are you busy right now?"

"I was working out." His tone is dry.

No kidding. Look at you. She shakes her nerves. *Focus. Think.* "Can I speak to you for just a second?"

Reluctantly, he motions for her to come in. "You don't have to hide. Tom isn't here." He closes the door.

She turns to face him as he grabs his towel and wipes down his washboard abs. Her senses are weakening as she gapes at him. But it is impossible not to.

"Okay. I mean, I wasn't going to hide." *Although, right now, I feel like I could die because I'm really uncomfortable, being here alone with you.*

"What's up?" he asks.

She doesn't have long before the girls will wonder where she is, so she decides to cut to the chase. Clearing her throat, she tries to summon some confidence as she blurts out, "Are you not hanging out with your sister—I mean, us because of me?"

"Who said that?"

"I'm asking you, Kelly."

He wipes the sweat from his brow. "No," he answers flatly.

"Really?" She digs her hands into her slender hips.

"I'm a little busy," he says, motioning to his weights on the floor. "I didn't feel like going tonight—that's all."

Feeling stupid yet again, she quips, "Well, good. That's all I wanted to know."

He mockingly laughs at her. "Really? You came all the way here just to ask me that?"

Confused and irritated at the same time, she says, "Yes, I didn't want that hanging over my head all summer. She's your sister and all."

"I see." He slightly rolls his eyes.

"See what?" she asks.

"Why you're here."

"I'm sorry if I bothered you. I only wanted to confirm what I thought."

He cocks his head. "Well, you did. So…"

Her cheeks burn. *I guess he's done with this conversation and with me.* "Okay then. Have a great summer."

"You said that already." He chuckles.

"I'm aware," she sighs. "So, fine, Kelly." Her hand flies from her side. "I'll see you around then. Is that better for you?"

She takes a few strides past him and toward the door when in a low, barely audible tone, he replies, "You can't ignore this forever."

It stops her dead in her tracks. She turns to face him. She wishes she could hide the shade of her cheeks as they flush the color of red apples ripe for the picking, but she can't. And although she is going to ask him, she fears she might already know the answer. "Ignore what?"

"This." He motions between them.

Feeling terribly uneasy and unwilling to admit anything, she simply states, "I'm not."

Please, world, swallow me up, make me disappear. I can't have him look at me the way he is right now.

"You've been at my house twice today, and what has that accomplished? Tell me, Abigail," he practically begs. "Because I really want to know."

"Accomplished?"

He inches closer to her. "Yeah, you came here to tell me you were sorry. But for what?"

Him being so close to her causes the thumping in her heart to pick up speed. "For running away, I think. I'm not sure," she whispers.

"And now, to make sure I'm not going to avoid you?"

In protest, she quips, "Well, no. I felt bad, thinking that maybe you were."

"Try not to think about it." He's purposely being mean, and it's not helping at all.

"*Kelly…*"

"What?"

Exasperated, she asks, "Why did you say those nice things to me the other day?"

"Because I thought you needed to hear them."

She tilts her head and asks, "So, you pity me? Is that it?"

"Pity you? *Oh, please.* You know right where you're standing."

"What do you mean?"

"That you're fully aware of what you're doing. So, no, I don't pity you."

Muddled more than ever, she asks, "Why do you seem mad at me?"

"Mad at you? I'm frustrated." He pokes his bare chest. "This is me, frustrated."

"I'm sorry if me coming here today has caused you to be upset or frustrated or whatever. It was not my intention."

"What is your intention?" he scoffs.

Her eyes soften. "To go back to how it was a few days ago." *I was less confused.*

He tosses the towel back on the couch, evidently displeased with her request. "You know that is not possible."

"What? Why?"

"Because it's not for you to decide that."

"I'm not. I'm asking you," she says, fidgeting with her fingers.

"Well, I'm saying *no.*"

"No?" she whispers.

"Yep, can't happen."

"Why not? You said yourself, nothing happened between us. So, I don't get it."

"Because you want it to. And that's that." He crosses his arms over his expansive chest.

And just like that, the air in the room changes, and so does her attitude. Again. She can't keep letting him play these mind games with her. Or whatever he's doing.

Her blood boils as she replies, "That is awfully presumptuous of you. But then again, it doesn't surprise me in the least."

"How's that?"

"You're full of yourself! Look at you." She points at him. "Standing here like that!"

"Would it make you more comfortable if I covered up?" he teases as his tattooed muscles contract, distracting her eyes away from his stare.

She shakes the cobwebs. "If I say yes, I know you won't do it, just to try and tick me off."

"You could not be more right." He digs his hands into his hips. "And you should be uncomfortable."

"That's a nice thing to say to someone."

"I'm saying it to *you*."

"But why?" she asks, nearly on the verge of tears.

"Because *this* is uncomfortable. You"—he points at her—"standing here, in my apartment, for the second time today."

"Boy, you really know how to make a girl feel welcome," she scoffs.

"Is that what you want? To feel welcome?" he asks.

"Well, it wouldn't hurt, would it?"

His smile is bordering on sinister as he steps closer to her. "I think no matter what I did, you'd feel uncomfortable, wouldn't you?" His green eyes darken as he locks eyes with hers.

She can smell the sweat on his skin, mixed with soap, and a feeling of euphoria washes over her. She needs to get out of here and fast. "As you encroach upon my space, yes," she whispers.

His stare is more than she can handle as her head swirls with uncertainty. She wishes more than anything that he did not look that way he does. It would make things so much easier on her.

He leans in to be within inches of her. "There is a part of you that regretted leaving the laundry room the other night, isn't there?"

She swallows down her lies and replies, "No."

"If you didn't care, you wouldn't have come here."

"Of course I care. But…"

"Then, kiss me and get it over with. It won't hang over your head all summer, right?"

"Kiss you?" She laughs. "I can hardly stand you right now."

He smiles. "Abigail, you're a terrible liar."

"Am I now?"

"Yes, awful. I know you've thought about it. Just admit it."

"Have I?" *Yes, I have, but I'd never admit it.* "So, now, you read minds?"

"No, but I can read you."

"Kelly…are you trying to get me in trouble?"

"No, I'm trying to get you to live a little. Because all I see you do is wait around."

She gasps. "I live."

He edges to within centimeters of her, and with an icy stare, he says, "Prove it."

Something about the way he challenges her sparks a fire within her gut that she cannot ignore. He clutches her hand, and the warmth of his skin draws up her arm as he pulls her into him.

Again, he says, "Prove it, Abigail."

Before she can comprehend what she's doing, she presses her lips onto his. Within seconds, he wraps his burly arms around her body and pins her against the wall. He holds on to the back of her head and kisses her with such passion that her knees buckle. He pulls her tighter around the waist, holding her body to his. She can't breathe or comprehend the ramifications of her actions in this moment. Their tongues dance around one another, and their lips fit perfectly, as though they had done this a thousand times before.

Then, without warning, he pulls her back. Leaving her at arm's length. She's startled, and her eyes flash open. He's staring at her, his eyes full of dark, wanton lust and annoyance.

Her knees are shaking as she tries to move. She is stunned by her gutsy move to kiss him, but more, she's in shock from his kiss back. She could have sworn she felt more alive than ever before.

He wipes the taste of her off on the back of his hand and then murmurs, "Now, you should leave."

"What?" she whispers.

"You have a boyfriend," he states.

Crushed by the mere thought of Nathan, she spins on her heel and lunges for the door, praying to God she doesn't trip or embarrass herself more as she attempts to exit.

She slams his front door, practically bursting into tears as she rushes back down the street and toward the fraternity house. Adrenaline is coursing through her veins, causing her feet to carry her quickly across the pavement.

What have I done?

She ducks behind a building on the way back to the party, too tormented by her choice and too devoted to her tears to be seen by anyone. She's a dead giveaway.

And this is a secret I must never tell. I just committed the ultimate sin. The one thing I prayed Nathan would never do to me. The one thing I've imagined him doing with Poppy that has driven me mad these past months.

Kelly has just been around so much. When Nathan hasn't. But that is a terrible excuse. I'm trying to make it work. I am. But Kelly said I wait around all the time. And I do.

I want to live.

But now, I can never take it back. But Kelly knew that, and he still provoked me.

I'll have all summer to feel this unresolved issue swarming inside of me. How could I do such a thing? I deserve my misery. I just earned it.

Fourteen

Junior Year 1997-1998

A late summer breeze billows into Abigail's room. She breathes in deeply and then exhales slowly and deliberately. With trepidation, she closes the window in her bedroom. Skyler, her faithful companion, has not left her side all morning. Her dog senses today is the day Abigail will be moving back to school and leaving her once again to a quiet and empty house.

Abigail spent the summer volunteering at a local animal shelter in Glens Falls, New York—the town she grew up in. She saw Nathan a few times by visiting him in his hometown of Halifax, Pennsylvania, but like most summers for Nathan, he has serious training to do in order to get ready for the football season. He's back on campus in the beginning of August for preseason. So, he spends what time he can with his dad and family, knowing he'll have a lot more time with Abby and his friends during the school year. And for the most part, their relationship seemed to be back on track, so there was less added pressure to see one another over the summer.

But there was a lingering feeling twisting in her gut that neither trips to Lake George to bask in the sunshine nor ice cream on Canada Street with her best friend, Rebecca, could erase. She couldn't stop thinking about her kiss with Kelly. And she most certainly did not tell Nathan. He has to focus on football. His scholarship depends on it. Besides, she decided that Kelly was just testing her, and that was all there was to it. She is positive it meant nothing to him.

Alex called her a few times over the summer, and Abigail did not have the gall to inquire how her brother was, although deep down, she was dying to ask. She promised Alex to keep in touch more, but every time she went to pick up the phone, she'd freeze and chicken out.

What if Kelly answers?

Abigail's car, now packed to the brim, is beckoning her in the driveway. She says her final good-byes to her mom and dad and gives a special hug to her dog before climbing into her white 1982 Volkswagen Rabbit convertible and reversing out of the driveway. Her parents eagerly wave as Skyler sits next to them, her ears drooped in sadness.

Abigail makes the two-and-a-half-hour drive to Syracuse without stopping.

The excitement of a new year is dawning as she pulls into the gates of Onondaga State University. She drives slowly through campus, nostalgically passing her old dormitory and peering out at the fresh-faced students unloading their parents' cars. She's fine with driving right by and toward her new, beautiful home awaiting her.

She pulls into the driveway. Parked in the first spot is Bree's Mercedes, next to that is Laura's Toyota, which is littered with bumper stickers of bands and the letters of the college radio station, WOUR97. Abigail pulls next to her and pops open her door. The sun is bright, and the air is damp.

She pulls out a box from the back and is about halfway up the driveway when she hears the squeak of brakes. She turns, steadying the box in her hands.

Kelly's Mustang comes to a stop at the end of her driveway. Abigail's heart rate doubles as she watches him climb out. He's wearing athletic shorts, a well-fitted T-shirt, and aviator sunglasses. His skin is tanned to a golden brown. He walks toward her, his pouty lips in a hard line. He barely acknowledges her until he is within a few feet of her.

"Hello," Abigail says.

"Hey. My sister said you guys needed some help?"

Confused, she states, "I just arrived, so I'm not sure."

He takes the box from her arms. "I'd say this is helping." He passes her and goes up to the stairs leading to the expansive wraparound porch.

She walks back over to her car and takes out her suitcase and rolls it up the driveway. She can hear a squeal of delight as Laura comes running out the front door to greet her.

"You're here!"

Abigail drops her suitcase and hugs her friend. "Hi! I've missed you."

"You, too."

"Did you call him?" she whispers as Kelly comes back down the stairs.

Laura cocks her head. "No. Thought you did?"

"Nope, literally just pulled in."

"Huh."

"This your ride?" he yells over.

"Yeah," she says back.

He pulls out a few boxes and then rests them on the grass. "Looks like you've got an issue."

Concerned, Abigail goes over to where he is looking. "What's wrong?" she asks, leaning in closer to look.

"See that?" he says.

"Yes."

"Brake fluid. Your car is leaking."

"Is that bad?"

He chuckles and then removes his sunglasses. Abigail could not have prepared herself for the contrast of his tanned skin and the way it makes his green eyes ignite. "Yeah, it's bad. But it can be fixed."

"Oh good," she exhales.

"Don't drive it for now, okay?" His tone is scolding.

"Okay."

He slips his glasses back on and picks up the boxes from the grass. She follows him inside.

She internally gasps. Bree has outdone herself. There is nothing left to be desired in this place. The living room is impeccably decorated. Everything is clean and bright. It's far too much for college students. But then again, OSU has never had the likes of Bree Van Tousen before.

"Nice place," he says.

Abigail, almost stunned into silence, replies, "Yeah, I can't believe I live here."

"Where are these going?" he asks.

"Third floor," Abigail says as she eyes the decor.

He raises his eyebrows at her. "Third floor it is."

Bree graciously offered the room on the third floor to the girls despite it being the largest of the four because she knew she'd be spending a lot of time at her boyfriend, Adam's, cabin. And then Laura said she'd be spending long days at the station, and shortly after, Melissa got the call over the summer to officially join *The Weekly Blue* as the new student editor, replacing Travis' spot, so she immediately called Abigail to not only tell her of the great news, but to also insist that she take the third floor.

"Bree," Abigail yells.

Bree comes hustling out of the back room.

"Hey, didn't know you'd arrived!" She gives her friend a big hug and kisses her on each cheek, like she does with all her model friends in the city.

"This place looks amazing!" Abigail boasts. "I can't believe we live here."

"Thanks. I've spent the last week getting it ready."

"It shows. It's beautiful."

"Your bed arrived yesterday. So, I had them set it up in your room. I made sure it was up to standards."

"Thanks." Abigail giggles.

"Of course."

Kelly comes bounding down the stairs with a whistle. "I'm impressed, Bree."

Her eyes get wide as she looks at him. Never one to shy away from the truth, she says, "I have to give you my agent's number. She would love you!" she boasts. "Have you modeled before?"

Abigail watches him blush.

"No, thanks. Not my thing."

"Everyone says that until they get paid to look good. If you change your mind…"

Changing the subject, he states, "I'll get the rest of your stuff." He walks out the door.

"Already having him doing your bidding." Bree smirks.

"Me?! He said Alex said you needed help," Abigail protests.

"Do I look like I need help?" Bree scoffs.

"Huh, weird." Abigail shrugs her shoulders. "Well, I can be useful and at least grab my stuff." She turns and walks down the stairs to her car.

He's leaning into her trunk, pulling out items and leaving them on the grass. An awkward moment passes by them as he steps around her, carrying her boxes to her room. She tries to shake it off, but she can't. She carries all her items onto the porch and leaves them there, emptying her car. One by one, he takes her stuff up to the third floor, never taking a break.

Abigail carries the last box to her room and is terribly warm from the combination of all the trips up and down two flights of stairs and the muggy weather. She whisks open the windows in the widow's walk, wishing for a breeze. She grabs the elastic from around her wrist and piles her hair atop her head, securing it in a messy bun. As she turns, she finds Kelly standing in her room, watching her.

She blushes. "Thank you, Kelly. You didn't have to do all this."

Ignoring her, he asks, "Are your keys in your car?"

She pulls out her car keys from the pocket of her jean shorts. "Why?"

"I'm going to take it and try to figure out if I can fix it."

More confused than ever, she says, "Kelly, I can't have you do that."

He steps toward her, and instantly, she is reminded of two short months ago, in his apartment. Her body shivers despite the heat.

"Bring my car by later—the keys are in the visor—and hopefully by then, I should have an idea about yours," he says, obviously not taking no for an answer. "Looks like you've got your afternoon cut out for you," he says, glancing at all the boxes.

Their fingers briefly touch as he takes the keys from her. She finds herself with a feeling of utter desperation and confusion.

Why don't I want him to leave?

"Okay, thanks."

He vacates without saying another word. She watches out her window as he climbs into her convertible car and backs down her driveway.

Focus, Abigail. You're a junior now. You've got a full semester of hard classes. Nathan and you are committed to making this work. And if there is any time that will tell us if it's going to work, it's now, during football season. So, you owe it to Nathan to support him and be there for him. And us. Not Kelly.

Kelly.

And just like that, the memory floods back across her mind. She can never stop it.

She runs the tips of her fingers over her lips. She closes her eyes as the sensation of that deep, sensual kiss warms her body yet again.

Fifteen

Bad Start

Nathan peels off his wet clothes and equipment and limps toward the shower. He stands there, letting the water run down his skin as he watches it swirl into the drain.

After rising off all the soap, he turns off the scalding hot water and grabs his towel, wrapping it around his waist.

"Coach wants to see you," one of the players says as he sits in front of his locker.

"Okay, thanks." Nathan dresses and heads to Coach Bromley's office.

"Close the door." He grimaces.

Coach Bromley is a man of few words, little tolerance, and has about as much patience as a child with a lollipop being dangled in front of him.

"Sit."

Nathan does as he was told and sits across from him.

"Listen, the school needs you on Wednesday at four for some photo shoot thing for the goddamn posters," he barks.

Coach doesn't like all the stuff that goes along with playing nice at the school. He wants to coach and his players to play. But with recognition of the program and scholarship money being awarded, he knows it is their duty to abide.

"Right. Sure, of course."

"Do your best to make it quick, so you're not late for practice. Understood?"

"Sure thing."

"And they need you to work at the local high school. Help the players this season." He peers over his glasses at Nathan. "Coach Stanfield can give you some drills to run with the offense there. And you'll need to do some community service work, too. I'll fill you in more next week."

"Okay, Coach."

He tosses his glasses on top of the pile of papers on his desk as he leans back in his chair. "There is a lot riding on you this season. You and your partner in crime there, McPherson. Cocaptains. Make this team proud, you hear?"

"Yes, sir."

"Good. Now, go find something to do away from here." He motions with his hand toward the door.

Nathan tries with all his might not to limp, but his ankle is sore. He took a wrong step at practice this morning and a shooting pain jolted up his leg. He'll ice it more at his apartment and see how it looks tomorrow before he says anything. But he refuses to let on to Coach that he might have tweaked it this soon in the season.

He drives back to Parkers Village and parks his car in his spot across from his apartment. Both Tank and Nathan decided not to live at the Ridge because their full scholarships afforded them the money to live on campus only. They got a quad with Webber and Logan. There's a living room, small eating area, kitchen, outside back patio area, and upstairs are four small bedrooms. It's nothing fancy—stock furniture, standard beds, and communal laundry in the basement. But it beats the heck out of spending money he doesn't have on rent.

Nathan keys into his apartment. Webber and Logan are sitting on the couch, playing video games.

"Hey," he says.

"How was practice?" Webber asks.

"Good. Tweaked my ankle," he states as he pulls a bag of ice out of the refrigerator.

"Shouldn't you be doing that with the trainers?" Logan asks.

"I don't want to set off the alarm bells yet. Besides, there are times when I just need to get out of there."

"Totally get it."

"Where's Tank?"

"Haven't seen him since this morning. But Abigail called twenty minutes ago. Left her new number by the phone."

Nathan strolls over with his bag of ice, rips the piece of paper off from the pad, and gingerly hobbles up the stairs and into his room. He plops down on his bed, placing the bag of ice on his ankle, and picks up the phone, dialing her number as he leans back on his bed.

"Hello?"

"Hey there," he says.

"Hi! How are you?"

"Good. You all settled in?" he asks.

"I'm getting there. This place is beautiful. Bree has really outdone herself."

"I can imagine. When can I see you?"

"Whenever. I'm almost finished unpacking."

He hesitates as he glances at his ankle. "Oh good 'cause I'm icing right now and I need to stay put."

"You okay?"

"Yeah, just my ankle is a little sore."

Relieved, she says, "Why don't I come by later? I'll bring takeout?"

"That sounds perfect. I'm looking forward to it."

"Me, too," she says.

"Bye," he says as he places down the receiver.

Nathan closes his eyes to rest his mind and body. Moments pass, and he hears the bellowing voice of Tank, entering the apartment.

"Get off the games," he barks.

Nathan can hear some commotion and other voices as Webber and Logan start talking to whoever is with him. Within minutes, Nathan's door swings open.

Tank bursts in. "What are you doing, buddy?"

"Resting."

"Come on. We're going out."

"Huh? I'm not going out." His voice is strained.

"Yeah, come on, for a little bit. It's a back-to-school party."

"Tank, I can't…"

Then, he hears a voice cooing in the background, "Come on, Nathan. Just for a little while?"

Poppy is standing in the doorway. Dressed in a tight white tank top, jean shorts, and tennis sneakers. Her tanned skin is glowing. He swallows hard. She grants him a tempting smile. He finds himself swinging his legs over the side of his bed. Taking the bag of ice in his hands.

"Where?"

"Shelby's house."

"Come on. We're going," Tank demands.

"*Fine,*" he concedes. "But I'm coming back in an hour."

Tank rolls his eyes at his friend. "Sure, buddy. Fine."

Nathan slips on his sneakers. His ankle feels decent but not great. He shouldn't be on it, but he can sit at the party.

I'll only stay for an hour, so I can be back in time to have dinner with Abigail.

He walks toward the common area of their apartment to find Morgan, Poppy, Tank, and Webber all waiting for him.

"You going with us, Logan?" Nathan asks.

"Nope. I'm going to see Melissa in a bit. Help her unpack and stuff. I'll catch you guys later." He turns back to his video game and very contently bangs his thumbs on the controller.

That's what I should be doing. Waiting for Abigail. But I won't be long. I'll just say hello and be back before anyone notices.

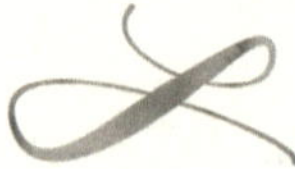

They pile in Tank's truck and drive the short distance to Shelby's apartment on Bayley Street. Radiohead booms from the speakers in the backyard. Morgan leads the way through the gate. Nathan does a quick survey, and there are about twenty people hanging out, drinking beer, and playing quarters at a table on the patio by the sliding glass door.

"Can I get you a beer?" Poppy asks.

"Sure," Nathan replies.

As soon as he is recognized, several partygoers surround him and start asking him all sorts of questions about the team, his thoughts on the schedule this season, how preseason went, and on and on. A burst of energy pulsates through him, as he is undoubtedly the center of attention.

Poppy returns with his beer and hands it to him.

"Thanks," he says.

"You're welcome."

She gives him a smile that makes his cheeks pink. He averts his eyes over to Tank to see what he's doing. It's no surprise he is surrounded by girls and loving every second of it. Nathan gets a funny feeling, as though his life is heading in a much different direction than where he was two short years ago. A shy freshman, trying to make his spot on the team and navigate his way through school. Now, he stands before a group of disciples as cocaptain and still QB1 at one of the most prestigious schools and highest-ranked football programs in the United States.

"Penny for your thoughts," Poppy asks, interrupting his lucid daydreams.

"What?" he whispers. "Oh, sorry. Just thinking about the season. Got a lot riding on us this year."

"I can tell." She links her arm in his. "Will you excuse us for a moment?" Poppy says to those surrounding him.

Poppy pulls him over to the side of the house, still in plain view but far enough away from everyone.

He sighs, "Thanks."

"I've got you." She smiles. "You're going to have a whole season of answering questions. The last thing you need is to be at a party and be surrounded by wannabe reporters."

He laughs. "I think they are just trying to be nice."

"Of course, but there is a time and place. You shouldn't feel badly about saying so."

"I don't, but I guess I feel like I owe it to people. If that makes sense."

She touches his arm. His skin prickles.

"Yes, it makes sense. You're so sweet."

"Well, I don't know about that," he shyly replies.

"I do."

His cheeks flame under her stare. "Thanks, Poppy."

"You deserve to relax and enjoy this beautiful afternoon."

Her eyes are alive as she smiles at him. He's seen this look countless times before, and as her fingers attempt to touch a curl near his ear, he politely steps a foot back.

"Poppy, listen, this year, I really need to concentrate on football, school, and Abigail."

The sound of her name is like a poisonous gas in the air. She doesn't even try to hide her dislike. "It's much easier to spend time with me, us, the cheerleaders during the season than worry about making time for her. Don't you agree?"

"I love her, so no."

"You're so young." She laughs. "Have some fun, Nathan."

"Isn't that what I'm doing right now?" he says.

"Yes, but I'm thinking about road trips this year. It'll be so much fun if we're all single."

"I don't want to be single." He pauses and squarely faces her. "What about you? Don't you get sick of being single, looking for just a hook-up?"

"Maybe I like hooking up," she says, her eyelashes batting.

"But you've got a lot to offer. I'm saying that as your *friend*," he quickly adds.

She flips her hair, and as if he hadn't spoken a word, she says, "Of course we're good friends, silly. Don't worry so much. Let me get you another beer." She takes his cup.

He smiles as he watches her stroll away and toward the pony keg.

Maybe it's me who is misreading things. Man, girls are so confusing.

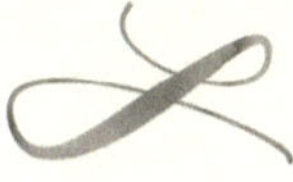

A few beers later, the sun is setting, and a wave of panic rips through Nathan.

"Oh shit," he slurs. "I have to run."

He drops his drink on the table and dashes through the gate. He can hear Poppy yelling after him, but he has no time to explain now.

Abby is going to kill me. I can't believe I got so caught up, but I started talking to Poppy and then Morgan, and then I played that stupid game with Tank. Oh shit, oh shit! The first day back, and I'm already in hot water. We had such a great summer, and I promised her I'd manage my time better, and I'm already screwing up. What is wrong with me?!

He pumps his arms, jostling his way through the woods and toward the back parking lot of Parkers Village. His foot throbs as he pushes off with each step. He finally approaches his front door and finds a bag of cold takeout food placed in front of his locked apartment. No note needed. He knows exactly who it's from.

"Shit," he growls. "I'm off to a bad fucking start."

Sixteen

Give Him Hell

Like a fool, Abigail waited for half an hour in front of Nathan's apartment. She saw Logan when he arrived at her place before heading over to Nathan's, so she already knew for a fact that he was at a party with Tank, Poppy, and her friends. But he said to meet him for dinner, so she did. And she waited. And waited. She thought for sure he'd return.

Her blood boils as she walks back to her place.

As she enters her apartment, Laura says, "That was quick!"

Cheeks bright as an apple, she quickly replies, "Yeah, quick dinner."

"Um, well, Kelly called. Said your car would be ready soon if you wanted to drive his over."

"Great," she replies. "I guess I'll head back out."

Angered and inconsolable, she treks down the driveway and to his car. As she climbs in the seat, she gets a tingling sensation shiver over her skin. The feel of the leather on her legs as she reaches in between them to pull the seat forward is a welcome one. She flips down the visor to locate the keys, and they fall on her lap along with a photo of a scantily clad girl. She recognizes her from last year—the tall brunette who would hang all over him. She quickly shoves it back in the visor and inserts the keys in the engine, roaring it to life.

Her mind is filled with a plethora of angry thoughts of Nathan. His blatant disregard for her. His willingness to blow her off on the first day back to school and how Poppy and her gang of Barbies always seem to be around to drive Nathan further away from the sweet, doting boyfriend she used to admire. And now, her mind shifts to Kelly and his incessant challenge of her despite having a girlfriend of his own. He has some nerve, showing up at her house on the first day, helping her move while Nathan was at practice, lying about Alex saying they needed help, and then fixing her car. Like she needs some knight in shining armor to keep an eye on her.

I'm doing fine on my own, aren't I?

She presses hard on the gas, and his car screams down his street. She spins the wheel. The tail of the car slides as she approaches his house. Something in her wants to keep going. To drive right out of the gates of campus and far away from here. But she can't. That would practically be stealing his car. She pounds on the brakes, bringing the car to a screeching halt. She swings open the door and steps out. Immediately, she sees Kelly slide out from under her car.

The expression on his face is unrecognizable to her.

"You like to drive fast?" he asks.

"Sometimes," she mumbles.

He cocks his head. Then, he wipes a bit of sweat from his brow. "I'm almost done," he says as he rolls back under her car.

She stands, tapping her foot as she waits for him to finish.

"In a rush?" he asks.

She wishes she had a good reason to say yes, but she doesn't. She bites her bottom lip. "What do I owe you for fixing my car?" she asks.

He slides back out from underneath her Volkswagen and smiles warmly at her. The little smudge of grease under his cheek looks sexy, and it hits her like a ton of bricks. She hates that he pulls her in so easily—and with a friendly smile no less.

Why is having him in my life complicating things so much? Every time things with Nathan get worse, Kelly is right there to make things better. It just doesn't make sense.

He stands up from the mechanics creeper and wipes his hand on the rag from his back pocket. "Let me wash my hands first."

She swallows the lump in her throat. Her cheeks are burning pink as she watches him walk toward his back door. The amazing shift of his hips toward his perfect backside is enough to make her jaw drop a little. He opens the door, and as he turns, he catches her in a stare.

"You coming?" he asks with a grin.

Abigail nods her head as her feet move underneath her. She enters, and then the memories from last semester rush through her, like a ghost from the past.

Don't think about the kiss, she repeats over and over in her head.

She tries to shake her nerves as she follows him to the kitchen. She watches in silence as he meticulously washes his large, strong hands. She steadies herself on the doorframe, awaiting his next move. He dries his hands, and then with one stride, he pulls open the refrigerator.

"You can pay me back by having a beer with me."

He pulls two Natty Lights out, and without waiting for an answer, he hands one to her. She takes it.

"I feel like I should be buying you a beer," she grumbles.

"Come and sit out back with me."

Out on the back deck, he takes a seat in a folding chair. She sits in the one diagonal to him. He takes a few gulps of his beer. She sips slowly on hers. He stares out into the woods in his backyard. She remains silent—for many reasons. One being, she's in a bad mood, and two, she doesn't really want to talk about, well, anything. He finishes his beer and then politely asks her if she cares for another. She has barely touched hers, so he enters and grabs one for himself.

He leans against the deck railing. "Listen," he begins, "about last year."

Her eyes grow wide, and her skin prickles at the memory.

"I said some things I shouldn't have, and I wanted to tell you that I'm sorry for that."

Slightly stunned, she slowly speaks, "Is that why you came to my house today?"

The corner of his mouth turns upward. "Sort of. I figured you all could use some extra help."

Her mood shifts toward darkness, and she replies, "Because you assumed I wouldn't have anyone to help me?"

"I didn't say that."

"But you're insinuating it."

Frustrated, he quips, "Maybe I am. And was I right?"

"Make you happy to be right?" she barks.

"No, Abigail, it doesn't."

She snickers.

"What? You don't believe me?"

She sighs. "I don't have the energy to argue."

"What's wrong with you?" he asks.

"With me?"

"Yeah." His eyes soften.

"Kelly, I'm in a bad mood," she admits.

"I can see that. What gives?"

She peeks her eyes up at him, trying to determine whether he's serious or not. She takes a gulp of her beer. "Look, you show up at my house to help me, us, or whatever, unpack, and then you fix my car. And, yeah, you did say some things that weren't very nice."

"Well, I'm not always going to be nice." His coolness is palpable.

She shakes her head. "Maybe I won't either then."

He chuckles. "You think you have it in you?"

"I'm getting there."

"So, what's that all about?"

"I'm getting tired of…"

"Waiting around?"

She whips her head up. "Why would you say that?"

"Listen, I called about your car, and Laura told me you were out for the night, having dinner with him. The next thing I know, you're pulling into my driveway."

Tears well in her eyes as she recalls her afternoon. She looks away from him. "I wanted to get my car," she lies.

"The last thing I wanted to do was upset you. But again, I find you in my apartment, and you're not reachable."

"Not reachable?"

"Yes, you're in this mood. And you tore into my driveway like a tyrant on the loose. And, yes, I do want to help you. Your car is a separate thing. I couldn't let you drive that. End of story."

"Fine, I'll agree to the car thing."

He rolls his eyes. "Good. Glad we could settle on one thing."

She lowers her head. She releases a heavy sigh, and as she does, she realizes her shoulders are hunched forward, and there is a stressful ache to them. Feeling the need to release it, she blurts out, "I waited in front of his apartment with a bag of takeout food for half an hour, only he was too busy to meet me because he was at a party."

"Jesus, Abigail. I'm sorry."

She looks up at him. "Are you?"

He takes his seat again. "Yeah, I am. I don't want you to be upset or in a bad mood. That doesn't make me feel good."

"Yeah, I wish I didn't feel this way either." She glances at her watch. She needs to address this issue, whether she wants to or not, but she can't avoid Nathan, nor should she let him off the hook. "I should go." She stands. "Thanks, Kelly. For fixing my car."

He stands as well. "If you have any trouble with it, call me, okay?"

Embarrassed by her interaction with him this afternoon and her admission about being stood up, she quickly tries to exit his deck. "Okay."

He calls after her, "Hey, Abigail!"

She spins around.

He leans back on the railing, and with an affirmative nod of his head, he says, "Give him hell."

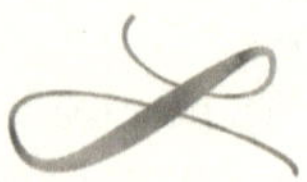

She can't give him hell because he's passed out on her bed when she gets home. Laura informed her he arrived an hour after she left, drunk and panicked. Laura told him he could wait in her room because she knew it wasn't going to be good. As Abigail watches him sleep, she wonders where their relationship is headed as she curses her vulnerable heart.

"If you can hear me, wake up," she whispers.

Startled, he bolts upward. "I fell asleep," he says, rubbing his eyes awake.

"You passed out."

He attempts to grab hold of her, but she quickly moves off the bed. Crossing the room to the large window looking out over the street, she folds her arms over her chest.

"I don't blame you for being pissed at me. I screwed up, and I'm so sorry."

She doesn't speak.

"Tank asked me to go for a bit, and I planned to come back to meet you and lost track of time."

"It doesn't matter," she whispers.

"Yes, it does." He climbs off the bed and approaches her. "Look at me, please."

Her voice chokes as she says, "You humiliated me…again."

"Abby, I didn't mean to."

She finally spins around to face him. Tears drip from her eyes. "How could you forget to meet me? The first day of school, and you're off at a party with…" It pains her to say it because green flashes before her eyes. She'll be admitting she is jealous of a girl she barely interacts with. A girl who can pull her boyfriend away from her and easily.

He attempts to hold her hand. She jerks hers back.

"Don't, please." She doesn't ever pull away from him. She can tell by the look on his face that he knows it, too.

"What can I do to make it up to you?"

"Don't ask me that. That's not fair," she snaps.

"You're right." Frustrated with himself, he runs his hand through his hair.

"There's something that is making you act this way, and I think you need to figure it out." She can barely grapple with her own words as they fly out of her mouth.

"What are you saying?"

"Don't string me along anymore, please."

Quickly, he responds, "I would never do that." He tries again to grab her. This time more forcefully around the waist. He pulls her in. "Where is this coming from?"

"Where? From *you*. You're not around, and when you say you will be, you aren't then either."

"I have to try harder."

"I don't want you to try harder. You shouldn't have to."

"You know what I mean."

"That's my point. I don't understand who you are anymore."

He releases her and steps back. "Can't a guy fuck up and get a break?"

"I've given you plenty, and maybe that's why you take advantage. You never would've stood me up before."

He hangs his head. "You're right. I wouldn't have." His omission surprises him.

"Last semester, you told me you didn't think of me." A tear falls on her cheek.

"That was stupid of me to say, and it wasn't how I wanted to say what was on my mind."

"Then, tell me now."

He walks over toward the couch in the corner of her room and drops into the seat, head in his hands. He sighs heavily. "Things have gotten busier for me, and I feel as though I'm being pulled in so many directions."

"We all are. But it's how we handle those moments that matter, Nathan."

"Every time I see that look of disappointment on your face, it makes me want to retreat, crawl in a hole, and die."

"But you…"

"Continue to do it, I know," he admits.

"So, what is it then?" she asks.

"I think that…" His voice trails off as he lowers his head.

She steps close to him. "Say it, Nathan."

He lifts his head and locks eyes with her. "I bet you're hard to get over."

She quietly gasps. "What?"

"And I love you so much. I do."

Her head swirls with indecision. Will anything change between them? "I love you, too. But this feels hard, and it shouldn't be."

"But I'm not ready to give up on us, and I think you feel the same, don't you?"

"Yes," she admits.

He takes her hand in his, pulls her gently onto the couch next to him, and in a tight embrace, he says, "I'm truly sorry, Abby. Can we start over now? Begin our junior year together on better terms?"

"Tell me what you're going to do differently, Nathan."

"I will keep my relationship with Poppy to on the field only. I promise you."

Her will to argue dissipates, and she agrees with a nod of her head. He pulls her back toward him as he stretches his long legs on the couch cushions. She settles into the bend in the couch as she pulls the blanket off the back, draping it over them. She closes her eyes, wanting desperately for this moment to be over and to wake up tomorrow with a different outlook.

He wraps his arms around her. He squeezes her tightly, unwilling to let her go. He kisses her on top of the head as he sighs with relief. He knows she could have given him hell, but instead, she gave him one more chance.

Seventeen

The Promise

Abigail is crouched in the large window overlooking campus, painting her toenails, listening to the muffled sound of Mazzy Star.

She hears a knock on her door. "Come in!" she yells.

She glances up at Laura and faintly smiles. "Hey."

Laura inhales another deep breath and then lets it out. "Hey."

Abigail scooches over to make room for Laura, but instead, Laura paces her room.

Abigail screws on the top of the nail polish and sets it down. She looks directly at Laura. "What's up? You okay?"

"Um, yeah. I'm good. It's just…" She plops down on the couch. "You remember last year?"

"You'll have to be more specific." She chuckles.

Laura doesn't smile. "You remember last year when we said we'd have no secrets?"

"I remember." She swings her legs off the window ledge and now directly faces Laura. "What's going on?"

"Um, well, I think…"

"You can tell me anything, Laura. You know that."

She nervously pushes her hair behind her ears. "You see, I—Wolfie and I were down at the fields, and…well, I at first saw them laughing and sort of bantering, but you know, I wasn't…"

"You saw who?" Her cheeks grow red.

Laura swallows hard. "Nathan and…Poppy."

Now, it's Abigail's turn to swallow, only her throat has tightened significantly. "I see, and?"

"Well, I wasn't going to say anything, but then we went into the training room. Long story, which I'll tell you later, but all of a sudden, some cheerleaders are rushing Poppy in. I guess she hurt her knee maybe, and then, like, out of blue, she *demanded* one of the girls go get Nathan."

"To get Nathan? Out of practice? For what?" Abigail barks. *Oh, this is making me so mad.*

"I didn't stay to see. It felt weird to me, so Wolfie and I left."

"So, Nathan never saw you?"

"No."

"Did she?" Abigail asks.

"No."

"But she wanted someone to get him?"

"Yes, more like commanded he come, and no one said anything to the contrary."

Abigail's eyes fill with hurt. Laura quickly jumps off the couch and sits next to her friend.

"I feel stupid," Abigail moans. "I mean, what the hell, Laura?"

"I hesitated to tell you but thought twice because I'd want to know. She's unsettling to me."

"Me, too. She keeps coming up in conversations with us, and that can't be a coincidence," Abigail says.

"Exactly."

She turns to Laura. "Thank you for telling me. I'm sure that wasn't easy." Abigail wraps her arms around Laura.

Laura rests her head on her shoulder. "You okay, Abigail?"

"Honestly, I'm tired, Laura."

"I can see it," she says, glancing up to meet her eyes.

"Is it that obvious?" Abigail asks.

"Yeah, unfortunately."

Sigh.

"Don't let anyone hold back on you, Abigail. You're too good for that."

"Yeah, I won't."

"No secrets. From anyone."

She tips her head, now resting it on Laura's shoulder, and as a tear drops on her cheek, she whispers, "No secrets."

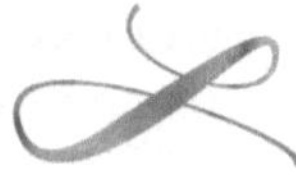

The Hawks are preparing for an away game against the team that knocked them out of postseason last year. She told Webber during their Advanced Kinesiology class that she would call Nathan soon and to make sure he gave him the message. She's trying not to overact about the news Laura shared. He did promise after all that he would keep his relationship with Poppy to on the field, and technically, that was in the field house, as disconcerting as it was to hear some other girl ask for her boyfriend. But she has been trying to study for a major test this week, and she really needed to concentrate on her academics and not all the drama in her life, as impossible as that might seem.

She wanders back toward Charlotte Street, alone with her thoughts. She takes out her headphones and plays the mix tape Laura made for her over the summer. The summer. When she felt better. Better than she does now.

She can't hear the car roll up next to her, but the slight beep of the horn makes her jump. She spins, ready to shoot daggers at the driver.

Instead, she sees Kelly roll down his window.

"Hey, stranger." He grants her an incredible smile.

She peels off her headphones. "What's that?"

"I said, hey, stranger." He laughs.

"Hey," she says with little reaction.

His brow furrows as he gives her a once-over. He stops smiling. "Hop in."

She opens her mouth to protest when he quickly says again, "Hop in, please." His expression tells her this is not a friendly invite but more of a demand.

She walks around the back of his car as he leans over, unlocks the door, and then pushes it open. She slides in next to him. He doesn't say a word as he speeds back down the road. He pulls down her street, but before he gets to her driveway, he stops the car.

"What's up?" she asks.

"I haven't seen you in a while."

"I've been so busy with school. Tough semester," she says.

"School, really?" he says with an edge.

"Yes, um, sorry I haven't seen you."

"You okay?"

She works her hardest to fight back her tears. "Yes, totally."

"I see."

She goes to grab for the handle when he grabs her hand. "Wait."

She turns. "What?"

"I want to know, are you okay?"

She tries to laugh him off. "I said I was."

His green eyes narrow. "My sister and I were at a party the other night."

"Good for you and Alex. Is that what you wanted to tell me?"

Kelly faces forward, and it's then that Abigail notices his uneasiness.

In no mood for chatting, she says, "Kelly, can we maybe pick this up some other time?"

He spins to face her. The anguish on his face is alarming. "Abigail," he says.

"What, Kelly? You're kind of freaking me out here."

"Abigail, I saw Nathan leave with Poppy," he blurts out.

Smack! Right in the face.

She swallows hard. She opens her mouth to speak, but nothing comes out. Her eyes mist, and she does nothing to fight back the tears. He tries to touch her hand again.

Suddenly, her sadness is replaced with anger. "Don't touch me," she hisses.

He veers back. "I'm sorry."

"Sorry? You're sorry? For what?!"

"For telling you, for seeing…"

"What? My boyfriend leave with another girl? Oh, please, you're loving this."

Shocked by her outburst, he says, "Abigail, I never…"

She flings open the door. "Leave me alone, Kelly." And before she can slam the door, she bursts into tears.

She runs full speed back to her house, up the driveway, and takes the rickety metal fire escape stairs all the way up the side of the house and to her bedroom. She climbs in the window. She has no idea what to do with all this information. She is in her right mind to march right over to his house and just get it over with. Break up with him. Once and for all.

But I love him too much to do that to him before a big game. Jesus, am I that much of a pushover? No, I'm not. I'm a good person. And if we're not meant to be, then I can at least end it like an adult, not some woman scorned. She won. I just have to accept that.

She sinks on her bed. Glancing down at her hands, she notices them trembling.

This is too hard for me. I can't do this anymore.

She lets sadness consume her, and at some point, when her tears have dried up, she passes out from exhaustion.

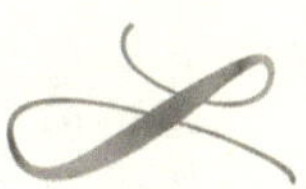

The loud ring of her telephone startles her. She stirs in her bed. Too tired to get up to answer it, she turns her back to the noise.

Her answering machine picks up. "You've reached Abigail. Leave a message."

"Hey, it's Nathan. Hoping to see you before I leave for my game. When you get this, swing by. I have something, um…just come by, okay? I love you."

Abigail groans as she rolls over and glances at the clock. It's quarter to seven, and she's been sleeping for hours. She rises out of bed and drags her body to the shower. Once out, she applies makeup around her eyes to mask the weariness that has permanently settled into them. She dresses in a pair of jeans and a flannel. She sighs deeply as she looks at her reflection, barely recognizing the person staring back at her.

She grabs her bag and heads down the stairs. She passes by Melissa's room and can hear a movie playing. With the door closed, most likely, she's in there with Logan, cuddled up and in for the night. Abigail does not disturb them. As she steps onto the first level, she's not the least bit surprised to find the rest of the big house empty.

Bree left a note on the large dry erase board in the kitchen: *Gone to Adam's for the weekend.*

Laura is in all probability out, doing something for the paper, at the station, or with Wolfie. It's a toss-up as to where she might be on a Friday night.

Abigail walks out onto the front porch, down the stairs to the driveway, and starts the engine in her Volkswagen Rabbit. She drives over to Nathan's apartment in Parkers Village. After she kills the engine, she rests her hands on the steering wheel, closes her eyes tightly, and prays silently that this pain in her heart will go away. After several minutes, she climbs out of her car and approaches the front door. She knocks twice, steps back, and waits.

Webber opens the door. "Hey there!"

"Hey, Webber." She steps into the entryway. "Nathan home?"

He cocks his head to the side, noting her somber demeanor, and replies, "Yeah, he sure is. Upstairs."

"Thanks." In no mood for small talk, she walks through a small hallway and right up the stairs to Nathan's room.

She can hear the soft hum of music playing through his door. She knocks.

He yells, "Come in!"

She exhales deeply and then turns the knob, trying desperately to shake her nerves.

"Hey, there you are!" His smile is bright and welcoming.

His reaction confuses her immediately.

She forces a smile. "Hey." She closes the door behind her. She hates that he is standing there in only a pair of sweatpants, leaning back on his bed.

"Where have you been hiding?" He laughs, sliding off the bed to approach her.

Her reaction is to step back, but she's frozen as he nears her. He wraps his arms around her and quickly seals their greeting with a kiss on the lips. He releases her.

"You've been busy?" he asks.

Snapping out of it, she mumbles, "Yes, so much schoolwork already."

"Well, I'm glad I got to see you before I left."

You are? she thinks.

He tips his head and asks, "You feeling okay?"

On the verge of tears and too overwhelmed to ask him anything, for fear she'll hear the awful truth, she lies, "Yes, not feeling well for a few days now."

"I'm sorry. Anything I can do?"

"No, just worn down maybe—that's all."

"Sit," he says, pointing to his bed.

She shuffles her feet over toward his bed, and she's about to say, *I need to talk to you*, when he quickly says, "Close your eyes." He goes over to his tall dresser and opens the top drawer. She can hear him move closer. "Open them."

She opens her weary eyes and looks upward. Nathan is standing before her, holding a small jewelry box with a wide smile on his face. He moves to hand it to her.

"What is this?" she stammers.

"Open it."

Her hands shake as she takes the box. His eyes are wide as she presses open the lid, revealing a silver band inside. Her body floods with confusion. She glances up at him with tears stinging her eyes.

"It's a promise ring," he declares.

"A what?"

He chuckles. "A promise ring. Try it on."

Her fingers tremble as she tries to remove the ring. She slips it onto her right ring finger. It fits perfectly.

"It's beautiful," she whispers. "But what's it for?"

He leans in front of her. "For you, silly."

A promise ring?

"I promise to always be there for you."

She watches his eyes dance over her face. His sincerity cannot be confused with anything else. His face is too honest for that. Which is why she practically bursts into tears.

"Abby"—he pulls her into him as he sits next to her on his bed—"I take it, you like it?"

She buries her head into his bare chest and nods her head.

"Good. I'm glad you like it."

She has never been more confused in her life and feels now, in this moment, that despite the information she might have been presented with, she can't outwardly ask him. They have too much history to try to destroy this moment.

He leans her back up after a few moments, and with unmasked passion, he kisses her deeply. He rests his head on her forehead. "I love you, Abby."

He leans in for one more kiss and then innocently asks, "Mind if I finish packing?"

"Of course not." She stares at the ring on her finger, but her mind is rushing with more questions than answers. *Maybe everyone else's assessment of the situations they witnessed were incorrect or innocent or can be explained?*

He snaps her back from her thoughts. "I'll be back Sunday," he says.

"If someone is injured, do they still travel with the team?" she blurts out.

He stops putting his clothes in the suitcase. "Not typically. No sense in them tying up a spot. Why do you ask?"

"Um, just curious."

He laughs. "Okay." He resumes putting his T-shirt in his duffel bag.

"So, what have you been up to these past few days?" she asks.

"You mean, besides buying you a ring?"

Did he buy me this ring out of guilt? she wonders.

"Not much. Typical football stuff."

She interrupts, "Any big news going on in your world?"

He chuckles. "No, I wish I had a better story to tell you."

Laura's and Kelly's words swirl through her brain. As queasiness rolls through her stomach, she is about to blurt out, *Did you sleep with her?* Then, his phone rings.

He picks up the receiver. "Hey, Dad. Yeah, I can talk. Abby's here."

"Tell your dad hello," she says.

"She says hello. What's up, Dad? Oh, really? Is it bad?" he asks. Then, there's a long silence as he listens intently. His brow furrows. "Uncle Dave, okay?"

Abigail approaches him. "Everything okay?" she whispers.

He places his hand over the receiver. "Someone broke into my uncle's fishing company."

"Oh, that's awful. Tell him I'm sorry. I'll let you talk to your dad and get some rest."

"Hang on, Dad." He places his hand back over the receiver. "You're leaving?" he asks.

"Yeah, you have to get up early, and I don't want to get you sick," she lies.

He smiles wide and winks. "You're the best." He leans down and kisses her on the cheek.

"Call me when you're back."

He waves good-bye to her, and without saying a word to Webber or Tank, she sneaks down the stairs and right out the front door.

She stares at her hand on the steering wheel the entire drive back to Charlotte Street. Thinking of the tremendous amount of guilt for doubting him, hatred in herself for not having the balls to straight up ask him, annoyed that Kelly had to be the one who saw them leaving together to place such doubt in her mind, and love for Laura for always looking out for her well-being.

But this ring tells me that Nathan is going to keep his promise to me. He's not the type of guy to do something like this to cover up his interest in someone else. I just have to trust him and start living my life without all this doubt clouding me. Only then will I truly be happy.

Eighteen

Love Hurts

Abigail slept like a rock last night. As though the stress of the past few days had finally caught up to her and she passed out from the sheer exhaustion of it all.

But now, as the sun shines into her window, she turns and hugs her pillow, not wanting to start the day. She lies in bed for an hour before she finally drags her body into the shower. After she is dressed, she heads out of the house on the gorgeous fall afternoon. With nothing planned for the day, she decides to go downtown and sit in Cool Beans and sip a nice cup of coffee. She sits in the window, staring out at the students walking by the store.

As she is about to pick up her book, she hears, "Hey there!"

Casey, Alex, and Jen approach her.

"Hey, guys!"

"Can we join you?"

"Of course." She slides into the booth.

"How come you're alone?" Casey asks.

"Oh, well, the girls are out, and Nathan has an away game." She immediately notices Alex's reaction. Her cheeks redden, and she lowers her eyes and plays with her coffee mug. Abigail tries to ignore it. "What about you guys? What are you up to today?"

"Not much," Jen adds. "I've got a game tomorrow afternoon, and that's about it for me."

"I plan to go watch her." Casey smiles.

"Great. I'll be there, too," Alex says.

Jen smiles. "Thanks, guys."

"Did I tell you, Abigail, that I got a job at Merrill Place the student health center?" Casey says.

"You did? Good for you," Abigail says.

"Yeah, now that we're off-campus, I need money, big time."

"I hear you. I should probably look for something, too," Abigail says.

The four sit and chat for another hour.

"Well, I've had my fill of coffee," Jen announces.

"We should get going anyway," Casey adds.

They all exit out of Cool Beans together.

"Abigail, you mind giving me a ride to campus? They have a bootleg CD table at the Union today, and I hear they have a bunch of awesome B-side stuff. I'm desperate for some new music," Alex says.

"No problem."

"See you guys, soon," Alex says as they all part ways. Alex climbs into Abigail's convertible. "I hear my handy brother fixed your car?"

Abigail swallows hard. "Yes, it was very nice of him."

"Yeah, he's good like that."

Abigail pulls into the center of campus and finds a loading zone close to the Union to drop Alex off.

Alex reaches for the handle but then stops. "My brother told me he saw you the other day."

Abigail's voice shakes. "Yes, he did."

Alex turns toward Abigail, and the expression on her faces says it all. She has something to say but can't.

"What?" Abigail asks.

Alex's eyes lower. "I saw them, too," she whispers. "Poppy and Nathan."

Abigail might throw up.

Alex places her hand on her leg. "We don't know what it meant, but we saw them leave together. It just seemed odd to us."

Abigail gazes forward. "I appreciate it, Alex. But if you'll excuse me now…"

Alex takes her hand off her leg. "Of course, Abigail. I'll see you later." She pushes open her car door and then closes it.

Abigail pulls out of her spot and heads straight home.

She knocks on Laura's door.

"Come in!" she yells. Laura is lying back on her bed, surrounded by CDs and her notebook. "Hey. I was making my playlist for next shift." She smiles, but it quickly fades.

Visibly despondent, Abigail sinks onto her bed.

"Oh no. What is it?" She tries to get a look at her face, but instead, Abigail buries it into her hands. "Abigail, talk to me."

"I…I think Nathan cheated on me."

"Oh no."

"Alex *and* Kelly both told me they saw him leave a party with Poppy."

"Shit. Really?"

"Yeah, and he gave me this promise ring yesterday." She lifts her head up.

"He bought you what?"

"This." She places her hand in front of Laura. "It's a promise ring, and I was so caught off guard that I didn't ask him anything."

"Oh, honey. I'm so very sorry. But until you know the truth, you can't assume anything, right?"

"But I already do, or I wouldn't feel like this." She drops her head again.

"Where is he now?"

"Away game, started at four."

Laura looks at the clock next to her bed. "Go to him."

"What?" Her head snaps up.

"Go to him. Make a grand gesture. Tell him that when you give someone a promise ring that it'd better be under the utmost considerate circumstances." She stands and takes Abigail's hands. "Because otherwise, it's just…" She pulls her up.

"Bullshit," she adds.

"That's my girl." Laura laughs. "Now, you go and confront him. Don't come back without a definitive answer, okay?"

With a renewed sense of purpose, Abigail nods her head firmly. "I won't."

"Good."

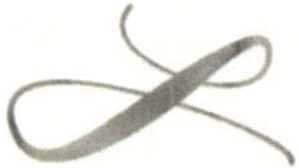

Abigail drives with the radio off the entire way. She recalls the first night she spent with Nathan in her dorm room.

They stood there together in the dark, watching the snow fall across the ground of the deserted campus. It was like they were the only two people in existence.

She pressed her head back onto his chest as he began to sway slightly to the music. He leaned down to one side of her face and kissed her on the cheek.

"I'm so happy to be here," he breathed, "with you."

"Me, too."

"Good. I'm glad you feel the same. I've been looking forward to some alone time with you since the day I laid eyes on you."

He started kissing her neck, and she could hear his breathing deepen. He ran his hand up her body.

He never let his arms go as she moved to face him.

"I almost feel like it's—"

"Too good to be true?" he whispered, finishing her thought.

"Yes, like it's too good. You're too good to be real, I guess." She bent her head as the intensity of gazing at his beautifully chiseled face was almost too much to handle. Then, she whispered, "It's you. You could pick anyone you wanted here—"

He cut her off, "Now, wait a second." He dropped his arms and backed up. His eyebrows bent in disappointment. 'No one can have anyone they want. Not me, not anyone."

"You know what I meant. I mean, you're—"

"Abby, stop, please. Think about what you're saying."

He seemed upset, and the more she tried to make it right, the worse she made it.

"Well, just because you're a football player. Your pictures are all over campus and—"

"Listen, and I only want to say this once. The first day I saw you, I never once thought a girl like you would be interested in someone like me. A jock, remember?" he said, sounding hurt. "So, just think about that the next time you look at yourself in the mirror and that you are someone that people—boys, guys, whatever—desire, Abby. And I'm not going to screw this up because I play football, understand? One has nothing to do with the other."

But now, she can't help but feel sadness as she knows things have changed so much. The way she felt back then was true. Dating a football player was going to bring her heartache. He was going to eventually become so popular that it would get in the way of their relationship. Only she can't blame him for it. When she had that conversation with him two years ago, he never could have known this would happen. And it's not his fault that it did happen. But what is his fault is how he has behaved despite it. He made his choices, and those choices have consequences.

And one of the choices she does not like is his friendship with Poppy. Abigail knows when a girl is on a mission to get someone. She makes no bones about it. And Nathan knows it, too. And if they are going to try and get their relationship back on track, Poppy can't be coming up in conversation. It's as simple as that. Abigail will just have to tell Nathan that tonight. And if he truly loves her, he won't think twice about asking Poppy to take a backseat. But then again, she feels like they have been here before.

Finally, Abigail pulls into the hotel lot. She spots the two large OSU football buses parked off to the side of the building. She parks her car and hesitantly walks into the lobby, praying she doesn't run into anyone who knows her. She approaches the front desk and asks for Nathan's room. She explains she's his girlfriend and that she drove all the way from campus to surprise him. The young woman behind the desk asks her for identification and then whispers to her the room he is staying in.

She winks. "Enjoy the night."

"Thank you."

She takes the elevator to the third floor and walks toward his room. Her adrenaline is rushing through her as she gets closer and closer to his door. Finally, she stands before number 327. Much like the day before, she knocks twice and then steps back, anxiously waiting for him to answer.

"Please be here," she whispers.

She can hear the door unlock, and then Nathan appears in front of her with nothing but a pair of sweatpants on. His cheeks pink immediately.

"Surprise," she whispers. "It's me."

"Abby, what are you doing here?"

He starts to close the door and step into the hallway when a voice asks, "Who is that? Is it Morgan? Tell that bitch to go away." She laughs.

Abigail can feel her heart start to pound. "Who's that?" Abigail says as she tries to get closer toward the door. She moves her head side to side, unable to get a good glimpse into the room.

"Let me explain." He tries shielding her with his body.

"Who is *that*?" But her gut is strong. Who else would it be? *Poppy.*

Poppy is sitting on the bed; she leans forward, and Abigail can see her peeking past the wall toward the door.

Oh my God. This cannot be happening.

Abigail looks into Nathan's eyes, and for the very first time, she sees someone she does not recognize. He pulls the door shut.

"How could you?" she says, her voice betraying her as it trembles low.

He tries to grab her arm, but she yanks it free.

"Don't touch me."

"Abby, please, it's not..."

"She's in your room, alone with you, and you're half-dressed—that is all I need to know," she spits out, unwilling to mask her anger.

She looks down at her hand. The ring. The symbol of short promises. She rips the ring off her finger, throws it in his general direction, and storms off down the hall. Nathan is hot on her heels. They reach the elevator nearly at the same time.

"Abby, please. Don't run away from me," he pleads. "Abby, please, I'm begging you to listen."

With venom in her voice, she blurts out, "I never want to see you again."

He's stunned into complete silence. He tries to catch his breath. "Abby, you can't..."

But she steps into the elevator, jamming her fingers to close the button, and says nothing. She won't even look at him. As the doors close, she can see in the distance a blonde figure peek her head out of his door. It's the last and only image she needs to see to say for certain that she is never taking him back.

It rains almost the entire way back. Fitting really. It's near one in the morning as her car careens back through campus. Her sadness is almost suppressed by her unwavering anger toward every man in her life—Nathan, Tank, and even Kelly, simply because he was right all along.

Too late to wake up Laura, she grabs a bottle of wine from the rack and doesn't bother with a glass, and she hides away in her room. There is a flashing light on her answering machine, but she can't get herself to listen to the messages. She forgoes any lights in her bedroom, opting to burn a few candles instead. The flicker of the flames better suits her mood. She takes several big swigs from the wine bottle as she stares out of the window overlooking the campus streets. The phone ringing breaks the silence of the night.

Thinking it is Nathan, she yanks the receiver off the base, and in a very stern voice, she answers, "Nathan, I told you, I never want to see you again!"

She starts to hang up when she hears, "It's Kelly."

Embarrassed and pissed off beyond belief, she completely has no words. She brings the receiver back up to her ear, listening to him breathe into the phone.

After a minute passes, she hears him say, "I'm coming over."

The line goes dead.

Right. Sure, he's coming over here. Well, I won't let him in!

She remains in her window, drinking from her bottle, when she hears the distinct muffled sound of his muscle car pull onto her street. Moments later, the sound is gone. She sits still in her window, praying he won't ring the doorbell at this hour and that he'll just go away.

But suddenly, she hears the clang of steel, one step at a time.

"Jesus," she mumbles.

She gets up and looks out her other window and sees Kelly climbing up the fire escape on the side of the house in the pouring rain.

She throws open the window. "What are you doing?" she whispers.

He looks up, having a few more stairs to climb. "What does it look like?"

She steps back inside her room, taking another long sip of her wine as she paces the wooden floor in her bare feet. She watches as he climbs into her window, as if any of this is normal.

The dimly lit room makes it impossible for her to see his expression. He doesn't move. Neither does she. He doesn't speak. Neither does she. An uncomfortable moment passes between them.

Then, he notices the bottle in her hand. "Going to offer me a drink?"

She holds out the bottle in front of him. "Have at it," she murmurs.

He gingerly steps toward her, T-shirt soaked, clinging to his pecs as he takes the bottle from her hand and takes a sip. He hands it back to her. She returns to her seat by the window, curling her legs up under her as she does. She stares back out into the miserable, rainy night.

He sits on the couch, facing her. There's a long pause.

Then, unable to mask her pain, she blurts out, "If you're here to tell me you told me so, you can save your breath, okay?"

He doesn't reply. Again, agonizing silence fills the room.

"You going to sit here and not say anything?" she finally asks as she turns to look at him.

The shadow from the candle casts a gloom over his handsome face. She hates that he looks sad as well.

Frustrated, she asks, "Why are you here, Kelly? To prove yet again that you can be the guy who's around?"

He lowers his eyes. But doesn't speak. He merely wipes the rain from his face.

She turns to face the window again, and tears drip down her cheeks. "Just leave, please," she begs.

Finally, he says, "You know I can't do that."

She wipes her cheek. "Why? So you can see me cry? *Again and again.*"

"Come on. I'm not an asshole. You know me, Abigail."

"Well, isn't that what you see? A girl who's always crying."

"What do you see?" he asks.

She tips her head back and sighs with frustration. "Yeah, that's what I see. A girl who is always sad…lately," she adds.

He leans forward on his forearms. "And me?"

"You what?"

"Want to hear what I see?"

As she wipes another tear, she tucks her long blonde hair behind her ear. She faces him.

"I see a beautiful girl trying hard to hold on to something that she should've let go of a long time ago."

His honesty catches her completely off guard. "Kelly, I can't…"

"Oh, no. No, don't mistake what I said. I'm not trying to win you over. I'm not here to sweep you off your feet."

I am so confused.

"I'm here as your friend. The sound of your voice on the phone. The sadness and anger I've seen. I hate it."

"You hate it?"

He chuckles. "Yeah, how could I like it?" He tries to get her to laugh but to no avail. He continues, "The other day, when you got out of my car, what I told you was huge, and it blew up in my face."

"It was…"

"Then, my sister said she saw you today, too. I had a feeling today was not a good day for you."

She places the wine bottle down with authority. "It was awful," she admits.

She faintly hears him say, "I'm so sorry."

"I feel like such a fool."

He leans back on her couch, resting his hands behind his head. "Want to talk about it?"

She sighs heavily as she finds herself yet again in the company of Kelly Conrad at a pivotal point in her life. He's the only one around to talk to.

"I went to his hotel room. And…" A tear drops down her neckline. "He came to the door, and then I heard her inside. They were alone. He seemed nervous. That was all I needed to see."

"That's awful. No bones about it."

"Yeah, first time for everything," she says at a poor attempt at a joke.

"If he tells you nothing happened, would you…could you take him back?"

Without hesitation, she sadly replies, "No."

"You'll get through this. I'm certain you will."

Something about his positive thinking in her condition aggravates her. She releases a long sigh and tries not to let her poor attitude cloud her vision. But she can't help it. "What about you? That girl I always see you with, where will you tell her you were tonight?"

"She's not my girlfriend. There's a difference."

"Is there? 'Cause I bet if you told her you climbed into my window"—Abigail's voice rises as she scrambles to her feet and motions toward the window—"that she'd be flat-out pissed."

"Maybe, maybe not. She wouldn't ask, and I wouldn't tell her."

"Typical."

He stands and moves toward her. In a very stern voice, he says, "Now, listen, I'm not the enemy here. I don't play games, and I don't lie to women. She and I know where we once stood. That's over and done."

She laughs. "Does she get that?"

"Listen, tonight is not about me…"

"It's always about you," she mumbles.

"I heard that." He steps closer. "I have it on pretty good authority to say that it's typically about *you*."

"Ha! How dare you."

"How dare me?" he challenges back.

"Yes, you are always pushing my buttons, making me feel like…why are you here now?"

His chuckle is deep, and it eggs her on more.

"You climb in my window like some knight in shining armor, but you're so quick to tell me you don't want to sweep me off my feet. Who does that?"

"I do," he hisses.

The alcohol mixes in her brain, and her words fly out of her mouth before she can catch them. This is unfortunate for her. "I'm not some charity case who can't keep a boyfriend."

"Oh, you didn't enter the pity party, did you?" His chest puffs.

"Pity party? Me?!"

"Yes, you."

"So, what if I did?" she says.

"You think because I didn't climb in your window specifically to get into your pants that I'm an asshole who has been leading you *and* some random girl I hook up with along? For what? What and where has that gotten me?"

She backs down. "That's not what I meant."

But he won't. "Sure it was. That is exactly what you were implying."

"I…I…"

He steps to within inches of her. She can sense the heat from his body and smell his cologne.

"You think I've done all this…for almost a year because we had one lousy kiss last semester? You really think that's what this is about?"

"Lo-lousy kiss?" she whispers.

She could not feel more stupid than she does in this very moment. She has thought about that kiss, like any college-aged girl would. But he brushes it off like it was simply another day for him. She should have known. He's probably kissed all his sister's friends since the moment he could.

"Yes," he says, exasperated. "You really think I envisioned our—a first kiss to be because I challenged you to live a little?"

Okay, so he remembers that part.

"You think I wanted to kick you out afterward? Is that how you saw this going? Come on. I can do a hell of a lot better…and by the looks of you, I'd say you can, too."

She's stunned. There he goes again. Stunning her into confusion. "See, what you did there, it confuses me."

He shakes his head. "Believe me, it's confusing."

"You're confused?"

"Abigail"—he laughs—"I've befriended a girl who happens to be dating the biggest athlete on campus. So, yeah, it's been a bit strange for me, too."

"Was dating," she adds sadly.

"Was," he whispers. He picks her chin up with his hand and looks her deep in the eyes. He takes a deliberate breath in and then adds, "Listen, get some sleep, please. I just really wanted to make sure you were okay. I swear."

She swallows hard. *I'm way too emotional for much more than climbing into bed and wishing this day away.* "All right."

He steps back toward the window. The rain has quieted, and cool air enters the room as he raises the window to climb out. He looks at her again. He hesitates. He seems like he's about to speak but says nothing; instead, he steps through the window.

"Be careful," she says.

He glances back at her. She notes the softness in his eyes, and before she can tell him that she appreciates him coming by to check on her, he's gone. And it's as though the last twenty minutes never happened. Her distraction is gone, and the wretched heartbreak that is Nathan Ryan consumes her again.

Nineteen

Saying Good-Bye

Abigail watches as Laura pulls out of the driveway, and shortly after, Nathan pulls in. She wanted to meet him on neutral ground, the front porch, in order to stay strong in her convictions. He climbs out of his car and shoves his hands deep into the pockets of his jeans as he makes his way toward the stairs. He slowly shuffles up the steps. She can't get herself to look at him.

"Hey," he says.

"Hey." Bile rises in her throat, and she forces it down with a hard swallow.

He steps in front of her. "Abby, please," he begs. "I am so sorry about last night."

"It's not about last night anymore," she replies.

"Look at me, please."

She turns her head and finally catches eyes with him. He looks worse for wear. But she assumes she does, too.

"Nothing happened between us."

"I don't believe you." As the words spill from her lips, she can't believe she is even saying them. She's never *not* believed a word he has told her.

He gasps. "You don't trust me? Wow."

"Why should I?"

"Because I'm telling you the truth." His voice is strained.

Her navy eyes fill with tears. "But it doesn't matter anymore."

"What? You've already made up your mind?" Sadness fills his voice. His eyes are lost and hollow, and he squeezes them shut, forcing back his tears.

"You made it up for me," she chokes out.

"I did?"

"Yes, you've proven over and over that now is not a good time for us anymore."

"I know what I've done, and I'm telling you, nothing would make me not want to be with you." He tries to take her hand, but she pulls it away.

"Don't ask me to rehash everything. This has been coming for a while. I think you wanted it to happen."

"No, don't say that!" He tries again to touch her, but she steps back from him.

"Then, you're not being honest with yourself, Nathan."

"I am. I swear."

"Have you kissed her?" she asks, wiping a tear from her face.

"What?" His face turns crimson.

Her lips quivers as she repeats the one question she has never wanted to ask, "I asked you, have you kissed her?"

"It's not what you think."

"Then, what is it?"

He nervously shuffles his feet. "It's that we're friends and the parties get crazy sometimes and it's harmless really…"

"Harmless to whom?"

"You know what I mean."

"If it was harmless, then it wouldn't hurt, but it does. Don't you see that?"

"She just…she likes me, and I keep telling her…it's not like she doesn't see I have a girlfriend…"

"Had a girlfriend, Nathan. *Had.*" Her voices fades.

"What?"

"You told me all I needed to know. And last night? Do you have any idea how humiliating that was for me? Do you?"

Her anger rises as he meekly stands before her, shoulders hunched, unwilling to tell her what she needs to hear. But if he did, she can't say for sure that her feelings would change. Words can't fix the hurt.

He reaches for her hand again.

"Don't," she begs, blinking back her sobs. "You had to recognize this wasn't going to work. You can't hang with her, be her go-to when she's hurt or whatever, and then return to me when you have time."

"Be her go-to? What?"

"Do you tell me every time you spend time with her or every time you party with her?"

He anxiously runs his hands through his hair. "No," he admits. "Because I know you'd get mad."

"Exactly. So, that tells me you know it's not right, but you do it regardless."

"What am I supposed to do?"

"Nothing. I don't want to pull you in one direction when you are so clearly heading in the other."

"Oh, Abby." A tear drops on his cheek. "I don't want this…"

Seeing him cry is killing her. But so is this horrible feeling, like someone is stomping on her heart repeatedly. "Nathan, we can't keep going in circles. I…I'm not happy anymore."

He gasps. "I don't make you happy?" he speaks to himself. "That is the last thing I ever wanted to do. Your happiness matters to me; it always will. I love you, Abby. I don't understand what is happening."

Tears fill her tired eyes, and it's painfully clear to her that if she doesn't end this, it will continue to cause them pain. God forbid they wake up one day with hatred for one another because they didn't have the strength to release it. "I think you do. It's over, Nathan. I'm asking you to respect that."

"Over?" he murmurs. "But…"

She's surprised at how crushed he looks. But regardless, she must shake the guilt she is feeling for breaking up with him. She must be free.

So, she thinks of Poppy peeking her smug face out of his hotel room last night, and it gives her the right amount of courage to look at the boy she once loved very deeply and say, "Good-bye, Nathan."

She spins quickly on her heel and runs full speed back into her house.

She bursts into tears, as the realization and significance of this moment is simply too raw for her.

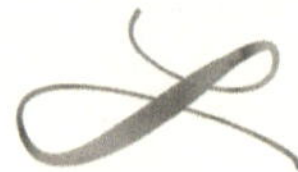

She closes the door to her bedroom, pulls the shades down tight, and crawls into her bed. She tosses and turns, knowing her internal clock is telling her it isn't time for bed, but her aching body and broken heart make her feel as though she is lost.

Where do lost people go? she wonders. *Aren't I supposed to be locked in my room? I can't burden society with my depressed mood. I should be confined to my bed. I'm too unstable to carry on as normal. Whatever that is anymore. All I know is, right now, I can't face anything or anyone.*

She stares at the ceiling as the realization of Nathan no longer belonging to her starts to sink in. She can't call him whenever she wants. She can't stop by his place or borrow his shirt. The red flannel one she used to wear around his room. She can't do any of the things she used to do, like meet him for coffee in between classes. She can't kiss him when he gives her a goofy grin. She can't cheer him on at the football games. She can't go to the Ridge. She won't see Webber or Tank as much. It's been her whole world for the past two years, and now, it no longer will be. Just like that. And she's in mourning, only she can't fully comprehend the magnitude of her breakup or the changes in her life still to come.

"Abigail," she hears faintly. Then, there's a knock on her door.

She waits. Her door clicks open.

"Abigail, it's me," Laura says.

"Come in."

Laura enters and crosses the room to her bed. She sits on the edge. "Are you okay?"

"No," she admits.

"Did Nathan come by?"

"Yes, and…" With tears filling her large navy eyes, she says the words that break her heart again, "It's over."

"Shit, I'm so sorry," she slurs.

Abigail wipes the wet from her eyes, sits up in her bed, and glances at the clock. It's three in the afternoon on Sunday. "You drunk?"

Laura smiles. "Maybe a little?"

Abigail flops back down on her bed, covering her face with her arm. "Ugh, I wish I were."

Laura giggles and pulls out a bottle of wine from behind her back. "Move over," she says as she climbs in next to Abigail. She hands her the wine. "Time to catch up."

Abigail drinks from the bottle. Laura places her hands behind her head and rests them on the headboard. A smile envelops her face.

"What are you so chipper about?" Abigail asks.

"I don't mean to be. I get you're sad."

"No, I need the distraction."

She sighs. "I realized today that I can't please everyone and that I'm really freaking sad about losing Travis. He was the first person I ever slept with, and he meant a lot to me."

"Wow. I didn't realize."

"Yeah, and I kind of play this fantasy in my mind that we are together and life is right back to where it was when I started the news segment on the radio. I liked those days the most. I couldn't admit that before today. But now, for some reason, I feel this weight has been lifted, and no matter what, I'm going to be okay."

She turns on her side and faces Abigail. She puts her hand on top of hers. "You're going to be okay, too. I guarantee it. I didn't want to come up here, all sad and blah. I wanted to come up here, look at you, and tell you, this will pass by, too."

Abigail lowers her eyes as a tear falls on her cheek.

"We're in college. We should be having fun, not worrying about all this relationship drama."

"Thanks," she whispers.

"So, what do you say, we take care of us?"

"I'd like that."

"I'll help you through this, I promise you."

Abigail laughs for the first time in weeks. "Who were you out drinking with that put all this perspective into that head of yours?"

Laura hesitates to tell Abigail about her running into Tank at the coffee shop earlier this morning. What could have been a friendly cup of coffee turned into a full day of drinking beer and discussing relationships and loss. Something they are both familiar with. The enlightened conversation they had put much of the past year into perspective for Laura.

But Abigail and Tank are having a tough time since their blowup about the trial. And if Laura says all this advice came from Tank, then Abigail will immediately dismiss it out of blind bias.

"It's amazing what can happen around here when you have a few hours to kill."

Abigail becomes noticeably quiet.

"Don't get trapped in your thoughts," Laura warns.

"I can't help it. I'm going to have so much time to kill now that it seems unreal to me. He was my world for two years."

"Oh, honey. It's going to be different. But there are other fish in the sea."

"Ha! Know anyone in particular?" she scoffs.

A smirk grows across her face, "Abigail, there has been a guy coming around for the past year, trying to get to know you. Please tell me you are not that oblivious?"

"You don't mean Kelly?"

Laura grabs the bottle of wine and takes another swig. As she winces, she says, "That is exactly who I mean."

"We're friends."

"I can see that."

"So, that's that."

"Sure it is," Laura says with sarcasm dripping off her tongue.

Abigail grabs the bottle back. "We are. He told me the other night."

"Other night?"

"Yeah, he came over after I got back from the hotel."

Laura shoots up in bed and turns her body squarely toward Abigail's. "I'm sorry. He was here, the other night? When?"

Her cheeks flame red. "Um, I don't know. It was, like, one in the morning."

"I didn't hear him come in."

"He came up the fire escape."

Laura bursts into a fit of laughter. "Kelly. Climbed up your stairs. At one in the morning. And you think you're just friends?"

"Um, yeah. He said he came by to see how I was. Well, he called first and…"

Laura cocks her head to the side and gives her a sympathetic gaze. "My dear, sweet friend. It's either that you don't know how many heads you turn or—and I'll give you some credit for this,—that you've been so consumed with Nathan that you haven't paid attention to what's been going on around you."

"*Laura.*"

"What? It's true."

"I don't know that."

"Oh my God. He came here in the beginning of the semester to help *you* move. What a sly little devil."

"What?"

"Yeah. Bree, Melissa, and I could not figure out why he said Alex said we needed help. It was because of you. Then, he fixed your car…"

"He drove me back and forth to the hospital when you were in there," she adds, subconsciously running through all the events in her head.

"Hot damn!" She giggles.

"Stop it. Seriously, we're friends."

Laura shakes her head. "If you say so. But, hey, do me a favor, okay?"

"What?"

"Don't wait too long."

"Wait too long?"

Laura winks. "Yeah, don't waste precious time."

Laura squeezes her hand, and in that moment, as they lock eyes, Abigail starts to understand the meaning behind her words. She cares about Abigail and doesn't want her to spend her junior year wasting her time…with just anyone.

Twenty

Bad Day, Worse News

Nathan can't begin to comprehend the awful sensation in the pit of his stomach.

What have I done? I just let the best thing that has ever happened to me slip right through my fingers. I have to win her back. But how? She doesn't trust me, and if she won't be with me, how can I get her to trust me?

The only thing he can think to do right now is to sweat out his misery in the gym. Rid himself of the past weekend. He must clear his head somehow. He wanders toward the field house, where he knows he'll be alone at this time of day. He gets on the bike and rides it for almost an hour, to the point where he's light-headed as he steps off, staggering to the weight bench and collapsing down on it. He puts his head in his hands, trying hard to calm the fast beat of his heart. Sweat profusely drips between his hands, pooling on the floor in front of him. Within seconds, nausea rushes over him like a tidal wave. He makes it to the nearest garbage can and tosses his last meal.

He slowly stands up and is on the verge of tears as the high from exercise is being replaced by the pain in his heart. He decides to hit the showers to try and cool his body down when he hears the slam of a door and the distinct cries of a girl in agonizing pain. He dashes toward the training room, and another loud crash can be heard over the music playing in the weight room. He pushes the door open, anxiously peering in the unlit room. He sees a figure leaning over the medicine cabinet, desperately trying to jimmy the lock with a tool of some kind.

He flips on the light as he yells, "Hey, you can't be in here!"

"Leave me alone," she yells.

"Poppy? What the hell?"

He races toward her and is about to hold her arm when she barks, "Don't touch me."

"Poppy, it's me!"

With hunched shoulders, she slowly turns to face him. She drops the tool in her hand, and it crashes toward the floor. "Just leave me alone."

But he can't. He sees the outline of his once-vibrant, well-put-together companion stand before him, and she is now pale, makeup streaking down her pretty face, her unkempt hair tied in a messy ponytail.

"What the hell happened to you?"

"Don't concern yourself," she says with bitterness.

"What the hell, Poppy? Tell me what's going on!"

She stumbles back toward one of the training tables and drops to the floor. He can now see clearly the damage she inflicted on the medicine cabinet.

"Were you trying to steal some drugs?" he asks.

"Jesus, you're such a do-gooder. You know that?" Venom escapes her mouth, and she makes no apology for it.

"I don't need this shit from you." He shakes his head. "You don't want my help? I won't give it to you."

He turns to leave. Suddenly, he can hear her sobs. The horrific cries of a girl undoubtedly in pain. He stops mere feet from the door. He waits for her instructions. If she really wants him to leave, she will tell him, as she holds nothing back.

But what he least expects her to say are the two words he hears her whisper through her agony, "I'm pregnant."

There is no way he heard her right.

"What did you say?" He spins to face her.

"It's true."

"Pregnant?" A horrifying chill runs down his sweaty body.

She nods her head.

"Jesus, Poppy." *Could this fucking day be any worse?!*

"I don't know when. But it's true."

He delicately glides toward her and drops to his knees in front of her. "How can I…I mean, what can I do?"

"I don't want to burden you."

He shakes his head. "Don't say that. Ever. Tell me what I can do," he says, his eyes softening as he takes in this pathetic creature piled on the floor of the training room.

"I need help," she admits.

He places his arms around her, and this time, she lets him. He holds her tight. He pulls her broken body into his, if only to let her know he won't leave her, no matter what.

He keeps her in his arms for quite some time until she finally says, "You're so sweaty."

Laughter is released inside them both, as though the realization of life is comical. That one day, you are one thing, and the next day, the biggest joke life could throw at a college student is hurled at you at lightning speed and you never bother to attempt to catch it.

"I'm sorry." He laughs.

But her laughter does not last long, and before she can speak, she is sobbing into his chest. "What am I going to do?"

"I think we should go to the student health center first and see what options there are."

"But I…"

Nathan releases his embrace and locks eyes with hers. He wipes the tears from her cheeks. "Poppy, you can't be in here, breaking into the training room. You could get in big trouble. You need to get help, okay?"

She drops her head. "I feel like I'm losing my mind."

"I can't imagine. But let me help you." He takes her hand, pulling her up with him. "Come," he says as he guides her toward the locker rooms. He peers inside the men's locker room, and once the coast is clear, he pulls her into the room. "Sit here and wait for me."

Her body shakes as she lowers onto the bench near the lockers. Nathan grabs a towel and then turns on the water in the communal showers. He undresses and rinses his body while shampooing his hair. He steps out and notices Poppy has leaned back on the locker, eyes closed, arms wrapped around her slender body. His mind races with all kinds of questions and depressing thoughts as he dresses into his dry clothes.

Quietly, he asks, "Ready?"

Without a word spoken, she stands and heads toward the door. Gently, he places his arm around her shoulders as they make the long walk to the health center.

Nathan approaches the counter.

"Can I help you?" the young woman asks. Her name tag says Justine.

"Yes, my friend would like to speak to someone privately."

"Please have her sign in." Justine points to the paperwork on a clipboard.

Nathan takes it and hands it to Poppy, who is sitting in the corner seat. Within moments of handing in the papers, Poppy is called.

"Please, come with me," Poppy begs.

"Of course." Nathan walks alongside her, taking her hand to steady her.

The doctor opens the door to their room, and both enter. The gloominess in the room is unmistakable.

"I'm Dr. Hale. Tell me why you are here today."

Voice shaking, Poppy replies, "I'm two weeks late."

"I see. Well, before we do anything, I'd like you to take a pregnancy test. Please follow me. You can wait here," she quickly says to Nathan.

Nathan, when left on his own, begins to panic. He went from standing on Abby's porch this morning, trying one last time to hold on to the one person he needs the most in his life, to now, being here with the one girl he shouldn't be with. If ever there was a time he felt his world spiraling out of control, it's now. He's on the verge of vomiting, and he wants so badly to run from here. Run from all of this. But he knows he can't. He can't leave Poppy in her condition. What kind of decent person would do that?

He paces the room, anxiously waiting for her return. Within minutes, she is back, the look of horror still gracing her face. And he knows, with just that one look, that he's trapped.

Nathan is about to ask her all the questions he's been holding back when Dr. Hale emerges into the room.

"Let me get some vital signs while we wait for the results."

It's been a few weeks since Casey got the position at the health center. So far, it has worked beautifully with her class schedule. She can manage both and socialize with her friends and, of course, spend time with her girlfriend, Jen.

She approaches Justine at the front. "Hey, I'm back from my lunch break."

"Great. Dr. Hale has a patient in room four. Can you grab the test results and bring them to her?"

"I'm on it."

Casey enters the back room, where the laboratory is, and approaches the lab assistant. "Hey there, you have the lab results for room four?"

The lab assistant hands the paper to Casey. Casey glances down and is struck by the brief note listed on the paper.

Pregnancy Test: Positive

It's almost impossible not to react, but a shiver runs down Casey's spine.

Poor thing, whomever she is. I'm assuming this news will not be good since everyone who comes in here is a college student.

Casey takes a deep breath in before she knocks quietly on room four.

"Come in," she hears.

She opens the door. Dr. Hale has her back toward the window. Casey steps into the room. The couple sitting in the chairs both have their heads down. His arms are tightly wrapped around the girl, who seems to be crying. As Casey approaches Dr. Hale with the paper in her hand, she steps by the two.

Her face burns dark red. *Holy shit! It's Nathan! And Poppy. Oh my God.*

"Thank you," Dr. Hale says.

Casey spins on her heel, and as quickly as she can, she exits the room without being seen. Thinking fast on her feet, Casey rushes toward the front desk.

"Justine, I must have eaten something bad. I am feeling so sick. Can you cover me?" she asks.

"Oh gosh, I'm so sorry. Anything I—"

"No, I really need to go. I can't stay here." She covers her mouth for effect.

Justine shoos her toward the door, and Casey grabs her bag and then bolts out the entrance. She drives quickly back to her house. She understands she can't say anything about what she saw. But she had to get out of there before they saw her. For all their sakes.

Twenty-One

Whatever It Takes

Abigail remained in her room for a few days. Leaving with only moments to arrive for class and then immediately leaving afterward. Making sure to take alternate routes whenever possible to avoid seeing anyone, specifically Nathan. But sitting alone in the big house is starting to get to her because all she thinks about is him.

Bree has her marketing work to do and is still head over heels in love with Assistant Professor Adam Cooper. Sneaking off as much as possible to steal time with him. Who can blame her? Abigail sure can't.

Laura is back into the swing of the radio station, reporting on the news, trying desperately to figure out who vandalized the soccer house. This means Melissa is right in the mix at *The Weekly Blue*. Laura, Melissa, and Wolfie are knee-deep in their work.

Naturally, this continues to create a noticeable absence in the house most nights.

After class, Abigail decides to borrow Bree's mountain bike, the one she bought to ride along with Adam, and take a ride herself. She finds herself zigzagging through the back streets of the campus and heading farther and farther away, feeling the freedom the distance between her and the university brings her.

The farther away from school, the farther away I am from him.

After riding for thirty minutes or so, she can see the back parking lot of Diesel Food in the distance. Parched and in need of some water, she decides to go in for a break.

The nearly empty bar is exactly what Abigail was hoping for.

The waitress, scantily clad in a tank top and cutoff jean shorts with purple hair, approaches her. "Hey, nice to see you again," she says.

"You, too."

"Have a seat," she says, pointing to a barstool.

"Thanks."

"What can I get you?"

"Water, please, and can I see the menu?"

"Sure thing, doll." She smiles and places the menu and water in front of her. "Hey, you waitress before? We're hiring if you're interested?"

Shocked, Abigail leans back on her stool. "Really? Me?"

"Sure, why not? You come in, and you're nice. They'd like you here."

I have been so bored lately, and everyone has something to do. I could use the money, and I could use the distraction. "I waitressed summers in Lake George."

"It pays okay, but tips are good."

Abigail smiles at the thought. "Sure, I've been looking for a job." *It's not a flat-out lie. I have been considering looking for some time now. Just happens that this came to me.*

"Great. Give me your number, and Norah will call you."

"Norah?"

"Yeah, she's the owner. Really cool lady."

"Oh, great."

She slides a piece of paper over to her. Abigail writes down her information.

She picks it up. "Abigail." She nods her head. "Chloe."

"Nice to meet you, Chloe."

"You like those Carbon Calms, don't you?"

Abigail smiles.

Chloe winks, and within moments, she places one in front of her.

The back door swings open, and as if on cue, Chloe says, "The usual?"

"Yeah, thanks."

"Your friend's here," she says with a peculiar grin.

Abigail's skin crawls with recognition of the deep voice that pierced the air. She peers over her shoulder toward the end of the bar. Kelly spins to face in her direction. He doesn't smile. Abigail faintly does. He strides toward her slowly and deliberately. Making it known he is in no hurry to get to her. She swallows hard as he approaches. His T-shirt is stained in sweat and grease. His face is a tad dirty as well.

"Doing a little day drinking?" He grants her a smirk.

"Um, well…more like a…"

"A welcome to the family," Chloe interjects. "She's going to be waitressing here. Toni left, and we need the help."

He looks at Chloe. "Toni left? I didn't know."

"Yeah, a few days ago. Had to move back to Florida. Family thing."

Kelly glances over at Abigail. "So, you'll be working here."

"Well, Norah still needs to call me and all, but…"

"She will," Chloe adds confidently. "Drink while you wait?" she asks.

"Sure, Chloe. I'll have what she's having," Kelly says.

She places a drink in front of him. "I'll go check on your order."

He takes the seat next to her. Silence again fills the room. "I didn't see your car. Everything okay?"

"Yes, I was riding Bree's bike."

He chuckles. "You, on a bike ride?"

"What's so funny?"

"Nothing. That's cute," he says with little emotion. "You eating?"

"Well, I came in for some water but was going to order…"

"Chloe!" he yells. "Can you make it two? To go?"

"Sure thing!" she yells back.

He picks up his drink and takes a big gulp. Nervously, Abigail does the same. Within minutes, Chloe is placing a large to-go bag in front of him on the bar. He stands up and pays, and then with a nod of his head, he motions for Abigail to follow him.

"Bye, Abigail. See you soon." Chloe disappears back into the kitchen.

"Bye," she whispers.

The draw toward Kelly is strangely undeniable. And she finds herself standing and walking out the door.

He pops the trunk of his car. "This yours, I assume?" He approaches the top-of-the-line Cannondale leaning up against the brick wall. He whistles. "You should lock this up."

"It was sort of a last-minute thing, and Bree was gone…"

He gently places it into his trunk. She stands and watches him, wondering what her next move is. But it's obvious to him. "You going to get in?"

Embarrassed, she quips, "Oh, yeah." She walks around and climbs into the passenger seat.

They drive in silence most of the way back. She realizes about midway back toward campus that he is going to his house.

He pulls into his driveway and kills the engine. "Can you grab the food? I'll get the bike out."

Abigail shoves her hand into her cutoff jean shorts as she grips the bag of food in her other hand and waits by the garage. He walks her bike in and leans it up by the back door. He opens the door, allowing her in first. Her nerves rush through her like a train off the rails.

"Beer?" he asks.

Desperate to calm herself, she nods. He goes into the kitchen and grabs two. He stretches out his hand but as she tries to take the beer, he pulls it away quickly.

He cocks his head. "You're quiet. What gives?" he asks.

Her cheeks flame red, and she's convinced he'll notice, so she lowers her eyes. "Um, it's nothing. I, um…" *Don't know what I'm doing here. And being alone with you is difficult for me. I can't explain it, Kelly so please don't ask me to.*

He hands her the beer. "I gotta shower before we eat. I'll be back. Please try to make yourself comfortable."

Again, she nods. She watches as he walks away from her. His broad shoulders give way to the tight shift in his hips, enticing her heart to race. Before he notices her stare, she turns and heads to the back porch. She sits in the chair, tucking her legs up underneath her as she watches the sun diminish. She hugs herself as the cool air replaces the sun-kissed autumn afternoon. She wishes she had brought a sweater with her. Her T-shirt is not keeping her warm.

Several minutes later, she notices a figure pass by in the kitchen. She catches a brief glimpse of Kelly as he walks by in only a faded pair of jeans. She swallows hard. She coyly eyes him from the porch as he pulls a T-shirt over his head. His body is something she has admired from afar for a long time, having caught sight of him briefly over the past year.

Kelly rummages through the kitchen, grabbing items for their meal. Almost finished with her beer, she gets up and approaches the entryway to the kitchen. She leans in the doorway and watches him.

He's a mystery. A very sexy mystery.

"Are you hungry?" he asks.

He never led on that he knew she was there.

She chokes out, "Sort of."

He turns, and for the first time, he smiles at her.

She bites her lower lip. Then, she quickly adds, "I mean, I'll eat or do what…"

He stops. "What I want?"

She could swear his eyes flashed a brighter shade of green. It catches her breath. "I mean, it's your…"

He comes closer to her, placing what he had in his hand on the table. "You seem nervous?" he asks.

Her throat is tight. "Nervous? Um, no…" *I'm lying. I'm wildly nervous around you.*

"Good." He steps closer. "I haven't seen you in a while." His expression softens.

"I've been in hiding," she admits as she takes a step to the side, distancing herself a bit.

"Are you still upset about me coming over that night?"

She shakes her head. "No, I'm not upset. Should I be?"

"I can't tell with you sometimes."

"Me?" she innocently asks.

"Yeah, one minute, you're all fired up at me, and the next, well, you're like this." He motions to her. "Quiet and nervous."

"I said I'm not nervous," she whispers.

"That's not what your demeanor is saying."

"Well, I can't control what you see."

He gives her a devilish grin as his eyes dance over her. She immediately turns.

"Can I have another beer?" she asks as she opens his refrigerator and grabs one.

He watches as she yanks off the cap and takes a very large gulp. "Help yourself." He laughs.

She releases her lips from the bottle but still can't meet his stare.

"Usually, when a girl won't look at me, it's because she likes me." He chuckles to himself.

Her face burns. But she must lock eyes with him for no other reason than to throw him off. "Did you really just say that?"

He comes a little closer. The sexy grin spread across his lips plays with her emotions. "See, you go from a little nervous—wait, *not* nervous." He laughs. "To fired up at me."

"Because you say all these things to me, and you're…" Frustrated, she puts her beer down on the counter and crosses her arms over her cleavage. "You're, like, trying to lead me on or something."

"Ha!"

"Kelly?" Her voice is strained. "Why are you doing this?"

"Doing this? What are you talking about?"

"This." She motions between them. "Buying me dinner, bringing me over here. Coming to my room. Telling me repeatedly that you don't like me but that…I…I am nervous. *Okay*. You make me *really* nervous."

He becomes very serious as he says, "You don't make me nervous."

"I never said I did. You're lucky to be so confident."

"No."

"No what?"

"I just know what I want."

She sighs, "Well, good for you."

His pecs twitch as he steps a little closer to her. "Aren't you a little curious as to what that is?"

Her heart beats hard in her chest. She wants to ask, but she can't speak. He's closer now. She senses the heat from his body. The smell of his clean skin entices her to breathe in deep.

"Can you take my hand?" he asks.

This completely throws her off. She gazes down at his open palm. Her hand trembles slightly as she hesitatingly takes his. The warm touch of his skin on hers is incredible. He delicately pulls her toward him.

"This is making me more nervous," she whispers. She lifts her large navy eyes up to meet his.

Without warning, he spins her around. She is facing the counter; his trunk is pressed up tightly to her back.

He shifts her hair off her shoulder and whispers in her ear, "It's only me."

Her skin prickles at the sound of his voice and the touch of his breath on her skin. He wraps his arms tightly around her waist. Her muscles tighten.

"Relax, Abigail."

She swallows hard. "You said I was a lousy kisser and that…"

He takes his hand, runs it up the front of her body, and to her chin, tipping her head back onto his shoulder. His face presses closer to her ear. He murmurs, "I said, *it* was lousy. Only because I couldn't do anything about it. I've been trying so hard to keep you at bay."

Her breathing deepens. She unequivocally desires to feel his lips on hers again.

He squeezes her a little tighter. "I don't want you to be nervous around me. Not anymore. Okay?"

Her breath catches as she tries to speak. Finally, she's able to whisper, "Kelly, the way you look makes me feel that way. You can understand that, right?"

"No, because when I look at you, all I want to do is fuck you."

She gasps, twisting to look at him. The darkness in his bedroom eyes is something she is not accustomed to. His confidence is brimming as he places his thumb and pulls down on her bottom lip.

"But right now," he says, "what I want to do is kiss you. Knowing you're here. With only me."

Tipping his head, he slowly parts his lips. Finally, his mouth presses onto hers, and a surge of electricity pushes through her. She grabs tightly around his waist as his hands drag through her hair.

She moans when his tongue drives into her mouth. His breathing is rapid. Her mind races with intense thoughts. Thoughts of him and her alone…*really alone.* Then, quickly, he lifts her up and carries her to his couch. Never letting his mouth leave hers.

He lowers them both down together. He is neither gentle nor rough.

He continues to kiss her over and over, trailing his kisses down her neck, tracing his lips over her collarbone. Her moans fill the quiet space. She is in disbelief that this is happening. Despite her trying repeatedly to put Kelly Conrad out of her mind, he's remained. As though he can sense her thoughts racing, he suddenly leans up, pulling her with him as he sits back on the couch.

Moments pass, and then he speaks, "Well"—he sighs—"we should eat."

She quickly looks up at him. She's somewhat confused. "Okay, but is something wrong?"

He squeezes her shoulder and kisses her atop her head. Then, rather abruptly, he releases his embrace and stands before her. Abigail swallows hard.

Here comes the bad news, right?

"Kelly?"

He starts to pace his living room. A terrible feeling rips through Abigail's gut. Kelly pauses and stares at her, and then he immediately starts to pace again. She watches him tear a trail into his carpet. She can't take it anymore.

She jumps up off the couch. "Okay, it's clear this was a mistake." She starts to pass him and head toward the garage.

Without warning, he lunges toward the door, blocking her from leaving. "You can't…I mean, please don't go."

"Kelly, tell me what's going on."

He releases a heavy sigh. He starts to back her up toward the living room again. "Listen, I need to ask you something."

Eyes wide, she asks, "What?"

He rubs his hand over his face. "Are you through with him?" he blurts out.

She hasn't thought about Nathan Ryan in the past few hours, but suddenly, he arrives smack dab into Kelly's living room…uninvited.

She stumbles a bit backward. "Kelly."

"I need to know."

"Do you think I'd be here if I wasn't?"

"I think we've been here a few times, and I need to understand where your head's at."

"Where my head's at?"

"Yes. Answer my question, Abigail."

She straightens up and sadly replies, "Yes, we are." *He's with Poppy—clearly.*

He spins toward the kitchen and walks in.

She follows him. "But that's not it. Is it?"

He starts to fiddle with the silverware.

"Kelly, talk to me."

"Abigail, I…"

"What, Kelly?"

"I'm—I'm not like him."

"Can we please talk about something else?" She grabs her beer off the counter. Obviously agitated.

He watches her drink. He leans back on the table, dropping the silverware back on top. She places the empty beer bottle back on the counter with authority. She goes to get another one.

"No," he says with conviction.

She freezes.

"Listen…"

"I'm waiting," she growls.

"I need you sober."

"I am!"

"Settle down."

She rolls her eyes. He straightens up off the table and nears her.

"Oh, be careful," he warns.

His demeanor is stern. She swallows hard.

"I'm serious." His eyes flicker.

She can't help but giggle. "You're *so* serious."

"Abigail, this is." He places his hand on her arm.

"Okay, okay. But I'm still confused."

"When I said I'm not like him, I need you to know, before this goes any further, that I mean it."

"But you hardly know him."

"I know enough. I know enough about you."

Slightly offended, she quips, "You think you know plenty about me?"

"I recognize who you are. Fundamentally."

"Really?" she challenges.

"I can tell a guy like me makes you blush a lot."

She tips her head back. "This again." She looks back at him. "It's like you want me to tell you that you're…"

"I'm what?"

"You need affirmation? Look in the mirror."

"The exact opposite."

"Then, what are you not telling me?"

He sighs heavily. "That I normally don't date girls like you."

Crushed.

"What?"

"Yeah, I don't."

Tears sting her eyes. She is merely at a loss for words. But she finds the courage to ask, "Why even look my way?"

"Are you fucking serious?"

"Yeah, I'm serious. I feel you push and pull me. All the time. And I don't know what to do about it," she confesses.

"I do."

"You do?"

He reaches over his head, grabs the edge of his T-shirt, and quickly pulls it over his head, tossing it on the table. He stands before her, chiseled to perfection and inked like a beautiful story. She can feel her skin warm as she takes in the view in front of her.

He comes a little closer. "But the question is, will you let it happen?"

"Will I let what happen?" she innocently asks.

"Listen, what I said before is true. I normally don't date girls like you because I don't date. And girls like you want to date." She goes to speak, but he quickly quiets her by gently tracing a strand of her hair, pulling it down between his fingertips.

"Kelly, if you don't want to date me, that is entirely up to you. But you aren't exactly pulling away." There is the challenging girl he's grown to admire. "Nor have you let me walk out the door."

"Come to my room. Will you?" he asks, presenting his hand to her.

She takes it, and he leads her up the stairs to his room. The entire time, her heart is beating so fast that she is positive it is going to burst.

He guides her inside and quickly closes the door. He braces her up against the door, passionately kissing her. Her understanding of his attraction to her is undeniable. He still wants her here despite their confusing conversations.

He leans his head onto hers. "Stay here."

He goes over to his bedside lamp and switches it on. He sits back on his bed, facing her. She remains leaning on the door.

In a deep, sultry voice, he says, "Can I speak freely? I don't want to offend you."

"It might be a bit late for that," she says with a little smile.

"Not funny."

"Kelly, do you not want me here? If I'm not your type or whatever, trust me, after everything I've been through, please just say it, so I can go," she says, trying desperately to sound confident and not like a little girl lost.

He rubs his face, and with marked frustration, he says, "No, the opposite. Because you're not usually the type of girl I'm with, it makes me want you even more. Christ, for the past year"—he stands up and approaches her—"I've watched you from afar, just wanting you so badly."

"What?" she whispers.

"Yes, and I'm not talking about going out on dates and movies and all that shit. I'm talking about…"

"Oh," she says, her skin flushing.

"Yeah, that's what I'm trying to tell you. I'm way more interested in what happens in here than any of that other stuff, and that doesn't always work for everyone. A lot of people in fact."

"I see."

"Have you thought about it?"

Her head is absolutely swirling with all kinds of thoughts. "Thought about what specifically?"

"Fucking me?"

She swallows hard. "*Kelly*?"

"What? I asked if I could speak freely." He takes her hand. He drags it down his chest to his waist, and her lips part. "Do you want this?" he asks.

She mumbles.

"Let me hear you." He slowly presses his hips into hers.

"Kelly," she moans.

"Abigail, tell me you want me."

Her body might burst. They've barely touched, but her hand caressing his massive chest only increases her lust for him. "I do want you."

He smiles. "Good." He starts to pull her toward the bed.

She freezes. She went from an innocent bike ride this afternoon to now being in Kelly's room. Her head spins with all kinds of frightening thoughts. One being that she's not sure she's ready to move on, and the other is that once she sleeps with him, he'll no longer see her. She's not ready for this to end. Whatever this is.

"I can't."

"What's wrong?"

She starts for the door.

"Talk to me, please."

"You said it yourself—we're different."

"No," he says, approaching her. "I said, we typically hang out with different people."

"Same thing."

"Okay, okay. Just please don't go." His voice is sincere, and she peers up at him.

"Why?"

"Because I've waited a goddamn long time to get you here, and apparently, I've done something to make you want to leave." He takes her hand.

She doesn't take his. Instead, she pushes her hair back off her face. "You were right. And you knew it."

"But what if I'm wrong?"

"I can't be some experiment for you."

He chuckles. "Is dating the only option for you?"

"No. But this isn't either."

She turns again, toward the door. He reaches over her head, pushing back on the door, preventing her from opening it.

"You going to keep me trapped in here?" she asks, placing her hand on the doorknob.

"Of course not. But if you leave now, we both know that's not a good sign."

He slides his hand down the doorframe and takes a step closer to her. She peers over her shoulder at him, giving him a twisted look. One glance from her, and he wraps his arms around her waist, pulling her back into his front. He softly kisses her on the side of her cheek, testing the waters again. She can't resist him and leans back into his frame. Running his hands over her slender belly, he traces the curves of her hips as he nibbles on her ear. Her skin prickles, and she can't—or doesn't want to—tell him to stop.

"Is this okay?" he asks.

She mumbles, "Uh-huh."

"What if I did this?" he whispers as he slides his hand into the waist of her jean shorts, barely touching her hip bone.

Her breath catches, and her belly tightens. "Kelly," she whispers. "I…"

Gliding his fingertips down further, they graze between her legs. "I want to make you feel great," he boasts.

His other hand releases the top button on her shorts. He eases his fingers into her as she braces herself on the door. She moans, her back arching in a perfect curve.

Oh my God, what is happening to me?

His free hand cups her breast over her T-shirt, squeezing it as her breathing becomes rapid.

He works his magic, and as her eyes flutter open, she sees he is watching her intently as she comes to life. Quicker than she thought she would.

But the pent-up sexual tension between them needed to be released—at least by one of them. And the way he's smiling at her tells her he is glad she didn't leave.

Twenty-Two

Dark Secrets

They finish dinner.

As Abigail sits back, Kelly touches her flushed cheek. "You good?" he asks.

"Yes, thank you for dinner."

"My pleasure," he says with a devilish grin.

He picks up the dishes as she puts the glasses in the dishwasher.

"Can I offer you another beer?" he asks.

She stumbles over her words, "If you—I mean, I'll have one if you are?"

"I offered."

"Okay."

He grabs two and heads toward the back porch. It's cool out, but cold air feels good on her warm skin. She hugs her body as she sits in a chair.

"Come here," he says. "I'll keep you warm." He pats his lap.

She walks over to him and lowers herself onto his lap. He wraps his large arm around her, pulling her in close. They sit, drinking their beer in virtual peace for nearly ten minutes, when he finally breaks the silence.

"You have beautiful hair," he says.

Her voice cracks. "Thank you."

"You averse to having it pulled?"

She nearly chokes on her beer. "Wow. Um…"

"I bet you'd like it."

He can tell by her reaction alone that this is unchartered territory for her. But that won't stop him from continuing. She turns on his lap to look at him. There is something about the way she is eyeing him, and he can't help but notice a tightness in his jeans.

This innocent girl-next-door thing you've got going on is too much for me. I don't know how much longer I can wait.

"Do you like to pull hair?"

He's mischievously joyful by her question. He takes the beer from her hand and places it on the table next to them. Bending her leg, he brings it onto one side of him while the other dangles around his hip. He sits up straight, bringing his face closer to hers. He pushes her hair off her shoulders, and it hangs beautifully down her back. He traces the thick waves with his fingers, and then he gathers it near the ends and gives it a slight tug. Her head leans back, exposing her neck. He watches her as she slowly brings her head back, and her eyes meet his. They dance across his face, and there is an eagerness to her stare. He can sense it. She has it. That thing no one talks about. But maybe she is not quite aware of it yet.

He wants to taste her again. "Kiss me," he says.

She leans forward, and he keeps a tight grip on her hair. Her beautiful blonde hair. Her lips touch his, and his heartbeat quickens. He runs his hand up to the back of her head, massaging the nape of her neck as he keeps his hand tangled into her hair. He can tell it feels good for her because she continues to kiss him. Then, when she least expects it, he twists his fingers into the thickness of her hair and pulls not hard, but not lightly either. Her head tilts back, her eyes rolling with pleasure. He leans into her, seizing her mouth. He captures her moans, savoring them as she enjoys her newfound pleasure.

Reluctantly, he pulls her back. Her eyes flash open.

He smiles at her. "To answer your question, yes."

She swallows hard. "Okay."

He doesn't want her to leave, but he can't have her stay. It's too soon. He wants her to be comfortable. "It's getting late. Can I bring you home?" He wishes he could take it slow with her, but a year has been slow enough. He knows he needs to let her call the shots, unfortunately.

He's glad to see she appears disappointed, but she agrees regardless. "Thanks."

With Bree's bike hanging out of the trunk, Kelly drives down Abigail's street.

"Um, you can drop me off here," she says as his car nears the driveway.

He chuckles. "You don't want your roommates to see me?"

Her cheeks redden. "No, I assumed you wouldn't want them seeing you."

He deserves that. "Okay. Here it is." Putting the car in park, he hops out and takes the bike out of the trunk. Every inch of him wants to take her in his arms and kiss her, but he recognizes he can't.

She grabs the handlebars of the bike. She bashfully glances at him. "I'll..." she starts to say.

"I'll see you around. I mean, soon?" he says.

Her smile is faint, and it's clear she has no idea that he is holding his breath, hoping for the answer he wants to hear.

"You know where to find me."

Crushed. That is not the answer I was hoping for. But I deserve it. I get this.

Trying to make light of the moment, he glances up the driveway and toward her house. "Yeah, I know where to find you. Night, Abigail."

"Good night, Kelly," she whispers.

He watches her walk the bike up the driveway. This beautiful girl-next-door that he understands, deep down, he should leave alone, but he can't. Or he won't. He waits for her to unlock her front door before he drives away and straight toward his sister's apartment.

He knocks twice, and Casey opens the door.

"Kelly. Hey, how are you?"

"Fine. My sis around?"

"Yep. We're just watching a movie."

"Cool."

"Come on in."

Kelly and Casey enter the living room. Alex is curled under a blanket on the couch.

"Brother," she says with a smile. "What's going on?"

"Nothing. You?"

"Chilling. What brings you over? You out tonight?"

"Um, I had to drop Abigail off." He notices as he says her name, Casey stops in her tracks.

She sits in the chair and immediately blurts out, "Is she okay?" with marked concern in her voice.

Both Kelly and Alex turn to look at her.

"Yes, she's fine. Why?" he adds.

It's obvious by her expression that there is more to her question than just friendly concern. "Oh, um, no reason. I want her to be happy—that's all." She chuckles uncomfortably.

Kelly is unsure how to read her response. *Does this have to do with me hanging out with her?* He jokes, "I get I'm not the greatest guy in the world, Casey."

Her lip quivers. "I didn't mean that." She quickly rises. "Would you excuse me?" She rushes toward the stairs and hurries up to her room.

Kelly turns to his sister and whispers, "What the hell was that about?"

Alex sits up and pushes the blanket off her. "Hey, what do you say we go grab a drink?"

Kelly looks at the clock. "Now?"

"Yes," she replies through gritted teeth. "I never get to see you."

"Um, sure, sis. Whatever you want to do." He follows her toward the front door.

She slips on her Dr. Martens boots and opens the door. They climb into Kelly's car.

"Where to?"

"Someplace close. Not Diesel Food."

He cocks his head. "Okay. Everything all right with you two tonight? You're both acting strange."

"I'll explain," she says as she urges him to drive.

They sit at a table at Monroe's, near the back. It's virtually empty, but Alex insisted on sitting far away from the bar. She carries over four beers.

Kelly shakes his head. "This had better be good." He laughs as she sits across from him.

Alex picks up a beer, and in one dramatic motion, she finishes about half of it. She places it on the table. Kelly doesn't touch his. Not yet.

"What's going on with you and Abigail?"

"Nothing. We had dinner." *And I finally got her alone and all to myself.*

"Dinner?"

"Yeah—you know, when two people eat a meal together."

She rolls her eyes. "I'm serious, Kelly. I know you. There's more to it."

"What can I say? She grabs my interest."

Alex smiles. "I knew it. I'm surprised, but I guessed it."

"Surprised?"

"Yeah, she's not exactly your type. Beautiful, yes. But…"

"Look, I get it. But maybe I need a new type."

Alex hangs her head.

"What is it?"

"It's just…I think she might have some *things* going on—that's all."

His heart drops. He fears more than anything that this is about Nathan. "*Things*? Like what?"

"I overheard something I wasn't supposed to," she blurts out.

"Yeah, and?" His heart rate quickens. *Is she back with Nathan? Couldn't be. She was with me a mere hour ago.* "Come on, Alex. Spill it. You brought me here. Now, tell." His green eyes narrow.

"You can't tell anyone. Promise?"

"A brotherly promise," he says, placing his hand over his heart.

"I'm serious, Kelly."

He takes his sister's hand. "I promise, sis."

Alex takes a sip of her beer. "I overheard Casey on the phone. She was crying, and I was about to go in her room when I heard her tell someone that..."

"That what?"

Alex swallows hard. "That *Nathan*...got Poppy pregnant."

Kelly's jaw drops open. A horrible sensation ripples through his gut. He takes in his sister's misty eyes and grasps unequivocally that she is telling the truth. The devastating and crushing truth. He leans back in his chair, grabbing a beer as he does. He takes a hard pull, swallowing several times until the bottle is done. He places it down. "I have no freaking clue what to do with this information," he barks.

"I know. Neither do I. But I'm guessing that's why Casey was so upset back at the apartment. She can't say a damn thing. She could get fired."

"Wait, fired?"

"Yeah, she works at the student health center."

Kelly bangs his fist on the table. "Jesus Christ. What a fuckup."

"Kelly, he's a really great guy. But I think he..."

"He got caught up in his popularity and caught with his pants down!"

"What?"

"Yeah, Abigail caught them in a hotel room," he sneers.

"Oh no! Poor Abigail."

"Yeah. Now, what?"

"I don't know. But how does she not find out?" Alex asks.

"You think she knows already?" Kelly says.

"You tell me. You're the one hanging out with her."

He contemplates the afternoon/evening they had. She seemed too relaxed to have something as grave as this on her mind. Cheating is one thing; getting the girl pregnant in college is a whole other type of hell.

He shakes his head. "No. No way she knows."

"Thank God."

"Shit!" he yells.

"Kelly! What?"

"I can't be around her. She can't know, and I can't look at her, having this kind of information. She'll be too broken to even...oh my God. This is awful. Just the worst. How can I keep this secret? Fuck." He places his hands over his face.

Alex grabs her brother's hand. "You have to. And besides, we can't predict the future."

His eyes tell her all she needs to know. "Mark my words. She'll figure it out. She'll see right through anyone that has this information. Something in my gut is telling me this secret will be impossible for anyone to keep."

I can see she's heartbroken. You don't just get over someone you spent two years within a couple of weeks. But I've had my eye on her for a year, and I've been watching her suffer. And now, she'll continue to suffer if she finds this out. Pregnant. You never want to hear you've been cheated on. But enough to get someone pregnant? Talk about a scandal you can't get out from under. I'll try and be there for her, but she might not want anything to do with men. Period. Nathan Ryan might have officially ruined my chances just by existing.

But this girl drives me wild. Like nothing I've felt before. She's so innocent-looking. But I get the sense there is something within her that's more like me than she realizes. I think she could use a little fun in her life. She needs to be free. She's been so tied up, playing the doting girlfriend to the star athlete, that she ended up being the one on the sidelines.

I want to make her center stage.

If only she'll let me.

But she's wary of me. I can see it. She thinks if I sleep with her, I'll forget about her. Which pisses me off. Because she completely underestimates how desirable is she.

If I get the chance to sleep with her, believe me, I'll want to do it again.

And again.

Twenty-Three

Testing Our Limits

Abigail walks into the Union in the hopes of catching Laura before her shift at the station. As she approaches the fireplace and couches, she sees Laura and Tank sitting close to one another, and they look to be in deep conversation.

Reluctantly, she approaches. She notices the expression on their faces, and immediately, she feels like the third wheel.

"Hey," she says.

Laura looks surprised to see her. Tank's expression is one of disappointment. "Hey," they reply in unison.

"I was wondering if you had a minute to chat?" she directs toward Laura.

Laura scrambles to her feet. "Sure. We can go into the studio?"

"That works for me."

As they start to walk away, there's a slight tug on Abigail's arm.

"Hey," Tank says. "You broke up with Nathan?"

She shimmies her arm free. "Yes, I did."

He shakes his head. "So, that's it, huh? You guys are over?"

"What are you asking me, Tank?"

"I'll see you inside," Laura interjects.

"I'm surprised—that's all. And I had to hear it from him. I expected to talk to him about it, but over, for good?"

"You live with him. And besides, you think I was going to dial you up and tell you?" Her tone is mean.

"Abby."

"What, Tank?" She's trying to remain strong, but her heart is so heavy.

"I thought we could get past all of this."

"Well, this is news to me."

"I think you need to reconsider the lawsuit," he snaps.

Her shoulders drop. "And now, you know why we can't get past it. I thought you were asking me about Nathan, and you bring this up?" She shakes her head in disgust.

"What?" he barks.

"It's just…the two of you. You always want to have it your way, and, well, life doesn't work that way."

He narrows his eyes at her. "Is that so?"

Desperate for a break from her life under the nose of the football team, she adds, "Yeah, this year is about me. Because it has to be." With that, she spins on her heel and heads to the station to talk with Laura.

"Abby, wait," he yells after her.

I can't do this right now. I just can't.

She marches in. Laura is waiting for her.

She greets the guys in the room, and then Laura, sensing Abigail's frustration, says, "We can meet in my studio."

Laura opens the door, and Abigail enters. As she closes it, she rests her head on the back of the door, closes her eyes, and sighs deeply.

"That bad, huh?"

"He is so maddening. They both are. Always about them and what they want. I'm sick of it."

Laura's eyes get wide. "Wow. What did he say?"

"Nothing. It's…"

"You can tell me."

"If I do, you can't say a word."

Laura tips her head in disbelief. "I'd never tell."

Abigail plops in the chair near Laura. "I'm sorry. I just see you guys talking and feel as if I have to say that." She pauses and quickly adds, "But obviously, I know I don't."

"What about Tank?"

"I need a break, Laura. I can't dance around his feelings anymore."

Laura's cheeks redden at her friend's confession. "But you still care about him, right?"

"Of course. I always will. But for right now, I need to distance myself from them. Football. All of it."

Laura is about to speak and then quickly stops.

Abigail continues, "I keep having this dream that Nathan gets hurt, is off the team, and leaves school, and I never see him again. I wake up with the weirdest feeling all the time. Like I'm empty." A small tear drips onto her cheek, and she catches it with the tip of her finger. "It seems so silly really. He was drifting away from me, so what was I holding on for so tightly? It only ended up making it harder for me. But I'd be lying if I said I didn't miss him, Laura, because I do. He was my best friend, too. I lost a lot that day."

"Oh, Abigail, I know you did. It'll take time to feel differently. Have you spoken to him at all?"

She shakes her head. "I can't. I don't even think I could hear his voice. I'd cry."

"I get it. It's too soon. But eventually."

She straightens in the chair and says with a bit of angry air in her voice, "And I'm mad at him, too, you know? He hurt me. So, I guess there's that, too."

"Yeah, there's that, too. It's good to let it simmer a little. For both of them. They need to know what they're missing and to understand there are consequences for their actions. They tend to receive a lot of privileges around here; a few bruises could do them both some good."

Abigail smiles. "See, this is exactly why I came to talk to you. You always make me feel better."

"I try," Laura says.

"I do have something else to tell you," Abigail says, her cheeks flushing.

Laura's eyes light up. "Oh, this should be good."

"I might have had dinner with someone the other night, and it went really well...I think...sort of."

Laura's eyes brighten. "Kelly?!"

She can't help her smile. "Yes, but I wanted to ask you before you freak out. Am I moving forward too fast?"

"What? No. I don't think so. Why?"

"I'm confused, I guess. Nathan and I were together a long time. And I'm still so hurt by how it all went down. I tried, Laura. I gave him chances to make it right. But that last straw was just too much for me."

"You gave him a lot of chances, Abigail. More than most people would, and believe me, he knows it."

Abigail cocks her head. "Why? Have you spoken to him?"

"Um, well, no. I see them around. Stuff like that."

Abigail's eyes lower. "Is he sad?"

Laura opens her mouth, but Abigail quickly adds, "Wait! Don't answer that. I can't—I mean, I don't want to know."

"Oh, Abigail," she whispers. "Just be happy. Whatever you do. Make sure you are taking care of you. You deserve it. And Kelly? Can I just say...damn! He is so fine. If you don't get with him, believe me, someone else will. He's so hot."

Abigail nervously plays with her fingers and says, "He's too hot. He's like crazy hot. I'm so edgy around him."

"Please. Get over it. You're totally hot, too. You've always been with hot people. So, just have fun. That's my advice!"

"Don't say anything, okay? It was just a quick dinner. Super casual. He's not a dating kind of guy. So, I'm just sort of doing my own thing, too."

"I won't. Secret's safe."

Abigail smiles wide. "Well, on that note, I have to go. Starting my new waitressing job, and I don't want to be late."

"I want details later," she says with a devilish grin, "about Kelly. I need to live vicariously through you."

Abigail leans over and kisses her friend on the cheek. "Lots of details…"

Laura smacks her on the arm as she hurries away. "Since I have your secret, I get the details, and I'm not letting this go!"

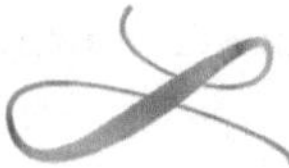

Abigail enters Diesel Food through the back door and clocks in. She is both excited and nervous for her first day on the job. She came last week for an hour and got all her paperwork filled out, followed by a quick run-through of the place, and she's as prepared as she could be to start.

Chloe sets her up in the front section of the restaurant, and before she realizes it, several hours pass by in a flash.

"It's busy today. You doing okay?" Chloe asks.

"I think so!" Abigail smiles as she picks up a few drinks and drops them off at a table of seven.

After she puts their food order in the window, she spins toward the bar and notices the girl with the dark hair who Kelly used to hang out with sitting on a stool, her hands wrapped around a cold beer. Abigail avoids making eye contact with her and goes about her work.

About half an hour later, the door swings open, and in walks Kelly. He doesn't see Abigail as she peeks at him from behind the host stand. He takes a seat next to the brunette, and it's obvious by their interaction that they were supposed to be meeting here.

Oh, I see how it is. He doesn't date, but he does this? Meeting girls here right under my very nose. No, thank you.

She hasn't heard from him in days, and she didn't quite know what to do about that. So, one day led into another, and she assumed at some point, she'd see him. But not like this.

"Order up, Abigail," the cook yells.

Her ears burn red as she goes behind the end of the bar to pick up her order for a table of four. She is dying to look at him but is too bent on seeing them together that the only thing she can think to do is to pretend they're not here.

As her shift winds down, she does her prep work in the back. Every so often, she glimpses out to see if they are still sitting together, side by side, drinking at the bar. A part of her doesn't want him to leave, but she's paralyzed with fear to approach him. At this point, it's beyond obvious.

She cashes out her receipts and unties the apron off from around her waist. She balls it up and then approaches Chloe. "Well, I think that's it for me." She musters a smile.

"Great job. Good hustle, girl," Chloe says.

"See you soon."

"Hold up."

Abigail stops in her tracks.

"You're not going to say hello to your friend?" Chloe gives her a nod in the direction of the bar.

"Oh, um…he looks busy so…I'll catch him some other time," she lies.

Chloe shakes her head. "Suit yourself."

Abigail ducks out into the back parking lot. She approaches her car and puts the key into the door. She rolls down the window, starts the engine, and pulls out of the lot, finally exhaling her breath. As she drives back to her house, she notes the worst feeling settling in her stomach. She knows she behaved like a fool, but she can't shake the sight of Kelly and his once-girlfriend-possible-current-lover sitting at the bar together.

When she arrives home, she's happy that all the cars usually occupying the driveway are gone. She parks and enters the house. She flicks on a few lamps, lighting her way to the kitchen. She grabs a glass of water and drags her tired body to the third floor. Flipping on the light in the bathroom, she turns on the shower to let the water heat up. She crosses to her room and notices the light flashing on her answering machine. She presses play.

5:23 p.m. Abigail, it's Casey. Call me when you get a second. Bye.

With the late time glowing on the clock, she decides to call her tomorrow instead, as she wants desperately to wash the grime of food and grease off her body. She undresses, flips on her stereo, and heads to the bathroom.

She tries to let the day wash away into the drain and relax herself. She had a busy day and wants nothing more than to put it behind her. Satisfied she's done just that, she steps out, wraps a towel around her, tucking it tight under her arms, and walks back into her room.

Her room is pitch-black, but he's positive she's home because her car is parked in the driveway, still warm from the ride home. He climbs the fire escape and enters through the window, which he's certain she keeps open for him. He can see the light under the door in her bathroom. He's about to switch on the lamp on her desk in her bedroom when she opens the door to her bathroom, crosses the hallway, enters her room, and flips on her light.

"Hey," he says.

She leaps about forty feet into the air at the sound of his deep voice in her room. "Jesus! You scared me." She clutches the towel to her bosom.

"Sorry."

"How did you get in here, Kelly?"

"Fire escape." He chuckles.

She glances at the open window. Then down at her wet body.

"Sorry, don't let me stop you from what you were doing."

She pauses, unsure what to do next. She walks to her bed and takes her jogging pants into her hands. "Can you turn around, please?"

He chuckles and barely turns, more like faces the window, and crosses his arms over his chest. Sensing her opening to dress is minimal, she quickly slips on her pants and then goes to her drawer and grabs a tank top. She faces the wall as she drops the towel and slips the cami over her head. She piles her wet hair into a bun, and as she turns to face him to tell him all clear, he is already looking at her.

Trying to play it cool, she says, "What brings you here?"

"I saw you at Diesel Food."

"Really?" she plays.

"Will you make it a habit not to greet customers?"

Heat fills her cheeks. "I didn't want to disrupt your date."

"It wasn't a date," he barks.

She nods and grabs the water off her coffee table. She takes a seat in the window. He approaches and sits on the couch.

"I was giving her keys to her."

Abigail nearly chokes on her water.

"Her *car* keys," he adds. "She had some work done at the shop, and I told her I'd drop it off there."

"How nice of you."

"I wanted to see you on your first day. She was having a beer, and I wanted one. I couldn't make her leave. Neither can you, by the way," he says with a smile.

She swallows hard, suddenly feeling like a massive jerk. "Thanks for the lessons on restaurant management."

With a slight roll of his eyes, he asks, "So, what have you been up to these past few days?"

Sensing a shift in the conversation, she decides to play nice. "Classes, working on a paper mostly. You?"

"Same. Work's been busy, too."

"Would you like a drink?" she asks.

He glances at the clock on her wall.

"I mean, unless you need to leave."

"I'll have a beer, if you have one."

She rises to her feet and pads to the door. He is leaning back on the couch, arms behind his head, waiting for her to return. His biceps push the limits of his T-shirt, and the smell of the motor oil remains on his skin. Her slim hips swing over toward him as she hands him the beer, and all he can think about is pulling the string on those joggers and letting them fall to the floor.

"Thanks." He slides over, making room on the couch for her. "Sit."

She lowers herself onto her couch. She seems nervous again as she sips her beer, unwilling to make direct eye contact with him.

"You like the job?" he asks.

"It was busy tonight. But so far, yes."

"Good." He places his hand on her leg. Her muscles tighten as he swirls his finger in a circle over the soft material. He puts his beer on the table and then takes hers and places it down as well.

As he leans toward her, she leans back, perfectly resting her head on the fold of the couch. His body hovers over hers.

"I never asked if you had plans tonight," he whispers.

She swallows hard. "No."

"Good."

He edges toward her, and his strong body presses onto hers. He licks his lips, and they glisten in the soft moonlight coming in from her window. He draws his hand up the side of her body, pulling her hips closer into his. Their eyes are locked on one another. He can see the pulse in her neck quicken as he continues to run his hand up her slender body. Lowering his head into her neck, he softly places his lips on her skin and up her jawline, breathing in her scent as he does. His hand finds its way into the tie in her hair, and he loosens it, allowing her wet hair to fall around her.

Her lips part as her breath catches. Her innocent eyes tell him she needs to feel his kiss again. With little warning, his mouth captures hers. She nearly gasps at his quick reaction to make her his. He releases the weight of his body on hers. She runs her hand into his sheared hair, causing his senses to shiver. Her bust heaves as his arm glides up her body, yanking the strap of her tank top off her shoulder. As her skin becomes available, his teeth graze it, and he notices the goosebumps all over her body.

"Kelly," she moans.

He nuzzles deeper into her. Not wanting words to disrupt the moment.

"Kelly, what are we doing?" she asks.

He releases a heavy sigh, hoping she'll stop using her lips for words and more for kissing. He leans back up. "I think we're having fun." He chuckles.

She rolls her eyes.

"Oh, that makes me mad," he adds with a menacing smile. "Someday, I'll tell you what I like to do to girls who roll their eyes."

She gulps.

He picks up his beer and takes a long pull.

She grabs her beer and sips it while he eyes her from the corner of the couch. His broad shoulders expand with each movement he makes. "Where are your housemates?"

"Not sure, actually. Laura is probably out, working on a lead with Melissa and Wolfie. That I can almost guarantee."

"And Bree?"

"She spends her time with her…boyfriend."

"Why did you hesitate?"

"Did I?"

He narrows his eyes. "Yes, as a matter of fact, you did."

"Oh. It's something we don't talk about."

He puts his empty beer on the table.

"Want another one?" she asks, hoping to change the subject.

His smile tells her he is onto her. "Sure."

She gets up and heads back downstairs. He glances down at his dirty T-shirt and realizes he needs a shower. She's been too kind up until now to not say anything. He gets up and walks into her bathroom. Turning on the shower, he doesn't wait for it to warm up since she was just in it. He notes all the products she has compared to his shower, but something about it makes him smile.

He hears the creak of the stairs and then notes the door open and then close, much to his disappointment. He was hoping she'd stay. Finishing quickly, he steps out to find she left him a fresh towel. Grinning, he dries off, slips on his jeans, grabs his T-shirt, and saunters back into her room.

"Can I offer you one of my T-shirts?" she asks as he tosses his on the back of her couch.

"Sorry. Working in the shop, I need a shower after."

She smiles. "I understand."

"Thanks for the towel." He winks.

She purses her lips together, trying not to smile. He sits back next to her, ignoring her question about a fresh shirt.

"So, does Bree still date that professor? Is that why you are all hush-hush?"

Her cheeks pink.

"You can trust me."

"Can I?" She smiles.

"I snuck into your room, had a beer with you, took a shower, and am now half-naked on your couch. I think you can trust me."

She gets up and walks to her dresser. She takes out her biggest gym shirt and spins around to face him, only to find him merely inches from her. She almost felt the heat from his body before she saw him. She swallows hard.

"Have I told you how sexy you look tonight?" He pulls on the strap of her camisole again. Then taking the shirt from her hands, he tosses it back on her dresser.

In one quick motion, he swipes his hands under her arms and lifts her, bringing her face closer to his. He spins her toward the couch again. Only this time, he lays her flat on the couch and crawls on top of her.

His eyes dance up and down her body. He told his sister that he'd have to stay away from her, but he can't. He gave it a few days to see if he could distance himself from her, but it proved to be impossible. Then, seeing her tonight at the bar, in her tight little jeans, moving around the floor, well, he knew he'd have to have her in his arms before the night was over.

As the tips of her fingers glide down his bare, tattooed chest, his eyes drop, and his lips part ever so slightly as he takes in the feel of her skin against his.

"You're gorgeous," she whispers.

His eyes flash open. "Careful, saying those things to me."

Her skin blushes. "I'm sorry."

He shakes his head. "No. It just makes me want to do unimaginable things to you."

She swallows hard. "Kelly."

"What? Am I not supposed to want to do things to you?"

She squirms under his stare. "I…I…think I'd like that," she pushes out.

His eyes widen as he leans back from her, pulling her gently with him. He takes her hand and stands her with him in the middle of the room. With eyes never leaving hers, he backs her up to the wall near her bedroom door. As she leans against the wall, he pushes her door shut and locks it. She is amazed by his confidence. He slowly rolls her cami up her sides, over her belly, lifting it over her bare breasts until it is over her head. He tosses it on her bed. She is exposed as the cool air from her open window touches her skin. His hands now rest on her hips, and he leans in, taking her mouth. His tongue explores her, nearly making her gasp for air as he eagerly owns her.

Pulling her closer to him, their fronts touch, and the feel of her soft skin on his is heavenly. He presses his body closer, pushing deeper into the wall. With no warning, his mouth releases hers, and he spins her to face the wall. His hands run up her belly, and before she knows it, her breasts are filling his hands. He wastes no time, teasing and possessing them.

His head buries into her neck as he moans. "My God, you have fantastic tits." His dirty mouth continues, "I can make you feel so good. I want to."

He presses his hips into her backside, and she can feel how excited he is. She braces her arms on the wall.

"I want you to," she says breathlessly.

That's the only invitation he needs. He reaches down the waist of her jogging pants and loosens the tie. Moving his fingers down to the hemline, she gasps as he whispers in her ear, "You're wet."

It's her turn to pant when his fingertips press firmly between her crease. Moving in and out and up and down. Each time a sound escapes her lips, he delves his hips harder into her.

Her legs get weak, and he flicks his thumb on her sex. She moans, tipping her head back onto his shoulder.

"I want to make you come." Just the thought of making her come makes him excited.

She lets out a half-moan, half-lip-biting-whimper as he breathes heavily in her ear. He's as completely turned on as she must feel.

She rests her forehead on the wall as she tries to catch her breath. He remains pressed up against her, his arms now tightly wrapped around her. When she finally starts to slow her breaths, she spins to look at him. He's completely pleased with himself as his eyes glimmer with mischief. He starts speaking, but she quickly shuts him up with a kiss and then trails a few down his neck. He twitches at the sensation of her lips on his skin. She continues, down to his collarbone, to his chest, tipping her head to kiss the muscles on his stomach.

Oh shit. Her lips down there. If she only knew how many times I've thought about this.

Then, in complete surprise, she lowers to her knees in front of him, and a faint sound of elation escape his lips. She places her hand on the button of his jeans.

"Abigail," he moans.

Unzipping his jeans, she can see the massive bulge dying to be set free. He shimmies his jeans over his hips and lets them fall to the ground. The waist of his black Calvin Klein boxer briefs is being pulled down on one side while he runs his hand over the side of her face. She takes ahold of the other side of his waistband until his boxer briefs are completely off. A tiny gasp escapes her lips as she views the size of his manhood. When she peers up at him, he can't help but smirk a little, and a part of him wants to ask her if she expected anything less. But her navy eyes flicker back at him, and he knows desire when he sees it. His eyes are wide in amazement and gratitude as she opens her mouth and takes him. He pants and tips back his head, his eyes rolling in the process. She grasps her hands around him and onto his backside as she helps guide him in and out. His hand gently rests on the back of her head, softly caressing her wet tendrils.

She glances up at him as he looks down at her, and he groans.

"Don't look at me with those innocent eyes," he pants. "Ugh, you're so good."

She smiles a little as she continues to please him. Within seconds, he is twisting his hand into her hair, pulling it gently, giving her a newfound sensation. He cries out along with his release in the most beautiful groan. His torso heaves, and he pulls in breath after breath until he collapses, bracing himself on the wall in front of him. He steps back as she rises to her feet.

"That was unexpected," he murmurs. He pulls up his boxers and jeans, zipping it and leaving the button undone.

"Just returning the favor." She grabs the cami off her bed and slips it on. She heads to the couch and sits down.

He plops down next to her, sipping his beer with complete satisfaction. Kelly is content and relaxed, and if he didn't know better, she seems quite ready to let go of her past history and have some fun tonight, too. Even if it's only for tonight. He's so glad he came over. He cannot stop thinking about her.

No matter what happens tomorrow, at least I had tonight.

"See, like I said," he finally speaks.

"Like you said what?"

Giving her a frisky glance, he says, "We're having fun."

Abigail extends her leg out to playfully kick him. He grabs it and slides her a bit closer to him. He massages her foot, to which she hums a welcoming note of appreciation.

"Must be hard to be on your feet, slinging drinks to admiring customers."

She smiles. "It must be hard for you to do what you do all day, fixing cars, plus going to school. How do you find the time?"

"I'm good at managing my time." He winks.

It's not a deliberate dig at her former relationship with Nathan, but it probably sounded that way to her. But it's true.

She needs a man who can find a few hours, like tonight, to show her how special she is.

They talk for another hour, which seems to surprise Abigail. But he told her she could ask him anything she wanted. And she had questions, so he answered them. He has a lot to say when he's one-on-one. He speaks about his amazing relationship with Alex and how he wasn't surprised in the least that if she was going to transfer to another school that she chose OSU. They are so close that it made sense for her to come here to be near him. He also speaks a lot about his parents but mostly his father and how he is hoping to follow in his footsteps and attend Harvard Law and become a lawyer, just like his dad. But that it hasn't always been an easy path for him. For a while in high school, he was getting into trouble and not wanting to study. Just fool around with cars and spend his money on tattoos and girls. He thanks his sister for setting him straight and showing him that he didn't have to choose one or the other. She is the reason he got his act together yet remained true to himself. He continues to admire her for her ability to stay real and not care what others think. It's why when all else fails in his life, he always has Alex by his side. No matter what.

"I like hearing the stories of the two of you. Having grown up in a household as an only child, I've always admired the close bonds of siblings. It's hard not to."

"Do you wish you had a sibling?"

"Absolutely. But it just wasn't going to happen. My parents tried for many years, and it just became too painful for them. So, they got stuck with me."

"Stuck? I bet they think they hit the jackpot with you," he says. "You're gorgeous, girl."

Her eyes lower. "Sometimes, you say things, and I—"

"Take a compliment. It's easy."

She smiles. "Why? Because you do it all the time?"

"It's different for guys. You know that," he says.

She yawns, leaning back on the couch. "Tell me why you want to be a lawyer. And not just because your dad is one. There has to be something else that drives you to want to crack a book open and study, no?"

"Yeah, sometimes, I think it's the only way to keep me on the right track. But that's for another time. You look tired."

Abigail's eyes grow heavy. He watches as they flutter as she fights to keep them open. Until finally, she surrenders. He stands and scoops her up, and then he carries her across the room, laying her gently on her bed.

He starts to pull the covers up when she murmurs, "You don't have to drive home."

"Are you sure?" he whispers.

She opens her eyes wider and looks at Kelly. It's the way she smiles at him that makes him feel okay about staying over.

"Yes, it's late."

And he wants to stay. He's wondered what it's like to be in her world, morning and night.

He slips off his jeans and climbs in next to her. The feel of her body is a welcome one. She rolls onto her side, and he scoots in closer to her, wrapping his muscular arms around her waistline.

He listens to this beautiful creature fall asleep in his arms. He can't believe he is in her bed. *Finally* in her bed. Earlier, when she dropped to her knees in front of him, he didn't think he'd be able to hold on. This woman has consumed his thoughts for the better part of a year. The day he met her by mistake in her room, he felt something he could never put his finger on. More like his hands…he wanted to put his hands all over her. To have her belong to him, unconditionally. But with the looming news of her dipshit ex-boyfriend lingering over him, he hesitated to make his move.

But he can't stay away from her anymore. It's not an option for him. When he wants something, he gets it. Surprisingly, he hasn't wanted much. Particularly, Aniston, the brunette who has followed him around the past year. Sure, he hung out with her, but she was way too into him for his liking.

"Good night, Kelly," she whispers, taking him out of his thoughts.

He pulls her over to face him. The soft glow of the moon peeking through her window lights her beautiful face, her hair twisting down past her shoulders. She smiles as her eyes flit open, nearly exploding his heart. He leans in, kissing her fervently. He might never be able to tell her what he really wants from her. He simply cannot scare her away. But she was at least willing to let him come over, unannounced, without all the fanfare. But he's not sure how much more slowly he can take this as his manhood twitches from only a delicate touch of her fingers as they run over his bicep.

His lips release, and squeezing her tightly, he says, "Good night, Abigail."

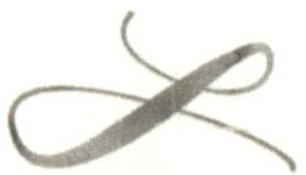

"Thanks for the ride. Sorry, it's so late," Laura says as Tank's truck pulls into her driveway.

"Anytime, Laura." He puts the car in park. "Whose car is that?" he asks as his truck lights reflect off the mint muscle car in the driveway.

Laura drops her head, unsure as to why she is hesitating. "That would be Kelly Conrad's car." She slinks a little in the seat.

She notices Tank's shoulders tense.

"Really?" He glances at the clock. "It's two in the morning."

Laura chuckles, trying to brush off his concern. "Yes, it is. And last time I checked, she's single."

Tank turns to face her. "Whose side are you on?"

"Sides? Really?" *Oh boy. Am I going to have to choose sides?*

He rubs his temple.

"Tank. Really?"

"I know. It's not my business," he concedes.

"No, it's not." She laughs with a playful punch on his arm.

He smiles wide. "I'll see you later, okay?"

Laura starts to get out of the truck and then adds, "I would have invited you in for a beer, but it's *two* in the morning." She giggles.

His eyes light up. "Next time."

"Night, Tank," she says with a wave.

"Later, girl."

Twenty-Four

The Day Brings

Abigail rolls over, her eyes fluttering open. She glances at the beautiful man lying next to her, sound asleep. Since her time at college, she has only woken up next to James, her high school boyfriend—which for the record, was only once—and then of course, Nathan. Now, as she gazes upon this man next to her, she can't help but feel excited at the prospect of being single for a while. And by single, she means, being able to be with someone new. Someone to excite her and to make her feel important again.

She waits patiently for him to wake up. She watches him breathe. The lines between his forehead are soft. He looks at peace. But she can't help but let her mind wander as her eyes trail down his exposed chest, his abdominal muscles stacked perfectly, down to where the trim of his boxer briefs traps the beauty below. Her thoughts travel to last night—Kelly pushing her up against the wall, him placing his strong hands down her pants, and then her wanting to drop to her knees to please him. Something about the way he takes care of her turns her on so much that she needs to return the favor.

As she stares at his stomach, she hears him clear his throat. She glances up at him, watching her.

"Deep in thought?" he asks.

Startled, she says, "I didn't want to wake you."

He tucks her hair behind her ear. His eyes, bright and green, tell her more than he could possibly articulate right now.

"Thanks for not kicking me out." He chuckles.

"Of course. It was late, so…"

He stretches his arms over his head. "Well, I should get going."

"Oh, yeah. I'm sure." She can't tell him why she's so disappointed, but more importantly, she hopes he doesn't sense it.

Kelly does not need another needy girl in his life. That I am sure of.

She watches as he gets up and puts on his jeans. He takes the T-shirt she offered him last night and puts that on. "This isn't some old boyfriend's shirt, is it?" he says, half-joking.

"No." She blushes.

"Good." He gives her a direct nod. It sends a chill up her spine.

He leans down and kisses her on the lips.

"I'll see you soon, okay?" The way he says it, it's as though he wants her to agree that she'll see him again. And while this confuses her, he did make it clear he doesn't date, so she's at least willing for now to enjoy whatever this is.

"Yeah." She gulps.

He pauses for a moment before pulling open the door and exiting her room. She flips on her back and faces the ceiling, smiling ear to ear.

Abigail dresses and then remembers she needs to return Casey's call. She dials her number, and after a few rings, Casey answers.

"Hey, it's Abigail."

"Hey, Abigail. How are you?"

"Great. You okay?" She's alarmed to hear the tone in Casey's voice. She doesn't sound sick per se, but she almost sounds depressed.

"Um, fine. You think maybe we could get some coffee?"

"This morning?" she questions, only because Casey doesn't sound in the mood for company.

"Are you free?" she asks.

"Yeah, I could meet you. Where to?"

"I'll come and pick you up. Say, in fifteen minutes?"

"Great, Casey. See you then."

Abigail grabs her bag and heads downstairs. Laura is curled up on the couch, sipping her coffee.

"Hey, Laura."

"Hey!" She smiles. "You seem cheery this morning." Laura grants her a sly smile.

Abigail laughs. "I am. Is that okay?"

She laughs. "Yes, it's better than okay. I saw his car here," she blurts out.

"In my defense, he showed up after work. I didn't know he was coming."

Laura rolls her eyes. "But I'm guessing you were not disappointed."

"To say the least."

"Good. I'm happy for you."

"Thanks."

There's a beep outside.

"Someone here?"

"Oh, Casey and I are going out for coffee. Care to join?"

Laura raises her mug. "Thanks, but I am all set for now. Tell her hello."

"Will do. I'll see you later."

"Bye, Abigail."

"Bye," she says as she opens the front door.

Casey doesn't smile as Abigail approaches the passenger car door.

She climbs in. "You okay, Casey?"

Casey fakes a smile. "Sure. You?"

"Great."

Casey drives east of campus, and then she almost immediately pulls into an empty faculty parking lot and parks.

"What are we doing?" Abigail questions. "Casey, what is wrong?!"

"Oh, Abigail," she says, unbuckling her seat belt and turning to face her.

"Casey, tell me." Her eyes widen.

"I can't keep this to myself. I just can't," she sighs.

"Okay. You know I'll help you." Abigail squeezes her friend's hand in anticipation of the terrible news she is about to share.

Her eyes soften. "There's nothing you can help *me* with," she stresses.

She swallows the hard lump forming her throat as she begins to sense the conversation shifting. "Okay."

"I got the job at the student health center," she blurts out. "And…"

"And what?"

"And Poppy came in."

Abigail's skin crawls at the mention of her name. *I don't want to know anything about her. Period.*

"And…Nathan was with her. They didn't see me, but I saw them."

"Them?" *No. Not Nathan. Please tell me this has nothing to do with him. PLEASE.*

"Yeah. *Them.*"

"Why were they there together?" Her stomach starts to churn. And the air in the car seems stale and suffocating.

"Oh, Abigail," she says, placing her hand on her friend's leg.

"What, Casey? Tell me," she barks. *Health center. Two people together. This cannot be good news.*

"I'm so sorry."

"Why are *you* sorry?"

"She's pregnant."

Boom.

And just like that, everything she ever thought up until that very moment changes. Forever. And there is no returning. The world surrounding her seems to swirl obnoxiously in the car. Flashes of anger, disgust, sadness, and disbelief wash over her.

What does that mean for Nathan? His career, his scholarship? Did he ever love me? Was it all an illusion? How far along is she? How could they? That poor girl. That bitch. What the hell is happening? This is the worst news possible. I think I'm going to throw up.

"Abigail, say something. You don't look so good."

"I...I have no words."

"I needed you to know because I couldn't keep this secret. I can get fired, but I thought you should be aware. If I can do anything, please tell me."

"Thank you, Casey. I'm sorry for you to know..." she utters words, but they're not exactly making sense because the world in itself no longer does.

"Are you okay?"

Am I okay? Absolutely fucking not.

"What can I do? They're adults. What else can I say?" *I want to scream at the top of my lungs!*

"That is very mature of you."

I'm dying inside. That bastard. What the fuck, Nathan?!

She senses Casey lean into her and hug her, but her mind has been removed from her body. She feels absolutely nothing as her friend wraps her arms around her.

Is this what it's like to feel nothing at all? Total numbness?

"Hey, could you drop me off on campus?"

"Now?" Casey asks.

"Yes."

"Are you okay, Abigail?"

"Casey, please," she begs as tears sting her eyes.

Casey turns the key, her engine roaring to life. She pulls out of the lot and heads back toward the main campus. They sit in agonizing silence.

As Casey approaches the campus, Abigail says, "Here is fine." She grabs the door handle, forcing Casey to come to a screeching halt.

She whips open the door.

"Abigail, wait. Are you going to be okay?"

"No, but then again, I don't have a choice." She hops out of the car. "Thanks, Casey. You're a good friend."

"Love you, Abigail," she says as the door slams shut.

Abigail hurries across campus. Making sure no one sees her, she crosses and heads directly downtown to the first place she thinks no one she knows will be. It's a dimly lit bar. As she pulls open the door, she notes only a few people drinking at the counter, eating brunch. She yanks out a seat at the bar and plops in it with authority. The bartender approaches.

"What can I get you, doll?" the pink-haired girl asks.

"Bloody Mary, please."

"Sure."

A minute later, a large Bloody Mary is placed in front of her. She takes a big sip. Then another. She drops her head as her emotions begin to take over.

"You okay, doll?" she asks.

"Yeah." She peers up. Her drink is gone. "I'll have another," she sighs.

"You got it, doll."

She's gone for a minute. Then, she places the new drink in front of her. "What's your name?"

"Abigail," she whispers.

She tips her head and gives her a good once-over. "All right, Abigail. You need anything, my name is Courtney."

"Thanks." She takes another sip of her drink.

Someone sits on the stool next to Abigail. She glances in his direction. He's a little older, maybe in his thirties—hard to tell with his baseball hat on.

He smiles wide at Abigail. "I hear the brunch here is pretty good," he says.

"I wouldn't know," she mumbles.

"Bloody Mary for breakfast?" He chuckles.

She can't help but smile a little. "My kind of breakfast today."

"Bad morning?" he asks.

Before she can respond, Courtney approaches him. "What can I get you?"

"I'll have a Bloody Mary." He glances over at Abigail's nearly empty glass. "Make that two, and I'll have some toast to start—wheat if you have it."

"Sure thing, doll."

She makes the two Bloody Marys and places one in front of him and the other in front of Abigail. "From your neighbor," she says, nodding toward the guy next to her.

"Thank you," she says to him.

"Welcome. My friends call me Dutch."

"Thanks, Dutch. I'm Abigail," she says.

"You a student at OSU?"

"Yes, a junior."

"Excellent. I'm in town for business. What are you majoring in?"

Obligated to answer his questions, she mutters, "I'm working toward veterinary medicine."

"Wow, impressive, Abigail. You must love animals."

She brightens a bit. "I do. Absolutely."

"Thinking back on my time at school, I wish I'd had more focus and gone for a business degree or something. Let me tell you, being an accountant is far from exciting."

"But that's a good job."

He smiles, and she notices how pleasant he appears when he smiles. "Yes, it pays the bills."

Abigail sips her drink. Courtney drops the toast off in front of Dutch.

Before he touches it, he slides it in front of Abigail. "Just a little something in your belly." He laughs.

Surprised by his kind gesture, she takes a slice. She is starving after all. "Thank you."

"You're welcome."

They talk for another hour, during which she consumes two more Bloody Marys.

Courtney collects the empty glasses in front of them.

"You know," he says. "there's a really nice bar in my hotel."

Courtney glances at Abigail.

"It must be a nice hotel then," Abigail replies.

"It is. You should come check it out with me."

Abigail whips up her head, surprised by his invitation. "Oh, I can't. I have work to do."

"After you've been drinking?" He laughs. "Just blow it off for a little longer." He smiles.

"I still have this drink." She laughs to curb the conversation.

"Good point."

"So, what hotel is it?" As soon as she says it, she realizes in her drunken state that she is absolutely continuing the conversation she does not want to continue. *You idiot.*

"The Ludlum Suites."

It's the nicest hotel in the area by far. She's driven by it before with her parents. It's far too expensive to stay in when they visit. They spend most of their time out—eating, shopping, and going around campus—to spend that kind of money for an empty room.

"Wow, I've only driven by it. I do hear it's beautiful inside."

He leans in closer to her. "Well, if you come back with me, I'll give you a tour."

Abigail blushes at his advancement. She takes another sip of her drink. She's tipsier than she wanted to get, but at the same time, she hasn't thought about Nathan Ryan since Dutch sat down next to her a few hours ago.

She laughs. "Tell me what makes it so special."

He places his hand on her thigh, and her entire body freezes. "You'd be there."

She can't help but laugh in his face. She blames it on the alcohol. "You know how to flatter a girl."

"So, I flatter you," he says with a sly expression.

Abigail wishes now more than ever that today had never happened.

Kelly pulls open the door, and like a moth to a flame, he notices some freaking guy's hand on her leg.

What the hell?

He walks up next to Abigail and says, "Courtney, can I get her tab?"

Infuriated, Kelly stares straight ahead, not looking at Abigail at all. Courtney comes over with the tab, to which Kelly glances at it, throws some cash down, and then steps behind Abigail toward the guy with the baseball hat on. He glances down at his hand on Abigail's thigh.

He's lucky he takes his hand off at the same time Kelly finally addresses Abigail, "Come on. Time to go."

A mix of emotions washes over Kelly as he locks eyes with her glassed-over, childlike navy blues. Part of him is grateful he is rescuing her from this guy. Another part of him thinks she should be getting in trouble for misbehaving. And then there is the fear that had he not been here, she would have undoubtedly headed toward danger, and she is clueless to that important fact.

Abigail starts to get off her stool.

"Leaving so soon?" Dutch quips.

"Thanks for the drinks, Dutch," she mumbles.

"You're not coming to the hotel with me? Remember the tour?" he says, reaching for her hand.

What?!

Kelly grabs Abigail's arm to hurry her and to help steady her. Neither of which he is happy about. "Abigail," he says through gritted teeth.

Courtney approaches Dutch. "Can I get you anything else?" she asks.

Kelly nods at Courtney.

"Bye, doll," she says to Abigail with a sympathetic glance. "See you, Kelly," Courtney says.

As Abigail walks away, she slurs, "You know her?"

"Yeah, we're friends."

"Is that why you knew I was here?" she asks as he pushes open the door.

He stares down at her, and his icy green eyes narrow. He doesn't answer her as he opens the car door and guides her in her seat.

"Buckle up, please." There is an unmistakable coolness in his voice.

He doesn't say a word as he drives out of the parking lot and back toward his house.

"Where are we going?" she slurs.

"Jesus, how much did you have to drink?"

"I was, um, having a Bloody Mary."

"Or several, I hear."

"Wait," she says. "Are you…were you snooping on me?"

He turns his head. "Really, Abigail? I was looking out for you," he says with irritation.

"Well, I don't think that's…I mean…you can't look at bars for me." She is making little sense.

He ignores her words completely. "Were you going to go to a hotel with that guy?"

She starts to laugh. This only increases his anger.

"I asked you a question."

She's never seen him so infuriated with her like this. He's so mad that it makes her giggle. Which is unfortunate for her.

"You're jealous." She laughs.

He pulls into his driveway and forcefully puts his car in park. He gets out and goes over to her side. He opens the door. "You need help?"

She stumbles to get out, and he grabs her arm.

"What are we doing?"

He guides her into his house and upstairs to his bedroom. She trips down the hallway as he pulls her along. Something about his silence worries her.

"What time is it?"

He turns to her as he pushes open his door. His expression is completely void.

"I'm annoying you, aren't I? Yep, I am."

He closes his door. He spins her back to the door and backs her up against it. With no warning whatsoever, he presses his body on hers, and with force, he kisses her. An incredible rush of emotions comes over him—fear, anger, hurt, disappointment. He pushes his tongue into her mouth and sucks her bottom lip as he kisses her again and again. Then, suddenly, he steps back. Leaving her breathless, pinned against the door.

He walks over to his window, and with this back to her, he says, "Tell me you were not going to go back to that guy's hotel."

"What? No. We talked about the place, and he said, you know, we'd get a drink, walk around. But I wasn't going to go."

She pushes off the door. With unsteady legs underneath her, she makes her way to his bed, sitting on the edge.

He doesn't speak.

Trying to lighten the mood, she laughs. "You seem jealous."

"No, I'm not. I was worried you were going to make a terrible mistake, Abigail. Obviously, you're not acting normal."

Feeling a touch rejected, she lowers her head a bit. The silence is painful.

Finally, he turns to face her, and seeing her slumped forward in defeat worries him, so he asks, "What's with the day drinking?"

She appears desperate to try and fight back her tears. She mutters, "No reason."

Not buying it, he presses, "Seriously, something's up. What gives?" He folds his arms over his front.

"Kelly, it's nothing, and why do you care?"

Visibly disappointed by her remark, he shoots back, "What the fuck is going on?"

She stands. "Nothing, I said."

But he isn't going to give up. "You're not leaving," he commands.

She laughs and mockingly says, "You going to stop me?"

He walks toward her. She starts to back up.

He reaches for her hand but takes her arm instead and pulls her toward him. "You're clearly not yourself. So, no, you're not leaving until you tell me."

"Kelly," she pleads.

But he won't let her go. He can't. His healthy obsession with her is growing by the day. Tears sting her eyes. She's surprised by his reaction as he pulls her into his chest and holds on to her tightly, and it's then the tears start to flow.

He strokes her hair. "I need to know that you are okay," he says softly. "Come on, Abigail."

She wipes the tears on her cheeks with the back of her sleeve. He doesn't let her go. She can't help but cry more.

Finally, she whispers, "I got some news about someone that I…"

"That you what?"

"Wish I hadn't," she admits.

"Like what?" His muscles tighten.

"I can't say it."

"Who is it about?" He fears the answer.

I can't tell her about Nathan. It will not only kill her. But she'll never be the same person. At least, not for a while. How could she be?

She buries her head deep into his chest, trying desperately not to burst into a horrible cry. It's awkward enough, thinking of your ex-boyfriend sleeping with someone else. But then to discuss his life with someone you currently have…well, feelings for…is overwhelming.

He remains holding her tight. He can't let her leave. He must try and make this right for her, but how?

"I don't understand. How I can get you to trust me?" he whispers.

"Why do you care so much about that?"

He draws her back enough to look into her eyes. "Are we not friends?" he says.

"Friends," she scoffs. "Sure, we're friends."

Trying desperately to curb his anger and give her a break today, he says, "So, tell me why you're crying."

"Kelly, you really want me to talk about him—"

Fuck. I knew it.

Selfishly testing her, he asks, "You're not over him, are you?"

Her face flushes red. She pushes off his front and wriggles herself free. "I'm over him, and believe me, he's over me," she barks.

"So, what's the issue then?" He must confirm what he fears.

She paces the room. Then, she blurts out with anger, "I found out he got a girl pregnant. Happy? Now, you know, and that, Kelly, is why yours truly was drinking her morning away!"

He tries to grab her hand to get her to stop moving. She yanks her arm back.

"My friends are aware. God only knows who else. I mean, what the fuck?!" she screams as she places her hands over her face.

He badly wants to touch her, to hold her tight, but he can't move. He can't imagine how this must make her feel. He's never loved anyone enough for it to be an issue in his world. But over the past year of knowing her, he's unequivocally positive that she must have fallen hard for Nathan and more so, him of her. But she had to realize that dating such a popular athlete on campus would, at some point in their relationship, cause her heartache. For God's sake, he's watched her suffer this past year.

Nathan Ryan is ruining everything. He's pushing his way back into my time with her. So help me God, I hope I never run into this guy on campus.

"Let me hold you," he begs. "Please, I can't imagine how terrible you feel right now."

She drops her hands. He gets a good look at her beautiful face, and he's sick to his stomach.

"Do you feel sorry for me?" she barks. "You could have just let me be today. Why did you want to come get me? Thought we could just have fun today?" she says with venom in her voice.

"Sometimes, you can be a real jerk, Abigail."

She gasps.

"It's true. And, no, I don't feel sorry for you. I'm just grateful it wasn't you that he knocked up."

Again, she gasps. "You have some nerve."

"What? To speak the truth?" He steps closer to her. "I came down to get you today because Courtney was worried about you. So, she called me. And this Nathan business fucking sucks, Abigail. Absolutely no doubt about it. But aren't you glad you're not a part of it? It's not you. It's not your life anymore. You broke up with him because you thought he cheated on you or was spending too much time away from you. So, in my eyes, you only reaffirmed what I think you'd felt the past few months. That your time was over."

She's speechless.

He adds, "And, yes, I absolutely thought about having fun with you today. I sure had fun with you the other night. I thought you did, too. So, sue me for thinking about you in that way. But try and stop me."

She swallows hard. "Wait, how did Courtney know to call you?" she asks.

"What?"

"You said Courtney was worried about me. But I just met her today."

His face blushes.

Noticing, Abigail presses on, "Why did she call *you*?"

He turns to his window. "She's my friend."

"You said that already."

He won't turn to look at her as he says, "I might have mentioned you in passing."

"Really? In passing? Enough that I give a stranger my name and she calls you?"

"Let it go, *Abigail.*"

"Ha! Like you would let me let it go earlier."

He spins to face her. "That is completely different, and you know it."

"There's something you're not telling me, Kelly."

Yeah, that I can't stop thinking about you and that Courtney saw right through me when I told her I was interested in someone, someone outside our circle of friends. But I'm not telling you that today. It's too obvious, and I need to be sure you're going to move on from Nathan for good.

When he doesn't speak, she says, "Can you take me home, please?"

There's a pang in his heart. His eyes soften. "Really?"

She recognizes the hurt. "I don't know what I want."

Crushed.

He grabs his keys off his desk. "Have it your way." He marches toward his door. "Come on."

He turns the doorknob and doesn't wait for her to follow him down the hallway. He gets to the garage and hops in the car. They drive to her house in silence.

Before she gets out, he says, "Just do me one favor? Don't put me in the same category as every other guy who has ever done you wrong."

She doesn't say a word to him as she climbs out and enters her house.

As he pulls away, he hates more than anything that she knows the secret now. Because look what it's done to her. He knew she'd be destroyed.

I feel so bad for her. I can't even imagine how horrible she must feel, knowing it was all true and he really was caught with his pants down. But thank God Courtney knew to call me today. Because she was drinking herself into a potentially dangerous situation, and if anything ever happens to her, I don't know what I'd do. But she might not let me be there for her anymore regardless. And that is what I've feared all along.

Twenty-Five

Friends Like These

Bree is sitting on the couch when Abigail bursts into the house. One look at her, and she says, "What the hell is wrong?" as she jumps up and meets Abigail in the threshold of the foyer.

Abigail accepts the hug from her friend.

"I'm beside myself, Bree," she cries.

Bree guides her into the living room. "What's going on?"

Abigail drops on the couch, head in her hands. Tears streaming down her palms. Bree grabs the tissue box from the coffee table and rests it on her lap, pulling out a few.

Abigail peeks up at her. "I can't believe what I'm about to say; it just seems so unbelievable."

"Please tell me 'cause you're starting to scare me."

She grabs a tissue and blows her nose. Finally, she blurts out, "I found out today that Nathan got Poppy pregnant."

A horrific gasp escapes Bree's lips almost at the same time as tears start to well in her eyes. Bree, Abigail, and Nathan have all been through so much together as friends—good friends—and to hear this news about him is difficult to digest.

"I can't believe it. Oh, Abigail. I'm so sorry. My God, I'm sorry for him, too. Have you talked to him?"

"Hell no. I'm so mad at him, Bree. But I'm also sad," she admits. "Devastated for him, and as much as I don't like her, I'm…I'm having mixed emotions about this, to say the very least."

"I'm sure you are. Oh, this is just awful news, right? Like your biggest fear coming true. Only it's Nathan. How could he get involved with her? Be so stupid? He's going to be a daddy at his age? Come on. A guy like him needs to be careful. We all do."

"Bree, I feel so sick to my stomach. I don't want to ever see him again. Or her!" she cries into a fresh tissue.

"Who told you?"

"You can't say a word because it was Casey. She works at the health center, and they came in…together. She saw the test results. It's true. No mistaking it."

"Holy shit."

"Who else knows?"

Abigail hesitates. "Um, Kelly."

"Kelly? Is that who just dropped you off?"

"Yeah, Casey told me this morning, and, well, he came and picked me up at the bar. I feel terrible. We argued, and I told him because I was crying. I couldn't hide it."

"Must have been so hard for him, too."

Abigail cocks her head. "Why do you say that?"

Bree shrugs her shoulders. "Isn't it obvious?"

"What?"

"He totally likes you, and now, he knows you're devastated by this, so that must totally suck for you guys."

"For us?"

Now, it is Bree's turn to look confused. "Yeah, I mean, must be hard to move forward in a relationship when you feel like you're in the shadow of someone else's ghost."

I'm. So. Stupid.

"Goddamn it!"

"What?" Bree asks.

"He dropped me off, and I didn't say a word to him. He told me not to put him in the same category as every other guy who has ever done me wrong."

"Listen, you can't push this guy away because Nathan has problems. You'd be a fool to."

"I'm just so…confused, hurt, maybe even a little scared."

"Scared?"

"Yeah, it could happen to anyone." Abigail dabs the corner of her eye.

"You're absolutely right. This is a good reminder to all of us."

Abigail hangs her head. "I'm exhausted, Bree."

"I know, honey. But you're moving on, right?"

She gazes up. "Yes, I was moving away from Nathan. Yes, that is true. But I can't help but feel a connection to him."

"Of course you do. He was your first true love. Anyone with eyes could see that. But now, he's moved on, and by the sounds of it, he has a lot of shit to deal with. And I thought you were trying to move on as well. Weren't you?"

Suddenly, a terrible sensation washes over her. She just pushed Kelly away. Like the past few months or whatever meant nothing to her. That Nathan's news would somehow have a direct impact on her future relationships. But why should it? He's already moved on. Enough so to get himself caught in his current situation.

"Can we not tell Laura right now?"

Confused, she asks, "Everything okay with you guys?"

"Yeah, but she hangs out with Tank—or at least, it seems that way. She doesn't really say. Tank and I are not on great terms either, and I don't want him to know I was given the information."

"Of course. Anything you need."

"What I need right now is a hot shower," she says, rubbing her tired eyes.

"Okay, Abigail. I'm here if you need me."

She rises from the couch and approaches the stairs. Through her sniffles, she asks, "You seeing Adam tonight?"

"Dinner. But I can cancel," Bree says.

"Please don't. I'll be okay."

Abigail enters her room and notes the blinking light on her answering machine. She dreadfully pushes play. Casey announces herself. She states how worried she is and wants her to call her back. There are no other messages.

Not quite ready to make the call, she undresses, leaving a trail of clothes to her bathroom. She is in desperate need of a hot shower to relax her tense muscles. She turns on the water, letting it steam the room before stepping in. She has no concept of how much time passes as she stares at the tiled wall, only that the water is now turning cold. She quickly washes her hair and turns off what is left of the room-temp water.

After she dresses, she decides to bite the bullet and pick up the phone to call Casey.

"Hey, it's Abigail."

"Hey, you okay?" Casey asks.

"Yeah, I'm okay."

"Good. I've been worried."

"I needed some time alone."

"Understandable," Casey says.

"You're a great friend. I'm sure that could not have been easy for you."

"I'm going to have to get used to this sort of stuff, I suppose." There is silence between them. Hesitantly, Casey says, "So, I'm having a party at my place on Thursday. You'll come, right? Jen misses you, too. So does Alex."

It does warm her heart to hear she is missed. "Of course. I'll see you then."

"If you need me, I'm here for you."

"Thank you. I'll see you guys soon."

Abigail hangs up the phone and goes over to the large window facing the front. She sits on the cushion and stares out over the campus in the distance. She pulls a blanket over her, resting her head on the wall.

Bree's right about Kelly. She wouldn't steer me wrong. He's always been there for me. Last year. This year. Right when I needed a friend, he was there to talk to. And pushing him away would be a bad decision, right? How can I be happy if I can never move on?

I hate more than anything that I still feel a connection with Nathan, but how could I not? I've spent those past two years loving him deeply, and now, I find out that maybe the past few months of me trying to make things right was all for naught. He was fooling around with her when he was telling me he wasn't. But there's a part of me that doesn't believe it's true. That is not the Nathan I know. At all.

And within minutes, her eyelids are heavy. As she starts to drift off, her mind unwillingly takes her back—to the first night she met Nathan Ryan and he walked her home after bringing a slightly intoxicated Webber home from her first football party.

Abigail started walking toward the door in Nathan and Webber's room when she heard Nathan switch off the light.

She went to open the door when Nathan stated, "Hey, you're not leaving alone."

She didn't want to bother him any more than she already had.

"Well, I don't know where you live, but I'm not letting you walk there alone." He grabbed his keys.

"Oh, thanks, but you should stay here with him." She placed her hand on the doorknob.

"Understood, but you don't live on the moon, do you?" He granted her an incredible smile.

"No, I live in Willis."

"Ah, Willis. Not too far. Easy. I'll be back before he notices." He peered over at Webber.

They walked down the hallway and then waited for the elevator. When they stepped into the elevator, she noticed Nathan rubbing his neck as he let out a big sigh.

"You okay?" she asked.

"Yeah, just been a long day, hasn't it?"

Before she could answer, she let out a huge hiccup. She gasped and put her hand over her mouth. He burst out in laughter, and she did, too.

"I'm so embarrassed. I don't ever drink, and I guess it's catching up to me!"

"Me, too." He chuckled just as the elevator doors were opening.

Jokingly, he grabbed her hand as she walked down the stairs, pretending to help steady her. Not even thinking, she played along. They walked out the door, still holding hands and laughing until they got to the sidewalk. It was as if they had known one another much longer than a few hours.

When they got to the front door of Willis Hall, he reached out his hand to shake hers. "Good night, Abby."

His palm was warm and large, and it practically crushed her small hand. A tingle went up her back, and she bashfully glanced away from him. She quickly dropped his hand even though, for some reason, she did not want to.

She started walking to the door. She pulled it open and then turned to wave. He was still standing there, watching her, and she was struck by his dashing features, his lean stature, and most of all, his beautiful smile as he remained under the streetlight near her dorm room. A quiet, unaffected freshman. So innocent. So untouched by college life.

As she pressed the button for the elevator, the strangest sensation came over her. As though they were supposed to meet.

Their lives collided that night before they could comprehend what was coming.

Only a collision brought together with such power tends to be torn apart with equal force.

And it has.

Twenty-Six

Moving On

Abigail hurries into the Union to grab a coffee before her class. She enters the coffee shop and places her order. She waits near the back for the barista to make her latte.

"Hey."

She whips her head up, and standing before her is Nathan. He looks happy, which surprises her.

"Hey," she says coolly.

"Haven't seen you in a while," he says like nothing is the matter.

"I've been busy," she quips.

"Oh, I see." Obvious sadness plagues his voice. "I didn't know if you'd heard."

She's on the verge of vomiting. She can't speak. Her face burns red.

"Got hurt last week. I'm out for the next game. First time for me."

The barista calls her name, and she is brought back to earth.

"No. I didn't hear that. Will you excuse me?" She spins toward the door as quickly as possible, grabs her coffee, and exits out the door.

What the hell?!

She rushes to her class and takes her seat near the front of the lecture hall. She sits there the entire time, trying desperately to concentrate as her professor reviews the cardiovascular system in felines. Watching the video of the dissection twists a wretched sensation in her gut. As much as she wishes it away.

But it remains for the entire class. It never leaves her. Because *he* haunts her. She figured at some point, she'd see him on campus. But not like this, having his horrible news swarming in her head.

Her day passes quickly, and as she finishes her last class and drives to the restaurant for her evening shift, she's more thankful than ever that she has this job. It takes her mind off her life as the fast-paced dinner rush leaves her little time to think about anything but serving her customers.

When she gets home, she undresses and showers before getting to her Microbiology homework. Thoughts of seeing Nathan in the Union consumed her today. She tried everything to shake them free. She tried writing what her professors said word for word. She tried doing extra work at the restaurant in the back to pass the time. She even parked her car as far away from the restaurant as possible and ran as fast as she could to the back door, just to stop her mind from thinking. But nothing worked.

And now, in the safe confines of her room, as she wanders around, getting ready to settle in for a long night of studying, she has no idea it is about to continue.

She hits play on her answering machine.

Beep.

Hey, it's me...Nathan. You seemed upset when I saw you today. I was hoping we could remain friends. I'd like to. Call me sometime, okay? Webber misses you, too.

Anger brews within her. He has some nerve, calling her. But there is a part of her that wonders if he might be desperate for a friend. But if he had any class, he wouldn't be seeking her out as his comrade. And she sees Webber in all her science classes. She hates that he used her friendship with Webber as a pawn. Does she go over to see Webber at his apartment like she used to? No. But with both Tank and Nathan there, she'll have to keep her social visits with Webber to places around the school for now. It's just how it has to be.

She has no other messages, and a part of her was hoping to have heard from Kelly. It's been two days, and it seems unnatural to have not spoken to him. But she hasn't called him either. She really needed this time to digest everything and to get her head screwed on right. She's not necessarily feeling better about it. Heck, seeing him sucked, but she can't change the facts, and if nothing else, Nathan has made it even easier for Abigail to move on.

No time like the present.

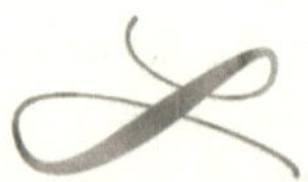

Bree, Melissa, Laura, and Abigail can hear the music pulsing as they approach Casey and Alex's place. They walk in to find the party in full swing.

"Girls!" Jen yells over the music. She hurries over and hugs each one of them. "Follow me," she says as she leads them over to the keg.

Each of the girls grab a beer as Casey and Alex find their way over to them.

"So glad you all came!" Casey smiles. She gives Abigail a special hug, and Bree takes notice.

She squeezes Abigail's hand and then whispers in her ear, "You're moving on, remember?"

Abigail smiles and nods at Bree.

They spend the next hour hanging out and drinking. There is a good mix of people at the party. Lots of the girls from the soccer house are here and lots of Alex's friends.

Abigail's relaxed and enjoying herself when she hears Alex yell, "Brother!"

The hair on the back of her neck stands up, and she is too afraid to look over in the direction of the door.

"Your hottie is here," Bree coos.

"Cut it out," Abigail barks.

"And he does *not* disappoint. Damn," she adds.

Abigail peeks over. Kelly is dressed in tight jeans and a light-blue sweater that makes his eyes pop from across the room. Bree is right; he is the most noticeable guy in this apartment by far.

He and his friends make their way to the keg. Not far behind them, Abigail recognizes Courtney and unfortunately Aniston, the brunette that Kelly dated—or dates? Abigail's blood boils at the sight of them following him like puppy dogs.

She starts to turn when a firm hold grips her hand.

"Don't you dare walk away," Bree says.

Abigail whips her head to look at her. "He brought the girl he used to sleep with. Really?" she says through gritted teeth.

"Have you called him since he dropped you off the other day?"

She narrows her eyes at Bree and then admits, "No."

"Can you blame him then?"

"So, I don't call because I need time, and he brings her?"

"I see your point, but I think you see mine as well. But we can't be sure it's a thing. Isn't she friends with Alex, too?"

"No idea. And I don't want to know."

As if on cue, Alex bounds over. "Hey, Abigail, my brother just got here!"

"Oh, really? Cool." She musters a smile.

"He'll be so glad you're here."

Huh?

Before she realizes it, Alex is pulling her by the arm toward the other side of the room, where he is standing with his group of friends and unfortunately Aniston. She tries desperately to shake her arm free, but Alex only laughs. It's obvious she thinks she is joking.

"Hey, doll," Courtney says with a huge smile as she approaches.

Faking a huge smile, she says, "Hey, Courtney!"

"Do you have Bloody Marys at this party, Alex? Abigail loves them," she jokes.

Abigail's face burns red at her comment.

"You like them? I could make one for you."

"That's okay," she stutters. *Oh my God. I want to crawl in a hole and die right now!*

She knows Kelly is staring at her. As she finally glances over, she notices Aniston is close to him—too close. "Hey," Abigail says out of social obligation. His smile, while pleasant, does give her pause. He's so hard to read. "Well, speaking of drinks." She tips her cup a little. "Going to grab a beer. I'll see you guys in a bit," she lies.

As she turns, guilt and hurt wash over her. *That sucked so bad!*

As she heads back to the keg, she catches Bree glaring at her. Abigail mouths, *What?*

Bree approaches. "Get your drink and come with me."

She fills her cup and follows Bree. Bree opens the bathroom door and yanks Abigail inside.

"Where's the fire?!" Abigail whispers.

"Ugh. You're blowing it."

"No. I was getting a drink."

"You stood over there—shoulders hunched, I might add—and lasted five seconds before running away."

Abigail starts to protest, "Did you see her all snuggled up next to him? What am I supposed to do?"

"Listen," Bree whispers, "what I'm about to say might temporarily bum you out, but I have to say it."

Abigail nods.

"Nathan has clearly moved on—to the point where there is no turning back for him. So, right now, I can see the way that guy out there looks at you, and I am telling you, Abigail, as your friend, to go for it. Forget your past."

Bree undoes the second-to-top button on Abigail's shirt.

"What are you doing?"

"What does it look like?" She tucks Abigail's hair behind her ear. Then, she takes out a lip gloss from her bag and goes to work.

"Bree," she tries to say under objection.

"Stay still," she commands. Once done, she says, "Now, look. I mean, no doubt, you're gorgeous, but now, you're irresistible."

Abigail can't help but laugh. "Oh, Bree, you're a great friend." She leans over and hugs her. "Now, get out, so I can use the bathroom."

Bree waves her hand. "Fine, fine, but you'd better not wipe that off your lips. There is more where that came from." She opens the door and then exits, closing it behind her.

Abigail stares in the mirror as she washes her hands. She wishes she had an ounce of Bree's confidence. But right now, she feels about two feet tall.

There is a slight bang on the door, bringing her out of her haze. She exits to find Aniston standing there.

"Oh, sorry," she says.

"No problem." Abigail says.

"I've seen you before," she says.

"I'm…" She can't find the words to say. *I'm friends with Kelly and Alex, and we've been at numerous parties together.*

"From Diesel Food. You're a waitress, right?"

Oddly relieved, she says, "Yeah, started a few weeks ago."

She smiles and then enters the bathroom.

As Abigail reenters the main party room, she should have known that the girls would be over, talking to Kelly and Alex. Bree obnoxiously waves her over. She drags her feet toward them.

"I was telling Kelly that your pesky little convertible is leaking oil all over our driveway and that the landlord is going to be pissed at us." She laughs.

She gives Bree a nasty stare. "I haven't had time to fix it."

"Bring it in," Kelly says. "I'll take a look at it."

"Take a look at what?" Aniston asks as she joins the group.

"Abigail's car," Bree says.

"Oh, yes. Kelly is the best at fixing cars," she coos. "He fixed mine, didn't you?" she adds, giving him her bedroom eyes.

Abigail's stomach churns.

Kelly glares at Aniston and then says, "Excuse me. I need a beer."

He marches over to the keg, leaving them all standing there in his wake.

"He's so moody sometimes." Aniston laughs.

Bree grabs Abigail's hand, getting her attention, and then nods in the direction of Kelly as he opens the back door of Alex's place.

"So, Aniston, is it? What year are you?" Bree asks to distract her.

Abigail takes a deep breath and then walks toward the back door. There are a dozen or so people in the back, hanging out. She notices Kelly is not out there.

Her heart sinks at the idea that he left.

"Hey."

She jumps.

Standing near the back of the house is Kelly.

"Hey," she says.

"Looking for someone?" he asks.

She steps closer. "Yes, as a matter of fact."

"Make sure you bring your car in. You can't ignore the issue," he barks.

Offended by his insinuation, she quips, "I don't ignore issues."

He shakes his head.

"What? You don't believe me?"

"Just bring it in, okay?" He starts to move off the wall.

She feels an urgency to keep him near her. "Did you come here with her?" she blurts out.

He stops. "What?"

"Well, did you?"

"Yes. We *all* came together."

She swallows. "Wow. Okay then."

She starts to turn when he says, "Does it make a difference to you?"

"Now, who's the jerk?"

He sharply inhales. "Me? You haven't called me. Not a word from you."

"You haven't called me."

"I was waiting for you."

"Really, is that so? Well, let me ask you something, Kelly. If I don't go home with you, will you go home with her?" She tries to mask the hurt with anger.

He narrows his eyes at her. Then, he notices the back door swing open, and Aniston steps out. Kelly grabs Abigail's arm and pulls her to the side of the house, out of view.

"Kelly! You out here?" she yells in a sickly-sweet voice.

Abigail starts to yell back, but he quickly puts his hand over her mouth.

"Don't you dare," he snips.

She starts to laugh.

He latches open the side gate and pulls Abigail through. His hand still over her mouth. He walks her to his car and releases her.

"I'm not your getaway," she says.

He opens the car door. "Quickly, come on." He delicately shoves her into the car. Then, he gets in and starts the car.

"This is not what I had in mind when I asked about you going home with her or me."

Kelly looks at her as he turns the corner. "Nice touch with that button undone, by the way," he says with raised eyebrows.

Her skin heats. She places her hand over her bust.

"Knock it off," he requests as he grabs her hand.

She smacks his hand away.

He drives a few minutes and then pulls into his driveway. She goes to open her mouth when he says, "Just come in."

"Look, I really don't want to be here when Aniston shows up."

He doesn't say a word as he opens his door and gets out. He comes around to her side, opens her door, and gestures for her to get out.

He enters his dark apartment, goes to the kitchen, and flips on a small light over the sink. He takes two beers out of his fridge and turns to walk back out when he sees her leaning in the doorway.

"Beer?" he asks.

She holds out her hand.

"Aniston is not going to show up here," he says.

"How can you be sure?"

"Because I am."

He starts to walk toward the stairs. She doesn't move, not knowing what she's doing.

He motions for her to follow. "Tom will be home any minute," he says.

She follows him up the stairs and to his room. She's incredibly nervous. Opening the door, he allows her in first. When he shuts it with authority, she immediately backs into the room, as he likes to pin her up against the door and she's not ready for that. Not yet.

"Sit," he says, motioning to his chair. "Listen, Courtney and Aniston are friends. And therefore, by proxy, she's my friend."

"I think the term is *girlfriend*."

"Girlfriend." He laughs. "Please."

"What's so funny?"

"She was never my girlfriend. And sometimes, she can't take a hint. And when we hang out with the same crowd, as friends, she makes assumptions. Despite what I tell her."

"If I wasn't there, would you have gone home with her?"

The sexy grin that grows across his lips makes Abigail blush.

"What?" she whispers.

"I'm interested to learn why you want to know the answer."

With a huff, she says, "Because I'm curious—that's all."

"Would it eat away at you?"

She puts her beer down on his desk. "Hey, you asked me the same question the other day." Sensing she's nowhere near closer to an answer, she adds, "Have at her, Kelly. In fact, what do you say we go back, so you can drop me off and you can pick up your little—"

He cuts in, "Your spicy attitude only encourages me."

She shakes her head. Her hair falls past her shoulder. "Your flippant attitude turns me off." She picks up her beer and takes a sip. All this talking is making her thirsty.

"No, it doesn't," he challenges.

She narrows her eyes. "Don't test me."

He grins.

"What are you smiling about?" she asks.

He snaps back to reality. "Nothing."

"*Kelly*."

"I was not going to bring her home, for Christ's sake, Abigail. I haven't laid a finger on that girl since last year." His admission shocks her silent. "I was, however, planning on taking you home. You coming into the backyard to find me simply put my plan into action much quicker."

"Your plan into action?"

"Yes." He nears the chair she is sitting in and reaches out for her hand. "I only want to talk, promise."

She narrows her eyes.

"I promise."

She takes his hand, and he swiftly pulls her toward him. He guides her to the edge of his bed, and they sit side by side.

"But you haven't called me, and I just have to ask, are you okay?"

She drops her gaze. "I…I really don't want to talk about it."

He gently places his hand on her chin. "Abigail, are you okay?" he asks again, lifting her jaw.

Their eyes meet. The sadness in her beautiful navy eyes is undeniable, but despite that, she forces a smile.

"I should have called," she says. "I know that."

"I guess you just needed your space," he says.

"I did," she admits. "But I want you to know that I never put you in any category. I just needed to figure out what I wanted."

"And did you?"

"Yeah, I did."

"What?" he asks.

"Well…you, Kelly."

A guy like Kelly doesn't get giddy or overjoyed or ecstatic even, but if ever there was a time for such emotions, he shows her with the way his eyes light up.

But the cool side of him overrules the juvenile side.

"Now," he says in a sexy voice, "we could spend the next hour bantering back and forth"—he playfully runs his fingers over the collar of her shirt—"or—and just hear me out—I could do things to you that would make you feel incredible."

She gulps.

He continues his teasing and skims the tip of his finger down the front of her neck to the opening left by her undone button on her shirt. "Thoughts?" he whispers.

She has no thoughts. Except for Bree's advice to move forward. *Forget my past.*

He undoes another button on her shirt. He pushes the neckline back, exposing her shoulder. He hooks his finger under her bra strap and eases it off. He leans in and softly places his lips on her skin. Her breath catches as her head slightly tips to the side. He continues to kiss her neck.

"Do you have any thoughts on what you'd like to do?" he tantalizingly asks.

She laces her fingers into the belt loops on the waist of his jeans. Her other hand draws up the side of his sweater, bringing it with her. His muscles twitch as he grasps for the material, pulling it up over his head and tossing it to the floor. His body is gorgeous. She bites her lip as she views this stunning man in front of her.

"I think we're done talking," she whispers.

The devious smile that hits his lips forces her to pounce on him. She throws her arms around him. Desperate to kiss him. He grabs the back of her head as he wantonly kisses her, pushing his tongue against hers. His body presses onto hers as he spins her back to his bed. She falls on his comforter. Seductively crawling on top of her, he kisses her hard as he unbuttons the rest of her shirt, pushing it off her shoulders as she wriggles free of it.

"That is a sexy bra," he growls. "But I need it off."

Wrapping his arms around her, he unhooks it with ease and then releases her breasts from the clutch of its beautiful black lace. He wastes no time licking and teasing her breasts. She moans as she runs her hands over his head. He places his hand on the button of her jeans, unhooks it, and then slides the zipper down. His hand eases into her panties. She gasps.

"I want to taste you," he says.

Biting her lip again, she nods her head. He slides her denim down her hips and legs until he can pull them off, leaving a heap of her clothing on the floor. Her stomach rises and falls as her breathing becomes rapid. He cannot wait to put his mouth on her, to own her in a place only the privileged can savor.

She parts her legs as he leans into her, his hand caressing her belly, the soft ridge of her hip. His lips part, and his tongue works magic on her. A soft whimper leaks out of her lips as her hips move up and down to meet his mouth, making her want to come quickly.

She wants to hold on, thinking, *This is amazing.*

His fingers gently tickle her skin as he teases her, and there is a part of her that wants them inside of her, but there is also a part of her that only wants *him* inside of her. The thought of having sex with him is consuming her thoughts more than ever.

"Kelly…oh, Kelly," she moans as her torso lifts off his bed and arches perfectly. Her breasts shimmering in the light from the streetlight outside.

She is unable to hold off anymore. He is just as she imagined he would be—really good in the bedroom. She collapses back down, trying desperately to catch her breath as she clutches tightly on to his sheets. He places his hands on her thighs and lifts his body toward hers, so he can be closer to her. He takes her mouth into his, kissing her deeply. She is shocked at how intensely he kisses her.

Moments later, he releases her swollen lips. They both lie face up, staring at the ceiling.

She peeks over at him as he turns on his side to face her and notes a slight smile on his face. He looks pleased.

"You look fucking gorgeous right now," he says.

She angles her head to look at him. She grins and takes her arms, draping them over her chest. He takes her arms and unwraps them from her body.

"Please," he insists.

Her voice is hoarse. "I feel vulnerable."

He traces the tips of his fingers down her neck and between the valley of her breasts, resting them on her stomach. He watches her intently.

She starts to giggle a little.

"What?" he asks.

"Nothing."

He playfully pinches her. "You can't laugh after what we did and expect my ego not to need to know what you're thinking."

"Your ego." She giggles again.

"Tell me, Abigail."

She leans to face him, her cheeks pink. "I thought the first time I met you that…"

"That what?" he presses.

"Fine, fine." She places her hands over her face. "That you'd be really good in bed."

He reaches over and removes her hands from her face. She is surprised to see such a serious expression. He's not laughing at all.

"What?" She can almost feel a chill in the air under his stare.

"I…"

"Did I say something stupid?"

"No, it's…" He shuts his mouth quickly.

"Oh." She climbs off the bed, desperately searching for her shirt.

"Hey, where are you going?"

"I'm so sorry about what I said. It was really dumb."

He jumps up.

"I'm mortified. I assumed you were okay with that or thought about it, being with me, but I never asked, and now, I'm so embarrassed that I could die."

She pulls her shirt on, trying to button it. He grabs her arm to stop her.

"Abigail, slow down."

She finally looks up and notes a different expression on his face.

"Just hang on a second. What I'm not doing a very good job of saying is that when you're ready…assume I'm *really* ready."

She swallows hard. "Oh."

"Yeah." He leans into her ear, and with a deep voice, he says, "And, yes, I am."

A tingle runs down to the tips of her toes.

He leans back and adds, "But no pressure."

Twenty-Seven

Wildflowers

Abigail pulls into the shop, as promised, to drop off her car to Kelly. Bree was right; the oil leaking from her car could not be avoided any longer. She shyly enters the main office, as she can't stop thinking about the last night she spent with Kelly.

"Can I help you?" the man asks, snapping her back to reality.

"Yes, I'm here to drop off my car."

"You have an appointment?"

"I think so?" She peers into the garage, hoping to catch Kelly's eye. No such luck. "Kelly told me to come by today."

Before another word can be spoken, the man yells, "Kelly!"

A minute passes, and Kelly comes around the corner. Her breath catches by the way his body moves toward her in his tight blue T-shirt and baggy jeans, wiping his dirty hands on a rag. He hasn't noticed her yet, but Abigail's heart drops at the sight of him.

Once he steps over a lift base, they catch eyes, and he smiles. "I got this, Frank."

"Sure thing, Kelly."

"Come on in," he says to Abigail.

"Okay." She follows him like a puppet on a string.

"Watch your step," he warns as she steps over and around equipment and parts.

He leads her out to the back driveway. "Got your keys?" he asks.

She reaches in her bag and hands them to him.

"You working tonight?" he asks, looking her up and down.

"Yeah, my shift starts in twenty."

"Okay, I'll take a look and let you know what I find out."

"Thanks, Kelly. I appreciate you doing this."

"I can't have you driving around in an unsafe car." The expression on his face lends one to believe his protection of her goes much further beyond a safe car.

"If you want to call the restaurant, that's great, too."

He climbs into her car and, before shutting the door, says, "see you later." He drives it into one of the empty bays and quickly gets to work on her convertible.

She turns and slowly meanders back down the sidewalk toward Diesel Food. Ten minutes later, she enters the side door and clocks in. It's not crowded yet, but the rush usually starts around three on Fridays. Her mind is relatively free as she goes in between customers, serving drinks and food. As predicted, things start to pick up, and more people are gathering around the hostess's station, waiting for the next table.

"Just sat table nine," Chloe says.

"Thanks!" She spins to face the restaurant with her pad in her hand, and she freezes. *You've got to be kidding me.*

At the same time, the group looks up and notices her, making it impossible for her to run.

With a stiff upper lip, she approaches the table, and in a professional tone, she says, "Hello."

Webber's expression beams. "Abigail! You work here?"

"Yes, I do." She shakes her notepad for effect.

Nathan frowns. "I wasn't aware you'd gotten a job."

"Got it a few weeks ago," she says.

"How did you find out about this place anyway?" Tank asks.

"Well, I used to…"

"Excuse me, miss?" another customer says.

Abigail looks at the table next to them. "Yes?"

"Can I get some ketchup?"

"Of course." She turns back to the situation at hand. "Um, what can I grab you guys to drink?"

"Beer," Tank says.

Nathan kicks him under the table. "Water. We'll have water."

Abigail turns and heads back to the bar. She grabs the water and the ketchup for their neighbor.

Placing them down, she says, "I'll give you guys a minute to look over the menu."

"Wait, wait," Tank murmurs. "What's good here?"

She slightly leans over the menu he is holding, and she notices Nathan has not taken his eyes off her. *Could this be any more uncomfortable? I'd assume for both of us.* "The pasta is excellent."

"No meat in it?"

"It's vegetarian."

He laughs.

She ignores him and continues, "The salad and the club sandwich are delicious." When they don't respond, she says, "I'll be back in a few minutes."

As she walks away, she notes they all lean into one another and whisper. *Ugh, why did they have to come in?*

She tries to keep herself busier than normal to keep her from their table.

After a few minutes, she rushes over. "Have you guys decided?"

They each order, and she hurries to the kitchen to place their order. She is about to pick up another table's drinks when she senses a presence behind her. She turns to find Webber standing there with the saddest expression on his face.

"Hey. You need something?" she asks with a forced smile.

"Just needed a napkin."

She turns to the spot where the napkins are kept, pulls a few out, and hands them to him.

As he takes them, he says, "He misses you, Abigail."

Her heart is crushed.

"We all miss you coming around."

Not willing to get in the middle of it now, she simply says, "I miss you, too, Webber. Call me for lunch, okay?"

He smiles. "I'd like that. It's really cool you got a job—"

Just then, Chloe says, "Abigail, table three's drinks."

"Sorry. We're slammed tonight," she says with sympathetic eyes.

"I understand."

She exhales as he walks away, and she carries the drinks over to table three. Trying not to seem like a total bitch, she swings by their table and refills their water.

"Your dinner should be up soon." She avoids eye contact with Nathan and Tank.

Their food comes out with no issues, which she is grateful for. They seem to be enjoying what they can of their time at Diesel Food. Then, the front door swings open, and in walks Kelly.

His smile is wide as he catches her eye. He approaches her.

"Hey, so your car is all set. Minor leak in the oil line. You shouldn't have any other issues. I gave it a good once-over. But at some point, you'll need new tires before the winter."

He notices she is not speaking and that she seems nervous. "Did you hear me?" he asks.

"Yes. Thank you." She turns her head slightly, and that's when Nathan's table comes into direct sight.

"They're here?" he says rather coolly.

"Um, yeah."

His expression darkens. "Did you know they were coming?"

"What? No."

He shakes his head. "I'm grabbing some food." And with that, he spins on his heel and takes a seat at the bar.

Chloe greets him warmly, "Hey, stranger. The usual?"

"Yeah," he mumbles.

Sensing her two worlds are colliding, Abigail makes a beeline for the break room for a much-needed minute to herself. Upon gathering her composure, she heads back out into the dining area and tries, albeit poorly, to avoid eye contact with all of them. She brings a few tables their food and then passes by Nathan's table.

"Ready when you are," she says as she drops the check on the table.

Shortly after, she notices them getting up and approaching the door. Nathan lingers and then turns to find Abigail.

"Hey," he says as she puts salt in a shaker.

"You need change?" she asks.

"No. Wanted to say I'm sorry for coming in. For us coming in. I can see it made you uncomfortable." His eyes soften, and it reminds her of the old Nathan, the kind, reserved guy she met their freshman year.

Her guard goes up as thoughts of Poppy and Nathan swarm in her brain. "It's a free country, and I can't stop anyone from coming in," she blurts out.

Her verbal whiplash nearly knocks him backward. He's visibly wounded, and something about her hurting him makes her feel victorious and sad, all at once.

He then peers over his shoulder; it's obvious he's glancing at Kelly, who is watching their interaction. "You, um…dating that guy?" His tone is unmistakably gloomy.

She can't care about his feelings right now, but she is also unsure how to define her relationship with Kelly. "We hang out."

"You hang out?"

"Yes, we see one another at times."

His shoulders hunch, and she is about to lash out at him and ask him how the fuck he could get someone pregnant, potentially ruin his career, his life, everything, but all she says is, "I'm really busy right now."

"Okay, Abby. Well, we left the check on the table." With a shake of his head, he turns and walks out the door.

She's left in the wake of her big mouth, and as she turns back to her work, Kelly is observing her. He's noticeably irritated, leaving her with an unsettling feeling in her gut.

Twenty minutes later, Kelly crumples his napkin onto his plate, takes his wallet out of his back pocket, and tosses cash on the counter for Chloe. He gets up and approaches Abigail near the hostess station.

"Your car is in the back," he says handing her the car keys.

She takes them as he brushes by her and exits rather abruptly.

Something in the advice Bree and Laura have bestowed upon her this year hits her quickly. She pads to the door and chases after him. "Kelly!"

He is about to cross the street. He stops.

"What's up?" he asks nonchalantly.

She steps within earshot. "What, um…" She hesitates as her nerves rise within her. "Do you have any plans tonight?"

He crosses his arms over his chest. "Nothing past a shower."

The thought of him in the shower makes her cheeks pink.

She finally gets the courage to ask, "Do you maybe want to do something?"

He plays it cool with a slight nod of his head. "Sure."

Relief washes over her. "I get out in an hour."

"Okay."

"I'll call you," she says as she turns and rushes back to the restaurant.

As she enters Diesel Food, Chloe is cleaning up behind the bar. Abigail approaches some of her tables and picks up the checks left. She noticed Nathan, Tank, and Webber gave her a huge tip, making her blue and uncomfortable.

Chloe gives her a concerned glance.

"Is it that obvious?" Abigail asks.

"You friends with those football guys?"

"Yeah. Wait, how do you know about OSU football?"

"Not my thing, but everyone in this town would recognize those guys."

Abigail releases a heavy sigh. "I used to date Nathan, and yeah, I was—am friends with Tank, too."

"Girl, you are in the mix!"

She drops her shoulders. "We had a rough breakup after the fact, if that makes sense?"

"Breakups are never easy. But it probably helps when you have someone waiting in the wings. Wouldn't you agree?"

"How do you mean?"

"I've been seeing you and Kelly do this song and dance since last year. It's none of my business, but I'd say a guy like Kelly won't be around for long."

"Song and dance?" she asks innocently with a tip of her head.

"You two have always had a connection. It's pretty obvious—well, at least to me it is."

"Oh, I didn't know that," Abigail says.

Chloe gently pats Abigail on the arm. "Listen, we're slowing down. Why don't you start to break down your section and get out of here?"

"Really?"

"Yeah, you worked hard tonight."

"Thanks, Chloe."

Before she turns her attention back to the bar, she adds, "He's a really good guy. Rough around the edges sometimes, but he's got a good heart. Don't ever tell Kelly I said that."

Shocked by her confession, she smiles at Chloe. "I won't."

Abigail does all her organizing and finishes her station. She cashes out her receipts, and as she walks out, she waves good night to Chloe. She approaches her car in the back and notes the gleam of the paint shimmering off the streetlight. Her car looks immaculate. Like an old penny that has been shone to its new state. She unlocks the door and gets in. The interior is just as pristine, and sitting on the passenger seat is a bunch of wildflowers tied together with a piece of string.

Kelly Conrad has struck again and when she least expected him to.

Twenty-Eight

Rebirth

Webber, Nathan, and Tank ride in silence on the way to the house party that is being put on by one of the football players.

"Hey, Nathan. You okay, dude?" Webber asks from the backseat of Nathan's car.

"Is she freaking dating that guy?" Tank asks.

Nathan's nerves rise as his friends throw a bunch of questions at him that he doesn't want to answer. Finally, he mumbles, "No, and I guess so."

"I saw his car at her house the other night," Tank admits. "Two in the morning."

Nathan flashes a nasty look in Tank's direction. "And you didn't fucking tell me?!"

"What was I supposed to say?" Tank says. "*Hey, dude, wanna hear some bad news?*"

"That she's moved on? Jesus, Tank!" Nathan barks. "It's worse, hearing it from her."

"Shit, it's not my job anymore," Tank growls back.

"Guys, guys. Hold up. She hasn't said anything to me," Webber adds.

Nathan looks in the rearview mirror at him. "You really think she'd tell *you*?" he blurts out. As soon as he speaks, he sees Webber's face grow glum. "Sorry, I didn't mean that, Spidey."

"Stop the car," Webber snarls.

"What?" Nathan asks.

"Stop the fucking car!" he yells.

This has been a long time coming. Webber has spent the last several months listening to Tank and Nathan complaining and pining over losing Abigail as their friend and girlfriend. Yet, he has never witnessed either of them do anything positive toward getting her back in their good graces. And because of their bad behavior, Webber's relationship with her has taken a major hit. He never sees her like he used to.

Nathan screeches to a halt.

Webber puts his hand on the door handle and pauses. "If you'd both stop to look at yourselves for one second, you'd realize this is all your fucking fault."

"What?" Tank quips back.

"Yeah. I was her friend first. Then, you two came along and consumed all her time. Only to treat her like shit when it didn't suit you anymore."

"Now, hold up a second, Spidey," Nathan says.

"No, you hold up. You had the best girl in the world, and you fucking blew it with those stupid groupie cheerleaders. So pathetic," he growls.

Tank laughs.

"And you! You're the fucking worst! You're a dick"—he pulls at his hair—"just to be a dick. Like tonight. You treat her like garbage all because she won't sue the school. Obviously, she didn't want to drag herself or you in front of the courts again! How could you not get that?! Do you have any idea what she and her friends went through? You disgust me. Sometimes, guys…" He pauses, seething with anger. "I get that you're, like, *kings* of this school, but sometimes, I question if it's worth it. 'Cause to me, losing someone like *her* wouldn't be."

"I didn't know you felt this way," Tank mumbles.

"Well, you never bothered to ask. So, do something about it, will you? I mean, she's clearly hurting—anyone can see it. I fucking miss the old Abby. And I blame both of you for that!"

With that, he yanks open the door and scurries onto the sidewalk. He rushes toward the house they were going to before Nathan has a chance to park the car. Webber is more than welcome in these parties at this point. He's been known as Nathan's roommate for going on three years now. But for the first time, the thought sickens him. He's one of *them* by proxy. He never asked for it. He's just always gone along with it.

I totally get how Abigail feels. It's high time that I stop being in the shadow of the football team because the way I see it now, they cast a pretty dark one.

He approaches the door as a guy attempts to high-five him.

"Spidey!" he says.

He doesn't reciprocate the love; instead, he walks right in and heads for the bar.

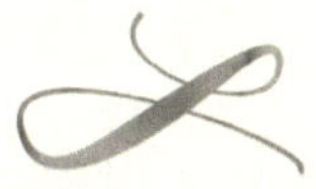

Abigail drives to her house with a peculiar smile on her face. This evening could only be summed up as a renaissance. There is a fire within her she can't quite place. She parks her car and enters the grand foyer. She can hear the TV playing in the living room.

"I'm home," she yells.

"Hey!" Melissa replies.

She walks in and finds Melissa and Logan snuggled up on the couch, watching a movie. Their relationship has always given Abigail a sense of fulfillment. They have stood the test of college life and continue to leave those around them believing that college relationships don't require drama in order to be interesting and worth talking about.

"Hey, Abigail," Logan says with a smile.

"What are you guys up to?" she asks.

"Watching a movie, about to order some pizza. You want in?" Melissa asks.

"No, thank you. I've got to shower and then…well, I might have plans tonight."

"Plans?" Melissa says with a smile.

"Yeah." Abigail glances at Logan.

"I do not speak of what happens here," he reassures her.

"I know you wouldn't, Logan. It's just…well, I might see Kelly." Her face blushes.

"Do we like him?" Logan asks Melissa.

"As long as she does." Melissa smiles back.

Abigail beams. "I'm heading up now. You two continue on," she says with a wave of her hand.

She climbs the stairs to the third floor. She undresses and gets into the shower. The hot water is a welcome feeling. She hums a tune as she shampoos her hair. Her thoughts drift to what she and Chloe spoke about earlier.

Within minutes, she's back in her room, towel on her head, and she takes great care to lotion her body.

She notices there are no lights flashing on her machine. She takes a deep breath and dials Kelly's number, not having any clue what will happen on the other end. It rings a few times, and her heart sinks.

He's probably gone out for the night. Why wouldn't he?

"A guy like Kelly won't be around for long," she remembers Chloe saying.

"Hello?"

"Kelly?"

"Yeah?"

"It's me, um, Abigail."

There is silence, and then he says, "I know."

Relief. "Um, what are you up to?"

"Not much. Having a beer with Tom and some friends."

Her heart sinks. *What friends? Aniston? Courtney?*

"Oh, okay. Well…" She hesitates, unsure of whether to ask him to hang out. *Is that too forward? Does he want to? He seems different today, and I'm not sure how to take his current mood.*

"Would you like to come over for a beer?" he asks.

Whew.

There is silence as she thinks of what to say. *What if I go over and Aniston is there? Won't that be awkward?* "Sure, I could come by."

"Okay, see you in a few." And almost immediately, he hangs up the phone.

She finishes getting ready and slips on a pair of jeans and a tight T-shirt. She inspects her makeup and hair before grabbing her bag and gingerly heading down the stairs.

"Going out to a party for a bit. I'll see you guys later."

"To Kelly's?" Melissa asks.

"Yeah, he's having some friends over," she says calmly, though her nerves are on high alert.

"You look really pretty," Melissa adds.

Shyly, she smooths down her shirt. "Oh, thanks. See you guys later."

"Night, Abigail," Logan says.

As she pulls into Kelly's driveway, she can hear laughter coming from the backyard. Not sure what to do, she knocks on the front door. When no one answers, she cracks it open and steps inside. She enters the hallway when she hears Kelly's voice. It's hushed but clear.

"What do you want me to say? Yes, I realize she is not like the others, but I can't help it. I can't stop thinking about her." There is a pause. "Yeah, maybe I am a little obsessed, sis. She's…"

Obsessed?

Sensing a flush to her skin, she quickly exits the house and goes around to the side to find several people sitting on the deck, drinking beer. She approaches the group.

Tom peeks his head out from behind a friend. "Oh, hey, Abigail. How are you?"

"Fine, Tom. And you?"

"Great." He smiles. Tom gets up and grabs a beer, handing it to her.

She tips back on her heels as she stuffs her other hand in the pocket of her jeans. She doesn't want to be obvious and ask where Kelly is because she already knows the answer.

"Kelly went to the store. He'll be back any minute," he says as he motions for her to join them on the deck.

"Guys, this is Abigail. Do your own introductions," he jokes to all their friends.

"Hey, I think you're in my science class," one guy remarks.

She looks at him and immediately recognizes the guy. "Oh, hi. Yes. Sorry, didn't see you earlier."

"Yeah, cool. Don't you date the quarterback, Nathan Ryan? Right? I used to see you guys together all the time," he says.

She is about to answer when she hears a clearing of a throat from behind her.

She surmises it's Kelly because Tom says, "Hey, bud, you get what we needed at the store?"

Too afraid to turn around, she tips back her beer.

He steps out onto the deck, carrying a case of beer. He empties it into the cooler. When he's done, he finally glances at her.

"Abigail." His tone is cool, and she questions whether she should have come.

"Hey," she barely whispers.

He makes me so nervous!

A breeze blows, causing her to shiver. Kelly enters the house, carrying the empty box. She's unsure as to whether she should follow him in. She doesn't have to wonder long, as he comes right back out and cracks open a beer. She stands in silence as all the guys chat. She peeks up in Kelly's direction, only to find him leaning on the railing, his body perfectly posed, staring at her. She must look away. Something in her feels like bursting into tears and running back to her car. The tension between them is palpable, to say the least.

What a night. Kelly is giving me the cold shoulder, and I'm not sure why. And the fact that Nathan, Tank, and Webber were in the restaurant tonight stinks. Then, the guy here just had to recognize me, right? And bring up Nathan. I just can't get away from my past.

A beer later, she is about to leave, as it has become inevitably clear she is the odd woman out. Kelly has not said a word to her in over twenty minutes, and at this point, she feels plain stupid for coming over tonight. Coupled with the fact that her T-shirt is no match for the late fall air and the bumps on her skin cause her to shudder again. Kelly disappears into the house, and within minutes, he returns with a flannel shirt.

He approaches her, and under his breath, he says, "Why are you only wearing a T-shirt?"

She glances up at him and swallows hard. "I…I didn't think we'd be outside."

He drapes the shirt around her shoulders, and in the process, the guy from her science class looks at her with a questioning expression.

She places her empty beer on the table and opens her mouth to speak when he says, "Let me get you another one."

He leaves her side and grabs two beers from the cooler. He returns to her. Confused and feeling a bit warmer, she takes the beer and sips it in silence, much like before.

"Kelly, you coming to Corey's?" Tom asks.

Without hesitation, he says, "Not tonight."

"Cool."

All the guys drop their empty bottles in the trash and start to walk in the backyard and toward the road.

"See you later, Abigail," Tom says.

"See you in class," the other guys add.

When they're officially out of earshot as their feet hit the pavement, Abigail steps closer to Kelly and asks, "Is everything okay, Kelly?"

He turns, his green eyes ablaze. "You tell me."

She cocks her head. "What I meant was, if you're not in the mood for company, then…"

"Then, what? You'll leave?"

Her heart thumps. "If you want to be alone, then yes."

"I asked you over," he replies rather flatly.

"Have I done something wrong? Is this about what the guy from my class said? Because I can't help that sort of thing, and besides, it's—"

"Did you know they were coming to the restaurant tonight?"

"What? Of course not."

He gives her a dark stare.

"You don't believe me?"

Ignoring her, he asks, "Besides what?"

"Besides, it is not my fault that the guy knew that."

"You didn't correct him."

She crosses her arms over her front. "Because I didn't have time to."

"Really?" he scoffs.

Now, it's her turn to get pissy. "Yes, really. You came out here, and I couldn't think…"

"Think of what?"

"What to say with you around, okay?!"

"The truth is a start."

"Kelly, that's not fair."

"Fair?!" He turns and goes back inside.

She rushes after him. "Kelly, why are you mad? What did I do?"

He's in his kitchen, grabbing a beer out of the fridge. He slams the door. She jumps.

"I'm leaving." She turns and heads back toward the porch.

There's a slight pull on her arm as she reaches the threshold.

He spins her toward him. "What did he say to you at the restaurant?"

"Let go of me."

"Not until you tell me," he says, his hand still on her arm.

"What the hell has gotten into you?" She shivers again.

He pulls her inside, shutting the door to the deck. He lets go of her. She leans back on the glass slider.

"He asked me if I was dating you."

"What did you say?"

Embarrassed she is having this conversation, she replies, "I said we hang out."

"Hang out?"

"Yes. Isn't that what we do?" she says with an icy edge.

His laugh is sinister, and it gives her the chills.

"You don't have girlfriends, Kelly. I'm not stupid."

He inhales sharply, and she notices his cheeks pink slightly.

"So, that's why I'm not understanding your mood," she admits.

"My mood?"

"Yes, you almost seem…"

"Seem what?" he asks as he takes a step closer to her.

She lifts her head, and as confidently as she can, she says, "Jealous."

"Jealous?" he questions as though the concept never occurred to him. Then, after some thought, he says, "I'm annoyed."

"With me?" Her navy eyes grow wide.

"That fucking guy had you, and he screwed it up. And every goddamn time I get an inch closer, he fucking rears his head again. I'm sick of it."

Now, it's her turn to inhale sharply. Tears sting her eyes as she asks, "You're sick of this?"

She pushes off the wall and passes by him.

"Where are you going?"

"I-I came here tonight to be with *you*, Kelly. And it seems like no matter what I do, I can't shake him, and I'm trying to. Today was not my fault, but for some reason, you think it is."

"Wait, please," he begs.

She stops in her tracks. "You guys are all the same, you know that?"

"Now, wait a second."

She spins to face him as a tear rolls down her cheek. "No, you wait. I've tried—obviously very poorly—to play this cool, but the facts of my past are indisputable. And I get pissed about it, mad about it, and, hell, even sad about it, but I have also tried like heck to find some semblance of happiness. I've accepted the fact that you don't date, and you could probably walk right out your front door and find a hundred girls who would want to screw you. But because I didn't spread my legs for you the moment you showed an ounce of interest in me, you're sick of it? Well, now, I'm glad I didn't waste my time." She wipes the fresh tears off her cheek.

He stretches his arm toward her. She quickly steps back.

"Please," he begs.

She shakes her head.

"Okay, okay." He backs up. "But you can't say that."

"Say what, Kelly?"

"You're not wasting your time. I can assure you of that."

She cocks her head and gives him a hard stare.

"I'm serious, Abigail. And I don't believe for one second that you really think that, or you wouldn't have come over tonight."

"Really? Tonight, where you made it so hard for me to feel comfortable? Where you played it cool and made me squirm to ask you to spend time with me? And then you bring him up as though I didn't come over here specifically because I didn't want to be with him. I wanted to be with you!"

His eyes light up.

"Kelly, is it not obvious?" She pauses and then adds, "But it doesn't matter anymore." She turns again to leave.

"Abigail, I'm not letting you leave, so stop this nonsense," he barks.

She spins to face him. "You stop *your* nonsense," she challenges.

"See, when you talk like that to me, it only makes me want you more."

"You're ridiculous."

He steps closer to her. "I'm warning you."

"Warning me?!"

"Yes." His eyes darken like nothing she has seen before.

"I don't get you at all."

Frustrated, he quips, "I know."

"See. Ugh, what am I doing here?!" she says, throwing her hands up in the air.

"If you walk away, you'll force me to forget about you."

"What?!"

"Yes, because I'm in deep with you."

Her skin chills. "In deep? What does that mean?" *Obsessed? Was he talking about me?*

"I'll show you."

Grabbing her around the waist, he pulls her to him. She has no time to react as his mouth finds hers. Fisting his hand tightly into her tresses, he holds his mouth to hers with feverish desire. His tongue assaults and twirls against hers, making her knees completely weak while an unmistakable urge settles between her legs.

What is happening to me? My God, this boy is maddening but so incredibly sexy.

Her knees drop slightly, so he rips her from his grasp, leaving her heaving before him. He wipes the wet from his swollen lips with the back of his hand.

"There," he says with a ragged breath.

"What…what was that about?"

"I can only wait so long to touch you."

She steadies herself on the wall. "Then, why did you stop?"

He draws near. "You didn't want me to?"

She gulps as his eyes pierce into her. "I said I came here to be with you. But I don't want to argue with you. That seems crazy to me."

"I just don't want him to keep hurting you," he says.

"Let me do this my own way because it's the only way I know how."

"Damn it," he curses under his breath. "You're right. I overacted, and I'm sorry, Abigail."

"Don't be so hard on me," she says. "Remember what you told me? I can't tell people to leave the restaurant." She tries holding back her smile, but she can't.

"Never thought that would come back to bite me, but well played." He takes her hand. "Can we start over tonight?"

"I'd like nothing more than to start this whole night over."

"Thankfully, it's still early," he says. "Can I take you up to my room?"

She nods.

He guides her toward the stairs. He is about to ascend when he grabs her by the waist and hoists her over his shoulder.

"Kelly!" she screeches.

He rushes up the stairs as she bounces on his trunk. They get to the top, and he gives her ass a firm tap.

"Ouch. Hey!"

"More where that came from," he says in a husky voice.

He opens his door and quickly shuts it behind him, placing her down against the frame. The unmistakable desire in his eyes quickens her pulse. There is an animalistic way about his manners, and she can feel a burn in her stomach with one glance from him. He leans forward, closer to her, and locks the door for good measure.

With no words needed, he presses his body onto hers. The sensation of his muscles on her slender figure excites her. He brushes her hair back off her shoulder, allowing him access to nibble at her neck. She tips her head to the side as he drags his tongue up to her ear. The heaviness in his breath deepens. She moans as he works his way to her mouth, his full lips finding hers, sensually kissing her. He takes control, and again, there's a weakness in her body she can't explain. He could own her, and she would not protest.

He pulls his flannel off her shoulders, letting it drop to the floor. Then, his hand drags up her T-shirt, and she moans in approval.

Once he pulls the T-shirt over her head, he reveals a baby-pink lace bra.

"Fuck, that's hot," he growls.

"Your turn," she whispers.

He grasps behind his back and pulls his shirt over his head. His body never disappoints. The muscles in his pecs twitch as she runs the tips of her fingers over his inked skin.

Wrapping his arms around her waist, he kisses her deeply but with force, as though he can't get enough of her.

My, he is a fabulous kisser.

Running her fingers over his sheared hair, she moans as he pushes his tongue deeper into her mouth. Then, he spins her toward the center of the room as she eagerly runs her hands down the sides of his waist and starts to unbutton his jeans.

Rejecting her advances by grabbing her hand, he whispers, "I want this to last." He steps back from her and sits on the edge of the bed. "Come here," he says, reaching out his hand.

She straddles his lap, watching him intently as he traces his hand up her back, unhooking her bra and easing it off her shoulders. He moves his mouth to one of her breasts, his tongue running over her soft skin while he takes the other hand and squeezes her nipple between the tips of his fingers. She arches her back as the most amazing sensation washes over her. He continues to feel her up as she groans deeper and deeper, her breathing becoming erratic. She starts to grind her hips on top of him. The carnality in her stomach grows with each push of her body on top of his.

Quickly, he stands up, taking her with him, and then he sets her back down on her feet.

"Undress for me," he begs as he steps back from her.

She shyly lowers her gaze.

"Now," he pleads.

She unbuttons her jeans.

"Slowly."

She lowers the zipper and then eases the edges of her jeans over her hips, swinging them side to side as they make their way down her slim, tanned legs.

He bites his lip as he watches her do as she was told. She steps out of them, sweeping them to the side of her.

"Put your hands behind your back," he says.

She gulps and clasps her wrists at her backside. He walks behind her, and as he does, she gets a chill down her spine. Normally, he'd grab a girl by her clutched hands, bend her over his bed or a couch arm, and have his way with her. It's in his sexual, consensual domination of another that he's the most himself.

She shudders at the feel of him so close to her. He runs his hand up one side of her body, tracing over one shoulder and back down the other side of her.

Is this finally going to happen? Does he have any idea how turned on I am?

She catches his eye as he places his hand around her waist to the front of her and down to her sex. She gasps at the touch of his finger.

"I've waited a long time for this," he whispers in her ear as she tips her head back onto his shoulder.

"Kelly," she moans. "Me, too."

He smiles a wicked grin as he releases his touch. With his hands now on her hips, he guides her back to the bed. She spins around to face him, and the look in his eyes is remarkable. He kisses her as he takes her hands from behind her back and clasps them around his neck. In one beautiful, fluid movement, he has her cradled in his arms and lies back with her on the bed.

He nuzzles a trail down her neck to the valley between her breasts and then lands soft kisses on her stomach. With eager but slow fingers, he takes hold of the lace on the edge of her panties and eases them over her legs. She's completely naked, lying on Kelly Conrad's bed, and she almost can't believe this is happening. He leans up and unbuttons his jeans, slipping them down his legs and onto the floor. He opens his nightstand drawer, grabbing a condom.

"Are you sure?" he breathes.

"Yes," she replies.

He rips the foil packet open with his teeth. Her chest heaves as he readies himself for her.

He climbs in between her legs. Then, he leans in seductively toward her face and kisses her deeply. She runs her hands down his back toward his buttocks and then pushes on his hips. She is telling him without words that she is ready to have him. He takes his hand and draws it down her waist to her thigh, lifting it toward him. Her leg bends and frames over his backside, and with one purposeful thrust, they finally become one.

So many thoughts swirl in her mind as he pushes deeper inside her. She, too, cries out with delight as he slides back out of her. Back and forth, back and forth, their bodies move as one. They're perfect together.

He is so good, and he feels incredible.

"*Mmm.*"

"Oh, Abigail," he whispers.

She moves her head to look at him.

He can't take his eyes off hers. Placing his hand on the side of her face, he leans in and kisses her deeply, and then he releases her swollen lips, again locking eyes with her. "Your eyes are intoxicating to stare into when I'm on top of you like this."

She cranes her head up a bit and nibbles a little on his ear, an enticing move on her part.

"Ooh," he moans in response.

"You like that?" she whispers.

"I like anything you do," he says.

She draws his lips to hers and kisses him as the thrusts deepen. They'd like to think this can last forever, but this has been built up for so long; neither one of them will be able to last much longer.

He buries his head into her neck as she cries, "Oh, Kelly."

This only makes him work harder for her. And he does. He shifts and turns his hips, pounding into her with a want she has never felt before. As her nails climb down his back, he tips his head up and moans as he is brought to the edge with her.

He collapses down on her, and she tightly wraps her arms around his back. Their breathing is erratic as they both slowly come down from their high.

She glances over at him. The glow of his skin and the satisfied expression on his face are perfect. He was amazing.

And almost immediately, she starts to think about when they can do it again.

Twenty-Nine

Don't Screw It Up

Abigail is sitting cross-legged on the bed, wearing only his flannel shirt, when Kelly returns from the bathroom.

"I'm going to the kitchen for some drinks. I'll be right back," he says as he exits again.

Abigail, needing a distraction, crawls off the bed and switches on his radio to a quiet hum. She surveys the posters of classic cars on his wall as well as the pictures of scantily clad models. Her skin flushes as she notices the stack of *Playboy* magazines on his desk. She retreats to his bed and sits where he left her.

Kelly enters the room, carrying two beers and a bag of pretzels.

"Thirsty?" he asks.

"Thank you," she says, almost unable to meet his eyes. The thoughts of them moaning together comes rushing over her mind, and her face blushes.

He sits on the bed next to her, placing the snacks between them. He rests back on the headboard.

"Everything okay with your car?" he asks.

"Yes, thank you. It looked beautiful. You didn't have to go through all that trouble."

"I know." He smiles.

"And the flowers…"

"What flowers?"

Immediately, her face drops. "There were—"

A wicked grin crosses his face. "I'm kidding."

She playfully punches him on the arm. "Don't do that to me," she whines.

He touches his arm. "Careful," he scolds with a look that gives her the chills. "I'll play if you want to play."

She gulps.

"Drink your beer first and eat." He opens the bag and offers her some.

"You're kind of bossy," she whispers.

"It's how I am."

She pops some pretzels in her mouth and takes a sip of her beer, all while smiling because he hasn't taken his eyes off her.

"I like when you do as you're told." He runs his hand over her thigh.

She peeks over at him. And her heart rate quickens as his eyes meet hers.

"Do you have any idea how sexy you look right now?" he asks.

"Kelly," she whispers.

"Do you?"

She pauses for a moment. *How do I answer that?* "Must be the shirt," she jokes.

"I like you in my shirt."

She wraps one arm around herself.

He tips his head. "But I like you out of it better." He tugs on the sleeve.

She inhales sharply at his comment. "Boy, you make me blush."

"A lot, I might add. Why do you think that is?"

She takes another sip of her beer and then turns to him. "For starters, look at you."

"Me?"

She laughs. "Kelly, be serious."

"I am."

She lowers her gaze. "Your looks are intimidating. And I don't think I'm telling you something you don't already get. People notice you."

He reaches up, raising her chin to face him. "I don't care if people notice me. Only you."

She chuckles. "Sure."

"I'm serious."

"Well, that's not for you to decide because it will just happen."

"When did you notice me?" he asks.

"Really?"

"Yeah, I'm asking."

"Oh, um, well," she stammers.

"It's a simple question," he muses.

"I-I noticed you when you came into the Union that day and we ended up sitting together. Up until then, I thought you were dating your sister."

"Gross. Really?"

"Yeah, you came into my room and were asking for her, so I assumed she was your girlfriend, but little did I know, you don't have girlfriends." She laughs.

"I'm ignoring your remark," he says with a scowl. "And besides, we hardly interacted, if I remember correctly."

"It's not the interaction with you that's noticeable." A small grin crosses her lips.

He can't help but smile. "Really?"

"Kelly, stop it. I watched a bunch of girls turn their heads as you walked by them toward the coffee shop."

"I didn't realize that you'd thought about that. You always seemed a little put off by me."

"I did?"

"Yeah, I could never quite get where you were coming from. You were a mystery."

"I'm not anymore?"

"Most certainly. But at least now, I can get you alone and talk to you."

She lowers her eyelids. "As I said, you've always intimidated me, so maybe that was it." She takes another sip of her beer.

"I'm glad you tried to move past that." He laughs.

"Are my feelings funny to you?" she quips.

"No. But I've told you not to be shy around me, haven't I?"

"And then you waved your magic wand." She chuckles.

He frowns. Taking her beer from her hand, he places it on his nightstand. He reaches over to her legs and uncrosses them. He crawls between them, his face now only inches from hers.

"I have been known to work some magic," he slyly says as he glances between her legs.

She gulps.

He traces one hand up her leg and stops at the top of her thigh. Her eyes dart back and forth as she intently watches him. His fingers dance along the crease of her leg and down the inside of her thigh. She inhales sharply as his fingers linger over her sex, moving back and forth.

"Would you like me to work my magic?" he asks.

She nods her head.

"Speak," he demands.

"Yes," she whispers. "Yes."

He slides one finger inside her, never taking his eyes off her.

My God, he is spectacular.

Her eyes roll back, and her mouth gapes open as her hips slant ever so slightly forward.

"Do you want more?" he asks.

YES!

She lowers her head down to look at him, a soft haze in her eyes as she utters, "Yes, please."

"How polite," he says as he swirls the tip of his finger over her flesh. "Can you please unbutton my shirt?"

She releases each button.

Her lips part softly as she tilts her head back, resting it on his headboard. The natural arch in her back sets her breasts free from the flannel for him to gaze upon. Her nipples harden as she becomes more aroused. He teases her with his fingers while she softly moans through the bite in her lip. It doesn't take him long to work his magic and bring her to climax. Feeling her tighten around his fingers gives him a massive hard-on.

She lets a huge sigh escape as her body relaxes. She's stress-free and content.

She catches his eyes, and with a laugh, she asks, "Can I have my beer back?"

He climbs off her and obliges. As he does, she notices the bulge in his shorts.

He looks down and laughs. "I'll get mine later."

"Later?" she asks, looking at the clock. It's almost midnight.

"You in a hurry to leave?" he asks.

"No, I assumed I'd…" She's not exactly sure what she assumed, but she didn't think she'd be sleeping over.

"It's still early," he says as he takes his beer from the nightstand.

She sips on hers, almost finishing it. She starts to slide off the bed when he grabs her hand.

"I said, it's early."

"I'm just going to use the bathroom," she says with a cock of her head. She places the beer on his desk and then slips her panties on despite his outward vocal disapproval.

"In case Tom comes home," she says.

"Fine. I'm grabbing another beer. Want one?"

"Sure," she says as she exits the bedroom.

When Abigail returns from the bathroom, Kelly is not back yet. She doesn't hear any noise coming from downstairs, so she assumes Tom is not back either. She gingerly walks down the steps, and as she enters the living room, she can hear the muffled sounds of voices coming from the garage. She takes a step or two closer and is about to yell for Kelly when she hears a female voice, although she cannot make out the words.

But then she hears Kelly say something, his voice heated. She draws near the door. It's cracked open enough for Abigail to see into the garage. Standing in front of Kelly is Aniston, and her hand is draped on Kelly's waist.

What the hell?! Is this a joke?

Aniston's eyes are filled with concern. And Kelly is now whispering to her as she gestures with her other hand. Abigail then sees Kelly grab ahold of the hand Aniston had on his waist. Abigail is immediately brought back to the party at Kelly's house on her birthday when she went into the basement and saw the two of them leaning up against one another. The sexual vibe emanating between them was not to be mistaken.

I can't let them see me spying on them. How embarrassing. Abigail turns without being noticed and hurries back up the stairs to get dressed.

Once in his room, she frantically searches for her bra and T-shirt. She slips on her jeans, and she finally locates her bra. Within moments, she hears the creak of the floorboards as Kelly approaches his room. He casually walks in.

"What's this?" he says as he motions to her. "You're leaving?" he asks.

Surprised by his tone, she glances up. He closes his door and approaches her. She turns to try and put her bra on with some privacy or dignity—she can't figure out which is more important to her at the moment. He reaches around her and snatches her bra.

"Knock it off, Kelly."

"Look at me, Abigail."

On the verge of tears, she says, "Just give it back."

"No."

"You think that will keep me here?" she says, crossing her arms over her chest.

He quickly moves around her, so she's forced to look at him. He places his hands on her shoulders as she tries to turn. His grip is firm.

"You're being irrational," he says.

"Am I?"

"Yes."

She chokes out a response, "Did you invite her here?"

He laughs and then says, "Were you spying on us?"

Abigail shakes free of him. "Spying? *Spying*? Oh, you have some nerve."

When his guard is down, she yanks the bra from his grip. She is shocked to see the expression on his face as she passes him. Annoyance.

"You did not just do that."

She ignores him as she takes off the flannel. With no warning at all, he throws his arm around her shoulders and pulls her to his chest.

"Kelly Conrad," she squeals. "Let me go!"

"Not until you have an adult conversation with me."

"You can't make me," she replies angrily. Only to quickly realize she is the one who sounds like a child.

He moves his lips to her ear. "I think that is exactly what I'm doing."

She tries to wriggle free.

"No use. I'm very strong."

Finally, she gives up.

"Good." His grip is still tight around her. "Now, listen, I had no idea she was coming over."

Abigail lets a noise of disapproval escape her lips.

He continues, "Really? I just asked you to stay. So, does that make any sense to you?"

She doesn't answer.

"She came by of her own accord."

"Why was she here?" she asks.

"Why do you think?"

She gasps.

"What do you expect me to say? That she *doesn't* want to fuck me?"

"Oh my God," she exclaims. "You *are* an asshole."

"Abigail, this is getting blown way out of proportion."

"Kelly, please let me go."

He leans into her ear again. "If I let you go, you have to promise me that you will simply have a talk with me and not leave."

She sighs. "Fine."

"Say it."

She rolls her eyes. "Fine, I'll talk and…"

"Not leave." He takes the bra from her grip and spins her around with the other hand to face him. "I heard someone in the garage, and she was walking back from a friend's house and wanted to see if I was free."

Her eyebrows arch as she crosses her arms over her bosom. "A booty call."

He laughs. "No, a booty call would mean I called her. Which I did not. I haven't dialed her in months."

"So, months go by, and she thinks you're simply waiting for her?"

He chuckles. "More like hoping."

"Oh, you son of—"

"Well, I'm being honest." His smile is infuriating.

"Were you honest with *her*?"

He places his hand on her neck and then brushes her hair back off her shoulder. His eyes soften. "Yeah, I was honest with her, Abigail."

She swallows hard. "What did you say?"

He steps back and runs his hands over his handsome face, and as he releases them, she sees his cheeks pink.

She presses him, "You asked me what I said to Nathan."

He narrows his eyes and then finally admits, "True. That's fair."

She taps her bare foot for effect as she waits for him to speak.

"I told her that if she ever cared about me, she shouldn't come around."

Abigail continues to tap her foot.

He rolls his eyes at her. "I also told her that nothing she could do would make me want to be with her again. That I'm only interested in…you."

Whoa. Heavy.

She gulps.

"Now, imagine if you got dressed and walked out the door." He crosses his arms over his front and taps his foot for effect. "Well?"

Her eyes soften. "It would've been a mistake," she admits. *I don't want to be played again. Casual is fine. But I don't want to compete with another girl. I simply don't have it in me after what I went through.*

He smiles and then tosses her bra on the floor. "Exactly."

"Did you have to grab me to stop me?"

"Absolutely. You can get a little feisty when you think you're right."

"Hey! So can you."

"Admit it," he says as she closes the gap between them. "You like it when I take charge of you. I think you need it."

She purses her lips. "You keep thinking that."

"Oh, that beautiful smart mouth of yours. You definitely need it."

He wraps his arm around her waist and pulls her into him. She can feel his bulge.

He's completely turned on by this.

He pushes his hips into hers. "See what you do to me?"

Her eyes dance over his, and suddenly, there's a burning in her stomach.

"I'm pissed you put your jeans back on," he says in a husky voice.

"I'm sorry," she whispers submissively. *It's been a roller coaster of a day. And of all the days for her to show up, it's the first night you and I sleep together? Can't I get a break today?*

He smiles wide. "So, make it right."

She steps back and shimmies her jeans back down her legs. She kicks them off with her foot into the corner of his room.

"Keep going," he urges.

She pushes the flannel off her shoulders, revealing breasts that are supple and full, and the curves of her naked body are flawless. He walks to his nightstand and takes out another condom. He takes her hand and walks her over to his desk. In one swift motion, he picks her up, placing her on top. He spreads her legs as he steps in between them, sliding out of his shorts. He kisses her hard at first, and then releasing her lips, he rips open the wrapper and rolls it over himself with a slight moan as he does.

With no warning, he thrusts himself deep into her. She cries out with pleasure, tipping her head back.

When he rotates his hips, she can feel the fullness within her, and his name escapes her lips. "Oh, Kelly."

"Come for me, please," he begs as he works harder and harder for her.

She digs her fingers into his back and hangs on for dear life as he pushes into her with such incredible passion that she can't think clearly.

Within moments, he pushes so hard that her body seizes, and her legs shake as her whole body climaxes. It is the most incredible feeling but so very scary that Kelly can do this to her.

He does have control over me, she thinks as she collapses into him.

He tips her head up to look at him as he continues to push into her despite her wanting to come down from this high. He kisses her hard and moans into her mouth as he reaches his climax. She can tell by the arch of his back that it's the one he won't soon forget.

He lifts her off the desk and carries her to his bed. She is exhausted, and her whole physique aches from the hard surface of his desk. He cradles her in his arms and kisses her softly on the head.

Her eyes grow heavy.

But he disrupts her drifting off as he asks, "Plain or blueberry?"

She lifts her head to meet his eyes. "What?"

"I want to know what kind of pancakes you want in the morning," he says matter-of-factly.

She yawns. "Blueberry."

"I thought so." He tucks her back into his arms.

She feels so safe in his arms, and although she's too tired to do anything, her mind won't rest as it should. She can't stop thinking about the day she had and the force pulling her toward him and much sooner than she expected it to happen.

But how can I get over my past? She can't imagine that taking place.

As Kelly holds on to her tightly, she listens to his breath as it shallows when he falls into a deep sleep.

I can't let my past ruin my future. And I can't let Kelly's past do that either. Aniston can't get in the way like Poppy did. If I start to see signs of that happening, I have to promise myself that I'll put my needs first, no matter how I feel about Kelly, because I can't go through another heartache so soon. I'll never survive another broken heart.

Thirty

His Girl

Abigail wanders across campus after her final class of the day. After another long week of school and waitressing, she is more than ready for the weekend.

Kelly had to pick up a few extra shifts this week because of staffing issues at the garage, so she hardly saw him. After their whirlwind night together last weekend, she has not stopped thinking about him. He's like a drug—once you get a taste, it's hard to stop wanting more.

"Abigail," she hears someone yell.

She spins around. Casey and Jen are holding hands as they hurry up to her. The sight of them brings a smile to her face.

"Hey!" she says as she leans in to give them each a hug. "So good to see you guys."

"You, too," Jen says.

"Where are you off to?" Casey asks.

"Going to the Union for some coffee. Do you want to join me?"

"We'd love to," they say in unison.

They walk along the brick pathway in front of the Union and enter the glass door.

Once inside the Union, they each grab a coffee and then find a cozy spot near the fireplace.

"It's getting cold out, huh?" Abigail asks as she shakes her coat off her shoulders.

"Don't I know it?" Casey says with a shiver.

"Is soccer almost over?" Abigail asks Jen.

Her face drops. "Yeah, and for the first time in my life, I'm kind of glad the season will be ending soon."

Casey takes Jen's hand in hers and lovingly glances at her girlfriend.

"Oh gosh, so sorry. Because of everything?" Abigail asks, referring to the vandalism debacle on campus last semester.

"Yeah, the house being vandalized really tore our team apart. A few of my teammates blamed others for their lifestyle and decisions, thinking those could have been the reasons we were targeted. We can't seem to get past all the stuff surrounding us, and it's affected our game," Jen says.

"I'm so sorry to hear that. I had no idea," Abigail says.

"Yeah, I hope they get the bastards responsible. Put an end to this once and for all," Jen adds.

A moment of silence passes between them, and then Casey asks, "So, how are you doing?"

Abigail can't help her smile. "I'm doing better. I mean, well. I'm doing really well."

"I can see that," she says as she looks her up and down.

"Thanks. The job is great. This semester is going well. And I'm happy."

Casey playfully punches her on the arm. "Happy?"

Abigail grins ear to ear. "Yeah, I've been hanging out with…"

"Oh, spit it out." Casey laughs. "We already know!"

Abigail rolls her eyes. "Of course you do."

"As you know, I'm gay, but holy shit is Kelly Conrad hot!" Jen boasts.

Casey laughs, too. "Anyone can see that. He must be so good in bed!"

Abigail blushes a deep red. "Stop it!"

"Well?" Casey continues.

Her friends' eager eyes tell her that, one, they desperately want to know, and two, they won't stop until they do. With crimson cheeks, she lowers her eyes and nods her head in acknowledgment.

"I knew it!" Casey cries out, and about five people in the vicinity look at them.

"Shh," Abigail warns.

And then as if by sheer dumb luck, a voice behind them says, "You girls causing a commotion?"

Nathan steps in front of them. Abigail's expression drops to the floor.

"Hey, Nathan," Jen says.

Casey meekly musters, "Hello."

Abigail, feeling as though the happy wind got knocked out of her, doesn't say much but a, "Hey."

His cheeks burn at the unwelcome greetings. "I saw you guys and thought I'd say hello," he says. His shoulders are hunched.

Jen breaks the ice by asking, "You playing this weekend?"

He perks up. "Yeah, finally got cleared to play." He glances at Abigail, trying to gauge if she knew that he was out for two weeks. But he sees no reaction.

"That's great news," Jen says.

He clears his throat and then nervously says, "Hey, Abby, mind if I chat with you for a minute?"

Thinking quickly, she raises her cup of coffee. "I was actually catching up with these guys over coffee. Maybe some other time."

Defeat drowns his face. And before anyone else can speak, he says, "Okay." He spins on his heel and hurries toward the exit.

"Ouch," Casey says.

"Harsh," Jen adds.

"What?" Abigail protests. "I'm supposed to go because he asks?"

"He seemed so desperate," Casey says.

"Well, that's not my fault." Abigail hunches back in the chair.

"No one said it was. Have you talked at all?" Jen asks.

"Not really."

"Considering the circumstances, I'm sure he could use a friend," Casey whispers.

Jen inhales sharply. "Casey, that is not *her* problem," she argues. "And besides, he can't know we all know."

"Well, they're friends, no?" Casey says as she looks at Abigail.

"Friends?" Abigail barks. "Friends? No, we are not friends. Not anymore."

"Wow, I didn't realize," Jen says.

"And you know why?" Abigail says as she puts on her coat and stands. "Because every time I see him or think of him, he breaks my goddamn heart all over again. And I'm sick of it."

"Don't leave," Casey begs. "We're sorry."

"It's not your fault, guys. I'm just not feeling social right now."

"We understand," Jen says sympathetically.

"I love you guys, and I'll see you at the party tonight."

Casey reaches for her hand and softly says, "Love you, too."

Then, as if she were never there at all, Abigail quickly disappears out the back entrance to the Union and walks at a snail's pace back to her house on Charlotte Street.

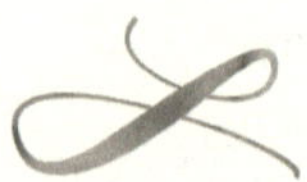

Abigail peruses through her closet after she showered, choosing a long-sleeved black V-neck and a pair of tight jeans with rips in the knees. As she dresses and then applies her makeup, her mind wanders to seeing Nathan in the Union and how she reacted to not only him, but also her friends. It's so unlike her to lash out, but she's simply never going to be okay with seeing him, and that is something she will never get used to until she is no longer at OSU.

How can I ever view him in the same light? Doesn't he get that? He keeps coming up to me like it's no big deal, and that in itself is bugging me, too!

After pulling her hair back in a ponytail and inspecting herself in the mirror, she's satisfied with how she appears on the outside, but on the inside, she knows she's dying a slow death.

Descending the stairs to wait for the girls, she sits on the couch and wonders if this horrible sensation in the pit of her stomach will ever go away.

Once Bree, Melissa, and Laura are ready, they grab their coats and lock the door. The four of them venture over to the party. As soon as they get close, it is when Abigail realizes it's the same house she was at last year, and she starts to put two and two together. Mike was one of Kelly's floor mates from the dorms, and he is also a part of the football team staff.

She really hopes more than anything that this is not another football party.

The girls enter the house, and after grabbing a drink, they head to the basement to find Alex, Casey, and Jen. They quickly spot them near the corner of the room.

"Hey, guys!" Jen yells over the music.

They all say their hellos.

"Is my brother coming?" Alex asks Abigail.

"Thought you might know?" She smiles.

"He said he was."

"Then, I'm sure he will," Abigail replies. *I hope he's coming.*

Abigail can't help but notice how quiet Laura is and, more importantly, how she keeps looking around like she's searching for someone.

Abigail is about to ask her when she departs from the group with Melissa to get everyone another drink.

"You think she's acting strange?" Abigail asks Bree.

Bree, never one to beat around the bush, says, "Yes, like she's on edge or something. She hasn't said anything to you?"

"Not a word. I've been a little preoccupied lately, and I haven't been spending as much time with her. I was hoping she said something to you."

"No, but I'll get it out of her," Bree says confidently.

Alex interrupts their conversation as she says, "There he is."

Abigail turns and sees Kelly walk down the stairs. There's a lump in her throat as she watches his body move fluidly across the room. He's wearing a tight red T-shirt, faded jeans, and a baseball hat on backward. He never wears a hat, but for some reason, the slightest change in his clothing makes him look hotter. Like she ever imagined that was possible. He spots her. She nervously waves and then lowers her eyes to the ground.

"Damn, is he hot," Bree says with a nudge to Abigail's ribs.

She blushes. "Holy cow."

"Yep. He's yours. No doubt. Look at the way he's looking at you," Bree says, elbowing her in the side.

"Stop it," she quips. "You're making it worse."

Bree drapes her arm around her friend and kisses her on the head. "You're so cute." She laughs and then releases her as Kelly nears.

"Ladies. Sis." He kisses Alex on the cheek, making Abigail's heart melt in the process.

"Hey, brother." She smiles.

He moves toward Abigail and leans into her ear. The smell of his cologne is a wonderful addition to her senses.

"You look fucking hot," he says.

Her cheeks flush as she finally looks up to meet his eyes. "Thank you," she stammers.

As he reaches around her waist, he takes a quick moment to tug lightly on her ponytail as he says, "More later."

Laura and Melissa return with their drinks. "Hey, Kelly," they both add.

He smiles. "Hey, ladies. Having fun?"

"So far," Melissa adds.

They stand around for an hour, mostly chatting and drinking. Then, they hear some commotion as a large group of people start to descend into the basement. Abigail starts to recognize the line of massive human beings as they walk down the stairs, one by one. Her worst nightmare is coming true; the football team is here, and so are the cheerleaders.

As Abigail tries to avoid staring, she can't help but notice Laura's eyes light up, and a smile she hasn't seen in quite some time graces her beautiful face. This deeply confuses her. She nudges Bree, and Bree takes notice as well.

Kelly turns toward Abigail. "I didn't know they'd be here."

"Me neither," she says.

"If you want to do something else, we can."

She glances up at him with her wide navy eyes. "I don't feel it's necessary for me to leave, do you?" she says with a bit of an edge.

Shocked, Kelly says, "I was only thinking of you."

She can hear people say Nathan's name as he gets deeper into the crowded basement. Poppy is only a few people behind him, and the sight of her makes Abigail's stomach churn.

It's no longer my concern. They are no longer my business, she tries to remind herself.

Laura keeps looking in their direction, and she waves enthusiastically at Tank. He smiles wide back at her. Then, he notices Abigail and Kelly, and his smile soon fades.

Laura nervously sips her beer and then says, "Going to grab another one." Only this time, she doesn't offer to grab the others a beer like she did the last time.

Abigail's on edge, and she can't seem to shake it. She's at a loss for conversation now.

Kelly takes her hand and pulls on it to get her attention. "Let's go find Mike. I'd like to say hello."

"Okay," she says. She follows Kelly back through the crowd and toward the stairs, grateful to leave her former friends behind.

As they get to the top of the stairs and enter the living room, Kelly soon spots Mike.

"Buddy," he yells to Kelly as they approach. Mike cocks his head to the side as he recognizes Abigail. "Don't I know you?"

"Mike, this is Abigail."

"Abigail Price?"

"Yes, I've met you before. A party here last semester." Her voice shakes, and then feeling Kelly's eyes on her, she adds, "I used to date Nathan Ryan."

He laughs. "Oh shit, right! Duh! For, like, a long time," he adds, not realizing how terribly uncomfortable this is making her.

Kelly drapes his arm around her shoulders and says, "His loss."

"Obviously." Mike smiles at the two of them. "I think I saw them come in. The whole team typically comes."

"We know," Kelly says dryly.

Feeling bad, he adds, "Hey, I've got something special for you two. Come with me."

They follow him to the bar in the front room, and he makes his way behind the wooden gate. He pulls out a bottle of vodka.

"This," he says, "is my special reserve. Only for my friends." He gets three cups and fills them with ice. "Lemon?" he asks as he pours the vodka into each cup.

"Please," Abigail says as Kelly nods his head.

They each fire back the shot.

"Mike. Mike." A guy frantically approaches. "We need more cups in the downstairs bar."

He rolls his eyes at his friend. "Everything is an emergency with you." He laughs as he pours another shot for each of them, taking his time to squeeze in the lemon. He raises his shot to them, and they take theirs. "Enjoy the party. Duty calls." He grabs a sleeve of cups and heads toward the stairs.

"Nice guy," Abigail says as she winces after the shot.

"Take it easy," he says. "We've got all night."

So bossy. She rolls her eyes at him.

"I saw that."

"I know," she says with a sly smile.

Kelly wraps his arm around her waist and pulls her in close. She likes that he's not afraid to show some affection in public and hopes it's for the right reasons.

If Aniston were here, would he do the same? she wonders.

"How was your week?" she asks.

"Busy. Yours?"

"Same. The restaurant was busy."

"I was hoping to see you this week," he says as his green eyes sparkle.

"Me, too."

"But then again, I'll take what I can get." He squeezes her backside, causing her to jump.

"Kelly," she coos.

His smile is wicked. "Yes?"

As he gazes deep in her eyes, a slower song comes through the speakers, and before she can protest, he has her pulled into his arms and is swaying with her to the beat.

She closes her eyes as the feeling of the vodka, mixed with the warm embrace of her tattooed guy, takes over her. For a little over two minutes, she completely forgets about everyone around her and everyone downstairs. More importantly, she has no idea that Nathan came up the stairs, saw them in a loving embrace, and immediately went back downstairs to drown his misery.

"I'm going to go find Bree before she leaves," Abigail says.

"Is she leaving soon?" Kelly asks.

"Yeah, she has other plans tonight."

Kelly takes her hand and guides her toward the basement stairs.

When they push through the crowd is when they see that Laura is over in a corner with all the football players and standing next to Tank. There is something about the closeness that seems out of place to Abigail.

They appear not only close by proximity but also close by the way they're interacting. Something is very different.

Poppy is near Nathan with a group of teammates, and Bree, Melissa, Alex, Casey, and Jen are off to the other side near some athletes clad in Starter jackets and, of course, the cheerleaders, much to Abigail's disappointment.

Poppy didn't win, right? So, what am I so concerned about? Kelly is awesome, and honestly, I wouldn't want to be her at all. Not for one second would I trade places…wait, is that a red Solo cup in her hand? Is she drinking alcohol? What the hell?! She's pregnant! Is she out of her damn mind?

"I need to talk to Bree," Abigail says to Kelly over the loud music.

"Sure thing," he says as he approaches his sister.

"Bree, can I talk to you?"

"Yep."

She shuffles Bree to a more secluded spot, and besides, it would be impossible for anyone to hear them over the music.

"Is she drinking?" she asks.

"Nobody knows what the hell is going on."

"And what's up with Laura?"

Bree's eyebrows rise. "She's been over there since you guys left."

Abigail narrows her eyes. "What the heck is happening?"

"No idea. But something is up. I'm getting strange vibes, too."

"This is unbelievable. I wish they weren't here."

Bree is about to respond when her eyes grow wide.

"What?" There's a tug on her shoulder, and she spins to face behind her.

Nathan is standing before her, swaying. "Will you talk to me now?" he slurs.

One look, and it doesn't take a genius for Abigail to conclude he's had too much to drink.

"What do we have to talk about?" she asks.

"I'll leave you two," Bree says.

"Hey, Bree," Nathan says sadly.

"Hey, Nathan," she says with a nod and then quickly leaves them.

"I wanted to say hello," he says to Abigail.

"Hello."

"I saw you before but wasn't sure I should approach you or not."

She doesn't speak. In fact, her eyes wander behind him, and she can see Kelly observing them. She also notices Tank and Laura head upstairs, just the two of them.

She desperately wants to ask him what is up with Laura and Tank but doesn't. "You're here with your friends, and I'm here with mine."

"They were my friends, too," he quips. "And *my* friends are still your friends."

Her eyebrows rise. "It doesn't feel that way anymore. Not for me."

"Why won't you talk to me anymore?" He tries to steady himself on the wall.

Jesus, how much has he had to drink?

Too afraid to say out loud that she knows about Poppy, she instead says, "Nathan, I need a break from this. Can't you see that?"

His eyes soften. "Boy, how did I fuck up so badly that you won't even be my friend? I lov—"

"I think you have an idea."

There's a loud crash heard over the music. Abigail's eyes grow wide, and Nathan spins to get a better look. Poppy is pinned in the corner by a very large, intimidating guy. He's flailing his arms at her. She looks frightened as he grabs her cup of beer and smashes it to the floor. The partygoers near them start to back up. Nathan rushes over, stumbling his way toward them. Abigail watches in horror as he pulls him back by his shoulder. An argument ensues.

Look at him, rushing to defend her. He was just over here, trying to get me to talk to him, and then he goes running back to her!

But soon, Abigail's attitude changes to concern when the guy grabs Poppy by the wrist and yells in her face. Nathan, on unsteady feet, shoves the guy, trying to break his grip on Poppy. And he does break free—free enough to swing and land his fist across Nathan's jaw. Nathan stumbles back and quickly falls to the ground. Blood dripping from his lower lip, he tries to scramble back up to his feet.

With Tank nowhere near them, the next person to jump into action is...Kelly?

Kelly?

Kelly lunges at the guy, knocking him back on his feet. He lands on the ground as Kelly leans over him and knocks him square in the chin—not once, but twice. Abigail can hear him yell something about not touching a woman like that. Only then do a few of the other players nearby come rushing in. One helps Nathan to his feet while the other two grabs the guy on the floor and holds him down.

Mike comes rushing down the stairs with a few other housemates. Tank and Laura are close behind.

"What the hell?!" Mike yells as he takes in the scene.

"No fighting in my house," the other guy yells.

Kelly says something to Mike as the players continue to hold the guy down.

The players lift the guy on the ground, his face gushing blood.

"Get him out!" Mike yells.

They escort him up the back stairs and toss him in the backyard. They follow him out, and one can only assume that what happens to him out there is his own fault.

Poppy is trembling as her friends try and console her.

Tank rushes over to Nathan as he wipes the blood from his mouth on the back of his hand. "What the hell happened?" Tank asks.

Nathan pushes past him as he makes his way to Poppy. Everyone around them watches as they both embrace, Poppy falling to pieces as he holds her tight. Tank turns and notices Kelly shaking the pain from his hand as Mike pats him on the shoulder.

Abigail is frozen as the scene unfolds in front of her.

Look at them holding one another. Nathan used to be my knight in shining armor. Now, clearly, he is hers. But tonight, he's too drunk to protect her, so my Kelly had to. He's no knight anymore.

So much has happened in the last few minutes that she almost can't comprehend it, nor does she have a clue what to do next. Then, as if he's reading her mind, Kelly turns to look at her.

Snapping back to it, Abigail rushes over to the bar. "Give me a bag of ice, now!" she yells over the music.

Sensing her urgency, the guy grabs a plastic bag and fills it with ice, handing it to her. She rushes to Kelly.

With tears in her eyes over the entire scene, she says, "Kelly, are you okay?"

"I'm fine."

She notes the sadness in his voice.

"He's one of the good ones," Mike says. "Now, let me get this party back on track," he says as he excuses himself.

She notices Mike approach Nathan and Poppy. Within minutes, Nathan has his arm around her shoulders and is being led by Mike up the stairs and away from all the prying eyes.

Alex runs over to Kelly, throwing her arms around him. "Kelly, are you crazy?" she says.

He puts his good arm around her, hugging her back. "It's fine, sis. I'm okay."

Abigail feels stupid, standing there, holding the ice. Once they let go, Abigail says, "I got you ice."

He takes the bag and puts it on his hand. And as soon as he does, the tears start to streak down her cheeks. Casey sees this and rushes to her side. She grabs her by the arms and escorts her to the bathroom. Once inside, Abigail bursts into tears.

"What the hell, Casey?" She shakes her head.

"Here." Casey reaches for the tissues. "That was so messed up!"

"I can't believe what Kelly did. And for Nathan and Poppy, no less."

Casey gives her an understanding glance as she helps wipe the wet from her cheek. "He's unbelievable."

"He could have gotten hurt. Did you see that guy?"

"What an asshole."

"Yeah, he was huge, but I didn't recognize him."

"Are you okay?" she asks.

"Casey, I can't believe he'd step in like that."

"Oh, Abigail, of course you can." She places her hand on Abigail's cheek. "Because he's a good guy—that's why."

"You're absolutely right. Kelly keeps putting up with this Nathan saga, and now, he got into a fight because of it, but that didn't stop him from defending Poppy..."

"And it's clear Nathan has his own shit to deal with, so just focus on Kelly right now."

There's a loud knock on the door, bringing them back to reality. Abigail tucks the tissue in her pocket as Casey leans in for the doorknob. As she pulls it open, she finds Kelly standing there, a bag of ice draped over his hand.

For once, Abigail doesn't think. She throws her arms around his neck and squeezes him as tight as she possibly can.

"Can we leave, please?" she begs in his ear.

He squeezes her back with one hand, and that is all she needs to comprehend that he's ready to leave as well.

Before she can speak, Casey says, "I'll tell them you left." She hugs her friend. "Take care of each other," she whispers in her ear.

Abigail and Kelly walk up the basement stairs and out into the cool night air.

"Kelly, should you go to the hospital?"

He chuckles. "No, Abigail. I'm fine."

"Well, how should I know?" she says defensively.

She feels so stupid for what happened at the party. Seeing Nathan try and defend his girlfriend. Getting punched because he was too drunk to come to her rescue, only to have Kelly jump in and save the day. She never in her wildest dreams saw this scenario unfolding.

A burst of cool air whips across her face. She hugs her body as they walk farther away from the party. She glances over at him. His face is twisted in anguish, and a contemplative expression grants his handsome face.

"I don't know what to say," she admits.

Ignoring her remark, he says, "Your place is closer."

They walk down Winter Street and onto Charlotte Street.

A heaviness rests in her chest, and she's on the verge of tears again.

Why is this so damn hard?

The house is dark as they approach the porch. She keys into the front door. "Will you come in?" she asks with trepidation.

He pushes open the unlocked door and goes straight to the kitchen. He tosses the melted bag of ice into the sink. His hand appears swollen. She grabs a bowl from the cabinet, opens the freezer, and fills it with ice and some water like Nathan taught her. Kelly sits at the kitchen table, leaning his head in his healthy hand.

She places the bowl on the table. "Soak your hand in the ice bath," she says.

He doesn't look up, only places his hand in the freezing water. She then goes to the cabinet where Bree keeps all the good liquor that she took with her father's permission. She grabs a bottle of scotch, pours two fingers, and sits at the table with him.

"Here," she says as she slides a glass in front of him.

He takes it, and without a thought, he tosses it back, wincing as he swallows. Her eyes grow wide. She stands and grabs the bottle of scotch from the counter. She fills his glass again. He picks it up and rolls the cool glass over his forehead. Abigail retrieves a glass, fills hers, and sips on it.

"Since when did you start drinking scotch?" he mumbles.

"Five minutes ago."

His green eyes gaze at her, obviously searching her face.

She swallows hard. "I'm sorry, Kelly."

"Sorry for what?"

"That you got involved tonight. I feel terrible. Just terrible."

"Not how I saw my night going."

"Me neither," she whispers.

"What were you guys talking about?" he asks.

"Me?"

"And Nathan."

"Nothing really. He was asking why I don't talk to him anymore."

"Did you tell him you know?"

"I didn't get the chance. It's a little awkward to talk about, Kelly."

"Fine," he says, narrowing his eyes at her.

She gulps, and her face flushes. "Fine?"

"I don't know what else to say."

Ouch.

"He was inebriated, and it wasn't right to speak of with others around who could hear."

"Of course."

"That's not fair. This isn't a typical scenario for me." Her voice rises an octave, visibly grabbing his attention.

"And you think it is for me?"

"Then, what made you do that? Get involved?" she asks.

"I saw someone being aggressive toward a woman, and I had to do something. Nathan wasn't going to get the job done."

Ouch again. But he's right.

"Like I said, he was intoxicated."

"Don't defend him."

"Defend him? I'm making a statement." He laughs, throwing back his second scotch.

"I'll never win with you, will I?" she asks.

"That's a question I'd like to ask you," he says with resentment as he gets up and tosses the bowl of ice water into the sink. "Maybe I should leave."

She sharply inhales. "Imagine if I said that to you."

He spins to face her. "Give me a reason to stay."

Her skin pinks with embarrassment and anger. She tries to think quickly, but her mind is blank. He pushes off the counter, and finally, she must react. She jumps up from her seat and blocks his way.

He doesn't speak.

"I don't want you to leave," she admits.

He backs up.

"It kills me that we're dealing with this. I never imagined that I would be. And tonight, I felt so many mixed emotions," she says with mist in her eyes. "I hated that they were there but not for the reason you think. I only wanted to spend time with you *and* my friends. That's it," she says as a tear drops on her cheek. Uncomfortably, she wipes it away. "But then you jumped in and helped them. And I was so appreciative that you did. That guy, whomever he was..."

"Clay."

"You know him?"

"Yeah, used to live on my floor in the dorm," he says.

She shakes her head. "I had no idea."

"He's always been a dick."

"Oh," she says. "Well, you helped someone who needed it, and I was so proud of you," she confesses.

His eyes grow wide.

"You're the type of person I am grateful to be friends with. You. Not someone too drunk to help a girl in need and *not* some asshole like Clay. But I froze, Kelly," she says as she decreases the distance between them. "I was scared for you. And everyone in the room. We're all lucky it only went so far."

"I wouldn't have let it get out of hand," he says.

She tips her head. "You think you have that kind of control?"

With a devilish grin, he says, "I do."

She rolls her eyes.

"Be careful," he warns.

"Kelly Conrad, stop intimidating me!" she barks.

He steps closer to her then runs the tips of his fingers down her cheek. "You ever think that maybe you intimidate me?"

She lowers her eyes "No, of course not."

"Well, you do. But in a good way. It keeps me on my toes. I wish I weren't so worried about losing you in all this confusion."

She nearly chokes. "Lose me? We've only just started, no?"

He smiles, dropping his hand to her waist. He pulls her into him, and she drapes one arm around his hip. She braces her other hand on his pecs.

"You said before that it's typical of me to not speak my mind. And I understand this about myself. It is one of my many flaws."

"Many?" he asks.

"Kelly," she continues, "I want to be with *you.* Only you. Not some ex-boyfriend who got the one girl I can't stand pregnant. And, yes, he asked me why we don't talk, and the reason was because I had seen him in the Union when I was having coffee with Casey and Jen. He asked to speak with me, and I said no. I just don't want to be a part of that drama."

Kelly smiles.

"What?"

"I'm sorry, Abigail. For being a jealous jerk. It's not cool of me, and I just want you to know that."

She smiles, too. "Wow. Kelly Conrad, did you just admit you get jealous and that you're a jerk?"

He laughs. "Sometimes."

His muscles contract as she wraps her arms tighter around his waist. "I've been waiting all week to see you," she says, tipping her face up toward his.

He licks his lips, the wet causing them to shimmer under the kitchen light above their heads. "And I've been waiting all week to get my hands on you."

Oh, that tightness in the pit of my stomach. How I've missed it this week, too.

"What are you waiting for?" she coos.

He owns her mouth, quickly and forcefully. A whimper catches in the back of her throat as his tongue swirls around hers. Wrapping his arms around her waist, he pulls her into him.

"I'm going to have my way with you—right here," he says as the adrenaline from the evening kicks in.

Her eyes flash open, stunned. He grabs a hold of her waist and unbuttons the top of her jeans and then pulls on the zipper.

He spins her toward the table, pressing her belly on the edge. He takes her hands and places them on the wood. "Hold on," he whispers in her ear, sending a shiver down her spine.

Placing his hand on her waist, he slides her jeans down her legs, only taking one leg out. He steps in between her feet, pulls a condom out of his pocket, and readies himself. "Hang on."

She glances over her shoulder at him, completely turned on from the events of the entire evening. Her knight in shining armor is now done with all his duties and finally has time for his lady in waiting.

He thrusts into her. She reacts by tipping her head back. One of her hands moves.

"I said to hang on," he instructs.

He places his good hand on her shoulder, the other gripped tight around her waist despite the pain radiating up his arm. He pushes in and out of her, harder and harder. Watching the table move with them, banging against the wall, knocking over some decorative thing that looks way too expensive to be in a college house anyway.

"Oh God, you feel good," he moans.

She leans her head forward, arching her back into him.

"Keep doing that," he says as he tangles his fingers in her tresses and pulls her ponytail. That beautiful mane of hair that she knows he loves yanking every time he sees her, especially when she wears that adolescent ponytail, like tonight.

She purrs, "Oh, Kelly," as her head pulls back toward him.

An incredible sensation ripples through her as he moves in and out. She tries to keep herself braced on the table until she finally collapses on top. He digs both hands into her hips, holding her right where he needs her in order to give her everything he has. As she cries out in complete and utter joy, he falls onto her back in a state of utter euphoria. Finally able to catch his breath, he traces his fingers around her waist, squeezing her tightly before standing back up. He steps back from her.

"Damn," he whispers.

"What?" She spins to look at him. She shimmies into her jeans and zips them up.

"That was amazing and something I desperately needed."

Shaking her finger at him, she says with a laugh, "Now, if you had left…"

"I know, smarty-pants."

Glancing up at the clock on the wall, she notices it is well after midnight. "We should go upstairs. My roommates and God only know who else will be home soon."

"Oh." He laughs, dressing quickly. "Are you asking me to stay?"

"Kelly…"

"What?"

"Yes, I am. Is that okay? Or is it breaking some new rule you've created?"

"There are no rules about that."

"Then, come on," she says.

They head up the stairs and to her bedroom. She switches on the small lamp near her desk.

"Mind if I change?" she asks.

"Please do," he says with a grin.

She takes out a T-shirt nightgown from her dresser, and after undressing, she slips it on. The sheen from the fabric shows the perfect outline of her figure underneath.

He approaches her. "Wow." He smiles.

"What?" She swallows, as his stare is intense.

"Look at you," he says. "You can make a T-shirt look sexy." He slips off his jeans and T-shirt and baseball hat, tossing them on her couch. "Man, you make this hard for me, you know that?" he says, backing her up to her bed and gently guiding her onto the mattress. She's about to speak when he places his finger on her lips. "Shh, don't say a word."

For a moment, he locks his piercing green eyes with hers. Something she can't quite put her finger on happens between them. Like a unique moment or change in the air. He wraps one arm around her back and cradles her into him. With lips parted, he leans in, his eyes still on hers, and kisses her. It's different, like he is savoring her, hoping it will last.

He releases his lips, and as he holds her in his arms, she sighs deeply, and her muscles relax.

With little warning, he hums in her ear, "That's my girl."

That's my girl? After the night I just had. The scene that unfolded. And he says three simple words to get me thinking in a completely different way. Never in my wildest dreams did I expect that Kelly Conrad would call me his girl.

Thirty-One

What Have You Done to Me?

Kelly strokes her hair as her head rests on his chest. The rise and fall of his body as she clings to him makes her smile. Morning has long come, but neither wants to admit it nor move from the warm bed.

"Do you have to work today?" she mumbles.

"No, thank God."

His answer prompts her to move and glance up at him. "Why do you say it like that?"

"Because I'm hoping to spend the day with you."

"How do you know that I don't have to work?"

"I asked Chloe." He smiles.

She can't help but return a smile. "I see."

"So, got any other plans?"

"No, I don't."

Typically, she would have made plans to attend the football game this weekend. The Hawks are in the semifinals, and it's looking pretty good for the team this year. But after last night—heck, the past three months—she's in no mood to watch football.

"It's going to be a beautiful December day. Let's get out of here and spend it somewhere else."

"I'd really like that."

He stretches his arms over his head. "Come on then. Let's get dressed."

She rolls off him, pulling the sheets to her chest as he slides out from under them.

He slips on his jeans. "I'll go get us some coffee," he says as he approaches her door.

"Like that?" she says.

"Like what?"

"No shirt?"

He laughs as he walks out.

Abigail shrugs her shoulders. *I suppose if I looked like that, I wouldn't wear a shirt either.*

She showers again, applies minimal makeup, and then blow-dries her hair. As she comes back into her room, Kelly is sitting on the couch, sipping his coffee. He gets up and hands a mug to her.

"Thank you."

"Welcome."

"Was anyone down there?"

"Just Laura," he says, and the thought makes Abigail uneasy.

"Alone?"

He cocks his head. "Yeah, alone. Why?"

"Just asking." She turns to face her closet. As she mindlessly rummages through her wardrobe, her thoughts drift toward Laura and the funny feeling she got last night.

I don't know what's going on with her these days, unfortunately. She seems preoccupied. And my time is definitely consumed by new things, like my job, a full class load, and...of course, Kelly.

"What should I wear?"

"I'd dress warm."

She takes out her favorite jeans, a long-sleeved shirt, and a green wool sweater. She lays them on her bed and takes a bra and panties out of her dresser drawer. Embarrassed, as she senses he's looking at her, she dresses quickly. He whistles, only egging on her uneasiness.

"You going to change?" she asks as she smooths down her hair.

"Thought you could drive me over. I'll change, and then we can take my car?"

"Sounds good."

"Bring an extra change of clothes," he says. "Just in case." He puts his T-shirt on.

"Just in case of what?"

He smiles and then nods toward the door. "Come on. Let's go."

He heads down the stairs. She grabs a bag and shoves some extra clothes inside along with some toiletries for good measure.

As she nears the bottom of the stairs, she notices Laura standing by the door.

"Hey, where are you off to today?" Abigail asks.

The expression on her face can only be described as a kid caught with her hand in the cookie jar, which seems peculiar.

"Hey. Oh, I'm going to the game," she blurts out.

"Ah. Well, have fun."

"You're not going?" she asks. "They're in the playoffs."

"I'm going out for the day with Kelly."

"All right. Well, see you later."

Abigail heads for the door as Laura pulls it open. They exit onto the porch.

"What happened last night?" Laura asks.

"Thought you might have more information than me." Abigail steps down a stair.

Laura's cheeks turn crimson. "Why would I know?"

"Well, you stayed after I left, so I thought you might have gotten the scoop." Abigail tips her head.

Laura looks almost relieved as she exhales. "Oh, right. Of course. No, I tried to stay out of it."

"Me, too."

Then, Laura whispers, "Kelly sure jumped into action."

"Yep," Abigail says as she lays her eyes on him as he leans against her car. "He's good like that."

"Well, have fun," Laura says as she climbs into her car.

"See you later." Abigail climbs in her car and starts it.

As she pulls out of her driveway, Kelly asks, "Everything okay?"

"It's fine." *I guess. But she sure acts like she's not telling me something. But what could it be?*

"Your body language—dare I say, both of yours—says differently."

"Can't put my finger on it. But something is off. I think she is hiding something."

His face twists. "Really? That's a pretty big accusation."

"I understand that," is all she says as she spins the steering wheel.

If she's still acting differently when I get back, I'll bring it up to her and see what she has to say then.

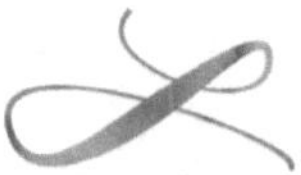

Back at Kelly's house, he showers quickly while Abigail talks to Tom in the living room. Within moments, he's coming down the stairs, and her breath catches as he comes into view. He's dressed in jeans and a tight, long-sleeved blue thermal shirt, and his eyes sparkle with mischief.

He grabs his ski coat and hat, completely unaware of how gorgeous he is. "Ready?" he asks.

She doesn't answer, so Tom taps her on the arm. "I think he's talking to you."

Brought back to reality, she says, "Yes, of course." Her fire for him ignites as the scent of his newly washed skin hits her nose. She grabs her bag and coat and follows him to the garage.

"See you later, Tom," he yells.

"Bye, Tom," she says as she starts to close the door behind her.

"Later, lovebirds," he yells.

Abigail shuts the door, face pink with embarrassment.

Kelly notices and mumbles something under his breath about Tom being a dick.

They climb in the car, and she asks, "You have a plan, or are we winging it?"

He winks as he starts the car. "I've got a plan."

Kelly drives west of campus for a little over an hour. Abigail observes the trees pass by as the soft hum of the music wafts out of his speakers. She gets a little kick out of his singing as he stumbles over the words.

He pulls into a convenience store. "Come on. We'll grab some lunch to take with us."

"With us where?"

"You'll see."

Once inside, they approach the counter near the deli and order two sandwiches, some water, and a bag of chips. Kelly insists on paying, so she lets him. Soon, they are back on the road, but not long after, Kelly pulls into a gravel lot on the edge of the road and parks the car.

"Let's go," he says with a smile.

She climbs out and puts on her jacket and hat. The air is cool, but the sun makes it seem warmer. He takes a backpack out of his trunk and puts their lunch inside.

Once his jacket and hat are on, he takes her hand. "You're going to love this."

Up ahead, there is a path, and they climb through some rocks. It's then she notices an iron fence near the ledge. As they get closer, she realizes how far up they are. The valley below is at least one mile, if not two, deep with a thick fog covering the gorge.

"Wow, this is beautiful. What is this place?"

"Huckleberry Point. Pretty amazing, huh?"

"Yeah. Do you come here a lot?" she asks as she leans over the fence to get a closer look.

"Careful. That fence is probably pretty old."

She steps back.

"This way." He leads her around the fence to an open clearing.

They step out onto a massive flat rock ledge. He drops his backpack on the rock and stretches his arms out and over his head. Something about his serene attitude grabs her attention. This is different from the mechanic-working, dominating, and mostly brutish Kelly she has come to know. She stands next to him, and as he lowers his arms, he wraps one around her and pulls her in for a peck on the lips.

"Hungry?" he asks.

"Actually, I am."

He leans down and pulls out a large blanket from his backpack along with the bag from the deli. He spreads out everything they need on the blanket and takes a seat. He pats the space next to him. She obliges, and he hands her a sandwich.

"Should I have gotten a veggie sandwich, too?"

He cocks his head. "Why?"

"Does it bother you when others eat meat?" she asks.

His eyes flicker, and he answers her with a warm smile. "Try it?" he says, leaning in toward her.

She takes a bite of his sandwich and covers her mouth with her hands. "It's delicious," she says.

"My turn," he jokes, taking a big mouthful of his sandwich.

They sit in silence, eating and watching nature play out in front of them. Birds flying overhead, trees swaying in the breeze, leaves falling at their feet. For once, there is no drama, no fights, no football to get in the way of her happiness.

After they clean up lunch and roll back up the blanket, he says, "There's a trail over here that takes us to a river. Want to see it?"

"Definitely."

"This way."

She follows him along the path. "How did you find this place?"

"My freshman year, I took an outdoor adventure class, and the professor took us here. Taught us some survival tips, how to navigate in the woods, that sort of stuff. When I get a chance, I come back here and spend the day."

"Wish I knew about that class when I was a freshman." She laughs. "I was taking Advanced Bio."

He turns and chuckles. "I wasn't slacking off. It was a tough class and very handy in real life, I might add," he says as she stumbles over a rock.

She laughs along with him.

She can hear the water running before she sees the river. But as they near an opening to the west, the most spectacular rushing body of water comes into view. "Oh, wow, this is beautiful."

"In the spring, we can come and rent some canoes."

In the spring? Already making plans for the future? How unlike him.

"That is, if you want to." He picks up a rock and tosses it in the river.

She smiles. "Can we get closer?"

He brightens up. "Yeah, we can. This way."

She follows him down a path. The decibel of the flowing water increases as they get closer to the edge. The cool air brushes across her face. She can see some ice forming on the rocks as the current of the river gets closer to them.

"Be careful," he warns as he turns to her.

She rolls her eyes. "I am."

"I saw that."

"I'm sure you did." She snickers.

The rocky path ahead has been carved by nature into a V-shape, narrowing as it nears the embankment.

"This is magnificent," she remarks.

The rushing water over the rocks is breathtaking as the fading wintertime sun touches the surface. She walks toward the bank, noticing a path of large rocks toward the rapids. A beautiful birch tree sprouts from the middle of a grouping of rocks.

"What is that underneath the tree?" she asks, straining to see better.

"Where?"

She ventures toward the first large rock, pushing off with her left foot and stepping gingerly on the top of it.

"Be careful," he says sternly. "What are you doing?"

"Is that a cardinal?" She hops onto another rock.

"Abigail, the rocks are slippery, please," he begs.

"It looks wounded," she says, ignoring his warnings. She remembers the cardinal whispering through the silence of that cold winter day when she and Will stood before Jonathan's gravestone. Since then, she has always believed that the sight of any cardinal was Jonathan's way of telling her he was looking out for her.

She hops to another large boulder, the river below lapping harshly against the stone.

"Do you hear me?" he howls.

She gambols to another rock. Almost immediately, she loses her back footing. Suddenly, she slips forward, scraping her hands down the rock, unable to catch herself. She crashes in between two large rocks, her body partially wedged in as the other part becomes emerged in the icy water.

"Kelly!" Her voice strains as the frigid water washes over her skin.

I can't breathe. I can't breathe. The pain! Is that my leg? Or the cold?

"Kelly!"

I can't move. I'm stuck. Oh shit, I'm scared. What if Kelly doesn't get to me?

"Jesus!" he yells, dropping the backpack and rushing from the shore's edge, jumping onto the first rock, nearly slipping in the process. "Abigail!" he yells, unable to see her behind the rock. He jumps to the next rock, crouching down, attempting to get a better view. He still can't see her. Fearing the worst, he jumps into the water, the freezing temperature nearly knocking the wind out of him. He swims around the rock. "Abigail!"

"Kelly, I'm stuck," she yells.

He finally catches sight of her. Her ankle is wedged in between the rock, forcing her upper body backward, and she is partially submerged in the water.

He swims around to the other side. "Does your foot hurt?"

"I…I don't know. I just can't reach it," she says as her teeth chatter.

He strains to reach her foot. "Hang on." In waist-deep water and against the current, he pushes his body toward the shore, in search of something to wedge under her foot to lift it. He grabs a large branch and carries it above his head back over to her.

She locks eyes with him as he approaches her, a stern expression on his face. He grabs her, holding her under the arm, relieving part of her body from the frigid water.

"I'm going to get this under your leg. Try and lift your foot," he says.

"Okay," she says, her body shivering uncontrollably.

"Ready?" he asks as he slides the branch under her leg. "I'm going to have to let you go," he says.

He releases her, and her body goes back into the water.

With tremendous force, he pushes on the branch. They can hear the crack and snap of the lumber as the force against the weight of her leg meets the wood. She tries with all her strength to pull her leg up.

"Come on," he snarls.

She notices how red his face is as his muscles bulge through his wet clothes.

With adrenaline coursing through her, she gives one last force with her leg, and between the two of them, her leg flies upward, becoming dislodged. A part of the branch goes airborne, landing on the rock she attempted to land on. As it crashes down, the cardinal scatters, soaring with ease into the sky. She takes in all of this in disbelief as she falls back into the water.

She wants to gasp for air as the alarmingly cold water washes over her, but she can't. *I can't catch my breath.* Thankfully, Kelly's hand reaches under the water. Yanking on her arm, he pulls her above water. She wheezes, desperate for air.

"Jesus!" he yells. "Are you okay?" His tone is scolding, and so is the look on his face.

She is almost too startled to speak. Her lips tremble as she tries to mumble, "Yes."

"Let's get out of the water," he says, placing his arm around her waist, guiding her to the edge of the river.

"Kelly, I'm so, so sorry," she stutters.

He doesn't speak, which is worse than scolding her. He takes the blanket out of the backpack and wraps it tightly around her. He guides her up the path and straight back to his car, never speaking to her the entire time.

He unlocks her side first. She shivers as she slides into the cold seat. He gets in, starting the car. His vintage car takes its time to heat up. He puts the car in drive and exits out of the lot.

She quivers, trying desperately to warm up. He turns down the street, heading in the opposite direction they came from earlier in the day.

"Where are we going?" she stammers.

"Someplace to get you warm," he says.

She notices the goosebumps on his skin.

"O-okay," she says, trying not to let her teeth rattle.

He heads down a long, winding driveway, a beautiful stone wall on the right side. A large colonial house comes into view, and it's gorgeous. Pristinely decorated, jaw-dropping landscaping, and a view of the mountains. He parks the car in a spot near the front.

"Come," he says, grabbing their bags.

Her hand shakes when she reaches for the door handle, and her jeans are practically frozen to her legs when she steps out to follow him up the walkway, passing a sign that says, *Mountain View Bed-and-Breakfast.*

Kelly holds open the door and allows her to go in first. The lobby of the B and B is spectacular, but Abigail is too cold to enjoy its beauty.

Kelly approaches the desk.

An older woman greets them, "Good evening—oh my!" She gets a good look at the two very wet patrons standing in front of her. "Are you okay?"

"Yes, we are. Fell in the river."

"My, it's freezing out."

"I'm well aware," he says. "I'd like to check-in, please. Conrad."

"Ah, yes, of course, Mr. Conrad. Your room is ready for you."

His room is ready for him? Was this his plan all along?

As quick as she can, the woman settles with Kelly and hands him the key. "Top floor, to the left. There's a fireplace. Please feel free to use it."

"Darling," she says to Abigail, "you must get out of those clothes immediately, or you'll get sick."

"I will," she chatters.

Abigail follows Kelly up the two flights of stairs to the top floor. He keys into the door. The room is just as wonderful as the rest of the place. This must be the suite because it is enormous. Kelly drops their bags near the door and closes it as Abigail hurries toward the fireplace.

"I'll do that," he says. "You get undressed."

He is obviously in a bad mood, so not wanting to upset him further, she peels off her clothes. She grabs the blanket off the back of the couch near the fireplace and wraps it around her.

I'm freezing, and he's mad at me. I'm pretty sure this is not how he saw this day going. But all I can think about right now is that my skin's like ice. Maybe if I rub it against the blanket, the friction will hurry the warmth process up because I can't remember the last time I was this chilled to the bone.

He moves quickly, building the fire. The flames produce heat. She stands close to it, shivering as both the warmth of the blanket and the fire battle with her frozen skin.

Come on, heat. Warm me up!

Out of the corner of her eye, she notices he starts removing his clothes. One layer at a time until he is only clad in his boxer briefs.

The silence is killing me. Or should I say, his silent treatment.

"You're mad at me," she whispers.

He turns to face her. His body looks amazing against the glow of the embers. She swallows hard.

"Do you know why?"

Think. Again, she swallows hard. "I-I'm not sure."

"Didn't think so," he quips.

He crouches down with the poker, moving around the logs. She just stands there, nervous and without an intelligent word on her lips. He straightens and puts the poker back. He leaves her side and wanders to the other side of the room.

"Are you going to talk to me?" she asks.

He turns, leaning on the desk. His eyes narrow. "I told you, I'm not like him, didn't I?"

Her mouth gapes open. "Yes."

"Well, I'm not going to coddle you. I told you not to go on the rocks, and look what happened!" he barks as he points at her.

"You're mad I fell?" she whispers. *I didn't do it on purpose.*

"Damn right I am. It's freezing temperatures, and you were stuck in the water. Do you not see the gravity of the situation?"

It never occurred to her that the situation could become dangerous. But why? She was jetting out across a rough river to see if a bird needed her help. She just went into action and didn't stop to heed his warnings.

"I'm sorry you had to help me," she blurts out. *I know I'm being defensive, but I feel really stupid right now.*

"Oh no, you don't. You're not going to turn this around on me."

Him reprimanding her like this brings tears to her eyes, but she fights them back. He's seen her cry far too many times. So, she tries with all her might to remain steady. But her mind is blank.

"Say something, Abigail."

He pushes off the desk and takes a step closer. Instinctively, she steps back.

"What? Are you afraid of an argument?" he scoffs.

"Your mood frightens me, so yes, I am."

"Let me guess. You want to leave, have me take you home?"

"What?"

"You thought about it, didn't you?"

Yes, I did.

"I know when I'm not wanted," she admits.

"Wanting you or not wanting you has nothing to do with what you did today."

"I see. So, which one is it?" she asks, crossing her arms over her chest.

He runs his hands over his face, clearly exasperated by her remark. When his eyes land on her is when she notices something change. She has never seen him look this way before.

"The only way I think you'll learn is if I teach you a lesson," he says. He strides closer to her.

She starts to laugh, but he is not. "Teach me a lesson? How to jump on rocks?" She snickers.

He comes close enough to her to where he is now peering down at her. With just her eyes, she nervously glances up at him.

"No. You put us both at risk, and you need to know that is not okay."

She gulps. He places one hand on her shoulder. Then, with no warning, he spins her toward the fireplace, and she braces herself with her hand on the mantel. He yanks off the blanket, tossing it on the floor. He pulls her body close to his, and his chiseled torso presses firmly against her back. His girth pushing into her backside.

He's turned on by this? What is happening right now?

"Kelly, what are you doing?"

He presses his face into the side of her. His breath ragged in her ear. "When I tell you not to do something," he starts, and she notices as he speaks, his hand is running down her belly and toward her waist, "you will listen to me."

He places the tips of his fingers into her panties. A gasp escapes her lips. He moves his fingers further down, and she's paralyzed to stop him.

I can't find my voice. I want to speak, but nothing is coming out. How is this happening to me?

He finds the right spot and eases his fingers up and down. She tips her head back toward his shoulder, her eyes closing in the process. Quiet moans escape her lips, and with each one, he presses his hips into her backside.

I've always been in control of what I want, when I want, but with him, it's completely different. He does something to me where my mind goes blank. And I don't want to say no. I don't.

"Kelly, what—"

The heat from the fire, along with the sensation creeping into her body, is more than she can handle.

He leans into her ear again and says, "You'll listen next time, right?"

She's closer to the edge.

"Right?" he whispers.

She moans, "Yes."

"Good." And just as the word releases from his lips, he pulls his hand away and steps back from her, literally leaving her on the brink.

Her brain snaps back into the present, and she spins to face him. *What?! That did not just happen!* She can't believe what he just did. But she has no words to confront him. Her jaw gapes a little, but not a single word is uttered.

He stands before her, arms folded over his chest, undoubtedly pleased with his ability to be in control. She grabs the blanket and hastily wraps it around her. She starts to walk past him toward the bathroom when he grabs her wrist and pulls her into him. Her face is crimson with embarrassment.

"You'll get used to it," he says kindly, as though any of this behavior is normal.

"The hell I will," she snaps, to which his eyes grow wide. "I'll let you know when I'm ready for dinner." She grabs her bag, walks into the bathroom, and locks the door behind her.

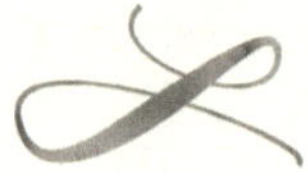

She can tell by just the way he's leaning up against the desk that he's waited long enough for her to come out of the bathroom. But Abigail needed to compose herself and take a long, hot shower, both of which she had to do alone.

"Ready?" she says sweetly.

Kelly nods his head and opens the door for her. They enter the large dining area. There are only two other tables occupied. It's beautifully decorated with seasonal colors, and the roaring fireplace on the back wall is encased by a gorgeous mantel.

"Hello," the woman says.

"May we sit by the fire?" Kelly asks.

She smiles. "Of course. This way."

They follow her to the back and sit at the table she placed their menus on. They look over them as she fills their glasses with water.

"Would you care for something to drink?"

"I'll have a vodka tonic," Kelly says.

"For you?"

"I'll have a red wine, please."

She stares a bit longer at Abigail. "You're twenty-one, right?"

"Yes." She smiles.

"Thought so," she says with a smile as she spins toward the direction of the kitchen.

Abigail crosses her arms low across her waist and glances at Kelly. "When did you make this reservation—or should I say, plan?"

"You caught that?" he says.

She narrows her eyes, and mockingly, she says, "Yes, I caught that."

"Last week."

"Oh, well, this is really nice. So, thank you. I'm having the best time," she says, practicing her sarcastic tone.

Narrowing his eyes, he responds with an equally cynical response, "You're welcome."

The woman places their drinks down on the table, and they order their food.

As the heat of the fire starts to relax Abigail, she sips her wine. Then, she says with a smirk, "Feels like a date though."

He nearly spits out his drink. "Wedging a stick under a girl's leg to try and get her out of freezing cold water is not my idea of a date," he snaps back.

"I said I was sorry."

"Not exactly."

"What?"

"I didn't hear you say to me that you were *actually* sorry."

He is unbelievable. He's lucky he is so damn gorgeous because he makes it hard to walk away.

"I'm sorry, Kelly," she says.

"There. Was that so hard?" He smiles.

She shakes her head, and thankfully, she sees the woman approach with their dinner. She is absolutely starving and can't wait to focus on her plate and not his piercing eyes.

"Looks delicious," he says.

"Agree."

They eat mostly in silence. Both hungry from a full day of craziness.

Near the end of dinner, she asks, "How did you know about this place? Been here before?" But quickly, she regrets it. *He's probably brought all his non-dates here.*

"If you're asking me if I've brought other women here, the answer is no, I haven't."

"Oh." She blushes. Then, almost immediately, she laughs. "So, this is a date."

He grins at her and then motions for the woman to come over to the table. "May we have two more drinks to bring up to our room?"

"Most certainly," she says as she clears their plates. "How was everything?"

"Delicious. Thank you," Abigail chimes in.

"Good. I'll be right back."

She returns with their drinks, and Kelly rises as she places them down.

"See you for breakfast," he says.

He takes the drinks and motions for Abigail to follow him.

They enter their room, and unfortunately, the fire has faded. Kelly places the drinks down on the desk and attends to it. She takes her wine and sits on the couch, curling her legs up. Once he is satisfied with his work, he joins her on the couch, drink in hand.

"Can I ask you something?" he says.

She swallows hard. "Um, okay."

"Does it make you feel better to think that this is a date?"

She crinkles her nose. "Feel better?"

"Yeah."

"I was only playing around."

"But is that what you need?"

"No, Kelly." She tucks her hair behind her ear, averts her eyes, and takes a sip of her wine.

"Huh." He chuckles. "You're not good at hiding things."

Irritated, she quips, "Does it make *you* feel better to know that it's not?" She starts to get up when his massive hand on her forearm forces her to stay put.

"Don't get up and walk away because the conversation isn't easy."

"Never is with you," she whispers.

"What did you say?"

"I said"—her tone rises—"nothing is easy with you."

"I told you."

"Yeah, well, you didn't exactly explain yourself."

"How so?"

"Let me see…that you're a control freak. That it's only your way. You think that's fair?"

"I think you like when I'm in control, don't you?" He smirks.

"Not at my expense, Kelly."

"I would never do something at your expense."

"You enjoyed your little torture session earlier, didn't you?"

"Like I said, you'll listen to me from this point forward, won't you?" The sly smile on his face falls somewhere between sexy and sinister.

"You're unbelievable. I'm not here to listen to your rules, Kelly."

"When you put me in harm's way, too, then I'd say, you should."

"You're maddening."

"Maybe it's you who needs to bend a little to meet *me* in the middle."

"The middle? I don't even know where that is with you."

"Well, for starters, let things go. I fucked with you. You were turned on. Now, let it go. It's done."

She gasps.

"See, that reaction right there," he says.

"*My* reaction?" She gasps again.

"Yeah, I spoke the truth, and you're acting as though I said something horrific." He pauses and then continues, "Can I ask you to be honest with me? Truly honest."

"Fine," she says.

"Were you or were you not turned on by what I did earlier?" She starts to scowl and talk quickly when he says, "Be totally honest. And I know you got mad at me, and I respect that. Regardless of your answer, I'll never do it again."

Oh. Well then. Huh. Being honest. I can do that. At least, I think I can.

"Well?"

She blinks again, trying to find the right words to a very simple question. In fact, there are only two answers. Yes or no.

Why am I struggling so hard to say it?

"Abigail, it's a yes or no."

"I know, Kelly," she blurts out, visibly frustrated. "I was, okay? And you know I was." She lets out an exasperated sigh. "We're so different," she whispers.

She takes a sip of her wine. She senses him get closer to her on the couch. She notices his hand reaching toward her face. He turns her chin, so he can look at her.

"We're not so different, you know."

Sarcastically, she says, "Really?"

"Yes, really. You want to be with me, don't you?"

She swallows as his beautiful eyes dance over her face. "Y-yes."

His lips curl upward. "And I want to be with you."

"You're just intense. I don't know…" she says.

"But you've always liked that about me. So, why the change?"

"How do you know that?"

He leans in closer. "We've played this cat-and-mouse game for the better part of a year, and every time, it's brought us right back to this."

"This what?"

"You wanting me and me being…" He pauses, searching her wide eyes.

In a rebellious mood, she blurts out, "Obsessed?"

Now, it's his turn to gasp. "Why would you say that?"

She immediately regrets her word choice, but it has been eating away at her. *Was he talking about me that day in his apartment or someone else? And is it okay to be obsessed with someone?*

"I-I was only kidding," she stutters.

"Not buying it."

And the expression on his face is definitely telling me so.

"Um, again, kidding." *How can I get out of this? Think quickly, Abigail.*

"Abigail, spill it." He places his hand on her arm.

He isn't going to let this go. "It was just a word."

He inches closer to her. His eyes darken as they scan her face. "Do I really have to ask twice?" The way he says it gives her pause, real hesitation.

"I-I…" she stammers.

Then, with no warning at all, he stands up, scoops her up, and flips her over his lap as he sits back down on the couch, restraining her as he does.

She squeals loudly. "Kelly, what the hell are you doing?!"

He raises one hand toward her backside. "Are you going to tell me?" he says.

Oh my God, he's going to spank me!

She tries to wrestle free but with no luck.

"Stop moving," he says.

She continues squirming.

"Abigail," he says with force.

"I'm so mad," she yells as the blood rushes to her head from being tipped over his knee. Keeping her head up is difficult, and slowly, the energy drains from her. The fight is gone, so calmly, she says, "Kelly, we need to talk about this."

"Tell me why you said that," he presses.

"You think I'm going to tell you while I'm like this?"

And then *smack*! A sharp noise shatters through the room, and then red heat emanates on her behind.

She whips her head to try and look at him. "You're in big trouble," she howls.

"No, darling, you are."

Smack!

She gasps in disbelief.

"Tell me and I'll let you go."

"Okay, okay!" she yells. "I heard you on the phone a few weeks ago." Her breathing is harsh from being bent over for so long.

"What did I say?"

"That you were obsessed with someone. Now, let me go!"

"Who was I talking to?" He loosens his grip on her.

"Your sister, I think." She regulates her breathing.

"Fuck," he whispers. "Obviously, it didn't scare you away," he says.

She tries to look at him. "No, but *this* will. Now, Kelly, please let me up." She lets out a deep sigh. "I promise I won't leave. But I'm mad as hell!" she screeches.

"That I can handle," he says as he swiftly pulls her up, placing her on the seat next to him.

She immediately springs to her feet. "You-you," she stammers, digging her hands in her hips.

His smiling face infuriates her more.

She starts to pace the room, her mind whirling with so many issues. What should she tackle first? She stops. Her mind has always been a good weapon for her when she can say what she needs to. So, she blurts out, "You have some nerve. I can't even tell you how mad I am right now."

"Remember that time I told you to live a little? I bet you wish you'd never kissed me that day, huh?" he says with a huge smile on his face.

And the flashes of red she sees before her eyes cannot be mistaken. "Kelly Conrad, I have never in all my life…" And then it hits her how much he is playing with her right now, and she's such a fool for walking right into his little game, each and every time. "Actually, you kissed me that day because you were the one obsessed with me, remember?"

His eyes flicker, and she notes the smirk form across his lips.

"Is that so?"

"Yep, your sister thinks so, too. Doesn't she?"

He looks away.

Ha! I got you!

"Well?"

He abruptly rises and makes his way to the fireplace. He adds another log. She glares at him from behind. Crossing her arms over her chest, she lets out an impatient huff.

He stands up, resting his hand on the mantel as he stares into the fire.

"I *was* talking to my sister," he admits quietly.

She steps closer. "About me?"

He spins to face her. The expression on his face is one she hasn't seen before. It's bordering on sad. "Yes," he admits.

"Oh."

"Yep."

She's shocked into silence as he stands before her, hands dangling down his sides, as though weighted. The silence in the room is horrific.

He breaks it. "Say something, Abigail."

She takes her wine off the side table, and in a few gulps, she downs the rest of it. She puts it back on the end table, and the sound of the glass touching the top is louder than normal. She peers over at him and then innocently asks, "Is it a bad thing?"

His face softens. "No, it's not."

"But what did you mean by it?"

His eyes drop when he says, "My sister knows me well, and she wanted to make sure that my head was clear."

"Why would it not be?" she asks.

"Listen, this is new for me. And my sister is just looking out for her brother." He steps closer, but his shoulders are still hunched.

"But why would you say that to her and about me?"

"Because that was the only way she could understand how I'm feeling."

She swallows and then chokes out, "How do you feel?"

His eyes dance over her, and in the moment, she can tell he's contemplating.

She brings him out of his thoughts by saying, "You can be honest with me, Kelly. I've been through a lot the past few years; I think I can handle what you might say."

His smile is slight but noticeable. "You're right. And you're a lot stronger than I often give you credit for. After I ran into you a few times," he begins. "I felt there was an edge to you. Maybe something that you didn't quite acknowledge either. It was as though you were also playing a part. But then I noticed some changes in you. And when I did, it was around the time I could no longer get you out of my mind. And I tried. I really did, Abigail."

"You did?"

"Over the summer, I worked all the time to try and think of anything but you standing in my apartment. Whether you knew it or not at the time, it was there. I tried to tell you it wasn't going to go away. But then that kiss, and holy shit, I couldn't stand it. Because I couldn't have you."

"I'm sorry."

He smiles. "That's life, isn't it? Sometimes, we get what we want, and other times, we don't."

"So, you showed up when I moved into my apartment for what exactly?"

He chuckles. "I wasn't expecting you to bring that up."

"Well?"

"Because I wanted to see you. As simple as that."

"Boy, do I feel stupid."

"What? Why?"

"Because I had no clue. Never would have assumed that at all."

He cocks his head and smiles. "I know. And that's what kept me coming back."

"Is your sister worried about you? Should I be worried about something?"

He laughs. "Not at all." He pads closer to her. "Listen, this is different for me. She cares for you a lot and just wanted to make sure I wasn't going to…" He looks frightened to speak further.

"Going to what, Kelly?"

He sighs and then admits, "Sleep with you and forget about you."

She gasps. "Really? But that's not what you did with Aniston," she says. She starts to back up. "I saw you hanging out with her. So, I'm calling bullshit on this whole act you've got going on." She points her finger at him for effect.

His eyes narrow. "Act?! Are you freaking kidding me?"

"Well, it's not you. So, is it me? Am I just too typical for you? Is that it?" The alcohol is starting to make her brave.

He puts his arms up. "Hold on. Just slow down, will you?"

She digs her hands into her waist and impatiently taps her foot. "I'm listening."

"You are like no one I've been interested in, and believe me, that's a good thing."

"Really?" she scoffs.

"Yes, smart mouth, it is. I've never thought about anyone else as much as I think about you. You're intelligent, kind, thoughtful, and…gorgeous, but you don't act like it." He comes closer to her. "I think you know it's true."

Gulp. "Do I?"

He smiles and steps even closer. "Yes, I know you do." He places one hand delicately around her waist. "And maybe I am a bit controlling. But you can't go around doing whatever you want and think I'm not going to say something about it." He pauses, and then with a devilish grin, he adds, "Or do something."

She gasps. "*Kelly*."

"*Abigail*," he says mockingly as he taps her backside with his hand. She is about to protest when he takes his palm and gently covers her mouth. "Shh," he says with a wide smile. "And being a little obsessed with you is not a bad thing. It just means being with you consumes me. And for me, there is nothing wrong with that. Not one bit."

Her eyes grow wide as his hand remains covering her mouth.

"Now, I'm going to let my hand go, and here is what is going to happen," he states. "I'm going to kiss you, and we aren't going to talk anymore. Sound good?" He notices her eyes soften. "Great. I didn't bring you here so we could talk all night."

He moves his hand, wrapping it around her cheek. He pulls her in and kisses her, and a soft whimper leaves her mouth.

Releasing her lips, he brushes his softly against her ear. "I've been waiting all day for this," he says.

As her eyes flit open and she catches him observing her, a smile spreads across her face. "Like you said, we've spent too much time talking."

She puts her arms around his neck and pulls him in closer to her, hugging him deeply. If nothing else, she needs to feel his embrace. Sensing it, he squeezes her tightly back, and they stand in the middle of the room for as long as they need, not talking, just being.

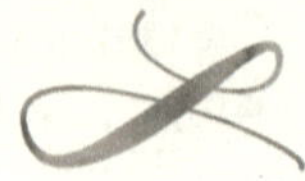

It's after two in the morning as Abigail curls into Kelly, snuggling her head into his chest. The warmth from the flames seems to melt her thoughts into a garbled mess. Her eyes grow heavy. This day has been a whirlwind of emotions, trauma, words spoken, and some taken back. And her brain would like nothing more than to shut down and restart tomorrow.

"This is nice," he sighs.

"Yeah, it is," she replies despite her head swirling from the last twenty-four hours spent with Kelly.

So, why do I feel so confused? So out of my element? Is it because my relationship with Nathan was so different than my relationship with Kelly? Of course, it is. If it wasn't, then could I ever truly grow as a person? But I am growing on the inside, right? Or am I just conforming to Kelly's rules in this relationship?

I am falling for him, no doubt. But I think many women would. But is that enough for me?

Am I equal in this relationship, or have I lost who I once was?

It's been such a crazy time of my life. College in itself is wild. I suppose I'm just trying to figure out who I am, and sometimes, I can't help but wonder whether or not he's molding me into his possession. He doesn't always respect my wishes.

But then again, this is a good escape for me. Maybe I need a little adventure in my life…but can it last long-term? Is it healthy for me in the long run? Can I really assert myself and gain equal control in the relationship?

What has he done to me?

Or am I doing this to myself?

Thirty-Two

Trouble

Abigail and Kelly enter the lobby of the bed-and-breakfast, carrying their bags. He holds open the door for Abigail to allow her to go out in front of him. The cold wind whips across their faces.

"Oh, Mr. Conrad," the woman behind the counter yells. "You have a call." She holds up the receiver for him to see.

Kelly takes his keys out of his pocket and hands them to Abigail. "Would you mind starting the car?" he asks.

"Sure thing," Abigail says as she exits the front door.

"Thanks."

He moves toward the front desk. She hands the phone to him.

"Thank you," he says to her. "Hello?"

"Kelly, it's Alex."

His heart skips a beat.

"What's wrong?" he barks.

"Everything is fine with Mom and Dad," she says, knowing his tone implied concern for their family.

"You?"

"I'm fine, too. Listen, I tried to tell her not to do it, but she wouldn't listen to reason."

"What? Who?"

"Aniston."

"Damn it. What did she do?"

He leans into the phone, anticipating bad news.

"She went to your house and saw Abigail's car."

His hand clenches around the receiver, his knuckles white as a ghost. "What the hell did she do?" he growls into the phone.

"Slashed her tires."

Kelly starts to slam the receiver down when the woman behind the counter glances up at him.

Kelly puts it back up to his ear. "She'd better not be anywhere near me when I get back. Tell her I know, and I'll deal with her."

"It's all my fault," Alex begins to cry.

"Slow down, sis. Why?"

"I told her you were away for the night. At the B and B. She put two and two together that you brought her. She was furious. She said that was your place."

"She's crazy. This was never our place!"

The woman clears her throat.

"She doesn't see it that way."

He takes a few deep breaths, trying to gain his composure. "Alex, if you see her, you tell her to stay away from Abigail. I'll come find her. Clear?"

"Yes, Kelly."

"Abigail's waiting in the car. I have to go."

"Okay. Sorry, brother."

"Me, too."

And with that, he hangs up the phone.

"I apologize," he says to the woman as he pushes the phone back across the counter.

"It's okay. Drive safe, Mr. Conrad."

He spins on his heel and heads to the door. The entire walk to the car, his mind races with terrible thoughts.

Stay calm, stay calm, he chants over and over in his mind.

He opens the door and gets in.

Of course, she asks, "Everything okay?"

"Yes. Tom locked himself out of the house and was wondering when I might be back."

She laughs. "Oh, that was a long conversation for that!"

He forces a smile. "He started babbling about some video game, too."

He puts the car in reverse and backs out of the parking lot.

The entire ride home, Kelly is seething inside. He plays music to try and distract her from wanting to talk too much.

They're approaching campus when Kelly says, "Hey, I'm going to drop you off at your house, okay?"

"Okay, but what about my car?"

His smile is genuine as he says, "It will be my excuse to come by later and see you."

She blushes. "I'd like that."

"Great." He swings down her street and pulls into her driveway.

She grabs her bag from the backseat. "I had a really interesting and nice time, Kelly."

He motions for her to lean into him. She does, and he presses his lips onto hers.

"So did I."

"Bye," she says with a push of his car door. She climbs out and waits in the driveway for him to pull away.

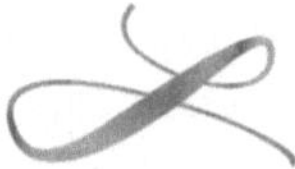

Kelly waits for her to go inside before he lays on the gas, maneuvering his car back toward his house. He pulls into his driveway.

His worse fear is now a reality. Abigail's car has four flat tires.

He yells, "Son of a bitch!" as he slams his hand on his steering wheel.

He puts his car in park and climbs out of the car. He inspects each tire carefully and then enters his door. Tom is sitting on the couch.

"Dude, what the hell?" Tom says as he rubs his hand over his face.

"Did you see her?" Kelly asks.

"No way. I would have stopped her. She had to have done it at night, when I was sleeping."

"I'm livid." He clenches his fists into tight balls. "She knows, no witnesses, no cops. It's just speculation."

"Total bullshit. Does Abigail know?"

He plops in the chair across from the couch. "Hell no. I dropped her off."

"How are you going to get out of this one?" he asks.

"No clue, but I'll tell you one thing: Aniston is going to pay for this."

"I don't want to be her." He chuckles.

"If you see her around here, you tell her I know where to find her." With that, he rises to his feet and bounds up the stairs two at a time.

Once in his room, he picks up the phone and dials his work. Frank, the manager answers. "Frank, it's Kelly."

"Hey, Kelly. What's going on?"

"Hey, I need a tow truck at my house right away."

His voice lowers. "What's the issue?"

"Four flat tires. Punctures."

"What the hell?!"

"Yeah, I'm in deep shit."

"Your car?"

"No, my girlfriend's…the girl I fixed the car for. The Volkswagen convertible."

"Damn, too bad. I can have Luke there in twenty minutes."

"Perfect. If you can fix them, great. If not, put some snow tires on it for me."

"You know that'll cost you, Kelly."

"I know, Frank. But what choice do I have?"

He sighs. "None, and that's the bitch of it."

With that, Franks hangs up.

Kelly slams down the receiver and paces his room, waiting patiently for the sound of the tow truck to pull into his driveway.

Only a few minutes pass when he hears Tom yell for him. "Kelly!"

Kelly hurries down the stairs.

"Someone's here for you," Tom says, pointing in the direction of the driveway.

Kelly goes out the garage door and starts to walk out to his driveway when he freezes in his tracks. Nathan's back is to him, but he most certainly recognizes him. He clears his throat.

Nathan spins to face him. "What the hell is this about?" he barks, pointing to her car.

"Hello to you, too," Kelly says.

"Why are all four tries flat—or should I say, slashed?"

"Jesus, like I need the good cop here. I'm trying to fix this, and I don't need you screwing it up more." He crosses his arms over his chest. "I'm handling it, Nathan. I don't know what happened, and neither does my roommate."

"Sure you don't," he says with a harsh stare. "Is she here?"

"No. I'm taking care of it."

"Big hero," Nathan snaps.

Kelly tries to remain calm. "What brings you here, Nathan?"

Nathan runs his hand through his hair, and doesn't answer.

"Well, if you don't know, then you're free to leave."

"I-I came here to"—Nathan shakes his head, clearly frazzled by Abigail's car—"to thank you for the other night."

"Not necessary."

His tone softens. "But it is. I'm sorry that happened and that you were involved."

Kelly steps closer to him. "Whatever issues you and that girl of yours are having, just do me a favor and leave Abigail out of it. I think you've hurt her enough."

"What?"

"You don't think it's hard enough on her? Why not just take your cheerleader and get the hell out of sight? Let Abigail actually have fun for a change."

"What the hell does that mean?" Heat fills his cheeks, and while he might not be as muscular as Kelly, Nathan is no slouch.

Football players in general have a toughness about them, just by playing the game. And quarterbacks? They're like tasty pieces of meat to a bunch of oversize hungry animals, but the crazy thing about QBs is that they step into that position, knowing that.

"Like you don't know."

"Poppy is *not* my girlfriend," he barks.

So, Kelly takes it all into consideration and chooses his words wisely but firmly.

"And that makes it worse," Kelly says, his chest puffing.

"Makes it worse? What are you talking about?" he says, taking a step closer to him.

"Listen, whatever issues you and Clay have with her, you need to fix it, and a girl in her con—"

"What?" he growls.

"I stepped in, Nathan, because you were too drunk to stick up for her, and she shouldn't be involved with anyone like Clay. Guy is an asshole. So, if you care about her at all, you'll get her away from him."

"Her relationship with Clay is complicated, and there's only so much…"

Just then, the beep of the tow truck pierces the air.

Kelly cuts him off, "And from where *we* sit, it seems like your relationship with her is complicated, too."

Nathan steps even closer to Kelly, his fists clenched. "Are you putting ideas in Abby's head?"

"Me? No." He shakes his head. "I didn't have to. Don't forget, Nathan, I've been around a while now, and I was the one who consoled her the night she found Poppy in *your* hotel room," he says with authority.

Nathan lunges toward him, grabbing Kelly's shirt. "You bastard. You couldn't wait to steal her from me!"

"Everything okay here, fellas?" Luke asks as he nears them.

"We're good, Luke," Kelly says as he pulls Nathan's hand free. "Nathan was just leaving."

He hands Luke Abigail's car keys. Luke goes toward his truck to release the cable and hook it to her car.

"I'll get her back," Nathan says under his breath to Kelly.

"Not after what you did, you won't." And with that, Kelly turns, leaving Nathan in his dust.

After Luke has her car on the flatbed, Kelly hops in his car and drives to Aniston's place. It's dark now, and he knows at some point, he'll need to call Abigail. He pulls into her driveway, noticing her car is the only one there. He doesn't bother knocking or ringing the doorbell. He walks right in. She's expecting him—that he is sure of.

He slams the front door for effect. Within moments, he hears her footsteps in the hallway. She peers around the corner.

"Come out here," he barks.

She steps into the dim light from the lamp near the couch. She's wearing only a long T-shirt and panties.

He crosses his arms over his chest. "What the hell were you thinking?"

"What did you expect me to do, Kelly?" she says.

"I don't give a shit, Aniston."

"How could you take her there?" she asks.

"I can do whatever I want—you know that."

"But *there*, Kelly?"

"We went there once, Aniston. It's not our place. You're insane if you think that."

"You hurt my feelings," she whines.

He shakes his head. "I can't hurt your feelings if we're no longer seeing one another, don't you get that?"

"But, Kelly—"

"No, Aniston. It's time to move on. How many times do I have to tell you that?"

"She's not right for you," she says, digging her hands into her hips.

"You know nothing about it."

"A few months ago, was she or was she not drowning her sorrows at a bar because her ex-boyfriend had knocked up some cheerleader?"

He strides closer to her. Angrily, he says, "You'd gossip about some poor girl all to prove a point about Abigail? How sick are you?"

"Well?" she says with big eyes.

"And you just proved once again why someone like Abigail is far better for me than you ever were!"

"Jerk," she hisses. "She'll never like the side of you that I like. I know you see it. She's too goody-goody for you. Squeaky clean. You need a dirty girl like me. You know you don't like vanilla, Kelly. It's so obvious. It'll never last with her."

"Well, it didn't last with us either." He laughs. "So, I guess you don't know everything about me."

She narrows her eyes at him, and in the moment, he completely regrets ever sleeping with her. And he's never felt that way about anyone before. But he's seen the ugliest side of her.

She twists her fingers together and says in a baby-like voice, "I'm sorry, Kelly. I think you're not seeing what others see."

His eyes drop to the floor. *Could this day get any worse? I'm simply trying to be normal, and nothing around me is.* "Just move on with your life, Aniston."

She steps closer to him. Her nipples pushing on the sheer fabric of the worn white T-shirt she has on. "Kelly," she coos, "I did a really bad thing, didn't I?"

He glances up at her. He recognizes the sultry gaze in her eyes. He knows exactly what she wants from him. He also knows the twitching below his waist is merely a reaction that he hasn't learned to control yet. But what he can control is what he does with it.

Kelly grabs Aniston by the wrist and pulls her toward him. He knows all too well that she wants him to flip her over his knee. To spank her and tell how bad she's been. Because that is exactly what he used to do. And they both loved it. That's the side he was able to set free with her. Which is now an unfortunate dilemma for him.

"And now, to the situation of her tires."

"Kelly Conrad," she says and doesn't struggle.

"You knew I was coming over," he says as he snaps the elastic on her panties.

She peers up at him then reaches down and grabs the bulge in his pants. "I see it still turns you on."

And then he completely changes, like Jekyll and Hyde, right in front of her very eyes. He grabs her arm. "I'm not playing with you anymore. You understand? That shit is over," he barks.

"I doubt it." The fact that she is smiling makes him even angrier.

"Four tires, really?" he roars.

"I hate her little convertible," she says.

His breath is ragged as he says, "Stay the fuck away from us, am I clear?"

He drops her arm, leaving her dumbfounded and unsatisfied. She's at a loss for words, so he storms off toward her door. He can hear her mumble something as he slams the door shut.

What the fuck am I going to do? I can't let this keep happening to me. Never again.

With adrenaline coursing through his veins, he drives in record time to the body shop, praying for good news.

When he gets there, Abigail's car is being worked on.

He walks in. "What is the damage, Frank?"

"Whoever did this did some job on them. Couldn't patch them. So, I'm putting on some snow tires; she needed them anyway. Especially around these parts."

He rubs his face. "Understood. How long?"

"Just need another hour."

"Appreciate it."

What the hell am I going to do? She's going to think it's odd that I got home and immediately put new tires on her car without even a conversation about it. I can't see her tonight and keep this all under wraps. How the hell am I going to spin this? And I can't believe Nathan knows. Aniston sure as fuck knows. And worst of all, either one of them could spill the beans. Sell me out on a dime.

"I'll be back, Frank."

He pulls open the door and walks to Diesel Food. Thankfully, it's not busy at this time of night. He sees Chloe behind the bar.

"Hey, Kelly." She smiles. "Stopping in for a drink?"

"Sure," he says, knowing he has an hour to kill.

She places the Carbon Calm in front of him. "You solo?" she asks.

"Yeah, and I need a favor."

She stops wiping the cloth over the bar top and leans toward him. "What's up?"

"I need you to come with me after your shift and help me at the garage. I have to drive Abigail's car back to my house, and I have mine, too."

She cocks her head and thankfully doesn't ask any questions. "Sure, Kelly. I'll be done in forty-five minutes." She returns to wiping down the bar and tending to what few customers she has left.

Kelly sits quietly, his mind racing as he finally has a moment to sit idle. He notices his hand shaking as he picks up his drink. He downs half of it in one gulp.

The thought of touching Aniston makes him want to vomit. He's always hated this side of himself. It's reckless. He vowed to never do something like that in an aggressive way again, and she almost pushed him to the edge, but Aniston knew that. She nearly forced his hand.

I can't lose Abigail. A girl like her isn't going to stand for shit like this. So, is my best course of action to keep her in the dark, or do I dare tell her what's going on?

Thirty-Three

Classic Scenario

Abigail spent the past two and a half hours in the library before heading to her last class of the day. With everything going on in her life, she needed to make up a lot of studying. She is satisfied that she is now caught up before class.

Abigail heads down the stairs in front of the library and toward the Draper building in a slight jog as she notes the time on her watch. She enters the lecture hall and grabs the first empty seat as Professor Rhodes begins talking. She barely made it by the skin of her teeth. She listens intently, trying hard to concentrate on school and not all the drama in her life.

"Okay, young minds," Professor Rhodes announces an hour later—he loves to say this. "Your paper is due next Thursday, and I'm expecting great things from all of you. If you have any questions, my office hours are posted on the syllabus. Have a great afternoon."

Abigail stands and gathers her items, and upon exiting the building, she wanders back from her final class of the day. She stayed up most of last night, thinking about Kelly and wondering why he never called her like he'd said he would.

Our weekend was definitely crazy, but I also feel like I got to know him a lot better. The good and the…well, I wouldn't call it bad. It's just Kelly. I always knew or at least thought that he had a mysterious side to him, and at any rate, he's not afraid to show it. There are lots of people who never show their true colors, never fly their freak flag, and we never get to know the real person deep down. So, I commend him for letting me in. I'm sure it can't be easy.

She enters the Union to grab a much-needed coffee and to get a little reading done near the warmth of the fire.

As she takes a seat in the chair and pulls out her textbook, her eyes land on Laura walking toward the radio station. She hasn't had a chance to see Laura much, as they have opposite schedules. She is about to call her name when, suddenly, someone else does. She'd recognize his voice anywhere.

"Laura," Tank yells and hurries up to meet her.

Abigail raises her textbook just up to her eyes and observes them interact. *They seem so friendly. And her smile…I think I'd describe it as flirtatious. But that seems way too unlikely. They used to be enemies when he was keeping all those secrets, so maybe they've just moved past that? Imagine if they became better friends than he and I once were.* She chuckles at the mere thought of it. *Again, very unlikely.*

But then she notices him whisper something to her, and her expression completely changes. She's concerned about something as the two discuss it further.

Something is going on with them. Oh, to be a fly on the wall. Those two are up to something. I wonder what it is.

Laura enters the radio station, and Tank heads toward the mailboxes. Abigail considers going into the station to pop in on her friend and see if she'll tell her.

But what if she doesn't?

Unexpectedly, two hands come from behind and are placed over her eyes. She puts her book down.

"Hey, who is this?" she asks.

"One guess," his sexy voice whispers in her ear.

"Kelly." She smiles.

He lets go and comes around to the front of her. He plops down in the chair next to her. "Studying?"

"Of course."

Before she can say another word, he says, "Sorry I didn't call you last night, but I have a surprise for you."

"A surprise?"

"Yeah, come with me." He stands and grabs her belongings before she can protest.

She hurries behind him as she rushes to put her coat on. "Where are we going?"

"You'll see." He holds open the door to the Union for her.

She notices his car is waiting in a loading zone out front.

"How did you know to find me here?" she asks as they approach his idling car.

"Let's see…you get out of class at three, and then you grab a coffee…usually." He smiles.

"Lucky guess."

He opens the passenger door for her, and she climbs in.

She blushes at the thought of him knowing her schedule and her habits. "Good intel, Kelly."

He pulls out of the loading zone and drives toward her house. Once in front of her house, he parks the car.

"Oh, my car is back," she says as she opens his passenger door.

He climbs out as well and walks up the driveway with her.

As he approaches, she squints her eyes. "What's different?" she asks.

"I thought you'd notice." He laughs. "I got you some snow tires."

Her eyes light up. "Kelly! But why?"

"You can't drive in this part of New York without snow tires," he says.

"But I can't afford—you can't pay for these," she says, inspecting the new tires.

"Of course I can. I work in a garage. I got a good deal on them," he lies. "It took me a little longer at the shop, and that's why I didn't get a chance to see you last night. Am I forgiven?"

"But why—I mean, thank you, but this is too much for me to accept." Her cheeks burn.

"It's a safety thing. You understand, right?" he says, crossing his arms over his chest.

"Yes, but, Kelly…" She trails off.

"It's a done deal," he says as he nears her, wrapping his arm around her waist.

She leans up on her tippy-toes and kisses him on the cheek.

"Thank you," she says. "You coming inside? It's cold out." She shudders.

"I need to help Tom with something tonight. Can I take a rain check?" he asks.

"No problem. Tell Tom I say hello."

"I'll call you later?" he says.

"Sure. Bye, Kelly."

Abigail goes into the house and finds Bree cooking in the kitchen.

"Hey," she says as she lowers the radio.

"Hey there."

"Why the smile?" she asks Abigail.

"Oh, Kelly bought me four new snow tires for my car!"

"Wow, isn't he charming?" Bree laughs. "Things are going well with him, huh?"

"Yeah, things are going great." *And dare I say, a little complicated, sexy, adventurous…and so on.*

"I'm glad to hear that. I'm making some pasta. Would you like some?"

"I'd love that." She takes a seat at the table. "Smells delicious," she adds.

"Adam's recipe."

"Speaking of going well, you two are really solid, aren't you?"

"Yep. Almost two years together."

"Wow, Bree. To think of where you first started and all the drama afterward, you guys made it. I'm so happy for you." *Maybe that will happen to me someday.*

"Thanks," she says, placing a bowl in front of Abigail. "I'm happy for you, too. It's good to see you moving on."

"It feels good, too. There was a while when I thought I'd never stop hurting over Nathan. But thanks to Kelly, it got easier."

Bree sits across from her with her own dish. She dives right in. They sit and eat, chatting about school and their lives in general. But if Abigail knows anything about Bree, it's that she is good for advice. She is a straight shooter, and that is something Abigail has learned to admire about her.

"So, I saw Laura at the Union today."

Bree peeks up from her dish. "What'd she have to say?"

"Nothing. I was about to yell her name, but Tank beat me to it."

"Okay?"

"It's just this feeling I can't shake."

"What feeling?"

"It's the way they look at each other. Something's different."

"Are you watching them?" Bree gibes.

"Funny, no. Well, yes. I couldn't help it. She went from kind of flirty to serious and…"

"You're not really friends with Tank anymore, right?"

"Sadly, no. But right now, it gives me a break from football…Nathan, too, I suppose. So, I've kind of been avoiding making up with Tank in a way. The whole trial debacle—what a mess that turned out to be."

"Right, so maybe this isn't such a bad thing, their newfound friendship. She's been through a lot this past year, and if I remember correctly, so has he."

"You're right. It's stupid of me to worry about this."

"Not necessarily. It's got to sting a little. He's now better friends with her—or at least, that's what you're feeling is happening. Am I right?"

Abigail nods her head. "You're always right, Bree."

She laughs as she twirls her long chestnut-colored hair around her hand. "Hey, at least you know deep down inside that they've found a good support system in one another, and that has got to make you feel a little bit better about it, no?"

"Again, you're right."

"Laura doesn't have Travis or Colin to lean on, and Tank doesn't have Jonathan—or you for right now—so they've found someone else. It's a classic scenario." She speaks so matter-of-factly that it gives Abigail an entirely new perspective on her analysis of the situation.

Abigail smiles wide at her friend. "I don't have to say it, do I?"

"You love me, I know." With that, Bree stands and puts her dish in the dishwasher.

"I'll clean up," Abigail says.

"Good, 'cause I've got to get some work done at the library. I'll see you later." She brushes her lips on Abigail's cheek. "Tootles."

"Absolutely."

So, they've found someone else to lean on. Just like I have. Maybe that's the recipe we've all needed this year. To spread our wings and see what else is out there for us. I've felt guilty for so long, not being connected to the football team and more importantly, to Nathan. But I can't any longer. He's moved on. I know this. And Laura and Tank have found a mutual friendship. It's clear they're doing just fine without me. I saw it with my own eyes today.

And I've got someone looking out for me, too. It might not always be perfect, but nothing is. And we're all doing okay, right? I'm doing okay. At least, I think I am.

If only there were a class I could take in college on all this relationship stuff, imagine what I could learn.

As Abigail clears the table, she can't help but laugh to herself as she wonders, *What kind of mythical creature would know enough to teach a class about all the lessons you could learn about love?*

Thirty-Four

Even the Best of Intentions

Kelly knew he'd hear from Clay at some point, so it was only a matter of time before he saw his old floor mate face-to-face. This time, under much better circumstances.

He pulls open the door to Monroe's and spots him immediately at the bar. He's slumped over, picking at the label on his beer bottle.

"I'll have what he's having," Kelly says to the bartender.

Clay glances up. His eyes bloodshot, dark circles around them. A bruise is evident on his cheek. "Thanks for meeting me, Kelly."

"Sure thing." He takes the seat next to him. "Ouch," he says, pointing to the shiner.

"Yeah, ya bastard. You always could hit hard, Kelly."

"Sorry, not sorry." He chuckles.

"Yeah, I know, Kelly. No hard feelings."

"What were you thinking?" Kelly asks.

"I wasn't."

"Well, if she's not your concern, then why get involved?"

"She used to be," Clay says.

"From what I hear, it's a good thing she's Ryan's problem now."

Clay peers over at him. "Why would you say that?" His fist clenches around the bottle, turning his knuckles white.

"Let him deal with her now. She's not your problem anymore. You said so yourself."

"He messing with her? Is that why he tried to step in on my business?"

"Your business?" A chill runs over Kelly's skin. "She's your business?"

Clay sits up and looks around the bar. He leans in toward Kelly. "Yeah, had a little situation a month back. But it's cool now."

Kelly swallows hard. "What kind of situation?"

Clay motions to his belly and mouths the word, *Pregnant.*

Kelly must react in order to keep up the charade. "Man, that poor bastard."

Clay cocks his head. "You mean, me."

"You?"

"Yeah, like I said, Poppy and I. But it wasn't even that long. She didn't care about me. I knew it. But I liked her. And then she lost the baby—miscarried or some shit like that. I mean, she'd called me and told me she was pregnant. Wouldn't take my calls and then called me the night of the party to tell me she lost it. I was so darn pissed at her for going to that party and drinking the way she was that I just reacted and took it out on her. What the hell is wrong with that girl?"

Kelly tries to calm him by patting him on the shoulder, "Okay, buddy. You can't imagine what she was going through, too. So, just take a deep breath. In hindsight, it's for the best. Don't you think?"

"Yeah, it's for the best. Who the hell wants to be a dad at my age? Scared me half to death. And I was hoping to see you to explain myself. Listen, I know I can be a jerk—"

Kelly interrupts, "I understand, but if I ever see you grab a woman at a party again, I won't go so easy on you."

"I should hope not," he says, hanging his head in disgust.

Kelly waves to the bartender for two more beers. "Because that shiner I gave you was me going easy on you. Just remember that."

Abigail hears the front door unlock. She sits up from the couch as Laura enters the foyer. "Hey," Abigail calls out.

Laura walks in. "Hey, Abigail." She has a concerned look. Abigail is about to ask her if she is okay when Laura says, "You okay?"

"I was about to ask you the same," Abigail says.

"Oh, I saw your car." But then she stops talking and hangs her bag on one of the hooks. She stays turned for a bit too long.

"What is it, Laura?"

"Nothing," she says rather quickly.

"Laura? What's going on?"

"You get new tires on your car?" she asks, now facing her. She leans against the credenza.

Abigail cocks her head. "You noticed? In the dark?"

Laura stammers, "Yeah."

She's known Laura a long time, having been roommates for three years now, and she knows when Laura can't meet her eyes that it's a dead giveaway. Something is not right.

"Laura Chase, what are you not telling me?" she asks.

"Who bought you the tires?" She seems nervous.

"Kelly. Why?"

"Oh." She averts her eyes. "I was just wondering."

"He said I needed snow tires. You think it's weird he bought me such a gift?" she asks, although she is not quite sure it matters.

"Maybe ask him that," she whispers and then nervously tucks her hair behind her ear.

"Why would you say that?"

"No reason, I guess. I, um, have a lot of work to do for the station," she says quickly.

"Really?" Abigail says, not hiding her sarcasm.

Laura breezes past the couch, pretending to look for something on the side table. She's acting jumpy. "You see my Discman?" she asks.

Anger brews inside Abigail, but she's trying not to take it out on her friend. Abigail stands and walks over to one of the hooks and pulls her jacket off it. "I don't care for the fact that you're being so cryptic with me. Not cool."

"Wait. Where are you going?!" Laura yells after her.

"Kelly's!" just before the door slams.

Abigail rushes to her car. She can hear Laura struggling with the old wood door to get it open. Finally, she yanks the door open just as Abigail shuts her car door. Laura shouts after her, but it's too late. Abigail has already pulled out of the driveway, and her car is screeching down the street.

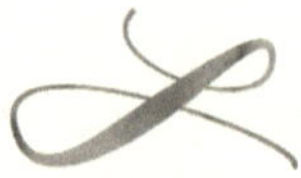

Abigail pulls into Kelly's driveway and parks next to his car. She goes to the front door and knocks, waiting for an answer.

Tom pulls it open. "Hey, Abigail."

"Hey, Tom. Kelly here?"

"Yeah, upstairs. Want me to get him?"

"No, I'll go up, if that is okay?"

"Be my guest." Tom allows her to go inside.

Abigail takes a deep breath as she nears the top of the stairs. She has no idea what she's doing here. She knocks.

"Come in!" he yells.

She pushes the door open and finds him sprawled out on his bed, wearing only a pair of sweatpants. Her heart rate quickens.

"Abigail, hey. Everything okay?" He slides to the end of his bed.

She paces his room.

"Abigail," he growls impatiently. "What's going on?"

He tries to grab her hand, and instinctively, she pulls away.

She stops. *Something about the new tires on my car and the way Laura was asking about them is very unsettling to me. It's a total gut reaction, but I'm going with it.* "Why did you buy me those tires?"

Abigail sees exactly what she was hoping not to see. The confident, often arrogant Kelly starts to squirm. The color from his lightly tanned skin drains and is replaced with a pale shade instead.

She steps closer toward him, making sure to lock eyes with him. And immediately, her body reacts to his physical response. "Kelly, tell me now."

"I can explain."

"I'm listening."

He rubs his hands over his face. "When I got back…"

"Got back from what?"

"When we got back from the bed-and-breakfast…your tires were flat."

"Bull!" she yells.

He stands in front of her. "Watch your tone," he barks.

"Oh, *please*, Kelly."

His eyes ignite.

"Was that the call you got? Was it about my car? What are you hiding?!"

"I'm not hiding anything," he lies.

"I don't believe you."

"No?"

"No! You're not telling me something, and I'm pissed."

"You're pissed?! He only told you to try and get you back!" he says.

She gasps. "What the hell are you talking about?"

He snaps his mouth shut. "Nothing. Forget it."

"Forget it?! Not a chance." She grabs on to his arm. "Kelly, tell me now, or I'm leaving."

Fear enters his eyes.

So, there is something he's not telling me, and it's big!

She releases her grip and strides toward the door. He steps in front of her.

"Aren't we past this?" she sneers. "You trying to block me from leaving? This is a free country, is it not?!"

His breathing is erratic, but he tries to calm himself. "Listen, he came here to say he was sorry I had to get involved…"

"Who are you talking about?" she yells.

"Nathan!" he yells back. "I'm sorry." Then, calmly, he says, "Nathan."

"What the hell does Nathan have to do with my tires, Kelly? Did he do something to my car?"

Completely puzzled, he says, "Wait, what are you asking me?"

"It doesn't matter." She heads for the door. "I can't be with someone who lies. Not again."

He can see the pain in her eyes. "Wait, listen. He came here to apologize for the fight at the party, and your tires were flat. He didn't do anything to your car. I assumed he was the one who had told you."

"Why would he even care?" she asks.

"I can't get in his head," he mutters.

"Wait, all *four* of my tires…were flat? That's weird, isn't it?" she asks.

He averts his eyes. Then, he whispers, "Slashed."

"What?!" She steps back from him. "Why the hell would someone slash my tires, Kelly?"

"Abigail, listen to me, please," he begs.

"What the hell is going on? I demand to know!" The smile that grows on his face only angers her more. "You think this is funny, do you?"

"No, it's just you…oh, never mind." He quickly changes his tune. "I don't think this is funny at all, but I handled it, didn't I?"

She crosses her arms over her chest. "Handled what, Kelly?"

"The tire situation."

"Oh, so in your eyes, hiding the truth from me was the right thing to do?"

"I was just trying not to upset you."

"Did it work?" she asks.

He shakes his head. "Obviously not. So, if he didn't tell you, then who did?" His eyes narrow at her.

"I'll tell you once I think you've told me the truth."

"I told you," he sighs.

"You have no idea who did it? Who would come to *your* house and slash *my* tires?"

He swallows hard, and just his slight hesitation tells her he knows exactly who did it.

"Abigail," he says as he touches her arm.

She pulls away. "It's clear to me that you don't know how to do this," she says, pointing between the two of them. "It should be easy. But you're hiding something, and the last thing I need is to be with someone who can't tell me the truth."

Abigail yanks the door open, leaving Kelly completely stunned. She bounds down the stairs and rushes out the door.

Abigail backs out of his driveway and can't think of anywhere to go. She wishes she could go see Alex and Casey, but she can't put this on his only sister. She doesn't want to go back to the house because she's pissed at Laura for being so obscure…and right, too. She can't go to Diesel Food; her coworkers would see right through her.

How could you lie to me, Kelly? You turned a nice gesture into something I just want to forget about. Actually, you took something terrible and tried to hide it from me, right under my very nose. And Nathan knows about this. Jesus, that's all I need.

And what scares me is that there's someone out there who hates me enough to destroy my property. Or to try to hurt Kelly. Is he that much of a heartbreaker that he leaves women in his wake, scorned and willing to do drastic things to get his attention? Or did he mess with that guy at the party the other night, and now, he's after him? Either way, it's not good.

She misses Webber. He's just the perfect friend to study with, talk about science or something to get her mind off her problems, but she'd be running right into the lion's den if she called their place. The last person she needs to pick up the phone is Tank or Nathan.

She drives downtown, passing the time as she crosses over one street to another with no place in mind. She finds her car veering into the local drugstore. She picks up some toiletries as she wanders the aisles of the pharmacy and then goes to another store to buy some wine and snacks for the house even though she is sure they don't need any more. As she climbs back into her car, she can't help but view her tires with a disgusted expression.

If nothing else, she learned today that even the best of intentions can sometimes come with a price. And in this case, the price was her finally losing her cool with Kelly. But she had to stand her ground.

If the tables had been turned, he'd have demanded answers, too.

Thirty-Five

It's Complicated

When she finally pulls into her driveway, Abigail is grateful that all the lights are out and the house appears to be sleeping. She puts her snacks away and then carries the other bags up to her room along with a bottle of wine and a glass from the cabinet. She has every intention of putting on a sappy movie and crying herself to sleep. She tiptoes past Laura's room and then up the second flight to her haven on the third floor. She pushes open the door and struggles to flip on the light. She drops her bags on the bed.

Her muscles ache from the tension built within them from her horrible, stressful evening.

Without warning, the lamp switches on, and a deep voice says, "Where have you been?"

She whips around, clutching her heart. "Jesus, you scared me!"

Kelly walks toward her. "I've been sitting here for hours. Where have you been?"

"You have some nerve, asking me that," she snarls.

"Really?"

"Yeah, really, Kelly. My roommates are sleeping, and you don't belong—"

"You stormed out of my house, and then you disappeared for hours to what?" He glances at her bed. "Shop?"

"I'm not doing this, Kelly. I'm tired, and I just want to relax."

"Not until we talk."

She opens the wine, pours herself a glass, and sits on her couch. "Talk."

He paces the room for a minute. His shoulders uncomfortably bent forward. "I know who did it."

"No shit," she whispers.

He stops and stares at her. It gives her a chill. "It was Aniston," he admits.

She gasps. "What the hell, Kelly? I thought you said there was nothing going on between you two. I should have known better. I'm such an idiot!"

"*Abigail.*"

"What?!"

"Stop yelling or—"

"Or what?" she challenges.

He clenches his fists. "Listen to me. She found out we were at the bed-and-breakfast—"

"Why would *she* know about that place?"

Kelly's eyes glass over.

"Oh my God. You took her there, too. You lied to me…again!"

"Let me finish," he growls. "That class I took, she was in it. One day, the bus broke down, so we all went there, and, well, you know…that's when she and I got together for the first time."

"I've heard just about enough for today," she says as she stands. She takes a sip of her wine. "You can leave."

"I'm not leaving. This is too important."

"You'll never listen to me, will you? This is only about what you want."

"When it comes to you…yes."

She inhales sharply. "So, you admit it."

"Yes, if I leave, this will never go away. You don't want that."

"Again, you think you can read my mind." *Control freak.*

"I know what your eyes are telling me, Abigail." He draws closer to her.

"Keep your distance."

He puts his hands up in a surrender-like fashion. "Okay, okay." Then, he continues, "She found out and was jealous. So, she reacted…poorly."

"*Poorly*? Poorly?!"

"I never saw this coming—you have to know that." He attempts again to get closer to her. "I would never put you in harm's way." His eyes soften.

She knows it, too, but she's still pissed off. "So, you thought by keeping the truth from me that you would be keeping me out of her crosshairs. What if I ran into her and never knew? She runs in your circle, right? Did you think your sister and others could know but not me?"

"I know I screwed up, and I'm sorry, Abigail."

"You're sorry?"

"Yes, I've never…" He stops and stares at her, unsure if he should continue or not.

"Never what, Kelly?"

"I've never had to care about someone else before, like this, and I messed up," he says quietly.

"Oh," she says.

"But she won't bother you anymore."

He states this as if it were a fact, and something about the way he spoke those words gnaws at her.

"How do you know?" she asks, unsure if she really wants to know the answer.

"Because I do."

Abigail steps closer to him this time, and in a low voice, she replies, "There's something you're not telling me. I can see it in your face. *Kelly*? How do you know she'll stay away this time?"

"You don't need to know all the details."

She laughs, egging him on, on purpose. "The hell I don't."

He tips his head, his eyes narrowing at her. There is a darkness about him that she's noticed in the past, but it's even clearer to her tonight, and she's not sure she can handle it.

But I must if I'm going to be strong about my decisions. I can still decide what I want, can't I?

"Did you go and see her?" Her voice shakes.

He runs his hands over his face, and when he releases them is when she notes pain in his eyes.

With trepidation, he answers, "Yes."

"What did you do, Kelly?"

He begins to pace in front of her. Her heart wants to explode, and her cheeks burn with heat as he tears back and forth in front of her, frustratingly pulling at his hair as he does.

"She…she needed to understand there are consequences for her actions."

"Kelly," she begs, "what did you do?"

"I had to talk to her," he says once he stops in front of her.

She gulps the rest of her wine down, sensing he is about to drop a bomb. He takes her glass and puts it on the coffee table. He takes her by the wrist, pulling her closer toward him. His grip is tight. She glances down at his hand, but he doesn't let go.

"I did it for you," he whispers.

"You did what for me?" Tears sting her eyes.

He swallows the lump in his throat. "I wanted to punish her," he admits.

A gasp leaks from her lips. The room begins to spin, and she senses the color drain from her face. Trying to find her words seems unlikely at this point.

"Say something," he pleads.

Snapping back to the present, she repeats, "You wanted to *punish* her?"

"Yes, but I didn't. Don't you see? She can't do something like that and not expect me to behave a certain way."

With anger, she voices her concern, "How the hell are you going to be a lawyer if you do behave that way?!"

"I know how to separate my personal life from my career."

She tries to free her wrist again, but she is unsuccessful.

"I can't let you go—you know that," he says in a nonthreatening manner. "This is too important."

"How-how were you going to punish her?" she dares to ask.

His eyes drop, and with a slight shake of his head, he answers, "I think you know."

Boom!

Immediately, she is brought back to the room at the bed-and-breakfast. When he said to her, "And maybe I am a bit controlling. But you can't go around doing whatever you want and think I'm not going to say something about it."

Aniston misbehaved. Badly. And he wanted to do something about it.

She has no clue how to react to this news. Never in her wildest dreams would she have envisioned her life would turn so drastically as it has these past six months. Her body starts to respond before her words come out, and tears drip onto her cheeks. With his other hand, he feverishly tries wiping them away.

"I-I…" But no other words come.

Then, he speaks the very last words she ever thought she'd hear from Kelly Conrad's lips, "I didn't do it because…I love you," he whispers.

She is snapped like a twig back to her reality. "What?"

"You have to know it, don't you?" His voice is so soft that she barely recognizes it.

What is happening?

Then, as if the past seventy-two-plus hours weren't strange enough, Kelly suddenly drops to his knees in front of her, releasing her wrist, only to tightly wrap his arms around her waist. "Please, I'm trying to change," he begs.

Who is this man?

He buries his face into her waist. "Please, tell me you can forgive me. I did it all for you."

He loves me?

"I promise I'll never lie to you again."

If she didn't know better, his voice caught as he spoke.

Is he crying?

Her hands find the top of his head. The tips of her fingers run over his hair. "Shh, Kelly," she murmurs. They find the side of his face, drawing it up to meet her eyes. The utter sadness in his beautiful green eyes breaks her heart yet again. Before she can comprehend what she is willing to accept, she says, "You need help, Kelly."

Relief doesn't wash over him. If nothing else, he remains as tortured as ever. Something in the way he regards her sparks a piece of her left untapped. *She* has the power. He is surrendering to her. She leans down toward him. His eyes dance over her face. He's uncertain what she will do next, and this is new for them. She's so close to him that she can feel his breath on her face.

"Please, Abigail," he pleads to her.

This difficult, controlling man loves me, and for some reason, I need him.

Her lips brush against his. A moan catches in the back of his throat. He tightens his grip around her body. Squeezing her with intent. She touches the side of his face as she presses her lips again onto his.

"I need you," he says as he releases his full lips. "You're the only one who calls me out on my bullshit."

"I'm here, aren't I?"

But I still can't imagine what would drive a woman to such jealousy that she would destroy my property. Is it Kelly? Or is she out of her mind?

"I know I screwed up."

"Yes, you did. But it's more than that. You need to be less in control of some things and more in control of other parts of your life if this is ever going to work."

His head drops. "I know," he whispers. "Just don't give up on me yet."

"Show me you mean it," she says, tipping his head so she can see it in his eyes.

And she does. She notes sadness, confusion, and disappointment. That overly confident Kelly Conrad is nowhere to be seen today.

If she had only known that day he mistakenly walked into her dorm room over a year ago that she would be so entangled in his complex web. But how could she have known? He seemed complicated, yes. But dark and controlling? No. It's a far cry from her former relationship. So far in fact that it's like another world away.

Thirty-Six

Off the Rails

After class, Abigail enters the Union to grab a coffee. Laura's shift at the station is starting within the hour, so she knows she'll be in her studio. She's been dying to clear the air since their spat a few days ago. Balancing her coffee, Abigail knocks on the station door. Patrick, the radio technician, pulls open the door.

"Hey, Abigail."

"Hello, Patrick. How are you?"

"Just super. If you're looking for Laura, she is in her studio," he says.

"Great, thanks." Abigail's heart picks up speed as she approaches the closed studio door. She hasn't been able to shake the unsettling feeling about her friendship with Laura over the past few months. She doesn't like how their separate social lives have driven a wedge between them when they used to be able to talk freely about anything with each other.

What if Laura doesn't feel the same and we are just drifting apart? What if her friendship with Tank is more important to her right now? But I'm still upset about the other day. It was so obvious she was hiding something from me. But what? She used to tell me everything.

Exhaling deeply, she knocks on the door.

"Come in!" she hears.

Abigail turns the doorknob and pushes it open.

"Oh, hey. Wasn't expecting you," Laura says awkwardly.

Just as I suspected. Things are not right between us.

"Thought this would be the best place to catch you." Abigail closes the door behind her.

"What's up?"

"I wanted to talk about the other night," Abigail says.

"Listen, I'm really sorry. I never should have said anything."

"But why did you?" Abigail asks as she leans against the wall.

"I'm not sure, to be frank."

Damn it. "I'm asking that you be really honest with me because you don't seem like you are."

A gasp escapes Laura's lips. "Well, tell me how you really feel."

It's crystal clear to Abigail that she's uncomfortable.

"How did you know Kelly bought me tires?"

"I really don't want to be involved in all this," she sighs.

"What are you involved in?"

"This." She motions back and forth. "I'm trying not to talk to both sides."

"What are you talking about?" *Both sides? Now, we are on sides? This is news to me.*

Her face burns red, and Abigail unequivocally knows she caught Laura in some sort of lie or predicament.

"I still see Nathan and Tank."

"How often?" she quips, but then in a gentler voice, she says, "I mean, I assumed you were still friends with them."

"I am, but it just feels like I can't talk about them around you," she blurts out.

Ouch. "Well, you don't, so how would you know?" she says with an edge.

"That's fair."

On the defensive and, more importantly, like the odd man out, Abigail shoots back, "So, let me guess…Nathan told you about the tires, and he wanted you to come running to me, so I'd question Kelly, possibly break up with him, and then Nathan could get me back?"

"*Abigail.*" Her eyes are wide with disbelief.

"What? You guys have no idea what these past few months have been like for me. I'm finally happy again, and Nathan can't have it both ways. He just doesn't want me to move on, but it's okay that he did with Poppy, right? What a twisted double standard that is. I can't find someone new, but he can—and right in front of my very nose."

"I have no—"

But Abigail quickly cuts her off, "Remember when you came in my room and told me not to wait forever to be happy? What happened to all that stuff you said to me?"

"I meant that," she whispers.

"Well, it doesn't seem like that from where I'm standing."

"I didn't know you were so upset with me."

"I wasn't until the other night. It was really crappy of you to be so cryptic to me and send me into a tizzy, don't you think?" *Even though that tizzy sent me straight toward the truth.*

"Yes, of course. I tried to come after you but—"

"I thought you'd be more supportive of me and not them, if I'm being honest."

"How have I not supported you?" she asks.

"Imagine the one friend who swore he'd always protect you telling you he needs a break from you! Can you imagine how that made me feel? All because I hadn't done what *he* wanted."

Laura crosses her arms over her chest and says protectively, "Well, you didn't exactly tell him the truth, now did you?"

"Why should I? He was going to do that regardless."

"You don't know that!"

"Are you defending what he did?" Abigail asks as heat fills her cheeks.

"Well, you care about him, don't you? Maybe he deserved better from *you*," she barks back.

"I see he's gotten to you now, too. You all must hang out a lot for you to feel so strongly. Is this what you guys do, sit around and discuss me?"

"Hardly," Laura says coolly.

Abigail laughs and then says in an unruffled voice, "Well, imagine if your ex-boyfriend got the girl he'd cheated on you with pregnant. I'd bet you wouldn't want to hang out with him, or his friends and you'd want to keep your distance. It might be the only way to try and find happiness. I'd bet a million dollars all of you guys would keep your distance."

Laura's eyes grow wide.

She can't speak, so Abigail continues to pile on. "I can tell by your silence that you've known all along, and you didn't think I deserved better from any of you. Were you all just going to ignore that elephant in the room and hope I'd just go away?"

"Abigail!" she cries as tears well in her eyes.

Abigail glances at the clock on the wall. "You're going to be late," she scoffs and then pulls open the handle and exits the studio. With authority, she bounds down the hallway and leaves the station.

The conversation between the two best friends and roommates went off the rails. But maybe it was time that someone knew how pissed off Abigail was. And since Laura wants to remain friends with a deserter and a cheater, then she, unfortunately, was the one to be there when Abigail finally let it all out.

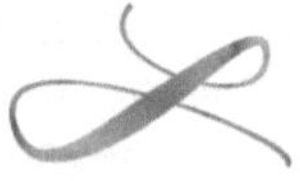

Laura, with tears in her eyes, picks up the phone and dials the one person she knows will help her. She masks her sadness when he picks up the phone.

"Tank, it's me. Can you pick me up after my shift?"

"Sure. You okay?"

She fake laughs. "Yeah, just about to go on the air. Gotta run. See you later."

"Sure thing, girl."

"Bye."

The hours pass by slowly. But as the final minutes tick off the clock, she closes her segment on the radio. She hurries out of the Union to Tank's waiting truck. She climbs in, and he leans over and swiftly kisses her on the cheek.

"What was that for?" she asks.

"Thought you needed it."

"What gave me away?"

"What didn't? The call, the radio…"

"Was I terrible?"

"No, not at all. I can just hear it in your voice."

She smiles at him. "Is Nathan home?"

"Yeah, just studying."

"Good. I need to talk to you both."

"Okay. Should I be worried?" he asks.

"No. I think it's time we clear the air."

Tank pulls into his spot in Parkers Village. Laura hops out and follows him through the front door.

"He's upstairs," Tank says.

Laura climbs the stairs, Tank close behind her. She knocks quietly on his door.

"Yeah?" he yells.

Laura opens the door as Nathan glances up from his book.

"Hey. What's up, guys?" he says with a smile.

"Laura needs to talk to us," Tank says as he takes a seat in the recliner in the corner.

Nathan closes his book and straightens up in his desk chair. Laura paces a few times and then stops and looks at them both.

Tank, never one for small talk, says, "Get to it, girl. Spill."

"Okay, um, Abigail"—the mere mention of her name changes the vibe in the room—"came to see me before my show, and…well, I wasn't expecting her to be so angry with me."

"What is she mad about now?" Tank huffs.

"One, I never should have asked her about the tires. It was none of my business or any of ours to meddle in her affairs."

"Screw that," Tanks quips. "If that guy is putting her in any kind of danger, it is *all* our business."

"Tank's right. You were within reason to bring it up to her. I saw it with my own eyes, for Christ's sake. Did he think we wouldn't step in?"

Laura contemplates their opinions. "I suppose we should be worried, right? Some person slashes her tires, and she doesn't think we should say anything?"

"Does he know who did it?" Tank asks.

Nathan laughs. "Of course he must. Why the hell would someone slash a random person's tires?"

"Okay, that was stupid to ask," Tank admits. "He some kind of player?"

"She wouldn't tell me who did it or what he knows," Laura says.

"Did you tell her I told you?" Tank asks.

"No, she thinks Nathan told me."

"Me? But why?" Nathan asks.

"Kelly must have told her he saw you."

"Wise move on his part," Nathan says, anger brewing on his handsome face.

"But there is more to all of this," Laura says as tears sting her eyes.

In a soft voice, Tank says, "Tell us."

Laura takes a deep breath in and releases it. She starts to cry.

Tank gets up and places his arms around her. "It's okay. You can trust us. You know that."

"I know. But we were all once good friends, and look at us now. It kills me. I hate the thought of us drifting apart."

"I know you do," Nathan says. "It's all my fault really."

"Don't say that," Tanks adds. "We all know it's my damn fault. I'm always to blame because I can't keep my opinions in check."

"Why didn't you fight harder?" Laura says.

"What?" Tank asks, releasing his hold on her.

"Why did you not fight harder to be her friend?" Laura says with a sniffle.

"I don't know," he admits. "I wanted to, but I just felt betrayed by her making decisions without consulting me."

Laura hangs her head. "Well, she did it to protect you. You should have known she'd do anything for you. There was reasonable doubt that it was just an encounter between two college students gone wrong. They even mentioned you being a jealous boyfriend. She feared the whole school would know about that." She turns and glances at Nathan. "She was worried about you, too. She didn't want you to be caught up in some campus drama either. A new trial would have only brought all this backup."

"Oh," Nathan says.

Laura continues, "Tank, her worst fear was that what you did for her would come into question. You know how rumors can spread. She wanted the story to remain that you were the hero and the reason *The Campus Creeper* was caught. That's all she ever wanted out of this. Not money, suing, or validation. What if a new trial produced the same outcome? Then, everyone would know. The whole world. It would all be for nothing!"

Tank's mouth drops a touch. "I had no idea."

"The worst of it? I promised her with all my heart that I would never tell you, but I just don't want to be in the middle anymore. I'm losing her, too, and that can't happen."

"I'm sorry if I've done that to you," Tank whispers.

"Me, too, Laura. I never meant to hurt either of you."

She glances over at Nathan. "I know this, but it's something else she said, too. She said something about imagining if my ex-boyfriend got the girl he'd cheated on me with pregnant. That I'd want to keep my distance, too, and try and find happiness someplace else. Why would she say that?"

The color in Nathan's usually rosy cheeks fades as his mouth drops wide open. He glances at Tank and then back at Laura.

"What's going on, guys?" she asks.

"You don't think…" Tank stops before speaking further.

"No way," Nathan whispers.

Tank replies, "But would she…"

"Someone, please fill me in here," Laura impatiently demands.

Nathan climbs out of his desk chair and paces the room, mumbling to himself. He pulls at his hair, stops, and then paces again.

"Dude, you okay?" Tank finally breaks the silence.

Then, with no warning at all, Nathan slams his fist on top of his desk, smashing something in the process.

Laura jumps. "You're freaking me out," she cries.

With hollow eyes, Nathan finally meets her stare. "It finally makes sense. She was so angry with me. Never wanted to even talk to me, look at me. I have been wondering *every goddamn day* what I could have possibly done to make the greatest love of my life hate me so much."

Laura swallows hard at his confession.

"How the hell did *she* find out?" Nathan adds.

Laura yells, "Find out what?!"

Tank takes Laura's hand, trying to calm her. "Nathan, you'd better tell this one."

He plops down on his bed, shielding his face from the world with his hands. One look at Tank, and Laura knows she must remain calm indeed, as the truth is about to be set free.

Finally, he sits up, and with no buildup at all, he blurts out, "Poppy got pregnant."

Laura gasps.

Nathan continues, "By Clay—that guy from the other night at the party. She got unlucky."

"Holy shit," she whispers.

"Yeah, and I knew she had a thing for me, but I told her from day one that it wasn't going to happen. So, she finally started seeing someone else. Part of me felt responsible for her troubles. I was *really* blunt with her."

"It's not your fault, Nathan," Laura says.

"I get that. But she's my friend. Aside from all the feelings crap, she's a good person," Nathan says.

"So, why would Abigail say that?" Laura asks.

"The night Abigail came to the hotel…" Nathan begins.

Laura starts to cry.

"Whoa, Laura. What's going on?" Tank asks.

"I…I told her to go that night. I said she should go to you and make a grand gesture. That when you give someone a promise ring, it'd better not be bullshit."

Nathan shakes his head. "It wasn't bullshit. I planned to be better than I had been because I knew she deserved all of me. Not just when football didn't need me."

"Football has been good to us," Tanks adds.

"I know this, believe me. My dad doesn't have to pay a cent for college because I play ball."

"See, it's a good thing," Tanks adds.

"But not when it cost me her."

Tank nods his head.

Nathan continues, "But, Laura, Poppy was in my room that night because she liked me. I knew it. Abigail knew it. I should never have let her in." Quickly, he adds, "Nothing happened. I swear on my mother. But at the time, Abigail never would have believed that. That told me a lot about where our relationship had gone. Off the rails."

"But she never asked you about Poppy and the pregnancy?" Laura asks.

"She could barely look at me, let alone speak to me." He shakes his head. "But it makes sense now. She hates me. Can you blame her? If it were true, she must have been devastated and filled with a lot of hate for me *and* Poppy."

"Why wouldn't she confide in me?" Laura asks Tank.

"It's the cycle we're in. She doesn't think you have her back, and that's partly because you hang out with us. She probably thought you had known all along, too. Or you'd run and tell us that she knew, if I'm being honest."

She gasps. "Oh, that's horrible."

"It is," Nathan says. "For all of us."

"But how did she know?" Laura asks.

"I found out the day Abigail broke up with me. I went to the gym to blow off some steam, and Poppy was there. She told me, and I took her to the student health…"

As soon as he speaks, they all stare at one another in complete disbelief.

"No," Tank whispers.

"Oh my God. *Casey*." Chills run down Laura's spine.

"It had to be. I know she works there. Who else would tell Abigail? As far as I know, no one really knew of her condition."

Laura cocks her head and asks, "But the night of the party? What was that all about?"

"Poppy told me she miscarried. And I guess she left Clay a message despite me pleading with her to talk to him. But she did it anyway. She's kind of strong headed like that. So, when he saw her at the party, drinking and acting like nothing happened, he snapped."

"Wow. I had no idea," she says, glancing at Tank.

Shrugging his shoulders, he says, "You understand it was none of my business to talk about that. Even to you."

Tucking her hair behind her ear, she says, "I understand."

"I can't believe she has been feeling this way for so long, and it was *never true*. What should I do?" Nathan asks them.

"I wish I knew the answer to that," Laura says.

"Yeah, me, too. I'm not exactly in her good graces."

Laura gives Tank a somber look after he says that.

Nathan cuts in, "I need to talk to her. But I know she won't see me."

"There is one person I know she misses and she'd be happy to see," Tank adds.

Laura gives him a pained expression.

"Not me, silly, but thanks for that," he mumbles.

"Sorry, I thought…oh, never mind. Who?"

"Come on, guys. Think! Who's the one person who's always been in her corner?" Tank asks.

Nathan slaps his hand to his forehead. "Of course. Spidey!"

Laura tips her head back. "Duh! Right. He'll help."

"But I'm going to have to convince him. Because he won't want to trap her into a conversation with me. He cares about her too much," Nathan says.

"But if we explain it all to him, I'm sure he'll see it's the right thing to do," Tank adds.

"He has to," Nathan says. "Webber is my only hope."

Thirty-Seven

Do Me A Favor

Nathan paces his room while clutching his lucky Nerf football in his hand. He knows Webber is due back from his class any minute, and this just might be the only time to catch him, as their schedules are typically opposite.

Finally, he hears the front door of their apartment open. Nathan's heart rate increases as he listens for the door to shut. He steps out of his room and goes slowly down the stairs. Webber has his nose deep in the refrigerator.

"Hey, Spidey."

Webber jumps. "Jesus, dude, you scared me."

"Sorry, buddy."

"You skipping class?" he asks.

"Um…well…"

Webber cuts in, "You okay, man?"

"Actually, I was wondering if I could talk to you."

Webber puts the cold cuts back in the refrigerator and closes it. "Sure."

Nathan motions for him to sit at their table. Webber does, and Nathan pulls out the chair adjacent to him.

"You're being kind of weird." Webber laughs.

"Sorry. I just need to tell you something."

"The suspense is killing me." He laughs again.

"Listen, over the past six months, I've done things that no one has known about."

"You rob a bank?"

"I'm serious, Spidey."

"Okay, okay. I'll keep my mouth shut."

"When Abby broke up with me—"

Webber cuts in, "I had a feeling this would be about her."

"It's always about her." Nathan tries to force a smile but can't. "I'm lost without her. I have tried to move on. I've even tried to pretend like I don't care that she is dating that guy. But every time I see them together, a knot forms in my stomach that never seems to go away. She doesn't notice that I'm around. But I see her all the time. I know which building her classes are in. I know when she gets coffee at the Union. I know which parties she'll be at and which ones she won't."

"Jesus, Nathan," he whispers.

"Pathetic, right?" he says, running his hand through his hair.

Webber tips his head, searching Nathan's face. "I'm not an authority on this kind of stuff—you know that."

"I know I screwed up. I got caught up in being so well-known on campus that, for a time, I took advantage of her."

"I think everyone does at some point."

"Maybe. Maybe not. But she deserved better than what I was giving to her."

"Sometimes, you need to lose something to realize how important it is to you." Webber chuckles. "Isn't that what people say?"

"Yeah, only, she started to hate me. She never wants to even talk to me. So, a part of me just gave up. She's dating someone new; she seems happy and all that, but still, I can't forget about her."

"Did you know she had gotten a job at that restaurant?"

Nathan nods his head. "I'm sorry I lied. I just needed to see her, and I wanted my friends with me for support."

"I get it."

"But the worst part of all of this is her inability to see me for the person she once knew. I never could figure out why she seemed to detest me."

"She did drop off pretty easily. It even surprised me. But throw Tank in the mix, and it was probably a good thing she got a break," Webber admits.

"I'll never disagree with that, but still, it hurts so bad. But I think I found out the reason."

"You did?"

"Yes. I'm asking you don't repeat this, okay?"

"Sure thing."

"She might have been given some misinformation on a situation I was involved in."

"What situation?"

"Poppy got pregnant, and Abby was told it was mine."

Webber slaps his hand over his mouth and then immediately drops it. "What the hell?!"

Eyes wide, Nathan quickly says, "I had nothing to do with it. I was just trying to help a friend in need, and the rumor got around that it was me."

"Dude, that sucks so bad."

"Yes. I feel terrible about the whole thing," Nathan says.

"That poor girl. Is she having the baby?"

"No. Miscarried, but I'm not even sure anyone knows that either."

"Wow. So, Abby thinks you got Poppy pregnant and that she's still having the baby?"

"Most likely."

"That's awful. I'm really sorry, Nathan."

"Me, too. But that's why I need your help."

"My help?"

"Yes. You need to find a time to get Abby alone. Then, I can finally talk to her."

"Wait. You want me to lie to her and trap her into seeing you?"

Nathan hems and haws for a moment and then finally says, "Yes, that is exactly what I want you to do."

Webber takes off his glasses, pinching the bridge of his nose. "How did you guys get so tied up in all of this?" he mumbles.

"But you can help me fix it. Please?" he begs.

"Fix it? What exactly are you trying to fix?"

"I'm not sure, but I have to at least see her face-to-face and tell her the truth."

"I agree, but what if it goes wrong, and then she's mad at me?" he says almost to himself.

Nathan pauses and waits for Webber to look at him. "Listen, I know how you've always felt about her. I realize the thought of her not being your friend is just as difficult. But this just might be the chance we all have in getting her back. Me, you, Tank, Laura. This might be what we need to mend all of our relationships."

"Even if that means nothing for you?" Webber asks.

"What do you mean?"

"What if she comes back to us, but…not you, Nathan?"

Nathan shakes his head. "It's all I think about. But I already lost her. The worst thing that could happen is she's over me, plain and simple. I can't do anything about that. I can't coerce her heart to feel something it doesn't." The sadness in his eyes is unmistakable. But the pain in his chest is far worse.

Over the past several months, he could have dated practically any girl at OSU. In fact, he's had more women throw themselves at him than he ever could have dreamed of. But not one of them compared to Abby.

Nathan couldn't recall a time in the past few months when Abby wasn't in the forefront of his mind. He knew she'd be hard to get over. But what he never could have expected was the way his pulse reacts each time he spots her on campus. The jealousy he feels when seeing her with Kelly consumes his thoughts. Particularly when he got injured this season and didn't have football to occupy his mind. Then, there was the matter of his body. After losing Abigail, he became so lonely. A few dates here and there did nothing for him. He compared everyone to her. Were they as sexy, as beautiful, as smart as Abby? Never. He couldn't find anyone who came close to all she was to him. He got laid only when he desperately needed to feel something other than despair. The number of women giving him the *you can have me if you want me* look truly nauseated him, but with the urging of his friends to move on, he'd bring home one after a party under the caveat that it would only be a one-night event.

The only one who really understands where he is coming from is his father. And even then, his own father only encourages him to try to find happiness while still young and in college. By no means does he tell him to sleep with random women, but he does lend advice that seeing what else is out there for him while he has the chance just might shed light on his future needs and wants. But he always feels so empty.

Until he can see her again.

Despite the pain that radiates in his soul, he still looks forward to catching a glimpse of her from across campus.

And now, he's desperate to see her. He must tell her the truth even if that exposes Poppy's secrets. He can't worry about that. Poppy is the reason their relationship ended. At least, that is what he has tried to convince himself. Because the truth of the matter is that with or without Poppy in his life, he still screwed up. You get a girl like Abigail Luna Price, and you don't mess that up by standing her up. Period. He must have known that eventually, despite her kindness, she wouldn't tolerate that from a boyfriend, which, if he's being honest, is exactly why he loves her.

With pitiful eyes, he glances at his friend.

"So, what do you say?" he asks Webber. "Will you help me?"

He can't blame Webber for hesitating. His stake in the game is great as well.

Finally, he says, "I will do it for you and…for her, so she can learn the truth. If nothing else, she deserves to know."

Nathan claps his hands together. "Thank you. You won't regret this. I'll make sure of that."

"I know you will. Now, where should we do this?"

"I need her in a place she'll feel comfortable and, more importantly, on neutral territory. But," he quickly adds, "I can't have anyone else around. What I need to tell her, no one else can hear."

Webber pauses, thinking to himself. The place he knows she won't hesitate to meet him at is the laboratory they work out of for their Chemistry class.

"Thursday, four o'clock, in the bottom of the Dixon East building. I'll tell her we need to work on our lab notebook."

"I'll be there. Thank you."

With that, Webber rises from the table, and with a gentle pat on Nathan's shoulder, he walks back to the refrigerator.

Nathan leans back in his chair. He knows that for Webber, the mere thought of lying to Abigail goes against everything he stands for. But Nathan must remind himself that what she thinks is the truth is a far greater crime than the one Webber is about to commit.

Thirty-Eight

Rumor Has It

Abigail rushes across campus after parking her car in the student lot. The wind whips across her cheeks, sending a shiver down her spine. She yanks the door ajar just in time to avoid another bluster of wind. The campus appears deserted in the winter mainly because if you are to survive in this part of New York, you must rush in between buildings to avoid the risk of frostbite.

The last days of the semester have forced her to spend endless hours studying for her finals. She wasn't the least bit surprised when Webber dialed her up, asking her to meet him to review their lab notebook before submitting it for their final grade. But she'd be lying if she said she wasn't looking forward to having dinner with Kelly tonight and *not* studying. She has put in enough homework time and has earned a night off.

She bounds down the stairs to the basement laboratory. Entering lab three, she finds Webber bent over a microscope.

"Hey!" she says.

His smile, while typically peculiar, notes a hint of sadness. But before she can ask him what is wrong, he says, "Hey there!" in a rather cheery voice.

"What are you working on?" she asks, placing her book bag on the bench across from him.

"I'm questioning our results on page seventy-two," he lies.

"Really?" she asks, pulling her notebook, a pencil, and her textbook out of her bag.

"Maybe," he lies again.

She reads over the page with great care. "I don't know, Webber; I think we got it right."

"You know me—I question our results. I can't help it."

"Well, I'd hate to think I'm right, and then we both get it wrong." She chuckles.

Abigail and Webber have been lab partners since they were assigned together first semester of their freshman year. They are both in the same major—veterinary science—and for the most part, by design, they have had every required class together for the past three years. They tend to know one another's work ethic, responses, and love of science.

"Let me look." She comes around the lab bench toward Webber.

He pushes the microscope toward her. She leans over, and with one eye, she reviews the slide with the specimen.

"I'm confident it's bacillus," she says as she stands back up.

"Oh, duh. I thought we wrote micrococcus," he says, forcing a laugh. He glances at the clock again.

After they review a few more pages, the door to the lab creaks open. The two glance up from their notebooks as Nathan enters the room. He's well dressed in a dark wool coat; his cheeks are flush from the cool air but are soft and shaven. His wavy, dark hair is pushed back perfectly from his face. It's the best she has seen him look in a long time. Nathan locks eyes with hers as he confidently walks straight toward them.

Webber hates the treacherous gasp that escapes Abigail's lips.

"What's he doing here?" she whispers.

"No idea," he lies and then adds loudly, "Hey, Nathan."

Abigail begins to close her book. "I should be going," she says to Webber.

As he approaches, Nathan replies, "Please stay for a minute."

"What's this about?" she directs at Webber.

With sorrowful eyes, he says, "I'm not sure."

"You're lying," she says.

He quickly gathers his things, and with a painfully swift move, he says, "I'm so sorry." Webber hurries toward the exit, nearly knocking over a lab stool in the process as he pushes open a door and leaves without looking back.

Abigail scrambles to get her belongings back into her bag, but by the time she's moving, Nathan is blocking her path to the exit.

"Can you please move?" she says.

"Abby," he begs, "you need to listen to what I have to say, and then you're free to go."

"You've got some nerve, asking me for anything."

"You have some nerve, treating me like shit for the past six months."

"*Me*?!"

"Yeah, you." He knows the only way to prevent her from storming out is to provoke her into conversing with him.

Well, he's not going to get that satisfaction today.

She's too proud not to stand up for what she thinks is fundamentally true. Even though she's wrong. Dead wrong.

"Just because I don't want to talk to you anymore…" She fades off.

"There was a time," he begins, "when you never would have *not* given me the benefit of the doubt. Oh, wait," he says. "Except the time you thought I was the reason Tank got kicked off the football team. Do you remember when jumping to such a conclusion seemed appropriate to you? And look how very far from the truth you were."

"That was a long time ago." She crosses her arms over her chest. "Why are you here, Nathan?" she says with narrowed eyes.

"Listen, I'm not here to try and win you back," he lies.

She scoffs at his words.

"But I am here to set the record straight. I might not have always been a good boyfriend. But I never cheated on you."

She interrupts him by asking, "How would you feel if you came to my house in the middle of the night and found someone in my room?"

"You mean, like the night you came to the hotel?" he asks.

"Exactly."

"So, are you saying Kelly didn't go to your room that very same night to console you?"

Her cheeks flush red. This happens when she is caught in a situation she knows she can't get out of. "What?" she says.

"Don't bother saying it didn't happen. I heard it from him."

"Well, I didn't invite him," she says gruffly.

"Like that matters."

"Nathan, you've obviously moved on and…"

"And what?"

She stutters, "So have I."

"I never slept with Poppy," he blurts out.

Her eyes get wide. "That's impossible," she adds.

"No, actually, it's not. I would know after all."

"But…"

"But what?" He wants to hear her say it.

"I…I…" She swallows hard. Her lips trembling.

"Whoever told you that I was the one who got Poppy pregnant should be in big trouble right now. But since that person is *your* friend—scratch that, *our friend*, I'm not going to say anything."

Her jaw drops.

He continues, "The magnitude of misinformation you got astounds me, Abby. But what hurts me the most is that *you* had a choice. You could have asked me about it, *or* you could have treated me like someone you never knew. The fact that you chose the latter almost breaks my heart as much as you did the day you broke up with me."

Finding her voice, she quips, "How could I have asked you that? Tell me!"

He leans in close to her, and with anger in his voice, he replies, "You didn't even try."

She steps back. "No, I didn't. I chose to believe what was presented to me, coupled with you disappearing on me to spend time with her and her groupie friends. So, yes, I believed it! I still—"

"It's not fucking true!" he yells.

She staggers back. "You know, you and Tank are both the same…"

He laughs. "You and I both know his heart is always in the right place. I get that you two are in some sort of tiff right now, but to throw him under the bus when he's not here to defend himself is beneath even you, Abby."

It's like a punch in the gut. But she recovers quickly. "Is that so?" she challenges.

"Yeah."

"Well, you forcing Webber to trap me in the lab so you can talk to me is beneath you!"

"You left me no choice!" he says with a frustrated bang of his fist on the lab counter.

"Just like you left me no choice. No choice *but* to believe the rumors."

He jerks backward. "Maybe, all along, it was you who gave up on me."

"What?"

"You had someone waiting in the wings to sweep you off your feet. I had no one."

"You're being crazy."

Only he's not. Like a light going off above his head, he steps away from her. And with a lower voice, he says, "No, it all makes sense to me now. You believed it because you wanted to make it easier on yourself. You needed to justify pushing us all away. It was easier for you to walk right into your new life than deal with the people who know you the best."

"So, I'm to blame for the choices you made? This is insane, and I don't have to stand here and listen to this anymore." She pushes past him, but he grabs her arm. Stopping her from leaving. "Let go of me."

"I will. But look at me before you storm out of here," he demands in a much softer voice, forcing her to gaze up at him.

"Say what you need to say." Despite her wishing them away, the tears sting her eyes regardless.

"I came here today to tell you that it wasn't me. But that I did want to help her. She needed someone's help to get through something so horrible and shocking. So, if that makes me a bad person, I can live with that. But what I can't live with is someone who used to love me believing for one second that I am such a careless person." His voice quivers. "So, now, you know the truth, and you can do whatever you want with that."

She swallows hard. "Nathan, I..."

He releases her arm from his grip and steps past her. She's at a loss for words as he walks away.

Before pulling open the door, he turns and says, "She miscarried, by the way. And the guy who was yelling at her at the party the other night? That's the guy who got her pregnant. He's a real jerk. So, now, you have the full picture. What was I supposed to do when she came to me for help? The worst feeling in the world is to think you have no one. I, more than anyone, know what that feels like."

He pushes open the door with force, and before she can even form a sentence, he's long gone. She sinks into the lab bench chair and buries her head in her hands as the tears pour through her fingertips.

The surmountable flow of information that was just thrown at her overwhelms her.

It's difficult enough when you've spent the better part of half a year believing that the person you once knew and loved is someone totally different, only to be confronted with the truth later. And by truth, it is exactly what your heart believed all along. But your head got in the way.

I believed he was someone else. But deep down, I knew I had to be wrong. Why didn't I trust my gut? Why didn't I confront him? Why didn't I dig deeper? Was he right in saying it was just easier for me to let them all go and to hang on to that anger for them instead of confronting my fears? My fear of the truth? No matter what that was?

But I'm with Kelly now. I'm happy. He loves me.

Then, the roller-coaster ride shoots off the tracks, and her sadness turns to anger as quickly as Nathan came and went.

How dare he come in here and blame it all on me! He was the one hanging out with Poppy all the time. So much so that I couldn't help but believe it was true. If he hadn't put himself out there like that, I never would have believed the rumor.

He has some nerve, turning this around on me.

She grabs her bag, wipes the wet from her skin, and exits the building. She must meet Kelly in thirty minutes for dinner. But the thought of seeing anyone right now seems painful to her.

All those rumors dispelled in the blink of an eye. And I'm left holding the bag.

Thirty-Nine

Truth and Lies

Abigail hopes that Courtney is bartending at Monroe's. She needs to take a minute or two to calm her nerves before spending the evening with Kelly.

She pulls open the door and waltzes in. Immediately, she goes to the restroom to touch up her makeup.

Once she's satisfied she no longer appears as though she has been crying, she heads to the bar.

"Hey, girl!" Courtney boasts.

"Hey." She forces a smile.

"You meeting Kelly here?"

"Nope. I just stopped in for a drink before dinner," she lies.

"What can I get you?" She tosses a coaster on the wood bar top as Abigail takes a seat.

"A Diet Coke, please."

"Sure thing."

Abigail mindlessly picks at a string on her sweater. The amount of information that she is forced to digest makes her want to choke on it.

Courtney places the glass in front of her, and without even glancing at it, Abigail reaches for it, drinking down half the glass in one gulp.

"Hey, I'm glad you stopped in because I wanted to say"—Courtney leans over the bar and uses a hushed voice—"it was really messed up what Aniston did. I'm so sorry you were on the receiving end of that."

With wide eyes, Abigail says, "It was more than *messed up*."

"I know. I know. I'm friends with her, but there's a dark side to her. It's not the side I care for."

"How could she do that? She's crazy."

"Yeah, well, jealousy is a nasty thing."

Abigail's blood begins to boil yet again today. "She'd better stay far away from me—*and* Kelly for that matter. She got away lightly this time," Abigail says with a pound of her fist on the bar.

"Bad day?" a voice queries from behind her.

She spins slightly. Her cheeks flush. Jason, the backup quarterback, is beside her, pulling out the stool next to her.

"Hey, Jason."

"Haven't seen you in a while," he remarks. It's clear he didn't hear her conversation with Courtney.

"Yeah, I know."

"What have you been up to?" he asks.

"Not much. School. Work."

"Yeah, you work at the restaurant, right?"

"Diesel Food. Yeah."

"Nathan told me." The mention of his name halts the conversation momentarily.

"Listen, I know it is none of my business…" She is about to tell him it most certainly isn't when he quickly adds, "But, damn, that guy is lost without you. I think the only reason I got to play this year is that he was so unfocused that he was doing shit no one could explain. He went from confident to total mush this season."

She gulps down her soda.

He continues, "I'm not trying to make you feel bad. You have every right to move on with your life."

She whispers, "Sometimes, it doesn't feel that way."

"You've been a good friend to the team for a few years now. That includes Tank when no one else would give that guy the time of day. So, I get it. We all need a break. But I guess I hope to see you around more. Honestly, they both seemed so much happier with you in their lives. Sounds corny, but it's pretty evident to anyone with eyes." He chuckles.

She turns in her stool to face him, and she asks, "Does he still talk about me?" In a million years, she'll never be sure why she asked Jason that question.

"You know, that's probably a better question to ask him."

"Please, just tell me."

"Yeah, Abby. He does. Often. It's like he can't help himself."

"But why?"

"Because he couldn't comprehend why you stopped talking to him, and I think it ate away at him." He crinkles his face. "This isn't meant to make you feel bad. It's just the truth."

"The truth," she whispers. She stares ahead. Her mind racing with all kinds of unpleasant thoughts.

Sensing the need to change the subject, Jason asks, "How's Bree?"

She whips her head up and notes the smile on his face. "You're really smitten with her, aren't you?"

"I've always held out hope." He laughs. "I figured if she knew I was interested, then maybe she'd come around."

Lying through her teeth so as not to shatter his dream, she says, "You never know, Jason."

Jason checks his watch, finishes his beer, and then pats Abigail on the back. "Well, I should get going," he says.

"It was nice to see you." She smiles.

"You, too. Don't be a stranger, okay?"

"I'll try." He goes to pay Courtney when Abigail adds, "I insist. It was nice chatting with you."

He nods at her and then exits out of the bar.

Abigail glances up at Courtney with a shrug of her shoulders.

"I take it, you know him?" she asks with a smile.

"Yeah, seems so long ago, but it really hasn't been," Abigail replies.

"Glass of wine on the house"—Courtney chuckles—"since my friend is an asshole." Courtney turns to grab the bottle of red off the shelf. As she spins back toward Abigail, her face drops.

"What is it?" Abigail says, following her stare toward the doorway.

"Oh no," Courtney mumbles.

The two women observe Aniston waltzes through the door, followed by another girl Abigail recognizes from a party, and then as if the day wasn't bad enough, Kelly follows them in.

"What the fu—" escapes her mouth.

Aniston notices her first, and the smile that spreads across her smug face is enough to make Abigail's fists clench. And then Kelly locks eyes with her. His expression could only be described as terrified.

Aniston and her friend take a seat at a table near the back. Kelly, while seemingly confident, approaches the bar.

"Kelly," Courtney says.

"Courtney." He reaches out his hand, touching Abigail's shoulder. She moves quickly. "Don't be like that," he says under his breath.

Not wanting to cause a scene, she peeks at him out of the corner of her eye and says under her breath, "Don't."

Looking up at Courtney, he says, "Three beers, please."

Courtney spins and heads toward the cooler.

A gasp escapes Abigail's lips.

"I can explain."

"Don't bother." She raises her glass to her lips.

"Don't you think you owe me more than this?" he hisses.

She whips her head up, fighting back her tears, as she is certain Aniston and her friend are watching them as though this were some sort of soap opera. "I tried calling you…twice," he scolds. "But I gather, you've been here?"

"I was about to leave. I thought we had dinner plans?"

"We did—I mean, we do," he corrects.

Just then a voice travels from across the room. "Kelly?" she coos. "Can we have our beers?"

Before he can respond, Abigail says, "Go, Kelly. Don't keep the girl who slashed my tires waiting."

Courtney pushes them closer to Kelly. "Take these," she says with an edge. "I don't want any issues here," she warns.

Kelly doesn't move.

Abigail pulls some money out of her pocket and places it on the bar. "You're making this worse," she says through gritted teeth. When Kelly still won't move, Abigail stands, says good-bye to Courtney, and walks straight out the door.

"What the hell was that about?" Courtney asks.

"I'll explain later," he says, taking the beers from the bar.

Courtney yells after him, "That's screwed up, Conrad."

He peers over his shoulder, a distraught expression on his face.

Aniston smiles as he approaches the table. "Little Miss Prissy upset?" she says with a pout of her lower lip.

"Shut up, Aniston," he barks.

"Whoa. Don't get all jacked up on me. It was your idea to come here."

"Like I had a choice," he whines and then pulls deeply on the bottle of beer.

"Slow down," she warns. "You'll get sick."

I wish that would happen. In fact, I wish much worse would happen to me right now.

Her friend gives Kelly a sympathetic glance, but that won't help his current situation. And the only reason he is in this current situation is because of Aniston. She stopped by his house, unannounced, this afternoon and threatened him.

"Kelly, if you don't hang out with me, then I will press charges. And you know me. I'll do it," she said.

"What the hell are you talking about?" he said.

"I have pictures. And I told several people about the things you did. Do you really want that hanging over your head? You think Harvard wants to know about this?"

"You wouldn't dare!"

"You sure you want to try me? I slashed her tires; you really think I wouldn't do this?"

"You know I hate you, right?"

"I like to think of our relationship as more of a love-hate."

"That's insane," he says.

"So, it's a date then."
"Fuck you, Aniston."

"So, listen to this," Aniston says, ignoring the tension between them all.

For the next twenty minutes, Aniston rambles on about how she and some girl in one of her classes became friends with this dork in order to steal his project thesis and use it for their own work. They pretend to like him, so they sit near him and cheat off his tests. It amazes Kelly that at this level, people still need to cheat. You don't know the subject matter? You shouldn't be in the class. But the sickest part of it all is that Aniston's friend said she'd pin it on this unsuspecting guy in her seminar in a heartbeat if it came down to it. A guy she describes as nerdy and in desperate need of getting laid. So much so that he'd do just about anything for a pretty girl.

Poor bastard. Guys will do anything for sex. It's sad.

The story sickens Kelly to his core.

At some point near the end of her story, he waves to Courtney to bring another round, much to Aniston's delight. He'll do whatever he can to make time pass.

But all the while, the only thing Kelly can think about is how badly he screwed up and that getting out of this one just might be the hardest thing he'll have to do.

Two hours later, several beers, and way past the dinner, Kelly rises to his feet. "I need to go," he says, pretending to wobble from side to side.

"Whoa, Kelly." Aniston giggles. "Let me help you home."

All too quickly, he answers, "No. I mean, not necessary. Tom is picking me up." He squints over in Courtney's direction and waves, keeping his charade going. "If you see Courtney, tell her good-bye," he says, stumbling, only to catch himself on the chair.

"She's right there, silly." Aniston laughs.

Again, he squints. "Oh, right."

He turns back to them. "Ladies, good night," he says with a fake tip of his nonexistent hat.

Kelly, trying not to rush toward the door, but yanks it open and steps into the freezing night air. Within seconds of beginning the long walk home, he hears, "Kelly, wait!"

Reluctantly, he turns. Aniston approaches him. "I think you forgot your promise," she says as she runs the tips of her fingers up his collar toward his rigid jawline.

Shit.

"Well?" she coos.

"Oh, right," he stammers. "Um…"

"Let me remind you."

Before his mind can catch up, her lips are pressed firmly on his. Her tongue pushes into his mouth, and he tries with all his might not to gag as she moans.

He squeezes his eyes so tightly, like a child wishing away a nightmare. She finally pulls back from him. He quickly retreats.

"You should get inside," he urges. "It's cold."

She smiles and winks at him. "See you later, Kelly."

As soon as she's gone, he spits on the sidewalk and then wipes away her taste with the back of his hand.

He pulls up the collar on his jacket as the snow begins to fall. He trudges up toward campus, cutting through the main walkways toward her house.

The alcohol has made his body temperature drop. No gloves or a hat don't help either. Finally, he approaches her driveway. Her car is where it was all day. Thankfully, all the other cars are gone. He can see the light in her bedroom is on, and a shadow of a slender figure is in the bay window. The window she likes to sit in when she is reading or needs to think. He climbs up the fire escape, nearly slipping and plunging to the earth as he scales up the side of her house.

He arrives at the top and taps on her window. With the snow coating thickly on the metal beneath his feet, he shivers and taps again. "Abigail, please. It's freezing out!"

He hears footsteps, and then he makes out her image as she approaches the window. She cracks it open just enough for him to get his fingers underneath and pull it open.

He steps inside, trying not to shake the snow off in her room. "Thank you for letting me in."

She scoffs, "As if I had a choice."

"Okay, I deserve that."

"What do you want, Kelly?"

He steps toward her. She looks down at her floor, and his eyes wander down as well.

He notices the wet on the floor. He kicks off his shoes and puts them on the rug near her door. Then, he takes his jacket off and hangs it on the hook on the back of her door. "Sorry."

She crosses her arms over her chest, scowling at him as he tries to take her towel and wipe the floor dry.

She sighs. He glances up at her, dropping the towel.

"Listen, I'm sorry about tonight," he says.

"Sorry for what exactly?"

"I never wanted you to see that," he says softly.

"See what?"

"Me...with her."

"How could you do that to me?" she asks as tears form in her eyes.

He steps closer. "Listen to me. She made me."

"What? How?"

"She told me she would press charges…for what I did." He hangs his head.

"Are you serious?" she yelps. "She's the one who slashed my tires. All four of them!"

"I know. But it doesn't erase what I did."

She narrows her eyes. "I don't care, Kelly. And besides, I'm the one she did it to, and then you went and hung out with her?"

"What should I have done?" he cries as he frustratingly pulls at his hair.

"Tell her I'll press charges. How about that?!"

"Abigail, that's not you, and I can't let her fuck with my future. That's what she is trying to do. Ruin me."

She sinks on her couch, resting her head in her hands. Then, she mumbles through her hands, "Were you just going to stand me up tonight?"

She can sense him move closer toward her. He leans down on his knees in front of her, taking one of her hands away from her face.

"I don't know," he admits.

Hurt fills her eyes as a tear drops on her cheek.

"I've made you cry," he sighs. "I fucked up so badly."

"Yeah, you did."

He wipes the wet from her cheek.

"Don't," she says.

"What can I do?" he asks.

"That's not fair to ask me, Kelly. You made your choices."

"But I truly felt like I had no option. She threatened us, and I couldn't let her do that."

She averts her eyes. "What did she ask of you…in return?"

"What do you mean?"

"A person like that doesn't do anything without thinking she'll get something in return."

"You're right. She wants me back. Plain and simple."

She gasps. "So, that is it then. That's how you were going to have me find out?!"

"No, no. I told her I couldn't."

"I don't understand. Why were you there with her?"

"To appease her. I told her I'd hang out with her. In a public place and…" His voice defies him and fades off.

"What, Kelly?" Tears drip down her face as she tries to blink them away.

He hangs his head, uncertain if he should tell her, but also, he's in fear Aniston will be all too willing to boast about it. "Abigail, you know how I feel about you. This has really gotten out of hand." He takes her hand. "Please."

She tries to pull her hand back. Instead of waiting for him to tell her, she asks, "Did you touch her?" Her bottom lip quivers.

"She…she kissed me." He squeezes her hand as she tries to pull away again. "But she knows I don't want her…that I only want you."

Abigail swallows hard, trying to fight back the urge to full-on cry. "What am I supposed to do with that information?"

"Nothing. Please," he begs. "You're supposed to know she means nothing to me and that I've only done this for you. To make sure she will leave us alone."

"But it's not working," she whispers through her sobs.

"Abigail, please let me make this right."

With all the information that has been thrown at her today, she can't merely contemplate what to do with all these feelings brewing inside of her.

He tries to wrap his arms around her waist.

"Kelly, you can't just make me forgive you, not this time."

He whips his head up. "Don't say that. I made a huge mistake—I get that. But you were at the bar, too. We had plans and—"

"It's not the same. I wanted some time alone—that's all."

He cocks his head. "Do you still feel that way?"

She stands up, pushing him off her. She paces her room. Leaving him sitting on the ground. Finally, she spins to meet his stare. "How would you feel if I told you that Nathan kissed me?"

His cheeks redden. "Why would you bring him up?" he barks.

"Isn't it the same?"

"Not even close. She never meant anything to me." He scrambles to his feet. "But you do."

"Then, why would you even allow her the chance to come in between us?"

"I won't anymore, I promise."

"How can you guarantee that?"

"I'll reason with her. That's all I can do."

"She's beyond reason."

"But I'll try," he whispers.

The silence between them is thick. They can only stand there, feet apart from one another, but it might as well be miles between them. Exhaustion is settling into Abigail's bones, and the thought of closing her eyes and putting an end to this day is more appealing than anything else. The streetlight across the way illuminates the hard fall of the snow.

As though it is putting her in a trance, she asks, "Is your car here?"

"No."

"Where is it?"

"Home."

"Did she pick you up?"

"Yeah."

"Wow," she says.

"I don't want to leave," he adds. "Please. I need to know that you don't hate me."

"Hate you? I don't hate you, Kelly."

He exhales. "Can…can I touch you?" he asks as he steps closer to her, reaching his arms out.

Everything in her soul tells her to just put him out of his misery and hug him. Reassure him that everything will be okay. But she can't. She can only envision Aniston and him lip-locked, and it kills her.

"She kissed you?" she says under her breath again.

"I hated every second of it. But don't you see? I would do anything to get her to leave me alone. I only want to be with you."

Abigail steps back toward the window she was sitting in less than an hour before, contemplating her next move. She sits back on the ledge and wraps the blanket back around her. She rests her head on the wall, noticing the heavy snow accumulate on the power lines leading to the house.

"You can stay here tonight. I just need some time to think," she says, never turning to face him.

"I promise you, it won't happen again," he whispers.

She doesn't respond or move.

Only silence fills the room. Until moments later, she can hear him undressing and then the creak of her bed.

A few more minutes pass, and then with marked sadness, he says, "Come to bed soon, please."

"I will," she lies.

My life used to be so much less complicated and carefree. And now, in a span of one day, I find out more information than my brain can possibly handle. Sometimes, I don't even know if I'm angry or sad and who I'm angry with or sad about. All I know is that the thought of being alone is more appealing to me than I ever imagined it would be. If only my heart would catch up to what my mind is thinking, I might actually be able to do something about it.

Forty

Time to Talk

Abigail sat in the window until she heard the soft hum of Kelly's breathing. She crawled onto the couch, pulling the blankets on top of her, and finally closed her eyes around three in the morning.

When she wakes only hours later, Kelly is still fast asleep. She dresses in warm clothes and then quietly goes down the stairs to find the house empty. She puts on a pot of coffee and waits for it to brew.

She thumbs through a magazine and finally hears the beep of the finished pot. She pours herself a large cup, knowing she'll need the energy to get through the day. Thankfully, she only has one final today, and then she will be done for the weekend.

She contemplates waking Kelly up. But she knows that might only start another deep conversation, and right now, she needs to focus on school. *The reason I'm here. I must put all the drama behind me and concentrate on my academics.* She forgoes waking him and leaves a note by the coffeepot instead.

Made coffee for you. Had to get to my final. I'll call you later.

Abigail

Her car is buried under a foot of snow. So, she decides to walk to campus instead of fighting over limited parking spaces, piled with snow. She gets to the science building with enough time to settle in and focus her mind on the subject matter.

The exam takes her less than three hours to complete. As she departs the building, she runs into Logan as he exits the adjacent building.

"Abby! How are you?"

She musters a smile. "Great. You?"

"Good. Just finishing up my finals today. Two more to go."

"I have a few more next week," she adds.

"Bummer. They'll be done soon enough. In fact, I'm heading to the Union to study before my next one."

"Cool." She pauses, and then for some reason, she asks, "Is Nathan okay?"

He cocks his head. "He's okay. I think."

"Oh, good."

"He doesn't have any finals today," he adds, giving Abigail a soft expression. "You know, I think he's just hanging out at the apartment."

"I see."

"Well, I'll catch you later," he says with a slight wave and then heads toward the Union.

Abigail trudges through the snow-covered pathways of campus and then stops in her tracks. She glances up the street toward the direction of her house and then almost immediately glances across campus toward Parkers Village. Her feet decide for her, and the next thing she knows, she is crossing campus and heading toward the student apartments. The storm last night made for a beautiful winter's day, one of those bright sun-shining days that almost makes you forget how cold it is. She pulls up the hood on her ski jacket as a puff of wind catches her across the face, quickly reminding her.

She nears Nathan's place and takes a deep breath in. She is uncertain as to why she is even here. A quiet knock is all she can muster on their apartment door. She can hear footsteps. With each one, her heart rate increases, and then the door pulls open.

Tank is standing before her in a T-shirt and sweatpants. His jaw drops open, and she is more than certain he never expected her to be at his door.

"Hey," he pushes out, a concerned expression on his face.

"Hey," she whispers.

She is about to ask if Nathan is here when she hears a familiar voice call from the living room. "Is that our food delivery?" Laura yells.

Tank's eyes get wide. Abigail leans past him and in disbelief sees Laura come waltzing toward her. Laura freezes in her path.

Before a word can be spoken, Nathan bounds down the stairs and adds, "Food here?" His eyes meet hers, but he blinks them hard, as if the vision in front of him is not real. Then, finally, he says, "Abby?"

She can't even think of a word to say as she takes in the sight of not one, not two, but three of her former friends all together.

"Um, I'll…I should go," she says as she spins on her heel and heads back in the direction she came.

"Wait, Abby," Nathan yells after her.

She can hear them all arguing that they should be the ones to chase after her.

But Abigail wants none of them to.

The sound of the hard crunch of the snow gains on her, and before she can react, a firm hand is on her shoulder, pulling her to stop.

"Wait, please," he begs.

But it's too late for her to try to stop her tears. She can't face him, so he steps in front of her.

"Please, Abby. Just wait for a second..."

With so many things to talk about and explain, she has no clue where to begin.

"Why are you here?" he asks. He starts to wipe away her tears, but he hesitates.

"I...I..." she stutters. "I made a mistake."

She tries to walk past him, but again, he grabs her arm.

"Please, just sit." He points to a bench under the enclosed shuttle stop on the edge of the sidewalk. He carefully guides her over to it. He zips up his jacket and secures his loose boot, as he was forced to dress so quickly to run after her.

Like strangers waiting for the bus, they sit and stare across Parkers Village.

He clears his throat. "Did you come to talk to me?"

"Yes," she admits. "But what did I see back at your place?"

He disregards her question and turns slightly on the bench. "I want to know why you came to see me," he pleads.

She looks up at him. His eyes are sad yet soft, and she knows she needs to at least answer him.

"I wanted to talk to you about the other day. The way we left it. I-I..." she stutters. "I needed to tell you that I'm sorry, Nathan. And that, yes, I believed what was told to me."

"I understand. But I don't, you know?"

"What?"

"See, for me, I can't help but think of all the times we could have spent being friends, and it was wasted on hurt feelings, anger, and for me, a lot of confusion."

"I don't know what to say other than I made a huge mistake."

"Yeah, but I did, too."

"You did?" she asks.

"I never should have taken you for granted. I'll forever be sorry for how I behaved. You deserved so much better than I was giving you."

"It's in the past," she whispers.

"Yep," he says sadly.

"Why was she in your hotel room that night?"

"Because I was a fool. I believed that I could still be friends with her despite her interest in me. Everyone hops from room to room after games to blow off steam and have some fun. But she was always waiting for me.

Wondering if or when I'd leave you for her. Regardless of how many times I told her it wasn't going to happen."

"You should've only had to tell her once," she scolds.

"I know, believe me. But I think she came to my room that night to tell me she was pregnant, and then when you got there, it sent the evening into a spiral."

"Sorry," she says sarcastically.

Ignoring her, he continues, "Somehow, I felt responsible for her. I'd kept pushing her away. Telling her to find someone. And so, eventually, she had, and she'd ended up with that jerk—and in the worst position possible." He hangs his head.

Before she can comprehend what she's doing, she gently touches his arm. A feeling, like a distant memory, rushes over her, and as soon as they lock eyes, she pulls her hand away. "Sorry."

He whispers, "No, don't be."

His face, still as handsome as she remembers it being, longingly stares at her, and she must look away.

"Does she know that I know?" she asks.

"No, I didn't tell her. I think she's been through enough."

"And what about Casey?"

"She should be fired for what she did. But because she was only looking out for you, I won't tell anyone."

"Thank you," she whispers.

"But next time you hear a rumor about me, will you please just come and ask me?" His voice pleads with her.

"Yes, I will."

"Good."

Abigail lets out a deep sigh. "But I also came here because something you said to me really hit me hard the other day."

"What was that?"

"You said I gave up to make things easier for me, so I could simply walk away. I've been trying to think hard about if that's what I did."

"I'm sorry I said that. I was angry."

"But maybe you were right."

"Oh."

"Because sometimes, being in your shadow or being known as *just* Nathan's girlfriend was hard. Being stood up while you were out being a social god on campus did suck for me. Or seeing girls like Poppy fall all over you weekend after the weekend was excruciating to watch. And I'd be lying if I said I was never attracted to Kelly while all this was happening. He paid attention to me, you know. And honestly, Tank bullying me did make me want to run for the hills, too. So, yeah, maybe the idea of starting a new life seemed appealing to me."

Nathan swallows hard.

"But if you think for one second that I've escaped any of it, you're wrong. I go into the Union, and your poster is hanging over my head. Poppy's, too. I turn on the radio, and they're talking about OSU football, you, Tank, and the game week after week. Melissa's writing articles about you in *The Weekly Blue* and talking to Laura about it on the radio. I live with both of them. Talk about not escaping it." She slightly chuckles.

"Oh," he whispers.

She continues, "And Webber is your roommate, but he's one of my best friends, and he's in all my classes. He's an extension of you. So, it's not possible there either. And then I stood in line at the grocery store three weeks ago, and the two kids in front of me were talking about your injury the entire time. I had to listen to every word of it. A student at the restaurant told me the other day to wish you good luck in the game. And the worst of it, I went to Kelly's, and some guy recognized me and said that he knew I was dating you. Talk about a slap in the face." She exhales. "Well, I think you get my point."

His steel-gray eyes soften. "Yeah, I definitely get your point." Then, she catches a slight smile from him as he asks, "Just curious, did Kelly hear the guy say that?"

"*Nathan.*"

"He did, didn't he? Bet that really got to him." He chuckles, and she playfully slaps him on the arm. "Sorry."

"But now, you get it. I never just walked away, Nathan. I couldn't. Everywhere I go, there you are. And you must know how hard it was for me to break up with you. It wasn't because I stopped loving you. It was because I didn't want to stop having good thoughts about you. And that night in the hotel, I did. But then when I heard that about Poppy, I had no choice but to rip you out of my heart. I can't even tell you how I felt. The thought of the two of you together…"

He puts his hand up. "Please don't," he begs, shaking his head. "I can't. I'm familiar with the feeling."

"Right." Her cheeks pink.

He's probably imagined her and Kelly. They've both felt it.

"So," he whispers, "here we are."

She sighs. "Yeah, here we are."

There is silence between them, but neither one of them wants to move.

Finally, Abigail starts to stand, but Nathan gently clasps her hand. She doesn't pull away. He stands with her.

"Can I ask you something?" he says.

She peers down at their intertwined hands.

He releases his touch. "Are you in some kind of trouble?"

"What?"

"Your tires? I saw your car. Who would do that to you?"

Her cheeks redden. "It's taken care of."

"I'm worried about you. How could anyone not like you enough to do that? Is he a bad guy or something?"

"No, it's complicated, Nathan. But I'm fine."

"Promise?" he pleads.

"Yes, Nathan." She contemplates telling him about Aniston, her jealousy, and all the confusion surrounding them, but knowing she has not resolved it all with Kelly first seems wildly unfair to him. "I should get going."

"Wait. Before you go, I need to know something."

She spins to face him. "What?"

"Does he make you happy, Abby?"

Before, yes. Now, not as much. But it's too involved of a story to tell you.

"I don't feel comfortable talking about this with you," she says.

"I understand. And this might sound crazy, but I really hope he does."

Her mouth drops a bit. "You do?"

"Yeah." He lowers his head, and his tall frame hunches forward. "Because you're the best, Abby. No one compares to you, and so I can only hope you're happy."

A breath escapes her lips. "I…I didn't know you felt that way."

He laughs uncomfortably and runs his fingers through his hair. She can see his cheeks flush as he says as quietly as possible, "You know I've always thought that. Nothing has changed."

A tear escapes her eye. She wipes it quickly, but he already noticed.

"That's not to make you sad," he adds. "It's my truth."

"Oh, Nathan," she says.

"It's okay. You don't have to say anything to me. You're dating someone else, and I have to respect that."

Trying to reduce the heat between them, she asks, "And you? Have you been seeing anyone?"

She holds her breath for the answer.

He again laughs uneasily. "Is it pathetic if I say no?"

Relieved, she says quickly, "No. Of course not. I guess I'm just surprised—that's all."

"A few dates here and there, but I just always compare them to you, if I'm being honest."

Now, it's her turn for her cheeks to turn pink. "I'm sorry if I've inadvertently stood in your way."

"Don't be. It was—I mean, it *is* my choice."

"I want you to be happy, too."

With a crooked smile, he says, "Someday, I will be. It feels good to talk to you like this. I always held out hope that we'd talk again one day."

"Me, too. Nathan. I hope you know that."

"I do now, and that's all that matters."

"Good. Well, I'll let you get back to your lunch."

He smirks and then asks, "Can I give you a hug?"

She smiles and says, "Of course."

As he leans down toward her, butterflies twist in her stomach, and a familiar sensation tingles over her spine. A touch as simple as a hug brings back so many memories for her.

Nathan lets a soft, satisfied moan escape his lips.

Neither is willing to let go first. She breathes in his familiar scent. Then, she places her hand to the back of his head, and on her tippy-toes, she softly brushes her lips onto his cheek.

A little startled by her affection, he releases her. "I'll, um, see you around?" he asks.

"Yeah, you will."

He gives her a slight wave and then turns, disappearing around the corner and back toward his apartment. She waits for a moment longer, trying to digest her thoughts and their conversation.

Then, she hears the soft squeak of car brakes behind her. She turns and is completely frozen as Kelly's car stops only inches from where she stands.

Forty-One

Are You the One?

Kelly rolls down the car window. The expression on his handsome face sends a shiver down her spine.

"Need a ride?" he asks jokingly.

Trying to seem upbeat, she says, "Sure." She walks around to the passenger side and gets in.

"How was your final?" he asks.

"Oh, fine, thanks."

He pulls out of the apartments and down toward his street.

"What are you doing today?" he asks.

"Nothing."

"I'd like to show you something."

"Really? Okay."

She observes him as he nervously strums his fingertips on the steering wheel. The car is filled with silence otherwise. Abigail is quiet because she is unsure of what Kelly might have witnessed transpire between her and Nathan and also due to the uncertainty as to where they stand, considering she never went to bed last night.

He pulls into his driveway and parks the car. He nods to her to follow him.

She gets out of the car, playing with her fingers as she enters the house, unsure of what she is walking into.

"It's upstairs," he says.

"All right," she says as she pads up the stairs behind him.

He pushes open the door, and unlike all the other times they have fought and ended up in his room, he quietly waits for her to enter. Then, he closes the door softly behind him. He doesn't pin her up against the door. He doesn't kiss her passionately. He's different, and it is completely freaking her out.

He motions for her to sit on his bed.

Trying to appear normal, she unzips her coat, pulls it off, and lays it next to her as she sits on his mattress. He pulls out his desk chair and sits to face her. The tension between them is obvious by his lack of affection.

He runs his hands over his face, rubbing the stubble on his chin. Finally, his eyes meet hers. "I'm just going to cut to it," he says.

She swallows hard. Her throat tightens as she nods her head.

"You never came to bed last night. Do you realize that was the first time you and I have not slept in the same bed while we were in the same room?"

"Oh," she says.

"And what I came to realize is that I hated it so badly."

"Kelly, I—"

"Please, Abigail. I need to get this off my chest."

"Okay."

"Part of the reason I hated it so much is because I've always feared it. Maybe so much so that I've unknowingly screwed up because, somehow, in the end, I figured it would all go south."

He sighs and then continues, "I've never told anyone I love them before. So, automatically, you have this hold over me, and a part of me is pissed about that."

She gasps.

"But don't you see why? It is a huge thing for me, and it belongs to you. You alone have the control of it, and that scares the shit out of me."

"I'm sorry."

"Don't be, Abigail. Please don't be."

"But I never meant for this to be so complicated."

"But it will always be, right? I'm…me, and you're…you, and together, we're intense, but I also think we're good for each other."

"You do?"

He cocks his head. "Yes. Of course I do. But before we go any further, I have to ask you if you think this is good for you."

Internally, she completely turns to mush. That is too specific of a question to answer. And more importantly, there is only one answer he is looking for.

"Kelly, I have had a very strange year. My former friends are all hanging out without me. I don't belong socially to the same group I used to. And honestly, the day I met you, I never thought in my wildest dreams that you would even remotely be interested in someone like me. Yet here we are."

"Okay, so tell me what you are feeling, Abigail," he begs.

Her brain ping-pongs between the new information from Nathan and her need to let go of all that anger toward him and then her desire for Kelly.

Two very different men. She has been away from Nathan and the team long enough to not miss it. She meant what she said to Nathan. She was, at times, *just* his girlfriend. Waiting in the wings, watching from the sidelines. That was not necessarily his fault—at least not all of it. But was her anger toward Nathan and Tank the reason she finally moved on, or was falling for Kelly the reason? Kelly Conrad, the sexy guy who turns everyone's head, including hers.

"What I'm feeling is, um…hurt."

"Okay, that's a start." He motions for her to continue.

"Hurt that you can't seem to stay out of trouble with Aniston. Hurt that you kissed her."

"She kissed me. I want to be clear on that."

"Fine. But it makes me nervous that she's around, taunting us. You. Me. Screwing with my stuff. I don't want that kind of—"

"It's done. I took care of it today."

Her eyes grow wide. "You did what?!"

"Please stay calm. Okay." He moves to the edge of his chair. "My prelaw major might have finally come in handy. Tom and I drafted a letter. He said he witnessed her on our property the night your tires were slashed. Along with Luke from the garage with the towing receipt, the cost of the four tires, and the pictures we keep on a file of the damage to the tires. I went over to her house and calmly presented it to her, and we came to an understanding. Courtney might have helped convince her, too."

"Really?"

"Yeah, she was being fucking crazy. Courtney got a good taste of that the other night, too."

"Jealousy is awful." She shakes her head.

Kelly gives her the most winning smile, and then with a chuckle, he says, "I know."

Abigail narrows her eyes. "Oh." But then she can't help but laugh along with him. "It's running rampant."

"Oh, I miss this part of us," he whispers after his smile fades.

"You had to go and be all serious and intimidating on me."

"I know. Believe me, I know. And that is also why I know…he'll try and get you back," he says.

"What?"

"I saw you both today. You kissing him on the cheek. It killed me. Even if it was innocent. But I'm guessing it didn't feel that way to you guys."

"How? I mean, why would you say that?"

"I could tell—that's all. You guys have history. Real history. Not the bullshit I'm accustomed to."

"We had some things to talk about."

"Like what?"

"Um, just needed to clear some things up."

"Is that why you went to the bar the other day?"

She tips her head. He's onto her. "Well, maybe."

"Wow," he says. "You need to be honest with me."

She scoffs.

"That's fair," he says.

She loosens the collar on her shirt. The air in the room has gone up a few degrees since she came in. "It all started with the tires. Nathan saw it with his own eyes, and I'm assuming he told Tank or Laura—someone else knew about it. So, in fairness, my friends are just looking out for me."

"Okay."

"But then Laura and I got into a heated discussion about some other stuff, and I might have voiced my feelings on everything that has transpired over the past months. The fight at the party. Him coming to see you to apologize and ultimately…" Her voice fades. As if by admitting that he is no longer responsible for Poppy's situation, it will somehow change things across the board.

"What is it?" he asks. Only his voice is quieter, less accusing than normal.

She peers up at him and tries to blink away her tears, but it seems far too difficult for her.

"Tell me," he pleads.

Much like before, the truth is crushing. Nathan, without even trying, can step back into their world with a simple clarification.

She hangs her head. "I made a mistake, Kelly."

His eyes get wide. "How so?"

"I believed…" she stutters, trying to catch her breath. "I believed Casey…"

His expression drops. "Casey what?"

"I believed it when she told me Nathan was responsible for Poppy…"

"And?"

"She was wrong."

He lowers his gaze. A moment passes, maybe two, when she clears her throat. He glances up.

She looks scared when he asks, "What is it?"

"Did you hear what I said?"

"Yeah."

"But you didn't have any reaction to that news whatsoever."

"What? I mean, it's crazy…"

"Oh my God," she gasps. "You already knew!" Her voice rises a few octaves.

She starts to stand.

He leaps off the chair, approaching her with lightning speed. "Abigail, please. Listen to me."

"You kept that from me? Why?" Disappointment replaces anger.

"I can explain."

She crosses her arms over her chest.

"Please just sit. I can't do this with you threatening to leave."

She lowers back onto his bed.

Again, he kneels in front of her. "I wanted to tell you. But that is what I was trying to say before. It's the fear of losing you that has gotten me all twisted and doing things I would never have had a conscience about before. I was so worried it would change the way you felt about me."

Who is this person? The same guy who, just months ago, gave me no indication he gave a crap about anyone but himself…except his sister.

"Do you doubt my feelings for you that much?" she asks.

"I just think you're someone who's hard to get over. And I don't want to know what that feels like."

It's the same thing Nathan said to her, and there is a part of her that wants to run. Be free from all of them. But how can she?

"Abigail, say something."

"You kept something from me to try to keep me? How could you do that to me?"

"I'm so sorry. But you believed it because Nathan pointed you in that direction."

He's right. I believed it because he led me to that. Whether anyone wants to acknowledge that or not. It was all too easy for me to think it was true.

"You're right," she whispers.

And if the tables had been turned, would she have been the bigger person and told Kelly something about Aniston? Maybe. Maybe not.

"I'm sorry. I should have told you, but it's hard to talk about him with you. I never gave a shit before about ex-boyfriends. And then you came along. And everything changed for me. *Everything.*"

She finally catches his beautiful green eyes. They melt her heart regardless of her confusion in the moment.

"I told my sister about what has been going on. It's my first step at getting help," he adds. "She won't let me fall. She never has. And she thinks the world of you…"

He leans up. His body presses onto her knees. Her attraction toward him is his greatest weapon. He sinks closer and slowly wraps his arms around her waist.

He nuzzles into her neck and whispers, "Abigail, I love you."

His scent and her longing to be touched by him completely overwhelm her in the moment.

A rush of emotions floods her body, and she whispers, "I love you, too."

I. Just. Want. To. Be. Happy.

He whips his head up. A calm smile adorns his handsome face. "I'm so happy to hear that."

"But can I ask you for one favor? No questions asked?"

"Of course," he says.

"I need to take a walk, clear my head."

He stands, taking her hand and pulling her with him. He opens his door, and with a slight smile, he says, "Call me, okay?"

She brushes her lips onto his and whispers in his ear, "Thanks, Kelly. I won't be long." And with that, she exits his house and walks slowly toward campus.

The OSU campus is quiet today, mainly due to finals week. There is a serene quality to the grounds. As if the library rules were sprinkled about the lawn. Students aren't rowdy or playful; they're serious and theoretical, noses buried in books, hurrying to absorb the last bit of information before they must regurgitate it for their final grade.

But it's still beautiful all the same. Pristine, old buildings with ivy vines growing up the sides. Brick walkways, encased by perfectly manicured shrubs.

Abigail recalls that wonderful moment when she knew this was the school for her. She came upon the science building during her tour just as a class was letting out. The students seemed alive as they scurried out of the doors, chatting and discussing what they had learned. And while that very same scenario could have happened at any school, during any tour, it hadn't. And she couldn't shake the way it made her feel.

She shoves her hands in her pockets and now stands in front of the very same building.

I've lost my way this year. I should have concentrated more on school and less on other things. Am I the only one who did this? Or does it just feel that way? I've got a few more finals next week to put all of my energy into. It's all I can do at this point.

"Take a picture. It will last longer," she jokes.

Abigail jumps. "Gosh, you scared me."

"Sorry." Melissa laughs. "But what are you doing, just staring at the science building?"

"Would you believe it if I told you that I was thinking back to when I took my tour of campus and how I thought coming to school would be so simple? Take classes, study, eat, sleep. Nothing to it, right?" She smirks.

Putting her arm around her friend's, Melissa says, "How could we have known how little we knew?" She squeezes her tight. When she doesn't get a reaction, she asks, "You okay, Abigail?"

Releasing a deep sigh, she says, "Melissa, can I ask you something? And I really want an answer."

She steps in front of her friend, taking in her serious expression. "Of course. You can ask me anything."

"How do you do it? All of it. School, work, Logan. You seem to move through life so effortlessly. What's your secret?" As she starts to laugh, Abigail quickly says, "I'm serious, and I want you to be, please."

"Oh." She swallows hard. "Well, nothing is as perfect as it seems."

"Agree. And believe me, I know that."

"But I guess, if I had to really answer that to you and you only?"

"Yes, only to me. I won't tell anyone what you say, I promise," Abigail says.

"All right. For starters, Logan and I put school first, above all else. That's why we're here. Second is my job. When I took over for Travis as a student editor, I knew it was a big job, and I take it very seriously. I have to. The school is counting on me, and so is Laura. It's a lot of pressure, and sometimes, it can keep me awake at night, thinking about it. So, if I don't have my grades in order, then I'll crumble at my job. It's a domino effect, and that leads right into Logan. He's so easy. He supports me, and most of all, he understands when I'm busy. I'm busy, and it's not because I don't want to see him. It's because there aren't enough hours in the day. But the hours I do have…"

"You make them count."

"Exactly. Having the right person by my side makes all the difference for me."

"He's a special person," Abigail says.

With a wide smile, Melissa says, "He sure is. He puts up with me."

"Stop it," she says. "You're the best, and he knows it."

Melissa, trying not to be obvious, glances at her watch. "Did I help at all?" she says.

"Yeah. My head has just been spinning lately. So much going on, and there are just days when I feel lost."

"Abigail, I can assure you, we all do. Logan does. I certainly do. Webber does. Laura. Bree. Not one single person is immune to the stresses, pressures, mistakes, or whatever it might be that happen here," she says as she swings her arm toward the sprawling campus. "But we love it here, right? And someday not so far from now, we will miss this place so badly that it'll hurt. All this will feel like a dream. Four years went by in a flash. And these thoughts you're having will be distant memories."

Abigail stares at her friend. Melissa has always had her way with the English language, the spoken word, yet she's considered the quiet one of the girls. The one who settled early with the same guy. Stays in a lot, doesn't party as much. Has a big job and tends to be the first one to go to bed. But as

Abigail locks eyes with her, she sees her in a new light. Her maturity has surpassed what she previously thought, yet her admiration for Melissa is even stronger.

"If I haven't told you in the past few days," Abigail says with a smile, "I love you, Melissa." She leans in and hugs her deeply.

"Oh, well, I love you, too, Abigail," she says.

Abigail lets her go and adds, "I don't want to be the reason you're late for work."

"Yes, I should go." She glances at her wristwatch again. "Oh, and one more thing."

"What's that?"

"I try not to repeat the same mistakes. Sounds simple, but it's a pretty good life lesson."

"Thanks, Melissa." Abigail chuckles as she proudly observes her friend head toward Rounds Hall.

And although this walk was meant to clear her head, she can't say for sure that clarity is exactly what she got. But what she did get is an understanding that not all is what it seems.

Not all is perfect. And more importantly, the choices we make in the short time we are here are all we can do to control the difference between one day and the next.

As long as we don't repeat our mistakes.

Forty-Two

Abigail's Lessons

Abigail knocks on Kelly's door. There is no answer, but Tom said he was home. She waits a minute and then knocks again.

After a few moments, she turns the knob and enters his room to find something she has never witnessed before. Kelly is lying on his bed, facing away from the door, curled in the fetal position, as still as can be. Fast asleep.

Quietly, she closes the door behind her. She slips off her coat, tiptoes over to the other side of the bed, and sits, watching him. How incredibly peaceful he appears. The hard lines on his face are softened. His muscles are relaxed, and his lips are a touch parted as he breathes ever so slightly, like a whisper to a friend.

Touching his arm, she says his name, "Kelly."

He stirs.

She leans in and softly kisses him. His eyes flutter but do not open as he wraps his arms about her, bringing her toward him. He kisses her deeply.

"Mmm," he says. "You're back."

Their eyes meet.

"I told you I wouldn't be long." She smiles.

"I'm glad." He leans upon his forearms. "Where did you go?"

"Just walked around campus."

"How nice," he says, and he can't seem to control his smile.

"What?" she says.

"I have something to show you." He yawns.

"Oh, right."

He stands and treads to his desk. Pulling the dresser drawer open, he retrieves an envelope. As he nears her, he holds it up.

"What's that?" she asks.

"Possibly our future."

Our future?

Eagerly, he pulls the letter from the envelope and hands it to her. The letter is addressed to Kelly from Harvard University.

"What is this?" she asks.

His eyes are wide as he replies, "Read it."

She mumbles the words as her eyes dance over the letter. "Oh my God, Kelly! You got into Harvard Law!"

"Yes." He smiles. "I've been freaking out these past few weeks because my friend got his letter and I—"

She can't help herself as she jumps up and swings her arms around his neck. Imagine your dream coming true with just a letter. It must be an amazing feeling. "Your father must be ecstatic!"

He releases her. "I haven't told him yet. I've only told you."

"What? Not even your sister knows?"

"No. I want you to come with me."

She is stunned into silence.

"Did you hear me?" he asks.

"What? Come with you?"

"Yes. After you graduate, come to Boston. They have the best veterinary program. We could live together."

Her head spins with numerous questions. "I-I don't know what to say."

"Just say you'll think about it."

I'm not even a senior yet. Kelly will be graduating in just a few short months and moving to Boston. I have one more year at OSU with all my friends and so-called friends. Is this right for me? Could I move to Boston? Live with Kelly? I haven't thought that far ahead. Have I even forgiven him for the whole Aniston debacle?

"Abigail"—he chuckles—"at least consider it?"

Her attention snaps back to reality. She gazes up at the man who just had the most remarkable thing happen, and the least she can do is relish in this moment with him.

"I'm so happy for you, Kelly."

He reaches up, and with the backside of his hand, he gently caresses her cheek. He leans in, and with soft lips, he delicately brushes them onto hers. He then whispers in her ear, "We can learn from our mistakes. You just have to take a chance."

Suddenly, the words from just an hour before rush over her. "*I try not to repeat the same mistakes. Sounds simple, but it's a pretty good life lesson.*"

"Did you hear me, Abigail?" he says.

Abigail gazes into his eyes and musters a smile as her junior year flashes before her eyes. Some of it like a bad dream. Some of it like an erotic fantasy.

And some of it taught her more about herself than any classroom, textbook, or lecture ever could.

She learned how to move on when it wasn't the easy choice to make and how to find happiness again.

She learned how to fight for herself and the people she cared for, even when her decision was not necessarily the popular one to make.

She learned how to hold her ground and that people, friends and foes, could be cruel, but striking back was not always the answer. Sometimes, walking away was the only way to truly get even.

She unfortunately found out that the truth could sometimes be the biggest lie of them all.

And it's true what they say—the truth hurts.

But most importantly, she learned that love in any form was without a doubt, the hardest lesson of them all.

Part Two

One

A Sophomoric Broken Heart

"Travis, why did you keep me waiting?"

"I was fixing my bike."

My heart pounds in my chest as another uneasy feeling dances over my skin. "You can't fix that motorcycle."

He laughs. "Sure I can. Don't you know I can do anything?"

"No!" I yell. "You can't."

He laughs again. "I thought you didn't care about me anymore."

"Don't say that. You know I do."

"Then, come for a ride with me," he says with a smirk.

"No. We are not getting on that motorcycle."

He discounts me. "Ruth," he says, tapping the seat, "will take us anywhere we need to go."

He named his motorcycle Ruth *because he told me the name means friend, a vision of beauty, which reminded him of me. But that still doesn't make me want to ride on it.*

"Please don't," I beg, but he simply smiles at me, virtually ignoring my warning.

Why won't he listen to me? *I reach out to grab his arm, but my hand slips through him. I try to reach for him again, but I can't grab his flesh. His eyes soften. He seems almost saddened by my attempt to feel him.*

"Why can't I touch you?" I cry.

"You know why." He pushes his hair back from his face and puts on his helmet.

"Please stop," I cry. "If I stay with you, will you not go?"

"It's too late for that," he whispers.

"No, no, no." I shake my head. "I can come back to you. I can."

He straddles his bike. The engine magically roars to life. "It's time I rest in peace."

"Don't say that!" I yell over the engine. "You know I hate that!"

He smiles at me.

"Please," I shout. "Don't say that," I repeat again and again.

He leans near me. He kisses me softly on the cheek. "Sweet dreams then," he murmurs.

He kicks the gear, and the bike jerks forward. I try and grasp him.

Then, like a flash, he's careening down the street. Away from me. Faster and faster, he goes. I try to scream, but my voice is silenced.

Laura bolts forward in her bed, the beeping of the monitors infuriating her. She yanks at the tubes in her arms. Her head throbs, but she swings her legs to the side of the bed regardless and attempts to stand. The nurse comes rushing in.

"I need to get out of here. I have to stop Travis!" she yells.

"Shh, darling," the nurse says. "This will make you sleep."

A rush of warmth from the drugs envelops her body. Her eyes grow weary, and again, she sees him. She attempts to grab ahold of him, to embrace him, but he slips away from her again. And again. And again.

"Travis, please…"

Colin Reed's hand is trembling as he tries to get the key in the lock cylinder. Finally, after multiple tries, he's able to jam it in and start the ignition. Laura's boyfriend is trying to hurry to the field to find her friends while she's still sleeping. Every time she wakes up, she panics, and the nurses come rushing in and give her more medicine, preventing her from ripping the IV tubes out of her arms. It was through these repeated events that Colin quickly realized he could not do this alone. And unbeknownst to Laura, as time seems to come and go as easily as she's floating in and out of consciousness, her friends are across town, waiting for her by the student entrance to Menton Field.

He pulls up to the field house. Droves of students are milling about, wearing the school colors of navy and white, making it virtually impossible for Colin to decipher one person from the next. Vendors are selling food, and booths with alumni and booster organizations line the entrance on the way to the gate.

You've got to be kidding me. I'll never find them. Damn it!

In no mood to play it safe, Colin parks in front, puts on his hazards, grabs his student ID, and pushes his way through the crowd and into the gate of the student section. The game has already started, and most of the people have made their way to the bleachers. But as luck would have it, today, the student section is completely jammed. He frantically searches the crowd, stepping over equipment and pom-poms on the sidelines as he forces his way along the section.

I know they said they'd be here. Abigail would never miss a game. Come on. See me, please.

His face is drawn and pale as he desperately scans the crowd, hoping to recognize someone. Anyone.

Then, he hears a female voice yell, "Colin!"

He glances up, shielding his eyes from the sun. Abigail is waving her hands at him.

He notices her and signals for her to come down to the field. He points toward the gate. Thankfully, he sees Bree coming with her.

I definitely need the two of them. I can't do this by myself.

They jump off the end of the bleachers, and Colin hurries toward them.

Before they can even ask, he says, "It's Laura. She needs you. In the hospital." His voice is strained, and he can see the look of despair on her friends' faces. It's no fun to deliver bad news.

But they don't even know half of it.

"What's wrong?" Bree asks.

"Come on. Let's get out of here, and I'll tell you on the way."

They ask zero questions as they hurry to his waiting car, which is parked, still running, in a tow-away zone in front of the stadium gates. Colin, Bree, and Abigail push their way through the latecomers to the game. Bree quickly hops in the front and fastens her seat belt as Abigail slides in the back and toward the middle.

As she leans forward, she asks, "Is she hurt?"

Colin does a three-point turn and then pulls out onto the main road. "She's okay. I took her to the hospital. She passed out." He tries to shake his fearful thoughts free, but he's terribly on edge.

"Jesus, what happened?"

"Her friend Travis, he died in a motorcycle accident last night," he chokes out.

He watches them as it quickly sinks in.

"Oh my God. That's horrible," Bree whispers.

"She's not doing so hot. They'd like to keep her for observation. She's sedated because once she woke up, she had a panic attack. They gave her some medication to calm her. But she keeps trying to leave the hospital. She needs you guys. I didn't know what else to do." He can't hide the strain in his voice. This is like nothing he's ever had to deal with before.

"I'm glad you got us," Abigail whispers. "She has been through so much…"

"With us. She's our rock." Bree's voice quivers.

Colin looks in his rearview at her. "I'm sorry. To both of you. It's been a hard year for you guys."

Laura was heavily involved in uncovering the conspiracy surrounding Dean Barrymore's attempt to bury the crimes on campus that were tied to Jeremy Gordon—aka the Campus Creeper. Travis was her partner at the paper and fed her the information, so she could successfully report the news on the radio. And through Laura, they—Bree, Abigail, and Colin—came to know how Travis was the one to break it all wide open. He wanted to ensure everyone was held accountable. Not just Jeremy. It's clear why Laura cared for him so much; he was an amazing person.

Colin pulls into the hospital parking lot. They hurry toward the entrance.

Colin leads them to the nurses' station. "I've returned for Laura Chase. Can we go in?"

"Let me check with her nurse." The woman disappears around the corner.

Thankfully, she returns promptly because Colin can't take the look of sadness on either of their faces as they anticipate seeing Laura.

"She said you can go in, but Miss Chase is sedated and very confused at the moment."

Colin hurries toward her room, eager to see her again. They quietly enter. Her head is turned toward the windows. Her eyelids remain heavy.

"Laura?" Colin whispers.

Her head moves, as if encased in molasses. As she takes in the view of her three guests, sadness washes over her otherwise frozen expression.

With a hoarse voice, she pleads, "I don't belong here. Please get me out."

Colin goes around to the other side. *Dear Lord, please say this won't be long. I hate seeing her in here.*

Abigail and Bree get close to her bedside. Abigail takes her hand. She squeezes it.

"It won't be long," she confides.

"But I have to go. I have to see him." Tears leak from her eyes.

Bree speaks up, "Okay, honey. We'll have the nurses get you better quickly."

Abigail glances up at Colin as he pulls the chair in the corner close to her bed, and as he eases into it, he takes her other hand into his, placing a kiss on top.

She turns. "Where's Wolfie?"

Wolfie is Travis's right-hand man. The definition of a wingman. He worked at the paper but remained solely in the background. He did lots of digging and research for Travis. But most importantly, he kept an eye on Laura when Travis could not. Wolfie was the one to bring Laura the news of Travis's passing. He knew right where to find Laura, and more than anything, he understood that she would need to hear the news from him and him alone.

While Travis and Laura's relationship grew, so did Wolfie and Laura's. He's a tough nut to crack and a character of sorts. A rather portly guy who typically sports a tweed jacket, no matter the weather, over a wrinkled button-down oxford. His nose is usually buried deep in a notebook as he scribbles down his thoughts, journalistic ideas, or observations, all to avoid eye contact with his fellow classmates. Yet Laura loves all his uniqueness.

The three of them made quite a team. They were the reason the radio station and the student paper were so successful.

"Wolfie wanted me to tell you he's thinking of you and he will come by as soon as he can," Bree says, tossing a little white lie at her, hoping it will ease her mind.

"But they need my help."

"They?"

"Yes." Her expression grows heavy again, and she turns to Bree. "You know they need my help."

Bree blinks the tears back. Laura is making sense but not within reality anymore. Bree leans in closer to her as Abigail steps back.

Her face mere inches from Laura's, she whispers, "I'll go to them. I know how to help."

"Please," she begs. "They need us, Bree. Tell them I'll be with them soon…"

Bree grabs Abigail's hand. "I'm going to talk to the nurse, and Abigail will get you some water."

"Thank you." Her voice is weak.

Abigail, Bree, and Colin leave the room.

Once out of earshot, Bree says, "Jesus, this is worse than I thought. But I know how to find Wolfie—or at least, I hope I do."

"Okay, what can I do?" Abigail asks.

"Stay here…for now. I'll come back."

"Okay." Abigail asks the nurse for a warm blanket and some water. She returns to her room, and Laura is now fast asleep. Abigail puts the blanket on her and the water on her table.

Colin waits for her and then asks, "Getting a coffee. Want one?"

"No, thanks."

Colin meanders down the hallway to the vending machine and gets a cup of coffee. Abigail is close behind. He rests the back of his head against the wall and closes his eyes as he clutches the coffee.

"What happened?" Abigail asks.

"That guy, Wolfie, he came to my apartment around six in the morning and said he needed to speak with Laura. The next thing I knew, I heard her screaming, and I came out. They told me he…he died in a motorcycle accident last night. That's all I know."

"I can't even believe it; he was so young." Abigail shakes her head.

"I know. It's horrible. I met the guy a bunch of times. He took Laura under his wing. I got the sense he truly cared for her." *I know she must be absolutely devastated.*

"How did she end up here?"

"Laura wanted to go with Wolfie to tell Professor Campbell about Travis—he's in charge of the paper—and she went upstairs to get dressed. I was going to make some coffee for us, and then we heard a loud bang and then total silence. I ran upstairs and found her passed out on my floor. She was white as a sheet and wasn't moving. I carried her down into my car and took off. I left that poor guy sitting at my kitchen table."

"Jesus, that's awful."

"Shit," he says as he lightly bangs his head on the wall. "Why does this all have to be so hard? It's just fucking sadness looming over all of us, and I'm …"

"Exhausted," Abigail says.

"Yes, the guy was twenty-two years old. What the fuck?" *I mean, gone. How can it be possible?*

"I know." She, too, leans up against the wall. "I should probably call her parents."

"She doesn't want them coming. I know that. But, yeah, they'll want to hear from you."

"Okay. I'll go back to our room. Get her some clothes and make that call. If she wakes, tell her I'll be back soon, I promise."

"Thanks, Abigail."

"Can I get you anything?"

"No, but take my car."

"You should keep it here in case she gets released or whatever. I'd feel better, knowing you're here with a car. It's a twenty-minute walk back to campus, and I could use the fresh air."

"Okay." He pushes off the wall. He gently wraps one arm around Abigail's shoulders and squeezes her.

Colin and Abigail have had limited interactions, but they have all been pleasant.

"I'll be back, soon," she says.

He releases his grip and enters back into Laura's room. He sinks into the chair next to her bed. He takes her hand gently into his, and with a pained expression on his face, he kisses her softly. Then, he mumbles, "Sleep, Laura. Sleep it all away."

Two

Reality Bites

Abigail exits the hospital. The sun is bright, but the air is cool. She shades her eyes as she strides down the ramp to the parking lot.

"Hey!"

She peeks up. Kelly Conrad is leaning against his black Mustang at the end of the ramp. Abigail can't help the way her pulse reacts.

She approaches him, concerned by his presence. "Everything okay?" she asks.

"You said your friend was hurt?"

"Yes, but you were just at the game."

"When I saw your friend's car peel out of Menton Field, I figured you might need some extra help—that's all."

"Gosh, I'm sorry. Yeah, my roommate's okay for now. I've got to call her parents, get her some clothes, stuff like that."

He looks around the lot. "You have a car?"

"No, I'm walking back to campus."

He shakes his head, laughing slightly. "Come on. I'll give you a ride."

"I don't want to impose. You were going to the game, and you should enjoy the day."

He goes around the front of his car and motions for her to get in. "You did me a favor." He winks.

Intrigued, she climbs in. "How so?"

"Now, I don't have to be at the game."

Feeling strange about his lack of interest in football and her necessity to care about football, she replies, "Then, why go?"

"Figured I could see my sis."

"Yeah, she was there."

"I know. She told me all you guys go down."

Her belly churns with an uneasiness.

Thankfully, he changes the subject. "If you don't mind me asking, how's your roommate?"

"We won't know until later."

"That's too bad." He pulls out of the parking lot and goes back to campus.

They drive in virtual silence. Abigail's mind wanders as she traces the vintage leather along the door with the tips of her fingers until she feels the knob. She rolls down the window, letting the cool air blow back her hair. It feels good as she tips her head closer to the window. She closes her eyes and takes in what few quiet moments she has.

He pulls into the side lot near her dorm. "I'll wait and bring you back," he says.

She's unclear why she can't reach for the door lever.

There is an urgency to get out of his car before she embarrasses herself, but then he asks yet again, "Are you okay?"

Tears sting her eyes and immediately she is brought back to last night at the party when she spilled her guts to him about the two non-guilty verdicts pertaining to her. So, crying in front of him is something she vowed she'd never do again.

The news last night and now Laura's tragedy are more than I can handle without shedding a tear.

She grabs the handle and exits in a hurry.

She can hear his door swing open as he calls, "Abigail, wait!"

She rushes toward the door to her dorm and yanks it open. He's hot on her heels. Once inside, she feels him tug on her hand.

"Hold up, will you?"

She stops. He steps in front of her and pushes the button for the elevator. He waits in silence next to her as she wipes her face. He says nothing as they step into the elevator. Mercifully, the doors open, and she can finally get out of the cage they were trapped in. As they walk side by side to her room, she notes the whole dorm is quiet. Almost everyone is at the game. She pauses at Bree's door and knocks. When she doesn't answer, she proceeds to her door and unlocks it.

"Come on in," she whispers.

He soundlessly follows her. She starts to rummage through Laura's drawers, taking out sweatpants and comfortable clothes. She enters the desk area, and with trembling hands, she reaches for her bag. Without warning, he takes her hand. The warm feeling that rushes over her is a welcome one because, right now, she feels helplessly alone. She sits in her desk chair as Kelly takes out Laura's and does the same. He releases her hand.

She owes him an explanation—yet again—for her emotions, so she raises her navy eyes to meet his and says, "Do you know who Travis Taylor is?"

"Travis Taylor…sounds familiar. Doesn't he run the student paper?"

A tear falls on her cheek. "He did. He died last night in a motorcycle accident."

"Oh my God. That's terrible." He shakes his head in disbelief. "I take it, you knew him? I'm so sorry."

"He was close with Laura. I guess she passed out after getting the news. But please don't say anything. I have no idea who knows yet."

"I won't. I promise. I feel awful for you…and your friends."

With a deep sigh, she confides, "I'm drained, Kelly."

His green eyes show a deep sadness. "I can only imagine. And after last night…"

She blinks back tears. "I need to call her parents."

He starts to stand. "I can go."

"No, please don't. I mean, could you stay?"

He lowers in his seat. "Yeah, sure."

"I can't be alone, you know?"

"Completely get it."

After she gets up and drags her feet toward her bed, she shoves Laura's clothes in the bag. Sitting on the edge, she reluctantly picks up the receiver. She dials Laura's home number.

Within a few rings, her mother answers, "Hello?"

"Mrs. Chase? It's Abigail."

Obviously concerned by her call, she says, "Are you two all right?"

"Well, I am but Laura." She takes a deep breath in and holds it. Then, with composure, she says, "Laura's friend passed away last night."

"Oh, dear God," she whispers.

"He was the student editor for the school paper. He died in a motorcycle accident."

"Oh, my Lord in heaven. Please tell me she's okay."

"Yes, the news was very difficult for her. They were close friends."

"Travis?"

"Yes?"

"Oh, that wonderful boy. He came here over the summer and had dinner with us. Rick and I found him to be such a smart and driven young man. Oh, how very, very tragic."

They knew him? Abigail had no idea. Laura never mentioned that she had seen him over the summer.

"I'm calling to tell you she passed out. The news was hard for her. It was too much for her to handle. She's in the hospital. She's going to be fine. But Colin wanted me to call you and tell you."

"Oh, Rick! Rick, come here!" Abigail can hear her yell in the background.

"Mrs. Chase, Colin said she specifically asked for you not to come. She's sad, very sad, but she needs to take care of some things regarding Travis and doesn't want to alarm you."

"I understand that, but we must see her."

"Can you call her first?" Abigail pleads.

"Laura's in the hospital. She passed out. That boy Travis was killed in a motorcycle accident," she mumbles to her husband.

"Oh God…no. What are they saying? Was Laura with him?"

"It's Abigail. No, she wasn't," Maureen says to Rick.

"Okay, we can call the hospital and get a report," Rick replies. Abigail can hear the strain in his voice despite the distance.

"Yes, Mrs. Chase, here's the number." Abigail reads her the number, and they say their good-byes. Abigail waits until she hears her hang up, and then she slowly places the receiver down.

The silence in the room is welcome but does give her a slight uneasiness that Kelly is waiting for her on the other side. She stands and crosses the room and peeks past the divider. He's standing in front of Laura's desk, staring out across the campus, deep in thought. She notes the sleeve of tattoos up his arm, the twitch of his muscles as he raises his arm and rubs his hand across his face. She finds his tranquility mesmerizing in her time of need. She also finds their unexpected time together to be confusing, yet here she is, with him again. Alone. She hardly knows a thing about him. Just his appearance, his love of animals, his tattoos, and apparently his interest in classic muscle cars.

She clears her throat. It startles him. When he turns to her, his eyes light up. Although it must merely be his awakening from his trance.

He gives her a small smile. "I'm sorry you had to do that." His voice sounds hoarse.

"Can I get you some water?"

"No, thanks."

"Well, I should probably get going," Abigail says.

"Yeah, hopefully, by now, she's doing better."

Abigail locks up her room. As she stops by Bree's door, she knocks again. No answer. She writes a note on the whiteboard on her door.

Gone back. Bringing clothes. Talk to you later.

She's cryptic on purpose, knowing that all the girls read the notes they leave for one another. It's not a bad thing—it's how they communicate—but Abigail doesn't want to alarm anyone about Laura until she knows more.

Kelly drives her back to the hospital. Abigail glances at her watch. The football game, at best, is finishing the second quarter. None of them will be back for hours.

Kelly kills the ignition.

"Thank you so much."

"Hey, why don't I wait here, just in case?"

Without hesitation, she says, "Okay." She grabs the bag of clothes and enters the hospital.

She notifies the nurses' station that she's here with clothes for Laura Chase. She enters the room and finds Colin resting relatively comfortably in a chair, his legs up on a stool. Laura is sleeping. Abigail taps his foot gently.

"Hey," he says.

"How is she?"

"Okay," he whispers. "She spoke to her parents, and I did, too. They're not coming. Thank you for that. The hospital plans to release her tomorrow."

"Tomorrow?"

"Yeah." He motions for them both to leave the room. "Sorry, hard to whisper. Yes, they had to sedate her a little more to calm her. Obviously, her parents knew about Travis. That sort of sent her back into reality, and that was rough."

"Understandable. Poor thing."

Colin cocks his head to the side. "Did you know Laura's parents knew him?"

"No. I had no idea."

Their relationship continues to be a mystery. And one much closer than we probably all thought. Including Colin.

"Huh, interesting. Regardless, the doctor said she should possibly sleep for another four hours. There is no use in both of us sitting here in silence. Why don't you and Bree try to figure out what happened, so when she's released, we can prepare her? She's going to want to know more from Wolfie."

"Okay. Should I let the station know she won't be coming in?"

"Already did. Sean is filling in for us both."

"Okay, great. I left the clothes in a bag on the floor. Can I get you anything before I go?"

"No, I'm good. My roommate, Stef, said he'd come by later, bring some submarine sandwiches and stuff."

"Okay. You have our number. Call my room if you need a break, and we'll be here."

"I know. You guys get ready for tomorrow. That will be a whole other thing."

Abigail hangs her head, knowing that he's speaking the awful truth. Because in the end, the mere veracity of it all is that reality can really suck.

Three

Last Good-bye

Abigail paces the room as she anticipates Laura's arrival. Within moments, she can hear voices in the hallway. She hangs back so as not to overwhelm her as she enters the room.

The door pushes open, and in walks someone resembling Laura. Her hair is matted and greasy. Her eyes are swollen and red. The shuffle in her steps would signify she's in the late stages of her life, an older woman unable to walk on her own. She glances up at Abigail, only her reaction is void. She barely indicates an emotion.

"Hello," Abigail whispers.

Laura acknowledges hearing a voice but does not speak. In fact, she moves past Abigail and goes straight toward her bed. As though her bones were broken, she lowers cautiously onto her mattress. Colin is a moment behind. When Abigail locks eyes with him, she's not the least bit surprised by his sadness.

"Here are her clothes," he says, placing her bag on Laura's desk. He gingerly steps toward Laura. He leans down and removes her shoes and then places the blanket from the end of her bed over her body. "Rest, okay?"

Leaning toward her head, he places a kiss on top. She doesn't interact with him.

When he enters the other room with hunched shoulders, it's clear he's not in the mood for chitchat. "In her bag is her medication. She can take one every four hours, as needed. It does make her sleepy, so just be aware of that."

"Okay. What can I do otherwise?"

"I'm not sure. She might need to talk to someone when she feels up to it. Here are some numbers she can call when she's ready." With a shaking hand, he gives Abigail the paper.

"You okay?"

"Me? Yeah. I just think I need to get some sleep. Tell Laura I'll call her later."

"I will, and thank you, Colin."

Abigail eases the door shut. With light feet, she enters the room and stands before Laura. Laura peeks up and then reaches out her hand for Abigail to take. As she does, Laura pulls her toward her. Abigail climbs on the bed and wraps her arms around her. When they touch is when Laura starts to weep with painful sorrow.

"I'm so sad," she cries.

Abigail strokes her hair, and then with the utmost sincerity, she replies, "I wish sewing kits could mend broken hearts, so I could fix yours."

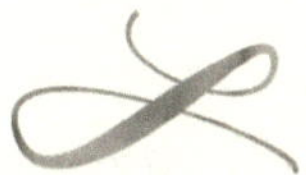

For eight long days, Laura remained attached to her bed. Colin stopped in periodically to check on her. He was pulling double duty at the station to help cover her shifts, so he did the best he could to continue to be by her side. It's clear he's sad that he cannot help her, but he remains to understand of her loss.

But now, on the day of Travis's funeral, she sits at her desk and stares out the window of her dormitory room, an emptiness in her heart so hollow and raw that she almost feels nothing at all.

And as the light from the sun is attempting to rise over the campus buildings on this early December morning, she can tell by the frost on her window that there is an unholy chill in the air. She shudders at the mere thought of going outside.

"Laura," Abigail whispers.

Without turning, she whispers back, "Yeah?"

"We'll be ready to go in a few minutes, okay?"

"Sure," she whispers.

Abigail's being quiet as she moves throughout their room while she finishes getting dressed, but this only leaves Laura with her depressing thoughts. This has been their routine for the past week since she was released from the hospital.

Laura has been staying in the room, barely showering or going to class. She only eats what Abigail brings her back from the cafeteria, and she has taken a leave of absence from the radio station and her classes. She spends most of her days sitting at her desk, staring out of the window, and has been very clear that she's simply not in the mood for company. It's not often but sometimes, in the middle of the night, Laura will get on the phone with Wolfie, and even then, they barely speak about Travis. Laura only wants to know what he's writing about for the paper or really anything in his world other than a word about Travis.

Laura can sense Abigail behind her as she gathers her wool dress coat and bag and then places her hand gently on her shoulder.

"We should go."

Laura rises from her seat, and Abigail helps her into her coat.

"I'll carry your bag," she says.

Laura barely nods.

Bree is waiting in the hallway. "Hello."

"Hey, Bree," Abigail replies.

Laura glances up at her and acknowledges her existence. It's a start.

As Laura passes them and waits for the elevator, Bree whispers to Abigail, "How is she today?"

"Worse."

I can hear them talking about me, but I don't have the energy to tell them they're terrible whisperers.

"I wish she'd talk to someone," Bree says.

I don't want to.

Abigail sighs.

They ride down the elevator in silence and head toward Bree's car in the student parking lot adjacent to their dorm.

"Do you want to ride in the front?" Abigail asks.

"No," Laura mumbles.

"Okay."

They drive the hour and a half to Travis's funeral in complete silence. Bree inconspicuously glances in the rearview mirror at Laura as she nervously pulls at the loose button on her coat. A trancelike state is plastered on her face, like an elderly woman placed in front of a television in a nursing home. Just there to pass the time, completely unaware of what's happening around her.

Bree parks the car. "We're here," she says.

Laura turns toward the voice, and she gives Bree a look, as if to say, *Where are we?*

Abigail climbs out of the car and opens Laura's door. Reaching in, she takes her hand. "Come. It's time to go in."

Laura follows the mourners dressed in black but then freezes at the door of the church. Her chest heaves as a wave of panic rush over her, like the realization of where she is, is now hitting her.

I can't breathe. I can't do this. Please don't make me go.

She grabs Bree's hand. "I can't go in. I can't," she says.

Bree squeezes it, allowing her dear friend this moment of sheer terror, but then she releases her hand.

Bree squares her body in front of Laura and places her hands on her shoulders, and for the first time in a week, she makes direct eye contact with her. "You have to."

"I-I can't do it."

Bree pushes back a strand of Laura's hair. "Yes, you can. Because you loved him, and now, you must say good-bye."

Laura's eyes are painfully red. "I did love him," she finally admits. *So very much.*

"I know you did, sweetheart. We all know you did and still do," Bree says.

Abigail touches her hand. "We are here for you. But *you* are here for Travis."

Travis. Oh, Travis. How can you be gone?

She lowers her lids as wetness pours down her cheeks. "Thank you," she whispers. "Thank you for being here."

"Come." Bree takes her other hand, and the three of them enter the church and huddle close to one another in the pew.

Don't look around at the sad people, Laura. It will only make it worse. Don't look at the picture of him either. Don't look. Don't look.

She lowers her head, glancing only at the tear-soaked tissue in her hands as Travis's cousin, Sam, delivers his eulogy, which is both funny and heartbreaking. He talks mostly of Travis's childhood and his passion for the student newspaper in high school. He says that while most people were running out to the field, Travis was running down the hall to meet a deadline.

"It meant everything to him," he says. "While others were worried about the big game on Friday night, Travis was worried about making sure the copy of the paper would be waiting for each student Monday morning, bright and early. Even if that meant giving up some of his social life on the weekends to make that happen. But he could see the bigger picture. He knew there was more out there for him. And so on it went at Onondaga State."

Laura shudders at the mention of their university.

Sam continues, "*The Weekly Blue* meant everything to him. And it showed. He was so proud of what he was able to accomplish there and at the radio station, too."

Laura squeezes her eyes tightly shut.

"He was finally able to find those like-minded friends he'd always dreamed about. And he had never been happier than he was this past year. And for that, I'm so grateful. Knowing he left this earth as happy as he could be."

Laura tries to listen to the remainder of the ceremony, but the numbness overpowers her body, and she sits there like a statue. Cold and merely a figure in the pew. The next thing she knows is Abigail's hand is on her arm, guiding her up.

"You ready to go?" Abigail asks.

It's over?

Nodding her head, she follows her friends down the aisle and out the doors of the church. Taking her place in the backseat of Bree's car, she returns her fingers to the loose button on her wool coat, and in the silent car ride home is when wonders if she'll ever be able to feel normal again.

Will I ever feel like the old me? Or am I dead and gone, too?

Four

Just Another Day

Colin knocks on the door, a sickening feeling in his stomach because he knows his girlfriend is in pain after returning from Travis's funeral and there's nothing he can do about it. But she didn't want him to go with her either. He simply can't seem to do anything right. No matter how hard he tries.

He waits for her to tell him to come in.

In a weakened voice, she yells, "It's open."

He enters, and immediately, he knows nothing has changed. Even the stale air in the room is getting to him. That stifling aroma that comes with not showering for days and wearing the same clothes seems to have even settled into the furniture at this point.

Colin cracks a window near her desk.

"Don't," she says.

"Laura, this room needs some fresh air—badly."

"That's insulting," she quips.

"You know what I mean," he says. "I'll close it in a minute."

"Why are you here?" she says.

His tensed shoulders drop. "I wanted to see how you were doing," he mumbles.

"How do you think I'm doing?"

"Not well," he sighs.

"No, Colin, I'm *not* doing well."

He wants to shake her, scream at her, hug her, kiss her, hold her, force her to shower, make her eat or do anything but what she has been doing the past weeks. But instead, he stands before her, just as broken as she is. In a completely different fashion, however. It's as though he's lost his lover, too.

Just like she has. Sure, she's standing before him, flesh and blood, but she's not Laura Chase anymore. That girl is gone.

"I…miss y—"

"Did you bring me the papers?" she curtly cuts in.

Either she doesn't care about the hurt his eyes are showing or her heart is so dark that she can't recognize that her lack of acknowledgment is eating away at him.

He extends his hand, holding the paper bag containing several copies of the latest edition of *The Weekly Blue.* She snatches them out of his hand.

"You sure this is a good idea?" he says.

The look of disgust she gives him forces him to swallow hard.

He takes a step back. "Fine, I'll leave."

But what I really want to ask you, Laura, is if you resent me for being around because Travis isn't?

Tears well in her eyes now, but this is not uncommon for her. She goes from angry to sad in the snap of a finger. It doesn't make him a jerk for not staying because when he has, the process of her getting mad and depressed simply begins all over again, and it's too painful for both of them.

He nears the door, placing his shaking hand on the doorknob. He starts to say, "I'll call you."

She says with bite, "Just leave."

She's angry again, and she has no idea as to why.

Colin opens the door and closes it, only he can't walk away. He takes several steps down the hall, and then sits on the carpet in front of Bree's door. He'll wait for Abigail to return.

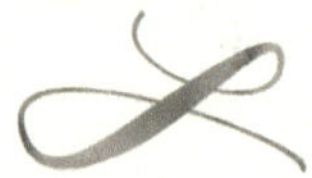

Laura's hands tremble as she retrieves the copies of the student paper from the bag. Her eyes land on his photo. Those big blue eyes she once loved to gaze into. And not always for the reason you'd think. He was so intelligent that he could often tell you most of what he was thinking by his expressions, too. It was part of who he was. Gifted, you might say. Travis preferred to speak in person than on the phone. He wanted that personal connection, as he, too, felt most of a person's story was in their eyes.

She unfolds the paper to reveal the entire photo of him, standing before the Rounds Hall and the office of *The Weekly Blue.* Arms folded over his chest, a slight grin on his handsome face, and his windswept dark hair tousled ever so slightly from the fall breeze.

He's beautifully captured. Just as she remembers him.

"Oh, Travis," she cries. "I miss you so much." Placing the paper down on her desk, she grabs a tissue.

She painstakingly reads every single word printed about him. With each inked letter, a tiny stab can be felt in her heart.

She was most certainly not prepared to open the paper. As the article continues, she sees the photo of the two of them from their first days together at the radio station.

A smiling, naive Laura sitting next to *the* Travis Taylor. Little did they know that in only a few short months from that photo being taken, Travis would win a major award, uncover a massive college scandal, take Laura's virginity, and tragically pass away in a motorcycle accident. It's almost too much to comprehend.

And it must be saved. Forever.

She grabs the scissors from her desk, and with feverish abandon, she begins cutting all the photos out of the paper.

Abigail huffs up to her floor, clutching Laura's dinner. She's seething with anger from her encounter with Tank and his little plan to drive her across campus in his truck to scold her about not getting a chance to tell him about the not-guilty verdicts. She's been a little busy, tending to Laura's needs.

As she heads down the hallway with the food for Laura, she notices Colin sitting on the floor, head buried in his hands. Unfortunately, this has happened more than once, and she's not surprised it's happening today, considering it was Travis's funeral. She clears her throat to gain his attention. Colin peers up, his face twisted with emotions.

"Hey," Abigail says as she nears him.

"I don't know what to do," he says, scrambling to his feet.

"I know. Let me talk to her."

"Be my guest." He storms past her, wiping the anguish from his face.

Their relationship has played out like this over the last few weeks. He stops by. She doesn't want him to. He stays to help her. This angers Laura. She lashes out. She calls Wolfie, or like in the case of this evening, Abigail steps in. The cycle continues until the following day.

"Laura?" she whispers as she quietly shuts the door behind her. "I brought you something to eat."

"I thought you said you'd be right back," she cries.

Abigail rushes to her. "I know; I know." *Damn you, Tank!* "I'm here now."

As Abigail approaches, she sees torment on Laura's normally beautiful face. Abigail places the food on her nightstand, as she knows this has nothing to do with hunger. This has to do with her pain.

Laura slumps into her mattress. Her once-voluptuous body now sits, frail and pale upon her bedding.

Her voice breaks. "I miss him so much, Abigail."

"I know you do."

"I don't know what to do. And Colin…"

"Colin will be okay. He's a big boy." Abigail has said this at least a hundred times.

"But…" And Laura always trails off. There is more to her thoughts; she just never seems to have the energy to articulate them.

"I know. You can only worry about one thing at a time, and right now…"

"How can he be gone?" she asks.

"Oh, Laura. I don't know."

She rubs her eyes, and then with defeat in her voice, she asks, "Can you just get me my medicine? I need to sleep."

Abigail takes the bottle of pills off their dresser and hands them to her. Laura tosses two back and quickly lies on her bed, shielding herself from the world with her comforter. Abigail stands over her bed, lost for how to help her friend. She wishes she could call Tank and ask him how he managed his pain when he lost his best friend, Jonathan. But she knows he didn't handle it well, and she's mad enough at him right now that the thought of dialing him up makes her blood boil.

Overwhelmed in the moment, she shuts off the light near Laura. She can hear the soft moan easing out of Laura as the medicine begins to take effect. Soon, she'll be fast asleep.

Wandering over to the desks and switching on the small lamp, she takes a seat. Immediately noticing a large pile of papers scattered on Laura's desk, she leans in closer to get a better look. She gasps at the sight in front of her. When left to her devices, Laura somehow got several copies of *The Weekly Blue*. The cover story was of Travis, and it took up the entire front and inside pages. Flipping through it, Abigail sees several pictures of him and his time at the paper along with photos of him on campus, a few with Wolfie, and a beautiful one of him and Laura in the radio station.

Oh, poor Laura. That must have been so hard to see.

Laura cut out most of the photos from the stacks of newspapers and glued them on individual papers. She cut out sections of the articles and taped them to her corkboard and on random places near her desk. It's downright depressing, and Abigail can't even imagine what Colin must have felt when he walked in and saw his girlfriend cutting and pasting photos, crying, like a child in a demented art class.

What is he supposed to do with this? How can he help her when she's like this?

Abigail can't let her start off another day in such darkness. So, she tidies up the clippings and throws the scraps in the trash. She puts the cap back on the glue and places Laura's scissors back in her desk drawer. She stacks what is left of the newspapers in the corner of Laura's desk and leaves the rest where it is.

Abigail grabs her shower caddy off the shelf and is about to leave to go wash her face when she hears a slight moan from the other side of the room. Abigail peeks around the wall and notes a sleeping Laura tossing and turning.

"Oh, Laura," she whispers with a shake of her head.

Another day of pain is gone, but unfortunately for Laura, there is one more day on the horizon.

Five

Dark Winter

Laura asked for a leave of absence from the station for the school break and opted to go home to Stockbridge instead of staying at school and working. Colin had all but begged her to stay, but she left anyway.

"I could help you if you stayed," he said.

She shoved more clothes into her laundry bag. "Colin, we discussed this. Tucker already covered my shifts at the station for the winter break. Tucker needs you at the station, not home with me. I need to go home. Get out of here. How do you not get that?" she said.

"I'm trying."

"I just need to get out of here."

Do you know how hard it is to look at you and not feel regret? Maybe if I hadn't left Travis for you, he'd still be alive today. I was his friend, and I knew he was working on that motorcycle. For God's sake, he gave it a name that reminded him of me. I would have made sure it was safe to drive. But I left him. For you. And now, I wish I could take it all back.

"Okay, but you'll call me, right?"

"Of course. It's just for winter break. I'm coming back next semester."

She spent most of her time at home in her room, talking on the phone to Wolfie about Travis, the dean, and what, if anything, they could do about the homophobic remarks spray-painted on the women's soccer house. As each day fell off the calendar, her codependency with Wolfie grew. She woke up with a phone call to him and went to bed, calling him. The times they weren't on the phone, she was writing him letters and sending them. She drove her parents crazy every time the mailman arrived.

She'd run down the stairs like the Tasmanian devil, shouting, "Anything for me?" every single day. Except for Sundays.

Colin phoned in between his shifts at the station, which were almost twice as many, as they all picked up extra shifts to replace Laura's show. She'd call him back half the time, if that, and their conversations were ones of mere strangers—with nothing to talk about but the weather and their mutual friends at the radio station. It was becoming abundantly clear to Laura's subconscious that her love for Colin was beginning to fade. She simply did not have the capacity in her heart to recognize it.

And as much as being home left Laura with some sense of peace and distance from her life at school, returning after a month suddenly crept up on her.

"You sure you're ready to go back?" Mrs. Chase asks as she folds another T-shirt and places it in Laura's suitcase.

"I think so. I want to. It's school, Mom. I can't drop out."

"No, no," Mr. Chase says. "That would not be a wise choice."

"But all that place does is remind me of him, and I don't know how to stop thinking about him. Or the pain I feel. I'm always sad, and I hate it so much. I just want to wake up and feel happy. But then again, if I do, I'll be forgetting about him. And I don't want to. I loved what we did at the station and the paper. I was so happy…really happy, and I'm just not anymore," she admits.

Her parents stand before her, dumbfounded, as this is the most she's spoken about how she's felt in the month she's been home.

"We think it's time you call one of those people the hospital recommended to you. Someone to talk to. Would you be willing to try that?" Mrs. Chase asks.

Laura's shoulders tense, but she tries to sound casual as she says, "Yeah, I'll definitely look into it. Promise."

"And lean on Abigail. She has been there for you and will continue to. She's such a great roommate. You two are so lucky to have found one another," her mom adds.

"We are. But she has a life, too, Mom. I'm going to try and not burden her."

"Friends don't ever think grief is a burden—you remember that," her dad says as he wraps his arms around her tightly. "Now, come on. We'd better hit the road if we're going to get there before dark."

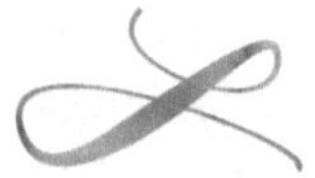

Staring out her dormitory window, Laura dabs the corner of her eye with a tissue. The soft hum of The Sundays plays through the speakers as the students shuffle in and out of the buildings spread out below her. The sun is attempting to make its way into the sky, which makes her glance at the clock on the wall. Class will be starting within the next hour, but the puffy bags under her tired eyes are begging her to stay hidden within her room.

A slight knock on her door catches her attention. Shoving the tissue in her pocket, she gets up and pulls open the door. Professor Tucker—the faculty head of the campus radio station, WOUR97—is standing before her with his hands clasped together. A serious expression on his face.

"Tucker. Hello."

He allows all the students in the station to call him by his last name.

"Laura." His expression immediately softens, and with him doing so, the tears sting her eyes. "May I come in?"

"Yes, of course." She opens the door wide and steps back toward her desk.

He follows her in and closes the door. "Rather unorthodox for me to come to a student's room, but under the circumstances, I thought this would be best. I hope you agree."

"Yes, yes, of course. Please, have a seat."

He pulls out the chair and lowers into it. Laura sits opposite him.

"I wanted to talk to you about the situation with the dean. This is highly confidential, but I feel it's my duty to fill you in, considering what you uncovered last year."

She swallows hard, and her pulse quickens. "I won't tell a soul."

"I know you won't. You're a very trustworthy young lady, and if nothing else, you have proven to me and those who know what really happened that your intentions are good. Now, after the documents were sent anonymously to law enforcement and the university president…"

"Wait, what?"

"The documents?"

"I don't know anything about that."

"Really? But I assumed…"

Laura drops her head, shaking her bob loose.

"What is it?"

She slowly raises her head, and although the notion of it all is tragic, she can't help but smile. She exhales deeply and replies, "Travis. He stopped including me toward the end because he'd lied to the dean and told her I knew nothing about what was going on. I only knew what information he fed me. And he promised her he'd stop, all to keep me out of her cross fire."

Tucker smiles warmly. "Well, he succeeded then. He sent pertinent information to those in a position to do something about her. I came to tell you that they have currently stripped her of her power at the university, and she's on paid leave until they can authenticate every fact. And once they do, the board has already indicated that they plan to publicly fire Dean Barrymore in a last-ditch effort to save face during this debacle."

"That is just the kind of news I needed to hear."

Over the past year, Tucker has become a mentor to Laura, someone she can go to for sage advice. And not just to Laura, but also to all the gang in the studio. He treats the staff at the station with respect and care, and he's always engaging and thoughtful. This makes it easy to work for him.

"I wanted to see you, aside from all of this garbage, because I need you to know that whenever you are ready to return to the airwaves, the spot is yours."

"Thank you, Tucker."

"We all miss you." He glances around her room. Taking in the scene of tissue boxes strewn about, clothes tossed on chairs, and the melancholy song playing in the background. But most importantly, the pale, unkempt woman who sits before him. "But I would be remiss if I didn't tell you that I strongly believe Travis would have wanted you to bounce back quickly and to keep going. I know I'm not telling you something you don't already know, but working hard and staying in school and fighting the daily battle of academia are imperative."

A tear falls on her cheek. "I know. But just when I think I'm ready to get back out there…I'm stunned by darkness I can't see."

He doesn't waver at her omission. "I understand. But the world doesn't. They won't feel your pain, so you have to push through it."

"I know you're right. People have already forgotten about him. It's like the days pass, and he's no longer in them, but the paper still gets printed, the records still spin, and I sit here, feeling alone…missing him," she whispers.

"You have every right to feel the way you do. I just want you to be able to step outside this room and live again. If you don't, you'll lose the part of you he liked the most. Trust me on this, Laura." He stands and strides toward her door.

"Tucker," she says as he pulls open her door, "thank you."

"Anytime, Laura. And how about you come by and have coffee with me? Next Tuesday at three. I'll meet you in the Union café."

"I will."

The door swings shut, and despite his pep talk, the gloominess falls back upon her. She spins and faces the window yet again and watches the crowd shuffle in and out of classes. Within minutes of the rush dying down, she hears the thud of footsteps approach her door. Abigail enters. Laura forces a smile at her roommate.

"You okay?" she asks.

Laura breathes a sigh of relief as she considers Tucker's advice on the world moving forward. "I'm okay. I think I'm okay," she repeats.

"Are you skipping class?"

"No, I'm going to go."

"Good. It might make you feel better."

She giggles. "Never thought school would be the medicine I needed."

"Right? I feel the same. Why don't you take a nice hot shower? And I'll run down to the commons and grab you a coffee and granola bar."

Laura smiles at her friend. "I love you, Abigail."

"I love you, too."

Laura grabs her shower caddy and towel and starts off down the hall toward the bathroom. "Let's start off this day right," she whispers to herself. "It can't get worse—I know that."

Six

Second Semester

Abigail and Laura enter the Union the following Tuesday, after the first full week of classes. The beginning of the semester is always relatively painless, like getting your syllabuses, hearing the expectations from your Professors, buying your textbooks, and so on. Laura made it through all of her classes but would immediately retreat to her room after each one. But Laura had promised Tucker she'd meet him for coffee, and Abigail was finally able to make plans with Tank to talk.

"I'm heading to the coffee shop to see Tucker. I'll come find you after, okay?"

"Sure thing."

"Good luck with Tank."

"Thanks."

Laura finds her way into the shop. Tucker is already sitting at a table near the back, his hands clasped around a cup. He waves when he sees her and points to the cup he bought for her. She takes off her coat, hangs it on the back of the chair, and sits.

"How was your first week of classes?" he asks.

"Okay. I made it to all of them." *If I can focus on classes, then I won't think about the pain I'm feeling all the time.*

"Proud of you."

"Thanks."

"We miss you at the station."

"I know. I miss you guys, too." *But station equals Travis. Not ready for that. At least, I don't think I am.*

"Any idea when you might be ready to come back?"

"Soon."

"We got some new equipment over the break."

Her eyes perk up. "Really?" *Okay, something good to concentrate on.*

"Yep, new microphones. State of the art. Sound quality is unreal. Some new recording devices. And a new computer."

"Wow, Patrick must really love that."

"You know, things have changed since Dean Barrymore was officially fired, and with the new administration, we were finally able to get some of our proposals reviewed."

The mention of Dean Barrymore thrusts Laura right back into the thick of it. Her face drops.

Tucker takes her hand. "It's a good thing, Laura. It's a good thing."

"I know."

"We got a new intern, too. A freshman, real eager to learn the radio business."

"Extra hands are always nice," Laura adds.

Tucker and Laura chat quietly for another fifteen minutes as they sip their coffee. He even gets Laura to laugh a few times as he tells her some of the crazy questions and requests that the student body has been asking when phoning into the station.

"One caller said, 'I heard if I'm the tenth caller, I get a free pizza.' Sean had no idea what to say to that."

"We do have to think fast sometimes because you never know what someone might say." Laura laughs.

"Sounds like you miss it," Tucker says as Laura places down her empty cup. "Come stop in for just a minute." He motions with his head toward the direction of the studio.

"I…I'm not…"

"Please. I think it will be good for you. Feel that energy again."

Maybe he's right. I'm missing so much normalcy in my life. Maybe seeing the guys again will bring me happiness. I'll never know until I try.

"All right."

"Great!" He claps his hands together in approval.

She follows him toward the door to the station. A rush of emotions plagues her. *What will I feel when I pass the threshold?*

Tucker opens the door, and as though she were being transported back in time, she steps in. Nothing looks out of place. It's like she never left at all. Ryker, one of the two engineers, is sitting at his desk in the main area. When he turns to see who has entered, his face lighting up is just what Laura needed to see. He jumps up and quickly approaches.

"Well, what an awesome surprise!" He gives her a hug.

"Hey, Ryker. Great to see you."

"It's nice to see *you.*"

"Thanks."

"Sean and Patrick are down in Studio A. They'll be so excited to see you."

"I'll be back," Laura says as she goes down the hallway toward A.

Patrick is the one Laura worked the most with. They sort of developed this unspoken appreciation for one another over the past year. And Sean is one of Colin's best friends, so they, too, had a close and trusting relationship.

She pushes open the door to the engineering room and is floored by Patrick's reaction. He hits silence on his board and jumps up with wide-open arms and squeezes her deeply. For someone who shows little emotion, this is extraordinary.

"My friend! Oh my God. How are you? You coming back? Are you back?" He throws so many questions at her that she doesn't know which one to answer.

"Hello, Patrick."

He pulls her back and gives her an anxious look, as though he's desperate for her to give him the answer he wants, that they all want.

"Soon. I'll be back soon."

She peeks into the room and waves at Sean. He gives her an enthusiastic wave and then blows her a kiss. She blushes and smiles back.

"God, we all miss you around here."

"Thank you. I miss you guys, too. I hear you got some new equipment."

"Yes! It's so awesome. But, hey, I gotta…"

But she already knows he's got to return to the board. "Of course. I'll see you later."

She leaves the room, and when she enters the common area, Tucker says, "Why don't you go check out your studio?"

"You trying to lure me in?" she smiles.

"That's the plan."

Ryker nods his head in agreement.

"Fine. I'll go." She wanders down the hallway and takes a deep breath before pushing her door open.

Over winter break, Laura spent less time talking to Colin and significantly more time chatting with Wolfie. Her grief over Travis seemed to come on stronger whenever she talked to Colin, so naturally, her desire to avoid time with Colin began to take its toll on their seemingly volatile relationship.

Colin had been patient in the beginning, but as time passed, so did his understanding for his girlfriend to not want to be involved in his world. Hence the voice message he left her. "Hey, Laura. It's me, calling again. Been a few days since I've heard from you. Could you call me back? A lot has been going on here, at the station, that I think you'll want to know about. Anyway, miss you, and I hope you're okay. Call me, please."

But what she's not prepared to see when opening the door is Colin sitting halfway on the desk, his long legs stretched out in front of him, and a young lady sitting in Laura's seat. Colin is showing her some buttons, and the girl laughs and coos at his remarks.

Colin seems so different. But I can't quite place it. He seems alive almost. Is he flirting with her? He's got a little spark back in him. I know I haven't seen him like that around me lately, but who can blame him?

Finally, Laura has seen enough, so she clears her throat.

Colin turns, and within seconds, he jumps up off the desk. "Oh, um, hey," he stammers.

The girl, on the other hand, remains in Laura's chair. A pompous air about her as she leans back, crossing her arms over her chest, as if Laura is bothering her.

"Hey, Colin."

"Zoe, this is Laura Chase."

It's then the girl realizes who Laura is. "Oh, Laura. So nice to *finally* meet you."

It's not clear if she meant that to sound insensitive, but to Laura, it did.

"Zoe is our new intern," Colin quickly adds.

"Intern." Zoe laughs. "I'm a little more than that," she says, giving Colin a sideways glance.

Ah, yes. The intern Tucker mentioned. Of course, he failed to say she was hot and a female. But why would he?

"Anyway, nice to meet you. I just wanted to stop in and see the new equipment. But I'll let you two get back to it." Laura spins on her heel and heads back down the hallway.

"Laura, hang on." Colin rushes to meet her. "Can we chat a second?" His tone is unnervingly casual.

She knows she can't say no, so she nods her head ever so slightly.

He grabs her arm and pulls her into the storage closet. His face softens. "I was waiting to hear from you."

"I know. I've been trying to get back into the swing of classes. I planned to call."

"When?" He's unable to disguise his irritation.

She drops her gaze toward the floor, knowing she should have at least reached out to him. "I'm sorry," she mumbles.

He takes her hand. It feels foreign to her. She tries not to show it.

"Are you coming back to the station?"

She lifts her head.

"They need you," he adds. "The student body needs to hear from you," he pleads.

He's right. She knows it. But her heart still hurts so much.

"I miss it," she admits.

"I'm sure you do. It wasn't the same over the break. Around here. Without you."

"I know it was a lot for all of you."

"Yeah, but Tucker is thinking of letting Zoe fill in some."

The hell he will. An intern? Interns never get on the air.

"She's ready to be on air?" she asks, masking her anger. She has no idea who she's even angry with—herself, for needing time off, or Zoe, for being the person who could fill in.

"She's a good study. But that's up to Tucker."

Oh, so now, you're a teacher?

"When did she start here?"

"Beginning of winter break."

The beginning? I thought she was a freshman. How did I not know this? Why am I so bothered by this? Who am I kidding? Everything bothers me these days.

"Cool," she lies.

With pleading eyes, he asks, "Can I see you later?"

She realizes she's hesitating. Last time she checked, Colin was still her boyfriend—or some version of one.

"Yes. Why don't…"

Just as she's about to invite him to her room, he says, "Come by my place at eight."

A lump forms in her throat. "Okay, I'll see you then."

She pulls open the door, leaving Colin standing in the closet.

Laura heads straight for Tucker's office. She can't fathom some newbie taking her place during all of this. She knocks on the door.

"Come in!" she hears him yell. Laura yanks open the door. "Laura, I was hoping you'd stop in before you left."

"I'd like to come back," she blurts out. "I think."

His eyes widen at her direct and unexpected news. "Oh, okay. When?"

"Soon."

"You sure?"

"Yes. I need this."

"All right. I'll let the guys know. Who will you be working with…" His voice trails off.

The Weekly Blue. The paper Travis ran. Travis. The news. Why this all hurts so badly.

She swallows hard. "Wolfie—er, Ainsley Atwood. He'll be helping me."

"I see. Okay, keep your nose clean."

"Of course."

"Good. Now, get some rest this week."

"I will."

God, I hope Wolfie is okay with helping me. I hope I didn't just bite off more than I can handle right now.

Seven

Wolfie's Den

Laura knocks on the door to Wolfie's apartment. He lives a little off the main streets of campus, tucked away down a tree-lined road.

Laura can hear laughter and music playing. She's surprised by this and even questions whether she has the right apartment. When she called Wolfie an hour ago and asked to see him, there was silence in the background, and he said she could come over anytime this evening. The door handle turns, and a slender guy with dreadlocked dirty-blond hair opens it. Laura does not recognize him at all.

"You must be Laura," he says with a sheepish smile.

Laura catches a whiff of the distinctive aroma of pot as she steps inside. "Yes, hello," she says.

"I'm Tripp."

"Nice to meet you, Tripp."

"You, too."

"Is Wolfie here?"

"Of course. Come in."

He leads her into the kitchen, where other friends are gathered. Wolfie sets his eyes on her and immediately approaches. He leans in and gently kisses her on the cheek.

Then, he turns, and unlike him, he announces in a grand fashion, "Everyone, *this* is Laura."

They all speak at once, and one girl with a knit cap, a nose ring, and a wrist full of silver bracelets gets up and hugs her.

"I'm Willow. We've heard so much about you. You've been an amazing influence on campus," she states.

Her cheeks burn with embarrassment as she replies, "Nice to meet you all."

Laura can feel the warmth emanating around the room. What a special group of friends he has.

Names are exchanged, and it becomes evidently clear to Laura that Wolfie has a secret commune of friends that she knew nothing about. She's intrigued, to say the very least.

"A drink?" he asks.

"Sure," she says, following him over to the counter in his kitchen.

"Wine, bourbon?"

No beer or sticky red punch? "Um, wine, please."

"This is a lovely French red. I think you'll like it."

Laura giggles a little as he pours her a glass and watches her enjoy the first sip.

"Delicious," she says.

"Indeed."

Willow motions for her to come into the eating area and join them at the table. As she sits down, Wolfie takes the spot across from her. She sips her wine as they continue the conversation she interrupted with her arrival. Laura listens as they debate the use of cannabis for medicinal purposes.

"What do you think?" Tripp asks Laura.

"Oh gosh, I wouldn't know anything about it."

Wolfie jokes. "Laura, you continue to surprise me."

She laughs. "How's that?"

"I thought for sure you would have smoked with…" Then, he pauses as he sees the look on her face drop. "Um, what I meant was…" He tries to break out of the conversation but is unable to recover.

Laura, cheeks fiery red, sips on her wine as she averts her eyes from all of those looking at her.

"Dinner is ready," a girl with dreadlocks in her blonde hair announces. She was standing in the kitchen, working away, while the others were deliberating at the table.

"I'm sorry. I didn't mean to interrupt," Laura says to Wolfie.

"Not another word. You have to stay for dinner."

She glances at the clock. It's a quarter past six. "Okay, but how can I help?" she asks. *I feel embraced in their company, and I really need more of this in my life.*

Everyone rises, eager to assist.

"Nothing," the girl notes. "Just grab a plate."

They all line up as she pulls out a baked lasagna from the oven and then slices the garlic bread and places it in a large basket on the counter.

Laura is in disbelief as they all inhale their dinner in record time. Some never even glancing up from their plates to breathe. Laura is not surprised since this is one of the best meals she's had while at school. It's light-years better than the cafeteria food.

"Who made this? It's delicious," Laura asks.

"Yours truly." Wolfie grins.

"I'm impressed."

"I have many talents, Laura."

"I'm starting to figure that out."

"He thinks he does." Tripp laughs. "But he's just a recluse who gets it right from time to time."

"I see." Wolfie smiles. "And is this the part where I say, it takes one to know one?"

Tripp laughs as he shovels in his last bite of food. He leans back. "Damn, was that good."

After they clear the table, Willow pulls out a bag and rolling papers. "Now, for dessert."

Laura, feeling uncomfortable yet curious, sits back and observes the events unfold in front of her. She has a choice to make—yes or no. It's not complicated. She eyes them as they all take a drag from the joint, and as Wolfie extends his arm to her, she reaches out to take it.

Willow places her hand on her leg. "Just inhale," she says with a whisper.

Laura does and then immediately coughs, and shortly afterward, she can feel her body relax, but her mind begins to race with questions.

They spend the next hour sitting around the table, discussing all kinds of topics, some leading to fits of laughter and others leading them to determine the meaning of life right here, in this very moment.

As the night wears on and the pot and wine seem to dry out, one by one, they disperse. As she hugs Willow and Tripp good-bye, she finds herself alone on the front porch with Wolfie. She wraps her arms tightly around her body. She sits in the wood chair facing the long dirt road in front of the house. Wolfie takes the seat next to her.

"Interesting night for you?" he asks.

With a cracked voice, she replies, "Yes, very. Never tried pot before, obviously." *This was a night of firsts for me, and I rather enjoyed myself.*

"These are kind of *my* people," he adds.

"I can see why you enjoy them. They tend to question a lot, which reminds me of you."

"Yes, we don't sit idle. They keep me motivated when times get tough."

"I can imagine."

"Like with you," he announces.

She turns, with the pot still influencing her mind. "How so?"

"Well, for starters, Travis had me keep an eye on you."

The mere mention of his name is enough to bring tears to her eyes. "He did?"

"Yes, he was worried about you and wanted me to make sure you were handling your role in all of this, and, well…"

"Well, what?"

Wolfie thinks long and hard about how he wants to say what has been eating away at him for months. "Travis cared deeply for you."

She bows her head.

"And he knew, although he never spoke it, that you weren't going to be with him forever."

She glances up. "You knew about us?"

"Yes. I knew he had strong feelings for you. Otherwise, he would have just left you out to dry. Made you blow in the wind, in no direction. He did nothing by accident. But you know that."

"I thought no one knew." She pauses, and then in a whisper, she adds, "About us."

"He was discreet. Not really a kiss-and-tell kind of guy."

"Of course. It's just…my friends barely knew." *I didn't want to kiss and tell either. It would have made what we had seem so juvenile, and it was so much more than that.*

"Which is why he loved you, Laura."

A tingle of the utmost wonder runs up her spine. *Love* is such a valued word yet used so frequently. When it's said in a manner such as this, it does remind one that there is everyday love, and then there is something more unspoken and profound. That is what Travis meant to her, and that is why she misses him terribly.

"I loved him, too."

Wolfie takes her hand. "He knew that. But he understood you could care for more than one person at a time. In a lifetime. Isn't that the beauty of living?"

"Yes, it really is. But I have so many regrets, Wolfie. I thought I'd have more time with him. More time to come back around and learn more from him. Because I wanted to. And I can't shake the feeling that if I had just held on longer, I could have saved him."

"What? You can't think that way."

"But it's true. That bike, I would have told him to wait. I might have even been there with him that night. I…I can't stop feeling guilty about it."

"Please don't. He was a really smart guy. He never would have taken a ride if it wasn't working right. You know that, Laura."

"But I miss him so much…"

"I want you to know he never stopped thinking about you. I thought you should be reminded of that."

"Thank you. It does help. Particularly when I'm having a bad day. I'll think of him. The way he looked at me. Pushed me to be better. Never letting me stop what I was doing."

"He did the same for me. I owe a lot to him."

"I guess we both do. You must miss him a lot, too, huh?"

Wolfie smiles and then turns to face the road. Clearing his throat, he says, "Let me walk you back. It's a nice night."

Laura smiles. "I'd like that."

As they walk back toward her dorm, Laura can't shake the sensation that for the first time since Travis left the earth, maybe, just maybe, he was there with them tonight. Sitting on the porch like they were, looking out at the road ahead, wondering where this all led to.

He'd tell me to go straight ahead and to never look back. No matter how hard it gets, I can't step backward, only forward.

As they approach her dorm, she says, "I'd like to go back to the station soon."

The expression on Wolfie's face is indescribable. It's somewhere between relief and anguish. "I'm happy for you, Laura, if you are happy with your decision."

"I will be. But only if you'll help me. I can't do it without you."

His shoulders slump. "Whatever you need."

She takes his hand. "Is that a yes?"

"What do you think?" He smiles.

"Thank you, Wolfie. You can start next week. I can wing it for a little bit, but I'll need you midweek at the latest."

The wind picks up, brushing across their faces.

"Get inside. It's getting cold," he says.

"Thanks for tonight." She keys into her dormitory door.

He just smiles at her as he pulls the collar of his tweed coat up. "I'll call you soon, okay?"

But she already knew that. They speak almost every day, if not twice a day. It's all they have.

She faces him once inside the glass door and waves. "Good night, Wolfie."

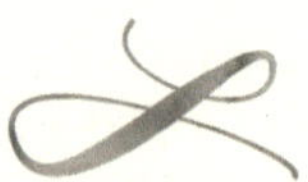

Laura arrives in her room.

Abigail is reading at her desk. "Hey," she says.

"Hey there."

"You okay?"

"Yes, just had dinner at Wolfie's."

"Oh." Abigail's brow is bent with concern.

"What's up?"

"You see Colin?"

"Oh shit!" Laura barks. "I completely forgot. I was supposed to see him." She looks at the clock on the wall. "Nine thirty. Double crap."

"Boy, the day my boyfriend forgets to see me…" Abigail laughs to make light of the situation.

"I know. I should go." She spins on her heel, and like a flash, she's gone from the room.

She practically stumbles down a flight of stairs as she poorly attempts to make up for missing hours. She pushes open the front door and jogs toward Colin's apartment. As she passes the Union, she looks in the open windows that run the length of the hallway toward the main area near the fireplace. She halts in her tracks. She squints, making sure she's seeing this correctly. Colin is sitting at a table across from the new intern, laughing and drinking coffee. He seems relaxed and happy. It kills her to see him appear this way without her. But he's been without her for a while now.

Can I blame him right now? I stood him up. I'm a terrible girlfriend. But, man, to see him with her, it feels like I've been replaced by a less troubled, younger version of a girl from the station. So, maybe I'm the one who got stood up. Maybe Colin's had enough, and he's ready to move on.

Laura, not wanting to make a scene, walks back to her dorm. As she enters her room, Abigail is right where she left her.

"That was way too fast. What happened?"

"Nothing. He wasn't home. Probably out, studying."

Abigail cocks her head. "Okay. Well, at least you tried."

"Yeah, I guess I did. Maybe next time, I won't."

Eight

Can We Be Friends?

Laura walks up to his apartment and takes a deep breath as she knocks with trepidation. Laura left Colin a message, asking if they could meet for coffee. Colin called her back in the morning to request they meet in a more private place—his apartment—in between classes. She waits a moment and then hears the door click open. Colin's expression is one of sadness as he invites her in.

"Hey. Come on in."

It's awkward when you must be invited in when you haven't had to be in the past months.

"Thanks."

"Austin will be home soon. Why don't we talk in my room?"

She follows him upstairs to his room. *Why do I feel so nervous? It's only Colin.*

He closes the door behind her and then leans up against it.

She stands in the middle of the room, bag still on her shoulder. *My God, is this strange, or is it just me?*

"I waited for you last night," he says.

"I know. And I'm sorry. I totally fucked up, and it's completely my fault."

"Made me feel pretty bad," he says, shoving his hands deep into the pockets of his jeans.

"I can imagine, Colin."

"What are we doing, Laura?"

"I don't know." Her eyes soften, and while she wishes more than anything that she had more to say, she simply doesn't.

"You have to know."

"I just…" She wants to ask him for more time. But he's given her plenty as is, and her sadness shows no signs of changing. *How much time will I need?*

"Talk to me," he pleads.

He pushes off his door and approaches her. Without thinking, she backs up.

"Wow, are you afraid I'm going to touch you?"

"What? No…" she says, shaking her head.

"You just moved away from me."

"I didn't mean to, I swear."

"Come here then."

He opens his arms to her, and with hesitation, she drops her bag on his floor and walks into them.

I guess I am afraid of touching you because I simply don't feel the way I used to, and I suppose I've known all along since the day he died that I'd never be the same. I'm too much of a coward to say it to you.

Her body tenses and she hates it. He places his fingers on her chin and slowly raises it, so their eyes meet. He leans in to kiss her, and as their lips meet, she gives him exactly what he needs. An answer.

He pulls back and takes her hand. He guides her over to his bed and motions for her to sit next to him.

"You have really great friends, Laura." She tips her head as he continues, "I don't think this is working out anymore, and I know your friends will keep an eye on you. Because I can't. Or better, I know you don't want me to."

"Is this about the intern?"

He cocks his head in confusion. "What?"

"I saw you guys last night in the Union."

"This has nothing to do with her. We work together. It has to do with *us*. You and me. What remains of us. Which we both know is barely anything at all."

Tears well in her eyes as he lays out the truth. "Really?"

"Laura, when I kissed you just now, I could tell it was over. The feelings you once had for me are gone."

"But I'm trying."

"You shouldn't have to try."

"It's just…I'm so…so depressed," she admits.

"I know you are. I know you miss your friend."

She whispers, "More than you know."

"Oh, Laura. I *do* know. I know a lot more than you give me credit for." He puts his arm around her and squeezes her tight. "Which is why I am hoping we can still be good friends. I think I could be there for you more, if the pressure is off you…off us. Don't you agree?"

She gazes up at him. She knows he's making total sense, but it still stings.

"So, we're not girlfriend and boyfriend anymore?"

He shakes his head. She notices the concern in his blue eyes, and it pains her to think she strung him along this far that it took *him* to say something. She didn't have the strength to do it herself.

"Wow. It's over," she murmurs. "I'm sorry it went on so long. Like this."

He drops his arm and takes her hand into his. "I'm here for you, okay? Please know I mean it."

"Okay."

He rubs the top of her hand, tracing his fingers over her skin. "I know coming back to the station won't be easy, but you can do it. I have faith in you."

"I'm trying not to overthink it."

"Good idea. We've all got your back."

As if completely taken out of the moment, she searches his face. "Since when did you grow a goatee?"

He smiles. "A few weeks ago."

She's embarrassed she never noticed. "Oh. Well, it looks nice." She touches it. "I didn't notice when we kissed." Her cheeks burn red.

He chuckles. "Well, you should have. It's scratchy."

"No. It can't be. Or I would have…"

"Noticed it."

She lowers her head.

"Laura," he pleads.

She looks up. "Am I that far gone that I notice nothing?" A tear drops on her cheek.

He wipes it away. "No, of course not."

"But you said when we kissed, you felt nothing."

"From you. Nothing from you. Not that I didn't."

"But how can I feel nothing?" she asks.

"You will again."

She grabs onto his hand. "But I need to now, Colin. Because all I ever feel is sad."

"What are you saying, Laura?"

She peers up at him. Her face beseeching him for help. She leans toward him. He doesn't move away from her like she did to him. Instead, he waits for her to let him know exactly what she means. She brushes her lips onto his, desperate for love.

"I need my friend," she says.

He runs his hand through her hair. He rests his hand on the nape of her neck. She wraps her arms around his waist. She kisses him again, only harder. He lets her set the pace, not knowing if or when she'll want to stop. She kisses him again and again, and each time, a more distinct feeling surges through her. She grips the edge of his shirt, and with enthusiasm, she pulls it up over his back. He lets her. She tosses it on the floor.

"This won't change anything," he whispers.

"I know. But I need you."

"I'm not going anywhere." And with that, he pushes her back on the bed.

He leans his long, slender body over hers. With one hand, he runs it up under her shirt, tracing her skin with his fingertips. She pulls her shirt up over her head. With reverence, he unhooks her bra, releasing her cleavage from their captor. She raises her back to meet his hands as they grab ahold of her full breasts. She moans. If there is one thing they are good at, it is this. Little does he know, it was Travis who taught her how to let go of her inhibitions and to simply enjoy sex.

"Don't think," he'd said. "Just feel your way through it, and you'll love it every time."

Colin licks and teases her nipple while she grasps down and starts to unbutton her jeans. His eyes flit open to meet hers, making sure she's in her right mind to want this. Or at least, in a space she won't later regret it. He sees a woman on the brink of satisfaction, wrapped tightly with a wanting he's never witnessed before. He knows he can satisfy her right now. He always has.

He undresses her. Taking in the beauty that lies before him. He gets up and takes a condom out of his dresser.

"Hurry," she says.

He stands before her, drops his pants to the floor, and readies himself for her. Like a tiger, he crawls on top of her, and with a hard thrust, he gives her exactly what she needs. In many ways, he needs it, too. He's missed her despite his fading love for her. He's had to stop loving her because it hurt so much. He's always known—ever since the day she collapsed in his driveway, crying in pain at the loss of Travis—that he'd never hold a candle to him. He never stood a chance.

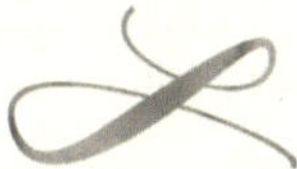

As she lies beside him, sheets crumpled around them, she releases her breath. "I guess I should go."

I really needed to feel something other than total sadness and be in the arms of someone I trust and will continue to trust—always. You're a good man, Colin Reed.

"Yeah," he says.

She sits up and starts collecting her clothes. He turns on his side, resting his elbow under his head. He eyes her while she dresses, and she doesn't protest because she knows it will be for the last time.

"I'll see you at the station," she says as she puts on her shoes.

He jumps up, quickly putting on his pants. He opens his arms to her. She steps in, only this time, her shoulders feel relaxed and comforted.

He squeezes her tight. "Take care of yourself, okay?"

"I will."

"If you need me, call me."

She gazes up at him. "I want you to know, this was never my plan. Any of this." *If I could change all of it, I would.*

"How could it have been?"

She smiles faintly as he releases his embrace.

"See ya." And with those last parting words, she exits Colin's apartment as an unattached woman for the first time in almost a year.

Nine

Advice and Memories

Laura finds herself heading downtown as opposed to back toward campus. Her mind is filled with disturbing thoughts of finality, death, loss, and breakups. She doesn't feel like going back to her dorm and rehashing the last tragic moments of her day with her floor mates. The idea of that nauseates her to no end.

Pulling open the door to Monroe's, she sees Bones, the beloved townie bartender, holding court behind the bar. He waves at her as she approaches.

"Stopping in for an afternoon libation?" he jokes.

"Yeah." She forces a smile.

He hands her a beer. She takes it and heads toward a secluded table near the darkened windows.

She picks at the label on her Natural Light as a group of rowdy football players enter and take over the pool tables. She takes out a book from her bag and tries to read, anything to occupy her mind.

Ten minutes pass when she feels a presence approach her table. She peers up. Tank is towering over her.

"Thought that was you."

She grumbles inside. "Hey, Tank."

"Alone at a bar." He chuckles.

"Yeah, and?" she gibes.

"Whoa, little lady. I meant no offense."

She peers past him. "With your Neanderthal teammates?"

He tips his head. "What's crawled up your butt?"

"Nothing, Tank."

He motions over to Bones, who carries over a few shots and beers. Bones places them on her table.

"Marcus!" Tank yells over his shoulder. "Play without me."

He invites himself to sit. "What is with you ladies these days?"

"What?"

"Nothing." He pushes the shot toward her. "Come on."

She takes it, and before he can clink glasses with her, she downs it.

"Jesus. Okay." He throws back his and motions for two more. "Keep 'em coming, Bones."

"Sure thing, Tank," Bones says.

"Look, I came here to…"

"To get away. Really? This place is crawling with OSU students."

"You know what I mean."

He picks up a second shot and motions for her to do the same. "Bottoms up."

She doesn't even flinch as she throws another back.

He's watching her, and she can tell he's hesitating, but then he quickly fires off, "Sorry about your friend. I meant to come see you."

Tears sting her eyes.

"Now…don't you cry on me."

As she blinks, a tear drops on her cheek. No use in pretending like she's not crying now. "Thanks for the kind words."

"Hey, I'm not good with this shit," he growls.

With venom in her voice, she says, "Really? You of all people?"

He gasps. "Now, look, I'm…" But he stops. He picks up his chair and brings it closer to hers. "I'm not trying to piss you off."

She laughs. "Isn't that what you do? Piss women off?"

His face is red. "Your roommate tell you to be an asshole to me?"

"Huh?"

"Nothing."

Apparently, Abigail didn't inform her roommate of their recent spat. He sits back in his chair and drinks half of a beer in one gulp.

She breaks the silence. "Don't feel like you have to keep me company."

"Well, let's be honest. I'm doing a lousy job of that." He smiles.

She finally cracks a tiny smile.

Bones puts two more shots down. This time, they clink glasses.

"Are you having a particularly bad day?" he asks.

She winces as she swallows. "Yeah, you could say that."

"What gives?"

"Let's see…Colin and I broke up."

"Wait, you and Colin broke up?"

"Yeah."

"When?" he asks.

"An hour ago."

"Jesus, girl. I'm sorry."

"It was long overdue. Like, months."

He interrupts, "Your cheeks were flushed earlier." He leans around to the side of her. "And your hair is a bit messy in the back. You just get laid?"

Her jaw drops open. Quickly, she attempts to regain her composure. "What?" She smooths the knot in the back of her hair that she was evidently unaware of.

"Let me guess…you two had a final screw." He laughs to himself.

Laura starts to stand.

He grabs her arm. "Relax. It's a joke."

Again, she rolls her eyes and lowers her butt back down.

He winks at her, and with a snide smirk, he says, "But it's true, isn't it?"

"Jesus, Tank." She tries to hide her grin.

"Hey, listen, I get it. Sometimes, it's the only way to say good-bye."

"You would know."

He chuckles and runs his hand through his blond hair. "Damn right. Sometimes, they just can't let me go."

"You are so full of yourself."

"Of course I am. But let's not focus on me. I know that's not all that is bothering you. So, what gives? Why are you drowning your sorrows?"

She releases a long sigh. "I suppose I'm nervous about going back to the station. And I…" *I miss Travis so much that I feel like I'm in physical pain. I don't want to eat, I can't sleep, I hate my life, and I wish more than anything that I could see him for just one more day. To tell him I fucked up. I never should have let him go.*

Much to her surprise, he takes her hand. "Is there anything I can do?"

She stares at the floor, her mind swirling from the alcohol, the taste fresh on her tongue. She whispers, "Can you bring Travis back?" She whips her head up, knowing her words slipped past her lips.

"Believe me, I wish I had that kind of power."

She realizes as he speaks that his words are deep. He experienced something similar when he lost his best friend, Jonathan, his senior year in high school. She quickly comprehends the painful connection they have.

"I'm…I'm sorry. I shouldn't have said that."

"Don't be. Trust me. Not talking about your feelings is about the worst thing you can do. Colin aside…you lost someone close to you, and you need to grieve. You owe it to yourself not to be too strong about it. It will bite you in the ass later if you do."

Laura contemplates his advice. "How do I do that without bumming out everyone around me?"

"Well, you won't bum me out."

"Really? Even after what you went through?"

"Well, I guess you could say, I've been there, so maybe I am the right person to talk to."

"I suppose." She conspicuously eyes him.

"So, why don't you start by telling me your favorite thing about him?"

Laura gasps. "My favorite thing about him?" *I can't tell Tank we were lovers, can I?*

He interrupts her thoughts with, "You can tell me anything because in the end, it won't matter, right? I'm a neutral party and a steel trap."

She thinks about the time he first held her. Just when she needed it the most, he seemed to know it. They connected without the use of words. His arms closed around her in a tight and warm embrace, and sometimes, when she closes her eyes, she swears she can still remember his scent. She noted the slight hint of tobacco on his shirt. At the time, she didn't know he preferred the taste of Parliament Lights over other cigarettes. He never really smoked around her. But when he ran the tips of his long fingers over her cheek, telling her how sexy he thought she was, she wanted to melt. No one had ever told her that, and she knew Travis would never waste words. He was too clever for that.

"He was so intelligent," she breathes. "And the way he looked at me…I knew I could trust him."

"Good."

"And…he smelled distinguished, if that makes sense."

"It does to you."

She continues as though she were alone. "He put me first, only he never had to tell me. I also admired what he'd created for himself at school. I knew he'd be successful…in life."

Tank grabs her hand.

A tear rolls down her cheek. "But you asked me what my favorite thing about him was. It isn't a thing. It was a day. The day we spent at my house last summer." The memory floods back, and she succumbs to it.

"Thank you, Mr. Chase, for showing me your radio equipment. Very cool," Travis said as he followed Laura and her father up the basement stairs.

"Call me Rick. Please."

"Sure thing."

"Can I offer you a beer?" her dad asked Travis.

Travis glanced at Laura, who was smiling proudly.

"Sure, Rick. I'd love one."

It was interesting for Laura to see her father be so friendly to a male friend of hers because it was really the first time Laura had a potential suitor in her home. Maybe it was because Travis just showed up today, or it could have been the fact that his involvement in the paper and the correlation with Laura's work at the radio station that had really intrigued her dad, but whatever it may have been, she was enjoying this time with the two of them more than she could have planned.

After the wonderful meal that Laura's mother, Maureen, prepared for them, Laura's parents excused themselves into the den to watch television. But not before her dad popped the caps on two bottles of beer and left them in front of Travis.

Travis grabbed them and started to head to the back deck.

"This way," Laura said, motioning with her head in the opposite direction.

Travis followed her to the stairs.

"I want to show you something."

She opened the door to her bedroom. Travis was in awe. Her room was a huge loft-style room overlooking the acres of land her family owns. She pushed open the large farm-style windows as the sun was setting over the hills in the distance.

"Beautiful."

"Isn't it?"

He nodded.

"But I wanted to show you this." On the large wood desk she had pushed up against the wall is an antique typewriter. "I was going to bring this back to—"

Before she could finish her sentence, he whistled as he ran his fingers over the keys.

"This is gorgeous—1923 Royal?" he asked.

She chuckled. "Figures you'd know."

"It's incredible."

"It's yours."

His face ignited. "What?"

"Yes, I planned to bring it back to school. Your senior year gift. For your last year at the paper."

His cheeks flushed. She noted she had never seen him blush before. He was way too confident for that.

"I don't know what to say."

"You like it?"

He glanced in her direction and shoved his hands deep into his jean pockets. His voice slightly quivered. "I love it."

"Good. I was afraid you'd give me some crappy argument on how you couldn't accept it."

He laughed. "No, I wouldn't do that. I really appreciate you thinking of me." He touched the keys again.

"You are most welcome."

She smiled at him, and with one look at her, he reached his arms toward her and pulled her into him. He wrapped a hand around her head, gently pulling it onto his chest.

She sighed deeply. They embraced while the sun faded toward another day.

They finally unwrapped themselves and chatted for hours as they sat on the floor in front of the large window.

"I'm so glad you came to my house." She yawned.

He draped his arm around her shoulders. "I've missed you this summer," he admitted.

She peeked up. "You have?"

"You seem surprised?"

"Can I say something?"

Intrigued, he let his arm go and swung his legs around on the floor to face her. "Of course."

She sat up, crisscrossed her legs, and faced him as well. "You, um, don't seem like the type of guy who talks about feelings. I mean…"

"You think I'm cold?" His brow was bent with concern.

"No. Oh gosh, no. It's more like you're all business." She winced as she finished her sentence.

"All business." He chuckled.

"I don't mean about all the work we have to do with the dean and all that but…well, maybe it is that. I shouldn't have said anything. I'm sorry."

He pulled his thumb and finger over her chin and raised her face to meet his. "Don't ever be sorry for having a thought, Laura Chase."

"But I…"

"I mean it."

"Okay," she agreed.

"And, yes, maybe I am mostly business. But I also haven't been around someone who has made me want to be more than what I'm wired to be."

Her eyes widened.

"I suppose I didn't know she was out there. Until I met you."

Laura tried not to gasp at his admission. "Travis, I…"

"We are more alike than I thought we'd be, and no matter what, your friendship is important to me, so I need to make sure that remains." He gave her a soft smile.

"I agree," she whispered.

He leaned forward and softly brushed his lips onto hers. She slid her legs over and tucked her body in closer to his. His long arms enveloped her, and she yawned deeply as the sound of his beating heart lulled and calmed her thoughts.

At some point, they fell asleep, curled on the rug, their bodies twisted together.

But when Laura woke up in the middle of the night, she found Travis leaning over her, his eyes were alive with lust. Without hesitation, she pulled his neck toward her face and kissed him deeply.

Within moments, they were both unclothed and in complete obsession of each other as they found another common ground their words had no match for.

"Earth to Laura," Tank says.

"What?"

"You drifted off, big time."

"Sorry. I…I should go." She stands, abruptly gathers her stuff, and heads toward the door.

"Wait up!" he yells.

She freezes at the door. Tank rushes over toward Bones, pays for their drinks, and meets her at the threshold of the doorway.

"You forgot your book." He holds her textbook in his hand.

She glances up at him with a glazed look in her eye. "Sorry."

"Don't be."

He pushes open the door to Monroe's. The cool air smacks them both in the face.

"Jesus, it's cold," he huffs.

She tries to pull her jacket tighter around her body. "Bye, Tank."

She heads toward the street, staggering a bit.

He jogs to meet her. "Hey, let me drive you home."

"I'm fine." Just as she says that, she stumbles forward.

His huge arm grabs her and pulls her into him, bracing her body.

"Laura," he whispers.

She glances up at him. This massive human hovering over her. *Why is he being so nice to me? My God, is he huge? Or am I standing in a hole? Man, too many shots. And now, I'm sad again because I know why I was here. But I can do this by myself.*

"Tank, I can make it on my own."

"Could have fooled me, and besides," he says as he steadies her upright, "I'm the one who supplied you with the shots, so let me make sure you get home."

She rolls her eyes, and before she knows it, he's scooped her up over his shoulder, and he's carrying her back to his truck. She tries to fight him, but it's no use. He's so damn big compared to her—compared to most people in fact.

"What the hell, Tank?!" she barks as he puts her down in front of the passenger door.

He unlocks the door and gently forces her in. He shuts it with a little force, and upon seconds of getting into the truck, he laughs. "You rolled your eyes a lot today. Am I that amusing?"

She laughs. "Really? And you think you can just hoist me up 'cause you're such a big guy…"

"To help you? Yes." He turns the key in the ignition, and the engine roars to life.

She crosses her arms over her chest and looks out the window. But her idea of the silent treatment does nothing to him. He's used to girls giving him this behavior, and he's learned to ignore it.

A few minutes pass, and he pulls into a parking lot.

"What are you doing?"

"Wait here," he says.

She glares after him as he climbs out. He's back ten minutes later, carrying a brown paper bag.

A welcoming aroma fills the cab as he pulls out of the lot. She'd never admit it to him, but she's starving. He parks in the student lot next to her dorm and reaches into the bag. He hands her what appears to be a submarine sandwich. In no mood for manners, she grabs it and starts to tear it open.

"Um, sure, eat it in my truck."

Having already taken a huge bite, she glances up at him, mustard on the corner of her cheek. He hands her a napkin.

"Sorry," she mumbles with a mouth full of food.

He finds some tunes on the radio and glances over at her with a smile as she continues to eat. "Relax," he says. "I'm not kicking you out or anything." He takes out his sandwich from the bag and takes a bite, too.

Laura's shoulders lower, and she starts to chew slower, savoring the food. They listen to music, eating their sandwiches, and watch random groups of students pass by every once in a while.

Out of nowhere, Tank says, "You're going to do great back at the station, Laura. You're a natural. Don't forget that."

"I'm nervous," she admits.

"Of course you are. I get that way before every game."

"You do?"

"Yep. But as soon as my feet hit the field, I know I'm right where I'm supposed to be, and I know all those thoughts before were just my way of getting me out there." He pauses and takes a huge bite, and then with a mouth half-full, he says, "Plus, I envision all the babes waiting for me after the game, and that doesn't hurt either."

"Give me a break," she says with a snort. "You're the worst."

"No, I'm dead serious, Chase. Have you seen the chicks after the games? They are the tens—easily. I'm not talking sixes or sevens—no way."

"I actually feel sick to my stomach right now. You're disgusting." She laughs.

God, I needed a good laugh today. Probably more than I needed this sandwich. Tank always seems to be there for our group of friends right when we need him the most. He never seems to disappoint. I'm sure glad he came over to me today.

He gives her the sweetest smile, and with a wink, he says, "It's nice to see you laugh."

Her cheeks flush slightly, and she crumbles her wrapper in her lap now that every morsel is gone. She looks over at him and says, "Well, I should get going. Um, thanks again, Tank."

"I figured you'd be hungry, and you shouldn't be going to the cafeteria tipsy," he states, throwing their trash in the bag.

Her hand rests on the handle after gathering her tote bag. With a slight glance in his direction, she says as she opens the door, "I wasn't exactly referring to dinner, but thanks for that, too."

Ten

She Is Back

Laura drags herself out of her dorm room after remaining frozen for minutes, anticipating her return to the airwaves.

I can do this. I have to move forward. I can do this. I can't go backward, she chants to herself the entire walk over to the Union as she blares music through her Discman.

Her heart pounds ferociously as she walks through the door. She is greeted by Tucker.

"Hello, and welcome back!" he says with a warm smile.

"Thanks, Tucker," she says, trying to put on a brave front.

He wraps his arm around her shoulders. "Ease into today, okay? Just get your sea legs back, and when you are ready, you can start the news segment again."

"Okay."

She refused to hear or entertain any information that pertained to the dean, Travis, or his motorcycle accident. She knew Wolfie would continue their work because he'd promised her he would, and that was good enough for her. Laura, on the other hand, needed to concentrate on getting back on air and reclaiming her spot at the station.

As she walks down the hallway, Colin is exiting Studio B, and she notes Zoe is close behind. Too close. Much to her surprise, Colin lights up when he sees her.

"Hey, welcome back!" He leans in and hugs her. "You okay?" he whispers.

"Yeah."

A squeaky, young voice says, "Welcome back, Laura."

"Thanks," she mumbles. Then, Laura asks, "Colin, can I talk to you?"

"Sure." He follows her back into her studio as Zoe heads toward the common area.

He closes the door as she drops her bag on the floor.

She spins on her heel. "You know I don't like people in my studio right before I'm supposed to go on," she snaps. "I can't have anyone touching the equipment."

"I was helping her cut a promo." He gulps.

"She's cutting promos?"

"Yeah. Tucker asked her to." Colin cocks his head to the side.

Laura shuts her mouth. She'll have to take that up with Tucker later.

"You all right, Laura?"

"Yeah, I just need to speak to Wolfie." She needs his support if she's ever going to get through today.

With sadness, he whispers, "Okay. Well, good luck today." Colin exits the room.

Moments pass, but it feels like years before she hears a slight knock on the door. She doesn't need to speak, as she knows Wolfie will merely enter, and he does.

He rushes up to her. "Are you okay?"

"I'm scared. I'm not sure I'm ready." *What if I suck? What if a caller asks me about Travis? Or the dean? Or where I've been? I haven't thought any of that through. Oh no! I can't do this!*

"Take a deep breath and let it out slowly."

She closes her eyes and does as he instructed. She can feel him touch her hand, taking it gently in his.

"He wants you to continue, Laura."

Her tear-soaked lashes flutter open. "I know, but I am so afraid that I'll crack."

"You won't. You're stronger than you think you are. He saw that in you. I see it, too."

She glances at the clock on the wall. Unfortunately for her, time is not on her side. "I said I'd do this, so I have to," she whispers.

"Come on. I'll stay while you get settled."

Laura turns toward the board and attempts to recall her routine. She runs her fingers over the panel and touches all the cataloged music, picking her first few songs. She sits and adjusts the height and the balance of her microphone. The audio console is ready. She leans over the board to make sure she can properly touch all the buttons.

"By the way," he says breaking her concentration, "why is Colin not in here?"

"We broke up."

Not one to really delve into the male-female relationship drama, he simply says, "Wow, okay."

"Long overdue."

"Yes, I think you need to concentrate on yourself."

"I agree."

He sits in the chair usually reserved for on-air guests, pulls out the small notebook from inside his tweed coat, and begins writing down his thoughts. He's often seen doing this; it's a part of his investigative nature.

"I can stay with you, if you want?" he offers.

Her shoulders completely relax, and she smiles for the first time in months. "I was hoping you would."

"I know," he says without looking up at her.

Patrick, the student engineer that Laura works with the most, walks into the room. At this point, he's used to seeing Wolfie around. Even more so these past few months now that Travis is gone.

"Hey, Wolfie. Welcome back, Laura." He gives her a warm hug, which is a new custom for Patrick. He only started hugging her after Travis's passing.

"Patrick, I'm so glad it's you today. I *need* you."

He blushes even though she isn't talking about a carnal need. "I'm always here for you. I'm just so glad you're back."

"Thanks."

"Get settled, and we are on in five." He enters the booth separated by soundproof glass.

Before she knows it, he's counting down to her. She places her headphones on her ears, as does Wolfie. Patrick switches on the *Silence* light. Laura cues up her first song. Then, she takes a deep breath and releases it. The *On Air* light illuminates.

In a concise, clear voice, Laura booms into the microphone, "Good afternoon, Hawks. This is Laura Chase, returning to you. I've missed you while on a brief sabbatical from the station, and thank you all for the words of encouragement and support. I will be bringing you the news segments at a later date, but for my first day back, I thought I'd go back to when I first started at the station and play some music for you. Hit me up at 555-WOUR and let me know what you'd like to hear. Until then, I'm going to start off the day with one of my favorites." She starts the music. "Here's 'The Day I Tried to Live' by Soundgarden."

Little does anyone know, that is the song Travis used to blare from the speakers in his room when he was trying desperately to rattle the trapped thoughts out of his head and onto the blank paper on his lap.

Thankfully, the next two hours fly by, and as she switches off the microphone, she spins around in her chair to shield her tears from Wolfie. Minutes pass before she can collect her thoughts. When she turns back around, the room is empty. There is a note on the chair where he sat. Curious, she gets up and picks it up.

Laura, come by my house—8 p.m. You did great.

Eleven

Dress Shirts and Typewriters

Laura enters her room to find Abigail, Bree, Melissa, Alex, and Casey all sitting on the floor.

Abigail jumps up and embraces her friend. "Laura, you were wonderful."

As they all get to their feet to approach her, Laura backs up again. *Touching is love, and I'm not ready for love again.*

They stop and instead quietly accost her with messages of a job well done.

"Thanks, guys. It was more exhausting than I remember it being."

"That's because you had the late shift for so long and were merely running on caffeine," jokes Bree.

Laura chuckles. "True."

"We were just waiting for you to grab dinner," Alex says.

"Thank you." She nods. "I am pretty hungry."

"You worked up an appetite," Melissa replies.

Laura has missed the trips to the cafeteria with her floor mates. She's craving the normalcy she once felt. *Maybe today is the day to start again.*

"Let's beat the crowd," Casey adds with an encouraging motion with her arms toward the door.

Laura follows them to the cafeteria in virtual silence. But this is really nothing new to her group of friends. Whenever Laura would get off work at the station, she would often lack a voice among her friends, having just spent the past few hours talking nonstop to thousands of students at OSU.

As they wait in line, Abigail turns to her. "Are you doing okay?" she asks.

"Yeah, I guess."

"Have you spoken to Colin at all? You guys cool?"

"Yeah. It's for the best. I'm no good for anyone these days."

Her friend's eyes soften. "You will be. Someday. He's out there. I just know it, Laura. It'll just take some time."

Dinner is uneventful, which is perfect for Laura. After she places her tray on the conveyer belt, the girls head toward the back room. Taking up a couple of tables in the corner are the players on the football team. She notices Tank almost immediately.

Abigail and Bree start to wander in their direction. "Come with us?" Abigail asks Laura.

"I've got to get back and get some homework done."

"Okay. See you back at the dorm," Bree says.

Laura starts to exit when she hears a familiar voice yell, "Laura, wait!"

Laura stops in her tracks. *What could he possibly want to talk to me about?* She waits for him to approach.

His large hand rests on her shoulder. "Laura."

Oddly, his touch doesn't alarm me. Why is that? She turns to face him. "Hey, Tank."

"I just wanted to say you did great today. I know that couldn't have been easy."

Duh, of course. My radio gig. "Thanks."

He looks out of his element. As though he has no clue what to do next. "Um, well, I guess I'll see you around."

"Bye, Tank." She turns back around and walks out of the cafeteria.

She spends the next hour trying to concentrate on her schoolwork, but most of the time, she's staring out the window, watching the students mill about, as though they have little to care about.

Wait, that is a major assumption on my part. Someone might assume a guy like Tank, big man on campus, has never suffered a major loss, and boy, would they be wrong. Then, there is Nathan. He lost his mother to a drunk driver in high school. How awful is that? No one's life is ever as easy as it might seem on the outside. So, I should remember that more. You never know someone's story until you ask them.

And everyone has one.

Abigail and Nathan's presence disrupts her thoughts as they enter the room.

"Hey, getting any studying done?"

"Not really," she admits.

"We're going down to the commons to study. Want to come with us?" Nathan asks.

"I can't. I'm going to Wolfie's." She looks at the clock on the wall. It's ten to eight. "I should go." She closes her textbook and stands. She pulls on her jacket. "I'll catch you guys later."

Laura wanders over to Wolfie's apartment. A cool breeze whips across the skin on her cheeks. She sniffles as she approaches the front porch of his house. She knocks a few times and waits for him to open the door.

"Come in," he says, stepping aside and allowing her to pass. Sadness clouds his features, but he often doesn't show much enthusiasm, as it's not his nature.

She watches him intently as he takes her coat, and then he asks, "Can I offer you a glass of wine?"

"Sure. Red, if you have it."

"Of course."

It's no surprise to anyone who knows Wolfie that he lives alone. Although Laura would worry more about him if she hadn't been invited to his dinner party and met his secret circle of friends. They were lovely and most definitely appreciate Wolfie for who he is, much like she does and Travis used to.

She takes a seat at his kitchen table as the glass of wine is placed in front of her. He pours another bourbon for himself and sits across from her.

"You left so quickly," she says.

"I thought you needed a moment."

"I get it." She smiles. "You don't know what to do when a girl cries."

His skin reddens. "No. No, I do not."

She sips on her wine, knowing Wolfie will get to why she's here when he's ready. Not that a social call isn't in order. They spend more time with one another than they probably do with anyone else. And she has a roommate, so that says a lot.

After some small talk and another drink each, Wolfie takes a deep breath and sighs purposely.

"I'll be right back," he says.

She gulps. There is something in the way he moves that strikes a note with her. "Sure thing."

He comes back shortly, carrying a box. He places it on the counter with great care and then takes his seat back across from her.

"So," he says.

"*Wolfie.*"

"Okay, okay. I know I'm stalling."

"You're freaking me out."

"Sorry." He swigs back his watered-down bourbon. "Travis's parents wanted me to speak with you."

The mere mention of his name sucks the air right out of the room.

"About what?"

"Do you remember when Travis got that letter from the Associated Collegiate Press?"

"Yes." She'll never forget him showing her that letter in his room.

Travis was notified that he was the recipient of the College Media Liberty Award, which recognizes students for demonstrating outstanding support for college press freedom and reform. This had all stemmed from his tireless work at the paper.

"Well, Travis will be honored at a ceremony at the university in April, and his parents would like you to give his acceptance speech."

She swears her heart temporarily stops. "What?!" *Me? Give a speech? On behalf of Travis?*

"Yes. You're the only one who can do it, Laura."

"Me?"

"Yes, you. You know it, and *I* know it."

"What about you?" she asks. "You're his…were," she corrects, "his best friend."

"And so were you. But you knew him differently than I did. You have that advantage. He would have wanted it to be you. You're the voice of this school. I'm not."

"Yes, you are," she argues. "The student paper is your voice. Just as much as it was his."

He deliberately ignores her pleas. "Laura, will you do it or not?"

She hangs her head. They both knew as soon as he asked her that she never really had a choice. Of course she'll do it. She cared so deeply for him that having anyone else do it wouldn't sit right with her or Wolfie. She's also positive that Wolfie would rather crawl under a rock than speak in front of a large crowd.

Barely able to push the words out, she says, "Yes. Tell them I will."

He clasps his hand over hers. "You know you're making the right decision."

"I know."

"More wine?"

"God, yes." She laughs.

He pours her another glass. They go over some specifics about what little Travis's parents were able to share with Wolfie. All she knows is, she's now tasked with the difficult job of writing what she thinks Travis would have written. Sort of.

Travis was a master of the written word. Laura has become a master at conversations and announcements on the radio. They're very different. But at least she has about six weeks to complete the speech.

That might seem like a long time, but to me, I can already feel the collar on my shirt tightening around my neck.

"Can I practice with you?" she asks.

"Of course. I won't let you go at this alone. I promise."

Something in the way he looks at her relaxes Laura. She knows she'll not be on her own. Wolfie would never let her be. He's proven that tenfold.

Finally, Laura downs the last sip from her glass and starts to stand. As she passes by his counter, she asks, "What's with the box? You moving?" She chuckles.

He gulps. "No. I have something for you."

Her cheeks are rosy red from the wine. "Really? A gift for me?" Her smile quickly fades as she notes the serious expression on his face.

"His parents had some things they wanted us to have. You to have. As a token for giving the speech."

"What?" A ghostly chill runs up her spine.

He opens the lid on the box. She leans in to get a better look. Neatly folded on the top is a navy-blue button-down oxford. She can see on the bottom of the pocket is an ink stain. Her eyes well with tears. "Put the lid back on, please," she stresses.

He immediately does. He stammers, "I didn't know how to do this."

"It's not you, Wolfie. You know that."

"Will you be okay?"

"Yes, of course," she lies. "Don't worry. I'll look at the stuff later." She brushes off his concern. "But I should go. Got an early class tomorrow." *It was so nice of them to think of me, to give me precious items of their sons. This is a really big deal, and I'm having a hard time even digesting this moment, let alone imagining touching his shirt.*

"It's a little heavy," she says, balancing the box in her arms. She assumes there are probably a ton of books in it, as Travis's room was filled with them.

Wolfie opens the front door for her.

As she steps out onto his porch, she turns slightly and says, "I'll see you tomorrow?"

"Of course. Want to meet in the Union. Say, two?"

"Great. See you then. And thanks for today, Wolfie. I couldn't have done it without you."

Laura unlocks her dorm room and finds a note on the door.

> *No class in the morning, so I'm staying at Nathan's. I'll meet you for lunch. Love, AP*

Thankful she has the room to herself, she quickly undresses and washes up in the bathroom. Then, she takes the box and places it on her bed. She's anxious because she already knows his dress shirt is waiting for her on the top. She can only pray that it still smells like him. She lifts the top off and tosses it on the floor. Her hands tremble as she takes the shirt in her hands. She brings it to her nose and inhales deeply.

The distinct aroma of woodsy pine with a hint of tobacco enters her nose.

It's him. It's him, she repeats in her head.

Her once-bright eyes are now rimmed in red. "How can you be gone?" she sobs, trying not to let her tears ruin his shirt. This is all she has of him. It's all she'll ever have. How very tragic.

She grabs several tissues as she places the shirt on her bed. As she tosses the tissues in the wastebasket, a shiny reflection from within the box catches her eye. She peers in. There are no books in the box. There is nothing but one heavy object. Her heart pounds. Sitting in the box is the 1923 Royal typewriter—the gift she gave Travis for the anticipation of his graduation from OSU. The only gift she ever gave to him has now been returned to her. With shaking hands, she takes the typewriter out, and pulled through the carriage is a note. She removes it, so she can read it.

Laura,

It would be a great honor for you to write Travis's acceptance speech on this typewriter. He loved it so much. He spoke of you often.

We look forward to hearing it.

Sincerely,

Buddy and Di Taylor

Laura carefully carries the typewriter to her desk, gently resting it down. She runs her fingertips over the keys, just like he did last summer in her room. As she thinks back to all the wonderful times she spent with him, she can't help but wonder if this pain will ever go away. Will she ever be herself again? She switches off the desk light illuminating the beautiful typewriter, and like a widowed lover, she reaches into her top drawer and dispenses two of the pills the doctor gave her.

Washing them down, she whispers, "At least this way, maybe I won't dream about you."

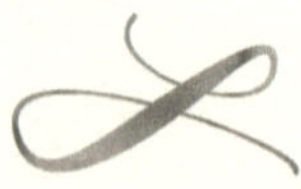

After tossing and turning all night, she skips her first class of the day and barely makes it to her second and third.

Finally, she approaches the door to the Union to meet Wolfie but not before grabbing a huge coffee on her way. The barista hardly recognizes Laura, as not only has her routine of grabbing a coffee before her shift at the station been nonexistent, but her appearance has noticeably changed, too.

She finds Wolfie near the back chairs adjacent to the fireplace. She plops in the seat.

"Jesus. Rough night, I take it?"

She barely glances up at him. She just grumbles as she takes a sip of her coffee.

"Understandable," he continues. "I might be able to help you with that."

She perks up. "Really?"

"Yeah, you need to be able to sleep at night."

"Those damn pills the doctor gave me are running out," she barks. "I can't sleep. I'm exhausted."

"Okay, I'll stop by later and handle that." He's so confident when he speaks; it's like he's ten years older than any other student she knows on campus, only he's not. It's just who he is. "But in the meantime, I've finally been able to come out from some other pressing issues at the paper and do a little digging into the vandalized house."

Her ears immediately perk up. "Really?"

"Yes, I think I'll have something for you—"

A deep voice interrupts their conversation, "There you are, *Radio Girl*."

Laura whips her head up to see Tank towering over them. The grin on his face fades once he gets a good look at the bloodshot-eyed and disheveled Laura slouched before him.

He starts to speak when Wolfie interjects, "Hey, you're Tank, right? I'm Wolfie."

Tank is a well-known figure at the school for not only what he does on the football field, but also for what he did in catching the Campus Creeper.

Wolfie extends his hand to shakes Tank's.

"Yes, nice to meet you. I've heard a lot about you from Laura."

"Tank, we are trying to have an *intelligent* conversation here," she growls.

Tank's eyes go wide as saucers, and he steps back from the table. Unable to mask his disappointment, he quips, "Well, don't let this dumb jock stop you." He turns on his heel and storms off through the crowd of students.

Wolfie, in too much shock to stop him and evidently not in the know as to why she would say that, remains silent. But it doesn't last long. He gently touches her arm. "Laura, why the heck would you say that?"

She drops her head. "I have no fucking clue. But he interrupted us and…" *I'm a terrible person, and my moods are all over the map. Up, down, left, right. Whiplash.*

"We are sitting in the middle of the Union. The probability of getting interrupted is likely. He was just saying hello."

"Just drop it, okay?"

Wolfie sits back and carefully chooses his words. "It's dropped."

"Now, what were you going to tell me?"

"That I'll have some research for you to help me with. I have some notes to pick up from a few of the junior reporters. I'll drop those off to you when I stop by later."

Desperate for help, she pleads, "And when will that be?"

"I can be by your place tonight—say, eight."

"Fine."

He glances at the clock on the wall. "I need to get to class. You going to be okay?"

"Yeah." Again, she sips her coffee as a diversion to avoid eye contact with him.

He slings his bag over his shoulder. He clears his throat to gain her attention. "Take care of yourself today."

Something in his tone gives her pause, but she refuses to acknowledge the implication in his remark.

"Today, I'll do whatever I want," she mumbles under her breath as he walks away.

Twelve

Something Has to Give

Wolfie, knocks on Laura's door at ten to eight obviously not wanting to piss her off any further after her little hissy fit this afternoon in the Union. Thankfully, Abigail is not home, so the two can take care of a little business without having to whisper and draw suspicion.

"Listen, these are some herbal vitamins I take in order to sleep," he says. "They can make your stomach a little upset so I'm giving you a few joints should you need to settle your stomach. Just be careful, okay?"

"I will. Promise." She snatches them from his hand and takes the herbal supplements and then quickly shoves the rest in the top of her dresser drawer.

"I'm serious, Laura. I need your help with all this stuff, too," he says motioning to the file folder containing information on the vandalized soccer house.

"Wolfie," she says quickly changing her tone to a much sweeter sound. "I'm a smart person, you know that."

"I know. If you need me, call me. Okay?" he says as he tucks her into bed, eyelids as heavy as rocks and as close to sleep as she's been in a while.

"I will," she murmurs.

He sits on the edge of her bed for a while longer, writing down his thoughts in his notebook as Laura drifts off into a deep, much needed sleep.

Laura stirs in her bed. She slept like a baby, but unfortunately, her stomach isn't feeling so great as she starts to swing her legs over the side of the bed.

She tries her best to get dressed and pull herself together to make it to her class.

During class, she can only stare at the front of the room of her lecture, not participating and barely taking a single note.

At the end of her mathematics class, she leans over to Logan. "Can I borrow your notes?"

With sympathetic eyes and without hesitation, he hands her his entire notebook. "If you need a catch-up session, just call me."

"Thanks," she replies as she takes the notebook.

She exits class and quickly puts on her shades. She takes the long way around campus to the library and finds a place off the beaten path to take a quick hit off a joint.

I need to settle my mind and the rest of me.

With a numb body, she slowly makes her way back toward campus. Her mind races as she tries—poorly—to develop a plan of action on how best to tackle all the information Wolfie gave her last night. She has a lot of schoolwork to catch up on, but this is all she can think about. Finish what Travis started by finding the bastard—or bastards—responsible for the next fresh-hell narrative taking place at OSU.

Why would someone vandalize the women's soccer house? Think, Laura.

She's about to near the other side of the street when she hears a *tremendously* loud car horn and what seems like numerous people yelling. Then, without warning, she feels her body become weightless as she's lifted off the ground and scooped into a massive set of arms.

"Jesus Christ, Laura. You trying to get yourself killed?!" Tank barks with her body still swept up into his clenched arms.

"What?!" She comes back to reality.

"You almost got hit by that car!"

As he places her down, she looks over at the other side of the street and notices all the other students are waiting for the crosswalk to signal, and some of them still have their hands clasped over their mouths or heart in disbelief.

She pushes off Tank. "I got it." She steadies herself. "I'm fine. I can handle myself."

Just then, the loud signal to cross erupts their hostile conversation, and all the students paying attention are now approaching them to enter the library. Laura tries desperately to blend in with them as they talk about her.

Tank is hot on her heels. "A *thank you* would suffice."

"Thank you," she mumbles. She shuffles into the library and signals the woman behind the counter. "Yes, I need to do some private research. Where's the microfiche?"

"Third floor. There are rooms there."

Laura swipes her card and makes her way up the flight of stairs. Tank also heads to the third floor. He sees her go into room thirty-two as he plops his book bag down in a cubby, shaking his head in disgust. Only he can't concentrate, even after his adrenaline has resumed to a normal level. He's still seething from the situation out front. So, without even knocking, he busts open the door to room thirty-two.

"It's occupied," she barks in the darkness.

He still marches in.

"You hard of hearing?"

He leans over the desk in the room and switches on the lamp. "No, but clearly, *you* are."

She whips her head up. "Tank, please. I'm working."

"I can see that." He steps close to her. His eyes widen now that he can get a good look at her bloodshot sclera. He glances at his watch for effect. "Really? This time of day?"

She averts her stare. "What?"

"Oh, I don't know. You nearly got killed out front because you were off in la-la land, and now, I can see"—he dramatically motions toward her face—"that it's because you spent the afternoon, what? Hanging with Cheech and Chong?"

She bursts into a fit of laughter.

"Not funny, Laura!"

But she can't stop. Her eyes start to water from laughing so hard. She slows to a chuckle. "What do you want from me?"

He pulls a chair up near hers and sits. "How about acknowledging that you nearly got slaughtered on the street in front of a dozen or so witnesses, and if I hadn't been there to save you, you'd be freaking dead?!"

"I said thank you." *Jesus, what does he want, a cookie?*

"Barely."

"You want another hero acknowledgment? Is that it? You saved Abigail, and now, you've saved me, too."

"Jesus," he whispers. When she doesn't retort, he adds, "Okay, so let's talk about your attitude in general."

"What attitude?"

His expression dramatically softens. "You embarrassed me in front of your friend at the Union."

Her face drops. *Ouch.* Being called out on your shit is never fun. "We were talking, and you interrupted."

"I get that, Laura. But I've heard so much about him, and with all your history, that was how you treated me the first time I met him? You made me look like an asshole. A nuisance. Is that how you talk about me?"

"No," she whispers. *I hate that he looks so wounded.*

"Could have fooled me."

"Tank, listen, I don't have time for whatever this is." She motions between them.

Offended again, he quips, "Whatever this is? You don't have time for a *friend*? You don't have time for Colin or anyone but Mr. Codependent? Do you not see how unhealthy that is for you?"

"Not fair, and we're *not* codependent," she lies.

"Okay, how many nights do you go to bed on the phone with him?"

Four to five nights.

She doesn't answer, so he continues, "How many times do you only talk about Travis, the paper, and the work you need to do?"

Most of the time.

"Okay, the silent treatment. So then, do you ever talk about how Wolfie feels about his death?"

Maybe. It's complicated.

"Or is he only reassuring you of Travis's affection for you, Laura?"

She rubs her eyes. *I guess.*

He continues the hammer of questions. "Do you see Wolfie healing?"

Perhaps. I don't know how to measure that.

"Did you learn *anything* from the debacle I had last year with Abby and Nathan? That by me isolating one person to rehash all my sadness with was *not* a good thing?"

Her mouth drops open slightly, but her silence remains.

"I lost someone very dear to me. Don't you think I might be a good person to talk to? Maybe I misread all this. Maybe you *do* just think of me as an asshole. You don't need me for interviews anymore, so you've rendered me inconsequential." He crosses his massive arms over his chest.

"*Tank*," she gasps.

"But what do I know? One day, you'll look back on all this crap with disappointment in yourself. The days you spent popping pills and oversleeping, missing classes and your shift at the station. It's not like I don't know what it's like to lose a scholarship and my place on the team after one painful conversation with my coach." He digs the knife in deeper. "Like getting high to go to the *library* instead of focusing on really researching whatever you're in here doing with a clear head—or better yet, writing the acceptance speech Nathan told me you're giving for Travis next month. You could actually be trying to celebrate him instead of acting like no one has any idea as to what you're going through."

Her mouth opens, but not a sound escapes, not a peep from her. Her glazed-over eyes appear almost childlike now. As if she had been playing house, only to crash through the roof of reality, realizing quickly that being an adult was too hard.

He stands. "Well, I see this is a one-way conversation, so I'll leave you. Just try and be fucking careful when you walk home. I won't be there to *save* you."

His sarcasm snaps her back.

"Screw you, Tank."

He lets out a very dark chuckle. "You know, at one point, I definitely thought about it but not with the way you're keeping yourself these days." He eyes her up and down. "Take a shower and eat a meal, for God's sake, before people on campus stop recognizing you." With that, he yanks open the door and storms out.

Laura's jaw nearly hits the floor as it drops. She wishes she'd had something to say in return, but she's completely void. She just sits there in the dim light of a secluded room in the library as her mind swirls uncontrollably. Unfortunately, the first thought that comes to her mind is, *I must tell Wolfie about this!*

Tank's heart is beating double time for the second time in an hour as his head rests on the desk in the cubby of the library. His eyelids close, and his mind replays him barely grabbing Laura in enough time to prevent her from getting hit by the SUV barreling down the street. The mere thought creates a ripple of nausea in his stomach.

And he had to give her tough love. Wolfie won't. That's not his role in all of this. He needs to do what he needs to do in order to keep her close. To keep their relationship together. No one can blame him for that. If that means supplying her with medication, well, better him than Tank. If it means that she needs a late-night chat to get past the darkness? It should be with Wolfie. If their dependency right now helps keep Travis's memories and his work alive, then so be it.

But it can't last forever. At some point, something has got to give.

Thirteen

Accept Where You Are

Laura calls Wolfie with some of the information she got at the library but also to fill him in on what happened with Tank. She leaves out most of the details about their argument, but she can't help but tell him about her near-death experience with an automobile. But then again, she downplays it quite a bit so as not to worry Wolfie that she was out of control.

"Make sure you thank him properly. He could have gotten hurt, too."

"I know. I might not have been so kind to him."

"Laura, you're too nice for this type of behavior regardless of what's going on."

"I know. I know."

"I'll come by tomorrow afternoon to the station to review the papers, okay?"

"Okay. Night."

The typewriter on her desk is calling her to touch it. The scolding from Tank got her thinking long and hard about taking the plunge to sit down and draft Travis's acceptance speech. She owes him something concise, heartfelt, and meaningful for all that he accomplished in his tragically young life. She sits down, pulls out a paper from her drawer, gets a box of tissues at the ready, and begins typing away.

After a long night of tossing papers on the floor and attempting several rough drafts, she finally gets dressed for bed, brushes her teeth, and crawls under her covers. She sets her alarm for an hour before she needs to leave tomorrow morning. Exhausted from all the commotion during the day, she's more than ready to close her eyes and go to sleep. She rests relatively well, considering the day was anything but restful.

All I can do is go from one day to the next. If I beat myself up over every mistake, argument, or feeling I have, I'll never get out of my own way. I have to give myself a break.

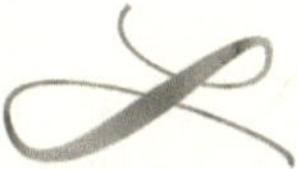

In the morning, she showers and dresses in something other than an oversize sweatshirt and sweatpants. She blow-dries her hair and does her best to look presentable today. She drags herself to Boyd Hall, and like a scolded child sent to her room, she climbs the stairs to Tank's room. She takes a deep breath in, and with trepidation, she knocks on his door.

She hears a commotion as the door jiggles and then opens. What she's not prepared to see is Tank standing before her with nothing but a pair of jeans on, still unbuttoned on the top. His smooth, hairless chest fills the doorframe, and his abdominal muscles ripple down to the top of his jeans, where the arch of his man V hits right where the button is left open.

She tries not to gape at him and quickly composes herself. "Tank, sorry to bother you."

He's just as surprised, shocked even, to see Laura standing before him.

"Everything okay?" He peeks past the door into the hallway, convinced there must be someone else with her.

"Just me," she whispers.

"Um, come in."

"I can't stay."

"Well, I don't feel like keeping the door open, so at least come in for a second."

She brushes past him and into his single room.

"You'll have to excuse the mess. My maid is off this week," he jokes.

She barely cracks a smile. She squares her shoulders toward him. "My mind is elsewhere, and there's not much more I can say about that, but I was way off for not thanking you for saving me yesterday. I know better than to treat anyone the way I've treated you lately. I'm sorry. I hope you'll accept my apology." She clasps her hands together to stop the shaking.

"Please have a seat." He pulls out his desk chair for her.

Reluctantly, she sits. He goes over to his dresser, takes out a T-shirt, and pulls it over his head and down his body. She can't even imagine what size shirt he must have to buy to fit over all those flowing muscles. He takes a brush and runs it through his platinum-blond hair and then secures it in a ponytail at the nape of his neck.

He spins to face her. "I accept your apology."

She starts to stand. He puts his hand up, telling her to sit back down. She lowers back into the chair. He sits on the edge of his bed.

"Listen, regardless of what's going on between your roommate and me…I still need to know that you're okay."

She cocks her head. "You said that the other day at Monroe's, but I have no idea what you are talking about."

"Let's just say that I feel as though Abigail made a pretty big decision not to pursue the non-guilty verdicts without even talking to me about it. It was a slap in the face to me."

Shit. Don't say a word, Laura. You promised Abigail. "But it's her choice." *You weren't in the room, Tank, when she got the call about the news. You can't possibly fathom how devastated she was.*

"Now, wait a minute. I'm not done. I do believe it's her decision but one we should have made together at least. Wouldn't you agree?"

"So, she didn't talk to you at all?"

"No, I found out from someone else."

"Who?" *Who would go behind her back?*

"That really doesn't matter."

"Okay, so you're mad at her? That's nothing new."

He narrows his eyes. "That's not fair either."

Laura lowers her head. "Sorry."

"I'm concerned she's not thinking clearly, and I worry that she made a rash decision."

"Really?" *She did it to protect your reputation.*

"Yes, I think it's because it was too close for comfort, and God only knows how she recoils quickly. It doesn't take much for her."

Laura does agree with this. It's not necessarily a bad quality. *We all have them.* "She was so upset when she got the call. I was in the room, and she was furious."

"Exactly, and then just like that, she wants to let it all go?"

"Makes no sense," Laura fibs. *I promised Abigail I wouldn't tell a soul, so I have to lie.*

She remembers Abigail's words to Claire Marion as clear as day. *"So, if I choose not to testify, that means Tank will never know that it was an option?"*

And then her direct comments to Laura were, *"I can't have the school thinking that I was caught up in some stupid jealousy triangle with Tank, Nathan, and that jerk. That would kill them. They can't know about this."*

"So, I told her flat-out that we needed some space."

"Ouch. A little harsh, no?"

"In hindsight, probably. But when it comes to us, I tend to be hyper-focused on her happiness, and lately, I think I need to find happiness on my own. I still love her, but she was pretty upset with me, so I'm looking at this as a mutual breakup."

"You definitely push buttons." Laura's face glows a beautiful pink hue.

"Sometimes, you need to push people." His silver eyes ignite as he says it, causing Laura to lower her gaze. He might as well be talking about her right now and not about Abigail at all.

She regains her composure by clearing her throat. "Well, thank you for hearing me out."

"You're welcome."

She stands and heads toward the door. "I gotta get to class."

He pulls the door open, and before she can exit, he adds, "I see you showered."

She whips around. "Yeah, about that, you were a bit harsh about my appearance yesterday."

He winks and then playfully adds, "Don't worry, Chase. I'd still screw you."

She chuckles as she walks down the hallway. "I was *so* worried."

Laura enters the station. Sean, the other DJ, is sitting at his desk. He glances over his shoulder as she approaches.

"Hey, Sean."

He spins in his chair. "Hey, um, Colin was looking for you. Said it was important."

"Okay. You know where he is?"

"Check his studio?"

Laura heads to Studio A and opens the door. She finds him sitting quietly in the room. His reaction to seeing her tells her all she needs to know. There is something he needs to get off his chest.

"What's up?"

"Close the door."

"Okay. You're kind of freaking me out." She laughs.

He stands before her now. "Listen, there is no great way to say this, but I wanted you to hear it from me. Um, Zoe and I are seeing each other."

The words hit her ears in slow motion. "Is that so? Since when?" She digs her hands into her hips and stares at him.

"Started a few days ago, and that's the honest truth."

"Really?"

"I swear, Laura. No one knows but the three of us. But I couldn't go on a moment longer without you knowing."

His expression is so earnest that she has no reason but to believe him.

"She's a bit young, no?"

"I know, but she's a super-awesome chick."

"It's your prerogative, Colin."

"Are you mad?"

Her expression softens as she reflects upon her conversation with Tank today. "No, Colin, I'm not mad. I just want you to be happy." *And I'm just in a perpetually crappy mood.*

"Well, I was trying to test the waters now that we're done."

"You should try swimming in another body of water," she jokes.

"Funny. What can I say? All the cool girls work in radio."

"I'm not so sure about that."

He takes her hand. "I am." Giving it a little tug, he asks, "How are you?"

"I'm okay. Trying to get Travis's speech done. Get back into the rhythm of the studio and hopefully start the news next week."

"You sleeping at all?"

"No. Not really."

"If I can do anything, you'll tell me, right?"

"Of course." *Sex always relaxes me. But from what you're saying, that ship has sailed for us. Probably a good thing not to fall back on something just because it's easy.* "I will. I'm happy for you, Colin. Thanks for telling me."

"Sure thing," he says.

She glances at her watch. "I do have to run."

He releases her hand. As she pulls open the door, he adds, "I'm sure your speech will be exceptional."

"You'll be there, right?"

"I wouldn't miss it. I'll be front and center." He gives her a kind smile.

"Thanks. I'll need to see friendly faces if I'm going to make it through."

Fourteen

Rock Bottom

Laura's performance on her show is the worst she's ever done. Hands down. No use in pretending otherwise. She is more than distracted; she is downright awful. Maybe Colin's news is bothering her more than she let on.

He moved on so quickly. And with the new girl at the station? Right under my very nose? I thought I could be cool about it, but the more I dwell on it, the more it rubs me the wrong way. Something about her bugs me, too.

But it could also be that Travis's speech is undoubtedly on her mind, and she can't recall a time when she felt so alone despite call after call, conversing with her fellow students.

"Next, I'm going to play—oh hell, I have no idea what song I've cued up. Sorry. Here's whatever is next. Let's hope it doesn't suck," she says while spinning the next tune.

And so the show continues.

Finally, her time has come to an end. "Well, that's it for me tonight, Hawks. I'm signing off. Thank God." *That was awful. I'm so embarrassed.*

She doesn't even bother recapping with Patrick as he switches off the *On Air* sign. She pushes open the door to her studio. "I'm outta here," she barks.

"Laura, wait," he says. "Where are you going?"

Why does he care? Why does anyone?

"That guy who called into the show said there's a party on Webster Street. Fuck it. I'm going there."

Patrick's eyes expand. "Absolutely not," he says.

"Why not? It's just a house party."

"With total strangers. Not safe, Laura."

She laughs. "What, you think you can tell me what to do?" *Just what I need, someone telling me what to do, not helping me freaking feel better.*

"Laura, be serious. You can't go to a caller's house party. You have no idea who they are!"

"Patrick"—she laughs—"don't be such a dork."

She's never spoken to him like this before.

"Hey, I'm just looking out for you," he hisses.

"Then, come with me," she says as she continues down the hallway.

He's hot on her heels, as he's too afraid to let her out of his sight. "I have a tech lab group I have to go to," he yells.

"Oh well," she says, pulling open the door. "I'll tell you all about it tomorrow." And just like that, she's gone.

Webster Street is only two blocks from campus, and by the time she gets around the corner, she hears the loud beat of the techno house music pulsating from the speakers. As she heads up the stairs, she's immediately recognized by some of the students, and a quick cheer erupts.

"She came!" one guy yells.

She's handed a drink, and she's immediately escorted into the main part of the house, where she's introduced to the guy who called the station and asked her to come.

"Holy shit! I'm Zack," he yells over the music. "You actually came. So fucking cool!" He gives her a quick hug and then points her out to all his friends.

When you're the only female DJ in over a decade and you also happen to be part of the reason the dean of the school got fired, your name and your face tend to be recognized around the school. She's bombarded with questions about the station, her favorite music, what it's like to work there, and on and on and on, all while she mindlessly sips on her drink.

Zack disappears and then finds her again. He hands her a few shots to toss back. Which she gladly does. Then, her doting host pulls her into the dining room, where everyone is dancing. She immerses herself in the rhythm of the club music as the flashing lights mimic the pounding of her heart. This is exactly the kind of distraction she needed in her life. To be somewhere no one knows the real Laura. Only the one they think they know.

"Another drink?" Zack asks as he tugs on her sleeve.

"Sure!" She takes the drink and resumes dancing up a sweat.

Tank is sitting in his desk chair, about to untie his sneakers, when the ring of his phone pierces the air. He grabs the receiver. "Hello?"

"Is this Tank?"

"Yeah. Who's this?"

"Wolfie."

"Oh. Hey, dude. What's up?"

"Listen"—he breathes heavily into the phone—"Patrick called me from the station." It's clear Wolfie is having a hard time catching his breath.

Tank's hair on the back of his neck stands up. "What's going on?"

"Some caller invited Laura to a party on Webster St—"

"You've got to be kidding me," Tank barks. *Please tell me she's not doing something stupid.*

"Nope. She apparently stormed out of the station after saying she was just going to show up at the house party. *Alone.* Patrick tried to stop her but couldn't go. And I've got to be honest with you. A guy like me showing up? Who the hell knows what could happen? I'd have no idea what I was walking into. I hope you know what I mean."

"Say no more, man. I hear you."

Tank is often asked to be the first guy to go into a place, break up a fight, et cetera. His size is a blessing and a curse. But he feels for Wolfie. He knows it can't be easy for him to ask for this kind of help. But it's necessary tonight.

"I can meet you there," Wolfie offers.

"Nah. She might freak out. You hear her tonight?" *What is going on with this girl?*

"Yeah. She was bad."

"I heard some of her show. Horrible. So, it'd be best if only one of us went," Tank says.

"You're a good friend, Tank."

"So are you. Thanks for the call."

Tank grabs his keys, puts on his jacket, and heads out of his dorm. He jogs the few blocks toward Webster Street. His heart races at the thought of her being alone, perhaps in trouble. Struggling.

Is she scared? Is she getting fucked up to the point where she can't function?

All he ever thinks about is her. Being with her, holding her, loving her—as a friend or sometimes as more. Whatever she needs. He's drawn to the little firecracker that she is—or once was. And someday, he has plans to tell her. When her head is screwed on right.

If it's ever screwed back on right.

It doesn't take a genius to find out which party she's at. From the street, he can see her through the window. She's dancing on the table with some guy grinding up on her, although she's barely dancing; he's more holding her up than anything.

Jesus, she looks smashed.

Tank bounds up the stairs two steps at a time and walks right inside without knocking on the door.

Much like Laura, Tank is always recognized around OSU. He's also feared. His size alone and what he does on the field leaves little to the imagination as to what it would feel like to have his body hit your body, let alone just his fist. So, most people with a smidgen of a brain know enough to simply back away and let him get what he wants.

"Hey, Tank!" a guy yells over the music.

A few students turn to look. But Laura doesn't. Neither does the guy dancing with her.

Tank glares at them.

"Want a drink?" one kid asks.

"I'm not here for a drink. I'm here for her," he growls.

"Zack!" his friend yells.

"What?" he yaps back.

"Zack!" Tank says. "Can you let go of my girl?"

Zack freezes, and Laura slumps in his arms, visibly intoxicated.

Tank springs into action. He grabs Laura. "What the fuck did you give her?"

Zack's eyes are enormous as he recognizes who's speaking to him. He stumbles backward, catching himself before he falls off the table as Tank scoops up Laura.

"Tank? What are you doing?" she slurs.

"Getting you the fuck out of here," he says.

"But I'm having fun," she says, trying to get out of his arms.

"Don't bother fighting me," he says angrily.

Her eyes roll back in her head.

"Jesus Christ. Someone tell me what she's had," he yells.

Zack puts up his hands. "Nothing. Nothing, I swear. Just some shots and a few drinks."

Tank looks Zack square in the eyes. "I know your name and where you live. If anything happens to her, I'll find you. You hear me? Watch yourself. The whole football team will know."

"I swear, we're cool."

"*Not cool*," he says as he spins and carries Laura out of the house.

Her body is curled in his arms the entire way back to his room. Even with his strength, it takes all his might to make the trek back to the dormitory.

Finally, back in front of his room, he sets her down to unlock his door. Unexpectedly, she tries to stumble down the hallway. Exhausted from his journey, he barely catches her as she nearly makes it to the first door to the stairwell.

"You have got to be kidding me," he says as he slings her over his shoulder while she screams. "Shut up!"

"You shut up!"

He gets her into his doorway and closes the door.

Just as he locks it, he hears his dorm monitor open his door and say, "Y'all better be quiet!"

Tank backs her up in his room, his hand placed gently over her mouth. His silver eyes are deadly serious as he says, "You listen to me. I just risked going to that party, not knowing what the fuck I was walking into, only to find you, nearly passed out with some stranger, so the least you can do is not get me written up, Laura Chase. You owe me that."

Her eyes are so bloodshot that he has no idea if she even comprehends what the heck he's saying to her.

"Now, sit down for a minute and let me catch my damn breath. I just carried you a couple blocks, and I think I'm having a freaking heart attack."

He releases his hand from her mouth and hovers over her to make sure she won't scream. She slumps onto his bed. Satisfied she's not going to bolt, he collapses on his mattress, his chest heaving as he tries to catch a lungful of air.

The room is quiet for a long time until Tank finally says, "What the hell were you thinking tonight?"

She doesn't say a word.

He sits up and grabs her arm. "Hey, I'm talking to you. You take something? They give you something?" He gives her arm a little shake.

Irritated, she quips, "No, Tank. I don't know."

"What do you mean, you don't know?"

"Drinks. He gave me drinks."

"You never asked what they were?" Tank says as he stands and starts to pace in front of her.

"No, okaaay?"

"No, *not* okay, Laura. *Not okay.*" He motions to her. "This is not okay. Don't you see? You have got to snap out of this before it's too late."

He takes in the woman sitting before him. Laura has always been a knockout—brown bob, always tucked neatly behind her ears; beautiful, piercing hazel eyes; pouty lips; a full figure with a slim waist. Always smiling and upbeat. Now, all he sees is a girl who is smashed, makeup around her bloodshot eyes, dressed like she's going to the gym. She's a far cry from the girl she once was.

He knows the signs. It was him. He never showered. He couldn't have cared less about clean clothes, being sober, or what anyone of any sex thought of him. He lost his scholarship, his friends, his girlfriend. All of it. Because after he lost Jonathan, he thought no one understood his pain, so he shut everyone out. And by doing so, he spiraled down deeply and quickly. Just as she is.

"Why can't you just leave me alone?" she mumbles.

"Because I can't. Is that a suitable answer?" he says, crossing his arms over his chest.

She peels off her jacket, and with a crooked smile, she says mockingly, "You're such a big hero. Big star." She pouts her lips for effect.

He narrows his eyes at her. "Oh, I see. So, you think you can be an asshole to me, and I'll just go away? Try again, Chase. I wrote the book on it."

She slurs, "You did, didn't you? Why don't you come here and show me what else you wrote the book on?" She slides back on his bed and motions with her finger for him to join her.

He uncrosses his arms, takes off his coat, and tosses it on the chair. He locks eyes with her and strides toward her. He notices her swallow hard as he nears the bed. Leaning in real close to her, he forces her back on his bed. With his massive body hovering over hers, he says, "I highly suggest you don't push my buttons tonight. I'll let this little shit-talking of yours slide tonight because you probably won't remember it in the morning. But hear me loud and clear right now. This"—he points his finger into her chest—"stops tonight. You understand? I've been in your shoes, and you're heading in the wrong direction. I won't stand for it any longer."

She goes to speak, but he presses his finger a little firmer into her chest. Although it's not the best way to handle things, he wishes someone had done this for him because he sure as shit would have saved himself a few months of torture if he'd just gotten some help.

"Now, you tell me, do you want to get help and feel better or get drunk and have a stranger at a party potentially assault you?"

Tears sting her beautiful eyes.

He releases the pressure from his finger on her chest and replaces it with the palm of his hand. "Your hearts beating so fast," he whispers. "Tell me, girl, what do you want?"

Wet soaks her cheek.

"Tell me," he repeats.

"I want help," she cries.

And with that, he lifts her up and into his arms, holding her tightly. "Attagirl," he says, stroking her hair. "I'll be there with you, for you, however you need. But this stops tonight, okay?"

"Okay," she whispers.

As Tank holds her, he can't help but wonder what might have happened had Wolfie not thought to call him. This stunning, amazing woman in his arms could have had the worst night of her life, all because she didn't know enough to stop putting coal on the fire.

She lifts her head. "Tank, could I stay here tonight?" she asks. "As friends?" Despite Tank being extremely attractive, she's far from ready to start anything new with anyone. At least she knows that about herself.

He can't help but roll his eyes softly. "Of course as friends. Your poor attempt at a drunk come-on washes right over me," he says with a chuckle. "I know you didn't mean it."

"I'm sorry about that," she says, letting him go and sitting back down on his bed. "Colin told me tonight that he's dating the new girl at the station. I don't know. Whatever," she scoffs, waving her hand in the air.

"Really? Ouch."

"No, it's fine. I think. I don't know."

"You sure?"

"Yeah. I think I'm just really lonely," she admits.

"No shit, girl. Look around. Tank's home alone. It's bad out there. Real bad." He laughs.

Laura laughs, too. "Man, this is pathetic."

"Yep." Tank gets up and grabs her a bottle of water. "Drink this and kick off those shoes." He pulls his sweatshirt off, slides off his jeans, and pulls back his covers. "Come on. No time to be shy. Let's be lonely and sad together," he says.

Too drunk to feel nervous and since it's evidently not the time or place for a hook-up—if there ever was going to be one—Laura tosses her jacket off the bed, takes off her shoes, and climbs into bed next to Tank.

He wraps his arm around her and places a friendly kiss on her head. "I know I'm tough on you."

"Don't," she slurs. "It's okay. I need it. Bad. You're a super friend."

"I think I got what you said, but just don't tell anyone. I have a reputation to uphold." He laughs.

Even if the details, words, and events are foggy to Laura tomorrow, at least Tank will have everything they talked about all locked in a vault, and he won't let her repeat this mistake. He'll keep it there to make sure she remains on track and moves forward. It's high time she starts to move in that direction instead of up and down, and what better time than just a week away from Travis's speech? Tank knows better than anyone when others are relying on you to keep it together and you don't; it can not only be costly, but it can also disappoint others when they're already going through so much.

But what Tank wants her to know more than anything else is that hitting rock bottom doesn't mean she can't get back up and fall again. It doesn't mean she can't still have bad days. It just means that today, with the help of Tank, she is finally forced to decide to find a better way to deal with the ups and downs before it really is too late.

Fifteen

Awards Ceremony

The rain is fitting today, she thinks as she approaches the podium to deliver the speech.

Despite knowing she's prepared well for today, she's still feeling like she needs more time. Her thoughts on Travis were hard to get on paper. So hard in fact that she paced the floor of her dorm room last night, questioning every sentence in her speech. She only realized it was light out because her clock had told her so. It had rained so hard the past few days that it seemed like the sun would never rise.

But finally, it's time to deliver her speech. The moment has arrived. And as she approaches the tent, she looks out across the crowd. She sees all her floor mates, all the guys from the station, even Colin. But no Wolfie. That is by design. He was with her earlier, and that was all that mattered to her.

Finally, the president introduces her, and she begins her speech. *The speech.*

"Good afternoon, Hawks. It's my great honor to be standing before you today to accept the Associated Collegiate Press College Media Liberty Award on behalf of my late friend, Travis Taylor. As I gaze out into the crowd today, I ponder two things. One, Travis would have loved the recognition for his work. I don't doubt that for a second. But more importantly, I see a lot of faces of people who didn't truly *know* Travis. Not many of us did. He was arrogant, complicated, driven, fearless, and calculated. Those qualities did not leave much for those around him to care for. That is, unless you were lucky enough to truly get to know him."

She pauses. "I had that distinct pleasure." She quickly dabs the corner of her eye with a tissue before continuing, "His idealisms were based solely on his future. He had grand plans to run his own newspaper someday, and that left little playtime for him. Hence, his tight inner circle. He would do anything for those close to him and stop at nothing to tear down an undeserving opponent. I came to admire this about him." She pauses again.

"He taught me to believe in myself. To stand strong when times were difficult and, more notably, to never let anyone get in the way of the truth. His integrity was second to none, and many of you are here today to pay your respects to him for simply *that* quality alone. He never backed down, even when his own college career hung in the balance. He refused to let that uncertainty stop him.

"His loss is something that this university will never forget. No doubt, his colleagues at *The Weekly Blue* and the radio station will never be able to replicate the hard work and dedication Travis had for uncovering the truth."

Laura breaks and places her hand over her heart. "And for me, it's quite simple. Every time I reflect on my time at OSU, I will forever and always remember *my* dear friend Travis Taylor."

With tears stinging her eyes, she recites, "Thank you to the Associated Collegiate Press for recognizing Travis's continued demonstration for college press freedom and reform. You have chosen a worthy recipient, and I accept this award in his memory. On behalf of Travis's family and his friends, thank you to the university for the plaque outside the doors of *The Weekly Blue*. It will be a reminder to us all that, when our days feel long and we just can't possibly push ourselves an inch more, if you do, you, too, will *earn* your success.

"Thank you all for coming here today. And…" She pauses, glancing up from her notes. She tucks her hair behind her ear and smiles, remembering the last time he smiled at her. "If I may, to Travis, wherever you might be…sweet dreams."

She delivered it flawlessly. And anyone who knows her knows it came only from the heart and those in the secret circle know it came even more from her love of him.

But she'd be lying if she said she wasn't glad it was over.

Thankfully, after the ceremony, Laura's friends and all the guys from the station invite her to the coffee shop downtown, where Laura and Travis used to spend time together. They all thought it would be nice to reconnect with her after the gut-wrenching day. They fill up a few tables at the shop and sipped on their coffee.

Laura sits in virtual silence.

"Your speech was wonderful," Melissa says.

"Truly," Bree adds.

"Thanks, guys. I appreciate all of you being there."

"Are you having dinner with his parents tonight?" Jen asks.

"Yes, and with Wolfie, too."

"That's special," Colin adds.

She turns to face him and smiles. "Thanks for being here. All of you. I couldn't have done this without you."

"Where are Nathan and Tank?" Casey asks.

Abigail's face flushes as she replies, "At a football meeting." Although she's felt all along that Coach should have postponed it for another day to allow them to attend.

Kelly, who was also in attendance with his sister and a girl named Aniston, pipes up, "Oh, I just saw them walk by."

Laura sees several large figures slip by the second window. She pushes back her chair and heads for the door after Abigail has already exited into the rainy afternoon.

"Will you excuse me for a moment?" Laura says.

"Nathan," Abigail yells over the loud drops of rain.

He turns. Tank turns, too.

Laura is now out under the awning, and he gives her a faint smile as he comes circling back.

"Couldn't make it?" Laura asks with disdain.

"I don't know what to say."

"How was your practice in the rain?"

He lowers his head. "It was brief, and by the time we got back up to campus, the tent was empty."

"That's too bad. Maybe next time."

"*Laura.*"

"What? It would have been nice for you, for all of you, to be there. After all he did for this school."

"I know you're right, and I feel like a jerk."

The rain picks up as she tries to shield herself from the drops with her hands. "Well, my *friends* are inside the coffee shop. Enjoy your day drinking with the groupies."

"They're cheerleaders," he mumbles. "I'll come find you later."

Laura passes Abigail and Nathan arguing, and as quickly as possible, she ducks back into the shop.

Abigail enters soon afterward and immediately runs into the restroom.

Nathan pulls open the door, faintly smiles, and says, "Hey, guys."

"Hey," they all mumble back.

He looks right at Laura when he says, "Sorry, we—I was unable to make it today. We had a mandatory football thing," he stares at the floor.

"It's okay," she says.

"I really am sorry. I hope it went well?"

"It did. Thank you."

"Good." He glances nervously around at all of them and quickly adds, "The team is up the street. Tell Abby I'll call her later."

"Bye, Nathan," they reply.

Sensing the mood shift even more, they all decide to finish their coffee and head back to the dorms.

"I gotta shower before dinner tonight anyway," Laura adds, trying to put everyone at ease. "I don't want to keep Travis's parents waiting," she adds, nervously playing with her hands.

She's both excited to spend time with them and wildly anxious. Every person walks around with a little bit of sadness within them, but his parents are on a whole other level.

I don't want to see in their eyes how much they miss him because if I do, I think I'll crack right in front of them, and I have to be as stoic as possible for them.

Once Laura is back in her dorm room and finishes showering and dressing, she sits on the edge of her bed, clutching Travis's shirt. She knows, as much as she'd like to, she can't skip out on tonight's dinner. Not because she doesn't want to spend time with them, but because she knows it's going to be difficult to sit there and not want to cry all night.

Finally, there's a knock on her door.

"Come in." Her voice cracks.

Wolfie enters, and with one look at her, he crosses the room toward her and says, "Listen, there's no way out of dinner tonight. They're expecting us, and you and I both know the right thing to do is to go and be with them, especially today."

Mist forms in her eyes.

"And so what if you cry in front of them? You wouldn't be the first, and you won't be the last. But, Laura," he whispers as he gently grasps the shirt in her hand, trying to get her to let it go, "we really do have to get going, okay?"

"All right," she says, releasing the shirt and placing it next to her on the bed. She gets up and puts on her coat.

Wolfie says with a playful wink, "Maybe try not to cry until at least dessert?"

Laughing, they walk down the hallway, and Laura replies, "I hadn't even envisioned me making it that long, so thanks for the vote of confidence."

"Please do. Because I'd really like dessert."

Sixteen

Unwanted Limelight

Laura enters Studio B and waits for Melissa to arrive. She's glad that Melissa took over as interim student editor. Despite his success at the paper, Wolfie had made clear that he had no interest in taking Travis's place. He likes being in the shadows. Travis liked being in the light. So, Melissa is a solid replacement, having interned at the paper before. Melissa knows just how to gingerly dance around Laura to keep it light and not a constant reminder of her devastating loss while filling Laura in on all the news segments for her show.

As she adjusts her board and microphone, she senses someone standing in the doorway.

"Hey," he says as he approaches her.

"Hey, Wolfie," she replies.

She deeply appreciates him due to his connection with Travis, even more so after the dinner with Travis's parents. The dinner in which Mr. and Mrs. Taylor confided to them that Laura and Wolfie were the only two people Travis ever really spoke about from OSU. This left them both dumbfounded, flattered, and confused, all at the same time.

"Wanted to say hello." He comes in and sits in the guest chair.

Laura stops what she's doing and rests her eyes on his. "I'm glad you did."

Every day that passes that she doesn't see or talk to Wolfie, her memories of Travis start to fade. But as soon as she exchanges words with Wolfie, she feels them rush back into her memory bank. She's never told him this, but she senses he knows.

"How are you?"

"I'm doing okay."

As soon as she got back from Travis's award ceremony, she called Wolfie to tell him how it went even though he was there briefly and she was having dinner with him in a few hours. She cried through most of it, and he just sat on the phone with her and listened. He's not much for words, aside from those he puts on paper; therefore, it makes him a great listener.

"I'm having a dinner party at my apartment next week. Before finals. I'd like you to be there."

She smiles for the first time today. Only Wolfie would have a dinner party. Most kids their age would have a kegger or toga party to end the year but not Wolfie. He marches to the beat of his own drum.

"I'll be there. What can I bring?"

"Nothing. I'll take care of everything."

Laura waits to see if he'll invite any of her friends to tag along. She's not surprised that he does not. It's not that they don't get along, but Wolfie is really her friend, and honestly, she likes to keep their friendship separate from her dorm relationships.

"Great," she says.

"I'll see you next Thursday at eight." He rises from his seat.

Nervously, Laura asks, "I'll talk to you before then?"

He pauses, giving her a sorrow-filled glance. "Of course. I'll call you later."

Relief washes over her as she adds, "Good-bye for now."

Moments after Wolfie leaves, Melissa enters Studio B. Her face is flushed as she anxiously fiddles with her hands.

"What is it?" Laura asks.

Melissa closes the door. She takes the seat recently occupied by Wolfie and exhales a deep breath. "I heard there was a meeting late last night with the administration to tackle the issue of the vandalism at the soccer house. From what I've been told, it was never really addressed to begin with," Melissa says.

Travis, Wolfie, and Laura had started to look into it when tragedy struck, leaving a duo with little appetite to continue without their fearless leader—until now.

"What the hell?" Laura barks. "This new dean had better have his shit together."

"I hope so."

"I wonder if Professor Tucker knows anything about it."

"Can't hurt to ask him. I have a meeting later with Professor Campbell to go over a few things. This is definitely on my list."

"Okay. I'll find Jen after my shift and see what she's heard, too."

"Sounds good. Until then, here are some of the topics for your segment."

As Laura and Melissa go over the list, there's a sinking feeling in the pit of Laura's stomach that there's a bigger issue brewing. The other day in the library, she was only able to find one other instance from two years ago about a vandalized car in front of one of the sorority houses. A sorority house that had mostly athletes as members. But what was so interesting about the article was that it was only reported by the local paper, not the school paper. She gets the sense there is much more going on.

This can't be good.

"You need me to hold off on this one?"

"Wolfie is on it. I'll keep you posted."

"I know." Laura smiles.

"You going to his dinner party on Thursday?"

Laura cocks her head. "Yeah, but how did you know?"

"Guess he likes me." Melissa smiles.

Laura is relieved that she is invited because it means Wolfie does like her—because God knows he's selective—and she's also glad that one of her best friends will be at one of the dinner parties with her, which is a first.

"I gotta run back to the paper and approve copy. I'll see you for dinner."

"Thanks, Melissa."

"Just doing my job." She smiles.

Laura knocks on Professor Tucker's door.

"Come in," he yells.

"It's Laura," she says, pushing open his door.

"Laura, how are you?"

His sympathetic stare makes her want to burst into tears. She has been getting a lot more of them since she gave Travis's acceptance speech. It really became evident to all those who might not have known that Laura and Travis had been much closer than they let on.

So, she answers like she always does when asked, "Fine."

"Good. Glad to hear it."

But now, I have something to focus on. The speech is behind me, and I need to do exactly what Travis would have wanted me to do. Get back to work!

She places her bag on her lap and takes the seat across from his desk. "Do you know anything about a car being vandalized a few years ago?"

He leans forward. "Yes, it was a car outside a sorority that belonged to a girl. Didn't *The Weekly Blue* report on it? Maybe you can get a copy from their archives." He pauses. "What's going on?"

"Well, they still have no idea who did that to the soccer house, and I'm guessing, at this point, we need to keep looking. But I'm getting the feeling there is a lot more to this."

"Well, you know how to dig. So, start digging. If I can help, I will."

"Dean Roland held a meeting to discuss campus safety last night. Can you find out who was there?"

He firmly nods. "I can."

"Thank you." Laura grabs her bag as she rises from her seat.

She exits the station and walks over toward the soccer house. She knocks on the door and can hear someone inside approaching it.

Shannon, the captain of the women's soccer team, opens the door. "Hey, Laura." She pulls it all the way and allows her in.

"Hey, Shannon. Jen around?"

"Yeah, upstairs."

Laura pauses. "Actually, you have a second to talk?"

Intrigued, Shannon responds, "Sure. Let's go into the kitchen."

"I wanted to ask you about the day the house was vandalized," Laura says as she sits across from Shannon at the kitchen table.

"You mean, when that scumbag spray-painted the words *dykes* and *lesbos* on our house?" Shannon spits out.

"Disgusting. But I wanted to know, who was home when it happened?"

"Um, me, Kate, Jen. The rest of the girls were at the student movie in Montgomery Hall."

"Okay. Who's working the case?"

"Some old guy," she huffs. "Officer Waters. He's so out of touch and barely spoken to any of us."

"What do you mean?"

"You know when someone talks to you, but they're looking right past you? That's how he makes you feel. He took our statements and then told us to paint over the derogatory comments, so other people didn't have to see them."

"Did he photograph them?"

"Not sure, but we did."

"When was the last time you got an update from the police?"

"Honestly, it's been so long that we just assumed they'd never catch them."

"That's awful."

"Yes, it is. So, why all the questions?"

"Not sure yet. I'm looking into a few things."

"Okay. Happy to help if you need anything."

"Could you get me negatives of the photos?"

"Sure thing."

Laura stands. "One more thing. You know anything about similar troubles a few years back?"

"No, never heard anything."

"Huh. Okay. Thanks, Shannon." She exits the kitchen and heads up the stairs.

Stories swept under the rug. But why? Are they connected? No police involvement in months? Do they have any intention of trying to solve this, or do they just let each one slip away year after year?

"Hey, Jen," she says. "It's Laura."

"Come in!"

Jen climbs off her green bedspread to greet her friend. "This is a nice surprise!"

Laura smiles warmly.

"To what do I owe the honor?" She laughs.

Laura sits on the edge of Jen's bed while Jen lies back next to her stack of textbooks.

"I wish this were a social visit," she says to her former floor mate. "But I need to ask you about the night the house was vandalized."

"Why?" Jen asks, trying to tidy up the stack of papers in front of her.

"Well, Melissa got word of some activity by the new administration, and I want to do my part to make sure this is done right."

Jen rubs her chin, trying to think back to that night. "All I remember is hearing some noises. Faintly, as if they were farther away. Then, I heard the shake of cans—you know, spray cans. Honestly, I didn't think much past that. Until the next day, when I went to leave for class. I was shocked. Scared really."

"What kind of noises?"

"Hard to tell. Like I said, I didn't think much about it. It was late. Thought it was some students, drunk and wandering around, causing trouble."

"I would have, too," Laura whispers.

"It's a tough place to be in," Jen says, averting her eyes and glancing at the poster on her wall.

Laura glances at her friend. The sadness in her voice is telling. "How so?"

"There is this part of me that wants to fight. To make a statement. To pave the way, so others don't have to. But then there is this large part of me that wants to let it go. It's a strange notion to put your sexuality on display for all to see. And it's scary to think that maybe they know who you are. Were they targeting me, Shannon, who? Someone was targeting the lesbians on the team. There are girls on the team with boyfriends and others with girlfriends. It's hard not to feel divided or to blame when the other half is thinking you brought this on them."

"No one thinks that."

"Not out loud."

Laura's stomach turns. "I suppose you could be right."

"With so much going on this past year, I'd say the police were occupied—and rightfully so. But there's an uneasy feeling about being a gay athlete."

"My hope is, that goes away."

"Me, too."

"Do you remember hearing from some of the other girls about a similar situation a few years back?"

Jen shakes her head. "No, nothing. Did it?"

"I'm not sure. I heard something today, and I'm trying to dig around a little."

"I know you'll be unobtrusive."

"Yeah, I kind of have to be. With all these things going on, it's important."

"Let me know what you find out."

"I will."

As Laura stands to leave, she can sense Jen's hesitation.

"You think Casey is doing okay?" she asks, seemingly out of the blue.

Laura cocks her head to the side. "Yeah, I do. Why do you ask? You don't?"

Jen's cheeks pink. "No, it's nothing. I'm just probably being paranoid."

"Paranoid about what?"

Jen shuffles some papers on her bed and very uncomfortably replies, "She kind of got thrown into the limelight of the gay culture here—or dare I say, lack of—and I worry about that. But it's nothing, honest. Probably all in my head."

"I'll keep an eye on her." *I guess I've never had to worry about that. But now, I do and will. Because these are my friends, and I must protect them.*

"I know you will. I appreciate that. I'll see you around, Laura." She smiles wide.

Understanding the notion of not being ready to dive deep into a subject matter that might or might not be bothering you, Laura pulls open her door and says, "Good night, Jen."

And without another word, she exits the soccer house. As she passes by the wall of the house, now with a fresh coat of paint, Laura can't help but fantasize about the type of despicable humans who would write such terrible things and what she'd say to them if she ever caught the bastards.

Seventeen

The Evening Awaits

A couple of days later, Laura and Melissa are in their respective rooms, getting ready for Wolfie's end-of-the-year dinner party. As she touches up her makeup, the phone rings.

"Hello?"

"Laura, it's Tank."

Her skin prickles. Laura has not spoken to Tank since the speech last week, nor has she seen him out and about on campus. But from what little Abigail has told her, there is trouble brewing among the football buddies and the girls in Willis Hall.

Boy, he waited a long time to call me after our little spat in the rain. Did he not get the message loud and clear about how disappointed I was that he was not there?

"Hey."

"Is it cold in your room? 'Cause I can feel the chill through the phone."

Trying not to laugh at his ridiculous remark, she pipes in, "Abigail's not here, Tank."

"I know that."

"Okay, well, I'm trying to get ready for a dinner party with Melissa, so I don't really have time to chat."

With disappointment in his voice, he says, "Oh."

"Bad timing."

There's a long pause, and then he says, "Can you call me when you get home? I'm not going out tonight, so whatever time is good for me."

Time is ticking off the clock, so she agrees and then hangs up. *Fine, I'll call you later but only because you asked.*

Laura inspects her fitted jeans and her tight black top in the full-length mirror. She places some large hoop earrings in and then smooths her bob behind her ears. She touches up her dark pink lip gloss, grabs her bag, and crosses the hall to Melissa's room. She is finally starting to resemble the old Laura.

"Dang, girl," Melissa says as she opens the door. "You look hot!"

"Thanks. So do you. It's not too much, is it?"

"You are single and ready to mingle!"

She throws her head back and giggles. "I guess I am!"

The girls head out of the dorm and make the short walk to Wolfie's apartment on the beautiful evening. The closer they get to the end of the school year, the warmer the nights get.

They can hear laughter and music as they knock on the door. As it opens, they catch a whiff of the distinctive aroma of pot.

"Hello, Tripp," she says as she gives him a warm hug. They step inside. "This is Melissa."

"Ah, yes, we've all heard so much about you from Wolfie. You're doing a bang-up job at the paper. I'm Tripp."

"I hope so, and nice to meet you," Melissa says.

"You, too. Come in."

He leads them into the kitchen, where about five or so people are gathered.

Wolfie immediately approaches them. He leans in and gently kisses Laura on the cheek. "You look stunning," he gushes.

"I showered." She laughs.

He gives Melissa a hug and compliment as well.

Then, he turns and announces in a grand fashion, "Everyone, you all know Laura, and this is Melissa from the paper."

They all speak at once.

Willow gets up and hugs them both. "Melissa, I'm Willow. We've heard so much about you."

Melissa's heart swells, and she's only been in the house a few minutes. "So nice to meet all of you."

Names are exchanged, and it becomes evidently clear to Melissa, like it once did to Laura, that Wolfie has a secret collective of friends. She has a whole new perspective on him. Melissa eyes the room, taking in the dark wood walls, the artwork hanging perfectly, the cookbooks lined up near the stove, and the plants in the window. It's a far cry from the frat houses occupied by many around campus.

Wolfie interrupts Melissa's thoughts. "A drink?"

"Sure," she says, following him over to the counter in his kitchen.

"Wine, bourbon?" These seem to be the only options allowed in his house.

"Um, wine, please."

"Me, too," Laura adds.

"This is a lovely red. I'm sure you'll like it." He pours them each a glass and watches as they savor their first sip.

"Simply exquisite," Laura says, winking at Wolfie.

"Indeed," he says.

Tripp motions for them to join the rest of the group at the table. And they do.

"Your speech was amazing," Willow gushes as she fixes the headband in her hair.

Melissa adds, "Doesn't she have such an amazing way with the spoken word?"

"Absolutely," she says.

"Wolfie, why didn't you go?" Melissa asks.

"Yeah, not my thing."

"I think what he's trying to say is, it's nobody's thing, but in particular, it's not his." Tripp pats him on the back.

Laura wants nothing to do with this conversation. "Could I have more wine?" she asks as she rises from her seat.

Wolfie quickly meets her near the bar. "You okay?"

"Are you?" she asks.

He seems surprised that she's asking him even though she feels like she has a thousand times before.

He smiles and says with a softness to his face, "I wish I were the type of person who could've been there for you."

"Believe me, I understand."

"I know you do. I just hope others don't think I'm a coward," he admits as he pours her more wine.

She places her hands on his shoulders. "Wolfie, your best friend died. No one questions your motives." If she didn't know better, she could have sworn she saw his eyes get misty.

He clears his throat. "We should get back to the others."

"Of course."

Within a short period of time after their first round of drinks, arrangements are being made by some of the others to start serving dinner.

"You never disappoint, Wolfie. This is so good," Laura says as she takes another bite of the homemade tofu pad thai.

"You made this?" Melissa says with a smile as the smell hits her nose.

He chuckles. "I do love to cook."

"I wondered why you never ordered out with the others at the paper. I wouldn't either if I could do this."

He grins.

Once everyone has cleaned up, they retire to the back porch of his house, which overlooks a small garden.

"I get a lot of my herbs from there." He points. "Super convenient, right?"

"You garden, too?" Melissa asks.

Willow laughs. "Tripp and I maintain most of it."

After they all finish their drinks, the night is winding down. Laura glances at the clock. It's much earlier than she expected it to be.

"Wolfie, thank you so much. This was amazing, as always."

"Yes, it really was," Melissa adds.

Good-byes are said all around, and then they exit Wolfie's house.

"I'm going to Boyd to see Logan," Melissa announces with a smile.

Laura is feeling a little adventurous herself on this wonderful evening. "I'll go with you. Tank called me earlier and told me he needed to chat tonight. Maybe I'll pop in on him."

Melissa cocks her head. "Everything okay?"

"Not sure. But I suppose I'll find out."

They enter the dorm, and Melissa heads to Logan's room. Laura takes a deep breath as she approaches Tank's room. This is by far an unorthodox move on her part, and she hopes he's not put off by it.

She knocks lightly on the door.

"Hang on!" she can hear him yell.

She takes a step back and waits for him to open it. He pulls the door open, and she can tell immediately that he's stunned to see her.

"Hey!"

He stands before her, wearing only a pair of OSU football shorts. His hair is tied loosely on top of his head.

She swallows hard. "Um, Melissa came here to see Logan."

Seemingly uninterested in her reasoning, he steps back into his room to allow her in. She steps in and closes the door.

Laura stands by his desk.

He blushes a little as he tries to find a T-shirt. "Sorry, wasn't expecting company."

He quickly pulls on a shirt over his head. The bun on his head becomes loose, and he pulls the elastic out of his hair. His shoulder-length hair falls around his face. Laura cocks her head to the side as she watches him struggle to tie it back.

She laughs. "I guess I never realized your hair was longer than mine!"

"Is that bad?" he asks shyly, which is so unlike him.

"Why would that be?"

"I don't know." He takes a seat on his bed and points for her to take a seat on his desk chair. "I'm really sorry about not being there to hear your speech," he blurts out.

Her face reddens. "Is that why you called me tonight?"

"Yeah. I mean, it's almost the end of the school year, and I didn't want you to leave, thinking no one gave a shit about what you had to do."

Her eyes get wide. "Well, I appreciate you calling me, but…"

"But what?"

She's more confused than ever. This is the guy who wouldn't hesitate to cut someone down if he didn't agree with them, but here, he's apologizing for not being there for her.

"I wasn't expecting you to apologize for it—that's all."

"Well, it's good to know I'm unpredictable." He laughs.

She smiles.

"You look great tonight, by the way," he adds.

"Oh, um, thank you," she stammers.

"Date?"

"God, no." Then, immediately, she stops. "I mean, no appetite for that."

His expression drops. "I get it."

Wanting to explain herself, she says, "I went to a dinner party at Wolfie's house. He invited Melissa and me as an end-of-the-year thing."

"Cool. I like him."

"Me, too." She smiles. "So, no date with Jessica?" she asks.

"No, we broke up—again. This time, for good."

"Really?"

"Yeah, we are too on- and off-again to make anything good out of it. I kind of always knew she'd end up hating me."

"Wow, you sound like a horrible person to date." She laughs.

His eyes narrow. "Like you're a peach."

She instantly stops laughing. "What the hell, Tank?" The smirk on his face tells her he is kidding, but still, she feels the need to defend herself. "I'm a catch, you know."

"Ah, the Radio Goddess finally gets a big head!"

"Radio what?"

"It's what they call you. Around school."

She laughs hard. "You've got to be kidding me!"

He puts his hands in the air. "Hey, don't shoot the messenger. I'm just telling you what I hear."

"If they only knew, right?" She giggles, and then it starts to fade. "I used to be something…"

"So," he says, his expression softening, "what else has been going on? You doing okay?"

"Well, that's sort of what I wanted to talk to you about…the other night…the night I stayed over." She notes his cheeks pink.

"Oh," he says.

"I really wanted to thank you for looking out for me. For coming to get me at the party, Tank. I took what you said very seriously, and knowing that you've been through something similar, well, I guess I just wanted to say thank you for being a good friend. Obviously, I've needed it."

"Anytime, Laura. There was a time I needed it, too."

She meets Tank's eyes and says, "So, thanks for pushing me to straighten out. I required a shove."

"Yeah, yeah," he says, dismissing her. "That's what friends are for."

"It's been good for me to talk to someone else, too. And it's helping me with Wolfie. I had to see that he can't be everything to me. He needs to heal as well. And I wasn't really able to let him, I suppose."

"Good. I'm happy for you. The both of you. It's important you stick together but find your own way to deal with Travis's death."

Desperate to change the subject, she says, "Anyway, I should be heading back to my dorm."

"It's late. I'll walk you."

Considering all the stuff that has gone down with the Campus Creeper and the vandalized house on campus and the crap she pulled the other night, she's in no position to refuse an escort home.

"Appreciate that."

"Look at that," he boasts. "It's not so hard to be agreeable, now is it?"

"What's that supposed to mean?"

He pulls on his coat and slips on his sneakers. "I just figured you'd give me some crap about how you could walk yourself home, blah, blah, blah. And then I'd get pissed and insist, and then you'd get even pissier, but in the end, I'd still be walking you home," he says as he motions for her to head out the door.

"Well, it's good to know I'm unpredictable." She laughs.

"Hey, that's my line."

She smiles. "I know."

They step out into the late spring evening.

"So, you going to the party next Friday?"

"Gosh, I haven't been out with my friends in so long," she sighs.

"You should go. Might make you feel normal-ish." He laughs.

"Yeah, whatever that is."

"Exactly. And, yes, I'll be there. Thank you for asking," he says.

She laughs. "I assumed since you'd asked me, that meant you were going."

"I see. Well, it should be a great way to end sophomore year."

"Where are you living next year?" she asks as they step onto the curb and near her dormitory.

"Logan, Webber, Nathan, and I will be in Parkers Village. Nathan Logan, and I have scholarship money, so free housing."

"Cool."

"You?"

"Not sure yet. But most likely, off-campus. Bree is sort of heading the charge on this one."

"Not surprised."

"Hey, works for me!"

"Well, Laura, I'm glad you stopped by."

"Me, too, Tank. Thanks for the chat."

"Take care of yourself," he says. With that, he turns and heads back to his dorm.

"See you Friday," she yells after him.

He doesn't turn as he yells back, "I figured that!"

She laughs as she keys into the dormitory.

And for just a brief time, she forgot all her woes regarding Travis. Tank's constant bantering and his sarcastic humor somehow take her away from her thoughts. He seems to have that effect on her. And more often than not these days.

Eighteen

End-of-the-Year Party

As the year winds down and everyone is so focused on their finals, the investigation into the soccer house has slowed, much to Laura's disappointment. She knows deep down that if Travis were still alive, he wouldn't have let his foot off the gas. But with Melissa only as an interim editor and all her finals to study for, it wouldn't be fair for Laura to say anything. But it is never out of her mind. Or out of Wolfie's, which is always reassuring.

Laura wanders back to her dormitory after her last final just as Brittney, their dorm monitor for the past two years, is gathering the girls on the floor in the common area to talk before they move out.

"I want to say thank you for some fabulous years together. I'm going to miss you girls," she says with a heavy heart. "You all went through a lot and have grown up so much. Thank you for being so wonderful and not setting anything on fire." She laughs.

The girls all say their good-byes to her.

"Come back and visit with us. Will you?" Melissa asks.

"I sure will. I'm only a few hours away. But after graduation, I must get a real job, so you know how that is."

"You were the best dorm monitor," Casey gushes.

"I wish all of you a great junior year." She smiles and then hugs each one of them before leaving the common room.

Maddie is sitting on one of the couches, clearly troubled, with her head hung low.

"You've been quiet tonight," Laura remarks.

Maddie lifts her head with an unsettling expression on her face.

"Jesus, what is it?" Bree asks.

"I'm, um…I'm transferring. I won't be here next year."

Maddie has been one of their quieter floor mates the past two years but always a solid friend, a true keeper of secrets and always a trusted study buddy.

"What?!" Casey says.

"I didn't know how to tell you guys, and I've just been so torn up about it. My parents are so disappointed in how the school has handled everything with all the lawsuits, the security on campus, and the vandalized building. They just feel like I need to be somewhere that is not riddled with controversy, and it was hard to argue with that. But as I sit here, looking at all of you, I'm ashamed for giving in and leaving you all."

Shock hits all of them in the face. No one says a word.

"Where are you going?" Alex asks.

"SUNY Buffalo. And in fairness, it's a lot closer to home."

"Wow. I'm surprised," Bree says.

Abigail notices the disappointment on Laura's face. She feels the need to break the tension. "Well, Maddie, we sure will miss you."

Maddie stands. "I'll miss you guys, too. I really will."

"We will see you this summer," Melissa adds.

"Promise?" she asks.

"Of course," Abigail says as she embraces her friend.

As Abigail thinks back, it did seem odd that when Bree, Laura, Melissa, and Abigail went apartment hunting, Maddie always had an excuse as to why she couldn't go. Casey and Alex decided to move forward as well, and they got a place together. Jen is remaining at the soccer house despite her parents' objections. The signs were there. But they didn't necessarily point to Maddie transferring.

"I've got to go finish packing," Bree says. "I'm going to miss you, Maddie," she adds as she heads toward the stairs.

"You, too."

The girls disperse and finish packing and cleaning before they head to the final party of the year at Delta Chi.

Laura aimlessly wanders around the room with no real sense of direction.

"You okay?" Abigail asks.

She looks up at her. Words escaping her mind.

"Something going on?"

Laura, still holding a sweater she can't figure out where to pack, stops. "About Maddie leaving," she blurts out.

"Hit hard, didn't it?"

"Yeah, I get her reasoning, but it just seemed like out of the blue. How long has she been feeling this way? Do a lot of students?"

"This way about what?" Abigail asks.

"That the school is a joke. A place you wouldn't want your daughter to graduate from."

Abigail sighs, "I know. Sure felt like her parents thought that way. Didn't it?"

"Yeah, all of a sudden, I feel like I didn't do enough. Could I, should I have sacrificed more to get the outcome…" She drops onto her bed.

"Oh, Laura. You've done so much. For the whole school. If Maddie's parents feel that way, there's nothing you can do to change it."

Laura ponders the thought. *I wonder how many students are transferring after this year because of everything that has gone on this past year and a half.*

"What's stirring in that brain of yours?" Abigail asks.

"The soccer house. What can I do to get things back to normal—whatever *that* is?"

"For starters, you can finish packing." She laughs.

"I'm serious, Abigail. I don't want to graduate from a place that's in total disarray."

"Neither do I. But I know you, and you can't have the weight of the world riding on your shoulders."

"No, you're right. I have Melissa and Wolfie to hold some of the heaviness." She tucks her bobbed hair behind her ear.

Abigail knows Laura well, and she knows she's contemplating something. She rests her hands on Laura's shoulders. "Whatever you are up to, count me in, okay?"

Laura's eyes widen. "You sure?" *Because I just might need all hands on deck for this one.*

"Yes, positive. You're going to need all of us."

She hugs her friend. As Laura releases her, Abigail can tell Laura's mind is already racing with thoughts.

"I have to go see Melissa," she pipes up as she tosses her sweater on her bed. "I'll see you before the party."

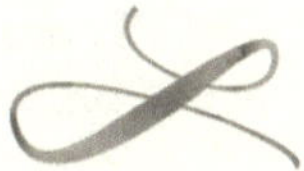

The party is in full swing when the girls arrive. At the door, they each pay their five dollars to get in and are welcomed into the grimy basement. They head to the bar and each grab a drink. They settle into the corner near the speaker.

There's a cloud of unhappiness none of the girls can quite identify. Ending their sophomore year with so many unresolved issues, is undesirable at best.

Maddie puts her arms around Laura. "I'm sad to be leaving OSU," she says.

"We are, too," Melissa adds.

"I hate the end of the year. I don't want to go back to the Hamptons and hang with all my bitchy friends." Bree smirks. "Plus, being without Adam is misery at its finest."

"I get to wallow in my own desolation before I can come back to the station. I hate the summer," Laura chimes in. "I feel like I have so much to do." *I have way too much to do.*

Although Tucker offered a full-time spot to Laura over the summer, she felt it was best to go home for at least a few weeks before being left to her own devices at school. She wasn't sure she was stable enough emotionally to handle the solitude. Her parents also encouraged her to come home, rest, and remove herself from the environment that was, naturally, a constant reminder of her loss.

Melissa, almost sensing her darkness, grabs her hand and says into her ear, "We will get to the bottom of this. We're too determined not to. But you must focus on your well-being, too."

Laura tips her head, resting it on her shoulder. "You're the best." She smiles.

But it isn't a guarantee that Melissa is going to be named the student editor next year. What if someone that Wolfie and I don't know becomes the new editor and we have to start all over again? What if they don't work the same as Travis did or Melissa does now? What then?

And believe it or not, this is me focusing on my well-being. By doing exactly what Travis would have wanted me to do, I'm healing in my own way. The only way I know how.

But we have to get to the bottom of this—and fast—before the student body starts to lose faith in us. Before they start to forget all that Travis built. The trust.

It's so hard to build.

But it only takes a second to wreck it.

The girls have another drink and all cheers to Maddie.

At some point, Abigail reappears from what must have been the longest line at the bathroom.

A half hour later, the entire football team descends into the basement. Laura spots Tank first, as it's impossible not to notice him. Nathan makes his way over to Abigail, and they sneak off to get another drink.

"Funny meeting you here," Tank says with a warm smile.

"I didn't know *you'd* be here," Laura jokes.

"You all packed?"

"Almost. It was hard to pack though. Leaving the dorms left me with a funny feeling," she admits.

"I can't wait to get out of that hellhole. Bring on apartment living!" he says.

"Yeah, I guess that's the positive, right?" She averts her eyes.

"You okay, Chase?" he asks.

She glances back at him. "Yeah. Maddie told us today that she's transferring next year. That bummed me out."

"No shit," he says. "That is a bummer."

"Yeah, but…"

Before she can continue, a guy stumbles into them and knocks Laura to the ground. As she peeks up to see what is happening, Tank is holding the guy up by the collar of his shirt against the wall. His face is red as he yells at him. It's almost impossible to hear what he's saying over the music, but it's clear he's angry.

Melissa reaches her hand out to Laura, helping her up off the dirty basement floor.

"You okay?" she asks.

"Did that guy just fall, or what the heck happened?" she asks.

"No idea. I was talking to Casey, and the next thing I knew, you were on the ground!"

Laura leans down, rubbing the pain out of the knee she just landed on. "Man, that hurt," she says.

Then, almost immediately, there's a large hand on her shoulder.

"Come with me," he demands.

Her hair has fallen over her face from bending down, but as she peers up, she sees Tank's expression is still one of anger.

"What?" she asks.

He grabs her hand and leads her to the stairs.

"Where are we going?"

He doesn't answer her but pulls her along up the stairs and into the kitchen.

"You've got to get ice on your knee," he says, reaching into the icebox with his hand.

He fists several cubes of ice and then wraps them in a paper towel. He commands a few students to move out of the way from the counter as he places the ice pack on top. He spins to Laura, scoops her up, and sits her on the countertop.

"What are you doing?" she says.

"You're too short for me to see, and I'm not bending down," he replies.

"I'm too short? Maybe you're too big," she boasts.

He ignores her and pulls up her jeans to where he can see her knee. A few guys at the party stare at them.

She whispers to Tank, "You're embarrassing me. I can…"

"I'm what?" he says rather loudly, catching her eyes.

She peers over at the nosy students, and Tank quickly spins to face whoever is making her uncomfortable.

"Scram," he says. "Nothing to see here."

"Sorry, Tank," one kid mumbles as they exit the kitchen.

"Ouch," she says as he places the ice on her knee.

"Yeah, it's going to hurt. That basement floor is unforgiving."

"What the heck happened? One minute, I'm standing…"

"Stupid guy, too drunk to stand, and, well, he wasn't going to knock me over," he adds, his chest puffing.

She rolls her eyes at him. "Really? So, I'm too short and too weak?"

"I never said that. Well, maybe the short thing, but everyone is short to me, so it's no offense."

Another kid enters the kitchen.

"Hey you. Go get me two beers. Quickly."

"Sure thing, Tank." The guy leaves and heads straight toward the bar.

"Tank!"

"What?" He smiles.

"You just make people do things for you?" she asks.

"Listen, I'm popular, and I know it. So, yeah, people do shit for me."

"Oh my God." She laughs. "You're unreal."

"That, too." He laughs.

"Don't let this," she says, pointing to him, "rub off on Nathan. He's a nice guy."

"Oh, please." He chuckles. "I'm nice, too."

The kid comes back with the two beers. "Here you go, Tank."

"Thanks, buddy." He smiles wide at him to make a point to Laura. "I really, really appreciate it."

"No problem, Tank. Anytime."

"See my friend here? She's too lazy to get a beer for herself, so she made me ask you. Can you believe her?"

"Tank! Shut up!" she says, trying hard to mask her laugh.

"Girls," the guy says as he exits the kitchen.

"Am I right?!" Tank yells after him.

Once they are alone again, Laura folds her arms over her chest. "Because of that, I'm not thanking you for helping me."

With a wink, he says, "I think you just did."

"No, I didn't."

"Yep, and I accept your praise." He leans on the counter. His massive body tipping close to her.

For the first time, she can smell his cologne—cedar mixed with notes of lavender and lemon. It's quite nice. It reminds her of being in the woods near her property back home,

"Hello? Earth to Laura!"

She shakes her head. “Sorry, spaced out for a second.” She gazes down at the ice melting on her leg. “Can I take this off now?”

“Give it a few more minutes. Finish your beer.”

“Okay.” She takes a sip. “Hey, question. When are you coming for preseason?”

“August 1.”

She laughs.

“What is so funny?”

“I’m coming back to work at the radio station…August 1.”

He smiles wide. “Well, what do you know?”

She smiles, and it’s in this moment that she realizes what an interesting person Tank truly is. He has such a massive presence, but when he wants to be, he can be quite charming, funny, and kind. Not at all how she used to think of him.

But maybe that’s why it’s so important to give everyone a second chance. He was so misunderstood last year. That, if nothing else, shows she owed him a second thought. God knows he’s given her one these past few months. He could have just told her to get lost. But he stuck by her.

She smiles at him and sips on her beer.

Tank rubs the back of his neck, and then with a deep sigh, he breaks the silence by saying, as though it’s completely normal, “Man, I need to get laid.”

And just like that, he’s back to the old Tank.

“Tank,” she says with a slap on his arm.

“What?” he says. “You interested?”

She blushes a thousand shades of pink.

Interested?

She thinks.

Um…

Maybe?

Nineteen

A Sophomoric End

Laura says her good-byes to the girls as her parents put the last bag in their car.

As she exits the dormitory, someone yells her name. "Laura, wait!"

She turns and sees Wolfie jogging toward her. The look on his face tells her he isn't here for a last good-bye before the summer.

"Wolfie, what is it?"

"I'm so glad I caught you," he says with a heavy breath. He leans on his knees as he tries to catch some air. "You need to see these." He takes out an envelope from inside his tweed coat and hands it to her. She goes to open it. "Not here," he barks as he lowers her hand.

"What is it?"

"Photos."

"Photos of what?"

"Places locally that have been vandalized in the last year." He leans in and whispers, "There's something strange in each one. But similar. Look and call me when you get home, okay?"

Laura's eyes grow wide as she stuffs the envelope in her back pocket. He gives her a quick hug. Then, as soon as he came, he's gone like a flash.

Laura turns and approaches her parents' car. She climbs in the back.

"Everything okay?" her mother asks.

"Yes. That was Wolfie, Travis's friend and, well, my friend, too."

"Oh, that's nice."

"Sorry. I would have introduced you, but he was in a hurry."

"Some other time," her father adds.

Laura waits for them to get on the road before she pulls out the envelope in her pocket. She's dying to see what he's talking about.

She slips the envelope on to her lap and retrieves the photos. The first one was of the side of an old house, roped off by police tape, with people gathered around, looking at the words spray-painted all over it—mostly swear words, nothing directly homophobic. She flips to the next photo and the next, and all of them are of a crude nature.

Is that what Wolfie meant? she wonders.

She eyes each one, trying to analyze the photos. Aside from the basis of the crimes, she can't find a commonality. Then, she starts to look away from the words. *What is going on around them?*

She notices a young man in one of the photos. His hands are shoved deep in his pockets. He's on the outskirts of the police tape, and he appears to be staring straight at whoever took the photograph. Laura flips to the next one. A similar man is standing, in relation to the previous photo. Again, his hands are deep in his pockets, and he's looking directly at the camera. An unfamiliar chill runs down Laura's spine.

Why is he looking directly at the camera when everyone else in the photo is looking at the graffiti?

She flips through pictures, and it's all the same. The young man is wearing a baseball hat. Laura leans in, trying to see what is written on his hat. The grainy quality of the photo makes it difficult to get any identifying features, let alone a logo on a baseball hat.

When she arrives at home, she unpacks and then calls Wolfie.

"Wolfie, it's me."

"Hey. You find it?"

"Yeah, the guy, looking at the camera."

"Good job."

She can hear him smiling with pride.

"You think he has something to do with it?"

"It's worth looking into. Criminals seeking power often come back to the scene of the crime to watch the chaos ensue. They get off on it. Either that or he's just really interested in the whole scene in general. Maybe he's building up the courage to do it himself. But it's no coincidence he's there."

"Sicko."

"Yeah, I know."

"I didn't know other houses had been involved."

"Yeah, I think the soccer house got some press because of their status on campus. I think the others were just off-campus, people who were targeted."

"How did we not know this?"

"It's amazing what you find when you dig."

"What can I do from here?" she asks.

"Can you talk to anyone at the police station?"

Laura's mind immediately goes to Officer Murphy and her terrible attempt at blaming the police this past year for the issues on campus. She offended him, and she's still licking her wounds. "I do know someone close to an officer I could ask."

"It's a start. I got a guy who can try to figure out something from these photos to give us a starting point."

"Of course you have a guy," she jokes.

"Hey, I play fair in all the departments at OSU. So, I have a guy *or* girl everywhere, all willing to help me in a bind."

Laura laughs. "I'll call you soon, okay?"

"Of course."

She places the receiver down and turns to face the bay window in her room, overlooking the farm. Her home is often a comfort to her. The expansive farmhouse, surrounded by acres of untouched land, glistens in the fading sun. She pulls open the window. An early summer breeze billows into her room. She breathes in deeply and then exhales slowly and deliberately.

"Regretting only staying for a few weeks?" her father asks, interrupting her thoughts.

She smiles to herself as she remains looking out the window.

"Don't take it personally, Dad," she jokes. "The radio cannot be silenced."

He chuckles. "Don't I know it?"

She turns to him.

"I'm real proud of what you did this year. You stuck your neck out for a lot of people."

She lowers her gaze. "I just wish it'd all ended better."

"I know, sweetheart. Losing someone will never be easy."

"Yeah, I know. I just have so much more to do and…" She wants to say, *I could really use him by my side.* But it's no use, saying the words. It wouldn't change a thing.

"Well, enjoy the time home while it lasts. Before you know it, you'll be back at school—and as a junior, no less. My, how the time has flown by." He shakes his head.

"Feels like just yesterday, I was walking into Willis Hall for the first time."

"Now, you'll be going to a fancy apartment with your friends."

She smiles at the thought of it. "Hard to believe."

"Get some rest while you're home, okay?"

"I will, Dad. Thanks."

She turns back to the window as her father leaves her room. She recalls the night she and Travis sat up for hours, working on their plan to uncover Dean Barrymore's involvement in the Campus Creeper nightmare.

"You look tired," she said as Travis feverishly rubbed his eyes.

"You know that's just code for, you look like crap."

Laura couldn't help but smile. "Is that so?"

"Yes, and besides, rest is for the weak."

"Travis, you need to take care of yourself."

"Are you worried about me?" he playfully asked.

Her cheeks burned, and she lowered her gaze.

He tucked a strand of hair behind her ear. "You do. You do care for me."

"Stop it. You're embarrassing me," she quipped.

He pulled her into him and rested his chin on top of her head. "Just remember this: I'll sleep when I know my work is done. And it's never done." He placed a kiss on top of her head and then released her. Able to switch gears effortlessly, he returned his focus on the pile of papers in front of him.

Laura undresses and pulls back the covers from her bed. Climbing in, she rests her head on the pillow, yet her eyes remain wide open. She realizes that thinking back on her time with Travis might not always bring her pain, like it once did. That maybe, time does heal some of the ache in her heart.

But then again, she knows herself better than anyone, and as she stares into the darkness, she wishes more than ever that she could simply turn off her brain. To stop it from spinning with thoughts.

"Will I be able to rest when my work is done?" she wonders aloud. "And more importantly, when will that be?"

Twenty

Junior Year 1997-1998

Bree convinced the girls to look off-campus for a better apartment than the cookie-cutter ones in Parkers Village, the on-campus student apartments. Bree picked the best house possible off-campus and assured the girls that her father insisted he pay most of the rent, considering this house was way out of their price range but was central to campus yet tucked back on a beautiful side road. They signed the papers at the end of last semester for the house on Charlotte Street.

Laura was excited to be moving into the three-story Victorian after spending the month of August in temporary student housing while she worked at the station. Thankfully, she was able to spend what little time she had with Nathan, Tank, and some of the other football players she knew as well as Jen, who was also at school for preseason soccer. She was grateful for the distractions, so she wouldn't be a third wheel in the Colin and Zoe saga. And by saga, it merely meant the strange vibe she kept getting from Zoe every time she was around. As if she was trying to compete with Laura. She wished more than anything that Zoe would just go away and that the station would go back to the way it had been pre-Zoe.

Wolfie, on the other hand, much to Laura's surprise, took the month of August to spend time in Prague with Tripp and Willow. At first, she had been saddened by the news of him not being around, but it honestly allowed Laura an opportunity to spin some records on the air and just enjoy the quiet life on campus before everyone rolled back onto campus in September.

Laura started moving her stuff into the house on Charlotte Street as soon as Bree called to say she was finished decorating and getting it up to her standard of living. The old Victorian had been upgraded and modernized, and each girl had their own massive bedroom. Melissa, Laura, and Bree were all on the second floor, and they had insisted Abigail get the third-floor bedroom, knowing that Bree would be at Adam's most weekends, Laura would be at the station, and Melissa would be at the student paper. Melissa deservingly got the call in July to say she was officially the student editor of *The Weekly Blue*. Practically the best news any of them had gotten in months.

Exhausted from all the work she did, unpacking and organizing her life, Laura is finally able to drag her body across campus to the one building she avoided at all costs this past month. As she encroaches upon the Rounds Hall, the home of *The Weekly Blue*, for the first time as a junior, the sensation of vomiting plagues her. She places her hand over her lips, trying to quell the awful taste in her mouth. She passes by a student smoking and breathes in the scent, reminding her of Travis.

Travis. Travis, is all she can think about as she pulls the heavy door open. But instead, she freezes. *I can't do this.*

She starts to turn to leave when an annoyed student behind her barks, "You going in or what?"

Ripped from her thoughts, she looks at this person and says nothing. He reaches past her and pulls open the door, letting it slam in her face. She doesn't care because she remains on the outside.

"It's better out here." She staggers back from the door.

An indescribable loneliness washes over her. She walks to the bench across from the building and sits, resting her head in her hands.

How can I go into the one building that was Travis's building? He made that place his. He owned it. Conquered it. Ran it. There is a fucking plaque with his name on it next to the door. And I'm expected to walk right through and not feel as though I want to die?

Minutes pass, and she remains, still attempting to kill the dark thoughts in her head. But her nerves get the best of her, and before she can stop it, she's running behind a large oak tree at the side of the building and spilling her lunch all over its trunk. She leans heavily on the tree for several minutes as she tries to steady her shaking legs. A few students walk by, mumbling comments. Embarrassed, she straightens up, removes a tissue from her bag, and dabs the corner of her mouth. Rummaging through her bag, she finds a peppermint and pops it in her mouth. She smooths down her shirt and tucks her hair behind her ears, and as though nothing transpired, she enters the building.

She passes the plaque memorializing Travis and purposely ignores it before entering the office of *The Weekly Blue*. She notes the clicking of the keyboards, and another memory flashes before her, much to her dislike.

"I'm here to speak with Travis."

Some kid yelled, "Travis!" down the hallway.

Travis—tall in stature with windswept dark hair and big blue eyes, well-dressed in an oxford with that sort of '80s disheveled-preppy style—came waltzing down the hallway toward her. Although he could barely get down the hall with everyone trying to get his attention.

"Travis," one girl said, "can you look at this?"

He took the paper and barely glanced at her. He scribbled something on it and then tossed it back to her.

Another guy approached. "Travis, this needs your approval for four thirty."

He grabbed that as well, peeked at it, scrawled something across the top, and then continued down the hallway toward Laura.

She had to blink several times just to make sure what she was seeing was real. This guy was the actual deal. His lemmings were falling all over him as he tried to make his way toward her.

"Laura, hello," he said in an overly confident tone. "I'm Travis Taylor." He extended his hand to her.

"Hello, Travis. Laura Chase."

Little did she know, that day was merely the beginning for them.

She doesn't bother asking anyone for assistance this time; instead, she heads straight down to the office once occupied by her dear friend Travis. Sitting in the chair is her *other* dear friend Melissa.

"Hey!" Melissa rises to greet her friend. "This must be so weird. You okay?"

With tears in her eyes, Laura admits, "It's strange. But I'm so happy for you. I couldn't have asked for a better person to be sitting in his chair. Err, your chair." She deeply hugs her. "Congratulations on the job."

Melissa squeezes back. "Thank you, my friend. I will do my very best to keep his legacy intact. I plan to make you all proud."

"I know you will." They release their embrace, and Laura takes her seat across from her.

Wolfie enters the room. "Hey, guys." He closes the door behind him.

Never one for good-byes or grand hellos, he shows little emotion in seeing Laura for the first time in nearly three months.

"How was Prague?"

"Fabulous. I'll tell you all about it," he says.

"No, you won't," Laura jokes.

He smiles at her and then gets right down to brass tacks. "I went down to the station and spoke to Officer Waters. After what happened last year with the school and the local police, I got the feeling that they are willing to work with us on this."

"What do you mean?" Laura asks.

"They have a few leads. He's hoping with our help in talking about it on the radio and printing it in the paper, we might get some traction."

Melissa adds, "Great. Let's make it the cover story this week. Start off the year with a bang. Let whoever is responsible for this know the summer did nothing to make us forget."

Wolfie's sly smile indicates to Laura that he's pleased with Melissa's direct approach.

"What do you have in the works?" Melissa asks Laura.

"I plan to interview a few more of the players, get their take on it. Shannon said she'd come on the air to show her support. I'd like to start with her," Laura says, referring to the captain of the soccer team and Jen's housemate.

"Agree. I'd like to see if anyone recognizes the guy in the pictures," Wolfie says.

"What pictures?" Melissa asks.

Realizing they haven't gotten her up to speed from the summer, Wolfie reaches into his bag and retrieves the pictures he gave to Laura. "Notice anything?"

Melissa shuffles through the pictures, conspicuously eyeing them until she reverts to the one at the soccer house. She takes out a magnifying glass from her desk and glances over each photo again. "Similar features. I can't make out the letters on the hat. Hard to tell."

"Yes, but it's clear to me, that is the same person. Same pose in each picture. The way he stands," Laura adds.

"Agree. I think it's the same person," Wolfie says.

"Okay, so let's get out there and see if anyone recognizes this guy," Melissa says.

"On it." Wolfie rises from his seat.

Laura quickly follows. "See you later, Melissa." She exits behind Wolfie.

Once they are out on the lawn, he turns to face her. "Hey."

"Hey."

"Good to see you," he says.

She leans in for a hug. "You, too."

He releases her. "How's your new place?"

"Beautiful. Wait until you see it. Bree outdid herself. Are you glad you stayed in the same apartment?" she asks.

"Yes, too busy to move around." He pauses, thinking deeply. "Look, I have an idea. The field hockey team is practicing now. I say, we walk down to the field house and do a little poking around. See if anyone stands out to us. Maybe this guy has a thing for all athletes. We can't let anything go unchecked."

"Sounds good."

They approach the fields and can hear the whistles and hollers from the coaches as they instruct the players during drills. Wolfie and Laura nonchalantly walk past the players, specifically looking for any male watching or near the practice.

"Do you really think he'd be here?" she asks.

"I don't know what to think about this," he admits. "My gut is telling me there's something else, but I'm unsure of what that could be."

"Trust your gut, Wolfie. It's usually right."

He smiles. "Come on. Let's go inside and poke around."

The field house is packed with athletes. The football team is getting ready to go out on the field. The athletic trainers are hurrying about, trying to get ready for the practice. The coaches are huddled in their offices, and the cheerleaders are about to walk into the gym for their practice.

Laura notices Nathan up ahead. Shortly behind him are a few of the cheerleaders, following him into the training room. Laura pauses as an unfamiliar sensation comes over her. Moments later, Nathan and Poppy exit, smiling and laughing. Poppy gently guides her hand down Nathan's arm, clearly a gesture she has done many times before.

Nathan heads to the back door, and Poppy yells in a high-pitched, sweetened tone, "See you later, Nathan."

Then she enters the gymnasium. Nathan turns, his cheeks flushed red, and smiles at her.

"Come on," Wolfie spouts, pulling on Laura's arm. "Quit staring," he jokes.

"I wasn't…" *Watching my best friend's boyfriend flirt with another girl, was I?*

"Sure, whatever. I'm going to see if any of the trainers will talk to us."

Laura shakes her thoughts free, refocuses, and catches up to Wolfie in the training room. The flurry of activity ceases as the two enter.

"Can I help you?" a guy asks.

"Yes, the head trainer, please," Wolfie says, brimming with confidence.

"Sure, right this way." He brings them to a back office. Knocks and then pushes the door open. "You have some visitors," he says.

"Come in," he bellows.

Laura and Wolfie enter the room. Standing before them is an incredibly well-built man in his mid-thirties, wearing head-to-toe OSU clothing.

"Jarvis Redburn. How can I help you?" he asks.

"Yes, Jarvis, my colleague, Laura Chase, and I are from the media team on campus, and we'd like to ask you a question for the paper."

Puzzled by his guests, he replies, "Okay."

Wolfie pulls out several cropped photos of the man in the pictures and hands them to Jarvis. "We were wondering if you might recognize the person in these photos. We believe he's a student on campus, and he might have an interest in the athletic teams."

Jarvis shuffles through the photos, his brow bent in concern. "Is this person in some kind of trouble?"

"No, not at all," Wolfie lies.

Jarvis looks again through the pile and then tosses them back toward Wolfie. "Don't recognize him."

"Of course," Wolfie says. "No problem. Sorry to take up your time."

"No trouble at all."

"Mind if we ask some of the others?" Laura asks, glancing over her shoulder at the bustling training room.

"Be my guest—as long as you don't get in the way of the treatments."

"Thanks."

Laura and Wolfie meander through the training facility, stopping and showing the photos to anyone who will give them the time of day. Laura is about to head into the back room when she hears a girl crying, entering the main room. Laura spins and sees the commotion erupting in front of her. Poppy is being carried in by a few of her teammates.

A trainer rushes over. "What happened?"

"She landed on her foot wrong," a girl pipes in.

Poppy winces as she's placed on a training table. "My ankle," she cries.

"Let me look," Jarvis says as he rushes to her side. He leans down and inspects her foot.

She fires off to one of the girls, "Go get Nathan—now!"

The girl spins on her heel and rushes out the door toward the football practice field. Jarvis glances conspicuously at her and then returns to assessing her ankle.

Laura, feeling uneasy, catches Wolfie's stare and motions for him to leave with her. They exit without announcement.

That was so strange. Why would Poppy mandate for Nathan to get pulled from practice because she got hurt?

"So, back to square one on the photos," Wolfie says as they walk back toward campus.

"Hey, mind if I meet up with you later?"

"Sure, no problem. I have a deadline at the paper anyway. I'll call you."

"Thanks. I'll keep digging," she says as she takes the path toward campus.

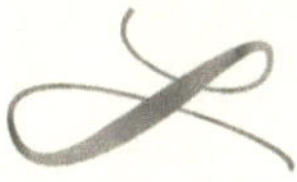

Laura has a nagging pull in her gut as she replays the scene of Poppy demanding to get Nathan from practice.

Huh, why would Poppy disrupt a football practice and have one of the cheerleaders get Nathan to come back to the training room for her? To what? Console her? That seems super odd to me.

He's the captain of the team and the most important player on the field, right? Would his coach even allow that to happen? Am I missing something? Her reaction to the situation makes zero sense to me.

I feel like what I just witnessed was not a normal series of events. My only job is to tell Abigail, right? As her friend, it's my duty to look out for her. If this girl is trying to steal her man, she should hear it from me.

Twenty-One

Allies

Laura stopped by a photo shop on her way through town. Wolfie had the right idea to isolate the person in the pictures and not show people the vandalism. It might sway their answer and reaction to the question, *Do you know the person in this picture?*

She makes copies and pays for them. She clutches the photos as she exits the store.

The sun is setting now, and a warm breeze dances across her skin as she makes her way through campus.

As she passes the Union, she catches sight of Colin and Zoe sitting near the window, laughing and drinking coffee. A surge of jealousy courses through her, and she spins quickly to avoid them catching her watching them.

As she turns, she's immediately bumped across her shoulder.

"I'm so sorry," she says as the photos fall from her hand. She leans down to pick them up.

And then she hears a voice she'll never forget.

"Well, well, Miss Chase," Officer Murphy says.

Laura stands, and Officer Murphy, wearing a plain white shirt and jeans, is holding one of the pictures in his hand. She tries to grab it when he pulls it away.

"Hello, Officer Murphy."

She hates that her voice shakes when she speaks to him. But how could it not? After all, she humiliated him last year on the radio, and unbeknownst to her at the time, it was completely off base. Man, did she eat crow for that. He was only trying to do his best to help the school catch the Campus Creeper; it was the powers that be that got in his way. It was never for a lack of him trying to keep the students safe.

He glances at the photo. "What are you up to now?" he says, peering at the others in her hand that she's trying to shield from him.

"What do you mean?"

His face softens. "Come with me. We need to talk—privately," he says as he heads in the direction toward the street.

She has no choice but to follow him, as he's still holding one of her photographs. He approaches a black SUV and gets in; he leans over and unlocks the passenger side and waits for her to climb in.

She opens the door and hops in.

"Listen," he begins, "if you want to be a detective..." She tries to interject, but he holds up his hand to silence her. "You can't go around, holding these in your hand. At least you had the smarts to isolate the person from the crime scene," he boasts as he holds up his photo.

"I just came from the photo shop—that's why," she mumbles.

"I see, but you just dropped them all over campus. What if he saw you?"

"Why do you care anyway?" she asks.

"Because I want to catch the guy just as badly as you do."

"You're working the case?"

"No, they gave it to someone else. Officer Waters, to be exact. But I have an interest in getting it solved." He hangs his head.

"You do? And why is that?"

He peers over at her, and for the first time, she sees his hard outer shell crack. "Obviously, I need to regain the trust of the student body. Last year was hard for me, both personally and professionally. It was evident that not enough was done and that politics got in the way of making an impact. A costly one."

It's obvious by his expression that he's painfully thought about it. So much so that Laura begins to feel his pain as well.

"But you tried to help my friend Bree. That much we know. You can't bear the burden of others' mistakes."

"We all made mistakes," he says.

She whispers, "Yes, we did." She turns to face him. "And that includes me."

"Well, Laura, if it wasn't for your willingness to stick out your neck, maybe nothing would have changed."

"It wasn't all me..." Her voice catches.

"I'm very sorry about your friend. What a tragedy."

She can only nod her head in acknowledgment, as the mere thought of speaking his name still makes her want to burst into tears.

Noting the shift in the air and sensing the need to change the subject, he asks, "So, what *is* your plan?"

"We're hoping that by talking about it on the radio and printing a cover story in the paper, we might get some traction this year. We must make the students aware it's still a priority, and we need to make it clear to whoever did it that we haven't forgotten."

"Okay, and the photos?"

"We showed some students in the field house this afternoon. We hoped an athlete would recognize him. But there was a bit of a commotion going on. In hindsight, it wasn't the best time to be down there."

He smiles slightly.

"What's that for?" she asks.

"You've got a good mind for this. And with my help, we just might find this guy."

"Really?"

"Yeah, but you'll need to listen to me, okay?"

"Okay. What about Officer Waters?"

"He's six months from retiring. I've got a feeling he plans to coast until the end."

"So, what can I do?"

"For now, do as you have planned. Run the article and keep your radio interviews. But what I'd like you to do is have the editor put in a footnote, indicating that anyone with a tip can send a note or call the paper. Same for the station. There is someone out there who knows something."

"Good idea," she says with excitement in her voice.

He smirks. "I am a professional," he jokes.

"Duh." She laughs and realizes this is the first time she's shared a laugh with him.

"Once those things are done, we can put these to good use," he says, pointing to her photos.

"How so?"

"More to come on that. But in the meantime, I'd like to keep this one."

"Sure," she says.

"And try and keep your nose clean."

"Me?"

"What I mean by that is, don't let people see you out and about, searching for a student. It could get ugly. This person is obviously not in their right mind."

"Right. I guess I didn't think they'd be dangerous."

"You never know."

She places her hand on the handle of the passenger door. "I'm glad I ran into you today," she says.

"Literally." He laughs.

"Right." She chuckles. "I'll see you around." She opens the door and steps out of his vehicle.

The sun has faded away her afternoon. She treks back toward her house on the hill, clutching the pictures tightly in her hand.

Another year, another campus crisis to solve.

Twenty-Two

Things Are Changing

Laura barely slept last night. She tossed and turned, thinking about her first attempt to go in to Rounds Hall, how she spilled her lunch all over an unsuspecting tree and her conversation with Officer Murphy. Trying desperately to relax and focus on her next shift at the station instead of all her troubles, Laura leans back on her headboard, surrounded by CDs and her notebook, sifting through them, making her next playlist.

But then she hears a slight knock on her bedroom door.

"Come in!" she yells. "Hey, Abigail," she says as she pushes open her door. "I was making some music ideas for my next shift." She smiles, but it quickly fades.

Visibly despondent, Abigail sinks onto her bed. "Oh no. What is it?" Laura asks as she tries to get a look at her face, but instead, Abigail buries it into her hands. "Abigail, talk to me."

"I…I think Nathan cheated on me."

"Oh no."

"Alex *and* Kelly both told me they saw Nathan and Poppy leave a party together."

"Shit. Really?" Laura nervously pushes her hair behind her ears. "Well, there's something else, too. You see, I…Wolfie and I were down at the fields, and, well, I, at first saw them laughing and sort of bantering, but you know, I wasn't going to say anything, but then we went into the training room. Long story I'll tell you later, but all of a sudden, some cheerleaders rushed Poppy in. I guess she'd hurt her knee maybe, and then, like, out of blue, she *demanded* one of the girls go get Nathan." *I'm rambling because this sucks, telling you all this.*

"To get Nathan? Out of practice? For what?" Abigail barks.

"I didn't stay to see. It felt weird to me, so Wolfie and I left."

"So, Nathan never saw you?" Abigail asks with hurtful eyes.

"No."

"Did she see you?" Abigail asks.

"Nope, not that I know of."

"But she wanted someone to get him?"

"Yes, more like commanded he come, and no one said anything to the contrary." Laura takes her friend's hand.

"I feel stupid," Abigail moans. "I mean, what the hell, Laura?"

"I hesitated to tell you but thought twice because I'd want to know. She's unsettling to me."

"Me, too. She keeps coming up in our conversations, and that can't be a coincidence," Abigail says. "But thanks for telling me. I'm sure that wasn't easy," Abigail adds as she stares at her hand. Then, in a whisper, she says, "And the worst part is, he gave me this promise ring yesterday." She lifts her head up as a tear drips down her cheek.

"He bought you what?"

"This." Abigail places her hand in front of Laura. "It's a promise ring, and I was so caught off guard that I didn't ask him anything."

"Oh, honey. I'm so very sorry. But until you know the truth, you can't assume anything, right?"

"But I already do, or I wouldn't feel like this." Her friend drops her head again.

"Where is he now?"

"Away game, started at four."

Laura looks at the clock next to her bed. "Go to him."

"What?" Her head snaps up.

"Go to him. Make a grand gesture. Tell him that when you give someone a promise ring that it'd better be under the utmost considerate circumstances." Laura stands and takes Abigail's hands. "Because, otherwise, it's just…" She pulls her up.

"Bullshit," Abigail adds with a firm nod of her head.

"That's my girl." Laura laughs. "Now, you go and confront him. Don't come back without a definite answer as to whether or not something is going on with Poppy, okay?!"

Laura can see a renewed sense of purpose in Abigail's eyes as she walks with authority toward her door. "I won't."

"Good. And drive safe!"

Nathan and many of the guys on the team have been more consumed with their popularity since the girls first knew them as wide-eyed freshmen. Laura saw this firsthand this August while at school with them. She spent her free time with her friends on the football team but was quickly reminded there was an entire population at this school that reveres them like they were gods. Particularly Tank and Nathan.

And to me, they will always be just Nathan and Tank. I consider myself lucky in that aspect. That I got to know them before all of the fanfare. Because I love them for who they are, not what they represent, and I know Abigail feels the same, too.

Last night, Laura waited up as long as she could, and when she didn't hear from Abigail, she assumed everything had gone great with Nathan and the two lovebirds had made up and had a fabulous night together in the hotel. Despite a better night's sleep, she's still forced to drag her tired body to the shower. Then, she dresses quickly, as her need to get out of the house and clear her head is propelling her forward, down the stairs and onto the large front porch.

"Hey," a voice from the side says.

Laura jumps. "Jesus, you scared me."

"Sorry," Abigail says as she wraps a blanket tightly around her body.

Laura approaches her. "Are you all right?"

Tears sting her eyes as they finally gaze upon her friend. "No. I am most certainly not."

Laura crouches in front of her. "What happened?"

Abigail bursts into tears. "Poppy was in his room, alone…when I showed up."

Laura gasps, "Oh, Abigail. That's awful!"

"Some promise, huh?" she sobs. Wiping the tears from her face with the blanket, she appears exhausted.

"Jerk," she says as she rubs her friend's knee to console her. "I'm so sorry. What can I do?"

"Nothing. He's coming over to talk—whatever that means. But I know how I feel…" she mumbles through her cries.

Thinking of her own heartache over the past year, she quickly adds, "Don't compromise. It will only pull you apart in the end anyway."

Abigail tips her head. And takes in her friend's advice. "Thanks, Laura. I…my heart hurts so bad."

"Obviously, I want the best for you. And him. He's my friend, too. But you must be happy together, right?"

"Yeah, and I don't feel so happy right now," she admits.

"I can see that. So, I'll leave you guys to work this out. I'm going to grab some coffee downtown. I'll give you your space, okay?"

"Appreciate that," she says as she sits up, brushing her hair back from her face.

Laura stands, and then she leans in and hugs her friend. "Love you."

With a tightness in her voice, Abigail says, "Love you, too."

Laura drives down to the coffee shop and takes a seat near the window. She stares ahead, trying hard not to think about Travis. But his memories consume her. She brought some work with her to try to pass the time, but she can't concentrate on much.

A voice snaps her back to the present. "Mind if I join you?"

Laura whips her head up. "Oh, hey. I was just…"

"Staring into space," Tank says as he pulls the chair across from her out and takes a seat.

"Yeah, something like that."

"You okay?"

"Me?" she asks.

Tank chuckles. "Yeah, you."

Laura lowers her eyelids, on the verge of crying. "I don't know," she admits.

"Why don't you try it out on me, and I'll tell you if something's wrong?" he says in his usual cocky tone.

Laura tips her head, and as she notes his serious nature, she realizes that he might just be the perfect neutral party to explain her predicament to.

After all, once I got here this summer and Wolfie wasn't around, he was pretty much my go-to when I needed a shoulder to cry on. I've just been busy lately, and I haven't had much time for anyone.

"Come on. Just start with one sentence to sum up how you feel right now." He crosses his massive arms over his chest and waits patiently. "Remember we used to do this over the summer, and it worked?"

First thing that comes to mind. The very first thing? "I miss Travis, and I don't think anyone realizes just how much that hurts me. I'm also unsure if I'll ever be able to find someone else. I know I drove Colin away. And it's clear he's moved on, and that's completely on me."

He uncrosses his arms and leans forward. "Yeah, I'd say you definitely have something wrong." He laughs, trying to get her to smile.

Only she doesn't. "I can't stop feeling sad. And I'm trying. I really am," she says.

"But it's with you all the time. I know; it's impossible to shake."

"It will get easier, right?" she asks.

"I know I still feel it constantly, and it makes me wonder if it will ever go away, too."

She gazes out the window as a tear falls on her pink cheek.

"But I get the sense, there's more to this?" he asks.

Laura sighs heavily. "I suppose I haven't been able to properly mourn over Travis because no one really knew about us. Does that seem weird to you?"

"No, not at all."

"And I have this friendship with Wolfie, and being around him makes me feel connected to Travis. Wolfie and I are only friends, but…"

Tank chuckles.

"What?" she asks.

"This sounds all too familiar," he says as he tucks his long blonde hair behind his ear.

She cocks her head, and then like a lightbulb went off, she says, "Oh my God, it's the same thing as you and Abigail."

The sound of her name makes him squirm. "Yes. I needed to be near her to feel the connection to Jonathan. It managed to tear apart my relationships, but I ultimately had to do what I felt was best for me regardless of the consequences. But you know that. And listen, Laura, you won't be able to make everyone happy. It's impossible. Particularly when you aren't happy."

His words resonate deeply with how she feels. She couldn't make Colin happy because she was not happy. It wasn't his fault. It was just the unfortunate circumstances they'd found themselves in.

"So, what do I do?"

"You take care of yourself. Allow yourself all the time you need. If being around Wolfie truly helps you both, then ride that wave for now."

"But I thought you said it was unhealthy?"

"I've gotten to know you both, and maybe I've changed my mind."

Laura picks up her cup of coffee and sips the now-cooled beverage. She tries to swallow the tightness in her throat. "What about you and Abigail? I don't see you guys around much."

Tank sighs. "We've hit a rough patch," he admits.

"How so?" she asks, wanting him to admit his part in their rocky relationship.

Tank leans back in his chair, taking his time to choose his words wisely. "I wish…" He rubs his face, wanting to make sure he says it right the first time. He's aware he is sitting across from her roommate and best friend. "I wish she fought harder for things. She tends to retreat and take the easy way out."

Now, it's Laura's turn to lean back in her chair. "You've thought about this, haven't you?"

"Yes," he says firmly. "I've thought about it a lot."

"So, you know what happened last night?"

He drops his head. "Yeah, it's why I'm here. Thought Nathan might need some alone time."

"You think it's over between them?" she asks.

"Honestly, I think it's not right for her anymore," he says.

"Really?"

"Yeah, Nathan has girls all over him. All the time. He can't have a girlfriend who will allow that to happen."

"*Allow* that to happen? You aren't suggesting it's her fault?"

He chuckles. "No, no. But like I said, she'll take the easy way out despite how she might feel about him."

"Are you fucking kidding me?" Laura barks. "Name one girlfriend you know who allows her man to have women drape themselves all over him and pays no mind to it? What world are you living in?"

Again, Tank laughs. "You're feisty, Laura."

"And you're a dick," she huffs and turns to face the window.

He laughs even more. "I can be. I definitely can be."

"Easy way out, my ass. He stands her up all the time. She finds him in a hotel room with *that* girl after giving her a promise ring, and he doesn't even notice that someone else pays more attention to her." Quickly, Laura shuts her mouth.

"What?"

Laura averts her stare.

"Laura, what are you talking about?"

"Nothing. Forget I said it. It's really none of our business." *I'm not saying Kelly's name. No way.*

"She likes someone else?" he presses.

"I have no idea. But maybe, like you said, this isn't right for her anymore."

He realizes that he isn't going to get any more information out of her than he already has. "Maybe. I guess we'll find out."

Laura squints at him. Then, without warning, her filter is off, and she blurts out, "And by the way, don't you find it a bit cliché that the head cheerleader goes for the quarterback or whatever is going on?"

"Hey, don't look at me. I'm not dating a cheerleader."

Laura rolls her eyes. "Like you wouldn't." *You wouldn't, right? Tell me you're better than that. God, I hope so. I mean, I know so.*

"Listen, if you must know, I'm looking for a girl who is intelligent, sexy, and gets under my skin. I like a little bit of a challenge."

Whew. Something about the way his eyes glimmer when he states this makes Laura's skin flush.

"Well, I hope you find her."

"Oh, she's out there. No doubt about that," he replies confidently.

She tips her head back and laughs.

He continues, "I've had enough coffee. You don't want to go back to your place. I don't want to go back to mine. What do you say we bust out of here for a bit?"

His proposal intrigues her. "What do you have in mind?"

"Come on. I'll show you. We'll take my truck."

Tank stops at the store and buys some beer before they head out of town. He drives about fifteen minutes on Route 20 and then turns down a long dirt road. He pulls into a clearing with a stone wall in front of it and a cabin off to the side.

"Abby ever tell you about this place?" he asks.

"No. What's this?" she says as she climbs out of his truck.

"My friend Jonathan drew pictures of this place before he died. Pictures with her. So, I come here when I feel like it. It brings me closer to him. When I need to make sense out of the days that don't add up."

"Like today."

"Exactly. Come, sit."

He goes over to the cabin steps and sits down. She takes the seat next to him.

"I know you're upset about Nathan and Abby. I am, too."

"It's like if they can't make it, who can?"

"But you have to understand, there are ups and downs in every relationship. That has become wildly apparent to me these past few years. I just try to go with the flow."

"I get that. I do."

"Good. So, let's pretend for the next hour that nothing else exists but this," he says as he motions to the surrounding area, and then he hands her a cold beer.

Laura's shoulders relax as she leans back on the step and takes a sip of her beer. She thinks of Travis handing her a beer in his place, and something about the comfort of being here, doing the exact thing with Tank, is new for her. But welcome all the same.

She peers over at him as he stares at the clearing ahead of him, and she can't help but smile to herself. There's a likeness to Travis that Tank continues to innocently emulate. And more importantly these days, he seems to be the person whose arms are held open to catch her, just before she's about to fall. Whether he knows it or not.

After dropping Laura off at her house, Tank pulls into his spot in Parkers Village. The apartment is quiet when he enters, but he notices the back door to the patio is cracked open. Pushing open the screen door, he isn't the least bit surprised to find Nathan, hunched over in a folding chair, head resting in his hands.

Nathan, startled by the noise, looks up. Tank immediately notices his eyes are bloodshot and swollen.

Using the back of his hand, Nathan quickly wipes away his tears.

"Jesus," Tank says. "What happened?"

"You don't have to be out here," he mumbles.

Tank eases into the folding chair next to him. "I know."

Nathan pushes his hair back from his face, trying to compose himself. "I fucked up," he begins. "She doesn't trust me, and I can't convince her otherwise. I'm such an idiot!" He lets out an exasperated sigh.

Tank squeezes his shoulder. "Having Poppy in your room, regardless of the situation, was the wrong move."

"You don't think I know that?!" he barks.

Knowing Nathan's anger is not directed at him per se, he continues. "Girls are going to want your attention, and it's a tough line to draw in the sand. I think, deep down, you saw this coming. Think about it. When you two met as freshman, you were such an unknown on campus."

Nathan picks up a rock and hurls it across the small yard. "Fuck!" he screams.

"What did she say?" Tank asks.

He abruptly stands and starts pacing. "She doesn't want this anymore. She knows about the parties, the girls—"

"But you haven't…"

He stops in his tracks. "No. God, no. But you know how the parties can be. Harmless flirting, maybe a kiss during a stupid game. I don't know. It never meant anything to me! Only she does."

"I know. I wish I could tell you this was going to be easy."

Nathan pulls at his hair. "But it is! Right? I love her, so how could I screw that up?!"

Tank adds, "It's my fault, too. That stupid back-to-school party. She won't tolerate being stood up."

"No, no," he says. "I went, and I knew I shouldn't have. But I also want to experience college life, you know. I thought I could do it all"—he kicks some dirt with his foot—"but, obviously, I can't."

"If I know Abby—and I do—she'll come to her senses. She loves you too much."

"She doesn't trust me, Tank. She thinks—or knows—I hang out with Poppy too much and…"

Tank quickly adds, "So, tell Poppy to piss off!"

Nathan freezes.

He's in no position to tell Tank that he just came from the health center, where Poppy was receiving the most horrible news a college girl could receive.

Yep, she's pregnant. So, of all the times to tell someone to piss off, now is not the right time. Regardless of my relationship with Abby, I can't leave a friend in need. If I'm being honest, yeah, I knew Poppy liked me. For God's sake, she's told me about a hundred times. And each time, the only thing I can tell her is to go find someone who cares for her. And that person is never going to be me. That I am in love with one girl and one girl only.

And so, Poppy finally did. She found someone else.

And look what happened.

I feel responsible for her.

I can't help it.

And it's all my fault.

Worse, I can't tell anyone either. It's not my business to talk about it.

"It's over, Tank. You should have seen the way she looked at me. Her mind is made up."

Tank stands and approaches Nathan. "Well, we finally have something in common."

Nathan cocks his head to the side. "What's that?"

"Abby hates us both," he says, trying to get him to smile.

"You suck!" Nathan boasts.

He chuckles. "You know you'll get her back. And me? Someday, we'll be friends again. This is the way it goes."

"You seem so certain," Nathan says.

"Something in my gut is telling me this isn't over."

"I hope you're right." Nathan pauses, and then it dawns on him. "Shit, Spidey is going to kill me!" he says.

Tank nods his head. "Yeah, Webber is going to be so pissed at you. He was mad at me for just arguing with her. Man, oh, man, you're going to have to do some damage control on this one."

Not only have Webber and Abigail been friends since their first few weeks of their freshman year, but it's also well known among the friends that Webber fell hard for her. Only to have her date his roommate. An unfortunate series of events, but ultimately, Webber has always felt that having her as one of his best friends is far better than what most people get.

"Thanks," he says sarcastically. "I needed that."

"Not to worry. Laura will look out for her and keep us in the know. That I'm sure of."

Nathan wipes his hands down his face and lets out a deep sigh. "I miss her already. Shit, I'm screwed."

Tank pats him on the shoulder. "Give her some time. You know she misses you, too."

"God, I fucking hope so."

Twenty-Three

Blue Devils and Hope

Laura is dropped off at her home after the long afternoon she spent getting to know Tank better, trying to put her thoughts of Travis out of her mind. More importantly, she is just in time to console Abigail in her room after her breakup with Nathan.

Her perspective on relationships is somewhat clearer after her conversations with both Tank and Abigail. But what becomes apparent to Laura is that it will take some time before both she and Abigail will get back to themselves. Or at least, as it applies to being someone's girlfriend.

So, for now, her only option is to devote her time and energy to her education, the station, and helping the police find the person responsible for the vandalized house.

The following day, Laura enters the offices of *The Weekly Blue* and heads straight for Melissa's office. Each time she enters the door, it gets a little easier for her—not that she doesn't think of Travis, but she chooses to focus more on Melissa. As she pushes open the door and is greeted by the smiling face of her friend, her heart can't help but feel full. The circle of life has most definitely made its way back around.

"Hey there. Thanks for coming."

"Anytime." Laura returns a smile.

"I was hoping you could look at my copy. It goes to print tomorrow," she says, handing the paper to Laura.

"Sure thing." She grabs the copy. "Did Wolfie review?"

"Not yet. He's coming in later. Said he had some work to do outside the office."

Laura reads the article while Melissa writes down some items in her notebook.

Upon finishing, Laura adds, "Speaking of work, between you and me, I ran into Officer Murphy the other day."

"Yikes," Melissa says with a crinkle on her face.

"Yeah, I was nervous at first. But it turned out to be a good thing."

"Really?"

"Yeah," Laura says. "He said he'd help me with the case. He kept one of my photos and was going to do some research at the station. He mentioned Officer Waters is retiring soon and not to rely on him for getting the job done."

"Interesting."

"Yeah, I thought so, too. Oh, that reminds me. At the end of the article, can you add how to contact the paper and the station should someone know something? Like a tip line, specific to this?"

"Of course," Melissa says as she jots it down on the copy.

"Officer Murphy is convinced someone knows something; they're just looking for a way to get it to us."

"Got it. I'll be sure to alert the staff and let them know to entertain all calls or letters we receive. I'll have the team give them to me, and I'll keep you guys informed."

"Appreciate that, Melissa. Well then, I must get to the station. I'll see you at home later." Laura rises and treads toward the door.

Laura hurries across campus to the Union. She enters the radio station and finds no one around, so she heads straight to Studio B. She pushes open the door and immediately shuts it.

Oh my God, are they screwing on my desk?!

She marches down to Tucker's office. She knocks loudly and hears him yell to enter.

"Laura," he says with a smile. Only it quickly fades as he sees her expression.

Her face is fiery red, and she can't even begin to mask her anger. "I'm going to need you to go down to *my studio* and tell Colin and Zoe not to use it as their personal…whatever I just caught them doing!"

Tucker's cheeks pink. "Oh," he says as he stumbles to his feet. "I'm, um, so sorry. I'll address it immediately." He walks past her and toward his door.

"And tell them both to stay away from me today," she growls.

"Of course," he says, closing her in his office.

She plops in the chair across from his desk, squeezing her hands together tightly to try and calm her temper.

It seems like forever until Tucker returns. "I told them to both leave for the day. They won't be bothering you."

Laura stands. "Nice intern you chose," she barks. "I mean, seriously, is she only here to screw the DJs?"

"Laura!" Tucker gasps.

"It's not the first time I've caught them!"

"Oh," is all he can say as he watches her storm out the door.

She's on the verge of heaving as she enters the studio. Her wanting to disinfect the entire room feeds her emotions as she scurries around the room, ridding it of anything and everything that is not hers.

Risking getting on the airwaves late, she stops her obsessive cleaning as she notes Patrick in the window, pointing to his watch. She stops and drops in her chair, and with masked disappointment in her voice, she begins her two-hour on-air show.

And she's awful.

Her mind is elsewhere, and she knows it. She stumbles over her words. She announces callers by the wrong name, and she barely reads the news articles with any care or emotion whatsoever. She absolutely sucks, and she's now on the verge of crying.

She ends the show by saying, "This is Laura Chase, signing off from *my Studio B* at station WOUR97. Come back soon for more news." And she switches off the microphone and can't even look at Patrick as he enters the room.

She puts her hand up in protest before he can even speak.

He sighs and finally says, "I'll have Sean talk to Colin."

Laura peeks up at him, marked sadness in her otherwise cheerful eyes. "Thank you, Patrick. You know I always appreciate you. Even if I don't always act like it."

"Anytime," he says as he quietly closes the door.

Laura exhales a deep breath, tucks her hair behind her ears, and rises to her feet. When she enters the main room, she's thankful it's deserted. She approaches Tucker's door but can hear him speaking to someone on the telephone. Not wanting to interrupt him, but knowing she owes him an apology, she exits the station and goes outside to the quad.

The breeze of the late afternoon and the fading autumn sun draw Laura into taking the long road home. Practically dragging her feet as she hangs her head, only watching the gravel below her, she never even notices Tank's truck pulling off the road across from her.

"Hey!" he yells.

She picks up her head, searching for where the noise originated from. She spots him. "Hey," she says back.

It's obvious to him that the fire from her spunky personality is gone, so he immediately motions for her to cross the street. As she does, he leans over and opens the passenger door.

She unenthusiastically hops into his truck.

"Where you headed?" he asks.

"Home," she says.

"Taking the long way?"

"Yeah. What about you?" she asks, unwilling to make eye contact with him.

"My apartment. Long practice. Got some ribs to throw on the barbeque," he says, patting the grocery bag in between them.

"How nice," she whispers.

He pulls out onto the road. "Dinner it is then." He chuckles.

"What? No. I mean, I can't see Nathan," she blurts out.

He chuckles uncomfortably. "He's at some school thing tonight. Won't be home until later."

"Oh," she says.

"But tell me, why can't you see him?" he asks.

For the first time, she looks at him. "You know. The breakup. I can't be around him if he's sad," she admits.

He nods his head. "But you can't avoid him either."

"No, I won't. It's just…today is not a good day," she says.

"Oh. Well, let's see if we can turn it around."

A silence settles between them as they ride in Tank's truck to Parkers Village apartments. She neither cares to be alone nor with someone.

I can't believe Colin would do that to me. Rub it in my face. Is he trying to get back at me? Prove a point? That he can move on before I can? That's such a messed up thing to do. And Zoe! Aren't we supposed to support one another as females on the job, working toward the same goal? She only seems like she is trying to derail my career. And screw my ex-boyfriend in the process.

"I grill them," Tank says, breaking the silence.

Laura has been staring at the television for the past half hour while Tank prepares the ribs.

"Okay," she says, stifling a sigh.

He enters the living area and switches off the television while simultaneously sitting in the armchair adjacent to her. "What gives, Chase?" he asks.

Her eyes betray her as they start to well with tears. "Dammit," she curses as she blinks them back.

"What's going on?" he asks, edging forward on his seat.

"I-I can't even believe I'm so upset about this."

"What?" he asks.

"I found Colin and Zoe in my studio, practically screwing on my desk."

"What?! No way."

"I wish. But—"

Tank interrupts, "The nerve of him. Not cool on his part."

"I know! Exactly!"

"So, don't be sad about it. Tell him to fuck off and be done with him."

"I wish I could but…"

"But what?"

"It's all my fault."

"How's that?" he asks, folding his arms over his enormous chest.

"I pushed him away, and off he went."

"Laura, you were going through a really hard time, and your relationship was just a casualty of reality. There is nothing you could have done."

"Nothing? Really? Don't you think I could have leaned on him and not ignored him?" Her voice rises as the memories of the first few weeks after Travis passed come rushing over her like a tidal wave.

"Hey, listen. There isn't a day that goes by that I don't wish I'd handled things better after Jonathan passed. But you know what? I did the best I could. And at the end of the day, I must be okay with that. Otherwise, I'll just drive myself insane, and what good is that? It sure as shit won't change what happened."

She hangs her head in her hands and whispers, "I know, but I lost so much. I lost Travis and Colin…"

"They say, someone cannot be lost if they aren't forgotten."

She picks her head up, staring at the large man across from her in disbelief. "I never thought of it that way."

He slightly smiles and says, "I've had more time to think about it, I suppose."

She stares back and says, "How unlucky of you."

He chuckles. "Indeed. So, what do you say that you learn from my mistakes and try and move on?"

"I could try harder," she admits.

"We all can. But you can't let Colin get to you that way. You two are over. Unless you still like the guy?"

"What? *No*. Not at all. I was just. I don't know. Felt like he was rubbing it in my face."

"I'm sure he wasn't. He never seemed like that type of guy. I'm not saying it's not messed up, what they did. Maybe it was all her?" He pauses and then adds, "But besides that, you know how it is when you first start dating. You want to screw anytime and anywhere."

Her face burns red.

"Are you blushing?" he asks.

"What? No?" she replies, turning her head. *I totally am!*

"Oh my God, you are!" He jumps up and nears her. He reaches his large hand and cups her face, turning it back toward him. "Ha! Can't believe it. I made you blush. What is it? The screwing part? Doing it? The horizontal mambo? Getting it on?"

"Stop it! You're being ridiculous," she says, pushing his hand away from her face.

He steps back, smiling ear to ear. "You'll get your groove back; don't you worry."

"Tank!"

"What? I'm sure you miss it."

I do miss it. I miss a lot these days. She stands, crossing the room toward the kitchen. She opens the refrigerator and grabs a beer. Twisting the cap, she says, "Yeah, of course I do. But what kind of…" She wants to say, *girlfriend would I be*, but it's more than that. It's just being mentally in the game that scares her the most. *Will I ever be ready again?*

He enters the kitchen and leans on the counter. "I'm not a terrible option." He laughs.

She nearly spits the beer from her lips. Wiping it away with the back of her hand, she laughs. "Tank, be serious." *Is he serious? Because he totally is not a terrible option.*

She notices his cheeks flame red, but quickly, he turns. "Don't think about it too much, just go with the flow." He opens the refrigerator and pulls out some items for dinner. "Mind making the salad while I check on the ribs?" He places the lettuce on the counter.

Welcoming the distraction and the change of subject, she nods her head and begins to wash the head of lettuce. The salad is prepared within minutes, and she carries it to the table, setting it down. She grabs the plates and silverware he left out and sets the table while Tank walks in with the platter of ribs.

"These came out perfect," he boasts, setting them down next to the salad bowl. "Sit, please," he says. "How many ribs?"

"I'll take a few," she says.

"Four it is." He jokes.

She picks one up and realizes she's starving. She tastes one bite and almost can't control the satisfying hum that escapes her lips.

"You like?"

"They're delicious," she mumbles.

She devours her meal. But she can't help but watch her handsome friend out of the corner of her eye as he enjoys his dinner.

I think what I'm really starting to like about him the most is that he's such wonderful company when I seem to need it the most. Like this afternoon. What are the chances of him driving by me? I feel so thankful now more than ever that I can lean on him when I've had a bad day. He makes me laugh with his crazy yet honest remarks. He's brazen and true to his word; he always has been.

And he might not even realize he's helping me.

But he is.

Like today.

He's given me so much more than just a homecooked meal.

He's given me hope.

Twenty-Four

Misplaced Suspicions

A few days later, Laura enters the station about thirty minutes before her scheduled shift. She knows Tucker will be in his office, and more than anything, she owes her mentor an apology.

His door is ajar at the end of the hallway, and she can see him sitting at his desk, reading the latest copy of *The Weekly Blue.* His eyes wander up as she peers in his doorway, nervously playing with her fingers.

He motions with his head for her to come in. She steps across the threshold and closes the door behind her.

With a shakiness in her voice, she says, "I am so sorry for how I acted the other day toward you."

He stands and comes around the desk and approaches her. He places his hands on her shoulders, looking her squarely. "You've been through a lot this past year, and while you won't always get a pass from me, I know where the hurt was coming from, and I made sure that it will not happen again."

Tears sting her eyes. "I promise I'll never let him—um, them get the best of me again."

His expression softens. "Have you spoken to him?"

"No."

"Well, Zoe is no longer working here."

Laura's breath catches. "I—that was not what I meant. I was wrong to say that, and I—please, Tucker," she begs as she steps back from him.

"She wasn't working out. You were right. She wasn't here for the right reasons, and this position is too coveted on campus to have it occupied by someone who doesn't take it seriously."

Her mouth gapes open. "Oh, I had no idea. I've had such little interaction with her besides…"

"You should talk to Colin. It's important for the dynamics within the team," he quickly adds.

"Oh, okay. I promise I will do that."

"I know you will." Tucker opens his arms and gives Laura a much-needed hug.

"Thank you, Tucker. For being so great."

"You guys are like my kids, and I only want the best for all of you," he says, releasing her. "Now, go have a great show, okay?"

"I will," she says as she pulls open his door and wanders down the hallway.

Sean is sitting at a desk near the main door.

"Hey, Laura."

"Hey, Sean. Can I ask you for a favor?"

"Sure thing."

"Could you see if Colin is free after my shift? I'd call him, but I'm going to be late," she says, glancing at the clock.

"Okay. What do you want me to tell him?"

"Ask him if he can meet me here, please? Tell him it's important."

"Sure thing, Laura. But are you okay?" he asks with a cock of his head.

She smiles a little and then says, "Yeah, I think so. Thanks, Sean."

Laura is much more on point today than she has been the past few times. She flawlessly makes her way through the show. But as it nears the end, she can't help but wonder if Colin will be there, waiting for her. In all honesty, she wouldn't blame him if he didn't show up. His girlfriend got fired, and he probably thinks it's because of her.

"I want to thank you all for your support today. Thanks for calling in *and* allowing me to come into wherever you are right now. But for now, Hawks, my segment is up for today. I'll be back on Monday with all the highlights from the weekend. Until then, be safe, be happy, and look out for one another. From all of us at WOUR97, have a great evening."

Laura turns off her microphone and switches off the board. Patrick gives her an enthusiastic thumbs-up. She returns a smile. She remains in her chair awhile longer, contemplating her show as she takes notes in her notebook about the callers, questions, where she might have stumbled for an answer.

There is a slight knock on the studio door.

"Come in," she yells.

Colin pushes open the door. She's surprised to see that he doesn't look angry at all; in fact, he appears subdued.

She stands. "Thanks for coming."

He swiftly closes the door and then leans back on it. "Sean said you wanted to see me?"

"I-I didn't ask Tucker to fire her," she blurts out.

He nods his head. "I know, Laura."

"You do?"

"Yeah, it wasn't working out here for her."

She cocks her head, and with furrowed brows, she asks, "It wasn't?"

"No. It was her idea"—he hesitates—"to come in here the other day. She told me she needed to talk to me, and the next thing I knew, she was throwing herself at me. It wasn't a normal thing either."

"What do you mean?"

"She was acting weird, trying to stir things up here, and I've had that feeling for a few weeks now. I told Tucker I wasn't sure she was right for the job, and then she pissed you off." He shoves his hands deep into his pockets and stares at the floor as he adds, "We pissed you off, and I know that wasn't cool at all."

"Oh," she whispers.

He peeks up at her. "I'm really sorry, Laura."

"I don't know what to say. I thought you did that on purpose."

"I would never hurt you like that. I meant what I said—I was hoping we could still be good friends. I think I could be there for you more, if you'll let me."

She gazes at him. "I'm shocked…"

A small smile spreads across his lips. "What do you say we go out sometime? Give us another chance?"

She tries not to react, but she's stunned. She wrote Colin off. He was a thing of the past. He had not only broken up with her, but he'd moved on. "Um, are you not with Zoe anymore?"

"No, I ended it with her the day that happened. I'm not into girls who make a point to hurt others. I left that shit behind when I broke up with Joey."

"Wow, Colin. I have no idea what…I'm…"

Just then, the phone on her console rings. It's like the awkward gods are shining down on her.

"Sorry, I should get that." She hurries around the desk and grabs the receiver. "WOUR. This is Laura."

"Hey, it's Wolfie."

"Hey, Wolfie," she says, glancing over at Colin.

His face drops at the mere mention of her friend.

"Officer Murphy called the newspaper and requested a meeting with us."

"What? Now?" she asks.

"Yeah. Can I come pick you up?"

"Yes, of course. I'll be out there in a minute."

" 'Kay. I'm leaving now," he says as he places the receiver down.

She hangs up the phone and grabs her bag. "I'm sorry, but I have to go. Officer Murphy requested a meeting with us."

"Sounds important," he jokes.

"I would say so," she replies. "I will talk to you later, okay?"

He reaches for her arm, gently holding on to it as she tries to walk by. "I'm looking forward to it." He leans in and kisses her on the cheek.

Her skin pinks. "Of course," she whispers as he releases his grip.

She pulls open the door and quickly exits the studio and heads out to the side entrance of the Union, just as Wolfie's car pulls up.

He beeps out of habit, and she rushes to his idling Honda Accord. With her messenger bag slung over her shoulder, papers spill out of it as she reaches for the door handle.

"What do you have in there?" he says as she picks up a few loose papers off the pavement.

She plops in the seat and pulls the door shut.

"You know I like to be prepared."

"Oh, I know," he sarcastically replies as he backs out onto the street.

Moments later they pull into the police station and enter the building.

"Can I help you?" the young clerk behind the counter asks.

"Yes, Laura Chase and Ainsley Atwood. We have an appointment with Officer Murphy," Laura says.

The guy gives Wolfie a smirk, and Laura can see his cheeks flame at the use of his birth name. "I'll let him know you're here."

As they walk toward the waiting area, Wolfie snips, "Do you have to use my real name?"

"You want me to tell a police officer *Wolfie* is here to see him?" She laughs.

"Yeah, I do," he says, trying not to smile.

"Fine, next time, you do it."

Before they can sit, they hear him say, "He'll see you now."

The clerk opens the gate and allows them down the hallway toward an empty conference room.

"Please have a seat," he says as he closes the door.

Moments later, Officer Murphy enters. His smile is genuine, and that immediately puts Laura at ease.

"Hello. Thanks for coming in straightaway," he says.

"No problem," she says.

He sits and places the folder on his desk. "Good news: I requested to work the case, and Officer Waters agreed."

"Oh, great!" Laura says.

"Good to know," Wolfie adds.

"So, here's what I came up with." Officer Murphy flips open the folder. "This guy right here," he says, as he points to the photo of the guy, "was identified as a student in the arts department."

"What? Really?" she says.

"Yes, I had a first-year officer—a young guy—go on campus and show the picture to the department heads, hoping someone might recognize him. We didn't tell them why."

"That worked?" Wolfie chuckles.

"It was all we could come up with without saying the police was looking for him."

"Interesting," Wolfie adds.

"Anyway, tonight, the art department is having their fall showcase, and I'd like you to attend," he says, looking directly at Laura.

"Me?"

"Yes," Officer Murphy says.

"You mean, us, right?" Wolfie says.

"Not just yet. For this one, just Laura."

"What? Why?" she asks.

"I need you to appear as though you're doing an entertainment piece on the event for the station. Casually go in and wander around. He's going to be there."

"How do you know?"

"His name is Guthrie Simmons, if it's the right guy. He's a senior, and this is required as part of his final grade."

"You think this is a good idea, just her?" Wolfie asks.

"Listen, it'll be crowded and fully staffed with faculty. The young police officer will be there, too. You won't know it, but he'll be there the whole time."

Laura interrupts, "What do you want me to do?"

Officer Murphy leans forward and says, "Guthrie has access to paint, right? Get a sense of what art he's doing. If given the opportunity, chat him up a bit. See what he has to say. Don't stay too long. Just enough to get a good look at him. See what he has been up to and then get out."

She turns to Wolfie. "I can do that, no problem."

He nods his head. "Yeah, just don't stay too long."

"I won't."

"Good. Starts at eight tonight. Silver building."

"Yeah, I know. Took my art elective there as a freshman," Laura adds.

"Okay, let me know what you find out," Officer Murphy says as he stands and moves toward the door. "And whatever you do, do not tell anyone his name. He's merely a person of interest currently. That is all."

Wolfie and Laura nod in agreement as they follow him out and back down the hallway to the main lobby.

"Talk to you soon," he says before disappearing behind another door.

Laura expects Wolfie will say something to her now that they are alone. But she's shocked when he doesn't say a word the entire way back to her house.

Finally, Laura clears her throat. "I'll be careful, and I won't stay long. I promise."

"I know," he says. "Call me as soon as you get back, all right?"

"You'll be the first one I call." She gets out of his car and waves as he pulls out of the empty driveway.

A heaviness envelops her, as it's clear by the lack of lighting that none of her roommates are home. These days, they all seem like ships passing in the night, never catching the same wind in their sails.

I suppose this is just another product of four busy women living together.

She opens the front door, and for good measure, she yells, "Bree, Melissa, Abigail! Anyone home?!"

Silence.

It's not like I can tell them what I'm doing tonight, so I suppose it's a good thing. I'm not sure I'd be able to hide the excitement I'm feeling. It's good to get back to the old me. This is what Travis would want me doing—digging deep, not sitting around anymore.

Twenty-Five

Dangerous Mind

Laura changes her clothes, putting on something a bit more professional-looking for her undercover mission. But as she tries to button her shirt, she notices her fingers are trembling.

"Come on, Laura. You've got this," she whispers.

The ring of her telephone pierces the air, and she jumps, like a nervous cat. Irritated at her lack of confidence, she leans over onto her desk and picks up the receiver.

"Hello?"

"Hey, Laura. It's Tank."

"Hey, Tank."

They have not spoken since their dinner a few nights ago.

"How are you?"

"Good, but kind of in a hurry," she says as she tries to balance the phone in between her shoulder while putting her notebook in her bag.

"Oh, where are you off to?" he asks.

"Can you keep a secret?" *I know he can, but I have to ask.*

He chuckles. "Of course I can."

"Officer Murphy asked me to check out the art showcase tonight because they think the guy who vandalized the soccer house is a student in the department, and I need to gather some intel."

She could not have expected Tank's reaction.

He speaks immediately, "I'm coming to get you. You're not going alone."

There is a click, and the line goes dead.

Crap. She stares at the phone in her hand and can still hear the dial tone. *Double crap.*

Finally, she places it down. She finishes getting ready because time is no longer on her side.

Ugh, why did I say anything?!

Less than three minutes pass, and she sees headlights shine in her driveway.

"He's crazy," she whispers.

She grabs her messenger bag and bounds down the stairs. Once she locks the front door, she approaches Tank's truck. He rolls down the window.

"What are you doing?" she asks.

With raised eyebrows, he whistles slightly. "Looking good tonight."

She finds her skin warming at his compliment. "I'm serious, Tank."

"Me, too. You clean up *real* nice." He laughs. "Come on. Get in."

"Tank, I can do this on my own. Err, I have to."

"One, I know that. Two, this guy is a real asshole, and you just might need me. I won't get in your way, promise."

She stifles a sigh. "Fine. But you have to absolutely swear to stay out of my way, got it?"

He chuckles. "I said I would."

She goes around the front of his Ford truck and hops in.

"So, fill me in," he says as he drives toward the art building.

"Apparently, he was recognized in a photo we had, and according to the department head, he's a senior, and tonight is their big art showcase. So, he has to be there. Officer Murphy wants me to go in, appear as if I'm doing a piece for the station, and maybe chat with him."

"Jesus, you sure about this?"

"Yeah, like you said, he's an asshole. I'm not convinced he's dangerous."

"Isn't the mind dangerous?"

She peers over at him while an obnoxious grin spreads across his face. "You amuse yourself, don't you?"

He chuckles as he pulls into a spot near the side door. There are numerous people filtering into the front entrance of the building, which is shaded from their view.

"Thanks for the ride," she says as she pulls on the handle.

He places his massive hand on her arm. "Hold up. I'm not leaving."

"What?"

"No. I'll stay here and make sure everything is okay. If you need me, step out and just wave to me."

She smiles, and with a wink, she says, "Don't you have anything better to do on a Friday night?"

"I like hanging with you," he replies shyly.

Oh, well, that was a nice thing to say.

"I'll be back soon." She pushes open the door and steps out. She takes a deep breath as she pulls open the heavy glass door to the art building.

Why is my heart beating so fast? It's not like this guy is a hard-core criminal, right? They don't even know if it's him. It's just a hunch. And I'm merely here to check out the scene and look around. Easy-peasy. No harm, no foul. In and out. Why am I saying all these stupid clichés in my head?

Concentrate, Laura. Relax. Deep breaths.

The main conference hall is packed with students, professors, and administration. Laura has not had a friend in her years at OSU in the art department, so she was unaware such an event took place. She scans the crowd as she arrives in the space. There are numerous sculptures in the middle of the room, displayed on tables and on the walls, and rows of student pieces are hanging on the walls along the corridor. A few catch her eye, and she steps in front of them to read a bit more about the artist and their inspiration. She pulls out her notebook and jots down what she sees, as she figures she could make this into a legitimate segment for the radio. She continues to wander around when she hears a voice behind her.

"You were in my freshman drawing class, correct?"

She glances up and recognizes her professor.

"Professor Baron. Yes, Laura Chase. Nice to see you."

"You, too. How have you been?"

"Great, thank you."

"You're on WOUR, aren't you?"

"Yes, almost two years now. I had a little hiatus in the middle, but it's been a great experience so far."

"Wonderful. I've listened, and it's been quite refreshing for the school." He pauses briefly and then asks, "So, what brings you here tonight?"

She smiles. "I'm doing an entertainment piece for the station."

He claps his hands together. "Fabulous. The arts don't get enough recognition at this school. Let me show you around. This way." He motions for her to follow him.

He takes her through the sculptures, and she notes the names of the students responsible for each. Nothing of interest to her, but she takes her cue from Professor Baron and writes down the ones he thinks are most notable.

"I'd like you to meet Guthrie. He's one of our seniors in the showcase this evening. Quite the artist."

Laura's skin pricks at the mention of his name. *Could this be him?* she wonders as his back is facing her.

Professor Baron taps him on the shoulder, and he turns.

Laura tries not to react as she gets a good look at the boy in front of her. He's not wearing a hat, and she's surprised to see a head of tight red curls pushed back off his face. His eyes lazily gaze over her.

"Hello," he says quietly.

"This is Laura Chase; she's doing an entertainment piece for the radio station."

She clears the frog from her throat and thrusts her hand toward his. "Hello. Nice to meet you."

He reaches his hand out, and noticeably covering his fingers are traces of paint. "Occupational downside." He chuckles as he shakes her hand.

"It must be." She laughs.

"Professor Baron," a young woman interrupts, "Michael needs your assistance in the back."

"Of course." He turns to Laura. "Miss Chase, if you need anything else, please don't hesitate to find me."

"Thank you, Professor Baron. It was nice to see you again."

"You, too." And with that, he turns and leaves toward the back of the hall.

"So, what work have you done?" Laura asks.

"What did Professor Baron say you were doing?"

"Oh, an art piece for my radio segment. I feature lots of different events happening across campus and in our community."

"I see. And what made you do this? I mean, this time. I've been here four years, and no one has ever bothered to cover this before." His expression is cold and unwelcoming, which immediately puts Laura on the defensive.

Thinking on her feet, she laughs. "I know. I've been asking for a year now for this and finally got the approval," she lies. "I took a class with Professor Baron and was hoping to be able to work with him on this piece."

He nods in approval and then says, "Here, this way."

She follows him through a small crowd toward the back wall. He steps aside as he says, "This is my senior piece."

On a massive canvas is a beautiful mountain view landscape of what appears to be the college town from afar, but what is most interesting about this is that over the top of the scene is paint splattered all over it in a rainbow of colors, nearly covering the work underneath. It's wildly interesting.

Laura jots down some notes in her notebook as he stands off to the side, staring at his own piece.

"What are you writing?" he asks.

"Just some notes."

He turns and says, "I know. But what are you writing?"

Trying to keep his interest and knowing he might be one to play games, she responds, "Do you reveal your painting before it's done?"

A dark smile spreads across his lips. "I suppose I do not."

She smirks and returns her eyes down to her pad and pen. "Do you have others on display?" she asks, scrawling down her last note.

"No, we're only allowed to choose one."

"That must have been hard."

"What?" he asks.

"To choose only one."

"Yes, it was. I love each one of them."

"Maybe I could see the others sometime?" she asks.

He tips his head, never taking his eyes from her. "I suppose, if you'd like."

"Cool," she says.

"Our studio is open on Wednesday nights at seven, if you want to check them out. On the third floor. There are a lot of really great artists here. Some better than others," he quickly adds.

"Is there a competitive thing going on in the art department?" She laughs.

Only he does not. "Yes, very."

"So, Wednesdays at seven?"

He looks past her, and his eyes narrow in disgust. "Do you know him?" he asks.

"Who?" She turns her head in the direction of his eyes.

"That meathead." He laughs coolly.

Laura watches Tank as he pushes through the crowd toward her, a concerned expression on his face. She lets him know with her eyes to stop moving toward her. She quickly turns her back to him.

"Not really. Spoke to him on the radio and stuff like that, but no idea why he's here."

"Why would he come to something cultural?" he says snidely.

"Not my day to figure it out." She laughs. Even though it makes her uncomfortable to put him down, she must. "Well, Guthrie, I'm sure you have other people to see tonight, and I'm going to continue to wander. Your piece is beautiful, and I look forward to seeing the others."

She steps past him and quickly attempts to blend into the crowd. She can see that Tank is back near the main entrance, and as soon as she's able to make eye contact with him, she motions for him to leave. Then, she, too, ducks out the nearest door she can find.

She hurries around the building and toward his waiting car. She opens the door and hops in. "Why did you come in?" she barks.

"You took so long, and I got worried."

"Worried? I was in a school building, surrounded by people," she says, letting out a frustrated sigh.

"Excuse me for caring," he says as he backs his truck out of the parking lot.

"I'm sorry. It's just…well, you're so noticeable!"

"I think the word is *handsome*."

She tries not to laugh but can't help herself.

"Want to grab a drink?" he says with a pleasant smile. "Unwind a bit?"

She glances over at him. "Sure, I'd like that. It's been a strange day."

Tank pulls into the parking lot next to The Cookie, a local bar. They climb out and walk in. He grabs two beers as Laura sits at a high-top table.

Placing the beer in front of her, he asks, "What happened at the show?"

She tries to relax her shoulders by taking a sip of her beer. Placing it down, she confesses, "Well, for starters, that guy I was talking to was the one the police asked me to check out."

"No kidding? Bastard."

"Yeah, he had a dark personality. His artwork was a little on the destructive side."

"How do you mean?"

"He painted this beautiful scene and then basically added graffiti over the top of it. It was cool, but knowing he could be the one, it all made sense. So, therefore, I hated it."

"Interesting."

"Yeah, and when he saw you coming toward us, he asked if I knew you and called you a meathead."

With a scowl on his face, Tank barks, "What a dick! The nerve of that guy."

"I know. Obviously, he does not think highly of sports or those who play them."

"So, what is your next move?"

"I'll tell Officer Murphy what I observed and see where he wants to go with it."

Tank leans back and says, "The only way he can be stopped at this point is to catch him red-handed."

"I know. But how do we do that?"

"I'm not sure. Let me think about it. If he hates athletes so much, there must be a reason."

"I need to talk to Jen again. Maybe something will jog her memory," Laura says.

"Yeah, there has to be something missing in all this."

"Unless," Laura says, "he really is just an asshole."

"Complete possibility." Tank chuckles. "So, how was the rest of your day? You said it was weird?" And as Tank eyes her, awaiting a response, her cheeks fill with heat. "Well?"

"Um, well… Colin broke up with Zoe over the whole debacle at the station last week, and on top of that, Tucker let her go. Apparently, she was trying to provoke me. Maybe she wanted me to crack and leave again. Try and take my spot."

"No shit?! That's crazy. See, told you Colin was a better guy than that."

She averts her eyes toward the floor.

"What? Was he a jerk about it all?"

"No, not exactly."

"Chase, spill it," he demands as he grabs her hand, shaking it to get her attention.

"Um, it was bizarre. He…he asked me out again. Said he wants to give us another try."

Tank drops her hand as if it were on fire. "What?! That's ridiculous," he barks.

"Ridiculous? Really?" she replies, visibly offended.

"Yes, you said so yourself—you're over him." His eyes soften, and he adds, "Right?"

"I haven't put any thought into it really," she admits.

"Oh," Tank says.

"You disapprove?" she asks.

His chest puffs as he sits up straighter on the barstool. "Yeah, actually, I do. It's a bullshit move to ask you out again."

Her expression dims. "Really? Bullshit move? That seems a bit harsh, don't you think?"

"Not at all."

"You've never been known to beat around the bush," she sighs, tucking her hair behind her ear.

"This isn't about me. This is about that guy—"

She interrupts, "Colin."

"Yeah, *Colin*, trying to get you back after he stopped…"

"Stopped what?" she says.

Now, it's Tank's turn to blush.

"What, Tank?"

"Well, he wasn't there for you. When you needed someone. He wasn't there. And now that you're…"

Her eyes narrow. "Now that I'm *what*?"

He shakes his head. "Better, okay? Now that he didn't have to do any of the hard stuff, he all of a sudden wants you back?"

Her eyes widen at his confession. "I see. So, you think he took the easy way out."

"You said it. Not me."

"You're unreal," she snaps. "I gave up on him, remember?"

"Did you? Or were you just going through what might have been one of the hardest things you ever will?"

Her expression softens. "I know but…"

"But nothing. Don't you see? You guys didn't survive it, and there's a reason for that. Don't go backward, Laura. Move ahead."

"You kept going back to Jessica, didn't you?"

He laughs. "Oh, please. We barely had a relationship. Come on. Do I really need to tell *you* that?"

"I suppose not."

"No, I don't, and when you really needed someone to love you, he wasn't up for the challenge, and I—" But he suddenly stops. As if his words got light-years ahead of his brain.

Internally, Laura gasps. *What did he just say?* She can see how uncomfortable he seems, and she can't help the pound of her heart as she watches her friend struggle for words. *This is so unlike him.*

The bartender interrupts their conversation. "Hey, Tank. These are on the house." He places two beers on their table and picks up the empty bottles.

Laura replies for him, "Thanks." She picks up her beer and takes a sip. Feeling the need to put him back at ease, she says, "I do appreciate you looking out for me."

He clears his throat. "Um, that's all I'm trying to do, Laura. I'd just hate to see you fall into an old habit and be unhappy again."

She contemplates his words. She hasn't really considered going back out with Colin, but she also wouldn't have considered that Tank's reaction would be as strong as it was. But he's right. They couldn't make it then, and that says more about them as a couple than she's guessing Colin realizes. Maybe he's just lonely, too, now that his relationship with yet another girl has failed.

I've never stopped caring for Colin, but I don't like him in a romantic way anymore. I must be honest with him and tell him the truth.

She kind of laughs to herself and says, "I never said I was going to go out with him."

Tank's eyes narrow at her. "You're a total poser, you know that?"

She playfully batts her eyelashes. "Me? Noooooo."

"I'll remember this," he gibes. "Steel trap." He points to his head.

"Anyhoo…how come you didn't have grand plans this evening? Where are all your football buddies tonight? Surely, you must have something better to do."

He leans back in the chair. "I could ask the same of you. You're a popular figure on campus, and *you* don't have anything better to do tonight? Kind of pathetic, Chase."

Almost as soon as he speaks, a throng of people shuffle into the bar.

"And here comes the party crowd." He laughs.

"Actually, these are all my friends," she jokes. "They're meeting me here."

"Sure, they are," he says.

"Honestly," she says, rubbing her temple, "I put in a long week. The last thing I wanted to do tonight was go to a party. Mentally, I couldn't handle it."

He winks. "Want to know a secret?"

She smiles. "Sure."

"I put in a long week, too, and the last thing I wanted was to be swarmed at another party and have to fend off all the babes. I just didn't have it in me tonight."

"If I could roll my eyes straight into the back of my head, I would." She laughs.

"Hey, you joke, but it's true."

She laughs loudly. "Give me a break." She sips the rest of her beer.

He tosses back the rest of his. "What do you say we get out of here before we get stuck all night?" he says as another large group stumbles into the door.

One guy shouts to Tank, and Tank politely waves back.

She glances at her watch. "Yeah, I'm exhausted. This girl is ready to call it a night."

"Cool. Come on," he says, leading her to the door, but as he does, for some reason, as if on instinct alone, he takes her hand and walks her out.

Why doesn't this feel weird? she wonders as she follows him toward his truck.

"Thanks for the ride. Sorry, it's so late," Laura says as Tank's truck pulls into her driveway.

"Anytime, Laura." He puts the gear in park. "Whose car is that?" he asks as his truck lights reflect off the mint muscle car in the driveway.

Laura drops her head, unsure as to why she's hesitating. "That would be Kelly Conrad's car."

She notices Tank's shoulders tense. "Really?" He glances at the clock. "At this hour?"

Laura chuckles. "Yes, it is. And last time I checked, she's single."

Tank turns to face her. "Whose side are you on?"

"Side? Really?"

He rubs his face.

"Tank. Really?"

"I know. It's not my business."

"No, it's not." She laughs and then pokes him in the ribs, trying to get him to lighten up.

He smiles wide. "I'll see you later, okay?"

Laura starts to get out of the truck and then adds, "I would have invited you in for a beer, but it's sooooo late." She giggles.

His eyes light up. "How about tomorrow night?"

She cocks her head. "What do you have in mind?" she asks.

"Swing by my place at seven, okay?"

Somewhat confused but too tired to ask questions, she says, "Sure, I can do that. Night, Tank."

"Later, girl."

Twenty-Six

Friendship on Fire

Laura bounds down the wood stairs from her bedroom to the main floor, well-rested, as she had no reason to get up before eleven.

She called Officer Murphy and filled him in for last night, saying that she didn't have time to call him before now despite the irritation in his voice. She explained all she'd found out and let him know about Guthrie's invitation to see more of his work and that her plan was to develop a story for the radio. In doing so, her time there would be viewed as legitimate and not undercover. He agreed and asked to see a copy of her piece before she talked about it on air. He also asked her to take some photos. She promised she would get Wolfie to come along with her, as a member of the paper to, again, solidify her legitimacy. Then, after her call, she took her time in her room, listening to music, showering, and dressing.

As her feet hit the bottom step, she hears, "Good afternoon, sleepyhead."

"Hey, Bree."

"You feel okay?" she asks.

"Yes, just needed some sleep—that's all. Where's everyone else?"

"Melissa went out with Logan. Abigail left with Kelly, and yours truly is doing nothing today," she says with a huge smile.

Laura lowers into the plush couch next to her friend. "So, is Abigail dating him or what?"

Bree chuckles. "You know her. She won't say it. She's always been a bit shy about that stuff. But, he stayed over, and they left together, so I'd say, at a minimum, they're hanging out."

"What's your take on him?" she asks.

"Honestly, we all love Alex. She's awesome. So, the apple can't fall too far from the tree. But I think Alex knows her brother can be a bit dark—it's noticeable. I do see that edge to him. But, man, when he looks at Abigail, it's like he sees stars." Bree laughs.

"Yeah, it's interesting. He did not seem like her type. But then again, it's probably good for her to date someone different than Nathan. They were so…I don't know…like picture-perfect or something, and it was almost hard to believe."

"Exactly," Bree adds. "This is good for her to branch out and not be so connected to the football team. She desperately needs a break from them. It was her whole life for over two years."

Desperate to change the subject out of her own guilty feelings about hanging out with Tank without discussing it with Abigail, Laura says, "Adam not around this weekend?"

And always more than happy to talk about Adam, Bree says, "Went to a bike race in New Hampshire with some of his old college roommates. He'll be back tomorrow."

"Hopefully, he got beautiful weather."

"He said it was going to be cool but sunny. Perfect for a ride. What are you doing the rest of the day?" Bree asks.

"Well, I'm heading out tonight at seven. Meeting up with Tank and I'm assuming the guys. Probably going to a party. The usual. Want to come?"

"Yeah, let me think about it. But that could be fun. Haven't seen them in a bit."

"Exactly," she lies.

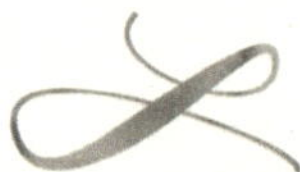

Laura sits on the edge of her bed and slips on her ankle boots. Something, yet nothing in particular, about this moment brings her back to her first time with Travis.

He took a deep breath in and then said, "I don't consider you a kid. If nothing else, I think you're an intelligent and sexy woman…if I'm being honest."

"Please, Travis. You don't have to say that."

"What? That you're sexy?"

"You're embarrassing me," she whispered, barely able to glance up at his handsome face.

"I don't want to embarrass you," he said in a sultry voice.

He reached down, now placing his thumb and forefinger on her chin, guiding her face up to meet his stare. She swallowed hard. A spark passed between them.

His expression became serious. His eyes danced with hers, and then he said, "I want to do this." Swiftly, he pulled her around the waist and up closer to him. Grasping the side of her cheek with his hand and gingerly placing his fingers behind her neck, he leaned in with fully parted lips and kissed her.

She stands and can't help but smile to herself as she grabs her bag and walks out her door, thinking of that moment with Travis.

Bree waits for her at the bottom of the stairs. The effortless gorgeousness that Bree exudes would make most people jealous but not when you love her, like Laura does. Her tall, model-like figure, flowing chestnut hair, and glowing skin are almost too much for this place, but as she stands by the staircase, wearing a gray T-shirt, blue jeans, and sneakers, Laura can't help but smile. She looks stunning in the plainest outfit known to man.

"Ready?" she asks.

"Sure am," Laura says.

They exit into the cool evening and make the short walk through campus and toward Parkers Village, talking about nothing more than the change of the leaves on the tress and a comment or two about a student passing by.

They arrive at Tank's apartment and knock on the door and step back. Within seconds, he opens the door. And he looks…*dapper?*

There's an enormous smile spread across his face. "You look pr—" But quickly, he pauses. "Hey," he squeaks, clearly surprised to see *them.*

Puzzled, Laura says, "Hey. What's going on?" She peers past him and notices the apartment is dark.

"Nothing. Um, you *guys* ready to go?"

Bree chimes in, unaffected by the weirdness, "Definitely."

"Cool. My truck is right here." He motions toward the closest lot to the building.

The girls climb in, and within the smaller confines of the truck, Laura can smell Tank's cologne. It's a heavenly scent. Maybe a bit of spiced citrus or sandalwood. It's pleasant.

He breaks the silence. "You guys in the mood for some dinner?"

Dinner?

"Oh, thank God. I'm starving. There is nothing good to eat in our house." Bree turns to Laura. "We need to go shopping tomorrow."

"Yeah, tomorrow," she whispers.

Tank pulls into the Italian Farmhouse on the edge of campus. It's not a typical place for college students to dine since most students' budgets are extremely limited.

"Oh good. Not a pizza shop," Bree says with a clap of her hands.

"A little expensive, no?" Laura adds, being one of those with limited income. The station pays her, but considering the leave of absence she took, her wallet has suffered for it.

"I've got you," they both say at the same time, causing all their heads to spin and look at one another.

Bree laughs and pulls open the door on the truck and climbs out. Laura follows closely behind. As Laura nears the door, she feels Tank's hand slide gently onto her back as he allows her to enter before him.

Tank approaches the young woman behind the hostess stand. He leans in and whispers something to the woman, and she quickly makes a few notes on the paper in front of her.

Tank joins them back by the door. "She said it will just be a few minutes," he says, removing his long wool coat, revealing a nice collared shirt and dark gray pants.

"You clean up nicely, Tank," Bree says as she straightens his collar.

"Thanks, Bree. It's nice to get out of my sweatpants occasionally."

Minutes later, they are seated at a table near the window. Bree does most of the talking, and once she has exhausted all her stories, she asks Tank a series of questions about the football team this year. As if the waitress knew he had finished all *his* stories, she places the check down in front of him.

Quickly, he grabs it. "I've got this."

"Tank, let me kick in," Bree says.

"No, ladies, I insist. I appreciate you putting up with me this evening."

Bashfully, Laura says, "Thanks, Tank."

He glances at her with an expression she can't place. "Welcome."

"So," Bree says as they stand, "what's your plan for the rest of the night?"

They exit the parking lot.

Tank unlocks his door and says, "Um, was just planning on having some beers at my house."

"Well, would you mind dropping me off? I'm not up for a party tonight," Bree says.

"Sure," he says.

"You should come for a beer," he says almost at the same time as Bree says, "Don't let me stop you, Laura…go for a beer."

Tank and Bree laugh.

Laura waits for them to stop and says, "Sure, I could have a beer."

"Excellent," Tank says.

Several minutes later, he pulls into their driveway.

Bree hops out. "See you later, Laura. And thanks again for dinner, Tank."

"Anytime. It was good to see you, Bree. Don't be a stranger."

She gives him a winning smile and then shuts the door and hurries up to the front porch.

Tank pulls back down the street to Parkers Village in complete silence.

Once he's parked and they are approaching the front door is when Laura says, "Where's everyone tonight?"

"They should be home soon," he replies, not actually answering her inquiry.

He steps into the kitchen, switches on an overhead light, and opens the refrigerator, taking out two beers. "Come have a seat." He nods toward the living room.

He hands her a beer and sits on the couch, not the reclining chair he usually claims as his own. She sits next to him.

"So, did you let Colin down easily?" he asks.

Surprised by his question, she says, "Um, not exactly. I haven't spoken to him."

"Oh," he says, visibly disappointed.

Feeling defensive, she says, "Well, I slept in and then had work to do, and then I came here—"

"With Bree."

She laughs. "Yeah, with Bree."

His cheeks pink.

"What's going on?" Laura asks.

"What do you mean?" He tucks his bright blond hair behind his ear.

She notices in the moment that his hair is not tied back, like it usually is. It's down and loose with a beautiful wave in it.

Laura springs off the couch and spins to face him, her hand digging in her hip and her other hand clutching the beer bottle. "You look nice tonight." She motions to him. "Your clothes are different. Your hair…"

He nervously smooths his hair down again.

"And dinner…"

"What?" he cautiously interrupts. "I can only wear jeans and a sweatshirt?"

"*Tank*?"

"Laura."

"Where is everyone tonight? Specifically, your roommates."

"They're out. Is that such a crime?"

"No. But why did you ask me to come here, to meet you at seven?"

"We talked about it last night, don't you remember?" He uncomfortably chuckles.

"Meeting here, yes. But…"

"But what?" He stands, towering over her.

She gulps. "Did you think…I mean…" And then her voice lowers. "Did you think this was…was a date?"

Again, he awkwardly laughs. "Yeah, a date. Me, you, and *Bree*."

She gasps. "Oh my God. Did you ask me on a date last night?"

He responds so swiftly with a, "No."

That makes Laura burst into a snicker.

"What?"

But soon, her smile fades. "Tank, do you want to go out with *me*?"

He places his beer on the coffee table and steps closer to her. She has never seen Tank look so out of sorts. It makes her feel bad for putting him through this conversation. But she must know the truth.

Because this is a big deal.

He takes her hand, and her reaction is to pull back a little. But he holds tight.

"I kind of thought you knew," he says in a husky voice.

She peers up at him under her lashes. "How would I know that?"

"Look, I just thought that if we had dinner and sort of just saw where the night went…that was kind of my unofficial plan."

"Why wouldn't you just ask me out?"

"Honestly, I thought you'd brush me off. Like you have before."

She steps back, eyebrows bent in concern. "Brush you off?"

"See," he says, closing the gap between them again, "you're starting to freak a bit. And, yeah, I've been tossing hints your way for a while now. But I get it. We're friends, and I don't want to lose that, but…"

"But what?"

"I'm…you're different than other girls, Chase. You're smart, cool, easy to hang with. I actually like you as a friend, and you know, I think you're a total babe, so it's kind of a bonus."

She sucks in a breath. "I had no idea you thought that way about me."

But when she starts to think back, it makes sense. And one clear conversation was his reaction to Colin wanting to go back out with her.

Ding, ding! Oh, I'm such an idiot.

"I'm a twenty-one-year-old male…in college," he says.

"Tank, I wasn't talking about *that.*"

The sexy grin that spreads across his face gives her goose bumps. "*That* is exactly what I'm talking about."

"Tank." She blushes.

He pulls her in close to him. "No pressure," he whispers. "Just think about it."

She swallows hard. Her eyes travel from his stare to his full, pouty lips as they form a seductive smile. She's mesmerized at the thought of him and her, tangled together. His massive body is something many women on this campus have admired. It's hard not to.

"Hello?" he says.

She snaps back to reality. "Sorry, um, what were you saying?"

He pulls her toward the couch. She sits, and he hands her the beer.

"Just think about it—that's what I said."

"Oh, yeah." She tosses back most of her beer. And then the awkwardness in the room is doubled as the door swings open, and Nathan, Webber, and a few other people enter.

"Laura," Webber says. "Good to see you." He wanders down the hallway toward her. "This is Heather, Noah, and Daisy." He points to each one of them.

Nathan comes over and pats Laura gently on the shoulder. "Hey there," he says with a hint of sadness.

She glances up at her friend. "Nathan, how are you?"

He sinks into the seat next to her. "Ugh. I've been better. But you know that."

She leans in. "I know."

With concern in his eyes, he asks, "How is she? Wait, don't tell me. I don't want to put you in the middle. But is she okay?"

"Leave the poor girl alone," Tank scoffs.

Laura says to Tank, "It's okay."

"No, he's right. I can't ask you every time you see me; otherwise, you'll never come around," he jokes.

Only Tank's response is more direct. "Exactly, and we don't want that."

Webber turns on the music and then can be heard rummaging in the kitchen fridge for beers. "Anyone needs another beer?" he shouts from the other room.

"Another one?" Tank asks softly.

"Sure," she whispers.

"Yeah, bring us all one."

Nathan leans up, resting his elbows on his knees. "Why are you all dressed up, buddy?" he asks Tank.

"Man." He laughs. He stands up and pulls the collared shirt up over his head. "A guy can't wear anything nice around here." He tosses it on the back of the couch.

Daisy yelps, "Whoa, look at you." She steps closer. "You're in unbelievable shape," she squeals.

He passes her but not before she glides the tips of her fingers over his abs. He reaches to one of the hooks by the front door and pulls a sweatshirt off it and quickly over his head.

"Don't cover up on my account." Daisy laughs.

Webber and Nathan simultaneously roll their eyes. Laura senses her body heat alongside a pinch in her gut.

He winks at Daisy. "Thanks, doll."

He takes a seat back on the couch, and immediately, Daisy swings her tiny hips over in his direction, sitting near him.

"So, Tank, Nate says you're doing a great job as cocaptain this year."

A smile draws his lips back. "*Nate* said that, did he?" He mocks the name Nate since no one ever calls him that.

"Dick," Nathan mumbles.

Tank clears his throat. "Yes, as a matter of fact, I'm one of the greatest captains this school has ever had," he boasts, causing Laura to choke on her beer.

Daisy shoots her a glare. "I'm sure you are," she coos.

Noah steps in. "Daisy, don't bother the guy."

"Shut up, Noah," she says, scrambling to her feet.

"It's cool," Tank says as he lets out a massive yawn.

"See, you're boring him." Heather chuckles.

"No, sorry. Just been a long week," he says, glancing over at Laura with a smile.

She smiles back and gets to her feet. "Well, guys, it was great to see you. But I'm going to head out."

"It was so good to see you, Laura," Nathan says as he gives her a hug.

"You, too." She spins and gives Webber a hug. "See you soon, okay?"

"Sure thing, Laura." Then, he whispers, "Tell Abigail hello from me."

"Of course."

Tank follows her to the door and leans in the doorway as she opens it. "You want me to walk you home?"

She squints. "That could be taken the wrong way," she says, looking back at their friends.

"Right. Well, I'm going to bed anyway."

"What about Daisy?" She laughs.

"Get out of here with that." He laughs back. "Let me rephrase that. I'm going to bed—alone."

Laura laughs, and then with a much more serious expression, she says, "Thanks for dinner tonight."

A quirky grin graces his face. "Next time…leave Bree at home."

She steps back from the doorway and waves to him as she walks on the sidewalk, through campus, and back home.

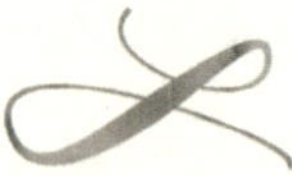

She pushes open the front door and finds Bree curled up on the couch, watching an old movie. The one she always watches when she's alone.

She sits up, rubbing her eyes awake. "You're home early. Everything okay?" she asks.

"Early? It's past midnight."

"I know, but this is early for a date, no?"

Thankfully, it's dark, so Bree can't see her cheeks flame red.

She chokes out, "Date?"

Bree cocks her head to the side. "Laura, are you serious?" Then, quickly, she claps her hand over her mouth. "Oh my God, did you not know?"

Laura flops on the couch and moans deep in a pillow. Bree pulls the pillow away from her face.

"I had no clue. But I felt stupid, so once Nathan and Webber came home, I left."

"I knew as soon as he opened the door, the apartment was empty, and he was dressed up. He was shocked to see me, and the worst part, he totally had a reservation made and had to make it for three!"

"Bree, why didn't you say anything?"

" 'Cause, sweetie, you were slowly catching on, and I didn't want to throw you deep into a date, unprepared. What was I going to do? Awkwardly bail on the dinner and leave you two standing there, feeling even more foolish? Besides, I was starving, and it's a great restaurant. I figured your first date will actually take place when it's just the two of you."

"This is crazy," she says a little to herself and a little out loud. "I can't go out on a date with Tank. Jesus, it's Tank. And Abigail and…" Her voice fades.

"Hold up," Bree cuts in. "Abigail has nothing to do with your decision. Unless you really don't like him. But if you do? I say, you figure that out before you place all the odds against you."

"But she's my best friend."

"Of course she is. But that only reaffirms that she would be happy for you. And look, they have a very complicated relationship. But in the end, no matter what, they love each other. They're just on a break."

"You won't say anything right now?" She tips her head, eyes softening, as she awaits her friend's response.

"There is nothing to say." Bree pats Laura's hand reassuringly.

"I don't know."

"About Tank?"

Laura shakes her head. "Um, I'm confused."

"I can only imagine. Look, he's been a great friend to you through a really hard time. Don't discount that."

She laughs as she recollects, "I blew off all his little remarks as Tank being Tank. He's flirty."

"I know, but he makes it about you, and that's nice to see."

Rubbing her temples, she whispers, "I need to think this through—alone."

"I get that. Having a sexy football player pining after you must be exhausting." She laughs as Laura throws the pillow at her. Bree picks it up and hugs it, and then she says, "Besides, you know what they say about true love…"

She chokes back her saliva, and then with a quivering voice, she says, "No, what?"

"True love is friendship set on fire."
Friendship set on fire…let's hope it doesn't char mine and Abigail's.

Twenty-Seven

Two Steps Forward

"Hello?" Laura says.

"Glad I caught you," Tank says.

She blushes at the sound of his voice. She has had a few days to think about their "date" and was flattered at his attention. But now, she's nervous to bring it back up to him.

"What's up, Tank?"

"Hey, so I'm thinking we should invite the art guy to a party. Get to know him a little better? And then we set our plan in motion."

"*Our* plan?" she replies.

"Yeah. How else are you going to get him in at the Ridge? You need access, baby."

She sighs. "But why would he want to go there?"

"Chicks. Grade-A, top-of-the-line ladies."

"Assuming he's into that."

With a dark sound in his tone, he says, "Trust me, that dickhead is a gay-hating hetero. And believe me, I don't want to hang out with that piece of trash, but we must get him out of this school."

She knows he's probably right. Unfortunately. But evil exists in the world. There is no use in pretending it doesn't.

She clears her throat. "What do you suggest?"

"We're having a party with the soccer team this Saturday. Work your magic, Chase, and get him to come with you."

"Me?" she squeaks.

"You're the only one who makes sense."

"Well, we're stopping by the studio tonight to check out his other paintings, but there's no guarantee he'll even there."

With a deep sigh, Tank replies, "He'll be there. Trust me. And if the hot girls don't bring him to us, tell him we want an artist to draw a mural on the wall of the house, commemorating the football team."

"A mural? You might be onto something there."

He laughs. "Of course I am."

Laura hears the faint honk of Wolfie's horn out front. "I gotta run."

Tank hesitates before adding, "Okay. Talk to you soon?" But it's with more of a question in his voice.

"Yes, of course," she says before placing the receiver down.

There is so much more I want to say to him. I just don't know how to spit it out.

Wolfie pulls in front of the Silver building. "Ugh, I hate this shit," he says.

With a slight chuckle, Laura asks, "Can you be more specific?"

"Being fake. I hate that I have to placate this guy."

"I know. Me, too. But we need to get to know him a little better. Which I hate even saying."

He rubs the scruff on his face and then whips open his car door. "Come on. The loser awaits."

Laura tries not to giggle, considering the crimes he's accused of, but it's all she can do to calm her nerves before seeing his face again. And then she thinks of her friends and former floor mates, Jen and Casey, and a nasty little storm starts to brew inside of her. Giving her just the right amount of courage to walk up to the third floor and trap this guy into showing his true self.

"Now, remember," Laura whispers as they near the threshold of the doorway, "you are only my photographer, here to take photos for the so-called piece I'm doing for the station and paper. Let me do all the talking."

"Yes, ma'am. I'm merely your humble servant, here to do as you wish." He smirks.

Rolling her eyes, she says, "Just be cool, will you?"

Immediately upon entering, Wolfie starts to snap a few pictures of the artwork and sculptures, jotting down the names of the students responsible in his notepad. Laura casually wanders around behind him, leaving enough space to make her available, should anyone want to approach her. And it doesn't take long.

"Hey," a male voice behind her says.

She spins and tries not to allow her pulse to react. With a nonchalant tone, she says, "Um, it's Guthrie, right?"

"Laura, right?" he replies with an icy edge.

"Yes. My photographer came with me to get some photos of the artwork for my piece at the station," she says with a yank on Wolfie's tweed coat sleeve.

He spins, and the flash from his camera erupts. Guthrie ducks.

"Sorry, man." Wolfie snorts. He narrows his eyes at Laura and says, "And that is why you can't pull on my coat. What if I dropped this baby?" he says as he cradles the camera gently in his hands.

You ham. "My bad," Laura says. "Anyway, Guthrie, which ones are your pieces?"

He doesn't speak as he begins to walk over toward the back of the studio. He stops in front of a desk. "The seniors get the back of the studio." He places a bottle of water on his desk. "My work is back here." He swings open a glass-paneled door and allows them to enter a beautiful loft space.

There is a girl sitting in front of an easel. She glances up briefly but doesn't speak. In fact, when she sees them walking in, her expression changes from content to troubled.

"These are being submitted for my final grade," he says but quickly puts up his hand toward Wolfie, "but they are not ready. So, no pictures."

"No problem," Wolfie says.

"You'll have to excuse me," Laura says in an uncharacteristically sweet voice. "But I'm still learning. What kind of art do you consider your work to be?"

He smirks somewhat. "I guess you could say postmodernism, but I'm more into street artists."

"Forgive me, but street artists?"

He tosses his head back in a dramatic laugh. "Yeah, they're kind of known for using the world as their canvas. It's actually pretty cool."

Out of nowhere, Wolfie chimes in, "Who's inspired you the most?"

He turns his attention to Wolfie, and with a snooty undertone, he says, "I like Keith Haring."

Quickly, Wolfie says, "Oh, never heard of him."

Guthrie's eyes widen, and then he adds, "So, anyway, Laura, let me show you some of my work I've already completed."

Laura and Guthrie spend a few more minutes looking over his work. It's clear to Wolfie that she's doing her very best to appear interested. Wolfie tries to keep his mouth shut, doing a damn good job of playing the part of the measly photographer, the hired help. He snaps a few photos of the sculptures and notices again that the girl is watching them.

Laura interrupts, "Did you hear me? We're all set."

"Sorry, just doing my job," he replies, to which Guthrie eyes him conspicuously. "I'll meet up with you guys out front. Just want to get a few more shots over there," he says, pointing to the opposite side of the room.

"Sure thing." Laura follows Guthrie out to the main studio.

Wolfie ever slyly moves over in the direction of the young woman painting. He sneaks a peek over his shoulder and says, "Your work is beautiful."

"Thank you." In a hushed voice, she asks, "Why are you guys taking pictures and talking to *him*?"

She stresses *him* with clear dislike that Wolfie spins to look at her.

"We're doing a piece for the paper and radio station. Trying to incorporate more of the arts."

"I see. And why, can I ask, did you choose him?"

"You seem to disapprove? I'm sorry..." He leans in closer to her work and notices the name. "Tammi, is it?"

"Yes."

"I'm Wolfie."

"Interesting name." She smiles for the first time.

"Thanks. Why the disapproval of Guthrie? You don't like his work?"

"No, each art piece is different, but it's...just...him, I suppose."

"I see. Well, I believe a professor recommended him. I'm not sure he was chosen by Laura per se."

"He's got a lot of people fooled," she whispers as she dabs her paintbrush into the paint. "If you'll excuse me, I do need to get this finished."

"Of course." Wolfie nods as he walks away.

Laura is waiting for him by the main door, and thankfully, she's alone. They exit the building and head toward his car.

Finally inside his vehicle and out of earshot of any prying ears, she says, "That was so uncomfortable."

"You're telling me."

"But I got him to agree to come to the football party this weekend."

"What?" he says, eyes widening.

"Yep. Said he'd come."

"Girls. All you have to do is bat your eyelashes, and boom, boys are putty in your hands."

"Fair. But I told him it was a not just a football party. It was a soccer party, too, and for reasons I'm unclear of, he seemed very interested in that."

"Sicko," Wolfie says as he starts his car and pulls out of the lot.

"Yeah, he seemed way too interested in that. Makes me question if it's really him. Why would you want to be around the people you targeted? You'd think he'd want to fly under the radar. It makes me question the entire thing. But I also told him the football team wants a student to paint a mural for them. But they don't, obviously."

"Good idea. That will pull him right along. By the way, I'll have the pictures developed by this weekend."

"Did you snap that one on purpose?" She laughs.

"Of course. Nice touch, by the way, grabbing my arm. It's as though we'd practiced it."

"What can I say, Wolfie? We've always made a great team."

He smiles as he pulls into the Union parking lot. "A couple of things. I spoke to the girl in the studio. Not a fan of his. She seemed quite bothered by him…as a person. So, food for thought on that. Also, his inspiration is Keith Haring?"

Laura shrugs her shoulders.

"Haring is a famous graffiti artist known for advocating safe sex and AIDS awareness. Hardly the type of guy who would approve of such hatred as written on the walls of the women's soccer house. Something is just not adding up here. Call me perplexed."

"That's very strange. All of this is. We need to find out more about this guy." Laura places her hand on the handle but hesitates.

"You'd better get going. You don't want to be late for your show," Wolfie adds as he points to the clock in his car.

"I know," she sighs.

"What's the matter?" he asks.

She leans back in the seat and sighs deeply. "Colin."

"Why?"

"He broke up with Zoe and asked me out again."

He's never one to be the gossiping type, but his eyes can't hide the surprise or the intrigue in learning more. "Shut up. No way. What did you say?"

"Nothing. It was the day you called me in the studio because we needed to see Officer Murphy."

"You're not…I mean…"

"No. At first, I was so shocked that I couldn't think in the moment, but given some time now, I know he'll agree this ship has sailed."

"Agree. Don't go backward."

"That's what Tank said," she replies.

A small smile spreads across his face. Laura tips her head and waits for him to say something.

Finally, he adds, "Now, you're really going to be late."

"Shit," she says, scrambling to get out. "I'll call you," she says, shutting the car door.

She rushes into the station. Patrick is sitting at his desk.

"Thought you weren't coming," he says.

"I know. Sorry, was out doing some research. I'm going to get settled," she says as she passes him and pads down the hallway to her studio.

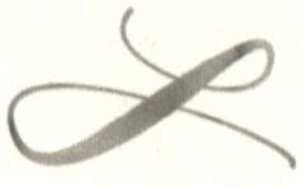

As she signs off from her show and turns off the On-Air sign, Patrick gives her an enthusiastic thumbs up from the booth before exiting. Not a moment passes when she hears a faint knock on her door.

"Come in!" she yells.

Colin opens the door, a wide smile on his face. She only wishes she could return the same expression. He steps in and closes the door.

"Hey, great show," he says.

"Thanks." She points for him to sit in the guest chair. "Got a second?" she asks.

He nervously pulls on the strings of his sweatshirt as he sits in the chair. "Sure thing."

She tucks a loose strand of hair behind her ear and then glances at him. "Colin, I thought about what you'd asked me the other day, and I think it's best for us to remain friends and coworkers."

He doesn't seem shocked by her words. "I figured as much," he whispers.

"I'm sorry about Zoe, but there was a reason you moved on with her. I have no doubt the right girl is out there for you, but what I know even more is that it's not me."

He hangs his head. "I know you're right. But I had to ask."

"Friends?" she says.

He stands and opens his arms to her. "Friends."

She rises and steps into his arms. "Thanks, Colin."

"No, thank you, Laura. And I'm sorry about everything that has happened between us. Minus the good parts." He chuckles.

She laughs. "Obviously."

He plants a quick peck on her cheek and releases her. "Let's grab a coffee soon, okay?"

"That sounds great, Colin."

Laura grabs her bag and follows him back into the main area of the studio.

She places her hand on the handle to the main door but not before turning to Colin. "I'll see you around," she says with a genuine smile.

With a wave of his hand, Laura exits the building, feeling free of the saga of her relationship with Colin. Finally.

It's time to move forward, she thinks. *No more looking back.*

Twenty-Eight

Purging Thoughts

Laura taps gently on the door. Webber opens it.

"Hey!" He smiles as he steps back, allowing her inside. "What brings you here?" he asks.

She nervously plays with her hoop earring. "Um, by chance, is Tank here?"

"Yeah, upstairs, studying." He motions for her to head up.

"Thanks."

Making her way up the stairs, she notices his door is ajar. Tank is sitting in his overstuffed chair, wearing only athletic shorts, his long, muscular legs stretched out before him. His stomach is flat and stacked, each muscle resting perfectly on top of the other. His huge bicep flexes as he turns the page in his textbook. His hair is touching his shoulders with his headphones acting like a headband. He appears content in his own world.

Laura swallows the lump in her throat. *My, he really is handsome.*

She takes another step toward his doorway, and his periphery picks her up as he glances in her direction. His expression softens as he peels back his headphones.

"Hey," he says as he sits up straighter in his chair.

"Hi, um, sorry to disturb you."

"No problem." He closes his textbook and then stands, placing the book and headphones on his desk. "Come in," he says.

She steps in and immediately freezes at the sight of this massive man standing before her. She completely loses her train of thought.

"What's up?" he asks as he reaches into his dresser drawer and retrieves a T-shirt.

"You don't have to do that every time I come into your room. This is your room, and I...I've seen men. I mean, you. It's just a shirt," she stutters. But her brain remains mush. *And if I'm being honest, which I'm not, I'd prefer you don't put one on, but I can't say that out loud.*

He steps past her and shuts his door. "Have a seat," he says, pointing to the chair recently occupied by him. He sits on the edge of his bed, leaving the shirt next to him.

She clears her throat and lowers into the chair. The warmth from his body remains on the cushion. "Wolfie and I went to the studio the other night."

He leans forward, eyes wide. "And?"

"Yeah, the guy is weird, no doubt. Well, maybe *weird* is not the right word 'cause a lot of people are, and it's not always a bad thing..."

"Ramble much?" He laughs.

She flushes. "I know, sorry. My brain is all over the place these days. But anyway, I could rephrase it by describing him as dark. There is a darkness about him."

"Okay, and?"

"Well, he's definitely inspired by graffiti artists, so that is red flag number one, but I'm not sure how the women come into play just yet. But I did get him to agree to come to the party with me on Saturday."

Tank nearly chokes. "Oh, um, you did?"

"Yep."

"With you?"

"Yeah. He asked me if I'd pick him up on my way," she replies shyly.

"Well then, we will see *you guys* at the party."

Laura's face burns red. "I, um," she starts as she plays with her hands, "I finally talked to Colin."

Tank sits up. "Yeah? How did that go?"

"Well, I told him we should be friends." She quickly corrects, "Just friends."

Tank's expression softens. "Really? How come?"

What do you mean, how come? She tips her head. "Because you were right. Going backward isn't the best thing for me." She wants to speak much more elegantly, but the words just aren't reaching the tip of her tongue.

He nods his head.

"So," she says, desperate to change the subject, "what have you been up to?"

"Studying, girl. I need to ace this exam tomorrow, so I can cruise into the weekend and focus on the game Saturday."

Oh. Have you thought about me at all? "Away game, right?"

He tries not to smile, realizing that she knows the schedule. "Yeah, Rochester. We should demolish RIT."

"Great. That's awesome."

The silence in the room is awkward, at best. Laura wants so badly to ask him about the other night now that her emotions have settled and she's come down from the shock of their unofficial first date. But he's not saying anything either, and he's not one to shy away from speaking whatever pops into that brain of his.

Maybe he's over it?

He disrupts her thoughts. "Well, I should get back to it." He rises to his feet and picks up the textbook off his desk.

She's startled at the abruptness. "Right, totally. I should be going anyway."

He pulls open his door, and as she passes by him, he reaches out, touching her arm.

"Hey, just be careful Saturday night, okay?"

"Well, if I don't show up, send out the search party." She laughs.

His eyes narrow. "Not funny."

"I'll be fine. I'll see you Saturday night."

And with that, she exits his room and goes down the stairs and into a dark front area. They all must have scattered to their own rooms to study, so she opens the door and quietly shuts it.

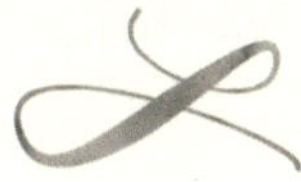

When Laura enters her house, Abigail and Bree are sitting on the couch, watching a television show.

"Hey, guys," Laura says.

"Hey," they both reply.

She sits in the chair adjacent to the couch. "How are you guys?"

"Good, just taking a break from studying. My classes got a lot harder this year," Abigail adds.

"Mine, too," Bree says.

"Yeah, I've got a test tomorrow," Laura says. "What do you guys have planned this weekend?"

"Not much. You?" Abigail asks.

Laura swallows hard. "Well, funny story actually," she begins, to which they both stop watching the TV and look at her. "We might have a lead on who vandalized the soccer house."

"What?!" Bree says.

"Yeah, and strangely enough, I'm escorting him to a party this weekend."

"Come again?" Abigail says with a slight laugh.

"Yeah, so I'm trying to find out more about him. See, on Saturday, there is a party at the Ridge…"

Immediately, Abigail's shoulders tighten at the mention of the house that her once-beloved team resides in.

"And with the women's soccer team, so oddly enough he was all gung ho to show up, if I go with him. I'm sort of doing a piece on him for the paper and station, but it's kind of a fake story. But it's real."

Again, I am completely inarticulate. Is this my new thing when I'm nervous?

"So, once he's at the party, I'm going to see his reaction or what have you. Tank"—she watches Abigail's face burn—"is going to try and trick him into thinking they want him to do a mural at the house."

Bree watches Laura squirm, knowing how strange it must be not to be able to speak so freely with your best friend. But in the same breath, Abigail, whether she realizes it or not, is displaying an intolerant vibe toward any mention of football or Tank.

"Well, sounds like a good plan and one that could really put an end to all this bad stuff at school once and for all," Bree exclaims.

Laura snaps back to her old self even if only briefly. "Exactly. I'll hang with the guy if I have to as long as he doesn't do it again."

"Just be careful," Bree adds.

"I will, and if you guys want to come with me…"

Abigail coughs on her own saliva. "I have plans with Kelly this weekend," she blurts out.

"Oh, okay," Laura says.

"Yeah, well, I gotta hit the books," Abigail says, abruptly standing and treading over to the stairs. "I'll see you guys in the morning," she calls as she hurries up the stairs.

Laura waits until she can't hear her on the third floor. "Jesus. What can I do? I don't know how the hell to talk about them to her. It's like it can't happen," she says, frustratingly running her hands through her hair.

"I know. It's painfully obvious it makes her upset. She seems very unwilling to even speak of them." Bree hates lying through her teeth, but after Abigail came home crying a few weeks ago and shared the news about Nathan and Poppy's pregnancy, Bree promised she would not say a word to Laura about it. And with news such as that, it's not her business to gossip about some poor girl getting pregnant. She will leave that up to Abigail to talk about it when she is ready.

"I'm glad it's not only me who sees it."

"No, it's as clear as day," Bree says.

"Ugh, speaking of muddied waters. I just came from Tank's, and it was so uncomfortable. I told him about the guy and I coming to the party this weekend. He didn't seem too keen on that even though it was his idea to try and get him to come. Then, I mentioned that I finally spoke to Colin."

Bree interrupts. "Colin?"

Laura smacks herself on the forehead. "Oh my God, I never told you. Colin asked me out a week or so back…I don't know at this point. But he broke up with Zoe, and then amid all of this, he actually thought we'd get back together."

"Oh, that boy is lost."

"Yeah, kind of. I think he just hasn't found the right girl for him. But we are friends and coworkers, and it's for the best."

"Did Tank have an issue with that?"

"No. If anything, I think he thought it took me too long to tell Colin. That maybe by me waiting, it was because I was unsure. But I've had so much going on that I just never had the time to sit down and talk with Colin. And in hindsight, I wasn't in a rush because I don't have any feelings for him beyond friendship."

Bree nods her head. "You do have a lot going on."

"But I was hoping Tank would have said something more about the other night. The date or whatever we are calling it, but nothing. It made me feel stupid."

"I'm sorry. I wish I could tell you what's in the boy's head, but if history has told us anything, it's that he's unpredictable, at best."

"I know. I just wanted him to say *something*."

"Maybe he wanted you to."

"True. Then again, maybe he was just looking for a hook-up. You know, a friend-with-benefits scenario. If that is the case, I just don't have the headspace for that." She pauses as a tear stings her eye. "I think I'd like to leave that special relationship to Travis."

Bree slides closer to her and rests her hand on her leg. "I think that is the best thought you've had since you came in the door. Leave that for Travis; it's a beautiful memory."

"Thanks, Bree."

"Anytime, sweetie," Bree says as she stands and shuts off the TV. She leans over to kiss Laura on the cheek. "Now, come on. We've got studying to do."

"Yes, I've got an Advanced Calculus exam calling my name." Laura smiles, following Bree toward the stairs. Before they go into their rooms, Laura grabs her hand. "Thank you," she whispers.

"Anytime."

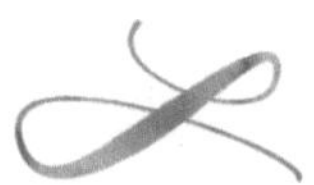

Abigail never had any reason to eavesdrop on her friends before. But something in their silence as she began to climb the second set of stairs to her room on the third floor made her pause. And she was right. As she slinked back down a few steps to be within earshot, she couldn't believe what she heard. Not one secret, but two and three and four all escaped their lips like it was nothing.

Colin asked her out again. She's clearly still hurting over Travis—and rightfully so. And now, she's inviting potential criminals to the football house as part of a sting operation that she and Tank devised. And did I hear her say she went on a date with Tank? That can't possibly be true. Of all the people at this entire school to go out with, and she picks my former so-called best friend. No way. My ears must have deceived me. Those two despised one another freshman year, and now, less than two years later, they are…I can't even think about it.

What is it like over there in Parkers Village? Is the happy foursome double-dating? Do they all know about Poppy's condition?! There's no way Laura would hang around Nathan and Poppy, right? She would never do that to me. Would she?

A horrific pain rolls through her belly.

Is this stress? Am I getting sick or…

And then, almost immediately, a terrible sensation washes over her. She, as quietly as possible, springs to her feet and rushes into the bathroom.

I think I'm going to throw up.

She splashes cold water on her face. Breathing in and out through her mouth, trying to quell the terrible feeling in her belly. And finally, it leaves her.

She only wishes she could purge the thoughts in her head.

Twenty-Nine

Kiss the Girl

Laura approaches the side entrance of the Silver building a few minutes before she's supposed to meet Guthrie to walk to the party together. Her heart is beating faster than normal as she stands under the lit doorway. She tries to calm her nerves by humming a tune, but it does little to relax her racing mind.

"Hey," he says from behind her.

She jerks a little at the sound of his voice.

He laughs. "A little jumpy tonight?"

"Sorry, Guthrie. I was in my own world there for a moment." She shoves her hands deep into her coat pockets as a chill hits the air. "Ready?"

"Sure am."

They cut through campus toward the other side of town, and as they pass the Union, he asks, "So, when do you plan to do the piece on us?"

"Soon," she says. "It's almost done."

"I see."

"Are you worried about it?"

"No, I'm not worried about it. What could you possibly say that would make me anxious?" He laughs.

"Well, art is subjective, is it not? What if I didn't like your work?"

"Of course it is, but isn't your work supposed to be subjective, too? You're not doing a piece on only the work you like or don't like. At least, that's what I assumed."

"True." *Man, is he irritating to talk to.* "We just need more time—that's all. The station's never really done this before, and I want to make sure we do it right. I'm a perfectionist when it comes to my segments."

"As am I," he says.

"So, what made you decide to come to the party tonight?"

"I didn't have plans this weekend."

"Why not? I mean, what do you usually do on weekends?"

"I do have friends." His tone is defensive, and to Laura, it feels out of place, considering her question wasn't meant to take a jab at him. "And those friends and I go to other parties."

"I wasn't insinuating that you had no friends," she quips.

"Seemed that way."

She stops about one hundred yards before the Ridge. "Are you always difficult to talk to?" she asks.

He crosses his arms over his chest. "Sometimes, yes."

"Tammi is not a big fan of yours," she blurts out. "Why is that?"

Despite the darkness, she can see his eyes grow wide. "What did that drip say?"

Now, it's Laura's turn to react similarly. "Whoa. That's a bit unnecessary, isn't it?"

"Why? Do you know her? Or should I say, know her like I do?"

"Well, no, but I…"

"Well then, she has a problem with everyone and can't stand when someone else gets recognized. So, yeah, I think she's a bitch."

Laura's breath catches. "Well, I guess there are—"

"Two sides to every story. I thought you, more than most, would know that."

Feeling stupid for jumping to conclusions and possibly being blindsided to the fact that he might be the person the police are looking for, she clamps her mouth shut.

"So, you still want to go in?" he asks in a much softer voice.

Abruptly brought back down to earth, she whispers, "Yeah."

He starts walking in front of her, and with a cocky sway in his steps, he approaches Junior. Junior glances past him, the clipboard tightly gripped in his hand.

"Hey, Laura," he says.

"Hey, Junior. Um, I was told Guthrie and me would be on the list."

He glances at the two of them and crosses them off the list. "You guys are all set. Enjoy the party."

Before entering the backyard, Laura asks Junior, "They win today?"

"Nope. Lost. Thirty-two to three."

"Wow, really?" she says.

"Nathan did not have a great game from the rumbling I heard before the party," Junior says, shrugging his shoulders. "But it's not a one-man game, last I knew."

"Right, right," Laura says aloud.

"But go in and enjoy the night." Junior pushes open the gate and allows them in. As soon as Laura walks in, she spots Jen and Casey. She walks over to them with Guthrie close behind. "Hi!" she says.

Casey leans in and hugs her friend. "Hey, Laura!" Casey says.

Laura leans over and hugs Jen, too.

"Guys, this is Guthrie," Laura announces.

Casey reaches out to shake his hand, and Jen noticeably retreats backward.

"I'm Casey, and this is Jen."

"Hello, Jen," he says rather coolly.

"Hey, Guthrie," she replies. Then, immediately, she says with a much more upbeat tone, "Oh my God, Laura, you are never going to believe who is here. They've been waiting for you." She yanks on her arm. "We will be right back."

"Drink?" Laura asks him.

"Sure."

"Okay, we'll be right back," she yells as Jen pulls her away.

"Where's the fire?" Laura whispers to Jen as she drags her up the stairs, to the deck, and then into the kitchen.

"What the hell, Laura?" she barks as she takes her over to the bar. "Four beers," she says to the guy behind the bar.

"What? What did I do?"

Jen peers past her, trying to get a good view of the outside. "Why the hell did you bring that guy with you? Please tell me you're not dating him."

"What? Gross. God, no!"

"Whew. Guthrie used to date Kate, and when I tell you it did not end well, it did *not* end well. The guy is a psycho."

Kate is one of Jen's teammates, and they both live in the soccer house.

"Shit," she mumbles as she takes two of the beers.

Jen motions for her to follow her, away from the bar. "Listen, we don't have much time, but keep an eye on him, and I'll give Kate the heads-up, okay?"

"What the hell happened?"

"Too much to get into now, but she will freak when she knows he's here. It's like the last place she thought he'd show up at."

"So, they used to date?"

"Yeah, last year."

Last year.

And maybe that is exactly why he came. He knew it was a women's soccer party, too. But does that make him the vandal or a jilted ex-boyfriend?

Laura puts on a brave face as she walks out of the sliding door of the kitchen and onto the deck. She approaches Guthrie with a beer. "Here you go," she says.

He takes it and takes a large sip. Then, he glances around the backyard. Laura does, too, hoping at least Tank or Nathan will see her and come over to say hello.

A whole hour goes by, but it feels like several as Laura stands near him, making awkward small talk. With no one she knows in sight and all the soccer team avoiding her because of who she's standing with, she finally says, "We should probably grab another drink and mingle a little?"

"Sounds good," he says as he follows her inside.

They wait in line at the bar. Slowly inching their way up toward the front. After grabbing two more beers, Laura turns to face the large crowd gathered in the living room. The beat of the music is almost vibrating the glass on the windows; it's so loud in here. As she's about to say something to Guthrie, she sees Tank across the room. He's leaning against the wall, his hand delicately draped on the slender hip of a gorgeous brunette. She's smiling up at him, tipping her head with laughter, as if he just said the most hysterical thing in the whole entire world.

"Is that your buddy who was at the art show?" he asks.

"What? Um, well, I know him, sure. But don't most people on campus?" she lies.

"I guess."

Quickly, she cuts in, "And besides, he was at the art show to look for student artists to see if maybe one of them would paint the mural, so he just might be the one to butter up to. That is, if you're interested in the project. He got us on the list after all."

"I might be," he flippantly replies.

It's as though Tank's ears are ringing because he looks across the room and straight at the two of them. When Laura catches his eye, he quickly drops his hand off the girl's hip.

An annoyance burns in Laura's gut. Mostly because she was right. He's just looking for a friend with benefits, and if Laura knows one thing about herself, it's that those days are in the past for her.

Tank whispers something to the girl and then crosses the room toward them. "Hello," he says. "Thanks for coming." His tone is formal. "You must be the artist? I'm Tank." He reaches out his hand to shake Guthrie's.

"Hey, Tank. Thanks for extending the invite," he says.

"Let me get you a beer, and I'll show you what we have in mind," he says, barely acknowledging Laura as he leads Guthrie toward the bar.

Laura spins on her heel and heads back outside, desperate to get away from them and spend some time with her friends after her evening of babysitting Guthrie. She notices Jen and Casey near the back fence, and as she approaches, there's a strong pull on her arm.

"Laura, can I talk to you?" Shannon, the captain of the soccer team, says.

"Sure."

"Over here." She glances over her shoulder toward the side of the house.

Laura follows, getting out of sight of the partygoers.

Stepping out of the shadow near the house is Kate.

Laura's pulse reacts. "Hey." Her voice chokes.

The three step further toward the fence.

"He can't know I'm here," she blurts out.

"Kate, I'm so sorry. I had no idea. I never would have invited him here."

"Why did you?" Shannon asks.

Unsure what to tell them, she reacts quickly. "The football team extended an invite…"

To fake trap him into thinking he'll paint a football mural at the house, but I can't tell you that.

"Weird," she says.

"Totally weird. I know it's none of my business, but we are doing a piece on the graduating seniors, and he's a part of it. Is there something I need to know?"

Shannon shakes her head. "Jesus, why can't he just go away?" she says.

"I'm so sorry," Laura says.

"It's not your fault, Laura," Kate says. "There is something—"

Shannon interjects, "He's an asshole of the greatest kind. When Kate said she didn't want to go out with him anymore, he freaked out."

Laura's skin prickles. *This could really be him.*

"Yeah, like, I caught him following me. Coming to my games, going to the places he knew I'd be at. He just couldn't take a hint."

"A hint! We found him in the house, after a party, drunk off his ass," Shannon says, visibly agitated.

Laura gasps, "Oh my God, he's crazy. I feel terrible. I'll try and get him to leave with—"

"No, you're not leaving with him," Shannon says. "Kate and I will go."

"Wait, before you go, did you ever file a report? Like, do the police know he was following you or in your house, uninvited?"

"Told you we should have filed a report," Shannon says to Kate.

"I know, but I was trying to let him figure it out. I haven't seen him at all this year. I assumed he'd moved on and learned his lesson. Rejection is hard, right?"

Do they not realize the coincidence in the house being vandalized and an ex-boyfriend who couldn't take a hint? But why the homophobic hatred?

"Okay, well, again, I'm really sorry. I'll do my best to keep him away from here."

"Appreciate it. We're going to slip out the gate and head back to our place," Shannon says as she takes Kate's hand and leads her into the darkness.

Laura remains there. She's completely unsure of what to do next. She brought the most unwelcomed guest to a party. She can't leave with him. She can't ask *him* to leave without being obvious, and she must find a way to convince Guthrie to be friendly with the football team in order to "catch" him…doing what exactly? If nothing else, she feels completely over her head and wishes so badly in this moment that Travis were here to talk to. He'd know exactly what to do.

She leans up against the house, closing her eyes as she tries to form an intelligent plan. But her mind is empty.

"Hey," she hears a deep voice say.

Her eyes flash open, trying to adjust to the darkness.

In a silky tone, Tank says, "You're not an easy girl to get alone."

Laura's laugh is cool. "Really? You seemed pretty busy tonight yourself."

He closes the distance between them, heat emanating from his body. "You've missed me, I gather."

She huffs, "Hardly." She's so butthurt from seeing him flirting with the pretty girl earlier, and it's quite reminiscent of Abigail and Nathan that she can't help connecting it all.

"Laura," he whispers as he tries to take her hand.

She pulls away.

"Listen, we don't have long to talk. Your friend is going to wonder where his hostess went."

"I'm not his chaperone," she scoffs.

"Easy, girl. I'm merely saying, he came with you, and naturally, he'll want to know where you are."

"Whatever," she says, trying to step past him.

He gently grabs her arm. "I get it, okay? But we don't have the time to do this right now."

She can't help the gasp that escapes her lips. But his comment has also made her more confused than ever.

"I think I convinced him to at least want to paint for us, but here is my plan. He's edgy, right? Hot under the collar?"

"Wait," she says.

"What?"

"Do you not know about him and Kate?" she asks.

"Kate?"

"Shh. Yes, they used to date. In fact, when we showed up, I thought Jen was going to kill me. They all hate him. He's done some creepy things with Kate, way too much to get into right now."

"Shit, so this could really be him."

"I'm leaning toward yes, but I'm not totally convinced," Laura whispers.

"Okay, so we have to get him to think he's going to do it and then pull it out from under him, really piss him off. And *boom*!" he yaps with a clap of his large hands. "We trap him!"

"Shh," she says again.

His eyes ablaze, he leans into her. His lips brush against her ear, sending a shiver down her spine, as he says, "There is only one way to shush me, girl."

Her heart pounds, and confusion washes over her. *Oh my.* She swallows the tightness in her throat. "I-I should get back then," she says.

He leans back up. "Hey, promise me you won't leave without me tonight, okay?"

"Wh-what?" she says, trying to compose herself.

"I don't trust that guy, and I'll make sure you get home."

Somehow, disappointment comes over her, but she's grateful all the same. "Okay, I will."

As Laura steps back into the crowded backyard, she notices Guthrie across the yard, standing against the fence, alone. She can't help but feel sorry for him. Maybe not knowing all the details of his situation with Kate has allowed her to be empathetic toward him. A broken heart can never be easy on a person. It's not possible.

"Hey," she says as she approaches him.

"Hey, was hoping to see you before I left."

"Oh, you're leaving?"

"Yeah, not really my scene," he says with a light laugh.

"I understand."

He pushes off the fence. "But thanks for inviting me."

"Wait, what did Tank say? I mean, about the mural?"

For the very first time since Laura met him a few weeks ago at the student art show, he smiles. "I think it could be pretty cool to have my artwork here long after I'm gone."

She freezes, completely unsure how to respond to that. There are so many questions she wants to ask him. *Is it you? How could you do that? What happened with Kate? Are you as troubled as the police think you are? Or are you simply misunderstood?* And more than ever, just simply, *Why?*

But all she can come up with is, "That could be cool. Well, I'll see you around, Guthrie."

And just like that, he's gone. But something about his desire to exit the party so soon leaves an uneasy feeling in the pit of her stomach.

She scans the crowd and spots Tank, as he towers over most of the people there. She pushes her way through the crowd toward him.

He's standing with Nathan and a few other players.

"Hey, Nathan," she says.

"Laura, I thought you were here."

"So sorry, but I can't talk. Tank, can I see you for a second?" she says.

His eyes widen, and without question, he spins and follows Laura as she rushes back through the crowd. She exits the gate.

"Bye, Junior," she whispers.

Tank is right behind her, and he shrugs his shoulders at Junior as he follows Laura down the driveway.

"Chase," he says, "where is the fire?"

She spins to face him. "Shh," she says, placing her finger over his lips.

He grabs her hand. "You keep shushing me tonight," he says with a sultry tone.

She's glad it's dark 'cause her skin pinks. Quickly, she regains her wits. "Listen," she says, pulling his hand toward the direction of the side yard near the hockey house, "try and be quiet. I have a weird feeling."

"Okay, okay," he says, following her.

They end up on the back side of the men's hockey team house. Thankfully, it's empty, and they're not having a party. Laura hurries alongside the house, through their fence, and leans against the inside post, squatting down as she comes to a stop. She motions for Tank to duck.

"What is going on?" he says.

"He left very soon after I saw him and not too long after Kate did," she says, motioning with her head toward the women's soccer house.

"You think he went there?"

"You can see over the fence. I can't. Peek?"

Tank slowly stands, just enough so his eyes peer over the top of the fence. Almost as soon as he does, he lowers back down.

He glances at her in awe. "How the hell did you know?"

"Is he there?"

"Someone is walking alongside the house. But hard to tell. It's so dark."

She grabs his arm. "Let's go," she says.

They duck alongside the back of the house the same way they came into the backyard.

She stops by their porch. "Go up to their house and pretend you need to talk to one of them. It will scare him."

Tank doesn't even question her. He hurries through the front lawn and up their porch, banging his feet loudly.

Startled, Shannon comes to the door. "Tank, what's up?"

"Hey, um, we need ice," he says. "Can I grab some?" He steps inside.

"Sure." She closes the door.

Once inside, he goes to their kitchen. "Is anyone else inside here?" he asks.

"Just Kate. Why?"

Tank steps out their back door and glances around their yard. It's empty. "I thought someone was walking through the back. Thought you were having a bender without us," he lies, closing the door. "Well, enjoy the night."

Shannon chuckles. "Jesus, Tank. Are you all right?"

He rests his hand on her shoulder. "As good as I can be."

"You're a strange dude."

"I know."

"God, this has been a weird night," Shannon says partly to herself.

"Tell me about it," Tank replies.

"You still need ice?"

"What? Um, no…all set," he says as he opens the back door again and steps out. "See ya, Shannon," he calls. He walks through their backyard, around the front, and back over to the next house to look for Laura.

She's hiding in the bushes.

And he can't help but burst out laughing. "You look like an idiot."

She stands up and brushes off her sweater. "Thanks," she says dryly.

"What's next?" he asks.

"Did you see him?"

"No. I walked around the house and nothing."

"Jesus, what a weirdo. Sometimes, I can't tell if I feel sorry for him or I'm angry with him."

Tank takes her hand as she steps over the shrubs. "Well, we don't know if it was him or someone just cutting through. People do it all the time."

"I know, but I just had this gnawing in my gut, and Tr—" she says but immediately claps her mouth shut.

"Travis what?" he scolds. "You can't stop talking about him, Laura."

She shakes her head. "It's just that he once told me I have good instincts."

"Duh." He laughs, draping his arm over her shoulders. "I thought that was common knowledge," he says as they start to walk back toward campus. "And no offense, but you sure you want to be a math teacher? I kind of don't see it."

"What do you mean?"

"It's just that you've got a knack for this kind of stuff, and maybe you need to reconsider your future."

She laughs uncomfortably. "That's a heavy statement."

He squeezes her shoulder before letting her go. "It's something I've thought about and wanted to share it with you."

"You've thought about my degree?" She chuckles.

He stops and faces her. "What's my area of concentration in?"

She completely freezes. "Oh," she stumbles for words. "I, well…"

"That's horrible. You have no idea," he says as he starts to walk again.

She catches up. "In fairness, you never talk about school."

"That doesn't mean you shouldn't ask me," he says, rather offended.

She sighs, "You're right. I'm sorry." In the sweetest voice possible, she asks, "So, what is your major?"

"I'll tell you in a minute," he says as he motions for her to follow him through the center of campus.

The center of the campus is truly stunning at night. The lampposts illuminate the brick walkway through the academic buildings and past the Union. The lawn is beautifully manicured, and it's nice to admire it before the ground is covered in a blanket of snow. Which, around here, could happen any day now. One afternoon, you're walking to class in a sweatshirt and jeans, and the next, you're dressed like you're going skiing in Switzerland. That's Syracuse, New York, for you.

"It's early still, right?" Tank asks while glancing at his watch. "Want to come back for a beer?"

It shouldn't make her nervous to be around him. It's Tank after all. They have been friends for years. But she'd be lying if she said her heart didn't betray her and flutter.

She shakes her nerves, and as casually as possible, she says, "Yeah, cool."

A quick jaunt through Parkers Village, and they arrive at Tank's door. Unlocking it, he allows Laura to enter first.

"Hit the light," he says to her.

She drags her hand along the wall until she feels the switch. "Where are the others?" she asks.

As he enters the kitchen and turns on the light, he says, "Let's see. Logan is at Melissa's tonight. Webber went home this weekend but is coming home late tonight, and I think Nathan should be back soon, probably in an hour or so."

"Who did he go to the party with?" she asks.

Tank chuckles as he twists off the caps on the beer bottles. "Me, silly."

"Oh, what I meant was, is he seeing anyone? Her?"

"And who is *her* exactly?"

"Poppy," Laura blurts out, unable to hide her disgust.

Tank plops down on the couch. "Honestly, between you and me, I think they're friends, and that's it."

"Really?" Laura says, sitting next to him.

"You're not disappointed, are you?"

"God, no!" she says. "I just thought they had a thing, and that's why Abigail broke up with him."

"He swears to me there is nothing going on between them, and he's a pretty honest guy. He seems really torn up about it."

"What about those girls who were here last weekend?"

"Webber brought them here, not him."

"Oh," she says. "Well, I don't want to be the one to tell him that *she* has moved on."

Tank takes a long sip of his beer and then adds, "Me neither."

"And I don't want to be the one to tell her I hang out with you guys," she admits.

He laughs. "Believe me, I get it, but why would you stop being our friend?"

"It's complicated—you know that," she says.

"What isn't these days?" he says with a spirited chuckle.

She cocks her head, and with a scowl, she says, "Yep."

"Why the face?" He reaches out and touches her hand.

Instinctively, she pulls away.

"Whoa, sorry." Then, he adds, "Is this about me not hanging out with you at the party?"

She can't hide the color of her cheeks as she lies and says, "No."

"Hey, that girl I was talking to when you saw me was Troy's girlfriend, and they just got in a huge fight. I was just trying to talk her down a bit."

"You don't owe me an explanation," she flippantly replies. The hurt in his eyes cannot be mistaken, and instantly, Laura regrets her words. "I didn't mean it that way."

He narrows his eyes. "Why don't you say what you really want to say then?"

Nervously, she stands, and without realizing she's pacing, she walks side to side and then takes a deep breath in. "I'm a bit frazzled about the other night, the dinner date or whatever you thought it was supposed to be."

He smiles slyly. "Well, it was not a very successful one if we are calling it that."

She stops, puts her beer on the coffee table, and then spins toward him. "Can't you just answer the question?"

He stands, too, putting his beer down as well. "That depends on what you want the answer to be."

She digs her hands into her hips. "I want the answer to be an honest one."

His cheeks warm as his eyes dance over her face. Then, with a slight smile, he says, "I was trying to see what it might be like for you and me to go somewhere unexpected and just relax and get away from the norm."

"But you didn't ask me?"

"Yeah, I know," he says, shoving his hands in his pockets. "I was worried you might overthink it and not come."

That's fair, she thinks. *Because I probably would have. In fact, I still am.*

"I don't want to come between you and Abigail. None of us in this apartment do, but the facts are the facts, and we're all kind of in a weird place. You just said as much a minute ago. So, I'm trying to be conscious of that."

She gulps. "I guess I didn't think of it that way. I was a little pissed off that night, thinking you were trying to…"

"To what?" he asks.

She tips her head and then softly says, "To blindside me, but that might be a bit harsh to say."

"Wow. Yeah, Laura, that is a bit harsh because that was definitely not my plan."

She reaches out to try and pull his hand out of this pocket, but he won't allow her.

She glances at this beautiful man standing before, and immediately, like a movie in reverse, she thinks about all the time they have spent together over that past year, whether that be him helping her through her grief or getting her back on track with school and the radio station or just trying to be a good friend. When she needed it the most, he was there for her. Her heart sinks as she realizes that all along, he was always right in front of her, being the good guy she has always known him to be.

"I feel really stupid right now," she admits.

He tips his head. "How so?"

She steps closer to him. "Because all this time, it was *you*."

Confused, he says, "Me? What do you mean?"

She tries to swallow the lump in her throat. She's about to confess her thoughts when they hear loud voices approaching the front door.

Quickly, he reaches out his hand to her and says, "Hurry, come with me."

They rush up the stairs at about the same time as the door swings open, and what sounds like ten or more drunk people come rushing in.

He pulls her into his room, closes the door, and locks it. "Sorry, I just know it will turn into a shitshow down there," he says as he switches on his desk light.

"It's fine."

"So, where were we?"

She nervously tucks her hair behind her ear. "I was trying to say that I'm sorry. I did freak out a bit. That I am confused. And I do worry about my friendship with her."

"All things that I already knew. But that doesn't really tell me where your head is at."

She drops her gaze toward the floor. "I know."

He laughs a little. "Well? Care to fill me in?"

"I'm really nervous," she whispers.

He steps closer toward her.

"And that isn't helping." She smiles as his enormous body towers over her.

"Maybe we don't need to talk," he says.

She swallows hard. *Oh boy. It's been so long since I've felt the warmth of caring arms around my body. I miss it so badly. Craving someone's touch on my skin. What I wouldn't give to feel alive again.*

"But I want you to know your friendship means a lot to me, and I won't take that for granted," he adds, to which a tiny gasp escapes her lips.

He reaches his hand toward her face, cupping her cheek in his palm.

As their eyes meet, an emotion Laura has not felt in ages ripples through her stomach. *Butterflies.* Honest and true. And there is no mistaking it.

He leans in close to her. "Can I kiss you?" he asks.

She nods ever so slightly. His full lips part and gently land on hers. A burst of vigor rushes through her. She can't remember the last time she felt so wanted. His lips move over hers as he wraps his other arm around her waist, pulling her in close.

A soft moan can be heard in the back of his throat, and his need for her drives her to envelop his body with her arms, pressing her figure resolutely on his. His kiss is wonderful, landing somewhere between incredibly sexy and fabulously sincere.

He pulls back from her, and finally, her eyes flitter open.

His face lights up. "That was—"

"Wonderful," she whispers, causing him to smile wider.

He reaches for her hand and pulls her with him toward his recliner in the corner of his room. She curls onto his lap as he lowers into the seat. His arms hold her tight, and she lowers her head onto his chest.

"This is nice," he says, stroking his fingers up and down the skin on her arms.

"Mmhmm," she hums.

He pulls the lever on the chair, lying them back in the seat. She's so comfortable in his embrace.

"I'm not nervous anymore," she says.

She can't see his smile, but it's beautiful.

"Good. You call the shots, girl, and I'll follow your lead." He laughs and then places a kiss upon her head.

She peers up at him. She can't let the evening end without another kiss. She notices the want reflecting in his incredible silver eyes. "Thank you."

Her eyes travel to his lips, and she watches as the corners turn up in a smile. She presses her lips to his, and he eagerly places the back of his hand onto her neck, holding it tightly as his lips smoothly trace over hers. She moans softly as his tongue plays tenderly with hers.

Oh my, he's an amazing kisser.

He releases her, and with a spirited laugh, he says, "I've waited a long time for that."

A tightness she hasn't felt in a while pulls in her stomach, and she welcomes it wholly.

"You have?" she whispers.

"Girl," he says with a frisky pinch on her waist, "you know what a sexy little thing you are."

"Oh, stop it," she says.

"I will," he says playfully. "For now."

The best part about tonight is that she knows Tank means what he says—he always has—good or bad. He's helped her through some of the darkest days, and he has continued to remain by her side, no matter what. And that is what it means to be a good friend.

She snuggles deeper into his chest as she traces her hands over his beautiful upper body. "So," she asks, breathing in his masculine scent, "what *is* your major?"

He laughs and replies confidently, "Liking you."

Thirty

Lies and Secrets Are One in the Same

Tank stirs in the chair, noticing a difference in the weight on his lap. He pats the arms and realizes she's gone, much to his disappointment. He lowers the recliner and stands in his room, stretching his long arms over his head. His body aches from the game yesterday and from sleeping all night in the chair with Laura curled on his lap. But it was worth it. Having her in his arms was a welcome feeling. One he had been wishing for, for quite some time.

She left a note on his desk.

Had to get up and go see Officer Murphy. I'll call you later.

After taking a hot shower and dressing, he bounds down the stairs, desperate for a cup of coffee. There is a half-full pot waiting for him. The living room is silent, but the back door is propped open. He fills a mug and walks out to see who might be up.

Nathan is sitting in a lawn chair, holding a cup, staring into space.

"Hey," Tank says as he steps out into the back.

Nathan barely picks up his head. "Hey," he mumbles.

Tank sits in the chair next to him, sipping his coffee. "Rough night?" he asks.

"Hardly," Nathan mumbles.

"What's up then?"

"Nothing." Quickly, he says, "You had an early night."

"Yeah, sort of," Tank says, pushing back his hair from his face. "I heard quite the crowd come in. Who was here?"

"Webber invited some friends back. Daisy, Noah, and Heather from the other night and some other people. Who was with you?"

"Huh?"

"There were two beers on the coffee table when we got home."

Tank laughs. "Oh yeah, forgot. Um, funny story, kind of," he says, averting his eyes away from Nathan's.

"If I had to guess, I'd say, it was Laura."

Tank tries not to smile, but it's inevitable.

"I know you like her," he says.

Tank whips his head up. "I'm sure it's weird for you. I know Laura thinks it's strange, too. Kind of hard not to."

"Don't let my misery get in the way," he says.

"We're taking it slow. There are a lot of feelings at stake."

"I get it," he grumbles.

Tank narrows his eyes at Nathan and then blurts out, "Okay, enough is enough. What the fuck is going on with you?"

Nathan's head drops into his hands. "I can't move on," he admits. "It seems impossible at this point."

"What do you mean?"

He picks his head up. "I had this gorgeous girl here last night. She was nice and all, but I kept thinking about how she wasn't Abby. How screwed up is that?"

"It's just going to take some time. You gotta give yourself a break. I don't know what else to say."

"There's nothing you *can* say. But sometimes, I can't help but think it's all my fault that she's gone."

"Because of Poppy?" Tank asks.

"See? Exactly. You think it, too!" he says with a raised voice.

"Well, dude, it's kind of hard not to think that."

Nathan stands and paces in the yard. "I know, and that's what I get for trying to be a good friend. Abigail won't even speak to me, and if I had to explain, I couldn't. I can't. I can't do that to Poppy."

With a furrowed brow, Tanks asks, "Why the hell not?"

Nathan stops. "I have a secret. And I mean, a *big* one."

Tank rubs his hand over his face. "Jesus, what could possibly be so huge?"

"Well…"

"Oh, for Christ's sake. Tell me and get it off your chest. You know damn well I'll never tell anyone." Then, with a chuckle, he says, "Unless of course, you murdered someone."

Nathan barely laughs. "God, no."

"So, what is it? Unburden your soul, man. You'll feel so much better."

"Okay, but you can't say a word, and Laura can definitely *not* know."

"You really think you need to tell me that?"

"This is serious, Tank."

"Okay, okay," he says, raising his hands in protest. "I get it. It's top secret. Now, spill it."

"Remember when you told me to tell Poppy to fuck off and I said I couldn't?"

"I say a lot of obnoxious things." Tank laughs.

Nathan rolls his eyes. "Tell me about it. But anyway," he says, releasing an exasperated sigh, "the day Abigail and I broke up, I saw Poppy in the training room, hysterical, and she told me that she's pregnant."

"What?!" he exclaims.

Holy shit! This is big news! And I most definitely will not tell Laura. What a horrible thing for her to carry and not be able to tell her best friend. No, thank you. I'd never put that burden on Laura. Ever.

"Shh," he says, peering toward the back door. "Yeah. It's true. Confirmed by a doctor and everything."

"Oh shit. That is awful. But it's not yours…"

"I've never laid a hand on her," he says with hurtful eyes. "I love Abby. Only Abby."

Whew. Didn't think so…but I had to ask in case he needs more from me.

"I'm sorry. I shouldn't have said that," Tank says.

"Look, I know she liked me, and she tried really fucking hard to get me to break up with Abby, but I was never into her. I kept telling her that. One stupid kiss during a game at one of our parties, but we all…"

"We all do it. It's pretty juvenile." *Those stupid drinking games they always insist we play.*

"Exactly. We all hang out with them, travel together, so it's hard to not be around them. And I always thought it was harmless, but I know now that I shouldn't have conformed and allowed it to happen. I feel so stupid, and maybe that's why I kept pushing her to find someone. And so, she did. And the rest is history."

"So, she knows whose it is?"

"Yeah, you know that guy Clay who is always hanging around?"

"No fucking way. That guy is a dick."

"Yep. And he freaked out when she told him."

"Poor bastard. And poor her. What is she going to do?"

"I don't think she knows," he says.

"This is heavy," Tank says. "I promise the secret is safe. This is not something to talk about."

"No, and it's killing me because as her friend, I, like, need to be there for her."

"Yeah, you kind of do," he sighs.

"But every day that goes by, being there for her, I get further away from Abby."

"Me, too," Tank admits. "I was really hoping that we'd all be friends again. But we seem to be getting further away from the good ol' days."

"I hate that you just said that, mostly because it's true."

"But at least Laura, Casey, Jen, Melissa, and Bree still like us. Hopefully, she'll come back around when she's more comfortable. A lot of it has to do with me, too. But I can try and fix that," Tank says.

"Worry about you and Laura for now. You deserve it," Nathan says, forcing a smile.

"We're taking it slow; it's the only way," he says sadly.

"Yeah, but a girl like her is worth it." Nathan smiles for the first time in the past hour.

Tank stands and pats Nathan on the shoulder. "I know, and you of all people would get that."

Thirty-One

The Truth of Coming Out

Laura is sitting in Officer Murphy's office, explaining the plan they came up with over the weekend and how she's more convinced now than ever that the person responsible for the horrible graffiti on the soccer house is Guthrie.

"I wish Kate had felt more comfortable and reached out to someone. We'd have a file on this guy by now."

"I know, but imagine if every girl or boy called someone to say their last breakup went poorly and they think the person can't get over it?"

He chuckles. "Sorry, it's not funny. But when you put it that way…"

"But on Saturday," she continues, "I can't say for sure it was him in their yard, but it would be a very weird coincidence if it wasn't him."

"Well, you sure did a lot this weekend," he says.

"I had help." She smiles. She reaches into her bag and pulls out all the photos Wolfie took at the studio.

Officer Murphy flips through them. "Do you see a similarity in his work?" he asks.

"I did, but what I'm struggling with the most is, why? Jealousy?"

"That is always the hardest to comprehend. Criminals, in general, have different minds than we do."

"Is he a criminal?" she asks.

"Defacing property is a crime. But without catching him in the act, it will be very difficult to prove and prosecute."

"So, why bother then? Why pursue this if nothing can legally be done?"

He nods his head. "I know what you mean. But I feel obligated to continue to look into this for the safety of the students on campus regardless of whether or not we will be able to prove it in the end."

"This is frustrating," she sighs.

"But there is a greater good. Sometimes, just calling someone out on their behavior is enough to make them want to change."

"But having him paint the mural might show us nothing, right?"

"I see where you guys were going with this idea, but I think you're right; it might end up being nothing. Do you want to glorify the work of someone with such little regard for people on campus? I guess you need to ask yourself that."

"Well, I already know the answer to that. And it's *no.* And the other instances?"

"You tell me. What do you think?"

Laura leans back in the chair, contemplating. "If I had to guess," she says, "he's interested in the act—or I should say, the art of it. So, he tends to show up when it happens—the graffiti. And as an observer, he looks around, watching others' reactions to the crime, how they are responding to it, hence why he's looking at the camera as the person is taking the pictures of the scene. I think that by him being there, he was just warming up to the idea. And when the time was right, he'd know what to do."

A gradual and sly smile spreads across Officer Murphy's face. "A very valid theory, Miss Chase. I think you might be correct in your assessment. But I still think there is something missing as to why. I think it's more than just a bad breakup. I think the answers are still out there for us."

She shakes her head just as there is a knock on the door, and immediately, it opens.

"Sorry to interrupt, but you're needed right away," the young man says.

Immediately, Officer Murphy stands. "Okay, let me walk you out."

Laura, sensing a true emergency, gathers her bag and hurries behind him.

He's greeted by someone in the hallway, and he motions for Laura to proceed ahead. "I'll talk to you soon. Great job, Laura."

Great job? I've done nothing, she thinks as she nears her car and unlocks the door. "But I know who to talk to."

She drives to the Union, parks, and enters the station. No one is in the main room, but she sees Tucker's door ajar, and the light is on. She knocks on the door.

"Come in," he says. His eyes light up when he sees Laura. "Hello there," he says kindly.

She closes the door and sits before him. "Hey. So, I have an idea, and I need your advice," she says.

He leans back in his chair, and without hesitation, he says, "Shoot."

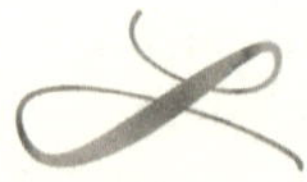

For the next hour, Laura tells Tucker all she learned over the past month and, more importantly, her crazy plan to catch Guthrie in the act. She doesn't go into detail about Kate or Guthrie since she isn't quite sure how their relationship plays into it, but she does her best not to be vague.

He rubs his goatee while listening intently to her detailed yet, at times, cockamamy idea.

"So, what do you think?" she asks.

"Wow, that is a loaded question," he says. "But I think if you can get everyone on board and you trust them one hundred percent, then I'd say you have a pretty good chance." There is a slight glimmer in his eye.

"Yes, I trust them. There's only one that is a long shot, but I think if I can reason with her, she'll see the light."

"All right then. I'll talk to Professor Campbell at *The Weekly Blue* for when you're ready. I want to be sure he's okay with the plan."

She hops up. "Thank you, thank you," she says. "I promise to run every step by you."

He laughs. "Yes, please don't be the reason they fire me from this wonderful place of higher learning."

She laughs. "I won't. I promise."

Laura exits the station, and with a renewed sense of purpose, she hops into her car and drives across campus to the soccer house. She pulls into the driveway, parks her car, and takes a deep breath as she walks up the walkway to their front porch. She knocks on the door and steps back, waiting for someone to answer.

She can hear someone yell, "I got it," and then the door swings open. As though perfectly planned, Kate stands before her.

"Hey, can I talk to you?" Laura asks.

Kate laughs. "If you've come to apologize again for the party, it's really not necessary, Laura."

"I'm not here to apologize," she says.

Kate's face drops a bit as she takes in Laura's serious expression.

"Would you mind taking a walk with me?"

Kate grabs her coat, closes the door, and follows Laura down the stairs.

They amble along the sidewalk, and finally, Laura says, "I need your help with understanding something. But I must be able to trust that you won't speak of this to anyone else."

Kate swallows hard. "Of course, Laura."

"Do you think Guthrie is…" Laura pauses as she thinks of not the guy who walked with her to the party, but the boy that spray-painted those words. Such contrasting personalities, and she wonders if he could be the same person, wrapped into one. "Well, I guess I'll just say it. Did he ever try and hurt you?"

Laura can tell by her reaction that she's shocked by the question. "No. Never."

"So, can I ask what happened between you two?"

She brushes her long brown hair off her shoulder and says, "Why do you want to know?"

"It's more important that I *do* know versus me *wanting* to know."

Kate laughs uncomfortably. "Sounds like you're not the only one with secrets."

Laura tips her head. "Secrets? More like a plan."

"What kind of plan?" Kate asks.

"Well, that all depends on what you really know about him. I need to make sure I don't put anyone in danger."

Kate sits on the rock wall around the corner from her house. "He won't. I mean, the guy I used to know isn't like that."

"Really? You certain?" Laura asks.

"Well…" she says, playing with her hands.

Laura takes a seat next to her, and with a deadpan voice, she announces, "I have reason to believe he was the one who vandalized the soccer house."

Laura gets a chill down her spine as she quickly realizes that Kate is not the least bit surprised by her accusation. Kate doesn't make a sound; in fact, she turns her head and stares blankly at the passing cars. Several moments of silence relinquish Kate from having any true thoughts of her own.

Until finally, Laura gently places her hand on her leg to bring her out of the trance she appears to be in and asks, "What is *your* secret, Kate?"

In the tiniest whisper, she admits, "I know it was him."

Laura tries not to react. "But how?"

Quickly, Kate spins her body to face Laura. "They don't know he's an art major. You can't tell the others."

Laura's head swirls with thoughts and questions. "But I don't understand. Why would you let him get away with it? Even an anonymous tip, anything?"

"Me?" she exclaims, her pupils dilating. "Why is this on me? No one else caught him. But somehow, I'm supposed to figure it all out?"

Kate starts to stand, but Laura grabs ahold of her wrist.

"I'm sorry. I'm just shocked that you knew." Laura's heart pounds in her chest. *I must take a step back, remain calm, and get the answers I'm seeking before she stops talking to me.*

"It's not like I saw him do it. I just had a feeling that it had to be him."

Laura shakes her head. "But I don't get it. Just because he's an art major and you broke up?"

"Yes. I mean, sort of." A tear drips onto her cheek.

Oh no, please don't cry. "I promise, you can trust me. But I'm in deep now, and I must find the truth because if I don't, someone else will. And, the graffiti was really directed at…"

"Lesbians. I know."

A tidal wave rises before Laura and then comes crashing down on top of her—at least, that's the sensation she has at this very moment. Completely overcome.

"Of course. I'm so stupid. How did I not put it all together?" she says quietly.

Kate quickly cuts in, "I knew something was wrong. He kept showing up at places that I was at. I ended it rather abruptly because…well, the night Shannon and I got together, he must have seen us because the next afternoon after classes, I found a note on my windshield, essentially calling me out. It had to be from him. No one else knew. Heck, I didn't even know. But it can't be a coincidence—the series of events happening. I was embarrassed and, more importantly, confused as hell. So, I ignored it. But one night, Shannon and I left a bar, and I saw him. The way he looked at me. It was indescribable. The next morning, we woke up, and there it was for everyone to see. It was horrible. It still is."

Laura takes her hand. "I'm so sorry, Kate. I never in my wildest dreams could have imagined…"

Kate says quickly, "But you can't tell anyone. My teammates would kill me if they thought I knew and never did anything about it. I live with so much guilt every day. I couldn't survive it if they hated me, too."

"I understand. I really do." She gives her hand a slight squeeze to get her full attention. "But herein lies the problem. The police are looking for a suspect, and they think it's him."

"What? They do?" Kate asks.

"Yeah. And I brought him to the party to see if he would paint a mural for the football team. As an attempt to trap him…sort of."

She starts to shake as she asks, "Will this all come out about me?"

Laura puts her arm around her. "I won't let this be about you. Only him. You have my word."

Kate's body trembles as she says, "But how can you promise that?"

I can't. Because if this leaks out, it will be everywhere. This campus is hungry for answers. And rightfully so.

"We have to think rationally." Laura stands and paces before a nervous Kate. "I…I wasn't expecting this today," she mumbles.

She tries to surmise what Travis would do. *What would Travis do right now? He'd remain calm, as cool as a cucumber, and reassure Kate that he'd get to the bottom of it.*

She kneels before Kate. "What I can promise you is that I won't say a word until I talk to you again. But I do have to ask for help. Because we've contacted him."

Kate wipes the wet from her cheek. "Thank you. And please make sure the girls don't know."

Laura can only nod her head as she rises. "I promise." *For now.* "I'll call you."

She hurries back to her car, leaving Kate alone to compose herself. She knows unequivocally that she must dig deep within herself and think how Travis taught her to. But she also knows that Travis never went at it alone; he relied on Wolfie and her as a sounding board. Since Wolfie is the closest thing to Travis that she has, she is on her way to him, heading straight toward his house, with a boatload of new information.

Thirty-Two

Stop the Presses

Laura bangs on Wolfie's apartment door. "If you're in there, it's me, Laura. I need to talk to you ASAP," she yells because Wolfie has been known to ignore people who knock on his door when he's not in the mood to converse.

She can hear movement, and then the door unlocks and swings open.

"Come in, come in," he grumbles.

"Listen, I have a major problem, and you're the only one who will know what to do."

"Let me put on some coffee," he says as he leads her toward the kitchen.

She takes a seat at the large table in the eating area. "Well," she begins, "I'm convinced it's Guthrie, but I don't think we should do anything about it."

He stops making the coffee and whips around. "What?"

"Listen to this. At the party we went to, it was as though I'd brought the Devil himself. All the girls on the team who saw us together couldn't wait to get me alone and ask me why the hell I came with him. Problem number one: I walked him right into the situation. But what I learned was that he used to date a girl on the team. And according to her, it was a very bad breakup."

Wolfie narrows his eyes. "There has to be more to this. Why would he write those things toward them?"

"Well, you see, she left him for someone on her team. And it sounds like he couldn't handle that."

Wolfie claps his hands together, and then in a disgusted tone, he says, "Of course not. What a pig."

"But here is the crazy part. She thinks it was him. She didn't say anything, for fear of it becoming about her being gay. She isn't ready to come out to the world. We covered it on campus, locally in the news, and she watched the whole thing like she knew nothing. I can't even imagine how much that must have frightened her. So, she remained in the shadows, and boy, was *he* glad about that. She didn't blow his cover, so eventually, he stopped harassing her. None of her teammates know he's an art major. So, she just tried to ignore it and hoped it would go away."

Wolfie hangs his head. "Now, I see the issue. She doesn't want you to pursue this."

"Wolfie, she cried. Really cried. How can I? How can we call her out like that if she's not ready?"

He sits across from Laura, sighing heavily. "I have no idea."

"What if I tried to talk to Officer Murphy? They practically know it was him; they're just trying to catch him in the act, right?" she says, questioning her own assessment of the situation.

"Let's not go to the police just yet, okay? Maybe we can reason with him. Or is that crazy?" he asks.

Laura shakes her dark brown bob loose and then tucks her hair back tightly behind her ears. Then, she rubs her hands over her face. She mumbles, "No, it's not crazy. *This* is."

He reaches for her hand, pulling it away from her face. "We can figure this out. We just need to think clearly, and obviously, that is not going to happen today. Give me some time on this, all right?" he says softly.

"Okay." She glances at the clock. She's already had about three days wrapped into one afternoon, and she still has her Mathematical Statistics class to get to. Her stomach rumbles despite nausea that ripples through it. "Thanks, Wolfie. I've gotta get to class," she says, standing and padding toward the door. Opening it, she steps onto his porch. "I'll call you tomorrow."

She enters the math building and heads into her lecture room, taking her usual seat near the front.

Professor Wilcox is writing on the chalkboard as Laura takes out her notebook and pen. Another gentleman, possibly in his late fifties, walks in and taps Professor Wilcox on the shoulder. They shake hands, pleasantries are exchanged, and then he steps to the side. Professor Wilcox places the chalk down, and as he moves forward, Laura can read what he has written. *Crime Rates and Assessments.* With a bunch of numbers and formulas underneath.

This immediately piques Laura's interest.

"Good afternoon, class. Today, Professor Haskell from the criminal justice department is here to assist us in discussing the use of math and statistics as tools in criminal investigations and police work."

This is the best news I've gotten all week! Well, aside from that kiss from Tank, but this is super awesome, too!

With her pen firmly pressed to her pad, she's eager to record whatever Professor Haskell wants to send her way.

"Thank you, Professor Wilcox, for inviting me to join your class today and discuss this exciting topic with you."

Exciting indeed, Laura thinks as she quickly glances around the room. *Is anyone else as pumped as I am for this?*

"Crime units across all functions use statistics collected from police reports, at the scene of a crime, surveys, measurements, and the like to determine areas where crime rates are the highest. This helps police departments determine where to increase their presence. Statistics and math used at a scene can also help them determine things, such as the rate of speed of a moving vehicle, trajectory of objects, and numerous other factors to help officers solve crimes. Professor Wilcox and I would like to run through some sample exercises with you today, using only math to solve some of these. And I say only math because in my classes, we tend to teach those to use deductible reasoning to solve issues, right? The most probable answer and to look from there. But in using math to solve, there can only be one true answer, and that is all we are looking for today."

Eagerly, Laura raises her hand.

"Yes, Miss Chase?" Professor Wilcox says.

"Will we be able to see the case study once we solve it?" *Please say yes.*

"Yes, we will review the case after we get to the correct answer," Professor Haskell answers.

Laura is barely able to contain her excitement behind her wide grin. "Thank you."

And just like that, her thoughts of Kate and the issues she had just an hour before are now gently placed on the back burner. Laura is able to get back to what she once loved. Applying the science of mathematics for logical reasoning—something she has surely missed.

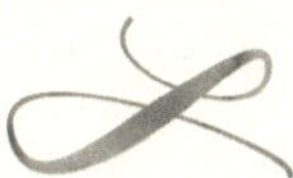

After class, Laura is finally able to take a break on the couch at home. She flips through the channels, trying to find something mind-numbing to watch, just as Melissa and Bree come home. The three decide to order pizzas before getting ready for the party they plan to attend tonight on Langdon Street. Laura promised Tank when they last spoke that she'd meet him there.

Within half an hour, Abigail opens the door and hangs her bag on one of the hooks by the front door. "What are you guys doing?"

"Nothing. Ordered some pizza. Want in?" Bree asks.

"I'd like that," Abigail says as she plops down on the couch next to Bree and stares blankly at the television.

"Earth to Abigail," Melissa says.

Snapping out of it, she says, "Sorry, long day."

"Well, it's Thursday night, and thank God for that!" Bree laughs.

Laura glances at her friend intently. "What do you have planned tonight?" she asks.

"Going to the party on Langdon Street. Aren't you guys coming? Casey, Jen, and Alex are going, too."

Laura's face blushes. "Yeah, I'm going there, too."

"I'm only going for a little bit because I'm going to see Adam," Bree adds.

"Going, too," Melissa says as she gets up to answer the doorbell.

She comes back in with two large pizzas and places them on the coffee table. The girls devour their pizza as they watch a movie.

"Well, I could watch that movie a thousand times," Bree says as she picks up the plates and wanders into the kitchen.

"Me, too, but I'd better get showered," Abigail says as she follows her with the empty pizza boxes.

"Me, too," Melissa says, turning off the television and making her way to the stairs. "Thanks for cleaning up."

"Yes, thanks. I'm showering, too, and I'll be ready in an hour," Laura says as she heads up to her room.

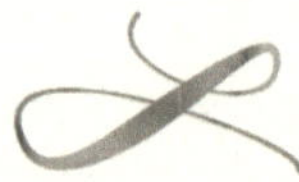

After Laura is all dressed up for the party, she finds Abigail ready as well, waiting in the kitchen, reading the latest copy of *The Weekly Blue.*

"Hey," Laura says as she pours herself a glass of wine. "I'll join you."

Abigail glances up from the paper. "Hey, you look great," she says.

"You do, too." Although she can't meet her eyes.

"What's up with you?" Abigail asks.

"How do you mean?"

"You seem off," Abigail says.

"I was thinking the same about you," Laura says defensively.

Abigail appears shocked at Laura's response, so she quickly replies, "I had a long day of classes, but I'm fine."

Laura's eyes soften. "Sorry, that came off wrong. I'm just…" *Trying to find the right time to tell you I've been hanging out with Tank more and more and I'm developing feelings for him. And I'm afraid you'll be mad about it since you've not made up with him, and it will just make this happy little bubble I'm in burst, and it's been so long since I've been happy with a man that I'm terribly anxious about opening myself back up to dating, let alone upsetting anyone else in the process.*

Melissa and Bree bound into the room, disrupting their conversation.

"You guys ready?" Bree says.

They have all learned over the years that when Bree is ready, she means it's time to go.

I guess it will have to wait for another time—yet again.

They grab their coats and lock the door, and the four of them venture over to the party.

The girls enter the house, and after grabbing a drink, they head to the basement to find Alex, Casey, and Jen. They quickly spot them near the corner of the room.

"Hey, guys!" Jen yells over the music.

Laura can't help but notice how quiet Abigail is and, more importantly, how she keeps looking around, as though the party is not complete unless Kelly arrives. Laura tries not to be offended because she's doing the same, searching the room for any sign of Tank.

Within moments, Melissa grabs Laura's arm. "Want us to grab you guys another drink?" she asks, pulling Laura along.

They nod, and the girls take off for the bar.

As they wait in line, Melissa suddenly turns to Laura. "Okay, so I know when something is bothering you. So, spill it."

Laura shakes her head in amazement. "How? I mean, am I really showing it?"

"Maybe only to me." Melissa smiles. "What is it, Laura? You just seem like you have the weight of the world on your shoulders."

They step up to the bar.

"Four beers, please," Melissa says.

He hands them the beers, and they each take two. Melissa motions for her to follow her away from their friends. They find a relatively quiet spot near the back door.

"Wolfie had to fill me in on some of it," she blurts out. "But you know why. We have deadlines. So, when I called him for his input on the copy, he had to tell me why he wasn't sure we should run it. He told me you guys needed more time."

Laura swallows hard. She's not mad at Wolfie; in fact, she knows he did the right thing by not keeping it from Melissa. They have an important relationship, just like Laura and Tucker do. It's common courtesy to keep your coworkers in the light.

"Now, you know why I feel the way that I do. I can't help but think that the only right thing to do is to let it go."

"You think you can convince Officer Murphy?"

Laura shrugs. "No clue."

"Maybe you'd feel better if you knew Guthrie had some good in him. Only then would you be able to make a better plan of action. After all, Kate is the only one you don't want to hurt again, right? She deserves the utmost consideration in all of this."

"What about the paper? Won't students inquire if you suddenly stop talking about it?"

She smiles. "Same for you, right? If anything, I'll be harder for you. You'll get calls on the air, on the spot, and you'll have to answer for it. The paper? We can hide a bit easier."

"I should have come and told you right away," Laura admits.

Melissa smiles. "Don't beat yourself up about that. Wolfie is your guy. I get it. You would have gone to Travis, and the next best thing is him. It's normal to seek out his advice. He's been with you a lot longer in this capacity than I have."

"I know, but I don't want to undermine you."

"Never. And you know that."

Laura sighs and takes a big sip of her beer. "Why can't I have a normal relationship?" She chuckles.

Melissa eyes her and then point-blank asks her, "You're not letting life get in the way of your happiness, are you? 'Cause if you are, I'll have to kick your ass."

Laura laughs. "Kick my ass? Really? Wow. Lay it all out there, why don't you?"

"I am," she howls. "You need a good man in your life, one who will treat you right, not this *Hardy Boys meet Nancy Drew* type relationship. I mean, a good old-fashioned, screw-your-brains-out, drama-filled, lusting, college-aged relationship."

Laura peeks into her beer. "How much have you had to drink tonight?"

"Enough to see a beautiful, smart, loving person in need of a fling."

"A fling?"

"Yeah, could be a lasting one, could be just tonight. But you'd better put yourself out there, Laura, and not care about anyone but you. You hear me?"

"Who says I'm not?" She laughs.

"If it's Tank," Melissa says just as Laura takes a sip of her beer, causing her to choke as she tries to swallow, "then don't wait. He cares about you as a person more than anything, and that is better than everything else. Travis would have wanted to know you were with someone who cared about you."

She leans in closer toward Laura. "Look over there." Melissa nods toward their friends.

Kelly is snuggled up next to Abigail, and the two of them look like they belong on the cover of a romance novel. Sexy, gorgeous, and completely enamored with one another.

"See Abigail? She's only thinking of her and Kelly. And if she can do it, anyone can."

Laura watches Kelly as he nuzzles into Abigail's ear, whispering God only knows what to her as she blushes a thousand shades of red.

Melissa is right. Tonight, I'm going to forget all my hang-ups and focus on myself.

Laura leans in and kisses her friend on the cheek. "Love you, Melissa."

Melissa winks and smiles. "I know. Now, let's give them these beers because Lord knows, they are warm as heck."

They return with the drinks.

"Hey, Kelly," they both add.

He smiles. "Hey, ladies. Having fun?"

"So far," Melissa adds.

They stand around for an hour, mostly chatting and drinking. Then, they hear some commotion as a large group of people starts to descend into the basement. One by one, Laura starts to recognize the line of massive human beings as they walk down the stairs. Laura keeps looking in their direction, and she waves enthusiastically at Tank. He smiles wide back at her.

Laura nervously sips her beer and then says, "Going to grab another one." Only this time, she doesn't offer to grab the others a beer, like she did the last time. She doesn't bother to look if any of her friends are watching her; she goes right over toward Tank and the other football players.

Tank's expression tells her more than he could realize tonight. A genuine smile spreads across his face. He leans in. "Hey, girl, you look hot," he says.

Her cheeks burn as she averts her eyes from his stare.

"What? Am I not allowed to say that?" he asks.

"No. I mean, yes, you can. It's just…" She struggles to find any words to form a sentence.

One of the players starts yelling for shots, and the crowd gets rowdy.

Tank grabs her by the hand. "Come on. I want to show you something."

He leads her over toward the stairs to the first floor. Once in the living room, Tank grabs two drinks from the bar and then motions for her to follow him out the front door. He steps on the porch with Laura closely behind. He hands her a drink and leans on the railing.

Laura glances up to a dark sky filled with stars.

"Nice night, isn't it?" Tank says.

Her voice cracks. "Yeah, it sure is."

"How was your day today?"

"Busy. I felt like I never stopped."

"I bet," he says just as she says, "I was going to call you."

Another genuine smile spreads on his face. "It's okay," he whispers. "I assumed you were busy."

"What did you want to show me?"

"Nothing. Thought you might be more comfortable if we talked alone."

She glances around the porch. They are, in fact, alone. Not a single soul is out here. She has so many things she wants to say, yet again, her words escape her. She wants to tell him all about her day. The conversation she had with Kate, Officer Murphy, Tucker, and Wolfie. But a part of her can't help but hear Melissa's voice in her head.

"Kate is the only one you don't want to hurt again, right? She deserves the utmost consideration in all of this."

She reaches for his hand. Feeling the warmth of his massive palm in hers, she squeezes slightly. "Thanks, Tank."

He steps closer to her. In his deep voice, he says, "Anything for you."

Her heart skips a beat as their gaze locks.

"I like your hair like that," she says in a stream of consciousness.

He shyly reaches for the bun at the nape of his neck. "Thanks. I could probably use a haircut at some point."

"Don't cut it," she says.

"Really? My hair is longer than yours."

"Well, most girls have long hair."

"I like that you're not like most girls," he says, releasing her grip and tucking her hair behind her ear.

She swallows hard. "And I like that your hair is long. It suits you."

He smiles and steps closer to her. The warmth of his breath is now on her face.

Suddenly, there is a bang, and the door swings open.

"Tank, Nathan…he needs you," someone shouts.

They both put their drinks on the ledge and run back inside the house, following the rushing crowd downstairs.

"What the hell?!" someone yells.

Tank forces his way down the stairs, like a battering ram prepared for combat.

"No fighting in my house!" Mike, the host, yells.

Kelly is in the mix somehow. He says something to Mike as some other members of the football team hold a person down on the ground. The players lift the guy up, his face gushing blood.

"Get him out!" Mike yells as they escort him up the back stairs and toss him in the backyard.

They follow him out, and one can only assume that what happens to him out there, he's got coming to him.

Poppy is standing there, shaking, as her friends try and console her.

Tank rushes over to Nathan as he wipes the blood on the back of his hand. "What the hell happened?"

Nathan pushes past him as he makes his way to Poppy. All eyes are glued to the unlikely couple as they embrace, Poppy falling to pieces as Nathan holds her tight. Tank turns and notices Kelly shaking the pain from his hand as Mike pats him on the shoulder.

Mike approaches Nathan and Poppy and escorts them upstairs and away from all the prying eyes.

Melissa rushes over to Laura. "Make sure they're okay, and I'll make sure Abigail is."

"What the hell just happened?" Laura asks, her breathing ragged from all the commotion.

My God, is that blood on the ground? What happened? Why is everyone fighting? Is Nathan hurt? This is bad, really bad.

"Some guy accosted Poppy. Nathan tried to step in, but he's super drunk. *Too drunk.* He needs to get out of here." Melissa immediately goes into reporter mode. "It's not good for him or the team. He can't be seen getting beaten up or whatever he's doing with that cheerleader. It will be the hot gossip all over town. The last thing any of them needs." She places her hands on Laura's shoulders. "Tell Tank to get him the hell out of here. *Fast!*" Melissa almost forces Laura with a slight shove.

But she's right. *Nathan needs to get the hell out of here. Pronto. He'll be crucified on Monday if anyone finds out he was in a fight—or Tank for that matter. This is not good for either of them. We all need to get out of here fast!*

Laura fights through the crowd and up the stairs. "Tank!" she yells.

He sees her get bounced back and forth as she tries to get near him. A goliath, he whistles so loudly that the people immediately stop moving. He yells, "Let her through," to the students as he points at Laura.

Like Moses parting the sea, they all step back, and Laura can easily move toward him.

"Melissa said we have to get him out of here, or it will be all over the news on Monday."

"Shit. What was he thinking?" He reaches for her hand and pulls her outside to a waiting Nathan and Poppy, surrounded by her friends and some of the players.

Laura tugs on his hand and pleads with Tank, "He's not thinking clearly. You need to do it for him."

Tank snaps to it. "Hey! Hey, guys," he says, forcing his way into the center of the crowd. "Shelby, Morgan, take Poppy home, *please.*"

"I'll drive them," Jason says.

"Thanks, Jay. Nathan, come on. I'm taking you home."

He reaches for his friend around the shoulders as he holds his T-shirt to his bloody lip. He's shaking from the cold air. It's a telltale sign he's had way too much to drink if he can stand out here in nothing but a pair of jeans.

Tank starts toward his truck in the driveway. "You coming, Chase?" he says.

Laura picks up the pace, leaving the crowd of students behind her. She can only hope this all goes away by Monday, or there will be a price to pay.

And this time, their friend Melissa might not be able to stop the presses.

Thirty-Three

Thieves and Lovers

Laura pushes the door open as Tank tries to hold Nathan upright.

"I'll get some ice," Laura says as she flips on the light in the kitchen.

Tank drags Nathan into the living room, lowering his cold, semi-naked body onto the couch. Laura hands him the ice pack.

"Here, buddy. You need to ice that."

Nathan grabs it and applies it to his lip. "He can't fucking grab a girl like that," Nathan slurs.

"I know, buddy. He's paying for it. Believe me."

Laura returns to the room with a blanket. She places it around Nathan's shoulders.

"Thanks," he mumbles.

Tank leans over and whispers something to Laura, and she immediately turns and heads upstairs to Tank's room.

Tank treads around the front of the couch and sits on the coffee table. He leans in as close as he can to Nathan. "Listen, man. You've got to get your shit together. This is not you. The scene back there? Not good for you. Or the team."

Nathan picks up his tired eyes and tries to focus on Tank. "You honestly think I don't know that?"

"*This girl*, I know you're trying to help her. But every time you do, you're one step further away from *her*. The one you really need to focus on."

Nathan knows exactly who Tank is talking about. Tank also knows that if he says Abby, it will only make Nathan spiral out of control even more.

Nathan leans back, and with an angered sigh, he says, "You see that fucking guy, *Kelly*…all over her tonight? They're like a goddamn couple. Then, he comes in and kicks the crap out of Clay. Could the guy look any better to her?!" He throws the ice pack across the room. "She'll never take me back. She won't even talk to me."

"Not like this, she won't. This isn't you. Don't you get that? She sees a guy losing his shit, rushing toward another girl. Can you blame her?"

"God, I'm so stupid."

"No," Tank says, patting his leg. "It's just that nice guys finish last."

He moans. "Why am I in this mess? I should have told Poppy to find someone else to help…" But his voice fades.

"But you *are* a nice guy. So, why change that? You know you would have helped anyone in her position, no matter what. Someday, Abby will see that."

He leans his head back on the couch, eyes barely open. "It's too late. She hates me."

"She doesn't hate you. She might hate me right now, but she doesn't hate *you*." Tank gets up and retrieves the ice pack. "Come on. Ice your lip."

Nathan barely lifts his hand to take it. "Go spend time with your friend. Leave me to wallow in my misery," he whispers.

"Come on, man. You can't beat yourself up like this."

"Leave me," he repeats. "Just fucking leave me."

Tank enters the kitchen, grabs a bottle of water and a few ibuprofens, and stands in front of Nathan. "I'll leave once you take these, and don't make me ask you twice," he says.

Nathan reaches out his hand. "Fine." He pops them in his mouth and drinks a gulp of water. "See? Gone. Now, will you leave me alone?"

"Don't sleep all night on the couch. Not good for you," he mentions as he walks over to the staircase.

The top step creaks as the weight of his tired body lands at the top. Tank pushes open his door and finds Laura sitting on the edge of his recliner, playing nervously with her fingers.

As soon as he steps inside, she stands. "Is he okay? Do you need anything?"

He closes the door. "He's all right for now, thanks." *I wish I knew how to help him more.*

"You have blood on your shirt," Laura says, motioning to the drops all down the front of his shirt.

"Shit," he says. He reaches over his head and pulls the soiled garment off, which loosens the bun in his hair, and a strand falls down the side of his face. He notices her swallow a lump in her throat as he stands before her, chiseled to perfection. His pecs dancing with each movement he makes.

"I didn't mean to kick you out before," he says. "I just needed to talk to him in private."

"I understand." She blushes as he steps closer to her.

He tosses his shirt on the floor, taking another step in her direction. The warmth in her cheeks creates a stunning pink hue.

"Are you blushing?" he whispers.

She struggles to speak. "Um, what? I-I think maybe it's warm in here," she lies.

He reaches out and takes her hand. "Hmm, but your hand is cold." He smiles.

"Oh."

He releases her hand and drags the tips of his fingers up the side of her shirt until he reaches the pulse point on her neck. "Your heart is beating quickly," he informs her.

"Is it?" she murmurs.

He leans into her, whispering in her ear, "Maybe it's from all the commotion tonight."

The heat of his breath is on her neck, causing goose bumps to trickle down her skin. "Probably," she mumbles.

His aftershave lingers on his cheeks as he seductively wraps his arms around her waist.

"I've been waiting all night to have you in my arms," he says, trailing light kisses up her neck.

His massive hand finds the back of her neck, and he draws her into him. Finally, his lips find hers. His heart rate skyrockets as he leans her back to the wall, pressing his body onto hers. She braces her arms on his firm chest. A moan escapes her as his tongue twirls around hers urgently. This is no ordinary kiss. He's hungry for her; he has a lusting desire within him to make sure this doesn't end here.

She drags her fingers down his chest and then traces her fingers over the perfect arches on his hips.

He shudders, and then barely releasing her lips, he mutters, "I like that." Then, he presses his full lips harder onto hers.

His skin's like glass under her touch. There is nothing but muscles stacked upon muscles, making his flesh so tight. Everywhere she touches, there is more of him to explore. Then, unexpectedly, he pulls back. She remains pinned to the wall, her lips swollen, her breathing ragged.

"What—what is wrong?" she asks.

A sexy smile grows across his lips. "Nothing, girl," he purrs. He softly caresses her cheek. "I just want to make sure you're cool with this." *'Cause I don't ever want you to change your mind.*

Her eyes dart back and forth. "Yeah, I'm cool with this," she says.

"Good. Because it's kind of hard to take it back." He laughs.

She bites her bottom lip. "Take what back exactly?"

He lessens the space between them as he reaches for the edge of her shirt, never taking his eyes off hers. He slowly rolls her shirt up over her head before tossing it on top of his on the floor. His eyes grow wide as he takes in her full breasts, beautifully captured in black lace. *Oh wow.*

"Being more than friends," he says.

He grabs her around the waist and spins her back toward the bed, cradling her as he lays her down. The weight of his body rests on hers.

"Damn, girl." He smiles. "You are gorgeous."

"Tank, stop it," she says, turning her head.

He touches her under the chin, moving her head to face him. "I'm serious, Laura."

She lowers her eyelids. "So are you," she whispers.

"So, you were blushing before," he teases.

"Obviously. Look at you." She reaches up and gently releases the band in his hair, letting it fall softly onto his broad shoulders. She pushes a strand back from his face.

I love the way she's looking at me right now. I've waited a long time to make sure she was healthier, and I finally see the old Laura, only far better.

"It's fun, being more than friends, isn't it?" he murmurs as he works his kisses down her neck, moving his way to the valley of her breasts.

Her skin's incredible as his lips trace the curve of her bosom.

She moans, "Uh-huh," as he continues to admire her with his mouth while she runs her fingers through his soft golden hair.

And for the first time since he can remember, he knows he's finally found someone in his life who's a perfect match for him. Someone he will always look out for, and in many ways, she'll be keeping an eye on him, too. And despite the pain, they have both endured in the past, it will make them stronger—together.

If only I could get Nathan on the same path because I see him heading down the darkened one we've been on before, and it leads to nowhere good.

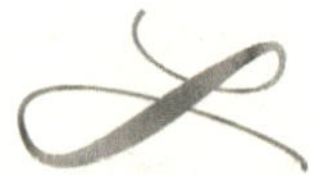

The smell of coffee hits Laura's nose, waking her from the best night's sleep. She turns onto her side and opens her eyes. They adjust not only to the sunlight streaming into the window, but also to the mug of coffee wafting its aroma near her.

"I made you a cup." He smiles.

She starts to sit up. Tank is leaning over her, his hair touching his shoulders, his bare chest molded to precision as he hands her the cup. His sweatpants hang low on his waist, and it's clear from her vantage point that sweatpants are the only article of clothing he's wearing.

"Mind if I join you?" he asks.

She reaches out to take the mug. "Thank you so much," she says. She scoots over, giving him some room on the bed. "How'd you sleep?" she asks.

"I slept great." He smiles as he rolls onto his side to face her. He bends his elbow and rests his head in his hand.

Laura thinks back upon their night together. Fooling around most of it, pausing for some time to talk and laugh. Never in her wildest dreams would she have imagined the two of them being so compatible. But she rarely allows herself to stop working long enough to think about it. And the thoughts of Kate, Guthrie, Abigail, Nathan, and everything in her world starts to creep back up into her consciousness, pushing away the sexy thoughts of the attentive football player lying next to her.

"Tell me what's on your mind," he commands. "Because I see you, Laura Chase. Your thoughts are far away from here."

She should have known Tank would notice.

She tries to hide behind the cup of coffee, taking a long sip while gathering her thoughts.

"I'd hate to take away your coffee." He chuckles.

She grunts. "I'm so obvious. Tell me how to stop doing that."

"No way. I need you to wear it on your sleeve."

She turns her head. "You do?"

"Yeah, girls are complicated, and if I don't know what you're thinking, I'll screw it all up." He laughs at himself. "Come on. You know me. I'll screw it up."

"Tank, stop it."

He rolls his eyes and says, "I'll stop when you tell me."

She knows she can trust him. He has proven that time and time again.

"Ugh, you and Nathan are the same," he says. "If you have something to say, just spit it out, and you'll feel better. And who knows? Maybe I can help."

Nathan. A lot of my thoughts have to do with Abigail and Nathan. But that's too much to get into right now, especially after last night.

"I know."

He reaches toward her. Gently takes the cup from her hand and places it on his nightstand. He swings back around to her and takes her in his arms. She rests her head on his chest. His other hand softly strokes her hair.

His soothing touch pushes the words out of her mouth. "I saw Kate the other day. She knows Guthrie is the one who graffitied the soccer house, only she doesn't want me to say anything because she doesn't want her name in the papers or anything."

"Really? Why?"

She releases a heavy sigh. "She's gay, and I gather, she's dating Shannon. I don't think her parents know. She doesn't want to be forced to come out because of Guthrie's actions, and she is hoping I'll stop looking into it. She said many of her teammates don't even know he's an art major, so no one suspects him. Kate knows they don't like him. Look how they reacted to him being at a party. She wants to keep him out of her world. And I think Kate kept it quiet because she had to. Isn't that awful?"

"Holy shit, that's heavy."

She peers up at him. "Yeah. So, what do I do?"

He brushes his hand down the side of her face. "If it were me? I'd tell Officer Murphy everything you know. I'd let him handle Guthrie under the caveat that Kate remains unmentioned. This guy is a semester away from graduating. He'll be putty in the hands of the police. I guarantee, Kate will never see his face again."

"You're right. I need to talk to him."

Tank cuts in, "Listen, Nancy Drew, you need to leave this to the big guns. I don't want you in harm's way. Understood?"

Hearing the name Nancy Drew brings up her conversation with Melissa. Maybe she has spent too much time uncovering problems and trying to solve them that she hasn't allowed herself to just enjoy more of her time at college.

But I like helping others by uncovering the truth.

"Do you think I don't know how to have fun?" she asks quietly.

He pulls her back to get a good look at her. "What? No way. I think you have a talent for this but not the authority to do much about it…yet."

"Yet?"

He smiles wide. "Yeah, I told you, you're in the wrong major, girl."

"Or maybe I'm just…I don't know."

He draws her body back in close toward his, squeezing her tightly. He rests his chin on the top of her head. A moment passes, and then he says, "Will you do me a favor?"

"Sure."

"Pack a bag tomorrow and meet me after the game, okay?"

"But—"

"No questions. Just do it, all right? Today, I need to rest and get Nathan's head straight. You understand, right?"

"Of course."

He lets her go and leans in, brushing his lips on hers. A warm sensation rushes over her skin. How quickly his touch can make her forget her woes.

The next afternoon, as Laura packs a bag, an unusual thought comes to her mind. As strange as this might be to some of her friends, she's really enjoying Tank's company. It's easy to fall for someone you already know. The *getting to know you* part is long past, but she gets butterflies when she sees him, and that's always a good sign. She throws her messenger bag around her shoulder and bounds down the stairs. As she nears the bottom of the stairs, she notices Abigail standing by the door.

"Hey, you leaving?" Abigail asks.

"Yeah. Going to the game," she shyly says.

She notices her cheeks flush at the mere mention of the football game.

"Oh. Well, have fun."

"You're not going?" Laura asks. "They're in the playoffs."

She brushes her hair back off her shoulder. "I'm going out for the day with Kelly."

"Oh, have fun. I'm sure I'll see you later," Laura says, trying desperately to sound upbeat.

Abigail heads for the door as Laura pulls it open. They exit onto the porch.

"What happened the other night?" Laura asks.

"Thought you might have more information than me." Abigail steps down a stair.

Laura's cheeks turn crimson. "Why would I know?"

"Didn't you stay after I left? Thought you might have gotten the scoop?" Abigail tips her head.

Laura looks almost relieved as she exhales. "Oh, right, of course. No, I tried to stay out of it."

"Me, too."

Then, Laura whispers, "Kelly sure jumped into action."

"Yeah," Abigail says as she lays her eyes on him as he leans against her car. "He's good like that."

Laura waves to Kelly. "Well, I should go. You guys have fun." She climbs into her car.

"See you later." Abigail heads to her car and climbs in.

Ugh. What is happening to us? We used to be so tight. As thick as thieves. And now? Our conversations are uncomfortable, filled with secrets, and only getting worse by the day. She barely talks about Kelly to me. And I'm too worried she'll be mad if I tell her I'm hanging out with Tank. What if Tank talked to her and smoothed their relationship out? Would she be happy for us then? But she'll be so hurt that she didn't hear it from me, too. I know I would be. The longer this goes on, the worse it will be. I must do something about this before it's too late.

Thirty-Four

Red Poppy

In the three years Tank and Nathan have been on the football team, today was the worst game the Hawks have competed in. And in a playoff game, no less. Last year, they'd had their best record in the past twenty-six years of the program.

This year is a mess.

A total mess.

Nathan was terrible. He threw three interceptions. *Three.* To put it in perspective, last year, he threw five. For the entire season.

They lost the game 36-7, and it wasn't even that close. Watching the Hawks struggle the way they did was almost unbearable for the fans.

Nathan looked unprepared, outmatched, and out of shape, all of which are normally not true. He just wasn't good on the one day he really needed to be.

Tank had a good game. He scored the only touchdown of the game. But in the end, it didn't matter. There was no way they could beat Georgia Tech.

And now, as they approach the end of December, the agonizing winter break looming, with no more football to keep them occupied, their idealistic ride to the NCAA finals has been shattered.

Nathan and Tank drag their tired bodies out of Menton Field. After the grueling media firestorm that took well over an hour, they're more than ready to put the season behind them.

Nathan's broken heart sinks yet again as he notices Laura waiting by the back door for them to come out. It should be Abigail standing there, eagerly anticipating his arrival. Nausea ripples through him as he sees Tank light up. Unfortunately, it's a feeling he used to have and no longer does.

Nathan attempts a smile as they approach.

"Hey, girl," Tank says, leaning in to kiss her on the cheek.

"Hey, guys. So sorry about the loss. It was a great season," she adds.

"It sucked," Nathan says. "But thanks," he quickly adds.

"Yeah, not a great one," Tank says.

"What do you say we get out of here?" Laura says, trying to force them away from the one place in the world that's giving them the most heartache.

"Hell yeah," Nathan replies.

Within seconds, they hear a faint voice say, "Nathan, can I talk to you?"

They all spin and find Poppy, shoulders hunched, dark circles under her pretty eyes, standing meekly by the door to the women's locker room.

Nathan turns back to his friends. "You guys go ahead without me. I'm not going out tonight anyway. So, I'll see you guys later."

"You sure?" Tank asks.

"Definitely."

"We can wait," Laura says softly.

"No, I insist. Really. I'll catch you guys tomorrow." With that, he turns and makes his way over toward Poppy.

"Hey, Poppy," he says once he hears the clang of the metal doors as his friends exit, leaving the two of them alone in the hallowed halls of the fieldhouse.

She smooths down her wool coat, trying to gain her composure. "I'm sorry about the game," she says.

"Me, too," he mutters.

She clears her throat. "But that's not what I wanted to say to you."

He releases a heavy sigh. "What's up?"

She sits on the bench outside the locker room. "I wanted to say, thank you for being a great friend." She starts to cry as she chokes out, "When I needed someone, you were there for me."

He lowers onto the bench next to her and gently places his hand on her leg. "Of course. You don't need to thank me."

"But I do. *You* were the one who held me that day in the training room. You were the one who took me to the health center. Whether you know it or not," she says, wiping a tear from her cheek, "you saved me that day."

He cocks his head. "What do you mean?"

"You know exactly what I mean," she whispers. "I've never felt so helpless in my entire life."

He sucks in a quick breath. "Oh."

"But I'm better. Well, I will be."

"That's great, Poppy."

She turns to him. "You really are one of a kind. You know that, don't you?"

His cheeks flame red. "I don't know about that. These days, I'm more like a dime a dozen."

"Don't do that, *please,*" she begs. "You're kind, thoughtful, sweet. And did I mention gorgeous?" She chuckles.

"Thanks," he whispers as he averts his eyes from hers.

She shifts in her spot. "And it's no secret," she says with a slight brush back of her hair. "Because like I've told you a thousand times, I have a total crush on you."

"Poppy," he whispers.

She laughs. "Worried you missed out, Nathan?"

And just like that, he sees a slight glimmer of the old Poppy.

He smiles sincerely at her. No one would dispute her striking looks. And someday, she'll make a guy happy with her outward, confident personality. But it's not for him. He's only had his eyes on one person since the moment he saw her on campus.

"It's my loss," he says.

"You're sweet to say that even though we both know it's not true." He starts to protest when she quickly adds, "But I have one more favor to ask."

"Sure," he says.

"You can't be friends with me anymore," she blurts out.

"*What?*"

"It's my own fault," she says with self-assurance. "I flaunted my feelings for you, and it cost you. I won't have it anymore. I'm so sorry, Nathan. Truly."

"It's my fault, too."

"I disagree." She abruptly stands and faces him. "Listen, maybe next season, we can be friends again when you're back with her. I'll keep my distance and make sure she knows I'm not a threat."

"I…I don't see that happening."

"At least if you're not friends with me, there's still hope."

He rises to his feet. "I don't want to be with anyone who doesn't like my friends," he states.

She smiles wide.

"Why are you smiling?"

"Because that's exactly why you are such a catch, Nathan Ryan." She leans in and softly kisses him on the cheek. "I've thought a lot about this, and it's the only way to get her back. I can feel it in my gut. You have to try." She takes his hand and pulls on it lightly. "You have to try again. You can't give up. Okay?"

"Why do you want me to try?" he asks with a frown.

"You think everyone likes to see you moping about all day long?" She dramatically sighs.

His muscular shoulders hunch forward in defeat. "I know. I'm a bummer."

She smacks him playfully on the arm. "See my point? She makes you happy." She turns on her heel and heads toward the exit. Before she pushes open the door, she says with just a wave of her finger, "And believe me, she's one lucky girl."

Then, swiftly, she steps into the cold night as Nathan remains still, in the spot where she left him.

Alone.

Yet again.

He immediately thinks of Abigail. *What is she doing tonight? Was she at the game? Does she even care about the team? Me? Tank? Who am I kidding? It's over. It's high time I accepted that.*

Thirty-Five

Nathan's Pain

He's been sitting in his car for almost half an hour, and he has no idea why. It's fucking cold, but he can't get himself to open the car door and haul his ass inside. He's not completely alone; he's got his friend Johnnie Walker by his side.

Maybe he fears going inside because he can see a light on, and that means either Logan or Spidey is home.

I don't want to be alone tonight, but I need to be. College is supposed to be fun, but for me, these past few months, it's been nothing but a huge downer. It's hard to be social when you feel like hell. And tonight, it's worse than hell, I'm shit. And on top of that, I'm completely embarrassed with how I played today. Hands down, the worst game of my career. I let everyone down.

He grabs his bag, shoves the bottle of JW inside, and pulls the handle on the car door. He closes and locks his car. Then, he drags his feet to the front door, hoping it's locked and someone just left the light on.

No such luck.

As he opens it, he can hear voices inside. Some female, too. He walks into the hallway, attempting not to draw any attention to himself.

Too late.

"Hey, buddy," Spidey says.

"Hey." He walks into the living room.

Spidey is with three girls and a few guys.

It's a goddamn party in my apartment, and all I want to do is go upstairs and be by myself.

"You remember Daisy, Heather, and Noah," Spidey says.

Of course he remembered them. Something about Daisy has always bugged him. But he can't quite put his finger on it yet.

"Hey, guys."

"And this is Amber, Tommy, and Hugh."

"Hey," he repeats with little enthusiasm.

Amber gives him a look that tells him she's not with these two guys.

Great, just what I need.

He pulls out the bottle from his bag and takes a swig. He's not trying to impress anyone. He should since any one of them could open their mouths about him, and it would get around the school in a millisecond. But fuck it. He just lost the most important game of the season, and right now, he doesn't care about anyone's opinion. Well, except one person. But she doesn't care about him anymore. So, that leaves him right back to zero. Zero fucks.

Amber gives him a sympathetic glance that makes him want to scream, but it gets worse when she says, "Sorry about the loss tonight."

Shit. Do we have to talk about it? "Thanks," he grumbles.

"Yeah," they all chime in their condolences as he nods and sips from the bottle, drowning out their words.

He hears nothing until Spidey says, "Let's leave the poor guy alone." He turns to him. "Let me make you a more sophisticated elixir. Something to release the serotonin. May I?"

Heather bursts out laughing. "Oh, Webber, only you would talk like that."

Daisy says mockingly, "Right, he's, like, sooo smart."

Nathan glances over at her and catches a hint of resentment in her voice. Maybe that's why he doesn't particularly care for her. She's pretty, and she knows it. Heck, last time she was here, she flirted with Tank and didn't think twice of it. But she's always with Webber.

Nathan can only hope Webber hasn't fallen for this chick. *Yuck.*

Spidey comes back with a drink for him, and as he reaches out to take it, he realizes he took the bottle of Johnnie Walker right out of his hand, and he didn't even notice.

"Thanks," he says.

"Have a seat," Webber says to him, pointing to the open chair in the corner, by the TV.

At least it's not on the couch, occupied by Hugh, Amber, and Daisy. So, he sinks down into it and sips on the drink Spidey made. And, man, it tastes awesome. He doesn't even question what is in it; it tastes so damn good. As a matter of fact, he's going to act like it's nothing just so Daisy won't ask Webber to make her one. He's keeping this little secret all to himself.

Until he must ask him to make another one.

And another one.

Until the next thing he knows is, they are all in the living room, dancing.

And Nathan never dances.

Ever.

The girls are having a blast. Heather and Noah are grinding up on one another. Hugh is spinning the tunes in the CD player, and he puts on a faster song, Amber twirls around in her skintight Guess jeans and body-hugging white T-shirt. Nathan is watching her move around. He hasn't looked at someone this way in a long time. That is, until Daisy spins into him and spills her bright pink concoction all down the back of his shirt.

"I'm sorry," she screeches over the music.

He can't even be mad at her; he's feeling too good right now. So, instead, he pulls his shirt up over his head and tosses it on the table. *Problem solved, right?*

Until Noah dims the lights, and Hugh puts on some slow jam he's never heard.

Nathan notices Daisy slip away as she yells, "Bathroom break."

Convenient.

It's clear to Nathan she's avoiding Webber, who is longingly staring at her. But then Nathan is pulled out of his thoughts by the soft touch on his arm.

"Want to dance?" she asks.

He turns to see Amber's eager eyes sizing him up. A drop of sweat drips onto his bare chest.

"I'm a sweaty mess," he lies as he wanders into the kitchen.

Thankfully, Webber is there to make another drink.

My last one, I think.

He knows it's rude to just walk away from her, but luckily, she follows him into the kitchen as he uses a paper towel to wipe his forehead.

"Sorry. I wouldn't do that to you," he says, forcing a laugh.

He swears she licks her lips.

Webber hands Nathan another drink.

My last one.

He glances at the clock on the stove. He can't believe it's already one in the morning. He's exhausted and drained and he's had way too much to drink.

"I've gotta shower this pink stuff off and get to bed," he says as he tips the drink back.

"Boohoo," she says with a pout.

"We'll get that dance soon," he says to Amber. "Promise."

"I'll tell them to turn it down," Webber says.

Nathan smiles at him and pats him on the shoulder. "Sure thing, buddy. And will you tell them all good night?" Nathan asks as he starts to back out of the kitchen to head to the stairs. "I don't like grand departures," he slurs.

It's usually about this time, when he's ascending the stairs, that the overall stress he's put on his body, on game days, begins to settle in deep in his body. Both physically and mentally.

He used to not notice it as much when he had Abigail around. She always made him so happy that he had such few moments to dwell on any negative feelings. It was probably why his first two years on the team, he performed much better than he did this year. He's just had too much of a mental block to get into any kind of good place.

Believe me, the team noticed, and my coaches noticed, too.

All he could do was promise them he'd do better. He tried. But apparently, he kept failing.

He flips on the light in his room and turns the radio on low. Sometimes, he needs it to drown out the noises in his head. He strips off his jeans and heads to the bathroom. He turns on the water and lets it run until the steam is fogging up the mirror. He steps in. The hot water feels so good on his skin as he washes away the horrible, sticky pink stuff Daisy was consuming. He shampoos and washes his body, and then he turns off the water and steps out. He wipes the condensation from the mirror, pushes back his hair from his face, brushes his teeth, and opens the door. He watches the steam waft into the hallway. He can hear them all downstairs, still partying, and to be honest, he's surprised he lasted as long as he did. Considering he had no intention of being near another human being tonight.

He pushes open the door to his room and freezes.

"What are you doing?" he asks.

"I wanted to bring you your shirt," Amber purrs.

"Really?" He chuckles.

She sits on the edge of his bed with her hands clutching his stained-pink T-shirt. She pushes her hair back with her free hand and says, "Actually, I was wondering if it was too soon for that dance?"

He stands in the room, clutching the towel around his waist, wondering what the hell to do next. He turns toward his dresser and pulls out a pair of sweatpants. He slips them on under the towel and then pulls the towel off like freaking Houdini, never showing his backside.

When he turns to face her, her eyes are lit bright, and she swallows hard.

"Wow, your body is, like, amazing," she says.

"Thanks," he says. He knows it's true. He works out constantly and eats what they tell him to eat, and the rest is good genes. "Here," he says as he approaches her. "I'll take that." He reaches for the shirt from her hands. He tosses it into his hamper.

As he turns back, she's standing mere feet from him. He can smell her perfume. He can't remember the last time he felt excited to be alone with a woman. Sometimes, he wishes it so much, but it simply does not happen. But something is happening now.

A slow song comes on the radio.

"How about now?" he asks her, reaching out his hand to her.

She leans in toward him and puts her hand in his. Her skin is soft to the touch. He pulls her into him, and she rests her other hand on his chest. It's a welcome sensation.

I've been so lonely. And she's right here. I barely need to try.

They slowly spin around in his room. At some point, he even closes his eyes as the soft hum of the music, the heat from her body, and the alcohol that isn't close to leaving his system make the perfect recipe for him to finally relax.

She leans her head on his chest and says, "I have a confession to make."

"Oh, really?" he replies.

She gazes up at him with these enormous brown eyes. "Yeah, I asked Heather to invite me tonight…so I could meet you."

That is not what he expected her to say. At all. It never would have occurred to him in the least. But now, she has his attention.

Being cocky, he asks, "And why is that?"

She traces her thumb over his palm and says, "I heard you were still single, and I thought maybe a girl like me might have a chance."

Her boldness does intrigue him. Although it's not his favorite quality. It reminds him of when he first met Bree. She was too forward for him. He loves her as a friend, but it was never going to be for them. At least Amber is a bit more subtle.

I have no intention of getting into the reason as to why I'm still single. I could say it's by choice, but deep down, I'd only be bullshitting myself, so why even bother?

He clears his throat and says, "Is that so?"

"Well?" she says with a smooth tone.

"Well what?"

"Do I have a chance?" Her eyelids grow heavy with lust.

His heart is telling him no, but his body is saying, *Why the hell not?*

So, he says to her, "Tonight, I'd say, you've got the best chance."

She giggles, and he notices how sweet her smile is. For the first time since he met her, he wants to kiss her. So, he leans in, and she immediately closes her eyes. His lips touch her soft, full lips. It's a nice kiss, but then her tongue pushes past his parted lips, and her body presses up against his. He wraps his arms around her slim figure, running his hands down to her tight ass. These jeans really know what they are doing because they hug everything just right. She feels good in his arms. He hears a slight moan in the back of her throat as he kisses her eagerly. He places a tender trail of kisses down her neck. Her skin alerts him with goose bumps letting him know that she really likes what he's doing. Her hands caress his back, tracing the tips of her polished nails up and down his muscles.

"You're so hot," she says, tipping her head back so he can get a better taste of her neck.

"So are you," he mumbles as he continues to brush his lips down the valley between her cleavage.

She moves him back toward his bed, pulling him, and his feet reluctantly move forward. He senses her calves hit the back of his bed, and she lowers her body onto his mattress, again forcing him to move with her.

With her body spread out before him, he can't help but open one eye again and peek at her.

And he wishes he hadn't because she's no longer interesting to him.

She's not Abby. As badly as I wanted her to be. In this moment, I know she's not.

"I can't believe this is happening," she whispers along with a nibble on his ear.

"What?" he says.

"Me and *Nathan Ryan*."

She said my name like it means something. But it doesn't. It shouldn't. Not to her anyway. She's not here for me. She's here to tell people she was here.

And as quickly as it came, his hard-on and interest in her are now gone.

He kisses her softly on the cheek and says, "I really need to call it a night."

He pulls her up off his bed and stands with her. The look on her face is enough to tell him how much he sucks, what a jerk he is, and how despite her own previous words, this is his loss. So, at the risk of standing here and having to endure a five-minute conversation reliving all these details, he simply goes to the door, opens it, and motions for her to leave.

Thankfully, she does. Without a word from her lips. But she does give him one more disappointed glance as she eases by him.

As soon as he hears her on the stairs, he shuts the door, locks it, and turns off the light.

As he closes his exhausted eyes, there is only one woman that he's thinking of.

Abby.

"Good night, Moon Pie," he says aloud, releasing a deep, intentional breath. "Wherever you might be."

Thirty-Six

It's Not What You Think

"Where are we going?" Laura asks as they drive past the gates of the university.

"Well, I was planning on hanging with the team. And you, of course. But after that miserable display, I have another idea, if that's okay with you?" he asks.

Her heart warms. "You sure do have my attention now." She giggles.

She loves the smile that spreads across his face. He should be despondent right now. But instead, he's taking the end of his season in stride. Yet another mystery that is Tank. His freshman year, he would have been drinking profusely, arguing with anyone around him, picking fights with teammates. But now, he's driving someplace with a girl, for an evening alone.

"Besides, it looks better if we don't throw a party at the Ridge right after losing in the playoffs. We'll plan something for next weekend."

A short drive later, they're pulling into the parking lot of a mini-mart.

"Wait here. I'll be right back," he says, opening the door to his truck.

A cool blast of air enters the cab as he closes it. Minutes later, Laura sees him exit, carrying two large paper bags. He puts them in the back of his truck and climbs back in.

"We're almost there," he says, rubbing his hands feverishly.

Back on the main road, there's a sign up ahead that reads, *Westvale Commons*. He turns into a complex of townhouses, then steers left, then right, and then left again until finally pulling into the driveway of a dimly lit townhouse. There are a few cars in the driveway. However, next door is another thing. It's filled with cars, and you can hear the beat of music thumping through the night.

"Um, whose place is this?" she asks as he kills the engine.

"Dylan's parents' ski place," Tank says, referring to one of the freshman players on the football team. Someone Laura is not familiar with, considering he's new to the team. "They said we can use it whenever we want to get away from the school scene. Dylan let a few of us know he was coming up here. These guys are cool. I'm kind of like their big brother. So, here we are" he says with a shrug. "You cool with this?"

"Sure, I'm fine with it."

He takes her hand in his. "Great, because I really couldn't go sulk at a party on campus. Or hear the negative whispers. We totally deserve to hear them, but you know how it is."

"What about Nathan? Is he coming?"

"No." Then, he quickly adds, "But he promised me he was going straight back to the apartment. He's in no condition to be around people tonight."

"You sure we shouldn't keep an eye on him?"

He smiles. "Trust me, he wants to be alone."

"So, is it okay for me to ask what happened tonight? Nathan seemed really off."

"He's been off for pretty much the second half of the season, but I think we know why."

Laura releases a heavy sigh. "That's so sad. I hate to see him struggle and in front of so many people, like he did tonight."

"The media lit him up pretty bad, too. But he took it like a man. He knew he sucked," he says with a shrug of his shoulders. "But it's a team effort, and we didn't exactly pull it together."

"There's always next year, right?" she adds with a slight smile.

He releases her hand and pulls open the handle on his car door. "Come on." He motions with his head as he gets out.

As they approach the front steps, the soft bump of the bass can be heard behind the front door. Tank doesn't bother knocking; he walks right in, holding the door open while Laura enters.

"You'll love this place." Tank drops their bags by the staircase to the second floor and carries the bags from the mini-mart down the hallway, toward the music.

"Hey, guys," Tank says as he places the bags on the counter in the kitchen. "You guys all know Laura," he announces.

Ah, so this is a couples type thing, Laura thinks as she surveys the room.

There are three other players snuggled up with their respective girlfriends. Laura recognizes most of them from the numerous parties she's attended at the Ridge.

"Drink?" Tank asks her.

"I made a pitcher of margaritas, Laura," one of the girls chimes in. She crawls off her boyfriend's lap and saunters over toward the refrigerator.

"Sure, that sounds great," Laura says.

"Maggie," she says. "I listen to your show all the time. You are so good," she says sincerely.

"Isn't she?" Tank adds.

His expression is so genuine that it makes Laura's skin pink. Tank has always been a guy's guy, but his appreciation for women is second to none. With just one look, Laura knows his thoughts are wandering, just like his eyes do, up and down her body.

"Dylan, come here," Maggie says. "My boyfriend is a huge fan of yours," Maggie says to Laura as she pours her a drink.

Dylan approaches Laura. "So nice to finally meet you," he says. His voice is much deeper than Laura expected for a freshman.

"Thank you, Dylan. I can't believe we haven't met before. But thanks for having us."

"I tried to keep my nose clean this season. Gotta make a good first impression on Coach."

Tank slaps him on the back. "You did, buddy. Just sorry we couldn't go further this year. Sucks. Really sucks."

"Yeah, it does. But anyway, cheers," he says as he raises his cup. "To next year."

They all cheer, and then Tank asks, "Who's next door? Looks like a banger of a party."

"Don't know. But my father said these condos rent out a lot during the year. Skiers, shit like that."

"I can see that," Tank says.

"Laura, come meet my friends," Maggie says as she pulls lightly on her arm.

"Would love to," Laura says with a smile as she's dragged away from the kitchen.

Laura is quickly introduced to the other girls there and is immediately bombarded with questions about the radio station. She never knew there could be so many questions about what it's like to work there and to be the only female on staff. But what she *least* expects is to be asked about all the controversy and chaos that took place last year as it pertained to Dean Barrymore and the Campus Creeper. It's as though these first-year students have been harboring all these questions until the very moment they met Laura Chase.

Much more at ease to talk about her past involvement with the Campus Creeper case, she politely answers their questions as they stare at her intently.

Suddenly, a voice can be heard from the hallway as the front door opens. "Knock, knock," a high-pitched voice says.

The guys turn and peer down the hallway as the girls remain steadfastly interested in Laura's words and pay no mind to the new houseguest. Laura peeks over with only her eyes, as there is a familiarity in the voice.

Then, she hears, "Is that Tank's truck in the driveway?"

He chuckles. "Depends on who is asking."

And then, like a bad teen movie, Jessica, Tank's ex-girlfriend, peeks her head into the kitchen. "Me," she says, oozing a sultry tone. She walks into the kitchen, without a care as to whose house it is, and approaches Tank. "I knew it!" She laughs with a flip of her curly brown hair. She runs to him and throws her arms around him. "My gosh, *Thomas*. I did not expect to see you tonight. So sorry about the game."

Tank hugs her back, and Laura's cheeks burn red as she observes the former lovers in an embrace.

They'd both tell you their relationship was unhealthy, but from what Laura knew about it, they were more into it for the physical component rather than the intellectual part.

Ugh, why does she have to be here? Of all the times, of all the towns, and of all the nights.

Laura only knows Tank in one of those ways; hence, while her jealousy starts to take over, she can barely concentrate on the questions still being asked of her by Maggie and her friends.

"What did he look like?" Laura hears on her left side.

She comes out of her haze. "Who?" she asks.

"The Campus Creeper, silly," the girl whose name she has already forgotten asks. "I heard he was like an ordinary guy."

"Yeah, you could say that in terms of looks. But he's no ordinary person. He's evil," she continues, trying not to pay attention to Jessica and Tank in the kitchen, chatting away, as the rest of the guys go back to their own conversations.

A few more minutes pass, and Maggie says, "Can I get you guys another?"

"Thank you, Maggie," Laura says. She investigates the kitchen for the first time in several minutes and notices that Tank and Jessica are gone. Her heart sinks.

Where did they go?

Maggie comes back, and Dylan is right behind her. He sits in the chair adjacent to Laura.

Trying to seem nonchalant about it, Laura asks, "Did Tank bring our bags upstairs or something?"

"No, I think he went next door. Guess there is a party with some OSU people. Said he'd be back, but feel free to put your stuff in the room. Second door on the left."

"Oh, great. Thanks. I will later."

Laura chats with the girls for what seems like forever with no sign of Tank's return. She finally gets up to use the bathroom, and she comes back to a room full of people but still no Tank. She grabs her bag from the hallway and makes her way to the room Dylan said she could stay in. She pulls out a sweater from the bag and pulls it over her head, tucking her hair back behind her ears.

Laura is about to leave the room when she hears voices outside. She goes over to the window, pulls back the curtain, and sees a bunch of partygoers on the front porch of the condo next door. What she cannot take her eyes from is Tank standing so close to Jessica with his arm draped around her waist. The sight sends a wave of sickness through Laura's gut. The casualness in his affection alarms Laura as she stands a mere forty feet from them.

Imagine if I wasn't right next door. How would he be acting then?

The thought consumes her as she releases the curtain and ventures back down the stairs. As she gets to the bottom, Maggie is putting something away in her purse.

"There you are," she says. "We're about to start a game of Asshole. Want to play?"

Laura can't help but chuckle at the name of the beloved drinking card game. "Sure, I'll play." *It will be good to get my mind off what I saw next door.*

It's not like Laura to play the part of the drama-filled girlfriend. And besides, her relationship with Tank, while close, is still undefined. They haven't even slept together. But regardless, she would never go across the way to cause a scene and embarrass herself. It's never been her style, so why start now? If Tank wants to be a major flirt while trying to get with her, it says a lot about his overall feelings, and that is something she won't address here among virtual strangers.

Laura sits at the long table in the open-concept dining room. The fire in the living room is now pumping a lot of heat, or it might be the tequila from the margaritas she has been consuming the past hour that is elevating her body temperature. She pulls her sweater back off and drapes it over her seat. She's now more determined than ever to have fun as she glances at the clock on the wall. She needs to take her mind off the missing guy she came with. No one has said a word about Tank being gone for quite some time now, and she isn't going to bring it up again.

The cards are shuffled and dealt. Round after round, they move seats until Laura is finally the President of the game.

With confidence brewing, as she now sits at the head of the table, she asks the group nonchalantly, "Who hasn't heard my show yet on WOUR97?"

"Your show?" the guy with the backward baseball cap asks. "Are you in a band?"

Everyone in the room laughs as Laura stands and yells, "Drink!"

As President of the game, you have the power to control the actions of everyone below you. It's why you play the game to begin with.

After everyone calms down, he leans into Dylan and says, "No, really, what show?"

Dylan tips his head back and lets out an exasperated sigh. "Dude. Laura Chase. DJ on our college radio station. Does the news, all that crap." He quickly turns to Laura. "No offense, but you know what I meant."

"Sure do." She smiles innocently and then points her finger at Dylan and says, "Now, you drink!"

Just as everyone bursts into laughter, the front door opens, and in walks Tank. Alone. He looks out of sorts. But not in an outwardly way. Maybe it's only something Laura would notice.

"Where the fuck have you been?" Dylan boasts.

Laura tries not to react as she concentrates on dealing the deck of cards.

"What are you playing?" he asks, his voice sounding hoarse.

With the courage of alcohol coursing through her veins, she peers up at him and says with a noticeably cool tone, "Asshole."

"Yikes," Maggie whispers under her breath.

Laura glances at her, her mouth in a hard, straight line.

"We can deal you in," the guy with the backward hat says. "But you'd automatically have to be the Asshole."

"No, thanks," he says. "I'm going to take a shower."

"Dammit," the Asshole curses.

"Ha-ha, you still have to be Asshole," Dylan chimes in.

Tank grabs a beer from the fridge and slips away upstairs as the heckling at the table continues.

As they all look over their cards, Maggie whispers to Laura, "He looks wounded."

Laura hates the sad eyes she's giving her.

"He disappeared for a long time," Laura whispers.

She shakes her head. "Men. Can't live with them; can't live without them."

Cliché, but oh-so-true.

Thirty-Seven

It's Even Better

Thank God Laura reigned as President for the next half hour because she was able to drink water instead of what the others below her had to consume. She wouldn't have been able to keep up. She has been waiting for Tank to come back down and join the party, or she's going to have to quit—while she's ahead, no less.

She glances over at Maggie and whispers, "I need to bail."

Maggie just winks and says loudly to the group, "Laura needs a potty break."

Laura laughs and says, "Yeah, I'll be back."

Before anyone can protest, she gets up and backs out of the room, passing the bathroom and heading directly upstairs. She can see a small glow of light under the doorframe. She takes a deep breath in before opening the door.

Tank is sitting in the overstuffed chair in the corner of the room. His eyes are closed, and he's holding the cold bottle of beer to his temple. He's not wearing a shirt. His arms look incredible as his defined biceps and broad shoulders move as he rolls the bottle across his forehead. His legs are stretched out before him. The sweatpants ride low enough on his hips that she can see the smooth man V arching perfectly.

Oh my.

Stop it, Laura. You're pissed at him.

She snaps back to reality despite truly not wanting to.

"Are you okay?" she chokes out as she closes the door.

His silver eyes flash open. His lips remain in a hard line as he brings the bottle down from his head to rest on the arm of the chair.

"You have fun playing?" he asks with little emotion.

"Yes. Did you have fun next door?" she shoots back.

"Ah," he says. "So, you are pissed."

Laura puts her finger up to the side of her cheek and sarcastically says, "Hmm, let's see. You left with Jessica and disappeared for an hour. Came back and went upstairs without a word about it. How would you feel if I did that?"

She hates that he smirks at her. But it quickly fades. With a serious expression, he asks, "Do you like me, Laura?"

Her jaw drops open. "What? Like you?"

"Yeah, you know what I mean."

Her anger begins to dissipate as she looks at his sincere expression. "I don't particularly like feeling the way I did tonight, but yes, I do. I'd like to think my answer does not come as a surprise."

He drinks the rest of his beer and places it on the small table next to the chair. He runs his hand over his face.

"Where is this coming from?" she asks.

Holding her gaze, he admits, "Jessica."

Laura tips her head back in response. That girl has always been dramatic, and Lord knows, she wasn't right for Tank.

"Really? So, when you had your arm around her, was she putting thoughts in your head that I don't care for you? Is that what's happening here?"

"I did what?" he says as he slides back into the chair, resting his elbows on his knees.

"Tank," she sighs. "I saw you out the window when I was getting my sweater. Are you trying to tell me something? Because if you are, I'd like you to just spit it out."

"When she introduced me to her new *boyfriend*, she made some comment about how being with me taught her everything that she *didn't* want in a relationship. She said it jokingly, but it fucking hurt because it was probably true. And…" He fades off.

Jessica had made several remarks about what a selfish boyfriend Tank was. How he left her alone most of the time. How he cared more about football and his friends in the dorms than he did her. Many of the things she said in jest, but in hindsight, it was mostly true, and the last thing he wants is to treat Laura poorly.

"And what?" Laura asks.

"And I don't want to do that to *you*." He stands and approaches her. "You've been through so much, and I don't want to bring you more heartache."

"That bitch," Laura whispers.

"Whoa. Down, girl," Tank says, motioning downward with his hands. "I know she rubs people the wrong way, but where's that coming from?"

Laura paces back and forth, gathering her thoughts. "You know, just because it didn't work out for her, it doesn't give her the right to assume it won't work with anyone."

He releases a spirited chuckle. "I see I've hit a nerve."

"Well, you've been through a lot, too, and you tried—" She wavers and then adds, "Oh my God, do you think that I'm the *you* in this situation? That I'm the vulnerable one, too fragile for any kind of relationship?"

He places his hand on his bare chest. "No. No, not at all. Let me back up here, okay? She just got me thinking that maybe I'm not very good at this, and I started to question"—he tips his head side to side—"our relationship."

She sits on the edge of the bed. It's funny when a person can see something so differently than how you do. Thinking back, she held back. Because she didn't know what else to do. She wants to open her heart wide, but there are so many scars getting in the way.

She giggles outwardly. "I can remember when I couldn't stand you," she begins.

"Hey"—he chuckles—"you were no picnic either."

"Oh, I know that. Believe me. But now, I feel so differently."

He smiles at her words.

"And I must put things behind me 'cause if I don't, I'll forever remain at a standstill. And I don't think it's fair of her to put doubts in your mind when she has no say in the matter anymore, right? Unless you told me that because you're second-guessing."

"I've been trying so hard to take it slow. To give you time to feel comfortable. But, Laura," he says, "you're all I think about."

Heat fills her cheeks. "Oh."

"Have I gone too slow?" he asks.

She shakes her head. "No, but I think we've both been holding back for everyone else but us."

"I'm sorry," he whispers.

Laura stands and goes over to the door and turns the lock. She spins back around, leaning against the door. "I don't want you to be sorry." She pauses. "I just want you."

Tank moves across the room to be within inches of her. In a deep, sexy voice, he says, "I love hearing you say that, girl."

He wraps his arms around her waist, leaning his large body closer to hers. She gazes up at him with her bright hazel eyes. Her lips part as she reaches her hand up to his hair and runs her fingers over his silky strands.

"It's just us now, right?" she asks.

"Absolutely. I care for you so much. This will be different, I promise you."

She smiles. "It already is."

She stands up on her tippy-toes and presses her lips onto his, wrapping her arms tightly around his neck. A sigh escapes him as he pulls her closer to him. He drags his fingers down the sides of her body, gathering her shirt at the ends and pulling it up over her head. He steps back, admiring her full figure. She's all woman, with curves for days.

She reaches behind her back, and with one quick movement, the hot-pink lace bra loosens around her sides. He reaches up and slowly pulls one strap off and then the other until her lingerie falls to the floor.

"My God, you are spectacular," he whispers.

Licking his lips, he presses them onto hers. Skin to skin, the warmth of their bodies intersects as they both explore one another with their hands. Tank spins her toward the bed, and in one swift motion, he scoops her up in his arms and lays her on the sheets. Seductively, he crawls on top of her, fisting his hands on each side of her as he trails kisses down her neck and to her breasts, sucking and teasing them.

A sexy smile grows across her lips. "Oh, that feels good," she purrs.

His silver eyes glance up to watch her as he continues to tease her with his tongue. The tip of her head and the moan from her lips are almost too much for him. But he wants to make this last. He's waited so long to be with her, and it must be perfect.

He grasps the button on her jeans and twists it open. He eases the zipper down the denim. He reaches for her hips as she wriggles her way out of them.

He's more than hard, and a tightness pulls in his lower body as he licks just below her belly, to the beautiful skin right above her panties.

Her breath catches.

He grazes the fabric with his teeth, teasing his fingers under the edges by pulling them down ever so slightly to expose more of her flesh. He wants to tell her how long he has waited for this moment. He needs her to know that their friendship through good times and bad is what will always make them right for one another. That he recognizes that now more than ever before. It's the only formula in their world for an honest and lasting relationship. Time has proven that for both.

But as he gazes up at this beautiful creature laid out before him, he can't find the words to express that now. The only thing he wants to do is make her feel good with his touch and with his body.

He eases her panties off, and his fingers slowly slide in between her legs. A sweet moan releases from her lips, and she tries to bite back the sounds by pulling her lips down between her teeth.

He kisses his way back up her flawless skin, resting at her side. He watches her softly turn her head side to side as the feeling of wonder lingers over her. He moves the tips of his fingers down further between her legs, his eyes only focused on her face. As he touches her pink flesh, her mouth opens, and she no longer tries to hide the sounds of pleasure.

She's a breathless beauty, he thinks as he watches her intently.

As he moves his fingers with intent, she cries out louder and louder as he brings her to the brink with ease. But the sexy grunts are too much for him, and he captures her mouth with his, twirling his tongue with hers, bringing her back to reality. She throws her arms around his neck, pulling him on top of her.

"I want you," she whispers.

"You sure you're ready?" he asks.

"Yes."

He can tell by her eyes that she's telling the truth, the way they soften and glisten in the dim light. "Let me get something," he says, reluctantly sliding off her and the bed.

He slips off his sweatpants, dropping them to the floor. She leans up onto her elbows to get a better look at the massive man standing before her like a chiseled Greek sculpture. She can't help her grin as she eyes her man.

He eases his enormous body back onto the bed after sliding the condom on. She reaches over and pulls him toward her. He kisses her.

"I've been waiting a long time for this," he says.

He inches his hips closer to her, and with his eyes never leaving hers, he enters her with a gentle thrust. And then another and another. Each time, her hands dig deeper into his skin. He nuzzles into her neck and lets out a groan. He starts to nibble lightly on her shoulder. She hums with approval. Her skin is like porcelain, smooth and flawless. He presses his hands deep into her hips and then pulls her up toward him, moving her along with him. He relishes the goose bumps that grace her skin as he teases her nipple, letting him know he's getting all the right places.

They move together, their legs tangled, hips rocking back and forth. The bed, with the force of Tank's body, pushes against the wall.

"Shh." She giggles. "You're knocking the bed against the wall."

He cradles her head in his arms as he deepens his movements, lust filling his eyes as a bead of sweat glistens off her brow. "What can I say, girl? I've got the moves."

This only entices her to want him more. She presses her hands into his backside, forcing his hips deeper into her. And he gives her everything he has got—and he does have the moves. Tank does not disappoint in the bedroom.

"Oh, Laura," he mumbles as an incredible sensation radiates through him, bringing him to the glorious edge.

He collapses onto her, shivering as his body slowly tries to regulate back to its normal state. He tries desperately to catch his breath. "Girl, you were wonderful," he says with a ragged breath.

Even better than I could have imagined.

Thirty-Eight

Trying for the Truth

"Thanks, Dylan and Maggie. I loved hanging with your friends. It was such a fun night," Laura says as Maggie leans in for a hug.

Dylan and Tank shake hands, and good-byes are said all around the room.

Tank packs up the truck while Laura waits in the cab, warming her fingers in front of the vent. Tank hops in and leans over, giving her a kiss on the cheek. Then, he backs the truck out of the driveway and starts the drive toward campus.

"So, can I say something?" Laura asks.

"Girl, spill it." He laughs.

"I'm going to tell Abigail about us," she blurts out.

His hand slips, jerking the wheel a bit, but he quickly regains control.

"Tank!"

"Sorry, but you just threw it out there." He lets out a deep sigh. "Wow, okay. What changed for you?"

"I don't know, Tank. Last week, last night, tomorrow."

With a devilish grin, he says, "Last night indeed." He rubs his hand on her leg. "Can I just tell you again how sexy you are?"

She blushes. "I do love that you keep telling me that…"

"It's true," he quickly adds.

"Anyway, can we focus, please? I really need to tell her. This just doesn't feel right."

He sighs deeply. "I agree. I miss her. This is so long overdue. We've both avoided talking to her."

"I know, and I miss her, too."

"It's the right thing to do, and I'm glad you're going to tell her, Laura. She'll want to hear it from you."

"So, it's settled. I'll talk to her. But before then, I need to chat with Officer Murphy and put an end to this investigation. At least, I hope to."

"Good luck with that."

"Could you drop me off at the station?" she asks as they near campus.

"Boy, you are one dedicated Nancy Drew."

She rolls her eyes. "What can I say? It's in my DNA or something. I have no idea where this all comes from."

"I feel the same about my passions."

"What's your major again?"

"Nice try. I haven't told you yet. You'll have to figure it out."

"You really want me to uncover another mystery?" She laughs, and then with a mischievous grin, she says, "Challenge accepted."

He pulls into the lot of the police station. "Should I wait for you?"

"Nah, Wolfie is meeting me here. I called him from Dylan's and told him to come. And then he said he'll drop me off at the station. I need to finish a few things there, too."

Tank shakes his head and smiles. "You continue to surprise me."

She leans over toward him, and her lips meet his. She whispers, "I'm glad."

He hums, "Girl, come see me later, will you?"

"A Sunday night sleepover?"

"Sleep? Meh. Other things? Yes."

Her breath catches as she locks eyes with him. Memories of last night flood her mind. "I'd like that," she chokes out. "I'll be by later," she says.

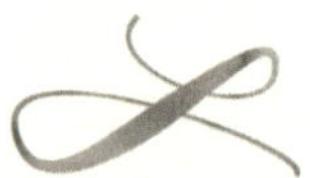

Wolfie is sitting across the desk from Officer Murphy, pleading with him to drop the investigation, when Laura is escorted in by an officer.

"Laura," Officer Murphy says, "do you agree with Wolfie's assessment of the situation?"

Sitting down adjacent to him, she says, "Yes, wholeheartedly. I think this is something that can't be proven but can be reconciled."

"Officer Murphy," Wolfie begs, "we cannot put this woman's sexuality on display to prove something that cannot and will not be verified. Unless you catch him in the act, right? It's clear to us he acted out of confusion and jealousy and, quite frankly, something his puny brain could not accept."

Officer Murphy rubs his face, contemplating his next move. "I have to talk to her if I'm going to close this case. So, whatever you need to do to get her in here, I need it done by Friday at the latest."

Wolfie and Laura exchange glances.

"I think I can get her to agree," Laura says.

Officer Murphy stands. "Okay, please tell her to come see me and that no one will know why she's here. We agree?"

"Agree," they say in unison.

Laura and Wolfie leave the station and climb into his car.

"What's with the bag of clothes? Am I dropping you off at home? Or the station?" he asks.

Her cheeks burn as she stumbles over her words, "The station. I-I had—I mean, I was away last night."

"Where?" He smirks.

"Well, I went with…" Saying it out loud makes it concrete, and while she knows he'll be happy for her, this is new territory. "So, Tank invited me to a friend's condo, and we went there…last night."

Without skipping a beat, he says, "Tough loss for them."

"It sure was. Did you hear what I said though?"

With a grin, he says, "Do you really think I don't know you hang out with him?"

"I have for years," she adds.

"Okay, so this now means you're dating?" he says.

"Maybe. What do you think?" she asks.

"I think I'm happy for you because I only *want* you to be happy, Laura. You deserve it."

"You're really happy for me?"

He chuckles and says with such kindness that her eyes well with tears, "*Our* Laura, dating one of the most popular football players on campus. Who would have thought? Be happy, Laura Chase. It's what you need in your life."

"Our Laura," she whispers.

As he pulls in front of the Union, he pats her leg and says, "Yeah, our Laura. You know he'd be so happy to know that you're moving forward. I'll never say you've moved on. Only forward. I'm happy for you. He seems like a great guy."

"He is," she says. "He's really good to me."

"Good. Now, let me know when you talk to Kate, and hopefully, we can put this debacle behind us. I'll chat with Melissa and see how the paper wants to handle putting this to bed."

She opens the car door. "Thanks, Wolfie."

"You are most welcome."

Laura enters the Union and heads down the hallway toward the station.

She nears the common area and is about to stop near the communal board, where the school posts the latest flyers and announcements of school activities, when she hears a familiar voice call her name, "Laura!"

She turns, and her face betrays her as it flushes a lovely shade of pink. Tank comes strutting toward her. Their eyes meet from a distance, only this time—for the first time—it's as lovers, and her heart is aflutter.

Look at him, my new man. Never thought this day would happen for me. And I am so glad it's with him. He's perfect for me. I'm so comfortable with him. Not a care in the world when it comes to us because, above all, we're friends, tried and true.

No sooner do these beautiful thoughts waft through her mind, like childish daydreams, than they quickly fade as she notices Tank's expression darken, the closer he gets to her.

Alarmed, she steps toward him as he leans in to whisper in her ear, and they speak at the same time.

"What's wrong?"

"I need to talk to you," he says.

"Okay," she says, remaining close to him.

"When I got home, Nathan was livid," he says.

"What? Why?" Laura's heart is pounding harder and harder in her chest.

"He went over to apologize to Kelly about the fight at the party, and Abby's car was in the driveway. All four of her tires were slashed."

Laura gasps; she's at a loss for words.

"He gave no explanation for it, and a flatbed truck was taking it away. That's all Kelly would say. How messed up is that?"

"That's so not right. What is going on?"

"No clue. But Nathan is not okay. He's so worried about her, and she won't talk to him."

"I'll try and get to her. But I'll need to be careful, too. Because that's bad news, and I'm concerned it could be serious, right?"

"Yeah. You'll know how to handle it. Let me know, okay? I'll see you tonight. I'd better get back to him."

"Bye."

Laura opens the door and is not surprised to find the house quiet, although she hoped it wouldn't be. Now that Wolfie knows about her and Tank, the necessity to fill in Abigail on her relationship weighs heavy on her mind.

Maybe if I share my news with her, I can convince her to be friends with Tank again. They can put all their disagreements behind them, and we can go back to how we once were.

But I also need to ask her about her car. I almost can't believe it's true. I believe Tank, but to slash all four tires of someone's car, right in someone else's driveway, is not only bold, but it is also evidently a serious cry for…what? I have no idea.

Laura climbs the stairs to the third floor. Abigail's bedroom door is ajar. She knocks once.

"Abigail, you in there?"

Silence.

Laura knocks again for good measure and then enters the empty room. The window near the fire escape ladder is slightly open, and it's exceptionally cool in her room. Laura finds a notepad on her desk, removes a piece, and leaves a note on Abigail's desk.

I have something important to talk to you about. Please come find me as soon as possible. This can't wait. Love you, Laura.

Out of habit, Laura closes the door upon exiting. The force of the door latching shut and the open window causes the note to fall delicately off her desk and back and forth until it finds its way under her bed.

Thirty-Nine

Can We Talk?

Laura is not surprised when Kate's expression drops when she opens the door to find her standing on her porch.

"Hey," Laura says. "Can we talk?"

She starts to close the door as she says, "I was wondering when I'd see you again."

"Sorry about that. I had to take care of a few things."

"Well, I wasn't eager, if that is what you're thinking." She smiles a touch. "Sorry, this is just not my favorite topic."

"For what it's worth, mine neither." She peers past Kate. "Do you want to take a walk?"

"Not necessary. Only Shannon is upstairs."

"Got you. I'll be brief. Officer Murphy would like to see you at the station before Friday—"

Kate's eyes grow wide. "Wait. I have to talk to the police?"

"Let me explain. We talked to him, and he will agree to drop this after he speaks to you. He's insisting. But he promised me he'd let it go."

"Really?" Kate says, relief on her face.

"Yes. Unless they catch him in the act, it's merely impossible to prove. I'd say, with one semester left in school, he has no desire to confess and throw his life away."

"So, I talk to the cops, and this whole thing goes away?"

"Pretty much."

"What about the paper?"

"We're going to work on that and try and squash it. I have my contact at the paper handling that."

"And what about him? He just walks away?"

Laura shrugs her shoulders. "I guess so. But then again, it's a hard thing to forget you've done. So, one could say he will carry that with him forever."

Kate's eyes soften. "I suppose you're right."

"I hope I am," Laura says.

"I'll go see Officer Murphy tomorrow," Kate says.

Laura smiles. "I'm glad to hear that. But one more thing before I go."

"What's that?" Kate asks.

"I'm so very sorry this happened to you and the girls. You deserve so much better."

"Thanks, Laura."

"But I've seen people, friends I care about, hide the greatest parts of themselves, and in the end, the only one who truly suffered was them. That, to me, is the saddest thing about it. I hope you don't go at it alone because there tends to be a lot more kindness in people than we give them credit for. They just need to be given the opportunity to show you."

Kate smiles for the first time. "Thanks, Laura," she whispers. "I suppose I didn't give my teammates a chance to be there for me."

"Well, that's not for me to say, but I just saw how much Shannon wanted to protect you the other night, and it dawned on me that given the circumstances, she seems like the person who would be there for you, no matter what. I know Jen would, too." Laura bounds down the stairs. Then, she turns and says, "I'll see you around."

She hops into her car and closes the door. Looking toward the porch, she sees that Shannon has joined Kate. With tears in her eyes, Kate says something to Shannon, and almost immediately, the two are embracing.

Laura hopes this was their opportunity for the truth because only then can they grow closer.

Laura might not have been entirely truthful with Officer Murphy and Wolfie about her plan. But she knew if she told them what she had in mind, they'd never allow her to go and talk to Guthrie. And sometimes, you have to take matters into your own hands. Like on this particularly cold and dark evening.

The lights on the walls illuminate the hallway inside the Silver building. Laura takes the stairs to the top level and wanders down the hall. From a distance and through the glass-paneled doorway, she sees him bent over his canvas.

Realizing her hands are balled tight, she shakes them free. *Relax. I've got this.* Laura takes a deep breath, counts to five, and then enters the space.

"What brings you here tonight?" Guthrie says.

"Nice to see you, too," she says, trying to appear unaffected by his presence.

A comment like that doesn't faze him in the least. He lives off sarcasm.

"Trying to get some more intel for your radio piece?" he asks.

"No," she says rather dryly. "I came to talk to you." Now, she has his full attention.

He grabs his rag, wipes the paint from his hands, and drops it on his desk. "Shoot."

Laura has envisioned this conversation taking place from the minute she met him that night at the art event. So, while never really being at a loss for words and occupationally gifted with a quick mind, she says, "I've studied your work. I've taken notes on your disposition. I remember things you've said. Expressions you've bestowed upon others. But what has stuck out to me the most is the reaction I got the night I brought you to the party."

"Reaction?" he says, his eyes narrowing at her. "How so?"

"It was clear to me that I invited someone who wasn't well-liked or welcomed, and while I tried my best to keep you from knowing that, I now *want* you to know."

He lets out a dark chuckle and then says flatly, "How kind of you."

"Are you surprised?" she asks.

"Of course I am."

"I'm not. Considering what you've done."

"What I've done?" he asks, his stare cold and hollow.

"Yes, you wanted to hurt her. You wanted her to know that you were still in control of her. You knew she was vulnerable, and you exploited that."

Clearly unruffled, he asks, "Who is *she* exactly?"

"Guthrie, you know exactly who I'm talking about. And the police know, too."

"The police? Are you fucking kidding me?"

Her radar goes off as he takes a step closer to her. "I wouldn't come an inch closer. Tank is right outside, and I scream once, and he's in here. Understand?" she says.

He scoffs, "I knew you were friends with him. Figures. You all stick together."

"I'd rather stick with them than the likes of you."

He leans back on his desk. "So, what, Laura? What are you going to do?"

"She doesn't want to see you. But the police have other plans for you, and if I were you, graduating in a semester, I'd try and make it right. If for nothing else than to save your rotting soul."

"Is that a fact?" he says.

"Yes, as a matter of fact, I was at the police station this morning."

"If they know so much, why haven't I been arrested—or even questioned for that matter?" he asks.

"Because I asked them not to. And while I think what you did is inexcusable, I also believe there is an opportunity to make this right. And not just for her. But for every student on this campus who has gone through enough the last year and a half. It's about time we put this all behind us and try and make this a better place."

"You expect *me* to do that?"

"Why do you think I'm here and the police aren't? It was no coincidence that Tank and I attended the art show. Or came back to look further into your work, or invited you to the party, or—"

"Enough!" he yells. "Are you even a student here, or are you some kind of undercover—" He rubs his temples.

"I only want to be proud of the school that I'll hold a degree from. Don't you?"

It's as though for the first time, he contemplates the ramifications of his actions. The dark stain he painted on the university. He did that through intolerable words. This is on him. And he knows it.

He folds his paint-spattered arms across his chest. "They have nothing on me, and I'll admit to nothing," he says.

"I didn't expect that you would. But mark my words, the police do, and they are trying to give you a second chance. And they are giving it *once*, and that is it. If you don't take it, they'll proceed, and I won't stop them nor would I want to," she mumbles.

He stares at her with disgust. "What are you proposing?"

Laura explains the only option he has. Agree to it, or she tells the police to do as they must.

Reluctantly, he agrees.

"I'll meet you outside by the picnic table. Eight o'clock. Alone," she says.

"Fine," he grumbles. "Now, kindly leave."

"Gladly," she says.

The silence in the hallways gives her the creeps, so she rushes down the steps until she's finally outside.

I can't believe I just did that. But I had to. I couldn't let him get away with what he did. Travis would have gotten this student body the answers they deserved, and without him, that left me to do it. Wolfie will handle the paper once I've gotten exactly what I need from Guthrie. But I knew he'd only trust me. I know he'll meet me at eight. He wants this erased from his life just as much as I want it inked on paper.

She hops into her car, hands shaking as she touches the steering wheel, and she drives, heavy-footed, straight to Tank's apartment.

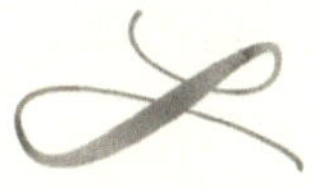

Tank pulls the door open and says, "Girl, where have you been?"

She steps in. "I know; I know. I'm sorry I'm late."

"Are you okay?" he asks.

"Yeah. Been a long day."

He takes the bag off her shoulder. "Let me get you a beer," he says, and she follows him into the living room. "Take a load off," he says.

Laura sits on the couch, nervously waiting for Tank to return. She knows she'll have to tell him where she was. "Where is everyone?" she asks.

"Nathan and Logan are at the library."

"How's Nathan?"

"He's as you'd expect. Confused and really frustrated that he can't help her or at least know what's happening with her. It's killing him."

"She wasn't home. I left her a note. I'll do my best to find out what happened."

"Thanks. I really want to know she's okay, too. It's really fucked up."

"Totally. Um, where's Webber tonight?" she asks, desperate to not think about Abigail for a while.

"Webber is helping that girl Daisy study or some crap like that. It's a scam if you ask me." He hands Laura a cold beer as he sits next to her, draping his massive arm on the back of the cushion.

"Scam? Care to explain?"

"Not a big fan of Daisy's," he says.

"Clearly. Why?"

"I don't like how she flaunts herself with Webber. I feel like she's using him."

"Really? Ouch. Poor guy."

"Yeah, she knows how to work her way into getting him to help her. He keeps inviting her here, and she acts like this is her apartment to party in. I don't like the way she talks to him. Or talks *at* him, like he doesn't matter as much as us. I just don't like it. She'd better not mess with him."

"Have you told him this?"

"How can I? I stay out of it. Guy has gotta get laid in college."

Beer spits from Laura's mouth. She wipes the back of her hand. "Tank! Warn me when you're going to say stuff like that!"

"Oh, come on. How long have you known him? It's so not cool that the guy can't find a girl. Shit, someday, we'll all be working for him. He'll be getting laid day and night."

"You really think Webber is the kind of guy who just wants to lose his virginity for the sake of losing it?"

"At this point, yes!" Tank laughs. "That's exactly what I think he wants."

"You guys are unreal!" She laughs.

"Can you blame him?"

"Haven't spent a lot of time thinking about it, but no, can't say that I can."

"Anyway," he says, inching closer to her on the couch, "enough about Webber. Let's talk about you. What kept you tonight?"

In hindsight, going to the art room alone might have been one of the dumbest things Laura has done in a while. She knew this when pulling into the parking lot, but she did it anyway. She needed to get answers. And she only knows how to do things one way. The way Travis taught her.

"I was in Silver," she says quietly.

Tank's brows bend, and his eyes narrow. "And why were you there, Laura?"

"Well…see, I needed to talk—"

"Please tell me you did not go there to talk to Guthrie," he says.

"Let me explain." She gulps.

"Was Wolfie with you?"

Now, she could lie, but what good would that do? "No, I was—"

"Alone?"

"Tank, let me explain. I had to tell him that the police know."

Tank immediately stands. "Wait a second. You went to see him and told him the police are onto him? Are you crazy?"

"I'm not crazy," she says.

"Okay, so not crazy but really out of your mind? The guy's a criminal, and you went there alone, at night, to tell him he might be arrested. What if he hurt you? Or what if—oh, I'm so mad at you. You could have gotten in trouble, and not a soul knew where you were!"

"I'm sorry," she says. "But I had to do it. They can't arrest him without evidence, and this needs to end."

"I'm just going to say this because I'm pissed at you, but I'm not certain if Wolfie—or dare I say, Travis—lets you do this kind of shit, Laura, but I won't."

Her cheeks burn red.

"I'm sorry if that is harsh to say. But you know how I feel about protecting my girls, and when I can't…it eats me up inside."

"Tank," she says, standing and taking his hand in hers. "I never even thought of that, and I'm even more sorry that I didn't let you know."

His eyes meet hers. "You know I would have gone with you. I could have sat in the car. Just in case you needed me."

She tugs on his hand. "If it makes you feel better, I told him you were outside, and that seemed to do the trick."

"Don't use my name if I'm not going to actually be able to do anything," he gibes.

"But just the mention of your name kept him in check. *And* I did get him to agree to put an end to all of this."

"You did?"

"Yep. While I admit it was stupid of me to go, I'd made a promise to Kate that I would do everything in my power to squash this once and for all."

"What did he agree to?" he asks.

"I gave him until Friday. Eight o'clock. I'm meeting him near Silver. By then, I'll know."

"This is the part where you ask me to go with you," he says.

"Yes, yes. I get it. But I'm quite capable of managing on my own. I've succeeded in surviving up to this point," she says, dropping his hand in protest, and she spins to walk away.

He quickly swipes his arms around her waist, pulling her back into his chest. He leans his cheek next to hers and whispers, "Oh no, girl. You're not walking away from me. I'm the one who's upset, remember?" He runs his other hand up the front of her stomach and her chest until he reaches her chin, tipping it back. He plants a kiss on her neck. "Now, listen to me. From now on, you need to fill me in on these little adventures of yours, okay?"

He pulls her earlobe into his mouth, grazing his teeth across it. Her breath catches.

"Laura?"

"Mmhmm," she replies.

His hand wanders from her neck down to the opening of her shirt, and he eases his hand inside the fabric, tracing his fingers over her cleavage. "I'll do anything for you, understand?" His tone is sultry as he slips his fingers over her nipple, pulling the bud between his thumb and forefinger.

She gasps, leaning her head back as she enjoys the attention. He continues to kiss her neck as he presses his body firmly against her back, letting her know how hard he is.

"Can…can we go upstairs?" she asks.

"Absolutely," he says as he spins her to face him, landing his mouth onto her pink lips, claiming what he knows to be his. He pulls back and scoops her up into his arms. "I'm going to make you feel so good," he says with an incredibly sexy smile.

She gulps. And then with a laugh, she says, "Maybe I should be bad more often."

Forty

It Hit the Fan. All of It.

A few days later, Tank and Laura bound down the stairs and into the dark kitchen. He switches on the light, and Laura immediately jumps.

"Jesus." She claps her hand over her heart. "Webber, why are you sitting in the dark?"

His expression can only be described as downtrodden. Unusual for him. "I didn't know you guys were home," he mumbles.

"Shit, girl," Tank whispers to Laura. "I really gotta go." He's already late for his meeting with his study group in the library.

"I got this," she says softly.

He leans down and kisses her. "Call me." He gives Webber a sympathetic glance before exiting their apartment door.

Laura enters the kitchen area and sits in the chair across from Webber at the kitchen table.

"You okay?" she asks.

"Not really. Abigail is super pissed at me. Nathan asked me to get her to come to the lab, so he could talk to her, and she knows I lied to her to get her to see him. Now, she hates me, too."

"I think you did what you had to do," Laura says. She recalls her conversation with Nathan and Tank, in which she informed them about the comment Abigail said to her in her studio about Nathan potentially getting Poppy pregnant, which had been news to Laura.

And Webber might be the only one who could corner Abigail into a conversation with Nathan. It's no secret he's had a crush on Abigail since the moment he laid eyes on her nearly three years ago. But what was a nerdy, generally awkward guy supposed to do when a beautiful blonde sauntered into his Advanced Biology class freshman year? The class wherein he was too shy to ask for a lab partner, so he thought it was better to go it alone. But then she came along, and the professor paired them up. No questions asked. Little did they know at the time, their partnership in *that* science class would be going on for six full semesters of school now.

So, when Nathan stood before him, begging his roommate of the same length of years to get Abigail alone, Webber couldn't say no. After all, Nathan had become one of his best friends, too.

Webber was paired with Nathan as a freshman, through a simple letter sent to both their homes the summer before their freshman year. Webber—the quiet, socially uncomfortable first-year student—happened to be matched with who would end up being one of the most popular guys on campus. And the guy who landed the girl of *his* dreams.

"And on top of all of that this past year, I feel completely out of the loop."

"Tell me about it." *Abigail and I might as well live on separate planets.*

Webber huffs, "Please, you guys know everything and don't fill me in on shit."

"That's fair," she admits.

"Is it? I'm nothing but a good friend. And where has that gotten me, huh?" His anger, while seemingly out of the blue for Webber, must be coming from someplace deep within.

"Webber, do you really want to know all of the crap people go through?" she asks. "Because, sometimes, I wish I knew nothing at all."

He tips his head. "I don't know. I couldn't say until I know it."

Laura eyes him and then slowly rises from the table. She removes two beers from the refrigerator and returns, placing one in front of him while she takes a sip of hers. With a peculiar grin, she says, "You know, there is a reason the expression *the shit hit the fan* exists. People use it a lot, but I'd say, it most definitely describes the series of disasters that have happened these past several months. This little world we live in here, while a nice bubble, sometimes can feel as though it's getting out of control. I think that accurately describes what has happened this past week, even more so. The bubbling over of it all and the small world encompassed at OSU in my mind finally burst."

"I've never known you to be so dramatic, Laura." He chuckles while leaning back in his chair.

"Oh, it's not me, Webber. It's this place."

"Really? Why?"

"Just remember you asked." She laughs. "Well, after the fight that involved Poppy and Clay at the house party, Nathan thought in order to at least look a little bit better in Abigail's eyes, he should go over to Kelly's place to apologize for his part in the fight with Clay."

"Fight?"

"Yeah, you were away, home for the weekend, but there was a scuffle at a party. When Nathan was too drunk to help Poppy, Kelly stepped in and kicked Clay's ass. Anyway, Nathan's plan was to thank Kelly for rushing into a situation that had nothing to do with him when Nathan was too intoxicated to react the right way."

"Nathan has only been drinking more 'cause he misses Abby. As sad as that might be. He doesn't handle himself well. And with Poppy around, he gets worse. Like, he can't get out of his own way with Poppy in the picture. I wish that girl would just go away. I don't care for her."

"No one really does, but you'll see why we all feel bad for her."

"Okay," he says, sipping his beer.

"But when Nathan got to Kelly's house, Abigail's convertible was parked in Kelly's driveway, and all the tires on her car were flat. Nathan quickly realized they were slashed."

"Slashed?!"

"Yep. And I guess Nathan showed up at the same time a flatbed truck was arriving to haul her car away. The two had it out, naturally. It must have been so weird for Nathan to see her car there and in that condition. So, it does make you wonder if Kelly is a bad guy. But then again, it's hard to imagine when we're close with Alex. But someone doesn't like the fact that Kelly and Abigail are an item. I think they were trying to send a message to Abigail to stay away from Kelly. But who?"

"That is messed up," Webber says, taking another sip of his beer.

"Totally, but with Nathan out of the picture, Tank out of the picture, and you not knowing, who could say something to her? Me."

"Makes sense."

"Right, so I got home the next day, and in the driveway was her car with four brand-new snow tires. So, I asked her about them, and she was visibly angry with me for some reason. Then, it dawned on me that Abigail had no idea why she'd gotten new tires."

"What?"

"Yeah, obviously, he never told her. By the way, Alex told me he works at a mechanic shop on Route 20."

"See, and you actually think I don't want to know this kind of stuff?" Webber says.

"Well, I'm on a roll now, so there's much more to tell you."

Shaking his head, he says with a slight chuckle, "Jesus, I can't even imagine."

"Oh, it's worse. So, Abigail hadn't stopped by the radio station in months. And she marched into the station to confront me about our conversation over the tires. But in hindsight, thank God she did because she blurted out why she had been avoiding Nathan and why you shouldn't feel bad for trapping her in the lab building."

"Really?" He perks up. "Wait, is this about Poppy and the pregnancy?"

"See! You know things, Webber. And, yes, the reason she was avoiding Nathan like the plague was that she was told by *Casey* that Nathan had cheated on her with Poppy and gotten her pregnant!"

"Casey?"

"Yeah, how could she not believe it, right?"

"Ouch. Casey is going to feel like crap for that huge drop of misinformation."

"Poor Casey. She was just trying to help, I think. But, now, you know all I do," Laura says.

"Well, I guess I don't feel as bad for getting her there for Nathan. He did tell me about Poppy. But Abigail was so mad at me. She didn't know the truth when he walked in, and you didn't see the look of hurt on her face. She was really disappointed in me."

"I'm sure she was. But you can explain it all to her. Trust me, she'll forgive you. She needs all the friends she can get. My gut is telling me something is off. Big time."

"I hate hearing that. She's such a special person," he whispers.

"Talk to her," Laura encourages.

"I will," he says.

"And about what you said before. You *are* a great friend Webber, and hopefully, if you ever need us to return the favor, we'll be there for you. No questions asked." Laura reaches across the table and squeezes his hand.

A massive grin spreads across his face, and then he adds, "I do know one more thing that you don't."

"What's that?" Laura says.

"My roommate Tank is *in love*."

Forty-One

Problem Nine

Two days later, a lab assignment forces Webber and Abigail back into the same building. This time, there is no ruse of any sort; it is merely the trappings of academia that brought them together.

"Please forgive me," Webber begs.

Abigail crosses her arms over her chest. "Why should I?" she grumbles.

"Because you know me, and you know I had to try and help. I can't stand this anymore," he says. He removes his glasses and squeezes the bridge of his nose. "I hate all of this so much."

"And you don't think I do?"

"Of course I do. But what is anyone doing about it?" he pleads.

"I went back over yesterday to talk to Nathan to try and smooth things over. I realize I believed something that wasn't true. But I was hurt. He hurt me, and it all snowballed into anger. Quite honestly, I felt isolated from you guys. I was no longer the former Abby. I was back to being Abigail, the girl on the outside of it all."

Webber puts his glasses back on. "Oh, Abigail, I need you to know that we have all missed you so much."

"Thanks, Webber." Her eyes soften. "I admit, I've missed all of you. But there was a part of me that needed the break in order to heal my heart. I was crushed. It hasn't been an easy year."

"Believe me, I get it. But the year isn't over, right?"

"No, but out of respect for Kelly, it's not exactly easy to say I'm going to my ex-boyfriend's apartment."

"Abigail," he says, "we're your friends. If he can't get that, then fuck him."

Her eyes grow wide. "Webber! Wow, tell me how you really feel."

"I think I just did."

"Well, what do you propose I do?"

"I don't have a clue. But all I know is, we need you back. And he will just have to learn to share you."

"I'm not so sure they all want me around."

"Yes, they do. Trust me. We've been friends, a group, for years, and now, you're the missing piece. It just doesn't feel right, not having you around. You must feel it, too."

"Laura and I are not on the same page. It's my fault. I should have made more of an effort, but a part of me was hurt that she'd teamed up with them."

"Teamed up? You have it all wrong, and you really need to talk to her. You're best friends. You can't let misunderstandings get in the way of that."

"I know you're right. I do. But I never see her, and if I do…well, it's seeing her at your apartment. It just felt so bizarre. So much time has passed, and now, I'm the odd man out. It's weird, Webber."

"Only because you guys are making it weird. Get over it and get back together…all of you…before I lose my mind!" He's sucking in the air like he can't catch his breath.

"Webber, are you okay?" she asks, gently touching his arm.

"Yeah. Yes, I'm fine. I suppose so. I'm meeting a friend here in a few minutes, and I have no idea what the deal is with us."

Abigail smiles. "Us? Do tell."

Webber's cheeks turn bright red. "I can't talk about it now. She'll be here any minute."

"Well then, I shall leave you to compose yourself." Abigail laughs.

"It's good to see you smile, smart-ass," he gibes.

"It's good to see you, my friend." She puts her notebook in her bag and slings it over her shoulder. "And whoever she is, she is one lucky girl. You just remember that." She backs away from the lab bench and heads toward the door.

"Come around more," he yells after her.

She waves and heads toward the stairs in the basement to the main level. As she glances up, she sees Aniston laughing with a friend as she pulls open the door to the building. Desperate to be unseen, Abigail ducks behind the wall to the left and waits for them to pass. She can hear their heels as they click on the staircase, descending to the basement.

"Does he know you don't like him?" Abigail hears Aniston ask.

"And ruin this good thing?" the other girl says. "No fucking way, and you'd better not blow my cover," she sneers.

"Now, why would I do that? I'm benefiting from this, too. Remember?"

"Good thing we're the only ones benefiting." She laughs as they pass the wall where Abigail is hiding behind. "Can you imagine?" the girl whispers. "How gross."

"Shh," Aniston warns. "Don't let him hear you."

"I'm in control," the girl says. "Now, put on a perky smile," she says to Aniston as she pulls open the door to the lab.

"Webby," she hears her say. "My favorite person."

Abigail's heart sinks. *Poor Webber. I hope this isn't the girl he's all hot and bothered over. She sounds like a real piece of work. But it's just like Webber to help people when they don't deserve his help.*

And Aniston…ugh. She's the worst person. I just despise her. I must find the right time to let Webber know he's hanging out with the wrong women. But is it really my place these days to crush his heart? The look on his face when he spoke about her…it was so obvious. If I can talk to Laura and make all things right with her, maybe she can help get the message to him before it's too late.

Forty-Two

Laura's Lessons

Laura exhales deeply as she pulls out of her driveway at ten of eight Friday evening.

"See," Tank says. "Imagine how nervous you would be without me by your side."

She bats her eyes at him. "My hero."

He smirks and playfully touches her leg. "Girl, I know I am."

"Men." She laughs.

"I think you meant, manly. 'Cause, that's what I am—manly."

She laughs as she turns east toward the academic buildings. Then, Laura notices quick reflections of light in her rearview mirror, drawing her attention to glance backward. "Who's behind me, flashing their lights?"

Tank spins in the seat to glimpse over his shoulder. "Just ignore them. We can't be late, or Guthrie might take off," he notes, pointing to the clock.

The car stops flashing but continues down the same road toward campus.

Before Laura pulls into the lot, Tank reclines the passenger seat, so he can't be noticed in the car.

"He's here," she whispers as she notices the shadow of a man sitting at the picnic table. As Laura is about to open her car door, a car pulls into the lot and parks next to her. She tries not to pay attention. "I'll be back," she says, opening the door.

She hears, "Laura, it's me."

Abigail has rolled down her window.

"Fuck, not now," Tank says.

"Abigail," Laura says quickly, "it's is not a good time. You have to leave. *Now.*"

Tank motions for her to leave. "Go," he says through gritted teeth.

Hurt settles in her eyes, and Abigail, embarrassed by the poor reception from her former friends, says, "Fine." She jerks her car into reverse and screeches out of the lot.

The commotion has caused Guthrie to be on the move, and Laura sees him scurry like a rat back along the building.

"Wait, wait," she yells.

He ducks around the building. Nervously, Tank gets out of the car and chases after Laura as she heads around the corner. He hides on the edge of the building as he hears voices.

"What was that about?" he barks.

"Nothing. My friend saw me driving and stopped to say hi. I didn't ask her to, and she left. It's cool. I promise."

"Whatever. Let's get this over with." He thrusts an envelope at her.

"Can I trust you that you've done the right thing?" Laura says.

"You'll have to," he quips, and then his tone softens. "I did the right thing."

"Good," she says and spins on her heel to leave.

"Laura," he calls after her.

She stops and turns back to face him. "Yeah?"

"I'm not the monster you all think I am," he says.

"No, you're just an asshole." And quickly, she dips back behind the building and to her car, where Tank is climbing back in.

Tank reaches over to her trembling hands. "You okay?"

"Yeah, that was just ten of the craziest and most intense minutes that I can remember," she says, shifting her car in reverse.

"What was Abby doing here?" Tank asks.

"Maybe it was her who was flashing the lights? Why was she trying to get my attention?"

"How strange that she was here," he says.

"But I can't deal with that now. I have to get this to Melissa," she says as she veers toward the Rounds Hall.

Melissa and Wolfie are waiting in her office. The room is lit only by the lamp on her desk. Laura and Tank enter.

"Did you get it?" Melissa asks.

Laura holds up the envelope.

"That is amazing," Wolfie says.

"Well, we still don't know what he said," Laura says as she tears open the seal and pulls out the handwritten letter on a torn piece of notebook paper. "Want me to read it out loud?"

"Yes," Tank says.

She tries to steady her quivering hands as she holds up the paper to read aloud. Clearing her throat, she glances briefly at the three very eager faces waiting for her to speak.

After concluding the letter, they all remain silent.

Until Tank says, "Wow. How did you get him to confess?"

"Simple. He writes the letter, or Officer Murphy moves forward."

"I'm impressed, Laura. I have to admit, I didn't think he'd do it," Melissa says.

"He'd be stupid not to write it. He remains anonymous still," Wolfie adds, to which Laura smiles wide. "What's with the grin?" he asks.

"Because what he never considered is that this letter," she says, shaking it in her hand, "will be printed in *his* school paper for everyone on campus to read. Imagine the bustle this is going to bring. He'll never be able to get away from it. At least, not for a long time. And the best part? It'll be out there forever. Other papers will pick it up. Years from now, it will still be in our archives. Once it's printed, it lives on for eternity."

Melissa tips her head back in laughter. "You could not be more right! It's a worse punishment than being questioned by the police."

"Exactly. They never had any evidence against him, and he never even asked me if they did. This, in my book, is how the punishment fits the crime. He's getting exactly what he deserves. And Officer Murphy thinks that all those other instances in which he was seen in the photos, he was simply interested as an artist and in some ways, gaining the courage to someday do it."

Tank glances over at her with admiration in his eyes. *My God, she's amazing, and she's all mine. How did a guy like me get so lucky?*

"Do we let Kate know ahead of time?" Wolfie asks.

Laura glances at her teammates and softly asks, "Would you guys let me handle that?"

"Of course. Is there anything I can do?" Melissa asks.

"Yeah. Can I get a clean copy before it goes out Monday morning?"

"Sure thing. We can leave together on Monday and come here. We can get the first copy then."

"Works for me," Laura says. Then, she turns to Tank, "We should go and find Abigail."

"She okay?" Melissa asks.

"She saw me driving and almost caused Guthrie to run. We had to tell her to leave without explanation, and she was clearly hurt by that."

"Yikes. Well, good luck with that. Wolfie and I have some work to do on this. So, I'll see you later?" Melissa asks.

"See you at home," Laura says.

"Bye, all. Great job on this," Tank says as he follows her out the door.

Abigail is perched in her window. The light on her desk and a few candles are all that can be seen from the driveway as Laura and Tank pull in and park.

"I'm nervous," Laura admits. "What if we waited too long to tell her and she doesn't forgive me? I'll die if that is the case."

"I'm nervous, too," he says.

"What? You can't be nervous. *I'm* nervous."

"She's mad at me for leaving her when she needed me. And rightfully so. I'm in real deep, and it scares the shit out of me that maybe I've failed her and she won't forgive *me*."

"Fuck," Laura says, running her hands through her hair. "We're screwed."

Tank grabs her hand, and with a gentle tug, he says, "There is only one way to find out. Come on."

He drops her hand and opens the car door. She reluctantly follows, dragging her feet up the stairs to the porch.

"If she browbeats us," Laura says, "we just have to take it, okay?"

"Agreed. Now, let's get this over with, so we can move on, hopefully."

The house is empty, and there are no signs of life. As they climb the stairs to the third floor, the soft hum of music can be heard through her door. Laura knocks, quiet at first and then a little louder.

"Come in," they hear.

Laura opens the door. Abigail is sitting on the sill, overlooking the campus sprinkled like tiny points of light in the night's sky. Her hair flows down her back, her arms wrapped tightly around her knees. A peculiar expression is on her face as she only turns her head to see who is at the door.

"Hello," Laura says.

"Hey," Tanks adds, his voice tight and strained.

She swings her legs over the edge of the wooden ledge and faces them. "What brings you guys here?"

Laura hurries over. "Abigail, I am so sorry about earlier."

"Yeah," Tank chimes in.

"I was there to meet someone, and he was very specific that I come alone. When he saw you, he started to run, and we couldn't let him get away," she blurts out.

Abigail narrows her eyes. "Is that so? Then, why were you there?" she asks, meeting Tank's eyes for the first time since he entered her room.

His skin flames red. He wants to answer her honestly. But his honest answer might send her over the edge. "I was there to protect—" he says at the very same moment Laura tries to save him by interjecting, "He was there to look out for—" But she stops.

"I see," Abigail says. "You were there to protect her. How nice of you."

"I deserve that," he mumbles.

"You're damn right you do," Abigail says.

Laura glances over at Tank as he takes his first blow, and then she says, "We came here to apologize for not only tonight, but also for the—"

"Laura, can I?" Tank asks as he passes her and takes a seat on the couch, facing Abigail.

"Abby, I want to apologize for not listening to you when you told me you wanted to drop the case. I should have known that you had your reasons."

"I did," she says.

"I know. I was just angry. Mad about a lot of things at that point in my life—about that trial and in general. Just because I'm not a female doesn't mean that I didn't—or don't—feel victimized by him, the school, and the justice system. All of it. Nothing about that was easy for me. But I asked Laura to bring me here tonight to ask for your forgiveness and that I would like nothing more than to try and be friends again."

Abigail remains still, but her eyes grow wide. "Just like that?"

"I'm not dumb enough to think it will happen overnight, but I can't go another day, not having you in my life, like it used to be. I miss you so much. We all do. There's a reason we are meant to be friends, and I just ask that you try and understand my point of view knowing that I did not handle the situation well with you. It's something I've been trying to work on."

On instinct, Laura reaches over and softly caresses his shoulder.

Abigail glances at her and then back at Tank and says, "Anything else?"

"Abigail," Laura says, "I hope you can understand that I never planned for anything to happen and not include you. Day after day passed, and I felt like I was going in one direction and you were heading in the other. I was struggling so badly about Travis, and quite honestly, Tank called me out on my bullshit more than once. From there, I just felt like I had someone who understood how I was feeling, and it made the pain easier to handle."

Tank adds, "You and I weren't on the best of terms, and then suddenly, you and Nathan broke up. It just felt like everything was crashing down around us. I needed to be there for him."

"What about me?" Abigail asks, her tone much softer.

"I know. I know I wasn't there, but you seemed so angry—with him, me, everything—and a part of me thought maybe a break would be good for you, too."

"I needed my friends, too, you know," she says. "It wasn't easy for me to suddenly be the odd man out. You guys were all continuing on as if I never existed," she says as the rims of her eyes water.

"Oh, Abigail. I'm so sorry. I didn't know if you'd understand," Laura says.

"Understand what exactly?"

Tank reaches over and takes Laura's hand. "I never saw her coming," he whispers.

Laura whips her head toward him. "*Tank*," she gushes.

"What? Well, I think she's getting the picture."

Abigail stands and says, "It would have been nice to hear it first from you," she scolds in Laura's direction. "You both can't fathom how stupid I've felt these past weeks, knowing you've been sneaking around behind my back. Regardless of my relationship with Nathan, I was there for you, Tank, when no one was on your side. And you not only left me when I needed a friend, but you also took my best friend away from me. You guys have no idea what I've been through this year. You don't think I miss him? I mean, this, all of you?" she corrects. "None of this has been easy."

"No, it hasn't," Laura says. "And I'm so sorry for not being there for you."

"So, come back to us," Tank quickly adds. "Because you can. You can walk right back into all of this, and…it's here, waiting for you. Nathan…"

"I have other people I have to consider, and I get no one wants to talk about Kelly. But he matters to me, and I—" She breaks off.

"What?" Laura asks.

"Never mind," she says, turning as a tear falls on her cheek.

"Abby, if you are in some kind of trouble…" Tank says.

"Not now, Tank, please," she begs.

"Okay, okay," he says, holding up his hands in protest. "But I'm here for you."

"Me, too," Laura says. "And I'm sorry we didn't tell you about us. It…"

"It came on fast because we've been friends for so long," he says. "But I meant what I said about—"

Abigail waves her hands in an away motion.

"I, um…okay, Abby," he stutters. "I get that this a lot. I'll give you guys some space," he says as he spins quickly and heads toward her door. He glances back briefly at Laura and waves good-bye.

Laura doesn't move. They can hear his large feet on the steps as he descends to the first floor. The door opens and closes.

"Do you want me to go?" Laura asks.

Surprisingly, Abigail shakes her head. She turns to face her friend. "I want to apologize if I haven't been there for you lately. I've been hurt. I've been avoiding you guys because, quite frankly, being around Tank and Nathan has been very difficult for me for a myriad of reasons. I was so embarrassed about the tire situation with my car, and I have just not felt like myself lately."

"I really do understand, Abigail. None of this has been a breeze."

"But I miss you, Laura. So badly."

Laura reaches for her hand. "I miss you, too."

"Are you happy?" she asks. "You and Tank?" Laura doesn't need to speak, as the smile that spreads across her lips is enough for Abigail to know the answer. "Wow, so that's it, huh? You and him?"

"Crazy, isn't it?"

Abigail chuckles. "Very." Then, her smile fades.

"What about you?" Laura asks.

Abigail sits back on the ledge. "Kelly asked me to move to Boston next year, after graduation."

Trying to keep her composure, Laura says, "Wow. Really? What do you think?"

"I don't—I mean, I haven't had much time to think about it, and it seems so far away to make a decision now."

"Yeah, it does seem far away. A lot can happen between now and then."

"I know. I'm just overwhelmed—that's all," she says with a yawn.

"And tired, too," Laura says. "Want me to stay or…"

Abigail smirks a little and says, "Even though I've just gotten you back, I think I'm going to go to bed."

"Me, too. It has been one crazy day," she says.

"Yeah, who was that guy you were trying not to get to run away?"

With a slight laugh, Laura says, "Mind if I fill you in tomorrow? It's a really long story."

"Yikes. That does sound better suited for tomorrow," Abigail says as she gets up and follows Laura to her door.

Laura leans in and places a soft kiss on her cheek. "I love you, Abigail."

"I love you, too. And, Laura?" she whispers. "I am really happy for you. With all my heart."

"Thanks." Laura smiles, and with a nod of her head, she turns and bounds down the stairs to her bedroom.

Lessons in Love

Laura sits on the edge of her bed. The room is dark, and the only noise is the clicking of the clock on the wall. She slips off her shoes as the ache in her body builds. Rubbing her tired feet as she stares ahead at nothing, she can't help but think back upon all the things she has been through this past year.

She's learned so much from Travis, Wolfie, Tucker, Melissa, Colin, Tank, Abigail, Bree, Nathan, and even Guthrie.

She's learned that losing someone doesn't always mean you have to lose yourself, too.

She's learned that hitting rock bottom doesn't mean she can't fall again; it just means she'll have to climb a little farther to get back up.

She's learned how to fight for the truth even if that means there is danger lurking around the corner and that people can be evil when they think no one is watching.

She's learned how to hold her ground when she believes she is right and to never stop searching for the answers.

She's learned how to move on when her heart is breaking and how, if she just allows herself time, she just might find happiness again.

But most importantly, she's learned that love is without a doubt, the greatest lesson of them all.

Forty-Three

Tank's Lessons

Tank unlocks the front door to his apartment after taking the long way back from Abigail and Laura's house. He needed the extra time to clear his head and to mull over the conversation he had with his former best friend.

It didn't go nearly as bad as he had feared it would, but they didn't exactly hug and make up either.

He shuts the front door, takes off his coat, and hangs it on the coat rack. He wanders into the dark kitchen and switches on the small light over the stove. Desperate to just flip on the television and veg out before bed, he grabs a beer from the fridge and then wanders into the living room. He curses as he hits his foot on the side table when he tries to find the chain on the lamp.

"Leave it off," a deep voice says.

Tank jumps. "Jesus Christ, you scared me," he barks. "What's with you guys sitting in the dark?" he mumbles.

Ignoring Nathan, he switches it on anyway. But he wishes he hadn't.

He did not expect to see Nathan with a bloody nose, red stains down the front of his T-shirt. A bottle of vodka in his hand.

"What the fuck happened to you?"

"Nothing," he slurs.

"You beat yourself up?" Tank growls.

Nathan peers up, and with disdain, he says, "Every damn day."

"Who'd you fight this time?" he asks.

"Some fucking guy made a comment about how I suck without her, and so they all started on me, saying how I ruined the season, which I did. I suck. I'm nothing without her."

"They," Tank whispers. "Jesus, man, you've gotta be more careful."

Nathan swigs from the bottle. "Maybe I don't care anymore," he says.

Tank sighs, "Oh, man," and takes a seat on the couch.

And that's the moment Nathan starts to cry. Head down, uncontrollable crying, like nothing Tank has witnessed before. Tank's heart sinks to depths beyond measure.

He can't mask the sadness in his voice when he asks, "How can I help?"

"Can you bring her back?" he asks.

Crushing. "I'm trying, buddy. I just came from her place. I apologized for everything, and Laura and I told her about us. I only hope she misses us as much as we miss her."

"Not possible. Look at me!" he yells. "I'm a fucking mess without her. She won't want me back. She's moved on, and I pushed her there. It's been months," he admits.

Tank gets up and takes the bottle from his hand. "Don't you give up, you hear me? The Nathan I know is a competitor and never gives up, no matter the odds."

"I'm not him anymore," he mumbles as he tries to get to his feet.

He staggers left and then right, and Tank realizes in that moment how completely drunk he is. He wraps his arm under Nathan's torso.

"I'm not him anymore," he repeats.

Tank helps him to the stairs, and slowly, one by one, they make their way to his room.

Tank pushes open Nathan's bedroom door and finds it in complete disarray. Clothes scattered about, papers all over the floor, a chair tipped over. But now isn't the time to bring this mess to his attention. Instead, he sits him on his bed.

"There is blood on this," he whispers as Nathan's eyes grow increasingly heavy.

Tank pulls the T-shirt up over his head, and Nathan slumps forward. Tank tips him on his side and swings his legs over on the bed. He wedges a pillow behind him, so he won't roll onto his back in the middle of the night.

Nathan's body succumbs to the alcohol, and he starts to snore. Tank grabs a blanket and pillow from his room and finds himself an empty space on Nathan's floor.

He tries desperately to stay awake, for fear Nathan might need him throughout the night. He hates the terrible sensation resting in his gut. He's never seen his best friend like this, and he's now concerned more than ever that he might never get past this.

What if she doesn't come back to us?

Nathan not only continues to spiral, but he also had a terrible football season, so much so that the coaches pulled Tank aside as cocaptain and discussed with him that if Nathan doesn't pull it together over the summer, they'll strip him of his captain's title next year. Nathan was Rookie of the Year for the entire conference two years ago, and now, they're debating on removing his title, kicking him off the team if necessary. Tough love if need be. They did it to Tank as a freshman, so he knows they mean business. It's not just talk.

Tank is waiting for the right time to broach the subject with him before the coaches are forced to.

Tank rubs his face and sighs. *How can I help him through this?* he wonders.

As he stares at the ceiling, he thinks back upon the year he's had and all the mistakes he made.

But more importantly, what he has learned from them.

He has continued to learn the importance of all his friendships and how imperative it is to savor each one. How he must always try and be a better friend, especially now that he knows what happens when he's not.

He's learned how to be there for one friend even if that means letting another have their space. But that it's so important to always love them, even from afar.

He's learned how to recognize when a friend is in desperate need of straightening their crooked arrow.

He's learned how to harness all those lessons of what to do and not do when you lose someone and help them crawl out of a hole should they find that they have fallen.

He's learned to look at someone differently than he has in the past, and by doing so, he is able to shake loose the misconception that he doesn't know how to be a good boyfriend. Because he does—with the right person.

He's learned a lot from his mistakes, and he continues to do so today.

But most importantly, after watching Nathan crumble, he's learned that holding on to someone you truly love, no matter the odds, might be the greatest lesson of them all.

But only if it works out in the end, right?

Forty-Four

The Letter

Kate is parked in her car in the lot at the mini-mart off Main Street, anxiously awaiting Laura's arrival. Laura pulls in, exactly on time, in the spot next to her and climbs into Kate's car.

"Hey, Kate. How are you?" she says.

"I'm doing good actually. My meeting with Officer Murphy went well, considering."

"Good to know. He's a good guy, and he really cares about the students at this school."

"So, what's this all about?" Kate asks.

"I thought a lot about the situation, and as I'm sure Officer Murphy told you, there was no way for them to arrest Guthrie without evidence. But the good news is, he didn't know that. And I felt he really needed to be held responsible for what he did." Laura hands her a copy of the paper. "This is coming out today, but I wanted you to see it first so that you weren't blindsided by it."

On the cover of *The Weekly Blue* is the caption, *Vandal Comes Forward*, and underneath it reads, *Anonymous letter sent to the editor, confessing to the crime committed at women's soccer house last year.*

Kate gasps as her eyes dance over the front page. "I can't believe this," she whispers.

She reads what is printed in his handwriting.

I made a terrible mistake. I took advantage of a situation and fed it with fear. But I write this letter as a changed person. I now see how awful my actions were. Defacing the women's soccer house last spring and writing words so horrible that I would not speak them aloud was an act of cowardice.

I have concluded that hiding and never coming forward only made what I did worse. I not only hurt those women, but also all the students on this campus. By creating mystery behind why such an act was done, it churned out more speculation and hatred than my small-minded brain could have imagined.

Therefore, I want to set the record straight. Once and for all.

I was too weak to properly express my feelings.

I was too uneducated to see past my own thoughts.

And I was too cruel to not see that what I was doing was criminal.

So, to all those I have hurt, I am sorry.

To the women's soccer team, I am very sorry I hurt any of you.

I do not expect to be forgiven, nor do I want to be. I should continue to live with what I did if I am ever going to be whole again.

Kate folds the newspaper in half and rests it on her lap. A lone tear drops on her pinked cheek. "Thank you, Laura."

Relieved by her reaction, Laura replies, "There is no need to thank me. I only wanted to do right by you, so if anything, I should be thanking you for trusting me to handle this."

"And I should have known that my teammates would understand, but I was so afraid of being outed that I kept it inside. So, I let Shannon know."

"You did?"

"Yeah, she deserved to know the truth, and she agreed that after I spoke to Officer Murphy, it'd be best to just let it go. If we try and fight every person who doesn't understand us, then that is all we'll end up doing our entire lives. We need to focus on the positive in our lives, not the narrow-minded people, like Guthrie."

Laura smiles. "Well said, and I wholeheartedly agree."

"And for what it's worth, I feel like I made a new friend out of all of this," she says. "I look forward to hanging out with you under better circumstances."

"Thank you, Kate. And me, too." Laura pulls open the door and climbs out.

Before Laura can close the door, Kate says, "I'll see you around, Detective Chase." To which, Laura giggles. "That's what Officer Murphy refers to you as," she says.

"Really?"

"Yeah," Kate says with a calming smile back at her.

Laura climbs into her car, and for the first time in a long time, she feels settled, perhaps having a new glimpse into her future.

"Huh," she says to herself as she turns the key, roaring the engine to life. "Detective Chase."

As she takes a left back toward campus, she knows there is only one person she wants to bounce this new idea off of. And that is Tank.

Maybe this is what he meant by me being in the wrong major? Travis also said I had a knack for this.

I suppose there is only one way to find out!

Forty-Five

Nathan's and Webber's Lessons

Abigail opens her bedroom door and drops her book bag on the floor near her desk. She takes a seat and hits the play button on her answering machine.

A moment later, there's a loud beep, and then a voice comes booming through the small speaker.

"Abigail, it's Webber." His voice is strained, and it's clear he's trying to catch his breath. "I need you to come over to my apartment as soon as you hear this message, please," he begs. "I assure you, this is not a trap of any kind. But I need your help. Badly. Please come. I'm here."

She hears the phone click, and then the machine beeps, letting her know that is her only message.

Webber has never in their over three-year relationship sounded so upset. She doesn't even bat an eye as she grabs her bag and bounds back down the stairs and to her car. She parks in the Parkers Village lot nearest his apartment and hurries to the front door. She knocks, and almost immediately, the door swings open. Webber is standing there, an indescribable expression of anguish on his face.

"Oh, thank God you came."

Terror envelops her body. "What's happening?" she says, fearing the worst. "Is everyone okay?"

"Yes, yes, sorry. Everyone is fine." He heads down the hall to the living room, and she follows closely behind. "I need you to listen to this," he says, his hand trembling as he presses play on his answering machine.

A beep, and then a deep, authoritative voice says, "Mr. Littman, this is the Jeffrey Woods, head of the Undergraduate Disciplinary Division. A matter has come to our attention regarding Professor Johnson's class." Just then they can hear the door open and close, voices being heard in the hallway.

"We will need to see you Wednesday at nine a.m. in Weston Hall, room 457. Failure to show at this time could result in a suspension from the university. We take these issues very seriously, and we are encouraging you to do the same."

Abigail's eyes are wide. She reaches over and grabs Webber's hands, which are still quaking.

"What is going on?" a voice says.

Abigail spins and finds herself face-to-face with Tank and Nathan.

"Who was that?" Nathan asks. "Was that for you?" he says to Webber. Nathan's eye is swollen, and there is a cut across the bridge of his nose.

"Talk to us," Tank encourages.

Webber sinks into the couch, and with his head in his hands, he says, "I have no idea. How could that be about me?" he asks, looking up at his friends. "Abigail, what the hell could that be about?"

She sits down next to him, rubbing his back. "I thought you got along well with Professor Johnson. He would have come to you first if he had an issue, no?"

"Yes, and you know I would never cheat," he protests.

"Smartest dude I know," Tank says. "Aside from Logan."

"The only thing you can do is wait until Wednesday, right?" Nathan says.

Abigail looks up and locks eyes with him. Her heart aches at the sight of him. He looks so unlike the vibrant guy she just saw in the lab.

"Knock, knock," they hear as the front door opens and closes. "Tank?" Laura calls out.

"In here, girl," Tank says with his signature pet name for her.

Abigail quickly averts her eyes from Nathan's stare as Laura comes waltzing in, clearly unaware of the mess she's about to face.

"Whoa." She laughs. "What's everybody doing?" She smiles as she notices Abigail. But quickly, it fades as she takes in the glum expression on their faces. "What's wrong? Nathan, what the hell happened to your face?"

He lowers his head and mumbles, "Got in a fight."

"Another one? Jesus," she says, which immediately makes Abigail look over at him, unable to mask the concern in her eyes.

"I'm fine," he says.

Tank quickly jumps in to change the subject. "Webber got a call, saying that he needs to…wait, who called?" he asks, realizing he did not hear the entire message.

Webber points to the answering machine. "Listen for yourself," he says, on the verge of vomiting.

Laura hits play and listens intently along with the others as the details are spelled out for them. Once the beep ends, she turns and goes right into character. "What class does Johnson teach?"

"European History."

"Okay, and what would make him think you cheated in that class?" Laura asks.

"I didn't, so I have no idea why."

"Wait," Tank says. "Isn't that the class you keep helping Daisy with?"

Webber's cheeks flame red. "Yeah, but no idea what that has to do with it."

"I don't know, man. I'm not a big fan of hers."

"What? Since when?" he says.

"Since the day I met her," Tank answers bluntly.

"Well, I like her, so…can we talk about something else?"

Abigail stands and walks over to the door near the back deck. She peers out the window, inhaling deep breaths.

"What is it?" Nathan asks. He knows her so well that he can tell when something is weighing on her mind.

She turns to face him. Her skin heats, as the mere act of him addressing her directly makes her uncomfortable.

"Do you know something?" Laura asks, trying to coax her into speaking. "You can tell us," she says.

Tank nods at her with approval.

"Webber"—Abigail's voice quivers—"the other night, when we were in the lab, was that Daisy who was coming to see you?"

"Yes," he says.

"And Aniston?" She hates even speaking her name.

"How do you know her?" he says.

Fiddling with her hands, she lowers her eyes and says, "Um, she used to date Kelly."

Nathan staggers back somewhat, as if the name Kelly knocked the wind out of him.

"Oh, yeah. She came the other night, too. But I don't know how this has anything to do with…"

And then it hits him. Hard. He abruptly stands and backs away from his friends.

"Webber, all I know is, she's not a good person—Aniston."

He protests, "But that doesn't mean Daisy isn't."

"Webber," she pleads, "she was the one who slashed my tires."

Tank gasps. "What?! You knew who did it, and you're okay with that?"

"No!" she says. "I'm *not okay* with it, Tank." She defensively crosses her arms over her chest.

"Guys, guys. Come on," Nathan says.

On instinct, he reaches out for Abigail. She eyes his outstretched hand, and he quickly lowers it.

"Sorry," he whispers. Then, he continues, "Spidey, maybe you need to consider that if a person is willing to hang out with someone like that, there has to be a part of them that might share similar qualities with that other person. We tend to surround ourselves with people of the same morals, don't we?" He looks around the room for confirmation, but little does he know that the speech he just gave weighed heavily with Abigail, probably more so than anyone else.

"Daisy didn't slash anyone's tires, and just because Aniston did—" he barks.

"*Webber*," Laura says, "don't."

"It's okay, Laura. I get it," Abigail says as she starts to move across the room. "I'm not sure what more I can do here anyway. And I have to be someplace," she lies as she heads down the hallway.

Webber runs after her. He pulls on her hand. "I'm sorry," he says. "I'm just so stressed out. I need you though. You really know what kind of student I am. It might come down to that."

"I'll always be there for you," she says as she pulls open the door and exits.

She hurries to her car when she suddenly hears, "Abby, wait!"

She halts and faces Nathan.

"I just wanted to say, if you need anything, please let us know."

"I'll remember that," she says.

He grabs her hand, unwilling to let it go. "I get that what you told us in there was a big deal. But I just couldn't let you walk away and not say that I'm here for you. Me. Because I want to be." He drops her hand.

"Looks like you need someone to take care of you," she says, pointing to his face.

"I'm fine," he says.

"You don't look it," she replies. "I mean—"

"I know what you meant," he says curtly.

She can see the hurt in his eyes. "Nathan."

"I should get back to Webber," he says. And before she can say another word, he turns and walks back to the apartment.

Nathan rubs the back of his neck and takes a deep breath as he hears her car drive past him. Every part of him wants to run after her to tell her he got in a fight over her. Because the mere mention of her name and any indication that he screwed up the best thing he had sets him off into another dimension.

He hasn't learned to not let people get to him.

But he *has* learned that every second without her gets more painful and not easier.

He's learned that there is such a thing as true love, and the worst thing you can do is lose it.

He's learned that the hard way.

But what he's also learned is that the right thing to do, no matter what, is to help someone when they feel like they have no one else. Because he knows what it's like to be alone and depressed, with no end in sight.

And he's also learned that it's okay to step back and let a friend find their own way.

But most importantly, he's learned that he needs to fight harder for what he wants, *whatever it takes*, and that just might be the greatest lesson of them all.

When he enters the apartment, Laura and Tank are nowhere to be found.

"Where did they go?" Nathan asks.

"They went to Wolfie's house. Said they would be back soon."

"Oh," he says with a cock of his head. "You okay, buddy?" he asks.

"No, obviously. I can get kicked out of school," he says. "I'm a nervous wreck!"

Nathan gets close to him, locking eyes, and says, "We won't let that happen."

"What if you guys are right? What if I did something to get in trouble?"

"You have to find out the details on Wednesday before you can push ahead."

"It might as well be a year from now," he says, rubbing his temples.

"I know," Nathan says. "But time could be on your side, too."

"I've got a bad feeling I'm going to need more than time."

"Anything you want to tell me?" Nathan asks.

"I need to think this through more. Retrace the past few months and see where it could have gone wrong."

"Okay, buddy. I'll just sit with you. In case you need to talk," Nathan says as he grabs the remote and switches on the television.

Webber leans back on the couch and sighs, "Thanks. I appreciate that." He closes his eyes, trying to forget the past few hours.

Impossible.

As he tries to shake this awful feeling in his gut, he reverts to this morning—when the sun rose across the campus, bringing an exciting new day of hope and promise for Webber. But as quickly as the sun began setting, it brought fear and worry to him like he never could have imagined.

But what Webber cannot comprehend in the moment is the monumental lesson he is about to face. A lesson that will teach them all what they could never have grasped when they met as wide-eyed freshmen. That their pending senior year is not a given for some, and for others, it will be the most challenging year of them all.

Forty-Six

Dynamic Duo

Wolfie is not expecting anyone at his door. But when he hears the urgency in her voice, he hurries to answer it.

"Are you okay? Oh, hey, Tank."

"Can we come in?" Laura asks.

"Of course," he says, allowing them to follow him into the kitchen. "Have a seat. What brings you two my way?"

"I need help with something," Laura says. "Our friend—"

Tank nudges her. "My roommate, Webber."

"Yes, Tank's roommate. Got a call from Jeffrey Woods, the head of the Undergraduate Disciplinary Division. Do you know him?"

"Heard of him, yes. Tough. A stickler for the rules."

Tank sighs, "Crap."

Laura continues, "Something regarding Professor Johnson's class, European History. He must appear on Wednesday at nine a.m. in Weston Hall, room 457. If he doesn't show, which he will, the message said he could be suspended."

"Just for not showing? That's major," Wolfie says.

"Right?" Laura agrees.

"Sounds pretty serious." Wolfie rubs his face and then reaches into his pocket and pulls out a small notebook about the size of his breast pocket along with a pencil. "Tell me more about Webber. The last name," he says to Tank.

"Littman."

"You guys live in Parkers Village, right? What number?"

"Five eight six."

"Okay, what is his major?"

"Veterinary science."

Wolfie's eyes rise. "Nice. So, this is an elective?"

Tank shrugs his shoulders. "I guess so."

"I'd say so," Laura adds.

"He does well in school?"

"Smartest guy I know. Well, one of them. My other roommate Logan is a brainiac, too."

"Logan is Melissa's boyfriend. The guy's here on that math scholarship. The one in lots of my classes."

"Not for long," Tank whispers.

"What?" Wolfie asks.

"Nothing." Laura blushes. "Yes, Webber is super smart. He's in the same major as Abigail, all the same science classes since freshman year. They're lab partners. He's so nice and just the greatest guy. He was shocked by the message. We all were."

Wolfie holds up his hand and nods at Laura, signaling to her to slow down a bit. "Drugs?"

"What?" Tank says.

"He do drugs?"

"Fuck no. He drinks, but that's it."

"Got a girlfriend?"

They both glance at one another.

Wolfie clears his throat. "You've got to tell me everything, even the things you think might mean nothing."

"I know. It's just…well, tell him," she says.

"There is this girl, Daisy. She's been coming around this year. She is—don't repeat this—but way outta the guy's league, and she knows it and treats him that way. He's always helping her with her schoolwork, and I just don't like her. I've never gotten a good feeling about her," Tank says.

"She in his class?"

"Yep."

"Daisy, huh? Know anything else about her?"

"Apparently, she hangs out with another girl that Abigail knows, Aniston. Abigail just told us she slashed her tires a month or so back, and, well, we just don't get good vibes about the company she keeps, so…" Laura says.

"Aniston slashed Abigail's tires. Not Daisy, right?" Wolfie asks.

"Correct," Laura says.

"But Aniston and Daisy are friends?"

"Yes," Tank says.

"Webber ever in any other trouble at school?"

"No, never," Tank says.

"Okay. So, they must have some reason to assume that Webber either cheated on an exam, plagiarized a paper, gave answers to someone by writing a paper for them, helped someone cheat essentially, or a variation of those scenarios, off the top of my head," Wolfie spits out.

"Damn," Tank says.

"Yes, none of those are good, and all of those are reasons to be expelled from the university."

Laura closes her eyes and then opens them. "Poor Webber. What can we do?"

"Let me do some digging, so whatever we are hit with on Wednesday, we can move quickly—as quickly as, I assume, they will want to move."

Laura stands. "Thank you, Wolfie."

Tank rises as well and reaches out his hand to shake Wolfie's. "Webber is a really great guy. So, I appreciate anything that you can do for him and, well, for me. He means a lot to me. He's like a brother."

Shyly, he accepts this hand. "Any friend of Laura's is a friend of mine."

If Laura's heart were on her sleeve, then Tank and Wolfie would have seen it grow twice its size in a matter of a moment. She can't believe she's standing in Wolfie's kitchen of all places with Tank, her boyfriend, watching the two of them essentially become friends. She never in her wildest dreams would have imagined this happening.

In the beginning of all of this, she leaned heavily on Wolfie. She felt she could only rely on him to help her turn Travis's memories from dark to light.

But eventually, without words spoken, Wolfie recognized Tank coming into the picture. And Tank's experience with losing Jonathan could also help Laura, and his tough love could only benefit her in ways she really needed—quickly. So, Wolfie and Laura transitioned their relationship back to how it used to be—friends who have common goals. After all, it's where it belongs. It's where Travis would want them to be.

"Well, if you need us, you know where to find us," Laura chokes out as she hurries to the door, trying to fight back her happy tears. As they exit his apartment, Laura turns and waves to Wolfie. "You're the best, Wolfie," she says.

And with a wave and a laugh, he says, "Keep your noses clean, Mulder and Scully, until I get back to you."

And with that, Tank wraps his arm around Laura's shoulders, and the two make their way back to Parkers Village to let Webber know that they've got the best guy looking out for him, someone no one in the school knows about.

And that's just the way Wolfie likes it.

"Mulder and Scully, huh?" Tank chuckles.

Laura glances up at him, a wide smile on her face.

"What's going through that beautiful brain of yours, girl?"

"As a criminal justice major, you should be able to find out."

With no warning, he scoops her up in his arms as she squeals, "Tank, put me down!"

He gently places her on the ground, wrapping his arms tightly around her. Leaning her back, he presses his lips to hers as a soft moan escapes her mouth. Releasing his kiss, he says with a wink, "See, you'll make a great detective."

Huh, imagine that.

What's Next for the Author?

In Last Semester, the final installment of the Onondaga State Series, Webber Littman is shocked to find out he has been accused of cheating and is faced with being expelled from OSU.

When a heartbroken Webber discovers his relationship with Daisy was nothing more than a ruse, his friends convince him that it's high time nice guys finish first and not last. They'll do anything to help prove his innocence—even if that means they must get their hands a little dirty in the process.

But when Webber's Student Union representative insists that Nathan be the only eyewitness Webber's allowed, everyone but Tank and Nathan thinks it's a good idea.

Nathan is spiraling out of control when he hears Abigail is moving to Boston. And he's one strike away from losing his football scholarship. Can he pull it together for Webber? Or will they both be forced to leave OSU?

But when Abigail discovers there were others involved in the cheating scandal, she's had enough. Could this be the final straw in her relationship with Kelly?

Join Webber, Abigail, Nathan, Tank, Laura, and friends as they tumble forcefully into their senior year. Some with bright futures ahead and a few not knowing if they'll even be able to graduate.

About the Author

Laurel (Kupillas) Ostiguy was born in Queensbury, a town sandwiched between Lake George and Saratoga Springs in Upstate New York, where she still visits with friends and family. She attended Plymouth State University and graduated in 1997. She also received her master's degree from Northeastern University in 2003.

She is now married to her college sweetheart, Jeff, and they have two sons. She currently lives outside of Boston, Massachusetts. When she is not working, she loves to spend time with her children, ski, practice yoga, write, or just enjoy the beautiful New England seasons.

www.ingramcontent.com/pod-product-compliance
Lightning Source LLC
LaVergne TN
LVHW041051080826
845145LV00007B/1528

* 9 7 8 0 5 7 8 9 5 3 9 5 3 *